Don Quixote

The Ingenious
DON
de

Hidalgo
QUIXOTE
la Mancha

Part I

Miguel de CERVANTES Saavedra

Translated with an Introduction and Notes

PENGUIN BOOKS

PENGUIN BOOKS

Published by the Penguin Group
Penguin Books Ltd, 27 Wrights Lane, London w8 5TZ, England
Penguin Putnam Inc., 375 Hudson Street, New York, New York 10014, USA
Penguin Books Australia Ltd, Ringwood, Victoria, Australia
Penguin Books Canada Ltd, 10 Alcorn Avenue, Toronto, Ontario, Canada M4V 3B2
Penguin Books India (P) Ltd, 11, Community Centre, Panchsheel Park, New Delhi – 110 017, India
Penguin Books (NZ) Ltd, Private Bag 102902, NSMC, Auckland, New Zealand
Penguin Books (South Africa) (Pty) Ltd, 5 Watkins Street, Denver Ext 4, Johannesburg 2094, South Africa

Penguin Books Ltd, Registered Offices: Harmondsworth, Middlesex, England

This translation first published, with Part II, in Penguin Classics 2000
Part I reprinted in this edition 2001

1

Translation and editorial material copyright © John Rutherford 2000
All rights reserved

The moral right of the translator has been asserted

Typeset in 10.25/13.5 pt Monotype Columbus
Typeset by Rowland Phototypesetting Ltd, Bury St Edmunds, Suffolk
Printed in England by The Bath Press, Bath

CONTENTS

❖

✠ CONTENTS ✠

❧ CONTENTS ❧

❖ CONTENTS ❖

❖ CONTENTS ❖

INTRODUCTION

WRITING *DON QUIXOTE*

> 'I do now have to say,' said Don Quixote, 'that the author of my
> history was no sage but some ignorant prattler, who started writing
> it in a haphazard and unplanned way and let it turn out however it
> would, like Orbaneja, the famous artist of Úbeda, who, when asked
> what he was painting, replied: "Whatever emerges."'
>
> (*Don Quixote*, PART II, CHAPTER III)

In the Prologue to Part I, Cervantes tells us that it was while he was in
prison that he had the idea for *Don Quixote*. It's probable that he's referring
to his incarceration in Seville (1597–8), for incompetence as a tax-collector.
Nobody knows whether he started writing while in prison, or later. But
what is clear is that the piece he envisaged was very different from what
he was eventually to produce. Cervantes was thinking of a short fiction,
something along the lines of his *Novelas ejemplares*, or exemplary novellas,
eventually published in 1613. This is indicated by the rapid pace and short
duration of the knight's first sally, undertaken alone and occupying just the
first five chapters, and by the fact that in the seventh sentence of the text
the narrator refers to it as a *cuento*, a short tale, something he does only
once more (see below): as soon as the fiction is fully under way Cervantes
calls his text a *libro* (book) and an *historia* (history or story), reserving *cuento*
for the tales contained within it. But by the time he reached the end of the
first sally, he'd begun to realize that he must explore this fascinating

fictional world he'd stumbled upon. So what perhaps started as a more or less moral fable, using parody to attack romances of chivalry for their pernicious effects on readers, turned itself, as it was being written, into the first modern novel. In his anecdote about Orbaneja, Cervantes tells us, with characteristic ironical self-mockery, how he created his great work.

Yet the moralizing content of even the first conception of *Don Quixote* is dubious. Its hero is as obsessed by the traditional Spanish ballads and their protagonists as by the romances of chivalry: stories about enamoured knights in shining armour wandering through exotic lands slaying giants and the occasional dragon and rescuing damsels in distress in order to prove their prowess as fighters and their perfection as lovers, despite all the worst efforts of evil enchanters. The romances of chivalry had enjoyed great popularity and had been attacked by moralists for turning readers' thoughts, in particular young female readers' thoughts, away from religion towards worldly matters. But all this had happened in the first seventy years of the sixteenth century. Since then the romances of chivalry had been superseded by the flowering of literature that we know as the Spanish Golden Age, and by Cervantes's time nobody considered them to be a threat any more. The theatre was the new literary moral menace. Yet at a time when, following the classical dictum, fictional literature was supposed not only to delight but also to instruct, and when the authorities could censor and ban books, it was wise to claim some orthodox moral purpose for what one wrote, particularly if its irreverent irony could suggest critical thoughts about certain aspects of Roman Catholic practice such as the trial and burning of heretics, the use of rosaries and the repetition of Hail Marys and creeds. But the evidence indicates that the delight interested Cervantes more than the instruction. What he relished was the joy of storytelling, the fun of parody, humour as something good in itself because of its therapeutic value. His allegation of an unconvincing and anachronistic moral purpose is perhaps part of the fun, yet another parody. And the joke is still funny today, because the book that claims to destroy romances of chivalry is the one that has kept their memory alive.

To read this lovely novel is to accompany its author in an exhilarating adventure as he improvises his story and watches it grow between his hands. It is also to understand that it would be mistaken to expect it to be a tightly structured book. Despite the best efforts of academic critics,

Don Quixote is an episodic work, as also are the romances of chivalry, consisting as they do of successions of chance encounters.

The first development after that brief first sally is to provide Don Quixote with a squire, Sancho Panza, which opens the way to the conversations that alternate with the action. The possibility of enlisting a squire had been suggested, but not put into practice, during the first sally. Long conversations between knight and squire are not a feature of the romances of chivalry, yet their contribution to *Don Quixote* is vital, allowing this novel of comic adventures to become a comedy of character as well. Quixote and Sancho first appear as two-dimensional figures of burlesque fun, both derived from recent Spanish literature: Quixote is an aging madman who thinks he's a knight errant and brings amusing disasters upon himself; and Sancho is the rustic buffoon, selfish and materialistic, who was a stock character in sixteenth-century Spanish comedies. Both are absurdly unsuited for their roles: in the romances of chivalry, knights and squires are young men of high birth, with the latter serving their apprenticeship before becoming knights themselves.

But these two clowns soon start to develop, as does the relationship between them. Each begins to show contradictory characteristics: Don Quixote is allowed his lucid intervals, derived from contemporary medical theories about the nature of madness, and Sancho acquires cunning and a certain sagacity, from the peasant figure in folk tales. They both gain depth and complexity – a sane madman and a wise fool – and the humour becomes more subtle, although burlesque is never abandoned. Above all, both Quixote and Sancho acquire the ability to astonish us, always however in convincing ways. Here two principles of Golden Age literary theory are relevant: the belief that *admiratio* (amazement) and verisimilitude are essential qualities of fictional literature underlies our two heroes' wonderful combination of unpredictability and credibility. *Don Quixote* is an experimental work far ahead of its times, yet it is also rooted in its times. Its protagonist's determination to turn his life into a work of art, which will reach its climax in his penance in the Sierra Morena, is the consequence of the crazy application of yet another Renaissance literary principle, that of *imitatio*, the importance of the imitation of literary models.

Cervantes was particularly proud of having created Sancho Panza, to judge from what he says at the end of the prologue. And as soon as Sancho has appeared, Cervantes relates what will become the most famous incident in the book, the adventure of the windmills. Readers wonder why it's narrated so briefly, but the reason is clear enough: the story has only just started to expand, it hasn't yet grown from a *cuento* into an *historia*. Readers might also wonder why it has become the most famous episode: simply because it's the first adventure that knight and squire have together?

The second stage in this spontaneous development into a novel is the invention of the narrators. Throughout the first sally the story has been told by an unnamed narrator to whom no particular importance has been attached. Here again, however, there are hints of what's to come as we're informed of differences of opinion on factual matters among the various authors who have written about Don Quixote, and as he himself anticipates how the sage who will chronicle his adventures will describe this first one. Hardly has Don Quixote left home again when Cervantes thinks of ways in which those ideas about different narrators can be exploited for further fun: at a most inconvenient point he claims that this is where the written source material, and therefore the story itself, comes to a sudden end. The mysterious second author who is now introduced together with the lying Moorish historian Cide Hamete Benengeli and his hardly more reliable Morisco translator manage, between them, to sort the problem out, enable the story to continue and provide opportunities for playing literary games throughout the novel. All this is another parody of the romances of chivalry, which were often presented as Spanish translations of ancient documents.

It is at this point, the beginning of chapter IX, that *Don Quixote* is called a *cuento* for the second and last time. The story is wriggling out of the hands of Miguel de Cervantes Saavedra and into those of Cide Hamete Benengeli. Cervantes also marks this transition by informing us that the second part is beginning here, and by referring to 'the great bulk of material that, as I imagined, was missing from this delectable tale'. 'It seemed impossible and contrary to all good practice that such an excellent knight shouldn't have had some sage who'd have made it his job to record his unprecedented deeds,' Cervantes continues, as he perceives the potential of this *cuento* and includes the act of perceiving it as part of his story. *Don Quixote*'s growth from novella to novel can no longer be checked.

So Sancho and the gang of narrators have now been incorporated, and Cervantes writes on, fast, not stopping to check or correct internal inconsistencies. After several more chapters it occurs to him that it would add to the amusement to have Sancho's speech characterized by accumulations of proverbs, and from now on this is how Sancho, famously, speaks. This idea could well have been suggested by Fernando de Rojas's *Comedia o Tragicomedia de Calisto y Melibea* (1499 and 1502), often known as *La Celestina*, a dramatic fictional narrative laced with proverbs, most of which are reused in *Don Quixote*. It wouldn't have been difficult to revise earlier chapters and put some proverbs into Sancho's mouth there, too, for the sake of consistency, but Cervantes won't stop for this triviality. He's writing an ephemeral comic novel for popular consumption, not some erudite classic work for future generations of learned critics to pore over and analyse. Yet he's also beginning to realize the full importance of this find he's making, and has one of his characters congratulate him: 'I can't believe that if anyone wanted to invent such a story he'd be clever enough to do it,' Cardenio says in chapter XXX.

But Cervantes has his doubts about his ability to turn such a simple subject as the relationship between two eccentric and nomadic friends into a successful full-length novel, and he includes some interpolated tales, which have tenuous connections with the main story, do not share its comic tone and can be skipped by the reader who finds them tedious, even though they have interesting qualities of their own. And once Cervantes has written his two hundred thousand words or so, he takes Don Quixote back home and brings his story to an end. This ending both closes the novel, by referring to the knight's death, and leaves it open for a possible sequel, by mentioning later adventures, in particular his participation in certain jousts in Saragossa, and by including a quotation from Ariosto's *Orlando Furioso* to suggest that someone else might like to continue the story, as often happened with the romances of chivalry.

El ingenioso hidalgo Don Quixote de la Mancha was published in Madrid, in a hurried, shoddy edition, between late December 1604 and early January 1605.

The book was an immediate popular success. Cervantes, born in 1547, was by now an old man, and yet, stimulated by the extraordinary flourishing of literature in early seventeenth-century Spain, he was at the height of his creative productivity. The encouragement given by *Don Quixote*'s popularity being irresistible, he takes up the threads of the open version of the ending and resolves to have his knight ride to Saragossa, as promised. Cervantes decides, in response to criticism, that any interpolated tales in this second part will be shorter ones, and more integrated with the main story by developing from the experiences of the two heroes.

Cervantes's imagination soon fastens on to a new circumstance, full of possibilities for enriching his novel still further: the publication and popularity of Part I. So Don Quixote now finds that he is the hero he had so improbably aspired to be, and Sancho also rejoices in unexpected fame. Neither knows the sad truth about the manner of their depiction, and so their self-assurance and self-importance grow, as does their complexity. Don Quixote attracts our sympathy and pity as well as our mockery, as he's made the butt of a series of elaborate practical jokes: our laughter at his expense is now more uneasy. Sancho Panza's growth from a bumpkin into a man of resourcefulness is accelerated, as he gains the confidence to deceive and manipulate his master, something he'd already begun to do in Part I: relationships between superiors and inferiors turn out to be more complicated than they might seem to be. And now Cervantes thinks of a way in which Sancho can astonishingly yet credibly become the governor of the island he's been promised ever since he made his first appearance; and Sancho amazes us yet again with the rare combination of wisdom and stupidity that he shows both in government and in departure from government.

In autumn 1614, as the weary Cervantes at long last approaches the end of Part II (not included in this volume), as he writes chapter LIX, comes a bolt from the blue: the publication in Tarragona of *The Second Volume of the Ingenious Knight Don Quixote de la Mancha*, by Alonso Fernández de Avellaneda, the pseudonym of an unidentified writer who has accepted the tongue-in-cheek invitation at the end of Part I and has produced an inferior imitation which narrates the journey to Saragossa and the events that take place there. Cervantes's anger is expressed in his prologue to Part II (which was the last section he wrote, of course). But he's too much of an artist to allow his anger to blind him to the comic possibilities opened up by this unexpected appearance of another Don Quixote and another Sancho Panza; so he writes them into his own story. And Don Quixote, still on his way to Saragossa, decides on the spur of the moment to change all his plans and ride to Barcelona instead, to demonstrate the spuriousness of Avellaneda's account. All this provides Cervantes with the momentum to carry him through to the end of his story, which for some time now has been foreshadowed in the growth in both characters' minds of doubts and disillusionment. Cervantes is careful to end Part II with a definitive and unambiguous closure. His own life has not many more months to run.

In this reconstruction of the writing of *Don Quixote* I've stressed its character as a funny book, because all the evidence indicates that this is what its author intended it to be. Some of the fun can be difficult for modern readers to appreciate, though, because it seems so cruel to us. In confronting this problem it will help to remember that until comparatively recent times laughter was the normal self-defensive reaction to the disconcerting discovery of gross deviations from the beauty and harmony of God's nature. Laughter distances us from that which is ugly and therefore potentially distressing, and indeed enables us to obtain paradoxical pleasure and therapeutic benefit from it. Over the last couple of hundred years the area of distressing experience with which it's possible to cope by enlisting laughter has shrunk, and nowadays it's the fashion to prefer humourless and politically correct euphemism, which could well prove even less effective; but in Cervantes's time madness and violence were among the many manifestations of ugliness that could be managed with laughter.

And yet works of fictional literature often develop, both in the writing and later, qualities other than those intended by their authors; and in *Don Quixote* we can also find much that provokes serious thought. We laugh at the antics of Don Quixote and Sancho; but when we discover that we're laughing in the company of the vacuous Duke and Duchess, we might well feel uncomfortable about our laughter; if so, the novel has become not just a funny book about madmen but also an exploration of the ethics of fun and of the hazy dividing-line between madness and sanity. It's clear, to take another example, that Cervantes made fiction itself a central theme of this work of fiction because of the comic possibilities with which this provided him. But there's nothing to prevent readers from moving on to a consideration of serious implications about the relationships between fact and fiction, and about the parallels between Don Quixote's response to romances of chivalry and current responses to televised soap operas or to televised violence. All this might even lead to a realization that self-conscious and self-referential fiction is not, as certain contemporary critics and theoreticians seem in their postmodernist parochiality to believe, a twentieth-century discovery.

With all its fun and all its seriousness and all its surprises, *Don Quixote* offers its readers a glorious journey of discovery in the excellent company of Sancho Panza, Don Quixote de la Mancha and Miguel de Cervantes Saavedra. ¡Buen viaje a todos!

TRANSLATING *DON QUIXOTE*

> It seems to me that translating from one language into another, except from those queens of languages, Greek and Latin, is like viewing Flemish tapestries from the wrong side, when, although one can make out the figures, they are covered by threads that obscure them, and one cannot appreciate the smooth finish of the right side.
>
> (*Don Quixote*, PART II, CHAPTER LXII)

Yet another *Quixote* translation? Isn't it an act of quixotry to write the thirteenth English version of the great Spanish novel?

Several of the earliest translations of Cervantes's masterpiece (those by Thomas Shelton, 1612 and 1620, John Philips, 1687, Peter Motteux, 1712, and Tobias Smollett, 1755[1]) are still of interest because they recapture much of the vivacity of Cervantes's writing. But they are inaccurate: their authors had only the most rudimentary dictionaries and other reference books, and their style of translation was much freer than is acceptable now. Motteux, for example, removes entire sentences or even paragraphs, and adds others of his own. He has a particular fondness for inserting his own jokes, which are more scurrilous than funny. He is an example of what we could call the cavalier tradition of *Quixote* translation.

Charles Jervas, whose translation was first published in 1742,[2] is important for initiating a different tradition. He follows the original text as closely as he can, and this is a welcome innovation. But his version lacks the energy and wit of Cervantes's prose, and turns *Don Quixote* into a solemn book. Jervas thus initiated the puritan tradition of *Quixote* translation, which was strengthened by the Romantic reading of the book, according to which

Don Quixote is no figure of fun but a noble hero fighting for his lofty ideals in a hostile and uncomprehending materialistic world. Like so much Romantic thought, this view of the book has remained influential to the present day. It's a misreading, because it underplays the fun; yet, as Anthony Close has shown,[3] it was what was needed to establish *Don Quixote* in modern times as a world classic.

Despite the Romantic revaluation, almost a century and a half passed without a new *Quixote* translation into the English language – and then three appeared in seven years in the 1880s. The puritan tradition, with its great strengths and its great weaknesses, is to be found at its best in these translations by Alexander J. Duffield (1881), John Ormsby (1885) and Henry Edward Watts (1888).[4] Each of these meticulous scholars devoted immense efforts to ensuring that every detail of his translation was as correct as he could make it, and Ormsby was particularly successful; but this was again at the expense of the humour. The twentieth-century English translations remain, on the whole, within the powerful puritan tradition.[5]

My intention in this latest addition to the large family of *Quixote* translations is to combine the virtues of the puritans and the cavaliers, and to avoid their vices.

But literary translation is difficult work, and translators often make it even more difficult by an understandable but mistaken attitude of reverence for the original artist, beside whom it's all too easy to feel like humble artisans who can only ever aspire to produce a pale shadow of the original or the reverse side of a tapestry: a self-fulfilling prediction. So whereas the artist dares to make the familiar unfamiliar and create fascinating strangeness, the timorous artisan-translator removes the strangeness and makes it all familiar again. Literary translators must conquer these fears. If, as we've been told over and over again, we're attempting the impossible, it follows that we aren't humble hacks but heroes. So I had to try to write as Cervantes did, and to be as creative and as playful with language as he was. By undertaking this translation I'd chosen to rub shoulders with the great man, so that was what I had to do, not grovel at his feet.

This is less immodest than it might seem. The original author's creative energies had to be spread over a vast area as he wrote his novel: the creation of characters, the construction of plots, the description of settings and the development of themes, as well as the writing of expressive sentences. But the translator can focus his creative energies on the sentences, because the rest is, in a sense, given. He does have to use his imagination in these other areas, because the novel must be for him not a string of words but a world in which he lives; yet this readerly re-creation is less of an effort than original creation. It is, however, an effort that translators must make. The translator is not a machine into which the original text is fed, to emerge in another language but in all other respects identical. What I tried to do was to let the Spanish words construct in my mind's eye the world of the novel, and to live in that world; to see and hear Don Quixote and Sancho and to make them my best friends (some loss of sanity is a price that any artist has to pay); and only then to search for the English words with which to describe what I found in my imagination.

I therefore had to reject the notion, implicit in the puritan tradition, that the translator must never impose anything of his own on his translation, and must use a neutral, transparent language through which the first author's brilliance can shine. This idea of the invisible translator depends on the discredited metaphor that presents language as the clothes for the body of the thoughts and the feelings. Watts expresses it with eloquence in his introduction:

The translator should efface himself, for it is not he whom the public have come to see, but the author. To intrude one's own nineteenth-century personality into such a book as DON QUIXOTE, is an offence as gross against good manners as against art. A worse crime than this, however, is to deck the author as well as his book in your own colours – to put on him your livery – to make him speak after a set manner – to torture and twist his character, as well as his work, into conformity with some fantastic ideal in the translator's brain.

But this self-obliteration, however admirable the modest sentiments underpinning it, is impossible. All that the principles outlined by Watts can achieve is a surreptitious imposition of their own dullness on the translator and the translation, which is the worst crime of all. The translator of the *Quixote* has no option but to deck the book in his own colours and make the author speak after a set manner, and it is better if he first decides what kind of *Quixote* he wants to write. In translating every sentence he must choose between a multiplicity of possible solutions, and his choices should be governed by his vision of the whole. This ideal of his doesn't need to be fantastic, and is more likely to be a reflection of current critical opinion, if the history of *Quixote* translation is anything to go by. My *Quixote* reflects a contemporary view that is a synthesis of the two opposing readings of the past, and that makes it possible, thanks above all to the work of Sir Peter Russell,[6] to see this novel as a funny book without this recognition interfering with its status as a world classic.

One instance of the unconscious imposition by translators of their own livery on Don Quixote is, as Russell has shown, the English translation of the most famous of the titles by which Don Quixote is known, 'el Caballero de la Triste Figura'. This title originates in Part I, chapter XIX, as a jocular coinage by Sancho, after some shepherds have stoned his master and knocked many of his teeth out of his head. When Don Quixote asks his squire why he has given him this new title, the reply is: 'I was just looking at you by the light of that poor bloke's torch and the truth is that at this moment you're the sorriest sight I've ever clapped eyes on. It must be because of being tired after your fight, or else losing all those teeth.' But Don Quixote disregards Sancho's explanation and accepts his new title as an appropriately lofty expression of his noble suffering, a heroic epithet rooted in the long and glorious tradition of the knights errant of olden days. Translators have decided that this ambiguity is untranslatable and have suppressed the joke: the early translators give us Sancho's jocular meaning, 'Ill-favoured Face' and 'Rueful Countenance'; and later translators, under Romantic influence, give us Don Quixote's solemn, heroic meaning, 'Sorrowful Figure', 'Sad Countenance', doubly unfortunate because it puts literary language into the mouth of an illiterate rustic. Yet 'The Knight of the Sad Countenance' is what has stuck in people's minds, a telling example of the power of translators: two badly translated words have perpetuated the false Romantic image of Don Quixote in the English-speaking world throughout the twentieth century.

To write my English *Quixote* I also decided that I must free myself from the insidious influence of the conventionally literary language of most nineteenth-century and twentieth-century English versions of the great novel, and use modern English, just as Cervantes had used the Spanish of his own day, not only in dialogues but in the narration. If my Quixote and my Sancho were to speak with living voices they had to use the varieties of contemporary spoken English that men of their age and background would use today, except where, for purposes of parody, Cervantes wrote a Spanish that was already archaic at the beginning of the seventeenth century.

It's absurd, for example, to have Sancho address his master as 'Your Grace' or 'Your Worship', literal renderings of the 'vuestra merced' that he always says in the original. Sancho uses this form because it was inconceivable for a servant to address his master in any other way. In the Spanish of the early seventeenth century there is no hint of archaism about it. To make Sancho employ those archaic English forms is to ensure that he's born dead; the same is true, for the same reason, when Quixote is made to call Sancho 'thou', as a translation of the 'tú' that he uses except when he is angry with him and moves into the more distanced 'vos'. The only form of address available in modern English to translate 'vuestra merced', 'tú' and 'vos' is 'you', and the different degrees of respect and familiarity expressed by the three Spanish terms must be conveyed in other ways.

Yet Cervantes's text imposes limits on modernization. It's impossible to prevent some of its non-modern features from seeping through into any faithful translation. One example of this is its narrative redundancy.

All narration contains redundancy, as does all language, since neither the conditions of reception nor the human memory is perfect. *Don Quixote*'s redundancy is, however, like that of other narrative texts of its period, more extensive than in modern novels. In part it reflects the rhetorical practice of those times. It may also be that with an extra four hundred years of accumulated novel-reading experience we need less help to follow the narrative thread than Cervantes's first readers did. It's also true that Cervantes wrote his novel with a listening audience in mind; there's more interference in oral reception than in visual reception, so the redundancy must be greater. Pleonasm is an insistent stylistic feature of this novel, most often taking the form of pairs of synonyms. Recapitulations are also more frequent and insistent in the *Quixote* than in modern narratives. Although the translator can do something to reduce the intrusiveness of the synonymous pairs and the recapitulations, he can't eliminate them and be true to Cervantes's text.

So I couldn't be consistent, and totally modernize the *Quixote*. Nor would it have been desirable to do so. Any translated literary work ought to retain marks of its origins, of its otherness in time and in space, of its historicity and its foreignness. Some of the unusualness to a modern ear of, for example, this novel's oaths and insults and its expressions of courtesy needs to be retained: it would be inappropriate to reduce the rich variety of religious and parental references in the characters' swearing to the unimaginative, repetitive scatology and sexuality of contemporary English expletives, or to turn graceful seventeenth-century courtesy into twentieth-century callowness. And many of *Don Quixote*'s themes and motifs are inescapably old-fashioned: there's no modernizing its concern with rank and with family status, or with feminine chastity.

Another non-modern, and non-English, feature of this novel is its many long and complex sentences. Now this is one aspect that it would be easy to modernize and anglicize, by dividing Cervantes's long sentences into the short ones preferred in contemporary English prose. This practice simplifies translation, and maybe makes for easier reading, but it destroys rhythms and emphases and relationships. It's wrong to take even those occasional long sentences in the *Quixote* with loose structures, and subdivide, tighten and correct them, because they are not instances of stylistic carelessness but examples of Cervantes's masterly creation of realistic dialogue: his amused observation of the deleterious effects of natural verbosity, or of passionate interest in the subject under discussion, on the speaker's grammar. One of Cervantes's many innovations is his exploitation of linguistic register to give all characters, even those who make the briefest of appearances, their own distinctive voices.

Chopping up the other kind of long sentence, the one formed with meticulous precision, is equally mistaken. Such syntactical structures are also projections of mental structures, and in particular of *discreción*, central to the value-system underlying the *Quixote* and much seventeenth-century Spanish thought. *Discreción* is manifested in speech in the ability to express profound and complex concepts in an appropriately complicated yet lucid manner, conveying a sense of the multiple relationships between them. Dividing a far-ranging sentence of this kind into a succession of simple short sentences overlooks this important fact underpinning the formal elegance.

So the translation of *Don Quixote* does turn out to be logically impossible, after all. The translator must both make his text modern and keep it old, make it English and keep it Spanish. There can be no coherence or consistency. But this doesn't matter. All creative literature exists as a defiance of rational logic. There's nothing more illogical or irrational than a metaphor, saying that something is something else.

Translation is only impossible as any worthwhile enterprise is impossible: impossible to perform with the perfection that we desire. What translators must do, like modern knights errant, is to come as close as we can to the impossible goal.

Notes

1. *The History of the Valorous and Wittie Knight-Errant, Don Quixote of the Mancha*, trans. Thomas Shelton (London, 1612) (Part I); *The History of Don Quichote* (London, 1620) (Parts I and II); *The History of the Most Renowned Don Quixote de la Mancha and his Trusty Squire Sancho Panza*, trans. John Philips (London, 1687); *The History of the Renown'd Don Quixote de la Mancha*, trans. Peter Motteux (London, 1712); *The History and Adventures of the Renowned Don Quixote*, trans. Tobias Smollet (London, 1755).

2. *The Life and Exploits of the Ingenious Gentleman Don Quixote de la Mancha*, trans. Charles Jervis (London, 1742).

3. In *The Romantic Approach to 'Don Quixote'* (Cambridge, 1978).

4. *The Ingenious Knight Don Quixote de la Mancha*, trans. Alexander J. Duffield (London, 1881); *The Ingenious Gentleman Don Quixote de la Mancha*, trans. John Ormsby (London, 1885); *The Ingenious Gentleman Don Quixote of La Mancha*, trans. Henry Edward Watts (London, 1888).

5. *The Ingenious Gentleman Don Quixote de la Mancha*, trans. Samuel Putnam (New York, 1949); *The Adventures of Don Quixote*, trans. J. M. Cohen (Harmondsworth, 1950); *Don Quixote of La Mancha*, trans. Walter Starkie (New York, 1964); *The History of that Ingenious Gentleman Don Quijote de la Mancha*, trans. Burton Raffel (New York, 1995).

6. P. E. Russell, 'Don Quixote as a Funny Book', *Modern Language Review* (1969); *Cervantes* (Oxford and New York, 1985).

FURTHER READING

I have only given a brief survey of Cervantes's life and works, because others have provided admirable accounts. Here is a list of some of the most useful recent books in English.

Byron, W., *Cervantes: A Biography* (New York, 1978)

Close, Anthony, *The Romantic Approach to 'Don Quixote'* (Cambridge, 1978)

——, Cervantes, 'Don Quixote' (Cambridge, 1990)

El Saffar, Ruth, *Distance and Control in 'Don Quixote': A Study in Narrative Technique* (Chapel Hill, NC, 1975)

——, (ed.), *Critical Essays on Cervantes* (Boston, Mass., 1986)

Johnson, Carroll B., *'Don Quixote' – The Quest for Modern Fiction* (Boston, Mass., 1990)

McKendrick, Mulveena, *Cervantes* (Boston, Mass., 1980)

Martínez Bonati, Félix, *'Don Quixote' and the Poetics of the Novel* (Ithaca, NY and London, 1992)

Murillo, L. A., *A Critical Introduction to 'Don Quixote'* (New York, 1988)

Nelson, Jr., L. (ed.), *Cervantes: A Collection of Critical Essays* (Englewood Cliffs, NJ, 1969)

Parr, James A., *'Don Quixote': An Anatomy of Subversive Discourse* (Newark, Del., 1988)

Predmore, Richard L., *The World of 'Don Quixote'* (Cambridge, Mass., 1967)

——, *Cervantes* (New York, 1973)

Riley, E. C., *'Don Quixote'* (London, 1986)

—, *Cervantes's Theory of the Novel* (Oxford, 1962)

Russell, P. E., *Cervantes* (Oxford and New York, 1985)

Williamson, Edwin, *The Half-Way House of Fiction. 'Don Quixote' and Arthurian Romance* (Oxford, 1984)

ACKNOWLEDGEMENTS

Thanks, from the bottom of my heart, to Tita Rutherford, to whom this translation is dedicated, for your wifely forbearance; to Peter Russell, because you showed me, and so many others, how to enjoy *Don Quixote*; to Peter Carter, because you showed me how to write a novel; a Ramón, Maruja e Pilar Cancio, pola sombra da vosa figueira e mais pola luz da vosa amizade; to Liz Kendall, David Longrigg, Ian Michael, Víctor Rodríguez Gesto, Laura Rutherford, Maruxa Rutherford, Rosa Rutherford, Xoana Rutherford, Janette Swain and Ron Truman, for all your kind help; to the legion of *Don Quixote* scholars, who made it easy to write the explanatory notes; to my fellow translators John Ormsby and Henry Watts, for many useful suggestions; to all the friends and colleagues who unconsciously contributed so much to the development of the characters' voices; to the Universities of a Coruña, Cork and Oxford, and in particular to Antonio Raúl de Toro Santos, Adolfo Luis Soto Vázquez, Terence O'Reilly, David Mackenzie, Ian Michael and Colin Thompson, for giving me audiences on which to try out my ideas; to the University of Oxford and The Queen's College, Oxford, for allowing me the sabbatical leave without which I could not have completed the translation; to Paul Keegan and Penguin Books, for giving me the enormous privilege of being a translator of *Don Quixote*; and to Don Quixote and Sancho Panza, whose ebullient company kept my spirits high throughout this long, long pilgrimage.

JOHN RUTHERFORD
Ribadeo (Galicia) and Oxford (England)
March 1999

CHRONOLOGY

1573	Takes part in a military expedition against Tunis
1575	Returning to Madrid with his brother Rodrigo by sea, is captured by Barbary pirates and sold into slavery in Algiers
1576	Tries to escape from prison Death of Venetian painter Titian
1577	Second attempted escape His brother Rodrigo is ransomed Birth of Flemish painter Rubens
1578	Third attempted escape
1579	Fourth attempted escape First permanent theatre in Madrid, the Corral de la Cruz, opens
1580	Ransomed for 500 ducats paid by his family and by Trinitarian monks, returns to Madrid Montaigne, *Essays* published
1581	Travels with Philip II's entourage to Portugal, newly annexed by Spain
1582	Death of St Teresa of Avila
1583	Sir Walter Raleigh's expedition to Virginia
1584	Marries Catalina de Salazar in Esquivias, La Mancha Illegitimate daughter, Isabel de Saavedra, born
1585	*La Galatea*, a pastoral romance, published Cervantes sells two plays (both now lost) Death of his father
1587	Appointed king's purchasing agent in Andalusia, responsible for provisioning the Armada against England
1588	El Greco paints the *Burial of the Count of Orgaz* Defeat of Spanish Armada
1590	Unsuccessfully petitions Council of the Indies for post in the West Indies Adds Saavedra to surname
1592	Charged with fraud, he is briefly jailed, but later cleared Signs contract to write six plays at fifty ducats apiece
1593	Death of his mother

1594	Briefly in Madrid, then returns to Andalusia as a tax collector
1595	Wins first prize in a poetry contest in Zaragoza
1597–8	Spends several months in prison in Seville, on account of discrepancies in his tax accounts; likely that he conceives *Don Quixote* during imprisonment
1598	Death of Philip II and accession of Philip III
1599	Birth of painter Velázquez
	The Globe playhouse opens in London
1600	Birth of dramatist Calderón de la Barca
1603	Death of Elizabeth I
1604	Cervantes and his family move to Valladolid, briefly the capital of Spain
	Finishes writing *Don Quixote* (Part I)
1605	*Don Quixote* (Part I) published
1606	Cervantes and family return to Madrid
1612	Thomas Shelton publishes the first English translation of *Don Quixote* in London
1613	*The Exemplary Novels*, a collection of short stories, published
1614	*The Journey to Parnassus*, a long allegorical poem, published
	The 'false' *Don Quixote II* appears, under the name of Alonso Fernández de Avellaneda
	The first French translation of *Don Quixote*, by Césare Oudin, published in Paris
1615	Cervantes published *Don Quixote II* and *Eight Plays and Eight Interludes*
1616	Finishes writing novel *The Trials of Persiles and Sigismunda*
	Death of Cervantes in Madrid
	Death of Shakespeare
1617	*The Trials of Persiles and Sigismunda* published posthumously

A NOTE ON THE TEXT

This translation follows the text of the first edition (Juan de la Cuesta, Madrid, 1604–5), as presented in the useful modern edition by Luis Andrés Murillo (Clásicos Castalia: Madrid, 1978) – except in the treatment of the narrations of the loss and of the recovery of Sancho's donkey. These passages were omitted from the first edition, through the oversight of either Cervantes or the printers, so that the reader suddenly finds Sancho without his donkey, and later in possession of it again, without any explanations. In Cuesta's second edition (1605), the loss and the recovery are inserted, in chapters XXIII and XXX respectively, but the former is the wrong place, because Sancho continues in possession of his donkey for another two chapters. So following Juan Eugenio Hartzenbusch's edition (Rivadeneyra: Argamasilla de Alba, 1863), I have, like several modern editors, inserted the loss where it belongs, in chapter XXV.

There are many other less important inconsistencies in the early edition. Some chapter headings, for example, don't belong to the chapters that they precede. I have left all these, without comment, for readers to spot and ponder on for themselves. Some critics think that they could be one of the games that Cervantes enjoys playing with his readers.

The original, in common with most books of the period, has hardly any paragraphing within chapters, so this has been my own work, often coinciding with Murillo's decisions.

The 1604–5 *Don Quixote* is divided into four parts (Cuesta's 1615 text was presented as Part II, but is not included in this volume. Occasional references to Part II in the notes refer to the 1615 text.) This translation does not include the formal dedication, which seems not to have been Cervantes's work.

Just before the Penguin Classics edition went to press, the critical edition directed by Francisco Rico (Barcelona: Instituto Cervantes, Crítica, 1998) became available, and its informative footnotes were used to make some important corrections.

The Ingenious Hidalgo
DON QUIXOTE
de la Mancha,
Part I

PROLOGUE

Idle reader: I don't have to swear any oaths to persuade you that I should like this book, since it is the son of my brain, to be the most beautiful, elegant and intelligent book imaginable. But I couldn't go against the order of nature, according to which like gives birth to like. And to what can my barren and ill-cultivated mind give birth except the history of a dry, shrivelled child, whimsical and full of extravagant fancies that nobody else has ever imagined – a child born, after all, in prison, where every discomfort has its seat and every dismal sound its habitation? Tranquillity, peaceful surroundings, the pleasures of the countryside, the serenity of the skies, the murmuring of the springs and the quietude of the spirit – these are the things that encourage even the most barren muses to become fertile and bring forth a progeny to fill the world with wonder and delight.

It can happen that a man has an ugly, charmless son, and his love blindfolds him to prevent him from seeing the child's defects: on the contrary, he regards them as gifts and graces, and describes them to his friends as examples of wit and cleverness. But although I seem like Don Quixote's father, I am his stepfather, and I don't want to drift with the current of custom, or beg you almost with tears in my eyes, as others do, dearest reader, to forgive or excuse the defects that you see in this my son; and you are neither his relative nor his friend, you have your own soul in your own body, and your own free will like anybody else, and you are sitting in your own home, where you are the lord and master just as much as the king is of his taxes, and you know that common saying, 'Under my cloak a fig for the king.' All of which exempts and frees you from every respect and obligation, and so you can say whatever you like about this history, without any fear of being attacked for a hostile judgement or rewarded for a favourable one.

I'd have liked to give it to you plain and naked, undecorated by any prologue or the endless succession of sonnets, epigrams and eulogies that are usually put at the beginnings of books. Because I can tell you that, although it was quite an effort to write the book, producing this preface that you're now reading was far worse. Many times I picked up my pen to write it, and as many times I put it down again because I didn't know what to say; and once when I was in this quandary, with the paper in front of me, the pen behind my ear, my elbow on the desk and my cheek in my hand, wondering what I could write, a friend of mine burst in, a lively and clever man who, on seeing me so thoughtful, asked me the reason, and I didn't keep anything from him but said that I was thinking about the prologue that I had to write for the history of Don Quixote, and that it had reduced me to such a state that I didn't want to write it at all, still less publish the exploits of this noble knight.

'Because how do you expect me not to be worried about the opinion of that ancient legislator called the general public when he sees that after all this time sleeping in the silence of oblivion, and burdened by the years as I am, I'm coming out with a book as dry as esparto grass, devoid of inventiveness, feeble in style, poor in ideas and lacking all erudition and instruction, without any marginalia or endnotes, unlike other books I see that, even though they are fictional and not about religious subjects, are so crammed with maxims from Aristotle, Plato and the whole herd of philosophers that they amaze their readers, who consider the authors to be well-read, erudite and eloquent men? And when they quote the Holy Scriptures! Anyone would take them for no less than so many St Thomases[1] and other doctors of the Church; and here they maintain such an ingenious decorum that having depicted a dissolute lover on one line they provide on the next a little Christian sermon, a pleasure and a treat to hear or read. There won't be any of this in my book, because I haven't anything to put in the margins or any notes for the end, still less do I know what authors I have followed in my text so as to list them at the beginning, as others do, in alphabetical order beginning with Aristotle and finishing with Xenophon and Zoilus or Zeuxis,[2] even though one was a slanderer and the other a painter. My book will also lack sonnets at the beginning, or at least sonnets whose authors are dukes, marquises, counts, bishops, ladies or famous poets; though if I asked two or three tradesmen friends of mine, I'm sure they'd let me have some, every bit as good as those written by the best-known poets in this Spain of ours. In short, my dear friend,' I continued, 'I have decided that Don Quixote shall remain buried in his archives in La Mancha until heaven provides someone to adorn him with all these attributes that he lacks – I'm not up to it, because of my inadequacy and my scanty learning, and because I'm naturally lazy and disinclined to go hunting for authors to say for me what I know how to say without them. This is why I was so perplexed and distraught when you arrived, my friend: there is justification enough for it in what I've just told you.'

When he heard this my friend slapped his forehead, burst out laughing, and said:

'Good God, my dear fellow, you've just corrected a misconception I've been labouring under all this time I've known you, considering you to be sensible and judicious in everything you do. But now I can see you're as far from being that as the heavens are from the earth. How can matters that are so trivial and easy to remedy have the power to engross and perplex a mind as mature as yours, accustomed as it is to demolishing far greater difficulties? I assure you this isn't caused by any lack of ability on your part, but by an excess of mental indolence. Do you want to find out whether I'm telling you the truth? Well, pay attention, and you'll see how in the twinkling of an eye I destroy all your problems and remedy all those deficiencies that, you say, are perplexing you and discouraging you from publishing the history of your famous Don Quixote, the light and mirror of all knight-errantry.'

'Tell me,' I replied once I'd heard him out, 'how do you intend to fill the vacuum of my anxiety and turn the chaos of my confusion into clarity?'

To which he replied:

'Your first problem, about the sonnets, epigrams and eulogies written by important and titled people that you lack for the beginning of the book, can be remedied if you take the trouble to write them yourself and then christen them and give them whatever names you like, fathering them on Prester John of the Indies, or the Emperor of Trebizond,³ of both of whom I know there's evidence that they were famous poets; and even supposing that they weren't, and some pedants and academics start their backbiting and their nit-picking about whether this is true or not, you mustn't care a hoot about that, because even if they do find out that you were telling lies they aren't going to cut off the hand with which you wrote them down. As for references in the margins to the books and authors from whom you take the sayings and maxims that you include in your history, all you have to do is to stick in a few relevant bits of Latin that you know by heart, or at least that you can look up without too much trouble, such as, when you're writing about freedom and captivity:

Non bene pro toto libertas venditur auro.[4]

And then, in the margin, you mention Horace or whoever it was that said it. If you're dealing with the power of death, you can trot out:

Pallida mors aequo pulsat pede pauperum tabernas,
Regumque turres.[5]

If you're talking about the friendship and love that God tells us to feel for our enemies, go straight for Holy Scripture, which you can do if you take just a little care, and quote the words of God himself, no less: Ego autem dico vobis: diligite inimicos vestros.[6] If you're dealing with evil thoughts, go for the Gospel: De corde exeunt cogitationes malae.[7] If your subject is the fickleness of friends, there's always Cato, ready with his distich:

Donec eris felix, multos numerabis amicos,
Tempora si fuerint nubila, solus eris.[8]

And with these scraps of Latin and other similar ones you'll be taken for a scholar, at least; and that brings no little honour and profit nowadays.

'As for providing endnotes, you can easily do it like this: if you include a giant in your book, make him Goliath, and this alone, which will hardly be any trouble for you, will give you a splendid endnote, because you will be able to say: "The giant Golias, or Goliath, was a Philistine whom the shepherd David slew with a stone from his sling, in the vale of the terebinth, according to what is narrated in the Book of Kings," in the chapter where you'll find it written.[9] After that, to show that you're erudite in the humanities and a cosmographer, you should contrive to name the River Tagus in your history, and there you have another fine endnote: "The River Tagus was so called by a Spanish king; it has its source in such-and-such a place, and it flows into the Atlantic Ocean, kissing the walls of the famous city of Lisbon, and it is said to have sand of gold, etc." If you deal with robbers, I'll tell you the story of Cacus,[10] which I know by heart; if it's whores, go to the Bishop of Mondoñedo and he'll lend you Lamia, Laida and Flora,[11] and this particular endnote will bring you great credit; if it's cruel women, Ovid will let you have Medea; if it's sorceresses and witches, Homer has Calypso and Virgil has Circe;[12] if it's valiant captains, Julius Caesar will lend you himself in his *Commentaries*, and Plutarch will give you a thousand Alexanders.[13] If love is your subject, with the slightest smattering of Italian you will find Leone Ebreo gives you full measure.[14] And if you don't want to go wandering in foreign parts, here at home you have Fonseca, *On the Love of God*,[15] containing everything that you and the cleverest of writers could ever want to find on the subject. In short, all you have to do is contrive to mention these names or touch on these stories in your own story, and leave it to me to provide the endnotes and marginalia; I swear by all that's holy to fill your margins, and use up reams and reams at the end of your book.

'Let us now consider the list of authors cited, which other books include and yours lacks. The remedy for this is simplicity itself, because all you have to do is look for a book listing them all from A to Z, as you say, then copy this list into your own book; and even if your deception is plain to see, this won't matter in the slightest, because you hardly need to use the authors anyway, and there could always be someone stupid enough to believe that you have used them all in this simple, straightforward story of yours. Even if it serves no other purpose, your long list will at least lend your book an instant air of authority. Besides, people aren't going to take the trouble to check whether you follow your authors or not, because they haven't anything to gain from doing so.

'What's more, unless I'm much mistaken, this book of yours doesn't need any of those features that you say it lacks, because from beginning to end it is an invective against books of chivalry – which Aristotle never dreamed of, St Basil never mentioned and Cicero[16] never came across; nor do the niceties of truth or the observations of astrology fall within the scope of its fabulous extravagances; nor are geometrical measurements of any relevance to it, or the confutation of arguments employed in rhetoric; nor is there any need for it to preach at anybody, mixing the human with the divine, a motley in which no Christian understanding should be dressed. All that has to be done is to make the best use of imitation in what one writes; and the more perfect the imitation the better the writing. And since this work of yours is only concerned to destroy the authority and influence that books of chivalry enjoy in the world and among the general public, there isn't any need to go begging maxims from philosophers, counsel from Holy Scripture, fables from poets, clauses from rhetoricians or miracles from saints, but rather to attempt, using expressive, decorous and well-ordered words in a straightforward way, to write sentences that are both harmonious and witty, depicting what is in your mind to the very best of your ability, setting out your ideas without complicating or obscuring them. You should also try to ensure that the melancholy man is moved to laughter when he reads your history, the jovial man laughs even more, the simpleton is not discouraged, the judicious marvel at its inventiveness, the serious-minded do not scorn it nor the wise fail to praise it. In short, always have as your aim the demolition of the ill-founded fabric of these books of chivalry, despised by so many and praised by many more; and if this is what you achieve, it will be no mean achievement.'

I listened in profound silence to what my friend said, and his words so stamped themselves on my mind that I accepted them without any argument and decided to use them for this prologue, in which, gentle reader, you will discover my friend's intelligence, my good fortune in finding such a counsellor at a time of such need and your relief on finding that there will be no deviousness or circumlocution in this history of the famous Don Quixote de la Mancha, reputed among all the inhabitants of the Plain of Montiel[17] to have been the chastest lover and the bravest knight ever seen in those parts for many a long year. I have no desire to extol the service I am rendering you in introducing you to such a noble and honourable knight; but I do want your thanks for making you acquainted with the famous Sancho Panza, his squire, in whom, I believe, I give you a compendium of all the squirely fun scattered throughout the whole troop of vain books of chivalry. And so may God give you health and not forget me. Farewell.

TO THE BOOK OF
DON QUIXOTE DE LA MANCHA

Urganda the Unknowable[18]

If you, O book, are duly hee —
To seek the company of pu —,
You won't be told by some prize du —
That you are but a fumbling gree —.
But if you aren't on pins and nee —
To go off into fools' posse —,
You'll no doubt see, when least expe —,
It is the wrong horse that they're ba —,
Although they will all be so fra —
To show that they're extremely cle —.

And since, of course, it's common kno —
That he who finds a tree that's lea —
Is well protected and well shie —,
So your good fortune kindly o —
In Béjar[19] a stout oak that's ro —,
And that gives princes as its a —,
And on which dukes were procrea —;
And one's a modern Alexa —,
So go henceforth to seek his sha —,
For Fortune always aids the bra —.

You will recount the sad adve —
Of a hidalgo, good and no —,
Who read during his idle mo —
And ended up mad and deme —.
Ladies and arms, loves and knights e —[20]
So made him swell with fond emo —
That, like some Orlando Furio —,
But tempered by his loving fo —,
By force of arms he went and co —

9

Fair Dulcinea del Tobo—.
        Don't print recondite illustra—
On the front page, on your fine scu—:[21]
Low cards can often win the ru—
When court cards are what all are pla—.
Be humble in your dedica—,
And you won't find some joker hoo—,
'Look, here is Álvaro de Lu—,
Look, here is Hannibal of Ca—,
Look, here is the new French King Fra—,
Complaining that Dame Fortune's stu—.'[22]
        Since it was not the will of Hea—
That you should have the erudi—
Of that wise negro Juan Lati—,[23]
You must avoid Latin expre—.
So don't you try to be too cle—
Or make out that you're some great thi—,
Because, with a dismissive gri—
From ear to ear, the knowing pe—
Who sees through all your bluff will mu—,
'And just who do you think you're tri—?'
        Don't go for needless complica—,
Or poke your nose in lives of o—,
Because when something's off the su—
What's wisest is to be eva—.
Those who indulge in random ja—
Will get a dose of their own me—,
But you must devote all your e—
To conquering renown and ho—,
For he who publishes his no—
Will leave it in this world for e—.
        You must remember that it's cra—,
If a greenhouse is your dwe—,
To go and pick up stones and pe—
And throw them at your next-door nei—.
The wise man should be most painsta—

And should proceed very discree—
In all the works that he relea—
For he whose fictional crea—
Are for young ladies' entertai—
Writes without any rhyme or rea—

Amadis of Gaul, to Don Quixote de la Mancha

SONNET

O you who lived the life of deep distress
I lived, far from my love and in disgrace,
Reduced to penitence from happiness,
Upon the Peña Pobre's rugged face;[24]
    O you, whose drink flowed freely from within
The salty reservoir behind your eyes,
And who scorned silver, pewter, plate and tin,
To eat on earth the food that earth supplies:
    Live on, secure that while the ages last
– At least, so long as that brave charioteer
Apollo drives his steeds in the fourth sphere[25] –
Your clear renown for courage must stand fast.
Your land in all lands will as first be known,
Your learned author stand unique, alone.

Sir Belianis of Greece,[26] *to Don Quixote de la Mancha*

SONNET

I cut and thrust and hacked and meddled more
Than all of chivalry's most valiant knights,
Was brave and proud and skilled in arts of war,
And set a hundred thousand wrongs to rights.
    I left my deeds to perpetuity;
In courtly games of love I was no fool;
The hugest giant was a dwarf for me;
And I obeyed the duel's every rule.

I made Dame Fortune grovel at my feet,
And my control, by calculating skill,
Of Opportunity was so complete
I dragged her by the forelock at my will.
But, though my luck soared up to highest space,
I'd love, O Quixote, to be in your place.

The Lady Oriana,[27] to Dulcinea del Toboso

SONNET

O Dulcinea, I so wish I could
Transport, and thereby banish all this care,
My Miraflores to the neighbourhood
Of El Toboso, moving London there;
     And then adorn my body and my soul
With what you wear, and what you long for, too;
And watch the famous knight whose heart you stole
Win some stupendous battle, thanks to you.
     And then if I could chastely take my flight
From my Sir Amadis, as you have done
From your Don Quixote, courteous and polite,
And so I'd envied be, and envy none:
Be sad no more – be happy without measure:
Not pay the bill, but still have all the pleasure.

Gandalín, Amadis of Gaul's Squire, to Sancho Panza, Don Quixote's Squire

SONNET

Hail, famous hero! It was Fortune's will
That you should be a squire; so she contrived
To shape her plans with sympathetic skill,
And you, triumphant and unharmed, survived.
     No longer does the errant enterprise
Regard with scorn the sickle and the spade;

To haughty knights who'd trample on the skies
Your unassuming modesty's put paid.
    I envy you your donkey and your name;
I envy you your food and wine galore
In saddle-bags that pregnantly proclaim
Your providence, O Panza. Hail once more!
Our Spanish Ovid's homage is unique:
To kiss your hand and let you cuff his cheek.

From the Witty Poet Streakybacon to Sancho Panza and Rocinante

    I am the squire called Sancho Pa—;
I took French leave, and scarpered pre—
To live a life of indepe—
Far from Don Quixote de la Ma—;
For Villadiego, though so gua—,
Would summarize all his state rea—
In the convenience of retrea—,
As is made clear in *Celesti*—,
A book than which none is divi—,[28]
Though of the human so revea—.

TO ROCINANTE

    I'm Rocinante, the world-fa—,
Great grandson of the great Babie—,[29]
Who, for my sins of macile—,
Into Don Quixote's power was ta—.
When last wins, I win all the ra—;
But when it mattered, I moved sma—:
I never missed my feed of ba—,
For this I learned from Lazari—
When all that wine the lad was stea—
And gave the straw to his blind ma—.[30]

Orlando Furioso to Don Quixote de la Mancha

SONNET

Among a thousand Peers you are our peer;
Though you are not a Peer, peer have you none,
Nor is there room for one while you are near,
Unvanquished victor, great unconquered one!

I, Quixote, am Orlando, one who, harried
By sweet Angelica,[31] roamed far seas, where
To Fame's high altars as a prize I carried
What valour dull Forgetfulness could spare.

I cannot be your equal. This respect
Is owed to both your exploits and your name,
Although, like mine, your sanity's suspect.

But you will be my equal if you tame
The haughty Moor and our fierce Scythian foe:[32]
Love binds us in a fellowship of woe.

The Knight of Phoebus[33] to Don Quixote de la Mancha

SONNET

My sword is not to be compared with yours,
Phoebus of Spain, strange courtier in disguise,
Nor with your glorious arm my arm that pours
Forth rays in which the day is born and dies.

I scorned all empire, and I scorned the throne
That ruddy Orient offered me in vain,
To see once more the fair face of my own
Most lovely dawn, my dearest Claridiane.

I loved her in a rare and wondrous way,
And, absent and beset by tribulation,
I tamed hell's fiends, who cringed under my sway.

Through Dulcinea, though, your reputation,
Great Quixote, is eternally secure,
And she, through you, is famous, wise and pure.

Solisdán[34] *to Don Quixote de la Mancha*

SONNET

Although absurdities have always played
Their havoc on your poor disordered mind,
There's nobody, Don Quixote, who'll upbraid
You, sir, for being abject or unkind.

    Your deeds themselves will be your judge and jury:
You righted wrongs, you freed the galley slaves
And in a thousand beatings felt the fury
Of many a wretched crew of arrant knaves.

    And if your Dulcinea were to slight
You or to play you false in some base way
Or were not sympathetic to your plight,
Your comfort in your woe would be to say
That Sancho had no pander's arts to move her:
A fool he, callous she — and you no lover.

Dialogue between Babieca and Rocinante

SONNET

B.   Why, Rocinante, are you thin and worn?
R. Because I'm overworked and underfed.
B. Are you not given any hay or corn?
R. No. Quixote wants to starve me till I'm dead.
B.   Your manners fill me, sir, with equine shame:
    It's ass's work to strike at one's sustainer.
R. Whoever's born an ass will die the same:
    See him, an ass in love. What could be plainer?
B.   It's folly, then, to love?   *R.* It's none too bright.
B. You're metaphysical!   *R.* My belly's rumbling.
B. Complain about the squire!   *R.* Why, in this plight
    Of mine, waste time on moans and grumbling
    When both my master and that squire of his
    Are hacks as much as Rocinante is?

CHAPTER I

❊

Concerning the famous hidalgo Don Quixote de la Mancha's position, character and way of life

In a village in La Mancha, the name of which I cannot quite recall, there lived not long ago one of those country gentlemen or hidalgos who keep a lance in a rack, an ancient leather shield, a scrawny hack and a greyhound for coursing. A midday stew with rather more shin of beef than leg of lamb, the leftovers for supper most nights, lardy eggs on Saturdays, lentil broth on Fridays and an occasional pigeon as a Sunday treat ate up three-quarters of his income. The rest went on a cape of black broadcloth, with breeches of velvet and slippers to match for holy days, and on weekdays he walked proudly in the finest homespun. He maintained a housekeeper the wrong side of forty, a niece the right side of twenty and a jack of all trades who was as good at saddling the nag as at plying the pruning shears. Our hidalgo himself was nearly fifty; he had a robust constitution, dried-up flesh and a withered face, and he was an early riser and a keen huntsman. His surname's said to have been Quixada, or Quesada (as if he were a jawbone, or a cheesecake): concerning this detail there's some discrepancy among the authors who have written on the subject, although a credible conjecture does suggest he might have been a plaintive Quexana. But this doesn't matter much, as far as our story's concerned, provided that the narrator doesn't stray one inch from the truth.

Now you must understand that during his idle moments (which accounted for most of the year) this hidalgo took to reading books of chivalry with such relish and enthusiasm that he almost forgot about his hunting and even running his property, and his foolish curiosity reached such extremes that he sold acres of arable land to buy these books of chivalry, and took home as many of them as he could find;[1] he liked none of them so much as those by the famous Feliciano de Silva,[2] because the brilliance of the prose and all that intricate language seemed a treasure to him, never more so than when he was reading those amorous compliments and challenges delivered by letter, in which he often found: 'The reason for the unreason to which my reason is subjected, so weakens my reason that I have reason to complain of your beauty.' And also when he read: '. . . the lofty heavens which with their stars divinely fortify you in your divinity, and make you meritorious of the merits merited by your greatness.' Such subtleties used to drive the poor gentleman to distraction, and he would rack his brains trying to understand it all and unravel its meaning, something that Aristotle himself wouldn't have been capable of doing even if he'd come back to life for this purpose alone. He wasn't very happy about the wounds that Sir Belianis kept on inflicting and receiving, because he imagined that, however skilful the doctors who treated him, his face and body must have been covered with gashes and scars. But, in spite of all that, he commended the author for ending his book with that promise of endless adventure, and often felt the urge to take up his quill and bring the story to a proper conclusion, as is promised there; and no doubt he'd have done so, and with success too, if other more important and insistent preoccupations hadn't prevented him. He had frequent arguments with the village priest (a learned man – a Sigüenza graduate no less) about which had been the better knight errant, Palmerin of England[3] or Amadis of Gaul; but Master Nicolás, the village barber, argued that neither of them could hold a candle to the Knight of Phoebus, and that if anyone at all could be compared to him it was Don Galaor, Amadis of Gaul's brother, because there was no emergency he couldn't cope with: he wasn't one of your pernickety knights, nor was he such a blubberer as his brother, and he was every bit his equal as far as courage was concerned.

In short, our hidalgo was soon so absorbed in these books that his nights were spent reading from dusk till dawn, and his days from dawn till dusk, until the lack of sleep and the excess of reading withered his brain, and he went mad. Everything he read in his books took possession of his imagination: enchantments, fights, battles, challenges, wounds, sweet nothings, love affairs, storms and impossible absurdities. The idea that this whole fabric of famous fabrications was real so established itself in his mind that no history in the world was truer for him. He would declare that El Cid, Ruy Díaz, had been an excellent knight, but that he couldn't be compared to the Knight of the Burning Sword,[4] who with just one back-stroke had split two fierce and enormous giants clean down the middle. He felt happier about Bernardo del Carpio, because he'd slain Roland the Enchanted at Roncesvalles, by the same method used by Hercules when he suffocated Antaeus, the son of Earth – with a bear-hug.[5] He was full of praise for the giant Morgante because, despite belonging to a proud and insolent breed, he alone was affable and well-mannered.[6] But his greatest favourite was Reynald of Montalban,[7] most of all when he saw him sallying forth from his castle and plundering all those he met, and when in foreign parts he stole that image of Muhammad made of solid gold, as his history records. He'd have given his housekeeper, and even his niece into the bargain, to trample the traitor Ganelon in the dust.[8]

And so, by now quite insane, he conceived the strangest notion that ever took shape in a madman's head, considering it desirable and necessary, both for the increase of his honour and for the common good, to become a knight errant, and to travel about the world with his armour and his arms and his horse in search of adventures, and to practise all those activities that he knew from his books were practised by knights errant, redressing all kinds of grievances, and exposing himself to perils and dangers that he would overcome and thus gain eternal fame and renown. The poor man could already see himself being crowned Emperor of Trebizond, at the very least, through the might of his arm; and so, possessed by these delightful thoughts and carried away by the strange pleasure that he derived from them, he hastened to put into practice what he so desired.

His first step was to clean a suit of armour that had belonged to his forefathers and that, covered in rust and mould, had been standing forgotten in a corner for centuries. He scoured and mended it as best he could; yet he realized that it had one important defect, which was that the headpiece was not a complete helmet but just a simple steel cap; he was ingenious enough, however, to overcome this problem, constructing out of cardboard something resembling a visor and face-guard which, once inserted into the steel cap, gave it the appearance of a full helmet. It's true that, to test its strength and find out whether it could safely be exposed to attack, he drew his sword and dealt it two blows, with the first of which he destroyed in a second what it had taken him a week to create. He couldn't help being concerned about the ease with which he'd shattered it, and to guard against this danger he reconstructed it, fixing some iron bars on the inside, which reassured him about its strength; and, preferring not to carry out any further tests, he deemed and pronounced it a most excellent visored helmet.

Then he went to visit his nag, and although it had more corns than a barleyfield and more wrong with it than Gonella's horse, which *tantum pellis et ossa fuit*,[9] it seemed to him that neither Alexander's Bucephalus nor the Cid's Babieca was its equal. He spent four days considering what name to give the nag; for (he told himself) it wasn't fitting that the horse of such a famous knight errant, and such a fine horse in its own right, too, shouldn't have some name of eminence; and so he tried to find one that would express both what it had been before it became a knight's horse and what it was now, for it was appropriate that, since its master had changed his rank, it too should change its name, and acquire a famous and much-trumpeted one, as suited the new order and new way of life he professed. And so, after a long succession of names that he invented, eliminated and struck out, added, deleted and remade in his mind and in his imagination, he finally decided to call it *Rocinante*, that is, *Hackafore*, a name which, in his opinion, was lofty and sonorous and expressed what the creature had been when it was a humble hack, before it became what it was now – the first and foremost of all the hacks in the world.

Having given his horse a name, and one so much to his liking, he decided to give himself a name as well, and this problem kept him busy for another eight days, at the end of which he decided to call himself *Don Quixote*, that is, *Sir Thighpiece*, from which, as has already been observed, the authors of this most true history concluded that his surname must have been Quixada, and not Quesada as others had affirmed. Yet remembering that brave Amadis hadn't been content to call himself Amadis alone, but had added the name of his kingdom and homeland, to make it famous, and had styled himself Amadis of Gaul, so Don Quixote, as a worthy knight, decided to add his own country to his name and call himself *Don Quixote de la Mancha*, by doing which, in his opinion, he declared in a most vivid manner both his lineage and his homeland, and honoured the latter by taking it as his surname.

Having, then, cleaned his armour, turned his steel cap into a visored helmet, baptized his nag and confirmed himself, he realized that the only remaining task was to find a lady of whom he could be enamoured; for a knight errant without a lady-love is a tree without leaves or fruit, a body without a soul. He said to himself:

'If, for my wicked sins or my good fortune, I encounter some giant, as knights errant usually do, and I dash him down in single combat, or cleave him asunder, or, in short, defeat and vanquish him, will it not be proper to have someone to whom I can send him as a tribute, so that he can come before my sweet lady and fall to his knees and say in humble tones of submission: "I, my lady, am the giant Caraculiambro,[10] the Lord of the Isle of Malindrania, vanquished in single combat by the never sufficiently praised knight Don Quixote de la Mancha, who has commanded me to present myself before Your Highness so that Your Highness may dispose of me as you will"?'

Oh my, how our worthy knight rejoiced once he'd spoken these words – even more, once he'd found someone he could call his lady! The fact was – or so it is generally believed – that in a nearby village there lived a good-looking peasant girl, with whom he'd once been in love (although it appears that she was never aware of this love, about which he never told her). She was called Aldonza Lorenzo, and this was the woman upon whom it seemed appropriate to confer the title of the lady of his thoughts; and seeking a name with some affinity with his own, which would also suggest the name of a princess and a fine lady, he decided to call her *Dulcinea del Toboso*, because she was a native of El Toboso: a name that, in his opinion, was musical and magical and meaningful, like all the other names he'd bestowed upon himself and his possessions.

CHAPTER II

Concerning the ingenious Don Quixote's first sally

Once he'd made these preparations he decided not to wait any longer before putting his plans into action, encouraged by the need that he believed his delay was creating in the world: so great was his determination to redress grievances, right wrongs, correct injustices, rectify abuses and fulfil obligations. And so, without telling anyone about his plans or being seen by anyone, one morning, before dawn because it was going to be one of those sweltering July days, he donned his armour, mounted Rocinante, with his ill-devised visor in place, took up his leather shield, seized his lance and rode out into the fields through the side-door in a yard wall, in raptures of joy on seeing how easy it had been to embark upon his noble enterprise. But no sooner was he outside the door than he was assailed by a terrible thought, which almost made him abandon his undertaking: he remembered that he hadn't been knighted and by the laws of chivalry shouldn't and indeed couldn't take up arms against any knight; and that even if he had been knighted, he would, as a novice, have been obliged to bear white arms, that is to say a shield without any insignia on it, until he'd won them by his own prowess. These thoughts made him waver in his plans; but, since his madness prevailed over all other considerations, he decided to have himself knighted by the first person he chanced upon, in imitation of many others who'd done the same, as he'd read in the books that had reduced him to this state. As for the white arms, he resolved to give his lance and his armour such a scouring, as soon as an opportunity arose, as to make them cleaner and whiter than ermine; and thus he calmed down and continued on his chosen way, which in reality was none other than the way his horse chose to follow, for he believed that in this consisted the essence of adventure.

As our fledgling adventurer rode along, he said to himself:

'Who can doubt but that in future times, when the true history of my famous deeds sees the light, the sage who chronicles them will, when he recounts this my first sally, so early in the morning, write in this manner: "Scarce had ruddy Apollo spread over the face of the wide and spacious earth the golden tresses of his beauteous hair, and scarce had the speckled little birds with their harmonious tongues hailed in musical and mellifluous melody the approach of rosy Aurora who, rising from her jealous husband's soft couch, disclosed herself to mortals in the portals and balconies of La Mancha's horizon, when the famous knight Don Quixote de la Mancha, quitting the slothful feathers of his bed, mounted his famous steed Rocinante and began to ride over the ancient and far-famed Plain of Montiel"?'

And it was true that this was where he was riding. And he added:

'Happy will be the age, the century will be happy, which brings to light my famous exploits, worthy to be engraved on sheets of bronze, carved on slabs of marble and painted on boards of wood as a monument for all posterity. O sage enchanter, whomsoever you may be, to whom it falls to be the chronicler of this singular history, I beg you not to overlook my good Rocinante, my eternal companion in all my travels and wanderings.'

Then he turned and said, as if he really were in love:

'O Princess Dulcinea, mistress of this hapless heart! Great injury have you done me in reproaching and dismissing me, with the cruel command not to appear in the presence of your wondrous beauty. Vouchsafe, my lady, to be mindful of this your subject heart, which suffers such sorrow for love of you.'

He strung these absurdities together with many others, all in the style of those that he'd learned from his books. This made his progress so slow, and the sun was rising so fast and becoming so hot, that his brains would have melted, if he'd had any.

He rode on almost throughout that day and nothing happened worth mentioning, which reduced him to despair because he was longing for an early encounter with someone on whom he could test the worth of his mighty arm. Some authors say that the first adventure that befell him was that of the Pass of Lápice, others claim that it was that of the windmills, but what I've been able to discover about this matter, and indeed what I've found recorded in the annals of La Mancha, is that he rode on throughout that day, and that at nightfall both he and his nag were exhausted and half dead from starvation; and that, looking all around to see if he could spot some castle or shepherds' hut where they might retire and find some remedy for their great hunger and dire want, he caught sight of an inn not far from the road along which he was travelling, which was as if he had seen a star leading him not just to the portals but to the very palace of his redemption. He quickened his pace, and he reached the inn as night was falling.

Sitting by the inn door there happened to be two young women, of the sort known as ladies of easy virtue, on their way to Seville with some muleteers who'd chanced to break their journey that night at the inn. And since whatever our adventurer thought, saw or imagined seemed to him to be as it was in the books he'd read, as soon as he saw the inn he took it for a castle with its four towers and their spires of shining silver, complete with its drawbridge and its deep moat and all the other accessories that such castles commonly boast. He approached the inn that he took for a castle, and at a short distance from it he drew rein, waiting for some dwarf to appear upon the battlements and announce with a trumpet-blast the arrival of a knight. But finding that there was some delay, and that Rocinante was impatient to get to the stable, he rode on towards the inn door and saw the two dissolute wenches sitting there, and thought that they were two beautiful maidens or fine ladies taking their ease at the castle gate. At this point a swineherd who was gathering together some pigs (begging nobody's pardon, because that's what they're called) from a stubble field happened to sound his horn to round them up, and Don Quixote thought that his wish had been fulfilled and that a dwarf was announcing his arrival; so it was with unusual satisfaction that he reached the inn and the ladies, who, on observing the approach of a man dressed like that in armour and clutching a lance and a leather shield, started to run in terror back into the inn. But Don Quixote, conjecturing their fear from their flight, and raising his cardboard visor to reveal his dry and dusty face, addressed them with courteous demeanour and tranquil voice:

'Flee not, nor fear the least affront; for in the order of knighthood which I profess it neither belongs nor behoves to offer any such, much less to high-born maidens, as your presence testifies you to be.'

The girls had been peering at him and trying to make out his face, hidden behind the ill-made visor; but when they heard themselves called maidens, a term so much at odds with their profession, they couldn't contain their laughter, which was so hearty that Don Quixote flared up and exclaimed:

'Moderation befits the fair; furthermore, laughter which springs from a petty cause is a great folly; but I say this unto you not to grieve you nor yet to sour your disposition; for mine is none other than to serve you.'

This language, which the ladies didn't understand, together with the sorry figure cut by the knight, only redoubled their laughter and his wrath, and things would have come to a pretty pass if it hadn't been for the appearance at that moment of the innkeeper, a man who, being very fat, was very peaceable, and who on seeing such an ungainly figure, with such ill-matched equipment as the long stirrups, the lance, the leather shield and the infantryman's body-armour, was more than willing to join the maidens in their merry-making. But he was also intimidated by all these paraphernalia and, deciding to address the knight in a civil manner, he said:

'If, sir caballero, you're looking for somewhere to stay the night, you'll find plenty of everything you need here – all except a bed that is, we haven't got any of those.'

Don Quixote, observing the humility of the governor of the castle, for they were what he took the innkeeper and the inn to be, replied:

'For me, sir castellano, anything will suffice, because

> My arms are my bed-hangings,
> And my rest's the bloody fray.'[1]

The host thought that Don Quixote had called him castellano because he'd taken him for one of the Castilian conmen, whereas in reality he was an Andalusian, a prime picaroon from the Playa district of Sanlúcar,[2] no less a thief than Cacus, and no less an evildoer than any experienced page-boy, and he replied:

'In that case,

> Your bed must be the hard, hard rock,
> And your sleep to watch till day

– and that being so, you go ahead and dismount in the certainty of finding in this humble abode plenty of opportunities not to sleep for a whole year, let alone one night.'

And with these words he went and held Don Quixote's stirrup, and the knight dismounted with the greatest difficulty, not having broken his fast all day long.

He then instructed the innkeeper to take great care of his horse, for a finer steed had never eaten barley. The innkeeper looked at the animal, which didn't seem half as good as Don Quixote had claimed, and, after housing it in the stable, went back to receive orders from his guest, whom the maidens, now reconciled, were helping out of his armour. Although they'd taken off his breast and back plates, they couldn't fathom how to disengage his gorget or remove his imitation visor, tied on with green ribbons that would have to be cut, since it was impossible to undo the knots; but he would by no means consent to this, and kept his helmet on all night, making the funniest and strangest figure imaginable. As these trollops unarmed him, he, thinking they were illustrious ladies of the castle, wittily declaimed:

> 'And never sure was any knight
> So served by damsel or by dame
> As Quixote was, one happy night
> When from his village first he came:
> Maids waited on that man of might,
> Princesses on his steed, whose name . . .[3]

is Rocinante, good ladies, and mine is Don Quixote de la Mancha; for although I had intended not to discover myself until the deeds done for your benefit and service should have made me known, yet the necessity to accommodate this ancient ballad of Sir Lancelot to our present purpose has been the occasion of your knowing my name ere it were meet; but a time will come when you will command and I shall obey, and when the might of this arm will manifest the desire I have to serve you.'

The girls, who weren't used to such rhetorical flourishes, didn't answer, but just asked if he'd like a bite to eat.

'I would fain eat anything,' replied Don Quixote, 'for, by my troth, much good would it do me.'

It happened to be a Friday, so there was no food in the inn except a few helpings of what is known in Castile as *abadejo*, in Andalusia as *bacallao* and in other parts of Spain as *curadillo* – in other words the humble salt cod; but in these parts it was strangely called *truchuela*. They asked him if he'd like some of this troutling, because that was all the fish there was.

'If you have a goodly number of troutlings,' replied Don Quixote, 'they will serve me as well as a trout, because it makes no difference to me whether I am given eight separate reals or a single piece of eight. What is more, it might even be that these troutlings are like veal, which is better than beef, or like kid, which is better than goat. But whatever this fish is, let it be served; for the travails and the burden of arms cannot be borne on an empty stomach.'

A table was set at the door of the inn, where it was cooler, and the innkeeper brought a dish of inadequately soaked and worse cooked salt cod, and a loaf of bread as black and mouldy as the hidalgo's armour; and it was a source of great mirth to watch him eat because, since he was wearing his helmet and holding up the visor, he couldn't put any food into his mouth with his own hands, and somebody else had to do so for him, a task performed by one of the ladies. But when they tried to give him some drink, they found this an impossible task, and he wouldn't have drunk a drop if the innkeeper hadn't bored a hole through a length of cane and put one end into his mouth and poured the wine into the other; and Don Quixote suffered it all with great patience, so as not to allow his helmet-ribbons to be cut. In the midst of these activities a sow-gelder happened to arrive at the inn, and as he did so he sounded his pan-pipes four or five times, which convinced Don Quixote that he was indeed in some famous castle, and that he was being served to the accompaniment of music, and that the salt cod was trout, the bread baked from the whitest wheat-flour, the prostitutes fine ladies and the innkeeper the lord of the castle; and it all confirmed that his decision to sally forth had been a wise one. Yet what most bothered him was that he hadn't yet been knighted, because he knew that he couldn't lawfully embark on any adventure without first having been admitted to the order of chivalry.

CHAPTER III

✠

Which relates the amusing way in which Don Quixote had himself knighted

And so, troubled by this thought, Don Quixote made short work of his meagre lodging-house supper, and then called for the innkeeper and, shutting himself up with him in the stable, fell upon his knees before him and said:

'I shall ne'er, O valorous knight, arise from where I kneel, until your courtesy vouchsafes me a boon which I desire to beg of you and which will redound to your own praise and to the benefit of humankind.'

The innkeeper, seeing his guest at his feet and hearing such pleadings, gazed down at him in perplexity, not knowing what to do or say, and kept telling him to stand up; but he kept refusing, and the innkeeper had to promise to grant his request.

'No less did I expect from your munificence, sir,' replied Don Quixote. 'Know therefore that the boon which I have begged and which your liberality has vouchsafed me is that tomorrow you shall knight me; and tonight, in the chapel of this your castle, I will keep the vigil of arms; and tomorrow, as I have said, what I so desire shall be accomplished, so that I can legitimately roam through the four corners of the world in quest of adventures for the relief of the needy, as is the duty of chivalry and of knights errant such as I, whose desire towards such exploits is inclined.'

The innkeeper, who, as I've said, was something of a wag, and had already suspected that his guest wasn't in his right mind, found his suspicion confirmed when he heard these words and, to have something to laugh at that night, decided to humour him; so he said that he was quite right to pursue these objectives, and that such desires were natural and fitting in such a knight as he seemed to be and as his gallant presence testified; and that he himself in his younger days had followed the same honourable profession, roaming through different parts of the world in search of adventure, without omitting to visit such districts as Percheles and Islas de

Riarán in Malaga, Compás in Seville, Azoguejo in Segovia, Olivera in
Valencia, Rondilla in Granada, Playa in Sanlúcar, Potro in Cordova and
Ventillas in Toledo,[1] and many other places where he'd exercised the
dexterity of his hands and the nimbleness of his heels, doing many injuries,
wooing many widows, ruining a few maidens and swindling a few orphans,
and, in short, making himself known in most of the law courts and tribunals
in Spain; and that he'd finally retired to his castle, where he lived on his
own means and on those of others, accommodating all knights errant,
whatever their status or position, solely because of the great affection he
felt for them and so that they could share their wealth with him, to repay
him for his kindness.

He also told Don Quixote that in his castle there wasn't any chapel
where he could keep the vigil of arms, because it had been demolished to
build a new one, but he knew that in case of need vigil might be kept
anywhere, and Don Quixote could do so that night in a courtyard within
the castle; and in the morning, God willing, the proper ceremonies would
be performed to make him into a knight, so very thoroughly that no knight
in the whole wide world could be more of a knight than he.

He asked Don Quixote if he had any money on him; Don Quixote
replied that he did not have so much as a single real, because he had never
read in histories of knights errant that any of them had ever carried money.
To this the innkeeper retorted that he was deluding himself – even if it
wasn't written in the histories, because their authors had considered that
there wasn't any need to record something as obviously necessary as money
or clean shirts, that wasn't any reason to believe that they'd travelled
without supplies of both; so he could take it as true and proven that all
knights errant, of which so many books are full to overflowing, kept their
purses well lined in readiness for any eventuality, and that they also carried
shirts and small chests full of ointments for curing the wounds they received;
because there wasn't always someone available to treat them in every field
or desert where they engaged in combat and were injured, unless they had
some wise enchanter for a friend, and he came to their aid, summoning
through the air, on some cloud, a damsel or a dwarf with a flask of water
of such magical properties that, on tasting just one drop, they were instantly
cured of their wounds and injuries, as if they'd never been hurt. But, just
in case this didn't happen, the knights of old had considered it wise to see

that their squires were provided with money and other necessities such as lint and ointments to dress their wounds; and if any such knight happened not to have a squire (a most unusual occurrence), he himself would carry all these supplies in small saddle-bags that were scarcely visible, on the crupper of his steed, as if they were something else of much greater importance because, except in such circumstances, carrying saddle-bags was rather frowned upon among knights errant; and the innkeeper therefore advised Don Quixote – although he could, if he wished, command him as the godson that he was about to become – never again to travel without money and all the other supplies just mentioned, and he'd discover when he least expected it how useful they could be.

Don Quixote promised to do exactly as he'd been told, and then he was given orders to keep the vigil of arms in a large yard on one side of the inn; and he gathered his armour together and placed it on a water-trough next to a well, and, taking up his leather shield and seizing his lance, he began with stately bearing to pace back and forth in front of the trough; and as his pacing began, night was beginning to fall.

The innkeeper told everyone in the hostelry about his guest's insanity, his vigil and the knighting that he awaited. They wondered at such a strange kind of madness and went to watch him from a distance, and saw that, with a composed air, he sometimes paced to and fro and, at other times, leaning on his lance, gazed at his armour without looking away for some while. Night fell, but the moon was so bright that it competed with the source of its brightness, and every action of the novice knight could be clearly observed by all. And now one of the muleteers staying at the inn decided to water his animals, and to do so he had to remove from the trough the armour placed there by Don Quixote, who, on seeing him approach, cried out:

'O rash knight, whomsoever you may be, coming to lay hands on the armour of the most valiant knight errant who ever girded sword! Take care what you do, and touch it not, unless you wish to pay with your life for your temerity.'

The muleteer wouldn't toe the line (it would have been better for the rest of his anatomy if he had); instead, grasping the armour by its straps, he hurled it to one side. When Don Quixote saw this, he raised his eyes to heaven and, fixing his thoughts, as it seemed, on his lady Dulcinea, he said:

'Assist me, dear lady, in this first affront suffered by this breast that is enthralled to you; let not your favour and your succour abandon me in this first moment of peril.'

And with these and other similar words he dropped his leather shield, raised his lance with both hands, and dealt the muleteer so powerful a blow to the head that he fell on the ground in such a sorry state that had it been followed by another blow he wouldn't have needed a doctor to treat him. Then Don Quixote replaced his armour and continued pacing to and fro with the same composure as before. After a while another muleteer, not knowing what had happened (because the first one still lay stunned), also came to water his animals and, as he went to remove the armour from the trough, Don Quixote, without uttering a word or asking anybody for her favour, again dropped his leather shield and raised his lance, and didn't break it over the second muleteer's head but rather broke the head, into more than three pieces, because he criss-crossed it with two blows. All the people in the hostelry came running at the noise, the innkeeper among them. When Don Quixote saw them, he took up his leather shield and, with one hand on his sword, declared:

'O beauteous lady, strength and vigour of my enfeebled heart! Now is the time for you to turn the eyes of your greatness towards this your hapless knight, on the brink of so mighty an adventure.'

With this he felt so inspirited that if all the muleteers in the world had attacked him he wouldn't have retreated one inch. The wounded men's companions, seeing them in such a state, began to rain stones on Don Quixote, who fended them off with his leather shield as best he could, unwilling to move away from the water-trough and leave his armour unprotected. The innkeeper was yelling at them to let him be – he'd already told them he was a madman, and as such would go scot-free even if he killed the lot of them. Don Quixote was shouting too, even louder, calling them perfidious traitors and the lord of the castle a poltroon and a base-born knight, who allowed knights errant to be treated in such a way and who, if he had been admitted to the order of chivalry, would have been made to regret his treachery:

'But to you, vile and base rabble, I pay no heed; stone me, come, draw near, assail me as best you can, for you will soon see how you are made to pay for your folly and your insolence.'

He spoke with such vehemence and spirit that he struck fear into his assailants; and this, together with the innkeeper's arguments, persuaded them to stop, and he allowed them to remove the wounded, and continued keeping the vigil of arms, with the same composure as before.

The innkeeper wasn't amused by his guest's capers, and decided to put an end to them by giving him his wretched order of chivalry before any further calamities occurred. And so he approached him and apologized for the insolent behaviour of that rabble, about which he'd known nothing; but they had been properly punished for their impudence. He said that, as he'd mentioned before, there wasn't any chapel in the castle, and in any case there wasn't any need of one for what was left to be done; because the essence of being knighted lay in the cuff on the neck and the touch on the shoulder, according to his information about the ceremonial of the order, and all of that could be done in the middle of a field if necessary, and his guest had already fulfilled the bit about keeping the vigil of arms, because two hours of it were quite enough, and he'd been at it for over four. Don Quixote believed every word; he was there ready to obey him, and could he please expedite the process as much as possible, for if he were to be attacked again, after having been knighted, he did not intend to leave a single soul alive in the castle except those whom its lord commanded be spared and whom, out of respect for him, he would not harm.

The castellan, thus forewarned and now even more concerned, hurried away to fetch a ledger in which he kept the muleteers' accounts for straw and barley and, accompanied by a lad carrying a candle-end and by the two maidens, he came back to Don Quixote and ordered him to kneel; and, after reading for a while from his ledger, as if reciting some devout prayer, he raised his hand and cuffed him on the neck and then, with Don Quixote's own sword, gave him a handsome thwack on the shoulder, all the while muttering as if praying. And then he commanded one of the maidens to gird on the novice knight's sword, a task performed with much grace and discretion, with which she needed to be well provided so as not to burst out laughing at each stage of the ceremony; but the exploits that they'd watched him perform kept their laughter in check. As the good lady girded on his sword, she said:

'May God make you a most fortunate knight and give you good fortune in your battles.'

Don Quixote asked what was her name, so that he should thenceforth know to whom he was indebted for the favour received, because he intended to bestow upon her a share of the honour he was to win by the might of his arm. She humbly replied that her name was La Tolosa, and that she was the daughter of a cobbler from Toledo who lived near the Sancho Bienaya market stalls, and that wherever she was she'd serve him and regard him as her lord. Don Quixote replied that, for his sake and as a favour to him, she should thenceforth take the title of a lady, and call herself Doña Tolosa.[2] She promised to do so, and the other maiden buckled on his spurs; there ensued almost exactly the same dialogue as with the lady of the sword. He asked what was her name, she said it was La Molinera, because she was the daughter of an honourable miller from Antoquera, and Don Quixote also asked her to take a title, and call herself Doña Molinera, and offered her further services and favours.

Now that these unprecedented ceremonies had been performed, at top speed, Don Quixote couldn't wait to be on horseback sallying forth in search of adventures, and he saddled and mounted Rocinante and, having embraced his host, made such extraordinary statements as he thanked him for the favour of dubbing him knight that it would be impossible to do them justice in writing. The innkeeper, concerned only to be rid of his guest, replied to his rhetoric in no less high-flown although somewhat briefer terms, and was so delighted to see the back of the man that he didn't demand any payment for his stay at the inn.

CHAPTER IV

About what happened to our knight when he left the inn

It must have been about daybreak when Don Quixote left the inn, so happy, so gallant, so delighted at being a properly dubbed knight that the very girths of his horse were bursting with his joy. But remembering his host's advice about the essential supplies that he should take with him, and in particular money and shirts, he decided to return home and equip himself with them and with a squire, resolving to take into his service a neighbour, a poor farmer who had a large family but was well suited to the squirely office. With this in mind he turned Rocinante towards his home village, and the nag, half sensing its old haunts, began to trot with such zest that its hooves seemed not to touch the ground.

He hadn't gone far when he thought he could hear, coming from a dense wood on his right, faint sounds as of someone moaning, and he said:

'I thank heaven for the favour it now grants me, providing me with such an early opportunity to fulfil the duties of my profession and gather the fruit of my honourable intentions. These cries come, no doubt, from some man or woman in distress, who stands in need of my protection and assistance.'

He turned right and rode over to where he thought the sounds were coming from. A few steps into the wood he saw a mare tied by the reins to an evergreen oak, and tied to another a lad of about fifteen, naked from the waist up, and this was the one who was crying out, not without reason, because a burly farmer was flogging him with a leather belt, accompanying each blow with a word of reproof and advice:

'Keep your mouth shut and your eyes open.'

And the lad replied:

'I won't do it again, sir, by Christ who died on the Cross I swear I won't, I promise that from now on I'll take more care of the flock.'

When Don Quixote saw what was happening, he fired up and said:

'Discourteous knight: it ill becomes you to assault one who cannot defend himself; mount your steed and take up your lance,' (for the man also had a lance leaning up against the oak to which his mare was tethered) 'and I shall force you to recognize that your actions are those of a coward.'

The farmer, seeing such a figure bearing down on him, encased in armour and brandishing a lance under his nose, gave himself up for dead and meekly replied:

'This lad I'm punishing, sir knight, is one of my servants, and his job is to look after a flock of sheep for me, but he's so careless that every day one of them goes missing; and although what I'm punishing is his carelessness, or his wickedness, he says I'm doing it because I'm a skinflint, so as not to pay him his wages – but I swear by God and by my eternal soul that he's lying.'

'You dare to use that word in my presence,[1] you villainous wretch?' said Don Quixote. 'I swear by the sun that shines down on us that I am minded to run you through with this lance. Pay him immediately, and do not answer back; otherwise, by God who rules us, I shall exterminate and annihilate you this very instant. Untie him.'

The farmer bowed his head and, without uttering a word, untied his servant, whom Don Quixote asked how much his master owed him. The reply was nine months at seven reals a month. Don Quixote worked it out and found that it came to seventy-three reals, which he told the farmer to hand over there and then, if he didn't want to die. The fearful countryman swore by the tight corner he was in and by the oath he'd already sworn (he hadn't sworn any oath at all), that it wasn't as much as all that, because an allowance and deduction had to be made for three pairs of shoes he'd given the lad, and one real paid for two blood-lettings when he'd been ill.

'That is all very well,' replied Don Quixote, 'but the shoes and the blood-lettings will be set against the flogging you have given him without due cause: for if he has done some damage to the hide of the shoes that you bought him, you have damaged his own hide, and if the barber bled him when he was ill, you have done the same to him in good health; so that on this account he owes you nothing.'

'The problem is, sir knight, I haven't got any money on me; if Andrés would like to come home with me, I'll pay him every single real I owe him.'

'Me, go with him, ever again?' said the lad. 'No fear! No sir, I wouldn't even dream of it – so that as soon as we're alone again he can flay me like St Bartholomew?'[2]

'He shall do no such thing,' replied Don Quixote. 'My command will be sufficient to ensure his obedience; and provided that he gives me his oath by the laws of the order of chivalry into which he has been admitted, I shall allow him to go free, and personally guarantee the payment.'

'Think what you're saying, sir,' said the lad. 'My master here isn't a knight at all, and he's never been admitted into any order of chivalry – he's just Juan Haldudo, the rich farmer from Quintanar.'

'That is of little consequence,' replied Don Quixote, 'there is no reason why someone with a plebeian name should not be a knight, for every man is the child of his own deeds.'

'That's as may be,' said Andrés, 'but this master of mine, what deeds is he the child of, seeing as how he refuses to pay me any wages for my sweat and toil?'

'I'm not refusing you anything at all, my dear Andrés,' replied the farmer. 'Please do be so kind as to come with me – I swear by all the orders of chivalry in the world to pay you, as I said, every single real I owe you, and with brass knobs on too.'

'You may dispense with the brass knobs,' said Don Quixote. 'Pay him in silver reals, and that will satisfy me; and take good care to do exactly as you have sworn to do, for otherwise, by that same oath, I swear that I will come back to punish you, and that I will find you, even if you hide yourself away like a lizard. And if you wish to know who is issuing these commands, so as to be the more obliged to obey them, know that I am the valiant Don Quixote de la Mancha, the righter of wrongs and injustices; and God be with you, and do not forget for one moment what you have promised and sworn, under pain of the penalties prescribed.'

And as he said this he spurred Rocinante, and before very long he had got under way. The farmer followed him with his gaze, and as soon as he was certain that he'd ridden out of the wood and was out of sight, he turned to his servant Andrés and said:

'Come here, my son, I want to pay you what I owe you, just as that righter of wrongs has ordered.'

'I swear you will, too,' said Andrés, 'and you'll do well to obey that good knight's commands, God bless him, because he's such a brave man and such a good judge, by all that's holy, that if you don't pay me he'll come back and do what he said he'd do.'

'And I swear I will, too,' said the farmer, 'but, since I'm so very fond of you, I think I'll increase the debt first, just so as to increase the repayment.'

And seizing him by the arm, he tied him back to the evergreen oak and flogged him half dead.

'And now, Señor Andrés,' said the farmer, 'you can call upon your righter of wrongs. As you'll see, he isn't going to right this particular wrong in a hurry. But I don't think I've done with the wronging quite yet, because I'm feeling the urge to skin you alive, just as you feared I would.'

But at length he untied him and told him he could go off in search of his judge so that this gentleman could carry out the sentence he'd pronounced.

Andrés crept sullenly away, swearing that he was going in search of the brave Don Quixote de la Mancha to tell him exactly what had happened, and that the farmer would pay for it sevenfold. But, for all that, Andrés departed in tears and his master was left laughing.

This was how the valiant Don Quixote redressed that wrong; and delighted with what had happened, and considering that he had made a most happy and glorious beginning to his knight-errantry, he rode towards his village full of satisfaction, and murmuring:

'Well may you call yourself fortunate above all women who dwell on this earth, O Dulcinea del Toboso, fairest of the fair, for it has befallen your lot to hold subjected and enslaved to your every wish and desire a knight as valiant and far-famed as is and shall be Don Quixote de la Mancha, who (as all the world knows) was but yesterday admitted to the order of chivalry and today has righted the greatest injury and wrong ever devised by unreason and perpetrated by cruelty: today he has wrested the scourge from the hand of that pitiless enemy who was so unjustly flogging that delicate child.'

As he was saying this he came to a crossroads, and this brought to his mind those other crossroads where knights errant would pause to consider which way to go; and, to imitate them, he remained motionless for a while; but after careful thought he let go of the reins, surrendering his will to that of his nag, which followed its original inclination – to head for its stable. After a couple of miles, Don Quixote spotted a throng of people who, as it afterwards transpired, were merchants from Toledo on their way to Murcia to buy silk. There were six of them, each beneath his sunshade, accompanied by four servants on horseback and three footmen. As soon as Don Quixote saw them, he imagined that here was the opportunity for a new adventure; and, wishing to imitate in every way he believed he could the passages of arms he'd read about in his books, he decided that one he had in mind was perfect for this situation. And so, with a gallant bearing and a resolute air, he steadied himself in his stirrups, clutched his lance, lifted his leather shield to his chest and, taking up his position in the middle of the highway, awaited the arrival of these knights errant, for this was what he judged them to be; and when they came within sight and earshot, Don Quixote raised his voice and, striking a haughty posture, declared:

'You will none of you advance one step further unless all of you confess that in all the world there is no maiden more beauteous than the Empress of La Mancha, the peerless Dulcinea del Toboso.'

The merchants halted when they heard these words and saw the strange figure uttering them, and from the figure and the words they realized that the man was mad; but they had a mind to stay and see what would be the outcome of the required confession and one of them, waggish and sharp-witted, said:

'Sir knight, we don't know who this worthy lady is; do let us see her, because if she's as beautiful as you claim she is, we'll most freely and willingly confess that what you say is true.'

'If I were to let you see her,' retorted Don Quixote, 'what merit would there be in confessing so manifest a truth? The whole point is that, without seeing her, you must believe, confess, affirm, swear and uphold it; if not, monstrous and arrogant wretches, you shall face me in battle forthwith. For whether you present yourselves one by one, as the order of chivalry requires, or all together, as is the custom and wicked practice of those of your ilk, here I stand and wait for you, confident in the justice of my cause.'

'Sir knight,' replied the merchant, 'I beg you, in the name of all us princes gathered here, that – so as not to burden our consciences by confessing something never seen or heard by any of us, particularly since it is so detrimental to the Empresses and Queens of La Alcarria and Extremadura – you be pleased to show us a portrait of that lady, even if no bigger than a grain of wheat; because the skein can be judged by the thread, as they say, and this will leave us satisfied and reassured, and leave you pleased and contented; indeed I believe we are already so far inclined in her favour that, even if her portrait shows that one of her eyes has gone skew-whiff and that sulphur and cinnabar ooze out of the other one, we will, just to please you, say in her favour whatever you want us to say.'

'It does not ooze, you infamous knaves,' replied Don Quixote, burning with anger. 'It does not ooze, I repeat, with what you say, but with ambergris and civet kept in finest cotton; and she is not skew-whiff or hunch-backed, but straighter than a Guadarrama spindle.[3] And you shall pay for the great blasphemy you have uttered against such beauty as that of my lady!'

And so saying he charged with lowered lance at the blasphemer in such fury that, if good fortune hadn't made Rocinante trip and fall on the way, things would have gone badly for the reckless merchant. But Rocinante did fall, and his master rolled over the ground for some distance, and he tried to get up, but he couldn't, so encumbered was he by his lance, his leather shield, his spurs and his helmet, together with the burden of all the rest of his ancient armour. And as he struggled in vain to rise he cried:

'Flee not, you paltry cowards; you wretches, bide your time. 'Tis my horse's fault and not my own that I am lying here.'

One of the footmen – not, it seems, a very well-intentioned one – on hearing all this bluster from the poor fallen fellow, couldn't resist giving him an answer on his ribs. And coming up to him he grabbed his lance and, breaking it into pieces, took one of them and began to give our Don Quixote such a pounding that, in spite of all his armour, he ended up as well threshed as the finest chaff. The muleteer's masters were shouting to him not to hit so hard, and to stop, but the lad was by now so caught up in his game that he wouldn't leave it until he'd played all the cards of his fury, and, picking up the other pieces of the lance, he shattered them, too, on the poor fallen man who, in the face of the storm of blows raining down, never stopped shouting as he threatened heaven and earth and those brigands, as he imagined them to be.

The lad grew tired, and the merchants continued their journey, supplied with enough to talk about throughout it on the subject of the poor pounded knight. Once he found himself alone, he again tried to get up; but if he hadn't been able to do so when fit and well, how was he going to manage it now that he was pummelled to pieces? Even so he considered himself lucky, in the belief that this was a fitting misfortune for knights errant, and he blamed his horse for it all; and it was impossible to get up, so very bruised and battered was his body.

CHAPTER V

In which the story of our knight's misfortune is continued

Finding, then, that he couldn't move, it occurred to him to resort to his usual remedy, which was to think about some passage from his books; and his madness brought to his memory the episode from the story of Baldwin and the Marquis of Mantua in which Carloto leaves Baldwin wounded in the forest,[1] a tale known to every little boy, not unfamiliar to youths, celebrated and even believed by old men, yet with no more truth in it than the miracles of Muhammad. It was perfect for the predicament in which he found himself; and so, with many manifestations of extreme suffering, he began to writhe about on the ground and to say in the faintest of voices what the wounded knight of the forest is said to have said:

> Where are you, mistress of my heart?
> Are you not pained by my distress?
> Maybe you know not of my plight,
> Maybe you're false and pitiless.

And on he went reciting the ballad right up to the lines that go:

> O noble Marquis, gentle sire,
> My uncle and my lord by blood . . .

Fortune decreed that at this point a farmer from his own village, one of his neighbours, happened to be returning home after taking a hundred-weight of wheat to the mill. Seeing a man lying there the farmer came up and asked him who he was and what was the matter with him, moaning away like that. No doubt Don Quixote thought that this was the Marquis of Mantua, his uncle, and so his only response was to continue reciting his ballad, informing the man of his misfortune and of the love that the Emperor's son felt for his wife, exactly as the ballad relates.

The farmer was astonished to hear all this nonsense; and, removing the man's visor, which had been battered to pieces, he wiped his face, which was covered in dust. And once he'd done wiping he recognized him and said:

'Señor Quixana,' (for this must have been his name when he was sane and hadn't yet turned from a placid hidalgo into a knight errant) 'who's done this to you?'

But he continued to reply with his ballad to everything he was asked. Sizing up the situation, the farmer took his back and breast plates off as best he could, to see if he was wounded, but couldn't see any blood or signs of any hurt. He managed to lift him up, and with great difficulty hoisted him on to the donkey, since this seemed the more tranquil animal. He picked up the armour and arms, including the fragments of the lance, and tied them on to Rocinante, which he took by the reins, and taking his donkey by the halter he set off in the direction of his village, deep in thought as he heard the nonsense being spoken by Don Quixote, who was no less pensive and so badly bruised that he couldn't keep his seat on the donkey, and every so often breathed sighs loud enough to reach heaven; so that the farmer again felt he should ask what was wrong, and it must have been the devil himself who made Don Quixote recall tales to fit the events, because at that moment, forgetting all about Baldwin, he remembered Abindarráez the Moor being captured and taken as a prisoner to his castle by the Governor of Antequera, Rodrigo de Narváez. So that when the farmer asked him again how he felt and what was the matter with him, he replied with the very same words and arguments used by the captive Moor to reply to Rodrigo de Narváez, as he'd read the story in Jorge de Montemayor's *Diana*,[2] making such appropriate use of it that the farmer wished himself to the devil for having to listen to such a pack of absurdities. He realized his neighbour was mad, and hurried on to the village so as not to have to put up with Don Quixote's interminable harangue more than necessary. It concluded like this:

'You must know, Señor Don Rodrigo de Narváez, that this fair Jarifa I have mentioned is now the beauteous Dulcinea del Toboso, for whom I have performed, do perform and shall perform the most famous deeds of chivalry that have been witnessed, are witnessed and shall be witnessed in this world.'

The farmer replied:

'Look here sir, as I'm a sinner I'm not Don Rodrigo de Narváez, nor the Marquis of Mantua, but Pedro Alonso, your neighbour; and you aren't Baldwin, nor Abindarráez, but the honourable hidalgo Señor Quixana.'

'I know who I am,' retorted Don Quixote, 'and I know that I can be not only all those whom I have mentioned, but every one of the Twelve Peers of France, and every one of the Nine Worthies as well,³ because all the deeds performed by them both singly and together will be exceeded by mine.'

With these exchanges and other similar ones they approached the village at nightfall, but the farmer waited until it was darker so that nobody could see the battered hidalgo so wretchedly mounted. When he thought the time had come he entered the village and went straight to Don Quixote's house, which was in an uproar: the priest and the barber, great friends of Don Quixote's, were there, and his housekeeper was shouting:

'And what's your opinion, Father Pero Pérez sir,' (for this was the priest's name) 'about my master's misfortune? Three days it's been now without a trace of him, his nag, his leather shield, his lance or his armour. A fine pickle I'm in! It's my belief, as sure as I was born to die, that his brain's been turned by those damned chivalry books of his he reads all the time – I remember often hearing him say to himself that he wanted to be a knight errant and go off in search of adventures. The devil take all those books, and Barabbas⁴ take them too, for scrambling the finest mind in all La Mancha!'

The niece said much the same and even more:

'And let me tell you this, Master Nicolás,' (for this was the barber's name). 'My uncle would often be reading those evil books of misadventure for two whole days and nights on end, and then he'd throw his book down, grab his sword and slash the walls of his room, and once he was exhausted he'd say that he'd killed four giants as big as four towers, and that the sweat pouring from him was blood from the wounds received in battle, and then he'd drink a pitcher of cold water and feel calm and well again, claiming that the water was a most precious draught brought by the famous sage Squiffy,⁵ a great enchanter and friend of his. But I'm the one to blame for it all, not telling you gentlemen about my uncle's madness so you could have done something about it and burned those unchristian books of his before it came to all this; he's got lots and lots of them, and they do deserve to be put to the flames, like heretics.'

'I agree with that,' said the priest, 'and I swear that before another day has passed they'll be put on public trial and condemned to the flames so that they can't make anyone reading them do what my friend must have done.'

All this was overheard by Don Quixote and the farmer, who could no longer have any doubts about his neighbour's illness, and so he began to shout:

'Open up to Sir Baldwin and the Marquis of Mantua, who's sore wounded here, and to the Moor Abindarráez, brought captive by the valiant Rodrigo de Narváez, the Governor of Antequera.'

These shouts brought all four running into the porch, and as the men recognized their friend, and the women their master and uncle, who hadn't dismounted from the donkey because he couldn't, they ran to embrace him. He said:

'Stop, all of you, for I am sore wounded through the fault of my steed. Carry me to my bed and, if you are able, summon the wise Urganda to heed and tend my wounds.'

'Just look at him, in the name of the devil!' cried the housekeeper. 'Didn't I know in the marrow of my bones what was wrong with the master? Up you go, sir, up you go to bed, we'll cure you well enough without any need for that there Ugandan woman. Damn those chivalry books, damn the lot of them, getting you into such a state!'

They took him to his bed and, examining him for wounds, couldn't find any; he told them that it had been a general, overall battering sustained when he and his steed Rocinante suffered a terrible fall as he was doing battle with ten giants, the most lawless and reckless giants to be found almost anywhere on the face of the earth.

'I see, I see!' said the priest. 'So there are giants in the game as well, are there? I swear by this Holy Cross that I'll burn them tomorrow, before the day is over.'

They asked Don Quixote a thousand questions, and his only reply was to request food and to be allowed to sleep, for this was his greatest need.

And then the priest asked the farmer to tell him exactly how he'd found Don Quixote. The farmer told him the whole story, including the nonsense that on being discovered and transported the knight had uttered, which made the priest even more anxious to do what the very next day he did do: call on his friend the barber Master Nicolás, with whom he walked to Don Quixote's house.

CHAPTER VI

About the amusing and exhaustive scrutiny that the priest and the barber made in the library of our ingenious hidalgo

Who was still asleep. The priest asked the niece for the keys of the room where the books, the authors of the mischief, were kept, and she was happy to hand them over. They went in, the housekeeper too, and found more than a hundred large volumes, finely bound, and some small ones; and as soon as the housekeeper saw them, she ran out of the room and back again clutching a bowl of holy water and some hyssop,[1] and said:

'Here you are, reverend father, you take this and sprinkle the room with it, just in case there's one of those hordes of enchanters from those books in here, and he puts a spell on us as a punishment for the torments they'll undergo once we've wiped them off the face of the earth.'

The priest laughed at the housekeeper's simple-mindedness, and told the barber to hand him the books one by one so that he could see what was in them, since he might find some that didn't deserve to be committed to the flames.

'No,' said the niece, 'there's no reason to let any of them off, they're all to blame. Better throw the whole lot of them out of the windows into the courtyard, and make a pile of them, and set fire to them, or take them to the backyard and make the bonfire there, where the smoke won't be such a nuisance.'

The housekeeper said much the same, so anxious were both women to see those innocents massacred, but the priest wouldn't agree without at least reading the titles. The first one that Master Nicolás put into his hands was *The Four Books of Amadis of Gaul*, and the priest said:

'This is a strange coincidence: I've heard that this was the very first chivalry romance to be printed in Spain,[2] and that all the others have their origin and beginning in it; so it seems to me that, as the prophet of such a pernicious sect, it should be condemned to the flames without delay.'

'No, no,' said the barber. 'I've also heard that it's the very best of all the books of this kind that have ever been written; and so, being unique in its artistry, it ought to be pardoned.'

'You're right,' said the priest, 'so its life is spared for the time being. Let's see that one next to it.'

'This,' said the barber, 'is *The Exploits of Esplandian*,[3] Amadis of Gaul's legitimate son.'

'Well, to be sure,' said the priest, 'the excellence of the father isn't going to be of any avail to the son. Here you are, ma'am, open that window and throw it into the yard, the first faggot on the bonfire we're going to make.'

The housekeeper was delighted to do so, and the good Esplandian flew out into the courtyard, where he patiently awaited the flames with which he was threatened.

'Let's see the next one,' said the priest.

'This,' said the barber, 'is *Amadis of Greece*, and all the books on this side, I think, are members of that same family.'[4]

'Then out into the yard with the lot of them,' said the priest. 'Just to be able to burn Queen Pintiquiniestra, and the shepherd Darinel, and his eclogues, and his author's devilish, contorted language, I'll burn the father that begot me, too, if I catch him going about as a knight errant.'

'I agree,' said the barber.

'So do I,' added the niece.

'That being so,' said the housekeeper, 'let's have them here, and out into the courtyard they all go.'

They gave them to her, and since there were so many of them she spared herself the stairs again and flung them out of the window.

'And what's that monstrosity?' asked the priest.

'That,' replied the barber, 'is *Don Olivante de Laura*.'[5]

'Its author,' said the priest, 'also wrote *The Garden of Flowers*, and to be frank I couldn't say which of the two is more truthful – or rather, less mendacious. What I can say is that this one shall go out into the yard, for its arrogant nonsense.'

'This next one is *Florismarte of Hyrcania*,'⁶ said the barber.

'Oh, so it's Señor Florismarte, is it?' replied the priest. 'I can tell you he's soon going to end up in the yard, too, in spite of his strange birth and famous adventures. No other outcome is feasible, given the clumsiness and dullness of his style. To the yard with him, and with this other one as well, ma'am.'

'With pleasure, sir,' the housekeeper replied, and joyfully she did as she was told.

'This is *The Knight Platir*,'⁷ said the barber.

'That's an old book,' said the priest, 'and I can't find anything in it deserving of mercy. Let it join the others without leave to appeal.'

And it was done. Another book was opened and they saw that its title was *The Knight of the Cross*.⁸

'With such a holy title as this book has, it could be forgiven its ignorance, yet as the proverb goes, "Behind the Cross lurks the devil": to the fire with it.'

Taking up another book, the barber said:

'This one's *The Mirror of Chivalry*.'

'I know this gentleman,' said the priest. 'Here we'll find Sir Reynald of Montalban and his friends and companions, worse thieves than Cacus, and the Twelve Peers, with the true historian Turpin.⁹ Yet the fact is that I'm inclined to condemn them to nothing worse than perpetual exile, if only because there are among them some of the creations of the famous Matteo Boiardo, from which the Christian poet Ludovico Ariosto also wove his tapestry – though if I find him in here speaking any language other than his own I won't show him any respect at all, but if he's speaking his own tongue I'll take my hat off to him.'

'Well, I've got that book in Italian,' said the barber, 'but I don't understand a word of it.'

'Nor would it be a good thing for you to understand it,' replied the priest, 'and we could have done without that captain bringing it to Spain and turning it into Castilian,¹⁰ because he left behind much of what was best in it, which is what happens to all those who try to translate poetry:

however much care they take and skill they display, they can never recreate it in the full perfection of its original birth. I say, then, that this book, and all others we find that are about these French matters, shall be thrown out and deposited in a dry well until, after further deliberation, a decision is reached about what to do with them – all except a certain *Bernardo del Carpio*[11] who's skulking about here somewhere, and another book called *Roncesvalles*,[12] because these will pass straight from my hands into the housekeeper's and from there to the flames, without any remission.'

This was confirmed by the barber, who thought it all very fit and proper, since he considered the priest to be such a good Christian and lover of the truth that he couldn't tell a lie if he tried. Opening another book he saw that it was *Palmerin of Oliva*,[13] and next to it was another one called *Palmerin of England*, and when the priest saw this he said:

'Let the olive be chopped into logs and burned, and not even the ashes remain. But let the palm of England be kept and preserved as something unique, and a casket be made for it like the one Alexander the Great found among the spoils of Darius and designated as a case for the works of the poet Homer. This book, my friend, deserves respect for two reasons: because it's excellent in its own right, and because it's said to have been written by a wise king of Portugal. All the adventures in Princess Miraguarda's castle are superb and splendidly contrived; and the speeches are courtly and clear, and have due regard for the character of the speakers, with great precision and sensitivity. I propose, then, that so long as you agree, Master Nicolás, this book and *Amadis of Gaul* should be saved from the flames, and all the rest should perish, without any further enquiry.'

'No, my friend,' replied the barber, 'because this one I've got here is the famous *Sir Belianis*.'

'That book,' replied the priest, 'and the second, third and fourth parts, too, need a dose of rhubarb to purge them of their excess of bile – and that section about the castle of fame and other more serious nonsense will have to be removed, for which purpose they are granted a stay of execution; and whether mercy or rigorous justice is applied to them will depend on how they mend their ways. Meanwhile, you keep them in your house, my friend, but don't let anybody read them.'

'All right,' said the barber.

And not wanting to weary himself any more reading chivalry romances, the priest ordered the housekeeper to take all the big books and throw them out into the yard. His command didn't fall on deaf ears, because she'd rather have been burning those books than weaving the finest and largest piece of fabric in the world, and, seizing about eight of them, she heaved them out of the window. But because she took up so many of them together, one fell at the barber's feet and, curious to know what it was, he saw: *History of the Famous Knight Tirante the White*.[14]

'Good heavens!' cried the priest. 'Fancy Tirante the White being here! Give it to me, my friend: I reckon I've found in this book a treasure of delight and a mine of entertainment. In it you'll discover Don Quirieleisón de Montalbán, a most courageous knight, and his brother Tomás de Montalbán, and the knight Fonseca, together with the fight that the brave Tirante had with the mastiff, and the witticisms of the maiden Placerdemivida, and the amours and the trickery of the widow Reposada, and the lady empress in love with her squire Hipólito. Let me tell you this, my friend: as far as its style is concerned this is the best book in the world. In it knights eat and sleep and die in their beds and make wills before they die, and other such things that are usually omitted from books of this sort. But in spite of all this I do have to say that the man who wrote it deserved to be sent to the galleys for life, for not knowing what he was doing when he was writing such nonsense. Take it home and read it, and you'll see that what I say is true.'

'That I'll do,' replied the barber, 'but what about these other little books here?'

'They can't be books of chivalry,' said the priest, 'but books of poetry.'

And, opening one of them he saw that it was Jorge de Montemayor's *Diana* and, convinced that they were all of the same sort, he said:

'These don't deserve to be burned with the others, because they aren't and never will be as damaging as those books of chivalry have been – these are books for the intellect, and do nobody any harm.'

'Oh sir,' cried the niece, 'please have them burned like the rest, because it could well happen that once my uncle gets over his chivalry illness he starts reading all these other books and takes it into his head to become a shepherd and wander about the forests and meadows singing and playing music and, what would be even worse than that, turn into a poet, which they say is a catching and incurable disease.'

'The girl's right,' said the priest, 'and it'll be a good idea to remove this dangerous stumbling-block from our friend's way. And as we're beginning with Montemayor's *Diana*, it's my opinion that it shouldn't be burned, but that the parts about the wise Felicia and the enchanted water[15] should be cut, as well as nearly all the poems in Italian metre, and that the book should be welcome to keep its prose and the honour of being the first of its kind.'

'This next one,' said the barber, 'is also called *Diana*, the second part, by an author from Salamanca. And this other one has the same title, too, and it's by Gil Polo.'[16]

'Well,' replied the priest, 'the Salamancan one can go to join and swell the ranks of the books condemned to the courtyard, but the one by Gil Polo must be safeguarded as if it had been written by Apollo himself. Look lively though, my friend, let's hurry up, it's getting late.'

'This,' said the barber, opening another volume, 'is *The Ten Books of the Fortune of Love*, written by Antonio de Lofraso, a Sardinian poet.'[17]

'As sure as I'm in holy orders,' said the priest, 'no book as amusing and as fanciful as this has ever been written since Apollo was Apollo, the muses were muses and poets have been poets. In its own way it's the best and most singular of all those of its kind that have ever seen the light of day, and anyone who hasn't read it can reckon that he's never read anything worth reading. Let's have it, my friend: I'm happier to have found it than if I'd been given a cassock of finest florentine.'

He put it to one side with great satisfaction, and the barber went on to say:

'These next ones are *The Shepherd of Iberia*, *The Nymphs of Henares* and *The Undeceptions of Jealousy*.'[18]

'Well,' said the priest, 'all you have to do is hand them over to the secular arm of the housekeeper, and don't ask me why, or we shall never be done.'

'The next is *The Shepherd of Filida*.'[19]

'That's no shepherd,' said the priest, 'but a clever courtier, to be cherished like a precious jewel.'

'This big book here,' said the barber, 'is called *The Treasury of Divers Poems*.'[20]

'If there were fewer of them,' said the priest, 'they'd be better thought of. This book needs some weeding, to rid it of certain vulgarities among its splendours. Keep it back, because its author's a friend of mine, and also out of respect for other more heroic and sublime works he's written.'

'This,' said the barber, 'is López Maldonado's *Book of Songs*.'[21]

'The author of this book,' replied the priest, 'is also one of my great friends, and when he sings his own verses his listeners are lost in admiration, because he does so in such a sweet voice that you could say he chants and enchants all at once. His eclogues are rather long, but then you can never have too much of a good thing. Keep the book with the chosen few. But what's this other one by its side?'

'*Galatea*, by Miguel de Cervantes.'[22]

'That fellow Cervantes has been a good friend of mine for years, and I know he's more conversant with adversity than with verse. His book's ingenious enough; it sets out to achieve something but doesn't bring anything to a conclusion; we'll have to wait for the promised second part; maybe with correction it'll gain the full pardon denied it for the time being; so while we wait and see, you keep it a captive in your house, my friend.'

'All right,' said the barber. 'And here are three more, all together: *Araucana*, by Alonso de Ercilla, *Austríada*, by Juan Rufo, the magistrate from Córdoba, and *Monserrate*,[23] by Cristóbal de Virués, the Valencian poet.'

'Those three books,' said the priest, 'are the best ever written in heroic verse in the Castilian language, and they can rival the most famous Italian ones. Preserve them, as the finest pieces of poetry Spain possesses.'

The priest grew tired of looking at books and ordered all the rest to be burned in one fell swoop, but the barber had already opened another one, entitled *The Tears of Angelica*.[24]

'I'd have shed them myself,' said the priest when he heard the title, 'if I'd had this book burned, because its author was one of the most famous poets in the world, not just in Spain, and an excellent translator of Ovid.'

CHAPTER VII

✠

*About our worthy knight Don Quixote de la Mancha's
second sally*

And now Don Quixote began to bellow:

'Come, come, you valiant knights; 'tis now you must display the worth of your mighty arms, for the courtiers are getting the better of the tourney.'

They ran to see what the commotion was all about, and this put a stop to the scrutiny of the remaining books; as a result it's believed that *Carolea* and *The Lion of Spain*, together with *The Exploits of the Emperor* by Luis de Ávila,[1] went to the flames without any trial at all, because they must have been among the remainder; and perhaps if the priest had examined them they wouldn't have received such a severe sentence.

By the time they reached Don Quixote's room he was out of bed, shouting and raving, laying about him with his sword in all directions with slashes and backstrokes, as wide awake as if he'd never slept. They wrestled him back to bed, and once he'd calmed down a little, he turned to the priest and said:

'Indeed, my Lord Archbishop Turpin, it is a disgrace for us, who call ourselves the Twelve Peers, so meekly to allow those knights courtiers to carry off the victory in this tournament, after we knights adventurers had won all the honours on the previous three days.'

'Hush, my friend,' said the priest, 'God will grant a change of fortune so that what is lost today is won tomorrow, and for the moment you should look to your health – you seem to be overtired, if not sore wounded.'

'Wounded I am not,' said Don Quixote, 'but weak and exhausted I am indeed, for the bastard Roland has been pounding me with the trunk of an evergreen oak, and all out of envy, because he can see that I am the only man who opposes his bravado. But my name would not be Reynald of Montalbán if, as soon as I rise from this bed, I did not make him pay for it, in spite of all his magic spells. For the present, however, bring me victuals, for they, I know, will be more to my purpose, and leave it to me to seek my revenge.'

And that's what they did: they gave him some food, and he fell asleep again, and they fell to marvelling at his madness.

That night the housekeeper burned to ashes all the books in the courtyard and the house, and some must have perished that deserved to be treasured in perpetual archives; but fate, and the scrutineer's laziness, wouldn't permit it, and in them was fulfilled the proverb which says that the just sometimes pay for sinners.

One of the remedies that the priest and the barber had prescribed at that time for their friend's malady was to have his library walled up and sealed off, so that he couldn't find his books when he got up – maybe if the cause was removed the effect might cease – and to tell him that an enchanter had carried them off, with the library and all; and this was done without delay. Two days later Don Quixote did get up, and his first action was to go and look at his books; and, since he couldn't find the room in which he'd left them, he wandered all over the house searching for it. He kept going up to the place where the door used to be, and feeling for it with his hands, and running his eyes backwards and forwards over the walls without uttering a word; and after some time doing this he asked his housekeeper where his library was. Well trained in her answer, she said:

'And what library do you think you're looking for? There's no library and no books left in this house, because the devil himself took them away.'

'No, it wasn't the devil,' replied the niece, 'it was an enchanter who came one night on a cloud, after you'd gone away, and he climbed off a serpent he was riding and he went into the library and I don't know what he got up to in there, because a bit later he flew away over the roof and left the house full of smoke; and when we made up our minds to go and see what he'd done, we couldn't find any books or any library. All we remember is that as that wicked old man flew away he shouted that because of a secret grudge he bore the owner of the books and the library, he'd done the house the damage that we were about to discover. He also said that he was called the sage Munaton.'

'Frestón[2] is what he must have said,' said Don Quixote.

'I don't know,' said the housekeeper, 'whether he was called Frestón or Piston or whatever, all I know is his name ended in ton.'

'That is indeed his name,' said Don Quixote, 'and he is a wise enchanter, a great enemy of mine, who bears me much malice, because he knows by his arts and his learning that the time will come when I shall engage in single combat a knight who is a favourite of his, and defeat him, without his being able to do anything to prevent it, and for this reason he tries to make as much mischief for me as he can; but I can promise him that he is powerless to gainsay or avert what heaven has decreed.'

'Who can doubt that?' said the niece. 'But uncle, why do you have to go and get involved in these arguments? Wouldn't it be better to stay quietly at home instead of looking for better bread than what's made from wheat, and forgetting that many a man's gone out shearing and come back shorn?'

'My dear niece!' replied Don Quixote. 'How wrong you are! Before anyone shears me I will pluck the beards off the chins of all those who even contemplate touching a single hair of mine!'

Neither woman answered him back, because they could see that he was growing heated.

And yet he did stay quietly at home for a whole fortnight without showing any signs of wanting to re-enact his former follies, and during this time he talked all kinds of amusing bunkum with his friends the priest and the barber, as he declared that what the world most needed was knights errant and a rebirth of knight-errantry. Sometimes the priest contradicted him and sometimes he gave in to him, because if he didn't make use of this tactic it would be impossible to restore his sanity.

During this fortnight Don Quixote set to work on a farmer who was a neighbour of his, an honourable man (if a poor man can be called honourable) but a little short of salt in the brain-pan. To be brief, Don Quixote told him, reasoned with him and promised him so much that the poor villager decided to go away with him and serve him as squire. Don Quixote told the man, among other things, that he ought to be delighted to go, because at some time or other he could well have an adventure in which he won an island in the twinkling of an eye and installed his squire as governor. These and other similar promises persuaded Sancho Panza, for this was the farmer's name, to leave his wife and children and go into service as his neighbour's squire.

Don Quixote immediately set about raising money, and by selling one possession, pawning another, and always making a bad bargain, he scraped together a reasonable sum. He also found himself a little round infantry-man's shield, borrowed from a friend, and, patching up his shattered helmet as best he could, he told his squire Sancho the day and time he intended to set out, so that he too could obtain whatever he considered most necessary. Don Quixote was particularly insistent on saddle-bags, and Sancho said that indeed he would bring some, and he'd bring a very fine donkey of his too, because he wasn't all that much given to going very far on foot. At this Don Quixote hesitated, racking his brains to try and remember if any knight errant had ever been escorted by a donkey-mounted squire, but none came to mind; yet for all that he decided that Sancho should ride his donkey, proposing to provide him with a more honourable mount at the earliest opportunity, by unhorsing the first discourteous knight he came across. Don Quixote stocked up with shirts and everything else he could, following the advice that the innkeeper had given him; and once all these preparations had been made, without Panza saying goodbye to his wife and children, or Don Quixote to his housekeeper and niece, they left the village unseen one night, and by daybreak they'd ridden so far they felt certain no one would be able to find them however hard he looked.

Sancho Panza rode his ass like a patriarch, complete with saddle-bags and leather bottle, longing to be the governor of the island his master had promised him. Don Quixote happened to take the same road he'd followed on his first sally, across the plain of Montiel, with less discomfort than before, because it was early morning and the sun, being low, didn't bother them. Sancho Panza said to his master:

'You'll be sure, won't you, sir knight, not to forget what you promised me about the island. I'll be up to governing it all right, however big it is.'

To which Don Quixote replied:

'I would have you know, my good friend Sancho Panza, that it was a custom much in use among the knights errant of old to make their squires the governors of the islands or kingdoms that they conquered, and I have determined that such an ancient usage shall not lapse through my fault. Quite on the contrary, I intend to improve upon it: for those knights would sometimes – more often than not, perhaps – wait until their squires were old men and, once they were tired of serving and of suffering bad days and worse nights, give them some title, such as count or at the most marquis of some valley or paltry province; but if your life and mine are spared, it could well be that within six days I shall conquer a kingdom with others annexed, any one of which would be perfect for you to be crowned king of it. And you must not think that there would be anything extraordinary about that: incidents and accidents befall us knights in such unprecedented and unimagined ways that I might easily be able to give you even more than I have promised.'

'And so,' said Sancho Panza, 'if by one of those miracles you've just said I became king, then Juana Gutiérrez, my old woman, would be queen no less, and the kids would be princes and princesses.'

'Who can doubt it?' replied Don Quixote.

'I can,' retorted Sancho Panza. 'To my mind, even if God rained kingdoms down on this earth none of them would sit well on my Mari Gutiérrez's head. Look here, sir, she wouldn't be worth two brass farthings as a queen – countess would suit her better, and even that'd be hard going for her.'

'Commend the matter to God, Sancho,' replied Don Quixote, 'and he will give her what is best for her; but you must not be so daunted that you agree to content yourself with anything less than being a provincial governor.'

'I shan't do that, sir,' replied Sancho, 'not with such a fine master as you, who'll be able to give me everything that's good for me and I can cope with.'

CHAPTER VIII

About the brave Don Quixote's success in the dreadful
and unimaginable adventure of the windmills, together
with other events worthy of happy memory

As he was saying this, they caught sight of thirty or forty windmills standing on the plain, and as soon as Don Quixote saw them he said to his squire:

'Fortune is directing our affairs even better than we could have wished: for you can see over there, good friend Sancho Panza, a place where stand thirty or more monstrous giants with whom I intend to fight a battle and whose lives I intend to take; and with the booty we shall begin to prosper. For this is a just war, and it is a great service to God to wipe such a wicked breed from the face of the earth.'

'What giants?' said Sancho Panza.

'Those giants that you can see over there,' replied his master, 'with long arms: there are giants with arms almost six miles long.'

'Look you here,' Sancho retorted, 'those over there aren't giants, they're windmills, and what look to you like arms are sails – when the wind turns them they make the millstones go round.'

'It is perfectly clear,' replied Don Quixote, 'that you are but a raw novice in this matter of adventures. They are giants; and if you are frightened, you can take yourself away and say your prayers while I engage them in fierce and arduous combat.'

And so saying he set spurs to his steed Rocinante, not paying any attention to his squire Sancho Panza, who was shouting that what he was charging were definitely windmills not giants. But Don Quixote was so convinced that they were giants that he neither heard his squire Sancho's shouts nor saw what stood in front of him, even though he was by now upon them; instead he cried:

'Flee not, O vile and cowardly creatures, for it is but one solitary knight who attacks you.'

A gust of wind arose, the great sails began to move, and Don Quixote yelled:

'Though you flourish more arms than the giant Briareus,[1] I will make you pay for it.'

So saying, and commending himself with all his heart to his lady Dulcinea, begging her to succour him in his plight, well protected by his little round infantryman's shield, and with his lance couched, he advanced at Rocinante's top speed and charged at the windmill nearest him. As he thrust his lance into its sail the wind turned it with such violence that it smashed the lance into pieces and dragged the horse and his rider with it, and Don Quixote went rolling over the plain in a very sore predicament. Sancho Panza rushed to help his master at his donkey's fastest trot and found that he couldn't stir, such was the toss that Rocinante had given him.

'For God's sake!' said Sancho. 'Didn't I tell you to be careful what you were doing, didn't I tell you they were only windmills? And only someone with windmills on the brain could have failed to see that!'

'Not at all, friend Sancho,' replied Don Quixote. 'Affairs of war, even more than others, are subject to continual change. All the more so as I believe, indeed I am certain, that the same sage Frestón who stole my library and my books has just turned these giants into windmills, to deprive me of the glory of my victory, such is the enmity he feels for me; but in the end his evil arts will avail him little against the might of my sword.'

'God's will be done,' replied Sancho Panza.

He helped his master to his feet, and his master remounted Rocinante, whose shoulder was half dislocated. And talking about this adventure they followed the road towards the Pass of Lápice, because Don Quixote said they couldn't fail to encounter plentiful and varied adventures there, as it was a much frequented spot. But he was dejected by the destruction of his lance, and he told his squire so, and added:

'I remember reading that a Spanish knight called Diego Pérez de Vargas, having broken his sword in battle, tore a weighty bough or trunk from an evergreen oak, and did such deeds with it that day, and thrashed so many Moors,[2] that he was nicknamed Machuca, that is to say, the thrasher; and from that day onwards his surname and that of his descendants was changed to Vargas y Machuca. I have told you this because from the first oak tree that comes before me I intend to tear off another such trunk, as good as the one I have in mind, and with it I intend to do such deeds as to make you consider yourself most fortunate to be deemed worthy to behold them, and to witness that which can hardly be believed.'

'God's will be done,' said Sancho. 'I believe every word you say. But do sit up straighter, you're riding all lopsided, it must be that hammering you got when you fell off your horse.'

'That is indeed the case,' replied Don Quixote, 'and if I do not utter any complaint about the pain it is because knights errant are not permitted to complain about wounds, even if their entrails are spilling out of them.'

'If that's so there's nothing more for me to say,' replied Sancho, 'but God knows I'd like you to complain if anything hurts. As for me, I can tell you I'm going to moan like anything about the slightest little pain, unless that stuff about not complaining goes for knight errants' squires as well.'

Don Quixote couldn't help laughing at his squire's simple-mindedness, and declared that he could moan as and when he pleased, whether he felt any pain or not, for he had not yet read anything to the contrary in the order of chivalry. Sancho pointed out that it was time to eat. His master replied that he didn't need any food yet, but that Sancho could eat whenever he liked. So Sancho settled himself down as best he could on his donkey and, taking out of his saddle-bags what he'd put into them, he jogged along and munched away behind his master, and every so often he'd take a swig from his leather bottle with such relish that the most self-indulgent innkeeper in Malaga would have envied him. And as Sancho trotted on, drinking his fill, he didn't remember any of the promises his master had made him, and reckoned that going in search of adventures, however dangerous they might be, was more like good fun than hard work.

To cut a long story short, they spent that night under some trees, and from one of them Don Quixote tore a dead branch that might almost serve as a lance, and fastened on to it the iron head that he'd taken off the broken one. He didn't sleep in all the night, thinking about his lady Dulcinea, to conform with what he'd read in his books, where knights errant spent many sleepless nights in glades and deserts, engrossed in the recollection of their ladies. Not so Sancho Panza who, with his stomach full, and not of chicory water either, slept right through until morning; and, if his master hadn't called him, neither the rays of the sun, falling full on his face, nor the songs of the birds that, in great throngs and with expansive joy, greeted the coming of the new day, would have been capable of awaking him. He got up, had his breakfast swig and found his leather bottle rather slimmer than the evening before; and his heart sank, because it didn't look as if this lack was going to be remedied as soon as he'd have liked. Don Quixote refused breakfast because, as we know, he had decided to subsist on savoury recollections. They continued along the road to the Pass of Lápice, and at about three o'clock in the afternoon they sighted it.

'Over there, brother Sancho Panza,' said Don Quixote when he saw it, 'we can dip our arms right up to our elbows in what people call adventures. But take note that, even if you see me in the greatest peril imaginable, you must not seize your sword to defend me, unless you should see that those who attack me are rabble and common people, in which case you can most certainly come to my aid; but should they be knights and gentlemen, it is on no account licit or permitted by the laws of chivalry for you to assist me, until you yourself be knighted.'

'You can be sure, sir,' replied Sancho, 'of being fully obeyed there, specially since I'm a peaceful man by nature and don't like getting involved in rows and brawls. Though I do have to say that when it comes to defending myself I'm not going to take much notice of those there laws of yours, because divine and human justice both let anyone defend himself against attack.'

'I do not disagree in the slightest,' replied Don Quixote, 'but as regards assisting me against knights, you must keep your natural impetuosity under control.'

'I'll do that all right,' replied Sancho. 'I'll keep that particular promise as strictly as the Sabbath.'

As they talked away like this, two friars of the order of St Benedict appeared on the road, each seated upon a dromedary: their mules were no less tall than that. They came complete with their riding masks and their sunshades. Behind them was a coach with four or five horsemen escorting it, and two footmen walking. In the coach, as was later discovered, there was a Basque lady on her way to Seville to join her husband, who was going to America to take up an important post. The friars weren't travelling with her, they just happened to be on the same road; but as soon as Don Quixote caught sight of them he said to his squire:

'Either I am much mistaken or this will be the most famous adventure ever witnessed; for those black figures over there must be and no doubt are enchanters abducting a princess in that coach, and I must redress this wrong to the utmost of my power.'

'This'll be worse than the windmills,' said Sancho. 'Look here, sir, those there are Benedictine friars, and the coach must just be taking some travellers on their way. Look, look, do take care what you're doing, this could be one of the devil's own tricks.'

'I have already told you, Sancho,' replied Don Quixote, 'that you know next to nothing on the subject of adventures. What I say is true, as you will soon see.'

So saying, he rode forward and planted himself in the middle of the road down which the friars were plodding and, when he thought they were near enough to hear him, he cried:

'Diabolical and monstrous wretches, release this very moment the noble princesses whom you are abducting in that coach, or prepare to be killed this instant as a just punishment for your wicked works.'

The friars reined in their mules and sat there in astonishment at the figure cut by Don Quixote and at the words he'd spoken, to which they replied:

'Sir knight, we aren't diabolical or monstrous at all, we're just two Benedictine friars going about our business, and we haven't the faintest idea whether there are any abducted princesses in this coach.'

'Soft words will not work with me, for I know you only too well, perfidious knaves!' said Don Quixote.

And without awaiting any more replies he spurred Rocinante and charged with levelled lance at the friar in front with such determination and fury that, if the friar hadn't thrown himself from his mule, the knight would have brought him to the ground sore vexed and indeed sore wounded, if not stone dead. The other friar, seeing how his companion was being treated, dug his heels into his castle of a mule and made off across the plain faster than the wind.

Sancho Panza, seeing the friar sprawling on the ground, slipped off his donkey, ran over to him and began to strip him of his habits. And now two of the friars' servants came up and asked what he thought he was doing stripping their master like that. Sancho replied that the clothes were rightly his, the spoils of the battle his master Don Quixote had won. The servant-lads, who lacked a sense of humour and knew nothing about spoils and battles, seeing that Don Quixote had gone off to talk to the ladies in the coach, fell upon Sancho, knocked him to the ground, gave his beard a thorough plucking and his body a merciless kicking, and left him lying there breathless and senseless. Without pausing for an instant the friar remounted, terrified and trembling and drained of all colour, and spurred his mule in the direction of his companion, who was waiting a good distance away to see what would be the outcome of this nightmare; and not wanting to stop for the conclusion of the incident they continued on their way, making more signs of the cross than if they had the very devil at their backs.

Don Quixote, as has been said, was talking to the lady in the coach, and saying:

'You may now, in your ineffable loveliness, my lady, dispose of your person as best pleases you, for the pride of your ravishers lies on the ground, o'erthrown by this mighty arm of mine; and that you may not pine to know the name of your deliverer, be informed that I am Don Quixote de la Mancha, knight adventurer and errant, and captive to the peerless and beauteous Doña Dulcinea del Toboso; and in requital of the benefit you have received from me, all I desire is that you turn back to El Toboso and on my behalf present yourself before that lady and inform her of what I have accomplished for your deliverance.'

Everything that Don Quixote said was overheard by one of the squires escorting the coach, a Basque; who, seeing that the man didn't want to let the coach continue on its way, but was saying that it must turn back at once to El Toboso, rode up to Don Quixote and, seizing him by the lance, said in bad Castilian and worse Basque:

'Go on way, knight, and go with devil. By God made me, if not leaving coach, you as killed by Basque as stand there.'

Don Quixote understood him perfectly, and with great composure he replied:

'If you were a knight and a gentleman, which you are not, I should already have punished your folly and audacity, you wretched creature.'

To which the Basque replied:

'Me not gentleman? I swear God you lie as me Christian. If leaving lance and taking sword, soon see you monkey making! Basque on land, gentleman on sea, gentleman for devil, and see lie if other saying.'

' "Now you shall see," quoth Agrages,'[3] quoted Don Quixote.

And throwing his lance to the ground, he drew his sword, took up his little round shield and set upon the Basque, intending to kill him. The Basque, seeing the knight advance, would have preferred to dismount from his mule, which was a hired one and therefore a bad one and not to be trusted, but all he had time to do was to draw his sword; and it was lucky for him that he happened to be next to the coach, from which he was able to snatch a cushion to serve as a shield; and then the two men went for each other as if they were mortal enemies. The rest of the party would have made peace between them but they couldn't, because the Basque was saying in his topsy-turvy tongue that if they didn't let him finish his battle he'd kill his mistress and anyone else who got in his way. The lady in the coach, astonished and terrified at this sight, made the coachman drive a safe distance off, and then settled down to watch the desperate struggle, in the course of which the Basque dealt Don Quixote such a mighty blow on the shoulder, over the top of his shield, that if he hadn't been wearing armour he'd have been split down the middle. When Don Quixote felt the impact of the terrible stroke he cried:

'O lady of my soul, Dulcinea, flower of all beauty, succour this your knight who, through his desire to satisfy your great goodness, finds himself in this dire peril!'

Uttering these words, gripping his sword, raising his shield and launching himself at the Basque was the work of a moment, as Don Quixote resolved to venture everything on the fortune of a single blow. The Basque, seeing Don Quixote advance, could see from his spirited bearing what a brave man he was, and decided to follow his example; so he stood his ground, well protected by his cushion but unable to turn the mule one way or the other because by now, exhausted and unaccustomed to such pranks, it couldn't budge a single step.

So Don Quixote was advancing, as described, on the well-shielded Basque, with his sword aloft, determined to split him in half, and the Basque was awaiting him with his sword also aloft, and upholstered in his protective cushion, and all the bystanders were terrified and wondering what was going to be the outcome of the prodigious blows with which the two men were threatening each other; and the lady in the coach and her maids were making a thousand vows and offerings to all the images and holy places in Spain for God to deliver their squire and themselves from this great peril. But the trouble is that at this very point the author of this history leaves the battle unfinished, excusing himself on the ground that he hasn't found anything more written about these exploits of Don Quixote than what he has narrated. It is true, though, that the second author of this work refused to believe that such a fascinating history had been abandoned to the laws of oblivion, or that the chroniclers of La Mancha had been so lacking in curiosity that they hadn't kept papers relating to this famous knight in their archives or their desks; and so, with this in mind, he didn't despair of finding the end of this delectable history, which indeed, with heaven's help, he did find in the way that will be narrated in the second part.

Second Part of
the Ingenious Hidalgo
DON QUIXOTE
de la Mancha

CHAPTER IX

✠

*In which the stupendous battle between the gallant
Basque and the valiant man from La Mancha is brought
to a conclusion*

In the first part of this history we left the valiant Basque and the famous
Don Quixote with naked swords aloft, about to deliver two such devastating
downstrokes that if their aim was true they would at the very least split
each other from top to bottom and cut each other open like pomegranates;
and at this critical point the delightful history stopped short and was left
truncated, without any indication from its author about where the missing
section might be found.

This worried me, because the pleasure afforded by the little I had read
turned to displeasure as I considered what an uphill task awaited me if I
wanted to find the great bulk of material that, as I imagined, was missing
from this delectable tale. It seemed impossible and contrary to all good
practice that such an excellent knight shouldn't have had some sage who'd
have made it his job to record his unprecedented deeds, something never
lacked by any of those knights errant

> Who go, as people say,
> Adventuring their way,[1]

because every one of them had one or two sages, made to measure for him, who not only recorded his exploits but also depicted his least thoughts and most trivial actions, however hidden from the public gaze they were; and such an excellent knight couldn't have been so unfortunate as to be totally lacking in what Platir[2] and the like had more than enough of. So I couldn't bring myself to believe that such a superb history had been left maimed and mutilated, and I laid the blame on malicious time, the devourer and demolisher of all things, which had either hidden or destroyed what was missing.

It also struck me that, since modern books like *The Undeceptions of Jealousy* and *The Nymphs and Shepherds of Henares* had been found in his library, his history must also be a recent one, and that, even if it hadn't been put into writing, it must live on in the memory of the people of his village and others near by. All these thoughts left me feeling puzzled and eager for exact and authentic knowledge of the complete life and works of our famous Spaniard Don Quixote de la Mancha, the light and mirror of the chivalry of that land, and the first man in our times, in these calamitous times of ours, to devote himself to the toils and exercise of knight-errantry, and to the redressing of wrongs, the succouring of widows and the protecting of maidens, those maidens who used to ride about, up hill and down dale, with their whips and their palfreys, carrying their maidenhead with them; for unless raped by some blackguard, or by some peasant with his hatchet and his iron skullcap, or by some monstrous giant, there were maidens in those times gone by who, at the age of eighty and not having slept a single night under a roof, went to their graves with their maidenheads as intact as the mothers who'd borne them. I say, then, that for these and many other reasons our gallant Don Quixote is worthy of continuous and memorable praise – which shouldn't be denied me, either, for all the hard work and diligence I devoted to searching out the conclusion to this agreeable history; although I'm well aware that if heaven, chance and fortune hadn't helped me, the world would have been left without the pleasurable entertainment that an attentive reader of this work can enjoy for nearly two hours. And this is how I found the missing part:

One day when I was in the main shopping street in Toledo, a lad appeared, on his way to sell some old notebooks and loose sheets of paper to a silk merchant; and since I'll read anything, even scraps of paper lying in the gutter, this leaning of mine led me to pick up one of the notebooks that the lad had for sale, and I saw it was written in characters that I recognized as Arabic. Although I knew that much, I couldn't read them, and so I looked around to see if there was some Spanish-speaking Moor in the street, and it wasn't very hard to find one, because even if I'd been looking for a translator from another better and older language,[3] I should have found him, too. In short, chance provided me with a man who, when I told him what I wanted and put the book in his hands, opened it in the middle and after reading a little began to laugh. I asked him why, and he replied that he was laughing at something written in the margin of the book by way of annotation. I told him to tell me what it was and, still laughing, he replied:

'As I said, this is written here in the margin: "This woman Dulcinea del Toboso, so often mentioned in this book, is said to have been a dabber hand at salting pork than any other woman in La Mancha."'

When I heard 'Dulcinea del Toboso' I was dumbfounded, because it immediately suggested that the notebooks contained the history of Don Quixote. So I told him to read me the title-page that very instant and he did so, making an extempore translation from the Arabic, and it said: *History of Don Quixote de la Mancha, written by Cide Hamete Benengeli,[4] an Arab historian.* I had to draw on all the discretion I possess not to reveal how happy I felt when I heard the title of the book; and, getting in ahead of the silk merchant, I bought all the papers and notebooks from the lad for half a real; and if the lad himself had had any discretion and had noticed how much I wanted them, he could well have expected and indeed exacted more than six reals. Then I went off with the Moor to the cathedral cloister and asked him to translate the notebooks, or at least all those that had to do with Don Quixote, into Castilian, without adding or omitting a single word, and I offered to pay him whatever he asked. He was satisfied with fifty pounds of raisins and two bushels of wheat, and promised to make a good, faithful translation, and to be quick about it, too. But to ensure the smooth working of our agreement, and not to let such a find out of my sight, I brought the Moor home with me, and in little more than a month and a half he translated the whole text just as it is set down here.

In the first notebook there was a realistic picture of Don Quixote's battle with the Basque, with both of them in the positions described in the history, their swords aloft, one protected by his little round infantryman's shield and the other by his cushion, and the Basque's mule so lifelike that you could tell from a mile off that it was a hired one. At the Basque's feet were written the words *Don Sancho de Azpetia*,[5] which must have been his name; and at Rocinante's feet were these other words: *Don Quixote*. Rocinante was depicted in such wonderful detail – as long as a wet week and as lean as a lath, with a jutting spine and far gone in consumption – that it was easy to see how appropriately he had been named Rocinante. Next to him stood Sancho Panza, holding his ass by the halter, and at his feet were the words *Sancho Zancas*; and he must, to judge from the picture, have had a short body, a plump paunch and long shanks, these last two features being expressed in the words Panza and Zancas respectively, because he's given both these surnames at different points in this history. Other details could be observed, but none of them is important, or relevant to the truthful narration of this history – and no history is bad so long as it is truthful.

If there is any objection to be made about the truthfulness of this history, it can only be that its author was an Arab, and it's a well-known feature of Arabs that they're all liars; but since they're such enemies of ours, it's to be supposed that he fell short of the truth rather than exaggerating it. And this is, indeed, what I suspect he did, because where he could and should have launched into the praises of such an excellent knight, he seems to have been careful to pass them over in silence, which is something he shouldn't have done or even thought of doing, because historians should and must be precise, truthful and unprejudiced, without allowing self-interest or fear, hostility or affection, to turn them away from the path of truth, whose mother is history: the imitator of time, the storehouse of actions and the witness to the past, an example and a lesson to the present and a warning to the future. In this history I know that everything anyone could want to find in the most delectable history is to be found; and if anything worthwhile is missing from it, it's my belief that it's the dog of an author who wrote it that's to blame, rather than any defect in the subject. At all events the second part began like this, according to the translation:

The keen-edged swords of the two valiant and enraged combatants, thus raised aloft, seemed to be threatening the very heavens, earth and watery abysses, such was the determination displayed by both men. The first to deliver his blow was the wrathful Basque, and he did so with such force and fury that, if his sword had not twisted in the course of its descent, that stroke alone would have been enough to put an end to the fearful fight and to all our knight's adventures; but fortune, which had better things in store for him, turned his opponent's blade aside so that, although it struck his left shoulder, all the damage it did was to disarm him on that side, carrying with it a large part of his helmet together with half his ear, all of which tumbled to the ground in hideous ruin, leaving him in a sorry state indeed.

By God, who could describe the rage that took possession of the heart of the man of La Mancha on seeing himself treated in this way? All that can be said is that it was so great that he rose at last in his stirrups and, gripping his sword with both hands, brought it down with such fury full on the Basque's cushion and head that his admirable protection was of no avail and, as if a mountain had fallen on top of him, blood began to trickle from his nose, and from his mouth, and from his ears, and he started to slide off his mule, from which he would no doubt have fallen had he not clung to its neck; but even so he lost his stirrups and dropped his reins, and the animal, terrified by the awful blow, began to gallop this way and that, and soon bucked its rider off.

Don Quixote was calmly watching this scene, and when he saw the Basque fall he jumped from his horse, ran up to him and, putting the tip of his sword between his eyes, told him to surrender or he would cut off his head. The Basque was so stunned that he could not reply, and his fate would have been sealed, so blind with rage was Don Quixote, if the ladies in the coach, who had been watching the fight in consternation, had not hastened to where he stood and pleaded with him to do them the great kindness and favour of sparing their squire's life. To which Don Quixote, haughty and grave, replied:

'To be sure, fair ladies, I am well content to do as you request; but I insist on one condition to which you must agree, which is that this knight promise me to repair to the village of El Toboso and present himself on my behalf before the peerless Doña Dulcinea, that she may dispose of him according to her pleasure.'

The fearful, disconsolate ladies, without stopping to think about what

Don Quixote was demanding or even asking who Dulcinea was, promised that the squire would do whatever was required of him.

'Since you have given me your word, I shall do him no further harm, even though he richly merits it.'

CHAPTER X

✠

About what happened next between Don Quixote and the Basque, and the peril with which he was threatened by a mob of men from Yanguas

By this time Sancho Panza had struggled to his feet, somewhat mauled by the friars' servants, and had stood watching Don Quixote's battle, as in his heart he prayed to God to be so kind as to give his master the victory and let him win some island of which he could make his squire the governor, as promised. So once Sancho saw that the fight was over and that his master was about to remount Rocinante, he went over to hold his stirrup and, before he started climbing, knelt down before him and, grasping his hand, kissed it and said:

'Don Quixote sir, please make me the governor of the island you've just won in this dreadful battle. However big it is, I'm sure I'll be strong enough to govern it as well as anyone who ever governed islands anywhere in the world.'

To which Don Quixote replied:

'I would have you know, brother Sancho, that this adventure and others like it are not island adventures but roadside adventures, in which there is nothing to be won but a broken head and a missing ear. Be patient, for there will be adventures that will enable me to make you not only a governor but something greater still.'

Sancho thanked him profusely and, again kissing his hand, and the skirts of his armour too, helped him on to Rocinante, and himself mounted his donkey and set out after his master, who, without a word of farewell to the ladies in the coach, rode off at a brisk pace into a nearby wood. Sancho followed as fast as his donkey could trot, but Rocinante's speed was such that Sancho fell further and further behind and had to call out to his master to wait for him. Don Quixote did so, reining Rocinante in until his weary squire caught up with him, and said:

'What I'm thinking, sir, is that it'd be a good idea to go and take refuge in some church somewhere, because that man you fought is in a really bad way, and it wouldn't surprise me if we were reported to the Holy Brotherhood[1] and they came to arrest us. And by God, if they do that, we'll sweat blood before we get out of prison.'

'Not at all, Sancho,' said Don Quixote. 'Where have you ever seen or read of a knight errant standing trial, whatever outrages he is accused of?'

'I don't know anything about getting out of rages, I've never been in one in my life – all I do know is that people who go fighting in the fields are dealt with by the Holy Brotherhood, and I'm not going to poke my nose into that other thing you said.'

'Do not worry, my friend,' replied Don Quixote, 'for I shall rescue you from the Chaldeans[2] themselves if need be, let alone the Holy Brotherhood. But tell me, pray: have you ever seen a knight more valiant than I on all the face of the earth? Have you ever read in histories of any knight who is or has been more spirited in the attack, more persevering in the pursuit, more dexterous in the wounding or more skilful in the unhorsing?'

'To tell you the honest truth,' replied Sancho, 'I haven't ever read a history, because I can't read or write, but what I will dare bet is that in all the days of my born life I've never served a braver master than you – and I pray God these braveries of yours aren't paid for where I just said. And what I pray you to do is to see to that ear of yours, you're losing a lot of blood from it. Here in my saddle-bags I've got some lint and white ointment.'

'All this would have been quite unnecessary,' replied Don Quixote, 'if I had remembered to make a flask of the Balsam of Fierabras:[3] for but one drop of it would have saved us both time and medicine.'

'What flask and what balsam is that?' said Sancho Panza.

'It is,' said Don Quixote, 'a balsam the recipe for which I carry in my memory, and if provided with it one need not fear death or contemplate dying from any kind of wound. And so, once I make some and give it to you, all you have to do when you see that in some battle I have been cut in two (as often happens) is to take the part of my body that has fallen to the ground and, before the blood congeals, neatly and carefully place it on top of the part remaining in the saddle, being quite sure to make it fit exactly. Then you will have me drink just two mouthfuls of the balsam, and I shall be as sound as a bell.'

'If that's so,' said Sancho, 'I here and now renounce being governor of the island you've promised me, and all I want in payment for my many good services is for you to let me have the recipe for that wonderful potion – to my mind it'll fetch more than two reals an ounce anywhere, so it's all I need to live an honourable and easy life. But first I'd better know if it costs a lot to make.'

'For less than three reals you can make twelve pints of it,' replied Don Quixote.

'Strike me blind!' replied Sancho. 'What are you waiting for, why not make some here and now and show me how?'

'Enough of that, my friend,' replied Don Quixote. 'I intend in due course to show you even greater secrets and do you even greater favours. But now let us see to this ear of mine, for it is hurting more than I should like.'

Sancho took lint and ointment out of his saddle-bags. But when Don Quixote saw his broken helmet he was on the point of going berserk, and, placing his hand on his sword and raising his eyes to heaven, he said:

'I swear by the Creator of all things, and by the four evangelists and all their holy writings, that I will lead the life led by the great Marquis of Mantua when he swore to avenge his nephew Baldwin's death, and until then "ne'er at table to eat bread nor with his wife to lie", and other such things that, although I cannot remember them now, can be taken as spoken, until I have exacted full vengeance on the perpetrator of this outrage.'

When Sancho heard this he said:

'I'd just like to point out, Don Quixote sir, that if that knight has done as he was told and has gone to present himself before my lady Dulcinea del Toboso, then he's done his duty and doesn't deserve another punishment unless he commits another crime.'

'You have spoken well and to the purpose,' replied Don Quixote, 'and so I hereby annul my oath as regards exacting fresh vengeance on him; but I swear anew and confirm that I will lead the life I have just described until I wrest from some knight another helmet at least as fine as this. And do not imagine, Sancho, that I am doing this without a solid basis, for I have a clear model to follow: exactly the same thing happened, down to the very last detail, with Mambrino's helmet, which cost Sacripante so dear.'⁴

'You just send all those oaths of yours to the devil, sir,' retorted Sancho, 'they're bad for your health and worse for your conscience. Or else tell me this – supposing days and days go by and we don't come across anyone in a helmet, what then? Have we got to honour the oath, regardless of all the inconvenience and discomfort, always sleeping in our clothes, never under a roof, and those hundreds of other penances in the mad old Marquis of Mantua's vow, that you're so set on reviving? Just think about it, sir – it isn't men in armour you'll find on these here roads but carters and muleteers, who not only don't wear helmets but have probably never even heard of them.'

'You are mistaken about that,' said Don Quixote, 'because before we have been riding along these highways and byways for two hours we shall see more men in arms than fell upon Albracca to carry off the fair Angelica.'⁵

'All right, then, so be it,' said Sancho, 'and please God we come well out of all this and the time soon arrives to conquer this island that's going to cost me so dear – and then I can die happy.'

'I have already told you, Sancho, not to worry about all that; for if finding an island presents any problems, there is always the kingdom of Denmark or the kingdom of Soliadisa,⁶ which would fit you like a glove, and still more so being as it is on terra firma, which should make you even happier. But let us leave these matters until it is time to deal with them; and now see if you have anything to eat in your saddle-bags, so that we can go without delay in search of some castle where we can stay for the night and make the balsam about which I have told you; for I swear to God that my ear is very painful.'

'There's an onion here, and a bit of cheese, and a few scraps of bread,' said Sancho, 'but that isn't food for a valiant knight like you.'

'How mistaken you are!' replied Don Quixote. 'I would have you know, Sancho, that it is an honour for knights errant not to eat for a whole month, and if they do eat, it must be what they find readiest to hand, and you would know this well enough if you had read as many histories as I have; for in all those very very many that I have read, I have not found any mention of knights errant eating, except when it happened that some sumptuous banquet was held for them, but otherwise they used to live on next to nothing. And although it is evident that they could not have gone without eating and satisfying all the other needs of nature, because, after all, they were men like us, it is also evident that since they spent most of their time wandering in woods and wildernesses, without cooks, their everyday food must have been country fare, like that which you are offering me now. And so, friend Sancho, do not be afflicted by what pleases me; do not seek to build the world anew, or to turn knight-errantry on its head.'

'I'm sorry I'm sure,' said Sancho. 'Not knowing how to read or write, as I said before, I haven't been able to find out about all these rules of knighthood. From now on I'll put all sorts of nuts and raisins into the saddle-bags for you, being as you are a knight, and for me, not being one, I'll put in feathered provisions of greater substance.'

'I am not saying, Sancho,' replied Don Quixote, 'that it is obligatory for knights errant not to eat anything other than those nuts to which you refer; but that they must have been their usual sustenance, together with certain herbs, known to them and to me, which they found in the fields.'

'It's a good idea,' said Sancho, 'to know about those there herbs. I fancy we're going to need that knowledge one fine day.'

Then he took out what he'd said he'd brought, and the two men ate together in peace and good fellowship. But anxious to find somewhere to stay that night they didn't linger over their dry and frugal meal. They remounted and hurried on, to try and reach a village before nightfall, but both the day and their hopes of doing so came to an end as they were passing some goatherds' huts, and they decided to spend the night there. Sancho's sorrow at not reaching a village was matched by his master's delight at sleeping in the open air, because he considered that each time he did so he performed an act of possession that provided fresh proof of his chivalry.

CHAPTER XI

✠

About what happened to Don Quixote with some goatherds

He received a hearty welcome from the goatherds. Once Sancho had accommodated Rocinante and the donkey as best he could, he set off on the trail of the smell being given out by some chunks of goat meat that were boiling in a pot over the fire; and, although he'd have liked to find out there and then if they were ready to be transferred from the pot to the stomach, this wasn't possible, because the goatherds took them off the fire and, spreading some sheepskins on the ground, made haste to lay their rustic table and, showing great goodwill, invited them to share their meal. There were six goatherds using that fold and they all sat down around the skins, after begging Don Quixote, with rough ceremony, to sit on an upside-down bowl that they placed there for him. Don Quixote did so, and Sancho stayed standing to serve him the drinking horn. When Don Quixote saw his squire on his feet, he said:

'So that you may see, Sancho, what great good there is in knight-errantry, and how close those exercising any of its ministries always are to being honoured and esteemed by the world, it is my wish that you should come and sit by my side in the company of these excellent people, and be one with me, your natural lord and master – that you should eat from my very own plate and drink from my very own cup: for of knight-errantry may be said what is said of love, that it makes all things equal.'

'What a great honour!' said Sancho. 'But just let me tell you one thing, sir – if I had plenty to eat, I'd eat it as well or even better standing up and by myself as sitting down next to an emperor. The truth is that what I eat in my own little corner without any fuss or bother, even if it is only bread and onions, tastes much better to me than all the fine turkeys on other tables where I'd have to chew slowly, drink hardly a drop, wipe my mouth all the time, never sneeze or cough if I felt like it, or do all those other things that being by yourself and free and easy lets you do. So, sir, as for these honours that you want to confer on me for being a follower and servant of knight-errantry, which is what I am as your squire, I'd rather you turned them into something more practical and useful, and I renounce all your honours from here to eternity – though I'm very grateful to you I'm sure.'

'You shall sit down all the same; for he that humbleth himself shall be exalted.'[1]

And seizing Sancho by the arm he forced him to squat by his side.

The goatherds couldn't make head or tail of this gibberish about squires and knights errant, and they just sat there eating in silence and staring at their guests who, with great elegance and even greater appetite, were stowing away chunks of meat as big as their fists. Once the meat course was finished, a quantity of sweet acorns was spread on the sheepskins together with half a cheese, harder than if it had been made of mortar. Meanwhile the drinking horn was being kept busy, circulating so often (now full, now empty, like a bucket on a water wheel) that it soon exhausted one of the two wineskins hanging near by. After Don Quixote had satisfied his stomach he took up a handful of acorns and, gazing at them, held forth as follows:

'Happy the age and happy the centuries were those on which the ancients bestowed the name of golden, not because gold (so prized in this our age of iron) was then to be obtained with ease, but because men living in such times did not know those two words *yours* and *mine*. In that blessed age all things were held in common; no man, to gain his daily sustenance, had need to take any other pains than to reach up and pluck it from the sturdy oaks, liberally inviting him to taste their sweet and toothsome fruit. The limpid fountains and the running streams offered him their delectable and transparent waters in magnificent abundance. In the clefts of rocks and in the hollows of trees, diligent and prudent bees formed their common-wealths, offering to every hand, without requesting anything in return, the rich harvest of their sweet labours. The sturdy cork-oaks, without any other inducement than that of their own generosity, shed their thick, light bark, with which men first covered their houses, supported on rustic poles, only as a defence against the inclemencies of the heavens. All then was peace, all was friendship, all was harmony; the heavy coulter of the arching plough had not yet ventured to open and enter the tender womb of our first mother, for she, without any compulsion, yielded from every part of her broad and fertile bosom everything to satisfy, sustain and delight the children then possessing her.

'Those were the days when artless, lovely shepherdesses roamed from dale to dale and from hill to hill, their hair in plaits or flowing loose, clothed in no more than was necessary to conceal with modesty that which modesty has always required to be concealed; and their ornaments were not those now in fashion, luxuries of Tyrian purple and martyred and tormented silk, but verdant burdock leaves and ivy intertwined, in which perhaps they walked as fine and elegant as our court ladies do now in the bizarre creations that idle curiosity has put before their eyes. In those times the amorous conceptions of the soul were expressed as simply as they had been conceived, without any search for artificial circumlocutions to enhance them. Fraud, deceit and malice were not yet intermixed with truth and plain dealing. Justice kept within her own bounds, and favour and interest, which now depreciate, confound and persecute her, did not dare assail or disturb her. As yet the judge could not make his whim the measure of the law, because there was nothing to judge and nobody to be judged. Maidens and modesty roamed, as I have said, wherever they wished, alone and mistresses of themselves, without fear of harm from others' intemperance and lewd designs: their ruin was born of their own will and desire. And now, in these detestable times of ours, no maiden is safe, even if she is hidden away in the depths of another Cretan labyrinth:[2] for even there the plague of love, with all the insistence of its accursed importunity, finds its way in through some chink, or wafted through the air, and infects and ruins her and all her seclusion. It was for the protection of such ladies, as time went by and wickedness increased, that the order of knights errant was founded, to defend maidens, protect widows and succour orphans and the needy.

'This is the order to which I belong, my brothers, whom I thank for the most friendly welcome that you have given me and my squire. For although every man alive is obliged by natural law to assist knights errant, it is nonetheless meet that, knowing as I do that in ignorance of this obligation you have welcomed and regaled me, I should acknowledge your goodwill with the utmost gratitude.'

This long harangue (which could well have been dispensed with) was pronounced by our knight because the acorns he'd been given had reminded him of the golden age; and so it occurred to him to offer these useless arguments to the goatherds, who listened without uttering a word, bemused and bewildered. Sancho kept quiet, too, and ate acorns, and paid frequent visits to the second wineskin, hanging from a cork-oak so that its contents could be kept cool.

It took Don Quixote longer to finish talking than it took the others to finish eating, and then one of the goatherds said:

'So that you can more truthfully say, sir knight errant, that we've welcomed you with a ready goodwill, we want to offer you some pleasant entertainment by getting a companion of ours, who'll soon be here, to sing to us – he's a bright lad, fond of the ladies, and, what's more, he can read and write and he plays the fiddle as prettily as can be.'

The goatherd had hardly finished speaking when the sound of the fiddle reached their ears, and soon after that the fiddler himself appeared, a well-graced lad of maybe twenty-two. His companions asked him if he'd had his supper, and when he replied that he had, the goatherd who'd offered Don Quixote the song said to the lad:

'In that case, Antonio, you could give us the pleasure of hearing you sing, just to show our guest here that there's someone among us who can, and that in these woods and forests there are people who know music. We've told him about your abilities, and now we want you to air them and show that we're right; so go on, sit yourself down and sing us that ballad about your sweetheart that your uncle the priest made up for you – everyone in the village thought it was very good.'

'All right,' the lad replied.

And, not needing to be asked again, he sat down on the stump of an evergreen oak and, after tuning his fiddle, soon began, with great charm, to sing this song:

Antonio

Although, Olalla, you love me,
    You never say you do,
Not even with those pretty eyes,
    Mute tongues that love speaks through.

I know that you're a clever girl,
So I'll say it yet again,
For once true love has been revealed
It never ends in pain.

It's true enough, Olalla dear,
You've sometimes made me feel
Your snowy bosom's made of stone,
Your soul is made of steel.

And yet amid your coy rebuffs
And modest dressings-down,
From time to time hope lets me see
The borders of her gown.

My hopes swoop on the fair decoy
And yet they've never savoured
The sadness of not being called
Or the joy of being favoured.

If love is kindness, as they say,
You're so endowed with this
That the conclusion to my hopes
Must be the longed-for bliss.

If loyal services can help
To turn a breast benign,
Some of the things I've done for you
Must surely make you mine.

For if you have been watching out,
You often will have seen
Me wearing my best Sunday suit
On Mondays, neat and clean.

As I well know, fine clothes and love
Walk down the selfsame way:
I've always wanted, in your eyes,
To look gallant and gay.

I shall not mention dancing, or
The singing, for your sake,
Of serenades, from darkest night
Till crowing cold daybreak.

I shall not mention all the praise
I've spoken of your looks;
It's true enough, but it's put me
In other girls' bad books.

    Craggy Teresa said, when I
Said you're as lovely as can be:
'There's them as thinks they loves a saint
When what they loves is a chimpanzee.

    Just look at all her flashy gewgaws,
Hair from someone else's head,
Just look at all her phoney glamour:
Love himself could be misled.'

    So then I told her she was lying;
Her cousin took her side;
He challenged me, and you know what
He did and I replied.

    It's love not lust I feel for you,
For it's not that I'm inclined
To slap and tickle, stuff like that:
I've better things in mind.

    The Church has got a solid yoke
Tied firm with silken twine,
You stick your head in your own half
And I'll stick my head in mine.

    If not, I swear it here and now
By my dead kith and kin:
I'll only ever leave these hills
To be a Capuchin.

With this the goatherd brought his song to an end; and, although Don Quixote asked him to sing them another one, Sancho Panza wouldn't agree to it, because he was more in a condition to sleep than to listen to songs. And so he said to his master:

'You settle yourself down straight away where you're going to spend the night, because the work these good people have got to do all day long doesn't let them spend their nights singing.'

'Yes, I understand, Sancho,' replied Don Quixote. 'It is plain to see that the visits to the wineskin demand requital in sleep rather than in music.'

'We all of us enjoyed the wine, thank God,' replied Sancho.

'I do not deny it,' replied Don Quixote, 'but settle down now wherever you like, for it is better for those of my profession to watch than to sleep. Nevertheless it would be a good idea if you dressed this ear of mine again – it is hurting more than it needs to.'

Sancho did as he was told, and when one of the shepherds saw the wound he told him not to worry, he'd apply a remedy that would soon cure it. And the shepherd picked a few leaves of the rosemary that was growing there in great plenty, chewed them and mixed them with a little salt, applied them to the wound and bandaged it tightly, assuring Don Quixote that no other remedy would be necessary; which proved true.

CHAPTER XII

About what a goatherd told Don Quixote and the others

And now one of the lads who brought provisions from the village appeared and said:

'Hey, do you know what's happened down in the village?'

'How are we supposed to know that?' replied one of them.

'Well, it's like this,' the lad continued. 'That famous student-shepherd Grisóstomo died this morning, and it's rumoured he died of love for that fiendish Marcela, rich Guillermo's daughter, that girl who wanders about all those God-forsaken places dressed up as a shepherdess.'

'Marcela you said?' asked one of them.

'Marcela I said,' the lad replied. 'And the best part is he's left in his will that he wants to be buried out in the wilds, like some Moor, at the foot of the rock by the cork-oak spring, because rumour has it that's where he first saw her, and they say he said so himself. And he's left other things to be done, too, but the village priests say they won't be done, and that it wouldn't be right to do them, because they're more like what pagans get up to. To all this, that great friend of his, Ambrosio – you know, that student who dressed up as a shepherd with him – replies that it'll all be done just as Grisóstomo ordered, and the village is in an uproar about it, but, to judge from what everyone's saying, they're going to end up doing what Ambrosio and all his shepherd friends want, and tomorrow they're coming to bury him with great pomp and ceremony where I said. And it's my belief it's going to be well worth seeing – at least I'm not going to miss it, not even if it means that I can't get back to the village tomorrow.'

'That's what we'll all do,' added the goatherds, 'and we'll draw lots to see who'll stay behind to look after the goats.'

'A good idea, Pedro,' said one, 'but there won't be any need for that, I'll stay behind with everybody's goats. And don't put it down to virtue or lack of curiosity on my part, but to me not being able to walk, because of that broken branch that went through my foot the other day.'

'Thanks all the same,' replied Pedro.

Don Quixote asked this Pedro to tell him about the dead man and the shepherdess, to which Pedro replied that all he knew was that the dead man was a rich hidalgo who lived in a village in the sierra and who'd been a student at Salamanca University for many years, after which he'd come back to the village with a reputation for being wise and well-read.

'In particular, people said he knew all about the science of the stars, and what the sun and the moon do up there in the sky, because he used to tell us exactly when the clips were going to come.'

'*Eclipse* is the word, my friend, not *clips*, for the obscuration of the two great luminaries,' said Don Quixote.

But Pedro, not troubling himself with trifles, went on with his story:

'And he also used to predict whether a year was going to be fruitful or hysterical.'

'You mean *sterile*, my friend,' said Don Quixote.

'Sterile or hysterical,' replied Pedro, 'it all boils down to the same thing. As I was saying, with all this predicting his father and his friends grew very rich, because they believed him and did as he advised when he said: "Sow barley this year, not wheat; this year you'd better sow chick-peas, not barley; next year there's going to be a bumper crop of olives, but the following three there won't be any at all."'

'That science is called astrology,' said Don Quixote.

'I haven't the faintest idea what it's called,' retorted Pedro, 'but what I do know is that he knew all this and more besides. In the end, not very many months after he came back from Salamanca, he took off his long scholar's gown one day and appeared dressed as a shepherd, with his crook and his sheepskin jacket – and this other man, his great friend Ambrosio, who'd studied with him, he dressed himself up as a shepherd too. I was forgetting to say that Grisóstomo, the dead man, was very good at writing poems – he even used to write the carols for Christmas Eve, and the mystery plays for Corpus Christi[1] that the village lads performed, and everyone said they were brilliant. When the people in the village saw the two scholars suddenly dressed as shepherds they were amazed, and couldn't work out what had led them to make such an odd change. By this time Grisóstomo's father had died and he'd inherited piles of property – royal estate, goods and cattles, cows and horses, sheep and goats, as well as masses of money, and the lad was left the absolute lord of it all, and the truth is he deserved it, because he was a fine companion and very charitable, a good friend to all good men, with a face like an angel. Later it was known that he'd only changed clothes to wander all about these wild places after that shepherdess Marcela the young lad mentioned before, because poor Grisóstomo, God rest his soul, had fallen in love with her. And now I'm going to tell you, because it's something you should know, who that lass is – it's possible, and more than possible, that you won't hear anything like it in all the days of your life, even if you live to be older than noses.'

'*Moses* you should have said,' interrupted Don Quixote, who couldn't abide the goatherd's word-mangling.

'Noses have been around for quite a while, too,' retorted Pedro, 'and if you're going to be picking on every other word I use, sir, we shan't be done in a twelvemonth.'

'Forgive me, my friend,' said Don Quixote. 'I only mentioned it because there is such a difference between noses and Moses; but your reply was an excellent one, for noses are indeed older than Moses; and do continue your history, and I will not interrupt you ever again.'

'I was about to say, my dear good sir,' said the goatherd, 'that there was one farmer in our village even richer than Grisóstomo's father, and he was called Guillermo, and God had given him not only vast riches but also a daughter whose mother, the most honourable woman in all these parts, had died giving birth to her. I can see her even now, that lovely face of hers with the sun in one cheek and the moon in the other. And what a fine housewife she was, and so good to the poor – I do believe that at this very moment her soul must be enjoying God in the other world. Guillermo was heartbroken at the death of such an excellent wife and he died, too, leaving his daughter Marcela young and rich and in the care of one of her uncles, a priest in our village. The girl grew up so beautiful that she put us in mind of her mother, such a great beauty herself, although everyone thought that her daughter was going to be even lovelier. And so she was, and by the time she was fourteen or fifteen all who set eyes on her praised God for making her so beautiful, and most fell hopelessly in love. Her uncle kept her shut up indoors, very bashful and demure, but the fame of her great beauty spread far and wide – and this, and her fortune, brought the men not only of our own village but of all the villages for many miles around, the very best of them too, flocking to ask, beg and pester her uncle for her hand in marriage. But even though he'd have liked to marry her off straight away, since she was of the right age, being a true and good Christian he was unwilling to do so without her consent – and no, he didn't have an eye on the gains to be made from delaying the girl's marriage and keeping control of her property. This, I can promise you, was said in praise of the good priest in more than one circle of commentators in the village. For I should tell you, errant sir, that in these tiny places everything's discussed and everything's gossiped about; and you can be quite certain, just as I am, that a priest has to be a saint to make his flock speak well of him, especially in a village.'

'That is quite true,' said Don Quixote, 'but do continue, for the story is a very good one, and you, my dear Pedro, are telling it with a certain stylish grace.'

'It's the grace of Our Lord God that I'm in need of, which is more to the purpose. Anyway, what happened was that although the priest described to his niece, in detail, the qualities of each one of her many suitors, begging her to choose and marry whichever she preferred, all she ever replied was that she didn't want to marry yet because, being so young, she didn't feel strong enough to bear the burden of matrimony. Faced with excuses as good as these appeared to be, her uncle stopped pressing her, and decided to wait until she was older and able to choose a companion to her taste.

For as he said, and said rightly, parents shouldn't provide for their children's future against their will. But lo and behold, like a bolt from the blue, meticulous modest Marcela appears one day converted into a shepherdess, and, despite all the efforts of her uncle and the other villagers to dissuade her, off she goes into the fields with the other shepherdesses in the village to mind her own flock. And once she came into the public gaze and her beauty was exposed to all eyes, I couldn't tell you how many rich youths, hidalgos and farmers dressed up just like Grisóstomo, and wandered about the fields wooing her – among them, as I've said, our deceased friend, who people said no longer loved her, but adored her.

'But you mustn't suppose, just because Marcela has given herself over to this free and easy life, with little privacy or rather none at all, that she's done anything to bring the least discredit upon her modesty or chastity; quite the opposite, she watches so closely over her own honour that of all her suitors and pursuers not one has boasted, or could boast without lying, of having been given the slightest hope of fulfilling his desire. Because although she doesn't avoid the company of shepherds, and treats them with courteous friendliness, as soon as any of them reveals his intentions, even if in a proper and holy proposal of marriage, she hurls him from her like a boulder from a catapult. And in this mood she's wreaking more havoc on these lands than if they'd been invaded by the plague; because her affability and beauty encourage those who know her to serve her and to love her, but her disdainful destruction of their hopes drives them to the brink of suicide; and so they don't know what to say, and only cry that she's cruel and an ingrate, and other similar words that describe her character all too accurately. And if you were to stay here awhile, sir, you'd hear these mountains and these valleys echoing with the laments of the broken-hearted wretches who pursue her.

'Not far from here is a place where there are almost two dozen lofty beeches, and there is not one on whose smooth bark is not engraved the name of Marcela, and above some a crown with which a lover affirms that Marcela wears and deserves to wear the crown of all human beauty. Here a shepherd sighs, there another moans; here songs of love are to be heard, there dirges of despair. There's one who spends every hour of the night seated at the foot of some oak or crag, and there, never allowing his tear-filled eyes a moment's rest, sunk and lost in his thoughts, he's found by the morning sun; there's another who, finding no relief or respite for his sighs, stretched out on the burning sand in the racking noonday heat of summer, sends his complaints up to merciful heaven. And over every single one of them the lovely Marcela triumphs, footloose and fancy-free, and all of us who know her are waiting to see where her arrogance will lead, and who will be the fortunate man to tame such ferocity and enjoy such perfect beauty. Since everything I've narrated is the proven truth, I can well believe that what this young lad here said they're saying about the cause of Grisóstomo's death is also true. And so I advise you, sir, not to miss his burial tomorrow – it'll be well worth seeing, because Grisóstomo has lots of friends, and it isn't a couple of miles from here to where he said he wanted to be buried.'

'That is indeed what I intend to do,' said Don Quixote, 'and I thank you for the pleasure you have afforded me by telling me such a delightful story.'

'Oh no!' replied the goatherd. 'I don't know half the things that have happened to Marcela's suitors, but it could be that tomorrow we come across some shepherd who can tell us about them. And now it'll be a good idea for you to go and sleep under cover, because sleeping in the damp night air could be bad for your wound – though the remedy you've been given is so effective that there's no fear of an infection setting in.'

Sancho Panza, who was wishing that the goatherd would take his endless talk with him to the devil, also asked his master to go and sleep in Pedro's hut. He did so, and there he spent most of the night remembering his lady Dulcinea, in imitation of Marcela's suitors. Sancho Panza settled down between Rocinante and his donkey, and there he slept the sleep not so much of a star-crossed lover as of a hoof-hammered squire.

CHAPTER XIII

Which concludes the story about the shepherdess Marcela, together with other events

But hardly had the day begun to show itself on the balconies of the east when five of the six goatherds got up and went to wake Don Quixote, to ask him if he still intended to go and see the famous burial of Grisóstomo, and to tell him that if he did they would keep him company. Don Quixote, who was longing to go, rose and told Sancho to saddle the horse and fit the pack-saddle on to the donkey immediately, which he did with great diligence; and with the same diligence they all set out on their way. And they'd ridden less than a mile when, as they crossed another path, they saw half a dozen shepherds coming towards them clothed in black sheepskin jackets and with wreaths of cypress and bitter oleander crowning their heads. Each had a stout holly stave in his hand. With them came two gentlemen on horseback, splendidly dressed for travelling, accompanied by three servants on foot. When the two parties met they exchanged courteous greetings, and when they asked each other where they were going they discovered that they were all on their way to the burial, so they travelled together.

One of the horsemen said to his companion:

'It seems to me, Señor Vivaldo, that we're going to count however much time we spend on this famous burial as having been time well spent: it is indeed going to be famous, considering the extraordinary things these shepherds have been telling us about the dead shepherd and the death-dealing shepherdess.'

'I think so, too,' replied Vivaldo, 'and I'm not talking about taking just one day over it, either – I'd happily take four days off for the sake of witnessing it.'

Don Quixote asked what it was that they had heard about Marcela and Grisóstomo. The horseman replied that they'd joined up with the shepherds earlier that morning and that, seeing them in such mournful attire, they'd asked why they were dressed like that; and that one of the shepherds had told them all about the secluded life and the beauty of a shepherdess called Marcela, and about the love she inspired in the many men who wooed her, and about the death of that Grisóstomo to whose burial they were going. In short, he told them everything that Pedro had told Don Quixote the day before.

So this conversation came to an end, and another one began when the man called Vivaldo asked Don Quixote what it was that prompted him to ride about such a peaceful part of the world armed in that fashion. And Don Quixote replied:

'The profession that I exercise does not allow me to ride in any other way. Easy living, luxury and repose were invented for effete courtiers; toil, disquiet and arms were created solely for those the world calls knights errant, of whom I, unworthy as I am, am the very least.'

On hearing this they all concluded that he was mad; and to make quite certain, and to find out what sort of madness he suffered from, Vivaldo went on to ask him what knights errant were.

'Have you not read,' replied Don Quixote, 'the annals and histories of England, which treat of the famous exploits of King Arthur, commonly known in our Castilian tongue as Artús, who, according to an ancient tradition divulged throughout that kingdom of Great Britain, did not die but was, by sorcerer's art, turned into a raven, and who, in due course, will recover his sceptre and kingdom, and reign again; for which reason no Englishman has ever been known from that day to this to kill a raven? Well, in the days of that good king the famous order of chivalry of the Knights of the Round Table was founded, and the love between Sir Lancelot of the Lake and Queen Guinevere was consummated as is there recorded, the go-between and confidante being that honourable duenna Quintañona,[1] all of which gave rise to the ballad that is so well known and so highly praised in Spain:

> And never sure was any knight
> So served by damsel or by dame
> As Lancelot, that man of might,
> When here from Brittany he came,

with its smooth and gentle unfolding of its deeds of love and war. Well, from that time onwards, handed on down the generations, the order of chivalry gradually extended and spread throughout many different parts of the world, and its members were famous for their exploits: the valiant Amadis of Gaul with all his sons and grandsons to the fifth generation, and the valorous Felixmarte of Hyrcania, and the never sufficiently praised Tirante the White, and the brave and invincible knight Belianis of Greece, whom we have very nearly been able to see and speak with and hear in our own times. This, then, gentlemen, is what it is to be a knight errant, and this is the order of chivalry, in which I, as I have said, although a sinner, have professed; and I do profess everything professed by the knights of whom I have told you. And so I roam these lonely and deserted places in search of adventures, with the firm intention to employ my arm and indeed my whole person in the most perilous adventures that fortune sends my way, in aid of the weak and needy.'

These words showed the travellers that Don Quixote was indeed out of his wits, and they could now see what kind of madness had taken him over, which astonished them as much as it did everybody else who made this discovery. And, to while away the time during the short journey said to remain, Vivaldo, who was a clever man with a cheerful disposition, decided, when they reached the sierra where the burial was to take place, to provide him with the opportunity to expand on his nonsense. So he said:

'It seems to me, sir knight errant, that you profess one of the very strictest professions in the world, and it's my belief that not even being a Carthusian monk is as strict.'

'It may be that it is as strict,' replied our Don Quixote, 'but whether it is as necessary to the world is something that I am within a hair's breadth of doubting. For, if truth is to be told, the soldier who carries out his captain's orders contributes no less than the captain who gives him those orders. What I mean to say is that monks, in peace and tranquillity, pray to heaven for the well-being of the world; but we soldiers and knights put into practice what they pray for, defending the world with the prowess of our arms and the blades of our swords, and not under cover but in the open air, the targets for unbearable sun-rays in the summer and for the piercing frosts of winter. So we are ministers of God on earth, the arms through which his justice is executed here. And since the business of war and all its associated activities cannot be conducted without guts, sweat and toil, it follows that those who profess it must labour harder than those who in tranquil peace and repose are forever praying to God to favour the weak and defenceless. I do not mean to say, nor does it even cross my mind, that the life of a knight errant is as virtuous as that of a cloistered monk; I merely want to argue, from my own sufferings, that it is, without a shadow of doubt, more laborious and more buffeted, hungrier and thirstier, more wretched, ragged and louse-ridden; for there is no denying that the knights errant of the past suffered much misfortune in the course of their lives. And if some of them rose by the strength of their arms to be emperors, I know that it cost them dear in blood and sweat, and if those who did rise to this degree had not had enchanters and sages to help them, they would have been baulked in their ambitions and cheated of their hopes.'

'That's what I think, too,' said the traveller, 'but there's just one thing, among lots of others, that I don't like about knights errant, and that is that when they're about to undertake some mighty and perilous adventure in which there's a clear risk of losing their lives, it never occurs to them to commend themselves to God, as every Christian's meant to do in such moments of danger, but instead they go and commend themselves to their ladies, with as much spirit and devotion as if their ladies were God himself – which seems to me to have a smack of the pagan about it.'

'My dear sir,' replied Don Quixote, 'it cannot be otherwise, and the knight errant who conducted himself in any other manner would be committing a grave misdemeanour, for it is an established custom in knight-errantry that the knight errant whose lady is present when he undertakes some great feat of arms turns his eyes to her with gentle lovingness, as if to implore her to favour and succour him in the parlous straits into which he is about to enter; and even if there is nobody there to hear him, he is obliged to whisper a few words in which he commends himself to her with all his heart; and of this we have innumerable examples in the histories. And one cannot assume from this that they do not commend themselves to God as well, for they still have the time and the opportunity to do so in the course of the subsequent action.'

'All the same,' replied the traveller, 'I still have my doubts – I've often read how two knights errant have words and, one thing leading to another, they lose their tempers and turn their horses and take up their positions a good distance from each other, and then, without any further ado, they charge, and in mid-career they commend themselves to their ladies – and what usually happens in these encounters is that one of them tumbles back over the haunches of his horse, pierced through and through by his opponent's lance, and the other one would fall off his, too, if he didn't hang on to its mane. Now I can't see how the one who died could have had any chance to commend himself to God, with everything happening so fast. It'd have been better if, instead of using up his words commending himself to his lady as he charged, he'd employed them on what he ought to have done as a Christian. What's more, it's my belief that not all knights errant do have ladies to commend themselves to, because not all of them are ladies' men.'

'That cannot be,' said Don Quixote. 'What I mean to say is that there cannot be any knight errant without a lady, because it is as natural and proper for them to be lovers as it is for the heavens to have stars, and it is quite certain that there has never been a history in which one can find a knight errant without a lady-love; because his lack of one would in itself be sufficient for him to be regarded not as a legitimate knight errant but as a bastard who had gained entry to the fortress of chivalry not through the main gate but over the wall, like a thief and a robber.'

'All the same,' replied the traveller, 'if I'm not mistaken, I think I can remember reading that Sir Galaor, the brother of the valiant Amadis of Gaul, never had any particular lady to commend himself to, and this didn't make people look down on him, and he was a very brave and famous knight.'

To which our Don Quixote replied:

'My dear sir, one swallow does not make a summer. Furthermore, I know that this knight did secretly burn with love, apart from the fact that, as everyone knows, he lost his heart to all those ladies who took his fancy, a natural inclination towards the fair sex that he could not overcome. But, in short, it is very well attested that he did have one special lady whom he made the mistress of his heart, and to whom he did indeed commend himself very often but very secretly, because he prided himself on being a secretive knight.'

'So if it's essential for every knight errant to be a lover,' said the traveller, 'we can assume you're one, too, this being part and parcel of the profession. And so long as you don't pride yourself on being as secretive as Sir Galaor, I beseech you, with all the urgency I can be permitted, on behalf of these good people and myself as well, to tell us all about your lady's name, home town, rank and beauty – I'm sure she'd count herself lucky to have the whole wide world know she's loved and served by such a knight as you appear to be.'

Here Don Quixote heaved a deep sigh and said:

'I cannot affirm whether or not my sweet enemy is pleased at the whole world's knowing that I serve her; all I can say, in response to what is so courteously requested of me, is that her name is Dulcinea; her homeland El Toboso, a village in La Mancha; her rank that of princess at least, for she is my queen and lady; her beauty superhuman, for in her all the impossible and chimerical attributes of loveliness that poets ascribe to their ladies become reality: her hair really is golden, and her forehead the Elysian Fields, and her eyebrows rainbows, and her eyes suns, and her cheeks roses, and her lips coral, and her teeth pearls, and her neck alabaster, and her breast marble, and her hands ivory, and her complexion snow; and the parts hidden to human gaze by modesty are such, I do think and believe, that wise consideration cannot find comparisons for them, but only extol them.'

'We should like to know about her family, lineage and ancestry,' said Vivaldo.

To which Don Quixote replied:

'She is not of the ancient Curtii, Caii or Scipios of Rome, or of the modern Colonnas or Orsinis, or of the Moncadas or Requeséns of Catalonia, nor yet of the Rebellas or Villanovas of Valencia, the Palafoxes, Nuzas, Rocabertis, Corellas, Lunas, Alagóns, Urreas, Fozes or Gurreas of Aragon, the Cerdas, Manriques, Mendozas or Guzmáns of Castile, or the Alencastros, Pallas or Meneses of Portugal; she is, rather, of those of El Toboso de la Mancha, a lineage that, although recent, is such that it could well be the generous rootstock of the most illustrious families of future centuries. And let no man contest this except on the condition placed by Zerbino under the trophy of Orlando's arms and armour:

Let no man move this armour or this sword
Who will not prove his prowess with their lord.'[2]

92

'My own lineage is the Cachopíns of Laredo,' replied the traveller, 'but I'm not going to be so rash as to compare it with El Toboso de la Mancha, even though, to tell you the truth, this is a surname I've never heard of.'

'Never heard of it my foot!' retorted Don Quixote.

The others were all ears as they listened to the conversation between the two, and even the goatherds realized just how crazy our Don Quixote was. Sancho Panza alone thought that everything his master said was true, having known him, and known what sort of a man he was, ever since childhood; and Sancho only hesitated a little when it came to the part about the lovely Dulcinea del Toboso, because he'd never heard of such a name or such a princess, even though he lived so near to El Toboso.

As they continued on their way engrossed in this conversation they saw, coming down a gorge between two great hills, about twenty shepherds, all wearing black sheepskin jackets and crowned with wreaths, some of which were later discovered to be of yew and the others of cypress. Six of the shepherds were carrying a bier covered with a great variety of flowers and branches. At this sight one of the goatherds said:

'Those men over there are bringing Grisóstomo's body, and at the foot of that mountain is the spot where he said he was to be buried.'

So they hurried there, just in time, because the shepherds had placed the bier on the ground and four of them had begun digging a grave beside a hard rock with their sharp pickaxes.

The two parties exchanged courteous greetings, and then Don Quixote and those who had come with him went to examine the bier, and on it, covered in flowers, they saw the corpse, dressed as a shepherd, of a man who seemed to be about thirty; and even though he was dead, it was plain to see that in life he'd had handsome features and a gallant disposition. Scattered around him on the bier there were some books and many papers, some open and some folded up. The onlookers, the grave-diggers and all the others kept an extraordinary silence, until one of those who'd brought the body said to another:

'You'd better make quite certain, Ambrosio, that this is the place Grisóstomo said, since you're so concerned for everything in his will to be carried out exactly as he instructed.'

'Yes, this is the place,' replied Ambrosio, 'because it was here that my unhappy friend often told me the story of his misadventures. He told me it was here that he first saw that mortal enemy of the human race; here that he first declared his love, as honourable as it was ardent; and here, at their last meeting, that Marcela sealed her scornful rejection, which led him to put an end to the tragedy of his wretched existence. And here, in remembrance of so many misfortunes, he wished to be laid in the bowels of eternal oblivion.'

And, turning to Don Quixote and the travellers, Ambrosio continued:

'This body, gentlemen, that you are contemplating with compassionate eyes, was the dwelling-place of a soul in which heaven placed an infinite portion of its riches. This is the body of Grisóstomo, who was unmatched in intelligence, peerless in courtesy, perfect in politeness, a phoenix in friendship, generous beyond measure, grave without presumptuousness, joyful without vulgarity, and, all in all, the first in virtue, and second to none in misfortune. He loved and was hated; he adored and was disdained; he entreated a dragon, pleaded with marble, chased the wind, cried out in the wilderness and served ingratitude, whose reward was to make him the prey of death in the midst of the course of his life, which was ended by a shepherdess whom he wished to make immortal in the memory of mankind, as those papers at which you are looking could demonstrate, if he had not instructed me to commit them to the flames as soon as I have committed his body to the earth.'

'If you do that,' said Vivaldo, 'you'll be treating them with even harsher cruelty than their owner himself, because it's neither just nor proper to carry out the wishes of a man who orders something that no rational arguments can justify. Augustus Caesar would have been out of his mind if he'd agreed to what the divine Mantuan poet ordered in his will.[3] And so, Señor Ambrosio, even though you are committing your friend's body to the earth, don't commit his writings to oblivion; for if he was so aggrieved as to command it, you shouldn't be so foolish as to obey him. Rather let these papers live, and Marcela's cruelty with them, for ever, as an example to the living, in times to come, so that they can avoid such pitfalls; because I and these friends of mine know the history of this enamoured and desperate friend of yours, and we know about your friendship, and what caused his death, and the instructions he left when he died; from all of which lamentable history it is easy to judge how great was Marcela's cruelty, Grisóstomo's love and your faithful friendship, and also to see what happens to people who rush headlong down the path that delirious love places before their eyes. Last night we learned that Grisóstomo had died and was to be buried in this place, and so, moved by curiosity and compassion, we departed from our route and agreed to come and see for ourselves what we'd been so sad to hear about. And in recognition of this compassion, and of our desire to do something about it if we could, we beg you, O Ambrosio, – or at least I for my part beg you – not to burn these papers and to let me have some of them.'

And without waiting for the shepherd to reply, Vivaldo stretched out his hand and took some of the papers closest to him. Seeing which Ambrosio said:

'Courtesy obliges me, sir, to let you keep the papers you've just taken, but it would be vain for you to think I shall not burn the rest.'

Vivaldo, longing to see what was written on the papers, opened one of them and saw that its title was *Song of Despair*. On hearing this Ambrosio said:

'This is the last thing the unfortunate man wrote. And so that all can hear, sir, to what a pass his misfortune had brought him, please read it aloud: there'll be time enough to do so while the grave is being dug.'

'That I shall do with pleasure,' said Vivaldo.

And since all the others were equally curious, they gathered around him, and he read the following in a clear and ringing voice:

CHAPTER XIV

※

In which the dead shepherd's verses of despair are given,
together with other unexpected events

Grisóstomo's Song

Since you would have me publish, cruel maid,
From tongue to tongue, in this and every nation,
The news of your implacable disdain,
I'll call on hell itself to come and aid

My grieving breast with howls of lamentation,
And bend and break my voice with grief and pain.
And as I strive and labour to explain
My sorrow and your cold and heartless deed,
Forth shall the terrifying clamour stream,
And in it fragments of my bowels shall teem
To make my torture exquisite indeed.
So give me your attention: listen now
Not to harmonious sounds, but to the row
That from my bosom's depths in desolation,
Stirred up by bitter frenzy without measure,
Flows for my pleasure and for your vexation.

    The roaring of the lion; and the raging
Howl of the vicious wolf; the scaly, craven
Snake's dreadful hissing; and the awful groan
Of some horrendous monster; the presaging
And cautionary croaking of the raven;
Across the tossing sea the gale's wild moan;
The furious bellow of the overthrown
And wounded bull; the pitiful lament
Made by the widowed dove; the dreary whine
Of the much-envied owl:[1] let all combine
With shrieks from the infernal regiment
To clamour forth from my tormented soul,
So mingling in one vast, tumultuous whole
That all the senses are soon overpowered;
For novel tones are needed to declare
This deep despair by which my heart's devoured.

    The doleful echoes of such great confusion
Shall not resound on Father Tagus' banks
Or famous Betis'[2] olive groves: for I
Shall spread my miseries in sad profusion
In mountains' deepest caves and steepest flanks,
With a dead tongue yet with a living cry;
Or in some hidden vale, or on the shy

Shores that from human dealings still abstain,
Or where the fiery globe was never seen,
Or where vast hordes of noxious creatures glean
Their baneful living from the Libyan plain;
For though, unto the barren wilderness,
Uncertain echoes of my heart's distress
Take word of your unequalled cruelty,
They shall, by favour of my wretched fate
Reverberate all over land and sea.

Disdain is death; suspicion, false or sound,
Defeats the patience of the firmest mind;
Base jealousy destroys with its despair;
Interminable absences confound
Our lives; faced by neglect, our hopes for kind
Or happy fortune don't reduce our care:
Inevitable death lurks everywhere.
And yet – a miracle! – I don't expire,
Jealous, disdained, far absent, fully sure
About suspicions that I can't endure,
Neglected by the one on whom I feed my fire;
And, racked by all this torture, I can't spy
A glimmer of those hopes that pass me by,
Nor do I, in my grief, seek hope – no, never:
Instead, to magnify my misery,
I swear to be bereft of hope for ever.

But is it possible to hope and fear
At once, somehow? And is it for the best
When arguments for fear have much more weight?
Why shut my eyes when jealousy stands here
And, through the thousand gashes in my breast,
Is something that I have to contemplate?
Who would not run to open wide the gate
To disbelief, when right before his eyes
Disdain's revealed, and wavering suspicion
Is changed to patent fact – Oh sad transition! –

While limpid truth is turned to murky lies?
Fierce tyrant of all Love's imperial lands,
O Jealousy, place cold steel in these hands!
Give me, Disdain, a rope of twisted thread!
But grief has gained a cruel victory:
Your memory, I fear, is long since dead.

    I die, and I despair of being blessed
In life or death with any joy at all,
So I'll persist in my fantastic dream.
I'll say that he who loves the most does best,
The freest man is he who's most in thrall
To Love's tyrannical and ancient scheme,
And my eternal enemy I'll deem
To have a soul as lovely as her face;
Say that forgetfulness is my desert
And that, by means of this most dreadful hurt,
Love builds his empire on a solid base.
With these ideas, and with a well-tied knot,
I'll put an end to my poor mortal lot,
Destroyed by her disdain and heartlessness.
I'll give my soul and body to the air
And know I'll bear no future palms of bliss.

    With your unreason you make manifest
The reason forcing me to bring to bear
This force on my own life, a baneful blight;
So, since this mortal wound deep in my breast
Is proof that must make anyone aware
How gladly I succumb to my bleak plight,
And if by chance you recognize my right
That the clear heavens of your lovely eyes
Should darken when I die, you must control
Your grief: when I leave you my shattered soul
I don't want kind responses as some prize.
Instead, with laughter on that grim occasion,
Show that my dying is your celebration;

But this request's a foolish waste of breath
For I well know it will increase your glory
That my life's story ends in sudden death.

And now the hour has struck: from deepest hell
Come, thirsting Tantalus, to my ordeal;
Rolling your mighty stone along its way
Come, Sisyphus; come, Tityus, come as well,
And bring your vulture; Ixion, bring your wheel;
Come too, you sisters toiling night and day;[3]
And now let all of you as one convey
Your mortal anguish to my breast, and sigh
(If it's allowed to victims of despair)
Your harrowing laments over my bare
Carcass, refused a shroud in which to lie.
Come, three-faced guardian of the dreadful gate[4]
And all hell's brood of fiends, and celebrate
And sing the doleful descant of your grief;
No better tribute can, I think, be due
To lovers who have won death's cold relief.

O Song of Desperation, do not grieve
Now that in desolation I must leave;
But rather, since the cause that gave you birth
By my misfortune grows and grows in gladness,
Be free from sadness, even in the earth.

The members of the audience quite liked Grisóstomo's song, even though the reader said he didn't think it accorded with the account he'd heard of Marcela's modesty and virtue, because Grisóstomo complained about jealousy, suspicion and absence, all to the prejudice of Marcela's good name and reputation. To which Ambrosio replied, as one who knew his friend's most hidden thoughts:

'To satisfy that doubt, sir, I should tell you that when this unfortunate man wrote this song he was far from Marcela, having taken himself away to see if absence would have its customary effect; and, since there's nothing that doesn't worry an absent lover and no fear that doesn't assail him,

Grisóstomo was worried by imagined jealousies and suspicions that he feared as if they were real. And so everything that fame affirms about Marcela's virtue is true: except for some cruelty, and a little arrogance, and more than a little disdain, there are no faults at all for envy itself to find in her.'

'That's true enough,' replied Vivaldo.

As he was about to read another of the papers he'd saved from the fire, he was halted by a miraculous vision (that was what it seemed to be) which came before their eyes: on top of the crag by which the grave was being dug the shepherdess Marcela appeared, so beautiful that her beauty was even greater than it was famed to be. Those who had never seen her before gazed at her in silent amazement, and those who were used to seeing her stood in no less awe. But as soon as Ambrosio saw her he said, with indignation in his looks:

'Have you come, perhaps, fierce basilisk of these mountains, to see if your presence will make the wounds of this poor man slain by your cruelty spout blood? Or have you come to gloat over the achievements of your barbarity; or to contemplate from those heights, like another pitiless Nero, the flames of burning Rome; or to ride roughshod in your arrogance over this luckless corpse, as the ungrateful daughter did over her father Tarquin?⁵ Tell us now why you've come and what you want; because knowing that Grisóstomo's very thoughts never failed to obey you when he was alive, I shall ensure that, even though he's dead, you'll be obeyed by the thoughts of all those who called themselves his friends.'

'I haven't come, Ambrosio, for any of the reasons you've mentioned,' replied Marcela, 'but to defend myself and to demonstrate how wrong are all those who blame me for Grisóstomo's death and for their grief; and so I beg all of you here to give me your attention, because it won't take me very long nor shall I need many words to bring the truth home to people of good sense.

'You all say that heaven made me beautiful, so much so that this beauty of mine, with a force you can't resist, makes you love me; and you say and even demand that, in return for the love you show me, I must love you. By the natural understanding which God has granted me I know that whatever is beautiful is lovable; but I can't conceive why, for this reason alone, a woman who's loved for her beauty should be obliged to love whoever loves her. What's more, it could happen that the lover of beauty is ugly, and since that which is ugly is loathsome, it isn't very fitting for him to say: "I love you because you're beautiful; you must love me even though I'm ugly." And even if they are well-matched as far as beauty goes, that doesn't mean that the attraction's going to be mutual, because not all beauty inspires love. Some beauties delight the eye but don't captivate the heart; just as well, because if all beauty did inspire love and conquer hearts, people's affections would be forever wandering this way and that without knowing where to come to rest – there's an infinite number of beautiful people, so the affections would be infinite, too. And, according to what I've heard, true love can't be divided, and must be voluntary, not forced on you. If this is so, as I believe it is, why do you think I should be obliged to give in to you, just because you say you love me dearly? Or else tell me this: if heaven had made me ugly instead of beautiful, would I have been right to complain about you for not loving me? What's more, you must remember that I didn't choose this beauty of mine – heaven gave it to me, exactly as you see it, quite freely, without my asking for it or picking it. And just as the viper doesn't deserve to be blamed for her poison, even though she kills with it, because nature gave it to her, so I don't deserve to be blamed for being beautiful; because beauty in a virtuous woman is like a distant fire or sharp sword, which don't burn or cut anyone who doesn't come too close. Honour and virtue are ornaments of the soul, and without them the body, even if it is beautiful, shouldn't seem beautiful. Well then, if chastity is one of the virtues that most embellish the soul and the body, why should the woman who's loved for her beauty lose her chastity by responding to the advances of the man who, merely for his own pleasure, employs all his strength and cunning to make her lose it?

'I was born free, and to live free I chose the solitude of the countryside. The trees on these mountains are my company, the clear waters of these streams are my mirrors; and to the trees and the waters I reveal my thoughts and my beauty. I am the distant fire and the far-off sword. Those who have loved me for my looks I have disabused with my words. And if desires are kept alive on hope, I have never given any hope to Grisóstomo or fulfilled any man's desires, so it can truly be said of all of them that they were killed by their own obstinacy rather than by my cruelty. And if it's objected that his intentions were honourable and that for this reason I should have been more responsive to him, I reply that when, in that very place where his grave is being dug now, he revealed those honourable intentions of his to me, I told him that mine were to live in perpetual solitude and to allow nothing but the earth to enjoy the fruits of my seclusion and the remains of my beauty. If, after I'd spoken as plainly as that, he still chose to persevere against all hope and sail against the wind, is it surprising that he sank in the middle of the gulf of his own folly? If I'd encouraged him, I should have been false; if I'd gratified him, I should have been acting against my own intentions, better than his. He persisted although disabused, he despaired although not hated: and now you tell me whether it's just for me to be blamed for his grief! Let the man I deceive complain, let the victim of broken promises despair, let the man I entice nurse hope, let the man I accept rejoice: but let me not be called cruel or murderous by any man whom I have never deceived, made promises to, enticed or accepted.

'Heaven hasn't yet made it my destiny to love, and it's vain to think I'd ever love out of choice. Let this general warning serve for the individual benefit of each of my pursuers; and let it also be understood from now on that if any man dies because of me, he isn't dying from jealousy or mistreatment, because a woman who doesn't love any man can't make any man jealous, and disabuse must not be confused with disdain. He who calls me fierce and a basilisk can leave me alone, as something evil and dangerous; he who calls me an ingrate can stop courting me; he who calls me distant can keep his distance; he who calls me cruel can stop following me: because this fierce basilisk, this ingrate, this cruel and distant woman is most certainly not going to seek, court, approach or follow any of them. If Grisóstomo was killed by his own impatience and uncontrolled passion, why should anyone blame my modest and circumspect behaviour for that? If I keep my purity in the company of the trees, why should anyone want me to lose it in the company of men? As you all know, I have wealth of my own and I don't covet anyone else's; I live in freedom and I don't like to be constrained; I neither love nor hate anybody. I neither deceive this man nor run after that; I neither toy with one, nor amuse myself with another. The innocent company of the village shepherdesses and the care of my goats keep me happy. These mountains mark the limits of my desires, and if they do extend any further it is only for the contemplation of the beauty of the heavens, the way along which the soul travels back to its first abode.'

And as she said this she turned and disappeared into the thick of a nearby forest without waiting for an answer, leaving everyone astonished as much at her intelligence as at her beauty. And some of them, wounded by the powerful arrows of the rays flashing from her lovely eyes, made to follow her, heedless of the clear warning that they'd heard. Don Quixote, seeing this, and thinking it a good moment to make use of his chivalry by succouring a maiden in distress, cried in a ringing voice and with his hand on the hilt of his sword:

'Let no man, of whatever estate or condition, dare to follow the beautiful Marcela, under pain of incurring my furious indignation. She has shown with clear and sufficient reasons that she bears little or no blame for Grisóstomo's death, and that she is far from reciprocating the desires of any of her suitors; for which reason it is right that, instead of being pursued and persecuted, she should be honoured and held in esteem by all good men, for she has shown that she is the only woman in the world who lives such a chaste life.'

Whether because of Don Quixote's threats or because Ambrosio told them to finish what they were doing for their dead friend, none of the shepherds left the spot until, with the grave dug and Grisóstomo's papers burned, they placed his body in it, not without shedding many tears. They sealed the grave with a thick slab of rock, to be replaced in due course by a tombstone which Ambrosio said he was going to have made, with the following epitaph engraved on it:

> In here, earth's cold and paltry prize,
> The body of a lover lies,
> A shepherd who was cruelly slain
> By one who paid love with disdain.
> Ungrateful, haughty, cold and fair
> Was she who drove him to despair:
> More triumph for man's deadly foe
> As tyrant Love's dominions grow.

They strewed flowers and branches over the grave, condoled with their friend Ambrosio and took their leave of him. Vivaldo and his companion did the same, and Don Quixote said goodbye to his hosts and to the travellers, who begged him to come with them to Seville, because it's just the place to find adventures – on every street and round every corner they're simply waiting for you, more of them than anywhere else in the world. Don Quixote thanked them for the information and for their disposition to extend such courtesies to him, but said that for the time being he did not wish to go to Seville and indeed could not go there, until he had rid all those sierras of foul robbers, with which they were said to be infested. In view of his firm intentions the travellers decided not to pester him any more and, repeating their farewells, they left him and continued their journey, during which they weren't short of things to talk about, what with Marcela's history and Don Quixote's mad deeds. He resolved to go in search of the shepherdess Marcela and offer her all the services in his power. But events didn't turn out as he expected, according to what is related in the course of this true history, the second part of which ends here.

Third Part of
the Ingenious Hidalgo
DON QUIXOTE
de la Mancha

✳✳✳

CHAPTER XV

※

Which relates the unfortunate adventure that came Don Quixote's way when he came the way of some wicked men from Yanguas

The wise Cide Hamete Benengeli says that as soon as Don Quixote had taken his leave of his hosts and of everyone else at Grisóstomo's burial, he and his squire rode off into the forest where Marcela had disappeared; and, after they'd wandered about it searching for her in vain for over two hours, they reached a meadow of fresh grass, with a cool, tranquil stream running alongside, which invited and indeed compelled them to spend the hours of early afternoon there, because the heat was beginning to be excessive.

Don Quixote and Sancho dismounted and, leaving the donkey and Rocinante free to graze as they pleased on the lush grass, they ransacked the saddle-bags; and, without ceremony, in peace and good fellowship, master and servant ate what they found in them.

Sancho hadn't bothered to hobble Rocinante, safe in the knowledge that the nag was so meek and chaste that all the fillies in the pastures of Cordoba wouldn't lead him astray. But as fate – or the devil, who isn't always asleep – would have it, there was also in that valley a herd of Galician pony-mares belonging to some muleteers from Yanguas, whose custom it is to take their siesta with their animals wherever there is grass and water. And that place where Don Quixote happened to find himself suited these men from Yanguas very well.

It happened, then, that Rocinante felt the urge to enjoy some fun and games with their ladyships the pony-mares and, abandoning his natural habits and his normal gait the moment he scented them, without requesting his master's permission, he broke into a lively trot and went to inform them of his needs. But it seems that they must have been feeling more like grazing, because they gave him such a welcome with their hooves and their teeth that his girths soon snapped and he was left saddleless and naked. Yet what must have affected him most was that when the muleteers saw the attack that was being made on their mares, they ran over with their walking-staffs and gave him such a good hiding that they left him sprawling on the grass. At this point Don Quixote and Sancho, having witnessed Rocinante's thrashing, arrived breathless on the scene, and Don Quixote said to Sancho:

'From what I can see, friend Sancho, these are not knights, but base and low-born men. I say this because it means that you can freely help me to take due vengeance for the affront to which Rocinante has been subjected before our very eyes.'

'How the devil are we going to take vengeance,' replied Sancho, 'when there are more than twenty of them and just the two of us – or just the one and a half of us, more like?'

'I am the equal of a hundred men,' retorted Don Quixote.

And without further thought he seized his sword and attacked the men from Yanguas, and so did Sancho Panza, encouraged by his master's example. Don Quixote dealt one of them a blow that slashed open both his leather smock and a large part of his shoulder.

The muleteers, seeing so many of themselves so rudely handled by only two men, resorted to their walking-staffs, surrounded the pair and began to lay into them for all they were worth. The truth is that with the second blow they knocked Sancho to the ground, and Don Quixote went the same way in spite of all his eager dexterity. As fate would have it, he fell at the prostrate Rocinante's feet, from which one can judge the furious pounding that walking-staffs can give when wielded by wrathful rustic hands. When the men from Yanguas realized what they'd done, they loaded their animals as fast as they could and hurried on their way, leaving the two adventurers looking a sorry sight and feeling in an even worse temper.

Sancho Panza, lying by his master's side, was the first to start groaning, and he said in a feeble, doleful voice:

'Don Quixote sir! Oh, Don Quixote sir!'

'What do you want, brother Sancho?' replied Don Quixote, in the same weak, languishing tones.

'If it's at all possible,' replied Sancho Panza, 'I'd like a couple of swigs of that Fairy Brass's drink, if you've got some handy. Maybe it's good for broken bones as well as for sore wounds.'

'If I had some here, wretch that I am, what more could we want?' replied Don Quixote. 'But I swear to you, Sancho Panza, on my word as a knight errant, that before two days have elapsed, if fortune does not ordain otherwise, I shall have some in my possession; given a modicum of luck I shall manage this in the turning of a hand.'

'And how long do you think it'll be before we can move our feet?' replied Sancho Panza.

'For myself,' said the battered knight Don Quixote, 'I must say that I cannot tell how long. But I am to blame for it all, for I should not have drawn my sword against men who are not knights, as I am; and so I believe that, as a penalty for having broken the laws of chivalry, the god of battles has allowed me to be punished in this way. For this reason, Sancho Panza, you must always bear in mind what I am about to tell you, because it concerns the well-being of us both: whenever you see rabble of this kind offering us some affront, do not wait for me to draw my sword against them, for I shall most certainly not do so, but you draw your sword and punish them to your heart's content; and if any knights come to their aid and defence, I shall then defend you and attack them with all my power. You have already had a thousand signs and demonstrations of how far the powers of this mighty arm of mine extend.'

This was how arrogant the poor gentleman had become after his victory over the brave Basque. But his warning didn't impress Sancho Panza enough to prevent him from responding, and he said:

'I'm a peaceful man, sir, meek and mild, and I can overlook any insult, because I've got a wife to support and children to bring up. So even though it isn't up to me to give any orders, you bear this in mind, too – in no way am I going to draw my sword against anyone, peasant or knight, and I hereby, before God my Maker, forgive all affronts that anybody ever has offered me or ever will offer me, whether the person who has offered them, offers them or will offer them is of high or low birth, rich or poor, a gentleman or a commoner, not excepting any estate or condition whatsoever.'

On hearing this his master replied:

'If only I had breath enough in my body to speak a few words to you at my ease, and if only this pain in my ribs would abate a little, so that I could make you understand, Panza, how wrong you are. Look here, you rogue: should the winds of fortune, hitherto so adverse, turn in our favour, driving the sails of our desire so that with a constant breeze behind us, and in perfect safety, we reach harbour on one of the islands I have promised you, what would become of you if, after conquering it, I made you its lord? Well, you would render things impossible for yourself, through not being a knight or even wanting to be one, or having the courage or the desire to avenge affronts and defend your dominions. For I would have you know that in freshly conquered provinces and kingdoms, the hearts of the natives are never so subdued or so well disposed towards their new master as to leave no fear that they might play some trick, to reverse the state of affairs once more and, as people say, try their luck again; and so the new master must have understanding to be able to govern, and courage to attack and defend in any crisis.'

'In this particular crisis we've just been in,' replied Sancho, 'I do wish I'd had that understanding and courage you're going on about, but I can swear, on my word as a poor man, that I'm in more of a state for plasters than for chit-chat. You try and see if you can get up, and we'll give Rocinante a hand, though he doesn't deserve it, because he was the main cause of all this battering. I never would have believed it of him, I always took him for a pure-minded character, and as peaceful as me. Still, as they say, you need time to get to know people, and there's nothing certain in this life. Who'd have said that after you'd cut that poor knight errant about like that, the follow-up was going to be this great storm of a thumping that's just rained down on our ribs?'

'Your ribs, Sancho,' replied Don Quixote, 'must at least be accustomed to such squalls; but it is clear that mine, nurtured as they were between cambric and holland-cloth, feel the pain of this misfortune more keenly. And if it were not that I imagine . . . – no, I do not imagine: I know for a certain fact – that all these discomforts are inseparable from the exercise of arms, I should be ready to die of sheer rage, here and now.'

To this his squire replied:

'Sir, seeing as how all these disasters are as you might say the harvest of chivalry, I'd be grateful if you'd tell me whether they happen very often, or just at certain set times, because to my mind after two harvests like this one we're going to be useless for the third, unless God in his infinite mercy helps us.'

'Let me tell you, friend Sancho,' replied Don Quixote, 'that the life of a knight errant is subject to a thousand dangers and misfortunes, and it is equally true that knights errant are potential emperors and kings, as is shown by the experience of many different knights, about whose histories I am fully informed. And I could tell you now, if the pain would allow me, about some who by the might of their arms alone have risen to the high estate I have just mentioned; and yet these selfsame knights, both before and afterwards, were engulfed in various calamities and misfortunes. The valiant Amadis of Gaul once found himself in the power of his mortal enemy the enchanter Arcalaus, who, it is attested, had him tied to a column in his courtyard and gave him more than two hundred lashes with the reins of his horse. And there is an anonymous author of no small credit who says that after the Knight of the Sun had been caught in a trap[1] by a door that opened under his feet in a certain castle, and found himself bound hand and foot in a deep pit underground, there he was given what is known as an enema, of snow-water and sand, which was nearly the end of him; and if he had not been succoured in that sore extremity by a sage who was a great friend of his, the poor knight would have fared very ill. So I can well have patience, being as I am in such good company; for they suffered greater affronts than those which we have undergone. And I would have you know, Sancho, that wounds received from weapons that happen accidentally to be in the assailants' hands are not dishonourable, and this is explicitly stated in the law of challenges: if a shoemaker hits a man with the last he is holding, that man cannot be said to have been birched, even if the last is made of this particular wood. I am only telling you this to prevent you from thinking that, just because we have taken a battering in this dispute, we have been dishonoured, for the arms borne by those men, with which they belaboured us, were only their walking-staffs, and none of them, so far as I can remember, was carrying a rapier, a sword or a dagger.'

'They didn't give me a chance to look into details like that,' replied Sancho. 'I'd hardly drawn my own trusty blade when they gave my shoulders such a thrashing with those pine trees of theirs that they knocked the sight out of my eyes and the strength out of my feet and left me where I'm lying now, and where wondering whether the beating was dishonourable or not doesn't bother me in the slightest – all that does bother me is the pain of those staff-blows, and they're going to be as deeply engraved in my memory as they are on my shoulders.'

'For all that, brother Panza,' replied Don Quixote, 'allow me to remind you that there is no memory that time does not efface, no pain that death does not destroy.'

'Well, what bigger disaster could there ever be,' retorted Panza, 'than the one that has to wait for time to efface it and for death to destroy it? If this mishap of ours was one of those that can be cured with a couple of plasters it wouldn't be so bad, but I'm beginning to think that all the bandages in a hospital aren't going to be enough to even begin to sort us two out.'

'Stop that talk, Sancho, and attempt to make the best of a bad business,' replied Don Quixote, 'because that is what I shall do; and now let us see how Rocinante is, because it seems to me that not the least part of this misfortune has fallen to the poor fellow's share.'

'There's nothing surprising about that,' retorted Sancho, 'seeing as how he's such a fine knight errant. But what does surprise me is that my donkey's still in the pink, while we're black and blue all over.'

'Fortune always leaves a door open in adversity, to provide a remedy,' said Don Quixote. 'I say this because that creature of yours can now replace Rocinante, and bear me to some castle where I can be cured of my wounds. Furthermore, I shall not count it dishonourable to ride on such a beast, for I remember reading that when good old Silenus, the tutor of the merry god of laughter, rode into the city of the hundred gates, he did so, much to his satisfaction, on a handsome ass.'[2]

'I expect it's true he rode on an ass, as you say,' replied Sancho, 'but there's a big difference between riding an ass and being slung across an ass's back like a sack of rubbish.'

To which Don Quixote replied:

'Wounds received in battle do not detract from honour, but bestow it; and so, friend Panza, stop answering me back and do as you are told, get up as best you can and put me on top of your donkey in the posture that most pleases you; and let us be gone from here before night falls and catches us in this wild place.'

'Well, well,' said Panza, 'I have heard you say that it's right and proper for knight errants to sleep on open plains and deserts for most of the year, and that they count themselves lucky to do it.'

'All that,' said Don Quixote, 'is when there is no alternative, or when they are in love; and this is so true that there have been knights who have remained on top of a crag, in sunlight and shadow and all the inclemencies of the heavens, for two whole years, unknown to their ladies. And one of these was Amadis, when he called himself Beltenebros and took up his quarters on the Peña Pobre, for eight years or eight months – I cannot quite remember which, but all that matters is that he was doing penance there for some vexation or other that the lady Oriana had caused him. But let us leave these matters, Sancho, and do make haste, before some misfortune like Rocinante's befalls the donkey.'

'Then there'd be the devil and all to do,' said Sancho.

And letting out thirty groans and sixty sighs and one hundred and twenty curses on the head of the person who'd brought him there, he hauled himself to his feet, but he was so exhausted that he stopped half way up, bent over in the form of a Turkish bow and incapable of straightening himself any further; yet despite all these troubles he harnessed his donkey, which had also taken advantage of the day's excess of liberty to go a little astray. Then he righted Rocinante, who, if he'd had a tongue to complain with, certainly wouldn't have been matched by Sancho or his master.

In short, Sancho settled Don Quixote on the ass, tied Rocinante behind and, letting the ass lead the way, set off towards where he thought the highway might be. And he hadn't gone a couple of miles when fortune, which was taking his affairs from good to even better, brought the road before him, and by the side of the road he saw an inn that, to his grief and Don Quixote's delight, was to be a castle. Sancho insisted that it was an inn, and his master insisted that it wasn't an inn but a castle; and their insisting went on for so long that they reached it before they'd finished, and Sancho walked in, without any further investigation, with his string of animals.

CHAPTER XVI

※

About what happened to the ingenious hidalgo at the inn that he took for a castle

The innkeeper, seeing Don Quixote slumped across the ass, asked Sancho what was wrong with him. Sancho replied that it wasn't anything much, he'd just fallen off a rock and got a little bit spifflicated in the ribs. The innkeeper had a wife who wasn't at all like most innkeepers' wives, because she had a charitable nature and sympathized with others in their calamities; and so she hurried to look after Don Quixote and made her daughter, a very attractive girl, help her. Another girl was serving at the inn: an Asturian lass[1] with broad jowls, a flat-backed head, a pug nose, blind in one eye and not very sound in the other. It's true that the loveliness of her body offset her other shortcomings: she didn't measure five feet from her head to her toes, and her shoulders, with something of a hump on them, made her look down at the ground more than she liked. This comely wench assisted the innkeeper's daughter, and the two of them prepared for Don Quixote a woeful bed in an attic that showed all the signs of having served for many years in former times as a hayloft. A muleteer was also staying at the inn, and his bed was a little beyond Don Quixote's. Although it was made up of his mules' body pads and blankets, it was far superior to Don Quixote's, which consisted of four bumpy boards on top of two tortuous benches, a mattress so thin that it was more like a bedspread, stuffed with what could be seen through rents in it to be balls of wool but which felt so hard that they could have been taken for pebbles, two sheets made of shield-leather and one blanket whose every thread you could have counted without missing a single one.

On this wretched bed Don Quixote lay himself down, and then the innkeeper's wife and daughter covered him in ointment from head to foot while Maritornes, for this was the Asturian's name, held the lamp; and, finding Don Quixote so badly bruised all over, the innkeeper's wife said that it looked more like a beating than a fall.

'No, it wasn't a beating,' said Sancho, 'it's just that the rock had lots of jags and sharp edges on it.'

And each of them had made its own bruise. And he added:

'I'd be grateful, lady, if you could see to it that there are a few bits of tow left over, because somebody else is going to need them – my back's a bit on the sore side, too.'

'So you fell off the rock as well, did you?' replied the innkeeper's wife.

'No,' said Sancho Panza, 'but from the shock of seeing my master fall my own body hurts so much it's just as if I'd been beaten black and blue all over.'

'That could well be so,' said the daughter. 'I've often dreamt about falling off a tower and never reaching the ground, and when I've woken up I've felt as weak and exhausted as if I really had fallen off it.'

'That's the funny thing about it, lady,' said Sancho Panza. 'I wasn't dreaming at all, I was wider awake than I am now, yet I'm almost as badly bruised as my master Don Quixote.'

'What did you say this gentleman's name was?' asked Maritornes the Asturian.

'Don Quixote de la Mancha,' replied Sancho Panza, 'and he's a knight adventurer, and he's one of the best and mightiest ones the world has seen for a long, long time.'

'What's a knight adventurer?' replied the wench.

'Are you so green you don't know that?' retorted Sancho Panza. 'Well, look here, my dear: a knight adventurer, to cut a long story short, is someone who's being beaten up one moment and being crowned emperor the next. Today he's the unhappiest creature in the world, and the poorest too, and tomorrow he'll have two or three kingdoms to hand over to his squire.'

'Well, you're the squire of this fine master,' said the innkeeper's wife, 'so how is it that, to judge from appearances, you aren't even a count?'

'It's early days yet,' replied Sancho, 'we've only been out looking for adventures for a month, and so far we haven't come across any worthy of the name. And sometimes you go looking for one thing and you find another. The fact is that if my master Don Quixote gets over his wounds or fall and it doesn't turn me into a cripple, I wouldn't swap my hopes for the best title in Spain.'

Don Quixote was listening to every word of this conversation and, sitting up in bed as best he could and taking the innkeeper's wife by the hand, he said:

'Believe me, beauteous lady, you may account yourself fortunate to lodge in this your castle such a person as I, whom I refrain from praising because, as is often said, self-praise is no recommendation; but my squire will inform you about me. All I do say is that I shall keep eternally engraved on my memory the service that you have rendered me, so as to remain grateful to you for so long as my life shall last; and if only it had pleased the high heavens that love had not so vanquished me and subjected me to its laws and to the eyes of that beauteous ingrate whose name I shall not speak aloud, the eyes of this fair maiden would have been the lords of my liberty.'

The innkeeper's wife and daughter and the worthy Maritornes were bemused by the knight errant's words, which they understood as well as if he'd spoken in Greek, although they did realize that he meant to compliment them and offer them his services; and since they weren't used to such language they stared at him in amazement, and thought that he wasn't at all like normal men; and then, thanking him for his offers in the most expressive innkeeperese, they left him, and Maritornes the Asturian went to see to Sancho, who was no less in need of help than his master.

The muleteer had agreed with her to have some fun and games together that night, and she'd promised him that as soon as the guests had settled down and her master and mistress were asleep she'd go to him and give him all the pleasure he could wish for. And it's said of this splendid wench that she never gave such a promise without keeping it, even if she gave it unwitnessed in the middle of a moor, because she prided herself on being a hidalga, and didn't consider it at all dishonourable to be serving at the inn, for she said that misfortune and unhappy events had reduced her to that situation.

Don Quixote's hard, narrow, wretched, perfidious bed was the first you reached as you entered that starlit barn, and next to it Sancho made his, which was just a rush mat and a blanket that looked more as if it were made of close-cropped hessian than of wool. After these two beds came the muleteer's, constructed, as described above, out of the body pads and all the trappings of the two best mules he possessed, although he owned twelve altogether, glossy, plump, superb creatures, because he was one of the rich muleteers of Arévalo,[2] according to the author of this history, who makes special mention of this man, because he knew him very well, some people even claiming that the two of them were related – quite apart from the fact that Cide Mahamate Benengeli was a careful and meticulous historian, something that's obvious enough, for he refused to pass in silence over the happenings related so far, even though they're so petty and trivial, which should serve as an example to those grave historians who recount events so very succinctly that we can hardly catch a taste of them and, out of carelessness, malice or ignorance, the most substantial part is left in their inkwells. All praise to the author of *Tablante de Ricamonte*, and to the author of that other book that narrates the deeds of Count Tomillas:[3] how minutely they do describe everything!

I was about to say that after the muleteer had visited his animals and given them their second feed, he stretched himself out on his body pads to wait for his dependable Maritornes. Sancho was poulticed and bedded down, and, although he was trying to sleep, the pains in his ribs wouldn't allow it; and Don Quixote's pains kept him staring into space like a hare. The whole inn was in silence, and there was no light except that of a lamp hanging in the porch.

This extraordinary stillness, and the thoughts, always occupying our knight's mind, of the events narrated at every turn in the books that had been his undoing, brought into his imagination one of the strangest whims that it's possible for anyone to imagine: he had arrived at a famous castle (as we know, all the inns at which he stayed were castles as far as he was concerned), the innkeeper's daughter was the daughter of the lord of the castle, and, overwhelmed by his charm, she had fallen in love with him and promised him to come that night, unknown to her parents, and lie with him for a good while; and, taking all these fancies that he'd constructed for the solid truth, he began to feel anxious and to ponder about the perilous predicament in which his virtue was about to find itself, and he resolved in his heart not to betray his lady Dulcinea del Toboso even if Queen Guinevere herself and her lady-in-waiting Quintañona appeared before him.

As he was mulling over such absurdities, the time arrived for the Asturian girl's visit and for trouble for Don Quixote: barefoot and in her shift, with her hair gathered in a fustian net, she tiptoed into the room where the three men were in their beds, in search of the muleteer. But hardly had she reached the door when Don Quixote heard her, sat up, in spite of all his poultices and the pains in his ribs, and stretched out his arms to receive his beauteous maiden. The Asturian girl, hunched up in silence, was creeping forward with her arms held out in front of her in search of her lover, when she bumped into Don Quixote's arms and he seized her by her wrist and pulled her towards him and made her sit on his bed, and she did not dare utter a word. He felt her shift and, although it was made of sackcloth, it was for him the sheerest sendal. On her wrists she was wearing glass beads, but for him they had the sheen of precious pearls of orient. Her hair was more like a horse's mane, but he saw it as strands of gleaming Arabian gold, the splendour of which made the very sun grow dim. And her mouth, which reeked of stale piccalilli, seemed to him to exhale the gentlest of aromas; and, all in all, he depicted her in his imagination with every attribute of that other princess he'd read about in his books who, overcome by love, came to see the sore wounded knight, arrayed in all the finery there described. And the poor hidalgo was so besotted that neither touch nor smell nor any of the good maiden's other attributes could make him notice his mistake, even though they'd have made anyone but a muleteer vomit; on the contrary, he thought that he was holding the very Goddess of Beauty in his arms. And as he clutched her he began to murmur in soft and loving tones:

'Would that I were in a condition, most beauteous and eminent lady, to be able to repay the singular favour that you have done me in allowing me the sight of your wonderful loveliness; but fortune, which never tires of persecuting the virtuous, has seen fit to lay me low in this bed, so weak and exhausted that, even if it were my desire to satisfy yours, such a thing would be impossible. Furthermore, to this impossibility is added another, which is the fidelity that I have promised to the peerless Dulcinea del Toboso, the sole mistress of my most secret thoughts; but if it were not for these obstacles, I should not be such a doltish knight as to let slip the happy opportunity that in your great goodness you have offered me.'

Maritornes was in a cold sweat of dismay at finding herself in Don Quixote's clutches, and, without understanding or even trying to understand the words he was directing at her, she struggled in silence to break loose. The good muleteer, who'd been kept awake by his wicked desires, had heard his woman as soon as she came in through the door, had been listening to Don Quixote's every word and, suspecting that the Asturian girl might have broken her promise to him in favour of another man, had crept up close to Don Quixote's bed and was waiting there to see where all that incomprehensible jabbering was going to lead. But when he saw the girl struggling to break free and Don Quixote doing what he could to cling on to her, he decided that he didn't like this little joke, raised one arm and delivered such a terrible punch to the amorous knight's lantern jaws that his mouth was bathed in blood; and, not content with this, he climbed up on top of his ribs and started to trot up and down from one end of them to the other.

The bed, being somewhat fragile and insecurely founded, couldn't bear the addition of the muleteer and came crashing to the floor and awoke the innkeeper, who immediately assumed that it must be some of Maritornes' goings-on, because he yelled out to her and there was no reply. So he got up and, lighting a lamp, went in the direction from which the racket was coming. The girl, realizing that her master was on his way and knowing what a fearsome fellow he was, took refuge, agitated and frightened, in the bed of the soundly sleeping Sancho Panza, and there she rolled herself up into a little ball. In came the innkeeper with the words:

'Where are you, you little tart? I know this is all your doing.'

Sancho awoke and, feeling that bundle almost on top of him and thinking he was in the middle of a nightmare, began to flail about with his fists and caught Maritornes with them several times; provoked by the pain, she threw modesty to the wind and gave him so many punches in return that he was soon wide awake, much against his will; and finding that some unknown enemy was treating him in this way, he struggled to his feet and grappled with Maritornes, and the two of them began the fiercest and funniest skirmish imaginable.

When, by the light of the innkeeper's lamp, the muleteer saw the plight that his lady was in, he left Don Quixote and went to give her the help she needed. The innkeeper went to her, too, but with a different intention – to punish the girl in the belief, no doubt, that she was the sole cause of all this harmony. And just as children chant that the cat chased the mouse, the mouse chased the rope, the rope chased the stick, so the muleteer thumped Sancho, Sancho thumped the girl, the girl thumped him, the innkeeper thumped her and they all thumped each other at such a rate that there wasn't a moment's rest for any of them; and the best part of it all was that the innkeeper's lamp went out and left them in the dark, and they all carried on thumping each other at random so mercilessly that wherever a fist fell something or other was broken.

As it happened, another guest at the inn that night was an officer of the Holy Brotherhood of Toledo who, also hearing the strange strains of the struggle, seized his staff of office and the tin box containing his warrants and burst into the dark room crying:

'Stay where you are in the name of the law! Stay where you are in the name of the Holy Brotherhood!'

And the first person he bumped into was the battered Don Quixote, who lay senseless on his back among the ruins of his bed; and the peace-officer felt for the knight's beard and grabbed it and kept shouting:

'Help an officer of the law!'

But realizing that the man he was holding didn't stir, he assumed that he was dead and that the others in the room were his murderers, and in a voice reinforced by this suspicion he yelled:

'Shut the inn door! Don't let anyone leave – a man's been killed!'

These shouts alarmed them all, and each abandoned his fight at whatever stage it had reached when he heard them. The innkeeper went back to his room, the muleteer to his body pads, the girl to her garret; only the hapless Don Quixote and Sancho couldn't budge from where they were. And now the peace-officer let go of Don Quixote's beard and went to look for a light to track down and arrest the delinquents; but he couldn't find one, because the innkeeper had taken the precaution of extinguishing the lamp in the porch when he went back to his room; and the peace-officer had to resort to the fireplace, where after much time and trouble he lit another lamp.

CHAPTER XVII

*In which a further account is given of the countless
hardships that the brave Don Quixote and his good
squire Sancho Panza underwent at the inn that,
unfortunately for him, he mistook for a castle*

By now Don Quixote had come to his senses and, in the same tone of voice
that he'd used the day before to call to his squire when lying in the Vale
of Staffs,[1] he called out to him with the words:

'Sancho, friend, do you sleep? Do you sleep, friend Sancho?'

'How am I supposed to sleep, damn it,' retorted Sancho boiling with
fury, 'when anyone would think all the devils in hell have been messing
with me?'

'You may well think that,' replied Don Quixote, 'because either I am an
ignoramus or this castle is enchanted. For I would have you know . . .; but
what I am about to tell you is something that you must swear to keep secret
until after my death.'

'I swear it,' answered Sancho.

'I am only saying this,' insisted Don Quixote, 'because I believe that it
is wrong to deprive anyone of her honour.'

'I'm telling you I do swear it,' Sancho repeated, 'and I will keep it a
secret until after you've died – and I hope to God I can spill the beans
tomorrow.'

'Do I harm you so much, Sancho,' replied Don Quixote, 'that you would
like so soon to see me dead?'

'It isn't that,' answered Sancho, 'it's just that I hate keeping anything
for very long – I wouldn't like it to go off.'

'Whatever the reason,' said Don Quixote, 'I trust your love and courtesy;
and I would have you know that I have this night experienced one of the
most curious adventures that I could ever celebrate; and, to be brief, you
must know that the daughter of the lord of this castle, who is the most
elegant and beauteous maiden to be found almost anywhere on earth, came

to me a short while ago. How can I paint for you the loveliness of her person? How describe her fine intelligence? How delineate other hidden charms that, to preserve the fidelity I owe to my lady Dulcinea del Toboso, I must leave untouched and in silence? I shall only tell you that – whether because the heavens were envious of the great boon that fortune had placed in my hands or (and this is more probable) because this castle is, as I have said, enchanted – just when I was engaged with her in the most tender and loving conversation, a hand attached to some arm of some enormous giant came down, without my seeing it or knowing whence it came, and delivered such a punch to my jaws that they are all bathed in blood; and then it so pummelled me all over that I am in an even worse state than yesterday, after the affair with those men from Yanguas who, because of Rocinante's excesses, inflicted on us the affront about which you know only too well. From this I conjecture that some enchanted Moor must be the guardian of the treasure of this maiden's beauteousness, and that it cannot ever be mine.'

'Nor mine neither,' said Sancho, 'because more than four hundred Moors have been giving me a going-over, and the hammering with the walking-staffs was chicken-feed beside it. But tell me, sir, how can you call it a curious and celebrated adventure, when we've ended up like this? You didn't do so badly, because you got your hands on that incomparable beauteousness you've just been on about, but what did I get out of it apart from the worst hiding I hope I'll ever be given in my life? Oh, what made my poor mother give birth to this miserable sinner? I'm not a knight adventurer and I'm never going to be a knight adventurer, yet I get more than my fair share of all the misadventures!'

'So you were beaten, too, were you?' replied Don Quixote.

'Isn't that what I've just been telling you, damn it?' said Sancho.

'Do not worry about that, my friend,' said Don Quixote. 'I shall now make the precious balsam that will heal us in the twinkling of an eye.'

The peace-officer had now managed to light the lamp, and he went to inspect what he thought was the corpse; and as soon as Sancho saw him walking into the room, in his shirt and nightcap, carrying the lamp and with an ugly look on his face, he asked his master:

'Sir, do you think this might be that enchanted Moor come to punish us again, with some extra punches he forgot to throw the first time?'

'It cannot be the Moor,' replied Don Quixote, 'because those who are enchanted do not allow anyone to see them.'

'Maybe they don't let anyone see them, but they let them feel them all right,' said Sancho. 'And if you don't believe me, just ask my ribs.'

'You could ask mine, too,' replied Don Quixote, 'but this is not sufficient evidence to make us believe that the man before us is indeed the enchanted Moor.'

The peace-officer approached and was amazed to find them coolly chatting to each other. It's true, though, that Don Quixote was still lying on his back, pummelled and plastered into immobility. The peace-officer went up to him and said:

'So how's it going then, you poor old fellow?'

'If I were you,' retorted Don Quixote, 'I should speak with greater courtesy. Is it the custom in this land to talk to knights errant in that way, you blockhead?'

The peace-officer couldn't tolerate being addressed so disrespectfully by such a sorry-looking wretch, and he raised his lamp, oil and all, and smashed it down on Don Quixote's head, leaving a good-sized dent there. The room returned to darkness, he hurried out and Sancho Panza said:

'I'm sure this is the enchanted Moor, sir, and he must be keeping the treasure for other people, and for us he just keeps his punches and his lamp-bastings.'

'You are right,' replied Don Quixote, 'and we must not heed these affairs involving enchantment, and it serves no purpose to grow angry about them: since they are invisible and chimerical, we shall not find anyone on whom to avenge ourselves, however hard we try. Get up, Sancho, if you can, and summon the governor of this castle, and have some oil, wine, salt and rosemary brought to me so that I can make the salutiferous balsam; I do believe I stand in much need of it now, because I am losing a great deal of blood from the wound that this ghost has inflicted on me.'

Sancho struggled to his feet with aching bones and groped his way in the dark towards the innkeeper's room; and bumping into the peace-officer, who was listening to find out how his enemy was faring, he said:

'Sir, whoever you are, please would you very kindly give us a little rosemary, oil, salt and wine that we need to heal one of the best knight errants in the world, who's lying in that bed over there sore wounded by the enchanted Moor that's staying at this inn.'

When the peace-officer heard this, he took Sancho for a madman; and, since day was beginning to dawn, he opened the inn door, called to the innkeeper and told him what this fellow had asked for. The innkeeper gave Sancho everything he wanted, and Sancho took it to Don Quixote, who was clutching his head in both hands complaining of the pain of the lamp-basting, which had done him no more harm than to raise two sizeable lumps; because what he thought was blood was only the sweat that had poured from him in the anguish of his latest storm.

So he took his ingredients and compounded them, mixing them well together and boiling them for a good while, until he thought they were done to a turn. Then he asked for a flask to put the mixture in, and, since there wasn't one of those in the house, he decided to pour it into an oil-bottle made of tin that the innkeeper gave him gratis. And then he said more than eighty Paternosters and as many more Ave Marias and Salve Reginas and Credos over the oil-bottle, and every word was accompanied by the sign of the cross, like a blessing. Sancho, the innkeeper and the peace-officer were present throughout, while the muleteer was calmly seeing to his animals' welfare.

Once Don Quixote had done all this, he was determined to test the virtues of that precious balsam, as he imagined it to be; and so he swallowed a couple of pints of what was left in the cooking-pot after filling the oil-bottle. Hardly had he done drinking than he began to vomit and didn't stop until there was nothing left in his stomach; and with all the retching and writhing he came out in a copious sweat, so he told them to wrap him up and leave him alone. They did so and he slept for more than three hours, at the end of which time he awoke feeling so soothed in his body and so much better from his beating that he considered himself cured. And he firmly believed he'd hit upon the recipe for the Balsam of Fierabras and that, provided with that remedy, he could now, without fear, undertake any fight, battle or devastation, however perilous they might be.

Sancho Panza, who also thought his master's recovery was a miracle, asked him for what was left in the pot, and there was plenty of it. Don Quixote granted the request and, taking up the pot in both hands, with great faith and even greater zeal, Sancho gulped down not much less than his master had swallowed. But the fact is that poor Sancho's stomach can't have been as delicate as Don Quixote's, and so, before he could vomit, he retched and gagged and sweated and swooned, and was fully convinced that his last hour had come; and in his anguish he cursed the balsam and the dog that had given it to him. Seeing him in this state, Don Quixote said:

'It is my belief, Sancho, that all your sufferings are caused by your not having been admitted to the order of chivalry, for it seems to me that this liquor does not benefit those who are not knights.'

'Well, I'll be damned, and all my kinsfolk too!' cried Sancho. 'If you knew that, why did you let me drink the stuff in the first place?'

But now the potion did its work and the poor squire began to gush at both ends at such a rate that neither the rush mat, on which he had lain down once more, nor the hessian blanket covering him could ever be used again. He was sweating and sweating, with such seizures and spasms that not only Sancho himself but all the others thought his end had come. This calamitous tempest lasted almost two hours, at the end of which he was left, not like his master, but so weak and exhausted that he couldn't stand.

But Don Quixote, who, as has been said, felt fit and well, decided to go out straight away in search of adventures, because he believed that every moment spent at the inn was time stolen from the world and from those in it who needed his favour and assistance, even more so with the sure confidence he felt in his balsam. And so, compelled by this desire, he himself saddled Rocinante and put the pack-saddle on the donkey, and helped his squire to dress and struggle on to the animal. Then he mounted and, riding over to a corner of the inn, seized a watchman's short pike leaning there, to use it as a lance.

All the people in the inn – there were more than twenty of them – were looking at him, among them the innkeeper's daughter; and he didn't take his eyes off her, every so often heaving a sigh that he seemed to wrest from the depths of his bowels, and that everyone thought was caused by the pains in his ribs. This, at least, was what was thought by those who'd seen him being anointed the night before. Once the two were mounted and stationed by the inn door, Don Quixote summoned the innkeeper and said in a calm, grave voice:

'Many and magnificent are the kindnesses, my lord governor, that I have received in this your castle, and I am under a great obligation to remember them with gratitude for the rest of my life. If I can repay you for them by taking revenge on your behalf on some insolent knave who has offered you some affront, I would have you know that my office is none other than to assist the helpless, avenge the offended and punish treachery. Search your memory, and if you find anything of this kind to entrust to me, you only have to mention it, for I promise you, by the order of chivalry that I have received, to bring you satisfaction and reparation to the utmost of your desire.'

The innkeeper replied in similarly tranquil tones:

'Sir knight, I don't need you to avenge any affronts for me, because I'm quite capable of taking whatever revenge seems fit when anyone insults me. All I need is for you to pay for your night's stay at my inn – your animals' straw and barley and your own suppers and beds.'

'What – is this an inn?' said Don Quixote.

'Yes, and a very respectable one,' replied the innkeeper.

'I have been in error all this time,' replied Don Quixote, 'for I truly believed it was a castle, and not a bad one at that; but since it turns out not to be a castle but an inn, the best procedure now will be for you to forgive me for not paying you, because I cannot contravene the order of knights errant, of whom I know for certain (never having read anything to the contrary) that they did not pay for their lodging or anything else at any inn where they stayed, because whatever hospitality they might receive is due to them as a right and a privilege, in recompense for the insufferable travails they undergo searching for adventures by night and by day, in winter and in summer, on foot and on horseback, thirsty and hungry, in the heat and in the cold, subject to all the inclemencies of the heavens and all the discomforts of the earth.'

'That hasn't got anything to do with me,' the innkeeper retorted. 'Just cough up what you owe, and don't come to me with tales about knights and errantry – all I'm interested in is being paid for my work.'

'You are a foolish, scurvy innkeeper,' replied Don Quixote.

And putting spurs to Rocinante and brandishing his pike, he rode out of the inn without anybody stopping him, and he continued for a good way without looking back to see if his squire was following.

Seeing Don Quixote leave without paying, the innkeeper hurried to extract the money from Sancho Panza, who said that since his master hadn't been willing to pay he wasn't going to either, because being as he was a knight errant's squire, the same rule applied to him as to his master about not paying in inns and hostelries. This enraged the innkeeper, who threatened that if he didn't hand over the money he'd make him pay in a manner he wouldn't relish. To which Sancho retorted that, by the law of chivalry his master had received, he wasn't going to pay a single farthing, even if it cost him his life, because the ancient and worthy custom of knight errants wasn't going to lapse through his fault, nor were the squires of the same yet to come into the world going to reproach him for the loss of such a just privilege.

As poor Sancho's bad luck would have it, among the people staying at the inn there were four cloth-teaselers from Segovia, three needle-makers from the Potro district of Cordova and two inhabitants of the Heria quarter in Seville,[2] cheerful, well-meaning, mischievous, playful fellows who, almost as if moved by a common impulse, sidled up to Sancho, pulled him from his ass, threw him into the blanket that one of them had run to fetch from the innkeeper's bed, looked upwards, saw that the ceiling was too low for what they had in mind, and decided to go out into the yard, whose limit was the sky. And there, with Sancho in the middle of the blanket, they began to toss him up and down and to amuse themselves at his expense, as people do with dogs at carnival time.

The wretched victim shouted so loud that his master heard him, and as he listened with rapt attention he thought some new adventure was looming, until he realized that the man who was shouting was his squire; so he turned about and rode back to the inn at a laborious gallop and, finding it shut, rode round it to see if he could find a way in, but before he reached the yard walls, which weren't very high, he saw the bad joke that was being played on his squire. He saw him rising and falling through the air so fast and so gracefully that, if his rage had allowed it, I do believe he would have burst out laughing. He tried to scramble from his horse on to the wall, but he was so weak and exhausted that he couldn't even get off the horse; and so, from where he was seated, he began to hurl such furious abuse at the men who were blanket-tossing Sancho that it's impossible to put it down in writing – but his cries didn't make them stop their laughter or their game, nor did flying Sancho stop his laments, sometimes mixed with menaces and sometimes with pleas, all of which served no purpose at all until the jokers stopped out of sheer fatigue.

They brought him his ass, sat him on it and threw his topcoat over his shoulders. And the tender-hearted Maritornes, seeing him so tired, thought it would be a good idea to come to his rescue with a jug of water, and she brought him one from the well, because the water was cooler there. Sancho took the jug and put it to his lips, but he stopped when he heard his master's cries:

'Sancho, dear Sancho, do not drink water! Do not drink it, dear Sancho, for it will kill you! Look, here I have the holy balsam,' – showing him the oil-bottle containing the potion – 'and with just two drops of it you will recover.'

At these words, Sancho rolled his eyeballs sideways in his master's direction and said, among other stronger words:

'Have you forgotten by any chance that I'm not a knight errant, or do you want me to spew up what guts I've got left inside me after last night? Keep your liquor, in the name of the devil, and leave me alone!'

Sancho's ending this speech and starting to drink was all one; but since at the first swallow he realized that it was water, he wouldn't drink any more, and asked Maritornes if he couldn't be brought some wine, which she was very happy to do, and paid for it herself; indeed it is said of her that, although she was of that old profession, there were some vestiges of a Christian about her.

As soon as Sancho had finished drinking he put heels to his ass, threw open the inn door and rode out, delighted at having had his way and not paid a farthing, even though it had been at the expense of his usual sureties, his ribs. It's true that the innkeeper kept Sancho's saddle-bags in lieu of what he was owed, but Sancho was so dazed that he didn't notice they were missing. Once the innkeeper had seen Sancho off, he went to lock and bar the door, but the tossers wouldn't allow it because even if Don Quixote had been one of the Knights of the Round Table these people wouldn't have cared a fig for him.

CHAPTER XVIII

*Which relates the conversation that Sancho Panza had
with his master Don Quixote, and other adventures
worth relating*

Sancho was so worn-out and droopy when he rode up to his master that
he couldn't even put heels to his ass. When Don Quixote saw him in this
state, he said:

'I am now altogether convinced, good Sancho, that the castle or inn is
enchanted, because what could those men who amused themselves with
you in such an atrocious way be but ghosts and creatures from the other
world? And I can confirm this by the fact that, when I was sitting beside
the yard wall beholding the acts of your sad tragedy, I could not climb on
to it, much less dismount from Rocinante, because they must have enchanted
me; for I swear, by my body and bones, that, had I been able either to
climb or to dismount, I should have exacted such revenge that those arrant
knaves would have remembered their prank for ever, even though it might
have meant contravening the laws of chivalry which, as I have already told
you several times, do not allow a knight to lay hands on anyone who has
not been knighted, except in defence of his own life and person, in dire
and urgent necessity.'

'I'd have had my revenge, too, if I could, regardless of the knighting,
but I couldn't, though to my mind them that were playing about with me
back there weren't the ghosts or enchanted men you say they were, but
men of flesh and blood like you and me – I heard them shouting to each
other while they were tossing me, and each of them had his own name,
one was called Pedro Martínez, and another Tenorio Hernández, and I
noticed the innkeeper was called cack-handed Juan Palomeque. So you see,
sir, not being able to get over the wall or even off your horse was caused
by something else, not enchantments. And what this makes me think is
that all these adventures we're looking for are going to end up by getting
us into so many misadventures that we aren't going to know our left legs

from our right. And what it would be best and most sensible for us to do, in my humble opinion, is to go back to the village now it's harvest-time and we ought to be looking to our own business, and stop gallivanting about from pillar to post and from the frying-pan into the fire, as they say.'

'How little you know, Sancho,' replied Don Quixote, 'about matters concerning chivalry! Come, say no more, and be patient, for the day will arrive when you will see with your own eyes how honourable it is to follow this profession. Or else just tell me this: what greater happiness can there be in the world, what pleasure can equal that of winning a battle and vanquishing an enemy? None whatsoever, none whatsoever.'

'That's as may be,' replied Sancho. 'I don't know, I'm sure. All I do know is that ever since we've been knight errants, or rather ever since you've been one, because I haven't got any reason to include myself in that honourable company, we haven't won a single battle, unless you count the one against the Basque, and you came out of that missing half an ear and half a helmet – and from then on it's been nothing but beatings and more beatings, punches and more punches, and I've got the advantage over you of one blanket-tossing, given by enchanted persons that I can't take my revenge on so as to find out how happy you feel when you beat an enemy, according to you.'

'That is what is worrying me and ought to be worrying you, too, Sancho,' replied Don Quixote, 'but from now on I shall endeavour to have at hand some sword made with such skill that whoever bears it cannot be subjected to any kind of enchantment; and it could even be that fortune brings my way the sword that belonged to Amadis, when he was known as "The Knight of the Burning Sword", which was one of the best that any knight ever possessed because, apart from having the power that I have just mentioned, it cut like a razor, and there was no armour, however strong and enchanted, that could withstand it.'

'Knowing my luck,' said Sancho, 'if that did happen and you did come across that sword, it'd only be of any use to knights, like that balsam, and the devil take the poor old squires.'

'Never fear, Sancho,' said Don Quixote. 'Heaven will deal better by you.'

As Don Quixote and his squire discussed these matters, Don Quixote saw that a huge, dense cloud of dust was approaching them along the road, and he turned to Sancho and said:

'This is the day, O Sancho, when will be seen the good that fortune has in store for me; this is the day, I say, when the might of my arm will be displayed as never before, and when I shall do deeds that will remain written in the book of fame for the ages to come. Do you see that cloud of dust rising up over there, Sancho? Well, it is being raised by a vast army from countless different nations, marching towards us.'

'In that case there must be two armies,' said Sancho, 'because opposite it, back there behind us, there's another dust cloud just like it.'

Don Quixote turned round and saw that Sancho was right; and then he was beside himself with joy, because he knew that these were two armies marching to clash in the middle of that broad plain. Every minute of every hour his imagination was filled with those battles, enchantments, adventures, extravagances, loves and challenges that books of chivalry recount, and everything he said, thought or did was channelled into such affairs. And the dust clouds were being raised by two great droves of sheep approaching from opposite directions along the same road, but the dust prevented the sheep from being seen until they came close. And Don Quixote was so insistent they were armies that Sancho believed him, and said:

'So what are we going to do now, sir?'

'What are we going to do?' said Don Quixote. 'Favour and assist the needy and helpless. And you should know, Sancho, that this army approaching from in front of us is led and directed by the great Emperor Alifanfarón, lord of the great island of Taprobana;[1] the other army coming up behind me belongs to his enemy, the King of the Garamantes,[2] known as Pentapolín of the Uprolled Sleeve, because he always goes into battle with his right arm bare.'

'But why do these two lords hate each other so much?' asked Sancho.

'They hate each other,' replied Don Quixote, 'because this Alifanfarón is a wild pagan, and he is in love with Pentapolín's daughter, who is a very beauteous and, moreover, charming lady, and a Christian, and her father will not give her in marriage to the pagan king unless this man first abjures the religion of his false prophet Muhammad and is converted to Christianity.'

'My eye!' said Sancho. 'Pentapolín's doing just the right thing, and I'm going to help him in every way I can.'

'Then you will be doing your duty, Sancho,' said Don Quixote, 'because to take part in battles of this kind it is not necessary to be knighted.'

'I'm very well aware of that,' replied Sancho, 'but where are we going to put this ass of mine so that we can be sure of finding it again once the fighting's over? Because I don't expect going into battle on something like this is what people usually do.'

'That is true,' said Don Quixote. 'What you can do with the ass is to leave it free to have its own adventures, whether it goes missing or not, because we shall possess so many horses when we emerge victorious that even Rocinante will be in danger of being replaced by another. But now pay attention to me and keep your eyes open, for I am going to inform you about the most important knights in these two armies. And so that you can see and observe them better, let us withdraw to that hill over there, from where both armies must be visible.'

This they did, and from the hill they would indeed have had a clear view of the two flocks that were armies for Don Quixote, if the clouds of dust they were raising hadn't interfered with the view. Yet seeing in his imagination what he didn't see and didn't exist, he began to proclaim:

'That knight you can see over there in yellow armour, with a crowned lion lying submissive at a damsel's feet on his shield, is the valiant Laurcalco, Lord of the Silver Bridge; the other one, with golden flowers on his armour, and on his shield three silver crowns on a blue field, is the much-feared Micocolembo, the Grand Duke of Quirocia; that other one on his right, with gigantic limbs, is the fearless Brandabarbarán de Boliche, Lord of the Three Arabias, wearing that serpent's skin for armour and, instead of a shield, bearing a door which is reputed to be one of the doors of the temple pulled down by Samson when in dying he avenged himself on his enemies. But look in the other direction and you will see at the front of the other army the ever victorious, never vanquished Timonel de Carcajona, the Prince of Nueva Vizcaya, with his armour quartered blue, green, white and yellow, and on his shield he has a golden cat on a tawny field with the word *Miau*, which is the beginning of his lady's name, for it is said that she is the peerless Miulina, the daughter of Duke Alfeñiquén of the Algarve; that other knight who burdens the back of that powerful steed, with armour as white as snow and white arms – that is to say a shield without any device on it – is a novice knight from France, called Pierres Papin, Lord of the

Baronies of Utrique; that other one, striking his iron spurs into the flanks of that dazzling, fleet zebra, and with armour of blue vair, is the powerful Duke of Nerbia, Espartafilardo of the Wood, who bears on his shield the device of an asparagus plant, with a motto in Castilian that says: "Divine my fortune." '

And he went on naming imaginary knights from one army and the other and, swept along by the fancies of his unique madness, he improvised armour, colours, devices and mottoes for all of them; and without a pause he continued:

'This other army, facing us, is formed of people of many races: here are those who have drunk the sweet waters of famous Xanthus;[3] mountaineers who tread the Massilian fields; those who sift fine gold dust in Arabia Felix; those who enjoy the famous, cool banks of clear Thermodon; those who bleed golden Pactolus along many different channels; and the Numidians, breakers of promises; the Persians, bowmen of great renown; the Parthians and the Medes, who fight as they flee; the Arabs, who move their dwellings; the Scythians, as cruel as they are pale; the Ethiopians, with pierced lips, and other infinite peoples, whose faces I see and recognize, even though I do not remember their names. In this other squadron come those who drink the crystalline waters of olive-bearing Betis; those who wash their faces in the liquor of the ever rich and golden Tagus; those who enjoy the beneficent waters of the divine Genil; those who tread the lush pastures of the Tartesian fields; those who take delight in the Elysian meadows of Jerez; men of La Mancha, rich and crowned with yellow ears of corn; men clad in iron, ancient relics of Gothic blood; those who bathe in the Pisuerga, renowned for the gentleness of its current; those who graze their flocks and herds on the broad meadows of winding Guadiana, famous for its secret course; those who shiver in the cold of the bosky Pyrenees and among the white snowflakes of the lofty Apennines: in short, all those whom Europe contains and encloses within its boundaries.'

Great God, how many provinces he mentioned, how many races he named, giving to each one of them, with wonderful readiness, its own attributes, steeped as he was in everything he'd read in his lying books! Sancho Panza was hanging on his every word, and didn't utter a single one himself, and every so often he'd turn his head to try to spot the knights and giants his master was naming; and since he couldn't see any of them, he said:

'Look sir, the devil can take any of those men or giants or knights you say there are hereabouts – at least I can't see them, perhaps it's all a magic spell, like those ghosts last night.'

'How can you say that?' retorted Don Quixote. 'Do you not hear the neighing of the horses, the sounding of the bugles, the beating of the drums?'

'All I can hear,' replied Sancho, 'is lots of sheep bleating.'

And he was right, because the two flocks were coming close.

'It is your fear, Sancho' said Don Quixote, 'that is preventing you from seeing or hearing properly; because one of the effects of fear is to muddle the senses and make things seem to be what they are not; and if you are so frightened, stand aside and leave me alone, for I am sufficient by myself to give the victory to whichever army I decide to support.'

As he said this he put spurs to Rocinante and, with his lance at the ready, he sped down the hill like a thunderbolt. Sancho shouted after him:

'Come back, come back, Don Quixote sir, I swear to God they're sheep you're charging! Come back! By the bones of my poor old father! What madness is this? Look, there aren't any giants or knights, or cats, or armour, or shields quartered or left in one piece, or blue vairs, or the devil. What are you doing? Lord have mercy on us sinners!'

But nothing would make Don Quixote turn back. Instead he galloped on, crying:

'Come, you knights, fighting beneath the banners of the valiant Emperor Pentapolín of the Uprolled Sleeve, follow me, and you shall see with what ease I give him his revenge over his enemy Alifanfarón of Taprobana!'

With this he rode into the army of sheep and began to spear them with as much fury and determination as if he really were attacking mortal enemies. The shepherds and farmers accompanying the flock were screaming at him to stop, but, seeing that this didn't have any effect, they drew their slings from their belts and started to salute him about the ears with stones the size of fists. Don Quixote didn't take any notice of the stones; instead he galloped this way and that, crying:

'Where are you, proud Alifanfarón? Come here: a lone knight am I, who wishes, in single combat, to try your strength and take your life, as punishment for the distress you have caused the valiant Pentapolín the Garamante.'

As he said this a large smooth pebble came and struck him in the side and buried two of his ribs in his body. This left him in such a state that he felt certain he was either dead or sore wounded and, remembering his remedy, he took out the oil-bottle, put it to his mouth and began to pour the liquor into his stomach; but before he could swallow what he considered to be a sufficient amount, another of those sugared almonds came and hit his hand and his bottle with such force that it smashed the bottle, taking out three or four teeth as well, and crushing two fingers.

Such was the first blow, and such was the second, that the poor knight couldn't stop himself from sliding off his horse. The shepherds came up to look at him, and thought they'd killed him, so they made haste to round up their flock, pick up the dead sheep, of which there were more than a few, and make themselves scarce, without looking any further into the matter.

All this time Sancho had been on the hill, watching his master's follies, tearing his beard and cursing the moment when fortune had brought them together. When he saw that Don Quixote was lying on the ground and that the shepherds had gone away, he ventured down the hill and approached him, and found him in a terrible state, although still conscious. And Sancho said:

'Didn't I tell you, Don Quixote sir, to turn back, because what you were attacking wasn't armies, it was flocks of sheep?'

'This just shows how my enemy, that scoundrel of an enchanter, can transform things and make them disappear. I would have you know, Sancho, that it is very easy for such people to make us look like whatever they want, and this villain who is persecuting me, envious of the glory he saw I was about to conquer in this battle, turned the armies of enemy forces into flocks of sheep. If you do not believe me, Sancho, I beg you to do something that will correct your mistake and make you see that I am telling you the truth: mount your ass and stalk them, and you will soon see how, once they have gone a little way, they turn back into what they were at first and, ceasing to be sheep, become real men again, just as I described them to you. But do not go yet, because I have need of your assistance: come here and see how many of my teeth are missing, for it seems to me that there is not one left in my mouth.'

Sancho came so close that his eyes were nearly inside his master's mouth;

and by now the balsam had done its work in Don Quixote's stomach, and, just as Sancho was peering in, he discharged all its contents with the violence of a shotgun and they exploded in the face of the compassionate squire.

'Holy Mother of God!' cried Sancho. 'What's up now? The man's dying, he must be – he's spewing blood!'

But when he examined the evidence more closely he could tell from the colour, taste and smell that it wasn't blood but the balsam he'd seen him drinking from the oil-bottle, and this disgusting discovery so turned his stomach that he vomited his guts all over his master, and both of them were left in the same fine mess. Sancho staggered over to his ass to look in the saddle-bags for something with which to clean himself and see to his master's wounds, and when he couldn't find them he almost went insane. He cursed himself again, and decided in his heart to leave his master and go back home, even if that did mean forfeiting what he was owed for services rendered and his hopes of governing the promised island.

Don Quixote now struggled to his feet, with his left hand clapped to his mouth to stop his remaining teeth from falling out, took hold with the other hand of the reins of the faithful Rocinante, who was so loyal and good-natured that he hadn't budged from his master's side, and went over to his squire, who was leaning over his ass with his hand on his cheek, in the posture of a man overwhelmed by thought. And when Don Quixote saw all these signs of deep distress, he said:

'Allow me to remind you, Sancho, that no man is worth more than any other, unless he achieves more than the other. All these storms falling upon us are signs that the weather will soon clear and that things will go well for us; for neither good nor bad can last for ever, and from this we can deduce that since this bad spell has lasted for a long time, a good one cannot be far away. So you must not be distressed about the misfortunes that I undergo, for you have no part in them.'

'No part in them?' retorted Sancho. 'The bloke who got blanket-tossed yesterday – was he by any chance any other than my own father's son? And the saddle-bags I've lost today, with all my valuables in them – do they belong to any other than the same?'

'You have lost your saddle-bags, Sancho?' said Don Quixote.

'Yes I have,' replied Sancho.

'So we have nothing to eat today,' replied Don Quixote.

'We wouldn't have,' replied Sancho, 'if it wasn't for those herbs you say you know all about growing in the fields, the ones that unfortunate knight errants like you go and pick to make up for lack of food in fixes like this.'

'For all that,' replied Don Quixote, 'I would sooner have a two-pound loaf of white bread or indeed an eight-pound loaf of bran bread and a couple of dozen salted pilchards, than all the herbs described by Dioscorides, even in Dr Laguna's magnificent edition.[4] But anyway, climb on to your donkey, good Sancho, and follow me, because God, who is the provider of all things, will not fail us, especially since we are engaged in his service; because he does not fail the gnats in the air, or the worms in the earth, or the tadpoles in the water. And he is so merciful that he makes his sun rise on the evil and on the good, and sends his rain on the just and on the unjust.'[5]

'You'd have done better as a preacher,' said Sancho, 'than as a knight errant.'

'Knights errant have always known and still must know about everything, Sancho,' said Don Quixote, 'for there were knights errant in centuries past who would stop to preach a sermon or deliver a speech in the middle of a fair just as if they were graduates of the University of Paris; from which we can infer that the sword has never blunted the pen, nor the pen the sword.'

'All right, I'll take your word for it,' replied Sancho, 'and now let's get going and find somewhere to stay the night, and God grant it's a place where there aren't any blankets, or blanket-tossers, or ghosts, or enchanted Moors – because if there are any of those, I'll send this adventuring lark to the devil, lock, stock and barrel.'

'You must pray to God for that, my son,' said Don Quixote. 'And now guide us where you will, for on this occasion I wish to leave the choice of a lodging to you. But first lend me your hand and feel with your finger how many teeth are missing on this upper right side, because that is where I feel the pain.'

Sancho put his fingers in and, as he felt around, he asked:

'How many back teeth did you use to have on this side?'

'Four,' replied Don Quixote, 'apart from the wisdom tooth, all of them whole and sound.'

'Are you quite sure of what you're saying, sir?' said Sancho.

'Yes, four, if not five,' replied Don Quixote, 'because I have never had any teeth extracted, nor have any fallen out or been destroyed by decay or infection.'

'Well, down here below,' said Sancho, 'you've only got two and a half now, and up above not even half a tooth, it's as smooth as the palm of my hand.'

'Oh, unhappy me!' said Don Quixote as he heard the sad news his squire was giving him. 'I would rather have lost an arm, so long as it was not my sword arm. For I would have you know, Sancho, that a mouth without teeth is like a mill without a millstone, and that a tooth is much more worthy of esteem than a diamond. But those of us who profess the order of chivalry in all its severity are subject to this. Mount your donkey, my friend, and lead the way, and I shall follow at whatever pace you prefer.'

Sancho did so, heading towards where he thought they might find a place to stay without leaving the highway, which was uninterrupted in that part.

As they plodded along, because the pain in Don Quixote's jaws didn't give him any respite or any inclination to ride faster, Sancho tried to amuse him and cheer him up by chatting to him, and said, among other things, what is recorded in the next chapter.

CHAPTER XIX

About the intelligent conversation that Sancho had with
his master, and their adventure with a corpse, together
with other famous events

'What I think, sir, is that all these mishaps of the past few days must have been a punishment for the sin you've committed against the chivalry order, not keeping that vow you took ne'er at table to eat bread nor with the queen to lie, and all that other stuff that came afterwards and you swore to do until you'd taken that helmet off Malandrino, or whatever the Moor was called, I don't rightly remember his name.'

'You are quite right, Sancho,' said Don Quixote, 'but, to tell you the truth, it had altogether slipped my mind; and you can be equally certain that the business of the blanket which you underwent was your fault, for not calling my attention to it in time. But I shall make due amends, for in the order of chivalry there are ways and means of redressing all such lapses.'

'And what vows have I taken?' retorted Sancho.

'It does not matter that you have not taken any vows,' said Don Quixote. 'It is enough that I believe you could be under suspicion of being an accessory after the fact, and it will be as well to seek a remedy, just in case.'

'Well, if that's the way it is,' said Sancho, 'you'd better make sure you don't go and forget about that, too, as you did with the vow, because the ghosts might take it into their heads to have some more fun with me, and maybe with you as well, if they see how stubborn you are.'

As they talked away like this, night came on and caught them on the open road, without a sight of anywhere to stay, and what made it even worse was that they were dying of hunger, being without saddle-bags and therefore without a larder or provisions. And, to complete their misfortunes, they had an adventure that didn't need any contrivance to make it look like one. The night was dark but they rode on regardless, because Sancho thought that, being as they were on the king's highway, there must be an inn not more than half a dozen miles off.

As they plodded on through the blackness, the squire famished and his master with a healthy appetite, they saw coming towards them along the same road a myriad of lights that looked exactly like moving stars. Sancho was frozen with fear at the sight of them, and even Don Quixote had the wind up: the one tugged on his ass's halter, and the other pulled on his nag's reins, and there they both sat motionless, peering to make out what it could be, and they saw that the lights were coming closer and closer, and the closer they came the bigger they looked; and Sancho began to quiver like a rabbit, and the hair on Don Quixote's head stood on end. But plucking up a little courage he said:

'This, Sancho, must be the greatest and most perilous of adventures, in which it will be necessary for me to show all my valour and resolution.'

'Oh, dear, dear me!' cried Sancho. 'If this is another ghost adventure, as

I'm beginning to think it is, where are the ribs that are going to be able to take it?'

'Ghosts though they may be,' said Don Quixote, 'I will not allow any of them to touch one thread of your clothes; for if they had their fun with you before, that was only because I could not climb over the yard wall; but now we are in open country, where I shall be able to wield my sword as I please.'

'And if they enchant you and put you out of action as they did the last time,' said Sancho, 'what'll it matter whether we're in open country or not?'

'All the same,' replied Don Quixote, 'I beg you, Sancho, to be of good courage, for the event will show you how courageous I am.'

'I will – if God helps me,' replied Sancho.

And standing a little to one side of the road, they peered again to try and make out what all those moving lights could be, and they soon saw a throng in white, a fearful vision that drained whatever courage remained in Sancho Panza, whose teeth began to chatter as if he had an attack of malaria; and they chattered even faster when he had a clearer view, because there were about twenty figures in white drapes, all mounted, with flaming torches in their hands, and behind them came a litter covered in mourning followed by another six mounted figures, in mourning too, right down to the heels of their mules – because it was clear, from their sober gait, that these were no horses. The men in white were murmuring in compassionate tones. This strange vision, at such an hour and in such a desolate place, was more than enough to strike fear into Sancho's heart, and even into his master's; and this could indeed have happened to Don Quixote, but not to Sancho, who didn't have any heart left for fear to be struck into. But what did happen to his master was the very opposite, because in his imagination he saw with total clarity that this was one of the adventures out of his books. He saw the litter as a bier on which must lie some sore wounded or dead knight, whose revenge was reserved for him alone, and without further thought he couched his pike, settled himself in his saddle, and with graceful and courageous bearing stationed himself in the middle of the road where the men in white were going to have to pass; and when they came up he said:

'Halt, you knights, or whatever you may be, and inform me who you are, where you have come from, where you are going and what it is that you are carrying on that bier; for it seems that either you have committed some outrage or you have been the victims of one, and it is right and meet that I should know this, either to punish you for the wrong you have done or to avenge you for the wrong done you.'

'We're in a hurry,' replied one of the men in white, 'and the inn's a long way off, and we haven't got time to stop for all that informing.'

And, putting spurs to his mule, he continued on his way. Don Quixote was affronted by such a reply and, grasping the mule's bridle, he said:

'Halt, and mind your manners, and inform me of what I have asked. If not, I challenge you all to mortal combat.'

The mule was a highly strung animal, and was so frightened at being seized by the bridle that it reared up and fell back on its haunches and on top of its rider. An attendant on foot, seeing the fall, started to shout insults at Don Quixote, who, beside himself with fury, couched his pike again and without more ado charged at one of the men in mourning and left him sore wounded on the ground; and as he continued charging about among the rest, it was wondrous to behold the agility with which he attacked them and knocked them off their mules, and Rocinante's movements were so swift and proud that it seemed as if he'd suddenly sprouted wings.

The men in white were timorous characters, and unarmed; and so they were only too happy to flee from the skirmish and run away across the plain with their torches blazing, looking for all the world like masked figures at a midnight party rushing hither and thither. But the men in mourning, swathed and tangled in their skirts and cassocks, couldn't run, so Don Quixote gave them all a good beating with impunity and made them quit the field much against their will, because they all thought he wasn't a man but a devil from hell, come to steal away the dead body they were carrying in the litter.

Sancho was watching it all, amazed at his master's courage, and saying to himself:

'It's true, this master of mine is just as brave and strong as he says he is.'

A torch was burning on the ground next to the man who'd fallen under his mule, and by its light Don Quixote could see him; and coming up to him he poked the tip of his pike at the man's face, ordering him to give himself up, or else he'd die. To which the fallen man replied:

'I've given up already – I can't move, one of my legs is broken. I beg you, if you're a Christian knight, not to kill me – you'd be committing a great sacrilege because I'm a master of arts and I've taken my first orders.'

'And what the devil brings you here,' said Don Quixote, 'if you are a man of the cloth?'

'What brings me here, sir?' replied the fallen man. 'My misfortune.'

'Another greater one awaits you,' said Don Quixote, 'if you do not give satisfactory answers to all the questions I asked you in the first place.'

'It'll be easy enough to satisfy you,' replied the master of arts. 'To start with, I ought to point out that although I said just now that I'm a master of arts, I'm really only a BA, and I'm called Alonso López; I'm a native of Alcobendas; I've come from the city of Baeza with eleven other priests, the ones that ran off with the torches; we're on our way to the city of Segovia with that litter containing the corpse of a gentleman who died in Baeza, where it's been deposited until now; and, as I said, we were taking his bones to be buried in his tomb in Segovia, his home town.'[1]

'And who killed him?' asked Don Quixote.

'God did, with a pestilential fever,' replied the bachelor of arts.

'That means,' said Don Quixote, 'that Our Lord has relieved me of the task I would have had of avenging his death, if anybody else had killed him; but seeing who it was that killed him, all one can do is shrug one's shoulders and be silent, for that is what I should do if he had killed me. And I would have you know, reverend sir, that I am a knight of La Mancha, Don Quixote by name, and my office and profession is to wander about the world righting wrongs and redressing grievances.'

'I'm not too clear about this righting of wrongs,' said the bachelor of arts, 'because I was all right, and you've done me the wrong of breaking my leg, which will never be right again in all the days of my life; and the grievance you've redressed in my case has been to leave me so grievously injured that I'll live in grief for ever; and it's been a terrible misadventure for me to come across you in search of your adventures.'

'Not all things,' said Don Quixote, 'follow the same plan. The trouble, my dear Alonso López BA, arose from your coming, as you did, by night, wearing those surplices, with your torches blazing, praying, and dressed in mourning, looking exactly like something evil from the other world; and so I could not fail to fulfil my obligation to attack you, and I should have attacked you even if I had known that you were the very devils from hell, which is what I took you for.'

'Since that's what my bad luck's arranged for me,' said the bachelor of arts, 'I entreat you, sir knight errant (whose errors I'm paying for), to help me out from under this mule, it's got my leg caught between the stirrup and the saddle.'

'But why didn't you say so in the first place?' Don Quixote exclaimed. 'How long were you intending to wait to inform me of your plight?'

He shouted for Sancho Panza, but Sancho Panza wasn't in any hurry to obey, because he was busy stripping the good gentlemen's supply-mule, loaded with food. Sancho turned his topcoat into a sack, crammed into it all the food he could, loaded his ass – and then he went to see why his master was shouting, and helped him to pull the bachelor of arts out from under his heavy mule, and sat him on top of it, and handed him his torch; and Don Quixote told him to follow his companions, whose forgiveness he begged for the grievance, which it had not been in his power to avoid. And Sancho said:

'If by any chance those gentlemen want to know the name of the valiant adventurer that did this to them, you can tell them he's the famous Don Quixote de la Mancha, also known as the Knight of the Sorry Face.'[2]

The bachelor of arts started riding away slowly, and Don Quixote asked Sancho why he'd called him the Knight of the Sorry Face, and at that moment in particular.

'All right, I'll tell you,' replied Sancho. 'I was just looking at you by the light of that poor bloke's torch and the truth is that at this moment you're the sorriest sight I've ever clapped eyes on. It must be because of being tired after your fight, or else losing all those teeth.'

'No, those are not the reasons,' replied Don Quixote. 'It is rather because the sage whose task it is to write the history of my exploits must have thought it right for me to take some appellation, as all previous knights have done: one was known as the Knight of the Burning Sword, another as the Knight of the Unicorn, another the Knight of the Damsels, yet another the Knight of the Phoenix, that one the Knight of the Griffin, that other one the Knight of Death;[3] and by these names and devices they were known all round the world. And so I believe that the sage I have mentioned must, a moment ago, have placed in your thoughts and on your tongue the appellation "The Knight of the Sorry Face", which is what I propose to call myself from now on; and to ensure that the title suits me all the better, I am resolved to have painted on my coat of arms, at the earliest opportunity, a very sorry face.'

'There's no need to go wasting time and money on a painting,' said Sancho. 'All you've got to do is lift your visor and let anyone looking at you see your face, and without any need of a picture or a shield they'll call you the Knight of the Sorry Face straight away. Believe you me, I'm telling the truth – I can promise you, sir (this is just my little joke, though) that what with being famished and not having any teeth your face is such a terrible sight that, as I just said, there's no need for any sorry painting.'

Don Quixote laughed at Sancho's little joke, but he still decided to call himself by that title as soon as he could have his round infantryman's shield painted as he'd said.

' – Oh, I almost forgot to tell you that you're excommunicated for laying violent hands on what is sacred, *iuxta illud: Si quis suadente diabolo*, etc.'[4]

'The Latin is beyond me,' Don Quixote replied, 'yet I know very well that it was not my hands but this pike that I laid on you; and furthermore I did not think I was attacking priests or anything to do with the Church, which I respect and adore as the good Catholic and faithful Christian that I am, but ghosts and phantoms from the other world. And even if I have done what you say, I can remember what happened to the Cid Ruy Díaz when he smashed the chair of that king's ambassador in front of His Holiness the Pope, who excommunicated him for what he had done; yet the good Cid's behaviour on that day had been that of a very honourable and valiant knight.'[5]

On hearing this the bachelor continued on his way, as described, without another word. Don Quixote would have liked to find out whether the corpse in the litter was a skeleton or not, but Sancho wouldn't allow it, saying:

'Sir, you've come out of this dangerous adventure more in one piece than out of any of the others I've seen, and, although you routed all those people, they could have spotted that it was just one person fighting them, which could make them feel ashamed, and they might pluck up courage and come back for us, and then we'd really have our work cut out. The donkey's well loaded, the mountains are near at hand, hunger's pressing and all we need to do is beat a dainty retreat and, as the saying goes, to the grave with the dead and the living to their bread.'

And pushing his ass along in front of him, he asked his master to follow; and Don Quixote, feeling that Sancho was right, obeyed him without a word. After walking a short distance between two hills they found themselves in a broad and secluded valley, where they stopped, and Sancho unloaded the donkey; and, stretched out on the green grass, they had breakfast, dinner, tea and supper all at once, accompanied by the best hunger-sauce, satisfying their stomachs from more than one lunch-box that the priests (such gentlemen seldom allow themselves to go short) had been carrying on their supply-mule. But another misfortune befell them, in Sancho's opinion the worst of all, and this was that they didn't have any wine to drink, or even any water to raise to their lips, and they were tormented by thirst. Seeing that the meadow where they were lying was thick with lush young grass, Sancho said what will be related in the next chapter.

CHAPTER XX

✠

About the unprecedented and unique adventure
undertaken by the valiant Don Quixote de la Mancha,
the one that with the least danger was ever brought to a
happy conclusion by any famous knight in the world

'All this grass, sir, must be a sign that there's a spring or a stream near here watering it, so it'll be a good plan to carry on a little further, and we'll find somewhere we can quench this terrible thirst of ours – I'm sure thirst hurts even more than hunger does.'

Don Quixote thought this was good advice, and he took Rocinante by the reins, and Sancho loaded his ass with all the left-overs and took it by the halter, and they began to feel their way up the meadow, because the darkness of the night prevented them from seeing anything; but they hadn't gone a couple of hundred paces when a sound of thundering water reached their ears, as if it were crashing down from some great cliff. They were overjoyed at this but, when they stopped to work out where the sound was coming from, they suddenly heard another noise that diluted the pleasure of the water, especially for Sancho, with his timid, fearful nature. What they heard was a steady pounding and some sort of a clanking of iron and chains that, added to the water's furious roaring, would have struck fear into any other heart than that of Don Quixote.

In this dark night they'd wandered in among some tall trees whose leaves, blown by the breeze, rustled eerily; and the combination of the solitude, the surroundings, the darkness, the noise of the water and the rustling of the leaves filled them with fear and dread, all the more so when they found that the pounding didn't cease, the breeze didn't die down and the morning didn't come; and, on top of all this, they had no idea where they were. But Don Quixote, steeled by his intrepid heart, leapt upon Rocinante, grasped his little round shield, clasped his pike and said:

'Friend Sancho, I would have you know that I was born, by the will of heaven, in this iron age of ours, to revive in it the age of gold, or golden age, as it is often called. I am the man for whom dangers, great exploits, valiant deeds are reserved. I am, I repeat, the man who will revive the Knights of the Round Table, the Twelve Peers of France and the Nine Worthies, and who will consign to oblivion the Platirs, the Tablantes, the Olivantes and Tirantes, the Phoebuses and Belianises, together with the whole crowd of illustrious knights errant of olden times, by performing in this age in which I live such prodigies, such wonders, such feats of arms as to eclipse the most brilliant deeds that they ever accomplished. You are aware, faithful and trusty squire, of the darkness of this night, its unearthly silence, the confused and muffled hubbub of the trees, the fearsome roar of the water that we have come to seek and that seems to crash down from the heights of the Mountains of the Moon,[1] and the incessant pounding that assails and wounds our ears; all of which together, and indeed each by itself, would be enough to infuse fear and terror and dismay into the breast of Mars himself, let alone one unaccustomed to such occurrences and adventures. Now all of this that I depict for you is an incentive and a stimulant for my spirit, making this heart of mine burst in my breast with a desire to launch out on this adventure, however difficult it seems to be. So tighten Rocinante's girths a little, and God be with you, and await me here for just three days, after which, if I should not return, you may go back to our village, and from thence, as a favour and a service to me, you shall go to El Toboso, where you shall inform my incomparable lady Dulcinea that her hapless knight died attempting exploits which would make him worthy to call himself hers.'

When Sancho heard his master's words he began to weep tears of infinite tenderness and said:

'Sir, I don't know why you want to take on this fearful adventure – it's night now, nobody can see us here, we can easily ride the other way and avoid the danger, even if we have to go for three days without a drink, and since there's no one to see us, there's no one to think we're cowards, either. What's more, I've heard our village priest, who you know well, saying in a sermon that danger loved is death won,[2] so it isn't a good idea to go tempting God by taking on such a tremendous feat that you can only get out of alive by some miracle – you ought to be content with the ones that heaven worked on you when it stopped you from being tossed in a blanket, as I was, and when it brought you out safe, sound and victorious from among all those enemies that were riding with that corpse. And if all this doesn't move or soften that hard heart of yours, let's see if this does – just think that as soon as you've gone away I'll be ready to give up the ghost to whoever wants to take it, out of pure fear. I left my village and my children and my wife to come and serve you, in the belief that I'd be better for it rather than the opposite, but greed breaks the sack and it's broken all my hopes, because just when they were brightest and I thought I was going to get my hands on that damned island you've promised me so often, I find that instead you want to leave me in a place like this, far from all human company. In the name of the one true God, sir, let not this wrong be done unto me, and if you just can't hold yourself back from doing this daring deed, at least put it off till morning – according to the lore I learned as a shepherd, dawn can't be three hours away, because the Little Bear's mouth is on top of its head, and at midnight it's in line with its left arm.'

'But Sancho,' asked Don Quixote, 'how can you tell where that line goes, or where that mouth or small bear is, when the night is so dark that there is not a star to be seen in the sky?'

'That's true enough,' said Sancho, 'but fear has many eyes, and it can see things under the ground so it's got even more reason to see them up in the sky, but anyway you only need to use your head to realize that it isn't long till daybreak.'

'However long it is,' replied Don Quixote, 'it shall not be said of me, now or ever, that tears and pleas deflected me from acting as I should, in a true knightly fashion; so I beg you, Sancho, to hold your tongue; for God, who has placed in my heart the desire to undertake this unique and dreadful adventure, will be sure to watch over my well-being and console your grief. What you must do is to make Rocinante's girths as tight as may be, and wait here, for I shall soon return, alive or dead.'

Sancho realized that this was his master's final decision, and that tears, advice and pleas weren't having any effect, so he decided to make use of his cunning to force him to wait until daybreak, if he could: as he was tightening the horse's girths he took his ass's halter and, ever so carefully and quietly so as not to be noticed, he tied Rocinante's hind legs together, so that when Don Quixote tried to set off he couldn't, because the only way in which the horse could move was in fits and starts. When Sancho saw that his trick had worked, he said:

'There you are, sir – the heavens, moved by my tears and my prayers, have ordained that Rocinante can't move, and if you keep on spurring him again and again like that you'll only annoy fortune and, as they say, kick against the pricks.'

Don Quixote was close to despair, and the more he gave his horse the spur the less it budged; and, not suspecting the ligature, he resigned himself to calming down and waiting either for dawn to come or for Rocinante to move, ascribing the problem to everything except Sancho's cunning. And so he said:

'Since the fact is, Sancho, that Rocinante cannot move, I am content to wait until dawn smiles on us, even though I weep at her delay.'

'No, you mustn't weep,' replied Sancho. 'I'll keep you amused by telling you stories till daybreak, unless you'd rather get off your horse and lie down for a little nap on the green grass, as knight errants often do, so as to feel nice and fresh when day comes and it's time to go off on that enormous adventure that's in store for you.'

'What do you mean, get off my horse and lie down for a little nap?' said Don Quixote. 'Am I, perchance, one of those knights who repose in the midst of danger? You can sleep, for you were born to sleep – indeed you can do as you wish – but I shall behave as I consider befits my aspirations.'

'Don't be angry, sir,' replied Sancho, 'I didn't mean it like that.'

And coming up to him he held on to the front of his saddle with one hand and on to the back of it with the other, so that he was left embracing his master's left thigh, not daring to stir one inch from it, so scared was he of the pounding, which continued unabated. Don Quixote asked him to tell a story to while the time away, as he had promised, to which Sancho replied that he would, if his fear of what he was hearing let him.

'But in spite of that I will try my hardest to tell you a true story that, if I manage to tell it properly and don't get interrupted, is the best true story there ever was, and now you must pay attention because I'm about to begin. "Once upon a time and may good befall us all and evil come to him that evil seeks . . ." And you can see, sir, that in those ancient times they didn't start their stories any old way, but with a saying by Cato the Senseless of Rome,³ who says "And evil come to him that evil seeks", which just about fits the bill here, to persuade you to stay put and not wander off seeking evil, and let's go the other way instead, sir, because nobody's forcing us to carry on in this direction, with all these terrors putting the fear of God into us.'

'Continue with your story, Sancho,' said Don Quixote, 'and leave me to worry about the direction in which we are travelling.'

'I was saying, then,' continued Sancho, 'that in a village in Extremadura there once lived a goat-shepherd, in other words a man who looked after goats, and this shepherd or goat-shepherd my story's all about was called Lope Ruiz, and this Lope Ruiz was in love with a shepherdess called Torralba, and this shepherdess called Torralba was the daughter of a rich stock farmer, and this rich stock farmer . . .'

'If that is the way in which you tell your story, Sancho,' said Don Quixote, 'repeating everything you say, in two days' time you still will not have finished; either tell it straightforwardly, like a man of good sense, or do not tell it at all.'

'The way I'm telling it,' retorted Sancho, 'is the way tales are always told where I come from, and I don't know any other way to tell it, and it isn't fair to expect me to learn new habits.'

'Tell it however you like, then,' replied Don Quixote, 'and since fate decrees that I cannot avoid listening, you had better continue.'

'And so, my dear good sir,' continued Sancho, 'as I was saying, this herdsman was in love with Torralba the shepherdess, who was a plump lass, unruly and a bit mannish, because she had the beginnings of a moustache – I can almost see her even now.'

'So you knew her, did you?' said Don Quixote.

'I didn't know her as such,' replied Sancho, 'but the person who told me the story said it was so very true that when I told it to anyone else I could swear blind I'd seen it all for myself. So the days came and the days went and the devil, who doesn't sleep and meddles and muddles in everything, made the love that the herdsman felt for the shepherdess turn into deadly hatred, and the cause, so the gossips said, was a dose of jealousy-pangs she gave him, that went well beyond the pale; and the herdsman hated her so much from then on that, so as never to see her again, he decided to leave that land and go where he wouldn't ever clap eyes on her. As soon as Torralba saw that Lope scorned her, she fell in love with him, even though she'd never been at all fond of him before that.'

'That is the way with woman,' said Don Quixote: 'to disdain the man who loves her, and to love the man who disdains her. Continue, Sancho.'

'What happened,' said Sancho, 'was that the herdsman put his plan into action, and he drove his goats in front of him through the fields of Extremadura to cross over into the Kingdom of Portugal. The Torralba woman found out and went after him, and followed him at a distance on her bare feet, with her staff in her hand and her two satchels hanging from her neck and containing, so it's said, a piece of a mirror and a piece of a comb and some sort of jar of face lotion, but whatever it was she was carrying, and I'm not going to start trying to find that out now, all I will say is that it's said that the herdsman and his goats reached the River Guadiana, and it was swollen almost to overflowing, and there wasn't any ferry or any other boat to take him and his animals across, which put him in a tizzy because he could see that the Torralba woman was getting close and she was going to make a nuisance of herself with all her pleading and moaning, but he kept looking so hard that he saw a fisherman with a boat by his side, so small that there was only room in it for one person and one goat, and in spite of this he spoke to him and bargained with him and they agreed that the fisherman would ferry him and his three hundred goats across to the other bank. The fisherman climbed into his boat and took one goat across, and he came back and took another goat across, and he came back again and took another goat across. You've got to keep count of the goats that the fisherman takes across, because if you let just one of them slip from your memory the story will come to an end and I won't be able to tell you another word of it. To continue, then, I ought to say that the landing-stage on the other side was very muddy and slippery, and the fisherman was taking a long time going to and fro. All the same, he came for another goat, and another goat, and another goat . . .'

'Just assume that he has ferried them all across,' said Don Quixote. 'Don't keep coming and going like that – you won't get them to the other side in a year.'

'How many goats has he taken across so far?' asked Sancho.

'How the devil do you expect me to know that?' replied Don Quixote.

'That's just what I told you – to keep good count. Well, by God, the story's over, I'm not going on.'

'How can that be?' replied Don Quixote. 'Is it so essential to the story to know exactly how many goats have gone across that if we are so much as one out you cannot continue telling it?'

'No, sir, not at all,' replied Sancho. 'It's just that when I asked you to tell me how many goats had gone and you replied that you didn't know, at that very instant I clean forgot what I had left to say, and it was full of good things, I can tell you that much.'

'So your story is finished?' said Don Quixote.

'As sure as my mother is,' said Sancho.

'I can honestly say,' replied Don Quixote, 'that you have just told one of the most original tales, true or false, that anybody could ever have dreamed of, and that your way of telling it and concluding it is something never heard before nor to be heard again, although I did expect no less from your fine mind. But this does not surprise me, because that incessant pounding must have turned your brain.'

'That's as may be,' replied Sancho, 'all I know is, that's the end of my story – it finishes where you start to make mistakes in counting the goats.'

'It is welcome to finish wherever it wishes,' said Don Quixote. 'Now let us see if Rocinante can move.'

He set spurs to his horse again, and again the horse jumped and froze, for Sancho's knots were good knots.

It appears that at this moment, either because of the cold of the morning, which was fast approaching, or because Sancho had eaten something loosening for his supper, or because of natural processes (which seems most likely), he felt the urgent need to do the job of work that nobody could do for him; but so great was the fear which had entered his heart that he didn't dare to move as much as a hair's-breadth from his master's side. Yet not doing what he had to do wasn't a possibility, either; and so what he did, for the sake of peace and concord, was to draw his right hand away from the back of Don Quixote's saddle and use it with great stealth to loosen the running knot that was all that held his breeches up, at which they slid down and encircled his ankles like fetters. Then he lifted up his shirt as best he could, and thrust two ample buttocks into the night air. Once he'd done this, which he'd thought was all he needed to do to escape from his harrowing predicament, he found himself in another even worse plight: he thought that he wasn't going to be able to relieve himself in silence, and he began to grit his teeth and hunch his shoulders and hold his breath for as long as he could, but in spite of all these precautions he was unfortunate enough, in the end, to make a small noise, quite different from the noise causing him such great fear. Don Quixote heard it and said:

'What murmuring is that, Sancho?'

'I don't know, sir,' he replied. 'It must be some new business, because adventures and misadventures never come singly.'

He tried his luck again, and such was his success that, with no greater noise than the previous time, he relieved himself of the burden that had been weighing so heavily upon him. But since Don Quixote's sense of smell was as acute as his sense of hearing, and since Sancho was clinging so very close to him, it was inevitable that some of the fumes, rising almost in a straight line, would reach his nostrils, whereupon he went to their rescue by squeezing them between finger and thumb, and said in somewhat nasal tones:

'It seems to me, Sancho, that you are very frightened.'

'That I am,' replied Sancho, 'but what makes you notice it now more than at other times?'

'The fact that now, more than at other times, you smell, and not of ambergris,' replied Don Quixote.

'You could well be right,' said Sancho, 'but I'm not the one to blame – you are, for dragging me into such wild places at these unearthly hours.'

'Move three or maybe four places backwards, my friend,' said Don Quixote, without taking his hand from his nose, 'and from now on be more careful with your person and with what is due to mine; for it is my familiarity with you that has given rise to this contempt.'

'I bet you're thinking,' said Sancho, 'that I've done something with my person that I didn't ought to have done.'

'The more you stir it the worse it gets, friend Sancho,' replied Don Quixote.

In this and other similar conversations master and servant spent the night; but when Sancho saw that morning was fast approaching, he very quietly untied Rocinante and tied his breeches. Once Rocinante found himself free it seems that, although he wasn't a high-spirited animal, the after-effects of his confinement made him begin pawing, because prancing (begging his pardon) was beyond him. And when Don Quixote noticed that Rocinante could move again, he considered it to be a favourable sign indicating, he believed, that it was time for him to undertake that terrible adventure.

And now dawn broke at last, and objects began to be clearly visible, and Don Quixote saw that he was beneath some tall trees, chestnuts, which cast a deep, dark shade. He also noticed that the pounding didn't cease, but he couldn't see what was causing it; and so, without further delay, he let Rocinante feel the spur and, saying goodbye again to Sancho, told him to wait there for three days, at the most, just as he had told him before, and, if by the end of them he hadn't returned, to take it as certain that it had been God's will that he should end his life in that perilous adventure. He repeated his instructions about the message to be taken on his behalf to his lady Dulcinea, and told Sancho not to worry about the matter of the payment for his services, because he had made his will before leaving home and in it he had made full provision for wages covering the time served, *pro rata*; and he added that, if God brought him out of that peril safe and sound and ransomless, Sancho could count with total certainty on receiving the promised island.

Sancho wept again as he heard his good master's doleful words once more, and he resolved not to leave him until the absolute final end of that particular incident. From these tears of Sancho Panza's and from this honourable decision of his the author of this history concludes that he must

have been of good family and, at the very least, of pure old Christian stock.
And his master was moved by his feelings, but not so much as to make him
waver in the slightest; on the contrary he hid his emotion as best he could
and began to ride in the direction from which he thought the noise of the
water and the pounding were coming. Sancho followed on foot, leading
his donkey – his perpetual companion in prosperous and adverse fortune
– by the halter, as he so often did; and after they'd advanced some way
under those gloomy chestnut trees, they came to a little meadow at the foot
of a high cliff from which a great waterfall came tumbling down. Beneath
the cliff there were some roughly constructed buildings that looked more
like ruins than anything else, and the two men realized that the ceaseless
pounding din was coming from over there. Rocinante started at the racket
of the water and the pounding, and Don Quixote soothed him and then
inched his way towards the buildings, commending himself with all his
heart to his lady and imploring her to favour him in this dreadful enterprise,
and while he was about it he also commended himself to God and asked
not to be forgotten by him. Sancho never strayed from his side, and he
poked his neck out as far as he could and he peered as hard as he could
between Rocinante's legs, to try to make out what it was that was filling
him with such dread.

They must have advanced another hundred paces when, as they came
round the side of a hillock, they saw, starkly exposed to their gaze, without
any room for doubt, the cause of that hideous and, for them, horrendous
din that had kept them so bewildered and scared throughout the night.
And it was (please don't take this amiss, dear reader) six fulling-hammers
making all the noise with their alternating blows.

When Don Quixote saw what it was he fell silent and stiffened from
top to toe. Sancho looked up at Don Quixote and saw that his head was
sunk on his breast in manifest mortification. Don Quixote looked down at
Sancho and saw that his cheeks were puffed up and his mouth was filled
with mirth, about to explode with it; and the knight's dejection was not so
great that it could prevent him from laughing at the sight of Sancho, and
when Sancho saw that his master had begun to laugh, he released his own
captive so suddenly that he had to press his fists to his sides so as not to
explode. Four times he calmed down, and four times he started laughing
again, every bit as hard as the first time, and Don Quixote was becoming

more and more enraged, particularly when he heard Sancho say by way of mockery:

'"I would have you know, friend Sancho, that I was born, by the will of heaven, in this iron age of ours, to revive in it the age of gold, or golden age. I am the man for whom dangers, great exploits, valiant deeds are reserved . . ."'

And he went on to repeat most of what Don Quixote had said when they'd first heard the dreadful pounding. Seeing Sancho making fun of him, Don Quixote was so furious that he raised his pike and struck him two such blows that if they'd connected with his head instead of his shoulders there wouldn't have been any need to pay any wages, except to his heirs. Now that his jolly jest had turned into ugly earnest, and fearful that his master might give him some more of the same, Sancho grovelled:

'Calm down, do, sir, please – I swear to God I was only joking.'

'You may be joking, sir, but I am not,' retorted Don Quixote. 'Look here, my merry fellow: do you fancy that, if these were not fulling-hammers but some perilous new adventure, I should have failed to display the courage needed to undertake and conclude it? Am I, perchance, sir, obliged – being, as I am, a knight and a gentleman – to identify and distinguish between sounds, and tell whether they come from fulling-mills or not? And furthermore it could be the case, as indeed it is, that I have never seen such things in my life, just as you must have seen them often, being a miserable peasant, born and brought up among them. Or else, sir, you just turn these six hammers into six giants, and set them on me one by one or all together, and if I do not topple each and every one of them, then you can laugh at me as much as you please.'

'Enough said, sir,' said Sancho, 'I will admit I was a bit free with my giggles. But tell me, now we're at peace again, and may God get you out of all your adventures to come as safe and sound as out of this one – wasn't it a great joke, and won't it make a fine story, this enormous fear of ours? My fear I mean, because I'm aware you don't even know what fear is, sir, or what it feels like to be afraid.'

'I do not deny,' replied Don Quixote, 'that what has happened to us is worth laughing at; but it is not worth telling, because not all people are intelligent enough to see things in the right perspective.'

'At least you got your pike in the right perspective,' replied Sancho, 'aiming at my head and hitting my shoulders, thanks to God and the care I took to duck. But there we are, it all comes out in the wash, and I've often heard people say "you've got to be cruel to be kind", and what's more, when important gentlemen give their servants a good talking-to, they normally give them a pair of breeches afterwards, though I don't know what they give them after beatings, but maybe what knight errants give after beatings are islands, or kingdoms on dry land.'

'The dice could well fall in such a way,' said Don Quixote, 'that what you say comes true; and forgive me for what has just happened, because you are intelligent and so you understand that man's first impulses are beyond his control; and pay heed from now on to what I am about to say, so that you refrain from talking to me excessively: in all the books of chivalry I have read, an infinity of them, I have never come across any squire who talked to his master as much as you do to yours. And in truth I consider it a great fault in both you and me; in you, because you show me scant respect; in me, because I do not make you respect me more. Yes, indeed: Gandalin, Amadis of Gaul's squire, was the Count of the Firm Isle, yet we read that he always addressed his master cap in hand, with his head bowed and his body bent double, in the Turkish fashion. And what shall we say of Gasabal, Sir Galaor's squire, who was so quiet that to convey the excellence of his miraculous silence his name is only mentioned once in the whole of that great and true history? From all that I have said you should infer, Sancho, that a distance must be kept between master and man, between lord and lackey, between knight and squire. So from now on we must behave with more respect, and not indulge in our little jokes, for in whatever way I become annoyed with you, sir, take note that it is always the pitcher that is broken. The boons and favours that I have promised you will arrive in good time, and if they do not arrive you will not, at least, forfeit your wages, as I have already informed you.'

'All you say is very well said,' replied Sancho, 'but what I'd like to know, just in case the time of the favours never does come round and I have to fall back on wages, is how much knights' squires used to earn in those olden days, and whether they were hired by the month or on a daily basis like builders' labourers.'

'I do not believe,' replied Don Quixote, 'that such squires were ever paid wages: they depended upon favour. And if I have provided for you to be paid wages, in the sealed will I left in my house, that was only because of what might happen; for I do not yet know how chivalry will fare in these calamitous times of ours, and I should not want my soul to suffer in the other world for the sake of a mere trifle. For I would have you know, Sancho, that there is no profession in this world more hazardous than that of knight adventurer.'

'That's true enough,' said Sancho, 'because it only needed the sound of some hammers in a fulling-mill to strike fear and terror into the heart of a really brave errant adventurer like yourself. But you can take it from me that from this moment on I won't open my mouth to make fun of your doings, but only to honour you as my master and natural lord.'

'In that case,' replied Don Quixote, 'your days will be long on the face of the earth, because next to our parents, our masters should be respected as if they were our parents.'

CHAPTER XXI

Concerning the sublime adventure and rich prize of
Mambrino's helmet, and other things that happened to
our invincible knight

And now it began to drizzle, and Sancho wanted them to shelter in the fulling-mill. But the mockery that Don Quixote had just suffered had given him such a grudge against those hammers that he wouldn't go in there on any account, so they veered off to the right and came to a road like the one along which they'd been travelling on the previous day. A little later Don Quixote sighted a man riding towards them with something on his head that shone as if it were made of gold, and as soon as he saw this man he turned to Sancho and said:

'It appears to me, Sancho, that there is no proverb which is not true, because they are all maxims derived from experience itself, the mother of all knowledge: especially the one that says, "When one door closes, another opens." I say this because if last night fortune closed the door to the happiness for which we were searching when she deceived us with the fulling-mill, today she is throwing open another door to a better and surer adventure, and if I do not succeed in entering this door I alone shall bear the blame, and I shall not be able to ascribe it to a lack of information on the subject of fulling-mills, or to the darkness of the night. I say this because, if I am not mistaken, we are being approached by a man who bears on his head Mambrino's helmet, about which I swore that vow.'

'Just be careful what you're saying, and even more careful what you're doing,' said Sancho. 'All I hope is that it isn't some more fulling-hammers to finish off the job of pounding and beating us senseless.'

'The devil take you for your perversity!' replied Don Quixote. 'What has a helmet to do with fulling-hammers?'

'I haven't the faintest idea,' replied Sancho, 'but by my faith, if I was allowed to talk as much as I used to, maybe I'd say that which would make you see how wrong you are.'

'How can I be wrong, you doubting Thomas?' said Don Quixote. 'Tell me, do you not see that knight coming towards us, upon a dapple-grey steed, wearing a helmet of gold?'

'All I can make out,' replied Sancho, 'is a bloke on a donkey, brown like mine, with something shiny on his head.'

'Well, that is Mambrino's helmet,' said Don Quixote. 'Move aside and leave me alone with him: you will soon see how, without uttering a single word, so as to save time, I bring this adventure to a happy conclusion, and the helmet that I have so desired becomes mine.'

'I'll move aside all right,' replied Sancho. 'But I'll say it once again – pray God this is what you say it is, and not more fulling-mills.'

'I have already told you, sir, never even to think of mentioning fulling-mills again,' said Don Quixote, 'or I swear my most solemn oath that I shall mill your very soul out of your body.'

Sancho held his tongue, fearful that his master might fulfil the vow he'd sworn with such verve.

The explanation of the helmet, the steed and the knight that Don Quixote saw is as follows: in this area there were two villages, one of them so small that it had neither a chemist nor a barber, while the other, close to it, had both; so the barber of the larger village also looked after the smaller one, where there was a sick man who needed bleeding, and another who wanted a shave, and the barber was on his way there with his brass basin; and fate ordained that as he was riding along it started to rain and, to prevent his hat, which must have been a new one, from getting stained, he put his basin on his head; and since the basin was clean it shone from more than a mile away. He was riding a brown donkey, as Sancho said. And this was what made Don Quixote think he saw a dapple-grey steed, and a knight, and a helmet of gold, because he was so ready to accommodate everything he saw to his delirious chivalry and his errant thoughts. And when he saw this poor knight coming close, he set off without directing a single word at him, and charged at him at Rocinante's fastest pace, his pike couched low, with the intention of passing him through and through; and as he came close, without checking the fury of his charge, he cried:

'Either defend yourself, base caitiff, or hand me of your own free will what is so rightfully due to me!'

The barber, seeing such an apparition descending upon him when nothing had been further from his thoughts or his fears, could only dodge the pike by throwing himself from his donkey; and he'd hardly touched the ground when he sprang back up nimbler than a deer and sprinted away across the plain so fast that the wind itself couldn't have caught him. He left his basin on the ground, and Don Quixote was delighted and said that the pagan had been prudent indeed in behaving like the beaver, which, when cornered by huntsmen, bites off what, by natural instinct, it knows it is being hunted for.[1] He ordered Sancho to retrieve the helmet, and Sancho picked the basin up and said:

'By God this is a good basin – it's worth a piece of eight if it's worth a maravedí.'[2]

He gave it to his master, who put it on his head and then turned it round and round searching for the visor, and not finding one he said:

'The pagan for whose measurements this famous helmet was first forged must have had a very large head; and what is worst of all is that half of the helmet is missing.'

When Sancho heard the basin being called a helmet he couldn't restrain his laughter, but then he recalled his master's fury and checked himself in full flow.

'What are you laughing at, Sancho?' asked Don Quixote.

'What I'm laughing at,' Sancho replied, 'is the thought of the big head on that pagan who was the owner of this here helmet that looks for all the world exactly like a barber's basin.'

'Do you know what I think, Sancho? I think that this famous piece of this enchanted helmet must, by some strange accident, have fallen into the hands of a person who did not understand or appreciate its value, and, not knowing what he was doing, he must, on seeing that it is made of the purest gold, have melted down the other half to sell it, and with the remaining half made this, which seems, as you say, like a barber's basin. But let it be what it will; for me, who knows it well, its transformation is of no consequence; I shall have it corrected in the first village where there is a blacksmith, and in such a manner that it is not surpassed or even equalled by the helmet that the god of forges made for the god of battles,[3] and in the meantime I shall wear it as best I can, because something is better than nothing, particularly since it will certainly be adequate to protect me against stonings.'

'So long as they don't use slings, that is,' said Sancho, 'as they did in the battle between those two armies, when they gave you that blessing on your jaws and smashed the bottle of that very holy concoction that made me spew my guts up.'

'I am not excessively distressed at its loss,' said Don Quixote, 'for as you know, Sancho, I have the recipe in my memory.'

'I've got it in my memory, too,' replied Sancho, 'but let me be struck dead here and now if I ever make it or drink it again. What's more, I'm not intending to be in the way of needing it, because I'm going to use all my five senses to avoid being sorewounded, or sorewounding anyone else. As for being blanket-tossed again, I can't make any promises, because those kinds of mishap can't always be prevented, and if they do come your way there's nothing to be done but curl up, hold your breath, shut your eyes and let yourself go wherever fate and the blanket take you.'

'You are a bad Christian, Sancho,' this prompted Don Quixote to say, 'for once you take offence you never forget. Well, I would have you know that noble and generous breasts pay no heed to trivialities. What lame leg, what broken rib, what shattered skull have you been left with, to make that little jest so unforgettable? For when all is said and done it was only a jest, an amusement; if I did not regard it as such, I should have returned there and avenged you by wreaking more havoc than the Greeks did for the rape of Helen[4] – who, if she had lived in our times, or if my Dulcinea had lived in hers, could be certain that she would not enjoy such a reputation for beauty as she does.'

And here he heaved a sigh that echoed throughout the heavens. And Sancho said:

'It'd better pass as a jest, then, since it isn't going to be taken in earnest and avenged – but I'm the one who knows what those earnest jests were like, and I also know that they won't fade from my memory any more than the sting of them will go away from my ribs. But putting all that aside, please can you tell me what we're going to do with this here dapple-grey steed that looks just like a brown donkey, left all defenceless by that Martino fellow who you knocked over and who, to judge from the way he scarpered, isn't ever going to come back for it? And, my eye, the dapple's a fine animal all right!'

'I am not in the habit,' said Don Quixote, 'of despoiling those whom I vanquish, nor is it a custom of chivalry to take their horses and leave them on foot, unless the victor has lost his own horse in the fray, in which case it is legitimate to take the defeated knight's horse, as a prize won in lawful war. And so, Sancho, leave that horse, or donkey, or whatever you want to call it, for as soon as its master sees that we have gone he will return for it.'

'God knows I'd love to take it,' replied Sancho, 'or at least swap it for mine, because I don't think mine's such a good one. These laws of chivalry are really strict, if they won't even stretch to letting you swap one donkey for another – could you please tell me if I can at least swap the tackle?'

'I am not very clear about that,' replied Don Quixote, 'and as it is a doubtful case, I should say that until I am better informed you can swap it, if your need is very great.'

'It's so great,' said Sancho, 'that if I'd wanted the tackle to wear it myself I couldn't have needed it more.'

And, now that he'd been granted official permission, he performed his *mutatio capparum*[5] and refurbished his donkey, a very great change for the better. Then they breakfasted on the leftovers of the camp-provisions plundered from the priests' supply-mule, and they drank from the river that powered the fulling-mill, taking care not to look in that direction, so great was the loathing inspired by the fear it had struck into them. Once they'd dulled the pangs of hunger, and even the pangs of melancholy, they mounted and, not taking any particular direction, as is appropriate for knights errant, their progress was dictated by Rocinante's will, which carried along with it that of his master, and even that of the ass, which always followed wherever Rocinante led, in love and good fellowship. Despite all this, they found their way back to the main highway, which they followed at random and without any fixed plan. As they jogged along, Sancho said to his master:

'Sir, would you very kindly give me permission to say a few words to you? With that harsh order of silence you imposed on me, quite a number of things have rotted away inside my stomach, and there's one I've got on the tip of my tongue at this very moment and I wouldn't want it to go bad too.'

'Out with it, then,' said Don Quixote, 'and be brief, for long speeches are never enjoyable.'

'What I'm saying, sir,' Sancho replied, 'is that for some time now I've been thinking about how precious little there is to be got out of going around like this looking for these adventures of yours in these wastes and along these remote roads where, even if you triumph in the most dangerous ones, there isn't anybody to see them or know about them, and so they're going to be hushed up for ever, which goes against what you intend and the adventures deserve. And so I think it'd be preferable, saving your better judgement, for us to go off and serve some emperor or other bigwig who's fighting some war, and in his service you can show off your personal qualities, your great might and your even greater intelligence, because once the lord we go to serve sees all this he'll be bound to reward us, each getting what he deserves, and you won't be short of someone to write down all your exploits, to be remembered always. I can't say as much about mine, because they won't go beyond squirely limits, though I will say that if it's regular in chivalry to write about the deeds of squires, I'm not intending mine to be left out of the story.'

'There is something in what you say, Sancho,' replied Don Quixote, 'but before one reaches that stage one must wander about the world on probation as it were, in search of adventures, so that, by bringing some of them to a happy conclusion, one gains such fame and renown that when one does go to some great monarch's court one is known as a knight by one's deeds; and as soon as all the boys in the street see one riding through the city gates, they follow one and come swarming around one and shouting: "This is the Knight of the Sun" or of the Serpent or whatever device it is under which one has performed great exploits. "This," they will say, "is the man who in single combat defeated the enormous giant Brocabruno of the Mighty Strength, the man who freed the Great Mameluke of Persia from the long enchantment in which he had languished for almost nine hundred years." And so they will go on proclaiming one's deeds from mouth to mouth, and then, upon hearing the noise of the boys and the other people, the king of that kingdom will stand at the windows of his royal palace, and as soon as he sees the knight and recognizes him by his armour or by the device on his shield, he is bound to say: "Ho, there! Let all the knights at my court come hither to receive the flower of chivalry, who approaches yonder!" At this command they will all issue forth, and the king will advance halfway down the staircase, and will give him a warm embrace and the kiss of peace on his face, and then lead him by the hand to the queen's chamber, where the knight will discover the queen with the princess, her daughter, and it will be difficult to find a fairer or more perfect maiden anywhere on the face of the earth.

'What will happen next, without a pause, is that she will fix her eyes upon the knight and he will gaze into hers, and each will seem to the other more divine than human, and without understanding how it has happened they will find themselves caught and enmeshed in the tight-knit nets of love and with great anguish in their hearts, not knowing how they can contrive to speak and make their feelings and desires known to each other. From there he will most certainly be taken to some richly furnished chamber in the palace, where, once his armour is removed, a fine scarlet robe will be brought for him to wear; and if he looked well in his armour, he will look as well or even better in his jupon.[6]

'Once night has fallen, he will dine with the king, the queen and the princess, and he will not take his eyes off her, stealing glances at her when the others are not looking, and she will do likewise, taking the same precautions because, as I have said, she is a most intelligent maiden. The tables will be removed and a tiny, ugly dwarf will appear in the hall door with a beautiful lady following him between two giants and bringing a certain adventure-game contrived by a most experienced sage, and whoever succeeds in it will be held to be the best knight in the world. The king will then order that all the knights there present shall attempt it, and none of them will bring it to a happy conclusion save the guest, to the great enhancement of his reputation, and the princess will be overjoyed and well satisfied to have set her sights so very high. And the best part is that this king or prince or whatever is engaged in a desperate war with another monarch as powerful as he, and his guest the knight asks him, after he has been at his court for a few days, for permission to go off and serve him in this war. The king will grant it most willingly, and the knight will courteously kiss his hands for the favour conceded.

'And that night he will bid farewell to his lady the princess through the railings in a garden by the room in which she sleeps, where he has often spoken to her before thanks to the mediation of a lady-in-waiting, the princess's confidante. He will sigh, she will swoon, the lady-in-waiting will fetch some water and be sore distressed, because morning is approaching and she would not like them to be discovered, worried as she is about her mistress's honour. Finally the princess will come to herself and will extend her white hands through the railings, and the knight will kiss them a thousand times and bathe them in tears. The two will agree on how they are to convey their news, both good and bad, to each other, and the princess will beg him to make his absence as short as possible; he will promise to do so, with many vows; he will kiss her hands again, and take his leave in such grief that he will be close to death. From there he goes to his chamber, throws himself down on his bed, cannot sleep from the pain of the parting, rises very early, goes to say goodbye to the king, the queen and the princess; after he has taken his leave of the king and the queen they tell him that the princess is indisposed and cannot receive any visits; the knight believes that this is because of her sorrow at his departure, he is broken-hearted and almost betrays his deep distress. The lady-in-waiting is present, she takes note of everything and she goes to tell her mistress, who receives her with tears, and says that one of her greatest griefs is not knowing who the knight is, and whether he is of royal descent or not; the lady-in-waiting assures her that such courtesy, gentility and bravery can only be found in illustrious royal persons; the distressed damsel finds some consolation in this; she attempts to be of good cheer, so as not to give her parents any cause for suspicion, and after two days she reappears in public.

'The knight has taken his departure; he fights in the war, defeats the king's enemy, conquers many cities, triumphs in many battles, returns to court, meets his lady in the usual place, it is agreed that he will ask her father for her hand in marriage, in return for his services. The king refuses, because he does not know who the knight is; but in spite of that, whether they elope or however it happens, the princess does become his wife, and her father eventually considers it a most fortunate match, because it is discovered that the knight is the son of the valiant king of some kingdom unknown to me, not being, as far as I am aware, anywhere on the map. The father dies, the princess inherits, in brief the knight becomes king. And now comes the time for bestowing favours on his squire and all those who have helped him to rise to such high estate: he marries his squire to one of the princess's ladies-in-waiting, obviously the one who was the helpful confidante, the daughter of a very important duke.'

'That's what I want, and no messing about,' said Sancho. 'And that's what I'm counting on, because it's all going to turn out just as you said, now you're called the Knight of the Sorry Face.'

'Do not doubt it, Sancho,' replied Don Quixote, 'because in the way and by the steps I have related knights errant rise and always have risen to be kings and emperors. All that is needed now is to discover which Christian or pagan king is waging a war and has a beautiful daughter; but there will be time enough to think about that because, as I have told you, one must win fame elsewhere before appearing at court. There is something else lacking, too: supposing that a king with a war and a beautiful daughter is found, and that I have by then won incredible fame throughout the universe, I really do not know how it could be discovered that I am descended from kings, or am even an emperor's second cousin, because the king will not give me his daughter to be my wife without enquiring very carefully into all this, however meritorious my famous deeds may be, and I am afraid that through this shortcoming I might forfeit what my arm so richly deserves. It is true, of course, that I am a hidalgo of known family and a man of property, and that the law protects my good name with a fine of five hundred shillings; and it could happen that the sage who writes my history deals with my family background in such minute detail that he finds me to be a king's grandson five or six times removed. For I would have you know, Sancho, that there are two kinds of lineage in this world:

those that sprang from princes and monarchs, and that time has gradually destroyed, and have ended in a point, like an upside-down pyramid; and others that began with low-born people, and have prospered little by little, until they have achieved the eminence of great lords. So the difference is that some were but no longer are, and others are who never were; and I might be one of the former, and it might be discovered that I had great and famous beginnings, which ought to be sufficient for the king my father-in-law-to-be; and, if not, the princess will be so enamoured of me that, in spite of her father – even if he has clear evidence that I am the son of some water-carrier – she will accept me as her lord and husband; and if this does not happen, it will be the moment to carry her off wherever I see fit, and either time or death will put an end to her parents' anger.'

'It will also be the moment,' said Sancho, 'for what some wicked people say, "Never ask as a favour for what you can get by force," although what's more to the point is "A clean pair of heels is better than a good man's pleas." I'm only saying this because if the king, your father-in-law, doesn't come round to letting you have my lady the princess, there's nothing for it but to cart her off and take her somewhere else, as you said. But the trouble is that until the war ends and you can enjoy your kingdom in peace and quiet, the poor old squire might well be starved of favours. That is unless the lady-in-confiding who's going to be the squire's wife goes away with the princess, and he shares his unhappy life with her until heaven decrees a change – because I suppose his master can give her to him as his lawful wedded wife if he wants.'

'Nobody can prevent it,' said Don Quixote.

'Well, in that case,' said Sancho, 'we'll just have to commend ourselves to God and let fortune take whatever course God wants it to.'

'May God provide,' said Don Quixote, 'as I wish and as you, Sancho, need; and he who thinks himself a wretch can stay a wretch.'

'I'll say amen to that,' said Sancho, 'because I'm of old Christian stock, and that's good enough for me to be a count.'

'It is more than enough,' said Don Quixote, 'and even if you were not, it would not signify; because as king I can make you a noble without your buying the title or serving me in any way. For once I make you count – there you are, a gentleman, say what they will; and, to be sure, they shall call you Lordship, whether they like it or not.'

'I bet I'd know how to live up to that handful all right!' said Sancho.

'I think you mean to say *handle*, not *handful*,' said his master.

'Whatever you like,' replied Sancho Panza. 'What I'm saying is that I'd be able to carry it off, because once, upon my soul, I was the beadle in a confraternity, and the beadle's uniform suited me so well that everyone said I had the presence to be the steward. So just imagine when I get the robes of a duke round my shoulders, or when I dress up in gold and pearls like all those foreign counts! I reckon people will come from hundreds of miles away to see me!'

'Yes, you will look well,' said Don Quixote, 'but you will have to shave frequently, because your beard is so thick, rough and unkempt that if you do not take a razor to it every second day at least, people will see in a trice what you are.'

'Why not just get a barber,' said Sancho, 'and keep him in the house on wages? And, if needs be, I'll even make him follow me around like a grandee's equerry.'

'And how do you know,' asked Don Quixote, 'that grandees are followed by their equerries?'

'I'll tell you how I know,' replied Sancho. 'A few years ago I was in the capital for a month, and there I saw a tiny little man that everyone said was a very big man because he was a grandee, going for a ride, and another man following him around on horseback wherever he went, as if he was his tail. I asked why this second man never caught up with the first one, but always rode behind him. They replied that he was his equerry, and that it was a habit of grandees to have these characters following them around. And that's how I know – I've known it so well ever since that I've never forgotten.'

'And I say that you are quite right,' said Don Quixote, 'and that you can take your barber with you in the same way; because customs did not arise all together, nor were they all invented at once, and you can be the first count to be followed by his barber; indeed, shaving a man's beard is an even more intimate duty than saddling his horse.'

'Let me see to the barber,' said Sancho, 'and you can see to becoming a king and making me a count.'

'So it shall be,' replied Don Quixote.

And raising his eyes, he saw what will be related in the next chapter.

CHAPTER XXII

*About how Don Quixote freed many wretches who,
much against their will, were being taken where they
would have preferred not to go*

Cide Hamete Benengeli, the Arab author from La Mancha, relates in this most grave, grandiloquent, meticulous, delightful and imaginative history that after the conversation between the famous Don Quixote de la Mancha and his squire Sancho Panza recorded at the end of the twenty-first chapter, Don Quixote raised his eyes and saw that some twelve men on foot, strung by the neck, like beads, on a great iron chain, and with shackles on their hands, were plodding towards them along the road. Two men on horseback and two others on foot were escorting them. The mounted men were carrying firelocks and the others swords and spears, and as soon as Sancho Panza saw them he said:

'Here comes a chain-gang of convicts, on their forced march to the King's galleys.'

'What do you mean, forced march?' demanded Don Quixote. 'Is it possible that the King uses force on anyone?'

'I don't mean that,' replied Sancho, 'just that they've been sentenced to serve the King in his galleys for their crimes, and they've got a long walk to get there.'

'In short,' replied Don Quixote, 'whatever the details may be, these people, wherever they are going, are being forced to march there, and are not doing it of their own free will.'

'That's right,' said Sancho.

'In that case,' said his master, 'this situation is calling out for the exercise of my profession: the redressing of outrages and the succour and relief of the wretched.'

'Look, sir,' said Sancho. 'Justice, and that means the King himself, isn't doing these people any outrages, only punishing them for their crimes.'

At this point the chain-gang came up, and Don Quixote, in courteous language, asked the guards to be so kind as to inform him of the reason or reasons why they were bearing those people off in that way. One of the guards on horseback replied that they were all convicts, detained at His Majesty's pleasure and on their way to the galleys, and that there was nothing else to be said and nothing else that he had any business to know.

'All the same,' said Don Quixote, 'I should like to hear from each one of them individually the cause of his misfortune.'

He added other such polite expressions to persuade them to tell him what he wanted to know that the other guard on horseback said:

'We do have here the documents and certificates with the sentences that each of these wretches has been given, but this is no time to stop to take them out and read them; so you'd better come and ask the men yourself, and they'll tell you if they want to – and they will want to, because these are fellows who really enjoy getting up to their evil tricks and bragging about them afterwards.'

With this permission, which Don Quixote would have taken for himself if it hadn't been given him, he approached the chain-gang and asked the first convict what sins had put him in that plight. The convict replied that he was there for being in love.

'For no more than that?' replied Don Quixote. 'If they send men to the galleys for being in love, I could have been rowing in them for a long time by now.'

'It isn't love of the sort you think,' said the convict. 'Mine was for a washing-basket that was chock-a-block with linen, and I loved it so much, and I hugged it so tight, that if the law hadn't taken it off me by force I still wouldn't have let go of it of my own free-will to this day. I was caught red-handed, there wasn't any need for torture, the trial's over and done with, they gave me a hundred of the best plus three in the tubs and that's that.'

'What are tubs?' asked Don Quixote.

'Tubs is galleys,' replied the convict.

He was a young man of maybe twenty-four, and he said he was a native of Piedrahita. Don Quixote put the same question to the second convict, who was so overcome by melancholy that he didn't offer a word in reply, but the first one answered for him and said:

'This one, sir, is here for being a canary-bird, that is to say for being a singer and musician.'

'What?' said Don Quixote. 'Do men go to the galleys for being singers and musicians, too?'

'Yes, sir,' replied the convict, 'because there's nothing worse than singing in your throes.'

'On the contrary,' said Don Quixote, 'I have often heard it said that one can sing away sorrows and cast away care.'

'Here it's the opposite,' said the convict. 'Sing just that once and you'll weep for the rest of your life.'

'I fail to understand,' said Don Quixote.

But one of the guards explained:

'Sir knight, among these ungodly people singing in your throes means confessing under torture. This sinner was tortured and he confessed to his crime – he's a prigger of prancers, in other words a horse-thief – and because he confessed he was sentenced to six years in the galleys and two hundred strokes of the lash, and these he's already been given; and he's always sad and lost in his thoughts, because the other criminals back there in prison and here in the chain-gang despise and mock and maltreat him and make his life impossible for confessing and not having the guts to keep saying no. They say, you see, that "nay" has no more letters in it than "aye", and that a delinquent's a lucky man if his life or death depends on his own tongue and not on witnesses or evidence, and it's my belief they aren't far wrong.'

'That is my understanding, too,' replied Don Quixote.

He moved on to the third convict and put the same question to him; the reply was ready and assured:

'I'm off to our old friends the tubs for five years, for the lack of ten ducats.'

'I will most gladly give you twenty,' said Don Quixote, 'to relieve you of such distress.'

'That looks to me,' replied the convict, 'like having money in the middle of the ocean when you're starving and there isn't anywhere to buy what you need. I'm saying this because if I'd had those twenty ducats you're offering me when I needed them, I'd have used them to grease the clerk's pen and liven up my lawyer's wits, and now I'd be in the middle of Zocodover Square in Toledo instead of in the middle of this road, like a greyhound on a leash. But God is good, and you've just got to be patient.'

Don Quixote went on to the fourth convict, a man with a venerable face and a white beard reaching below his chest who, when asked why he was there, began to weep and didn't reply; but the fifth convict acted as interpreter and said:

'This honourable man is going to the galleys for four years, having been paraded in state through the customary streets, all dressed up and on a fine horse.'

'That means, I think,' said Sancho, 'that he was exposed to public shame.'

'That's right,' said the convict, 'and the crime he was given this punishment for was stockbroking, or to be more exact bodybroking. What I mean to say is that this gentleman's here for being a pimp, and also for having a touch of the sorcerer about him.'

'If it were not for the touch of the sorcerer,' said Don Quixote, 'for being a pimp alone he does not deserve to go to row in the galleys, but rather to be the admiral in charge of them. Because the pimp's trade is no ordinary trade; it must be carried out by intelligent people and it is absolutely essential to any well-ordered society, and only the well-born should exercise it; and there should be an official inspector of pimps, as there is of other trades, and a maximum permitted number of them established and published, as is the case with stockbrokers, and this would be the way to forestall many evils that arise from the fact that this trade is in the hands of untrained and unqualified people such as little strumpets, page-boys and other scoundrels of no age or experience who, when at a critical moment some decisive action is called for, make a mess of the whole thing because they cannot tell their right hands from their left. I should like to go on to give the reasons why it would be advisable to make a careful selection of those who do such a necessary job in society, but this is not the place: one day I shall present my ideas to the proper authorities. All I shall say now is that the distress caused me by the sight of these white hairs and this venerable face in such a plight through his being a pimp is dissipated by the addition of his being a sorcerer. I know, of course, that there are no spells in the world that can control a person's will, as some simple people believe; for our free will is sovereign, and there is no herb or enchantment that can control it. What some silly little strumpets and deceitful rogues do is to make certain poisonous mixtures that they use to turn men mad, claiming that they have the power to make them fall in love, whereas it is, as I have just said, impossible to coerce the will.'

'Right you are,' said the old man, 'and honestly, sir, I wasn't guilty of being a sorcerer, though I couldn't deny the charge of being a pimp. But I never thought I was doing any harm, all I wanted was for everyone to be happy and live in peace and quiet, without any quarrels or sadness – but these good intentions weren't any use to prevent me from being sent where I don't expect to come back from, what with my advanced age and my bladder trouble, that doesn't give me a moment's peace.'

And here he started weeping again, and Sancho felt so sorry for him that he took a real from inside his shirt and handed it over. Don Quixote moved on to the next man and asked what was his crime, and he replied with no less brio than the last, indeed with rather more of it:

'I'm here because I fooled around too much with two girl-cousins of mine, and with two girl-cousins of somebody else's; and, in short, I fooled around so much with the lot of them that as a result the family tree's become so complicated that I don't know who the devil would be able to work it out. It was all proved against me, there weren't any strings for me to pull, I hadn't got any money, I was within an inch of having my neck stretched, I was sentenced to the galleys for six years and I accepted my fate: it's the punishment for my crime, I'm still young, long live life, while there's life there's hope. If, sir knight, you've got anything on you that you could spare for us poor wretches, God will repay you for it in heaven, and here on earth we'll take care to pray to God that your life and your health may be as long and as good as you obviously deserve.'

He was wearing a student's gown, and one of the guards said that he was a great talker and a first-rate latiner.

Behind all of these was a man of thirty, very good-looking except that he squinted a little. He was shackled in a different way from the others: he had a chain on his ankle so long that he'd wound it all round his body, and two neck-irons, one linking him to the other convicts and the other, one of the sort called a keep-friend or friend's foot, from which descended two bars to his waist, where his wrists were manacled to them with great padlocks, so that he could neither raise his hands to his mouth nor lower his head to his hands. Don Quixote asked why this man was wearing so many more fetters than the others. The guard replied that it was because he'd committed more crimes than all the others put together, and that he was so reckless and such a villain that, even though he was shackled up like that, they didn't feel at all safe with him, and feared he was going to escape.

'What crimes can he have committed, though,' asked Don Quixote, 'if he was not given a worse punishment than the galleys?'

'He's going for ten years,' replied the guard, 'which is civil death, more or less.[1] All you need to know is that this man is the famous Ginés de Pasamonte, also known as Ginesillo de Parapilla.'[2]

'Look you here, sergeant,' said the convict, 'just watch your step, and don't be in such a hurry to fix names and nicknames on to people. I'm called Ginés, not Ginesillo, and my family name is Pasamonte, not the Parapilla you said, and I'd advise you lot to stop poking your noses into other people's business.'

'Less impudence, you double-dyed villain,' replied the sergeant, 'unless you want me to shut your mouth for you.'

'It isn't hard to spot,' replied the convict, 'that at the moment I'm reduced to what God has seen fit to send me; but one day somebody's going to find out whether I'm called Ginesillo de Parapilla or not.'

'Isn't that what people call you, then, you liar?' said the guard.

'Yes, that's what they call me,' replied Ginés, 'but I'll stop them calling me that, or else I'll pull out every single hair from my I know what. If you've got something to give us, sir knight, let's have it, and then you can clear off, because you're beginning to get on my nerves with all your prying into other people's lives – and if you want to know about mine, let me tell you I'm Ginés de Pasamonte, and my life has been written by these very fingers here.'

'Now he's telling the truth,' said the sergeant. 'He's written his own life-history himself and a good one it is, too, and he pawned the book in prison for two hundred reals.'

'And I mean to redeem it,' said Ginés. 'And I would, even if I'd pawned it for two hundred ducats.'

'Is it as good as all that?' said Don Quixote.

'It's so good,' replied Ginés, 'that I wouldn't give a fig for *Lazarillo de Tormes*[3] and all the others of that kind that have been or ever will be written. What I can tell you is that it deals with facts, and that they're such fine and funny facts no lies could ever match them.'

'And what is the title of your book?' asked Don Quixote.

'*The Life of Ginés de Pasamonte*,' replied the man of that name.

'And have you finished it?' asked Don Quixote.

'How can I have finished it,' he replied, 'if my life hasn't finished yet? What's written so far is from my birth to when I was sentenced to the galleys this last time.'

'Have you been to the galleys before, then?' asked Don Quixote.

'I have, serving God and the King for four years, so I know what biscuits taste like and I know what the lash tastes like,' replied Ginés. 'And I'm not too worried about going back, because it'll give me a chance to finish my book – there are lots of things left for me to say, and in Spanish galleys there's more than enough peace and quiet, not that I need much of that for what I've got left to write, because I know it all by heart.'

'You seem to be an able fellow,' said Don Quixote.

'And an unfortunate one, too,' replied Ginés, 'because misfortunes always pursue men of genius.'

'They pursue villains,' said the sergeant.

'I've already told you, sergeant,' replied Pasamonte, 'to watch your step – you weren't given that staff to ill-treat us poor wretches, but to guide and take us to where His Majesty commands. Otherwise – by the blood of . . . ! – all sorts of things might come out in the wash one day, like those stains that were made at the inn, for example. So everyone keep his mouth shut, and live a good life, and speak even better words, and let's get moving, because this little joke has been going on for far too long.'

The sergeant raised his staff to hit Pasamonte in reply to his threats, but Don Quixote thrust himself between them and begged the sergeant not to maltreat the fellow, for it was only to be expected that one whose hands were so tightly bound would loosen his tongue a little. And turning to the chain-gang he said:

'From everything that you have told me, dearly beloved brethren, I have gathered that, although it is for your crimes you have been sentenced, the punishments you are to suffer give you little pleasure, and that you are on your way to receive them with reluctance and against your will; and it could be that one man's lack of courage under torture, another's lack of money, another's lack of strings to pull and, to be brief, the judge's perverse decisions, were the causes of your downfall and of his failure to recognize the right that was on your side. All of which is now so powerfully present in my mind that it is persuading, telling and even obliging me to demonstrate on you the purpose for which heaven sent me into this world and made me profess in it the order of chivalry that I do profess, and the vow that I made to favour the needy and those oppressed by the powerful. But because I know that one essential part of prudence is never to do by force what can be achieved by consent, I hereby request these guards and this sergeant to be so kind as to release you and allow you to go in peace, for there will be no lack of other men to serve the King in happier circumstances, and it does seem excessively harsh to make slaves of those whom God and nature made free. What is more, guards,' added Don Quixote, 'these poor men have done nothing to you. Let each answer for his sins in the other world; there is a God in heaven who does not neglect to punish the wicked and reward the virtuous, and it is not right for honourable men to be the executioners of others, if they have no personal concern in the matter. I am making my request in this mild and measured manner so that, if you accede to it, I shall have reason for thanking you; but if you do not accede voluntarily, this lance and this sword and the might of my arm will force you to comply.'

'That's a good one that is!' said the sergeant. 'That's a fine joke he's come out with at long last! He wants us to hand the King's prisoners over to him, as if we had the authority to let them go or he had the authority to tell us to! You'd better clear off and make tracks, sir, and straighten that chamber-pot you've got on your head, and don't go around trying to put the cat among the pigeons.'

'You are the cat, and the rat, and the villain, too!' retorted Don Quixote. He matched his deeds to his words and his attack was such a sudden one that he tumbled the man to the ground with a pike-wound before he had a chance to defend himself; and it was fortunate for Don Quixote that this was the guard with the firelock. The other guards were amazed and disconcerted by this unexpected development, but they rallied, and those on horseback seized their swords, and those on foot their spears, and they all fell upon Don Quixote, who was calmly awaiting them; yet he'd have fared badly if the convicts, seeing their chance to be free, hadn't succeeded by breaking the chain on which they were threaded. The hurly-burly was such that the guards, trying both to control the convicts, who were unshackling themselves, and to attack Don Quixote, who was attacking them, chased around in circles and achieved nothing.

Sancho, for his part, helped with the freeing of Ginés de Pasamonte, who was the first to spring into action as he launched himself at the fallen sergeant, snatched up his sword and his firelock and, pointing this at one man and then at another, without firing it, made all the guards disappear as they fled both from the gun and from the stones being hurled at them by the escaped convicts.

This incident saddened Sancho, because he supposed that the fleeing men would go and inform the Holy Brotherhood, who would sound the alarm and come out in pursuit of the wrongdoers; and Sancho said so to his master, and begged him to agree to a quick getaway to hide in the forests in the nearby sierra.

'That is a good idea,' said Don Quixote, 'but there is something I must do first.'

And he called out to the convicts, who were creating a furore as they stripped the sergeant naked; they gathered around to see what he wanted, and he said:

'It is a mark of well-born people to be grateful for benefits received, and one of the sins most offensive to God is ingratitude. I am saying this because you have seen, gentlemen, manifest before your eyes, the benefit that you have received from me; in payment of which it is my wish and desire that you should set out without delay, bearing that chain that I have taken from your necks, for the city of El Toboso, and present yourselves before the lady Dulcinea del Toboso, and tell her that her knight, the Knight of the Sorry Face, presents his compliments, and relate to her, stage by stage, every detail of this famous adventure up to and including my restoration of the liberty that you so desired; and once you have done this you can go wherever you like, and may good fortune attend you.'

Ginés de Pasamonte replied on behalf of them all, and said:

'This that you order us to do, dear lord and liberator, is utterly and totally out of the question, because we can't travel together – we've got to split up and go alone, each along his own road, and try to find a way into the very bowels of the earth so as not to be caught by the Holy Brotherhood, who'll be coming out after us, for certain. What you can do and what it'd be right for you to do is to replace that toll or tax payable to the lady

Dulcinea del Toboso by a certain number of Ave Marias and Credos, which we'll say for your kindness, and this is something that can be done by night and by day, running away and resting, in peace and in war; but to think that we're going back to the flesh-pots of Egypt,⁴ in other words picking up our chain again and setting off for El Toboso, is like thinking it's night-time already when it isn't yet ten in the morning – it's like trying to get figs from thistles.'

'By my faith,' cried Don Quixote, by now in a fury, 'you little bastard, Don Ginesillo de Paropillo or whatever you're called – now you shall go there alone, with your tail between your legs and the whole chain on your back!'

Pasamonte wasn't a long-suffering sort, and from Don Quixote's absurd desire to set them free he'd realized that the man wasn't very sane, so when he found himself thus addressed, he tipped his companions the wink and they edged away and began to rain so many stones on Don Quixote that, however he ducked and dodged behind his little round shield, he couldn't fend them off; and poor Rocinante paid no more attention to the spurs than if he'd been made of bronze. Sancho sheltered behind his ass from the hailstorm falling on them both. Don Quixote couldn't prevent countless stones from hitting his body with enough force to knock him to the ground, and as soon as he did fall the student leapt on him, snatched the basin from his head and smashed it three or four times on his back and as many more times on the earth, pounding it almost to pieces. Then they stripped him of a surcoat he was wearing over his armour and would have stripped him of his stockings, too, if his leg armour hadn't made this impossible. They took Sancho's topcoat and left him in his shirtsleeves, and they shared the rest of the spoils of battle, and each went his own way, more concerned to escape from the dreaded Holy Brotherhood than to burden himself with the chain and go to present himself before the lady Dulcinea del Toboso.

The ass and Rocinante, Sancho and Don Quixote were left alone: the ass hanging its head, lost in its thoughts, flapping its ears every so often in the belief that the storm of stones wasn't yet over, because it was still raging inside its skull; Rocinante stretched out by his master's side, because he'd also been brought down by a stone; Sancho in his shirtsleeves and fearful of the Holy Brotherhood; and Don Quixote sulking at being left in such a sorry state by men for whom he had done so much.

CHAPTER XXIII

✠

About what happened to the famous Don Quixote in the
Sierra Morena, one of the strangest adventures recounted
in this true history

Finding himself in this sorry state, Don Quixote said to his squire:

'I have always heard, Sancho, that to do good to low-born rabble is to cast water into the sea. Had I believed what you said, I should have avoided this vexation; but the damage is done now, so one must be patient and learn one's lesson for the future.'

'If you've learned your lesson for the future,' retorted Sancho, 'I'm a Turk. But since you're saying that if you'd believed me then you'd have avoided all this mayhem, just believe me now and you'll avoid worse — because I'd like you to know that chivalry doings won't wash with the Holy Brotherhood, they don't care a fig for all the knight errants in the world, and let me tell you I can almost hear their arrows whistling towards me even now.'

'You are a coward by nature, Sancho,' said Don Quixote, 'yet to prevent you from claiming that I am obstinate and never do as you recommend, just this once I shall take your advice and keep my distance from the fury that so frightens you, but on one condition: never, in life or in death, will you tell anyone that I retreated from this peril out of fear, but rather acceded to your entreaties; and if you say anything else, you will be lying, and I give you the lie from now until then and from then until now, and I affirm that you lie and you will lie whenever you think or say it. And do not answer me back; for the mere thought that I am retreating from peril, especially this peril, which does appear to have some faint shadow of fear about it, is enough to make me take my stand here and await alone not only that Holy Brotherhood whose name you speak in such terror but the brothers of the twelve tribes of Israel, and the seven Maccabees, and Castor and Pollux,[1] and all the brothers and brotherhoods in the world.'

'Look here, sir,' replied Sancho, 'withdrawing isn't running away, and waiting isn't prudent when danger outweighs hope, and the wise man saves himself for tomorrow and doesn't risk everything on one day. And I'd just like to say that although I'm an uncouth peasant I do understand a bit about this business they call right conduct, so don't repent of having taken my advice, but climb on to Rocinante if you can, and if you can't I'll help you up, and follow me, because my old grey matter's telling me that at the moment one pair of heels is worth two pairs of hands.'

Don Quixote mounted without another word, and Sancho led the way on his ass into a nearby part of the Sierra Morena, his idea being to ride right across it as far as Viso or Almodóvar del Campo and hide out for a few days in that rough country, so as not to be found if the Holy Brotherhood did come after them. He was encouraged to do this by the discovery that the provisions on his ass had escaped untouched from the skirmish with the convicts, something that he considered miraculous, considering how they'd searched and pillaged.

As Don Quixote rode in among the mountains, his heart rejoiced because these seemed like ideal places for the adventures he was seeking. The marvellous events experienced by knights errant in similar lonely and rugged spots were returning to his memory. He rode along musing on all these matters, so absorbed and carried away by them that he didn't have a thought for anything else. And as soon as Sancho believed they were safe, his only concern was to satisfy his stomach with the remains of the clerical spoils, and along he rode behind his master, sitting side-saddle on his donkey, and out of the saddle-bag came the food and into his belly it all went; and so long as he had this to keep him busy, he wouldn't have given a brass farthing for another adventure.

But then he did raise his eyes, and saw that his master had stopped and was using the tip of his pike to try to prise up a bundle that was lying on the ground, so he hurried to help; and he reached him just as he was lifting on his pike-tip a saddle-pad with a travelling bag attached to it, half-rotten or rather entirely so and falling to pieces; but they were so heavy that Sancho had to dismount and take them from the pike, and his master told him to see what was in the travelling bag. Sancho hastened to do so and, although the bag was secured with a padlock and chain, it was so torn and decayed that he could see what was in it: four shirts of fine holland-cloth, other articles of linen, as exquisite as they were clean, and, wrapped in a handkerchief, a sizeable pile of gold escudos. When Sancho saw them he exclaimed:

'All heaven be blessed for sending us an adventure that pays!'

Some more rummaging yielded a richly bound notebook. Don Quixote asked for it, and told Sancho to take the money and keep it for himself. Sancho kissed his hands for the favour and removed all the linen to his provision bag. Don Quixote observed his actions and said:

'It seems to me, Sancho (and this is the only possible explanation), that some lost traveller must have wandered into this sierra, and been waylaid and killed by robbers, who brought his body here to this remote spot to bury it.'

'That can't be right,' replied Sancho, 'because if they were robbers they wouldn't have left all this money behind.'

'That is true,' said Don Quixote, 'so I cannot guess or imagine what has happened. But wait, let us see if there is anything written in this notebook that can help us to trace and discover what we want to know.'

He opened it, and the first thing he found written there, as if it were a draft, although very neatly set out, was a sonnet, which he read aloud for Sancho to hear, and found that it went like this:

> Love's blind – or, rather, ignorant, I'd say,
> Or cruelty must be his guiding passion;
> For it's unjust to make a lover pay
> With torture on the rack for indiscretion.
> But if Love is a god, I must confess
> That he has boundless knowledge and, what's more,
> A god cannot be harsh and pitiless.
> Who, then, has sent this pain that I adore?
> My Chlöe? No, that couldn't ever be:
> Such ills could never have a source so dear,
> Nor have the gods sent suffering to me:
> That I am soon to die is all that's clear.
> For when the cause of the complaint's unsure,
> A miracle alone can bring a cure.

'We aren't going to discover anything from that rhyme,' said Sancho, 'unless that clue is something we can follow up.'

'To which clue do you refer?' said Don Quixote.

'I thought,' said Sancho, 'you mentioned something about his clue.'

'What I said was Chlöe,' replied Don Quixote, 'and this must be the name of the lady of whom the author of this sonnet is complaining; and to be sure he is a very fair poet, or I am no judge of that art.'

'So,' said Sancho, 'you know all about rhymes, too, do you?'

'More than you think,' replied Don Quixote, 'as you will see when you take a letter, written in verse from beginning to end, to my lady Dulcinea del Toboso. For I would have you know, Sancho, that all or nearly all the knights errant of past times were great troubadours and great musicians, because these two skills, or, to be more accurate, gifts, are essential to knights errant in love. It does have to be admitted, though, that the verses written by the knights of old are distinguished more by spiritedness than by elegance.'

'You go on and read some more,' said Sancho, 'I'm sure you'll find something to help us.'

Don Quixote turned the page and said:

'This is prose, and it looks like a letter.'

'A personal letter, sir?' asked Sancho.

'To judge from its opening it is a love-letter,' replied Don Quixote.

'Do read it out aloud, then,' said Sancho. 'I'm very fond of love stories.'

'Very well,' said Don Quixote.

And he read it out aloud, as Sancho had requested, and found that it went like this:

Your false promise and my true misfortune carry me to a place from whence you will sooner hear the news of my death than the sound of my complaints. You rejected me, ungrateful woman, for one more wealthy but not more worthy than I; yet if virtue were a valued treasure, I should not now be envying another's good fortune or lamenting my own misfortune. What your beauty raised up, your deeds have laid low: your beauty made me believe you were an angel, your deeds make me realize you are a woman. Peace be with you, who have sent war to me, and may heaven keep your husband's deceptions concealed for ever, so that you are not struck with remorse for what you have done, and I do not reap a revenge that I do not desire.

When Don Quixote had finished reading the letter, he said:

'All that one can discover from this and from the poem is that the man who wrote them is some slighted lover.'

And, thumbing through the book, he found other verses and letters, some of which he could read and others not, but they all contained complaints, laments, suspicions, longings and sorrows, favours and slights, some celebrated and others bemoaned.

While Don Quixote was going through the notebook, Sancho was going through the travelling bag, leaving not one corner of it or of the saddle-pad unsearched, unscrutinized or unexplored, not one seam unripped and not one tuft of wool unpicked, to make sure that he wasn't overlooking anything through haste or carelessness – such was the appetite that finding the escudos, of which there were more than a hundred, had stimulated. And although he didn't find anything else, he knew it had all been worthwhile – all the blanket-flying, the spewed-up balsam, the benedictions from the walking-staffs, the thumping from the muleteer, the disappearance of the saddle-bags, the theft of the topcoat, and all the hunger, thirst and exhaustion that he'd been through in his good master's service: all worthwhile because he'd been so well repaid by being allowed to keep that treasure trove.

The Knight of the Sorry Face was left with a great desire to know who was the owner of the travelling bag, and he conjectured from the sonnet and the letter, from the gold coins and the fine shirts, that they must belong to some lover of high rank, reduced to a desperate decision by his lady's disdain and ill treatment of him. But since there was nobody in that rugged and uninhabitable country to inform him, his only concern was to press on whichever way Rocinante wanted to go – in other words wherever Roci-nante could manage to plod – always imagining that some wonderful adventure must be awaiting him among those briars and brambles.

As he rode along, then, with this idea in mind, he saw on a hill in front of him a man leaping with unusual agility from rock to rock and from bush to bush. He seemed to be half-naked, and he had a thick black beard, long hair tied in a pony tail, bare legs and feet; he wore short breeches that seemed to be of light brown velvet, but they were so torn that in many places his skin showed through. He was bareheaded. Although the man moved at such speed, the Knight of the Sorry Face took note of all these details, and he tried to follow him but without success because Rocinante's feebleness wouldn't allow him to gallop over such rough terrain, and furthermore he was a sedate and phlegmatic horse. It immediately occurred to Don Quixote that this man was the owner of the travelling bag and the saddle-pad, and he decided to go in search of him until he found him, even if this meant wandering through the sierra for a year; so he ordered Sancho to dismount from his ass and cut across one part of the hill, and he himself would go the other way, as by such measures they might find the man who had so swiftly disappeared from their sight.

'No, that'll be beyond me,' replied Sancho, 'because as soon as I leave your side the fear comes over me and attacks me with all kinds of alarms and visions. And what I'm telling you now can serve as a warning so that you never again expect me to budge so much as an inch from your side.'

'Very well,' said the Knight of the Sorry Face, 'and I am delighted that you are resolved to rely on my courage, which will not desert you, even if your very soul should do so. And now follow me slowly, or however you can, and keep your eyes peeled; we shall ride all round this hill and maybe come across that man we saw, who is beyond doubt none other than the owner of the objects we have just found.'

To which Sancho replied:

'It'd be much better not to look for him, because if we do find him and the money does turn out to be his, it's clear I'll have to give it back – so it'd be better not to go to all these uncalled-for lengths, and for me to keep the money in good faith until its real owner turns up in some other way, without so much poking around for him. And by then I might have spent it all, and the King would let me off.'

'You are deluding yourself there, Sancho,' replied Don Quixote, 'because now that we have formed a suspicion of who the owner might be – and he is virtually standing here in front of us – it is our duty to seek him out and return his money; and if we did not go in search of him, our strong suspicion that he is the owner would make us as guilty as if we were altogether certain that he is. So, Sancho my friend, you must not let searching for him grieve you, in view of how finding him would relieve me.'

So he put spurs to Rocinante, and Sancho followed him on his donkey, as usual, and after they'd ridden some of the way round the hill they found a dead mule lying in a stream, complete with saddle and bridle, half devoured by dogs and pecked by crows, which confirmed their suspicion that the man who'd run away from them was the owner of the mule and the saddle-pad. As they contemplated this sight they heard a whistling, like that of a herdsman rounding up his animals, and suddenly, to their left, a number of goats appeared and behind them on the top of the hill the goatherd, an old man. Don Quixote shouted to him and invited him to descend. He shouted back asking what had brought them to that place, seldom if ever visited by anything other than goats and wolves and other wild beasts that lived in those parts. Sancho replied that if he came down they'd explain everything. He did so and as he approached Don Quixote he said:

'I bet you're looking at that hired mule lying dead in that ravine. To be sure it's been there for a good six months now. Tell me, have you come across its owner?'

'We have not come across anyone,' replied Don Quixote, 'just a saddle-pad and a travelling bag that we found not far from here.'

'I found it too,' replied the goatherd, 'but I never picked it up or even went close to it, for fear that it might bring bad luck, and that I might have to return it as stolen property – the devil's a cunning one, and things are always showing up at a man's feet to make him trip and fall when he's least expecting it.'

'That's what I say, too,' replied Sancho. 'I found it as well, and I wouldn't have touched it with a bargepole, so I left it just where it was, and there it lies exactly as it did before – I don't want a dog with a bell round its neck.'

'Tell me, my good man,' said Don Quixote, 'do you know who is the owner of these articles?'

'All I can tell you,' said the goatherd, 'is that one day roughly six months ago, at a goat-fold about ten miles from here, a good-looking young man turned up riding the mule that's lying down there dead, with that same saddle-pad and travelling bag you say you found and didn't touch. He asked us which part of this sierra was the most rugged and remote, and we told him that this part was where we are now, and so it is, because if you went in another mile or two maybe you'd never find your way out again, and I'm astonished you've got this far, because there isn't any road or path to bring you here. Anyway, as soon as the young man heard our reply he turned his mule and went off in the direction we'd said, leaving us all admiring his good looks and amazed at his question and at the speed at which he'd ridden away towards the sierra, and we didn't see him again until a few days later he waylaid one of the goatherds and without a word came up to him and punched him and kicked him and then went over to our supply-donkey and took all the bread and cheese there was on it, and ran away at an incredible rate to hide in the sierra. When we found out about this, some of us goatherds went looking for him for almost two days in the remotest part of the sierra, and in the end we found him hiding in the hollow of a fine, stout cork-oak. He came out very quietly, with his clothes ripped and his face changed and sunburned so that we could hardly recognize him – except that his clothes, torn as they were, were the same ones we'd seen him wearing earlier and showed he was the man we were looking for.

'He greeted us courteously, and with a few well-chosen words he told us not to be surprised at seeing him going about like that, because he had to do so to fulfil a penance imposed on him for his many sins. We asked him to tell us who he was, but we couldn't get this out of him. We also asked him, when he needed food, to tell us where we could find him, because he couldn't survive without it and we'd be more than willing to take it to him, and, if he didn't like this idea either, at least to come and ask us for it rather than snatching it from us. He thanked us for our offer, apologized for his past attacks, and said that from then on he'd beg us for his food, without annoying anybody. As for his dwelling-place, he said he had none but whatever chance offered him when night fell, and he ended his words with such tender tears that those who'd been listening would have had to be of stone not to weep with him, considering how he'd looked before and how he looked now. As I said, he was a very handsome and well-graced young man, and in his courteous and thoughtful words he showed himself to be a real gentleman, so that, although all of us listening were simple country folk, even we could tell that he was a person of high rank.

'He was in full flow when he stopped and fell silent and stared down at the earth, and we all waited in a puzzled hush for a good while to find out how this trance was going to end, saddened to see him like that – because from the way he was opening his eyes wide, glaring and glaring at the ground without batting an eyelid, then suddenly shutting his eyes tight and clenching his lips and arching his eyebrows, it was easy to spot that he was in the grip of some fit of madness. And he soon showed that we were right, because he sprang in fury to his feet from where he'd slumped to the ground, and launched himself at the man nearest him with such wild determination that if we hadn't torn him away he'd have beaten and bitten him to death, and he was saying:

'"Ah, perfidious Fernando! Now, now you shall pay for the wrongs you've done me! These hands of mine will tear out your very heart, the den wherein all evil dwells, and the greatest of them trickery and deceit."

'And he added other words, all of them abuse of this man Fernando, calling him perfidious and a traitor. We managed to pull him off our companion and, without another word, he ran away and hid among the brambles and the thickets, and we couldn't follow him. We reckoned that the madness comes on him every so often, and that some man called Fernando must have done something terrible to him, something awful enough to have brought him to that state. It's all been confirmed since, on the many occasions he's come down from the hills, sometimes to ask the goatherds for food, at other times to take it from them by force, because when the fit of madness is upon him he won't let them give him food, even if they do so willingly, but punches them and takes it; when he's in his right mind he begs them for it in a courteous, restrained way, and gives profuse thanks and even sheds some tears. And to tell you the truth, sirs,' continued the goatherd, 'yesterday I decided with four young lads – two servants of mine and two friends – to go in search of him until we find him, and once we find him to take him, whether he wants to go or not, to the town of Almodóvar, twenty-five miles from here, and have him cured there, if there is a cure for his illness, or find out from him, when he's in his right mind, who he is, and whether he has relatives we should inform about his misfortune. This, sirs, is what I can tell you in reply to your question, and you can be sure that the owner of the things you found is the same person you saw running by so nimble and so naked' – because Don Quixote had told him how he'd seen the man leaping from crag to crag on the hill.

Don Quixote was amazed at what the goatherd had told him, and was even more anxious now to know who the unfortunate madman was, and decided to do what he'd been contemplating: search the whole sierra for him, leaving not a cave or a cranny unexplored until he'd found him. But fortune was kinder than he'd dared to hope, because at that very moment, in a gorge that opened on to the place where they were talking, the young man himself appeared, muttering words that were incomprehensible from close up, let alone from a distance. His clothes were as they've been described, except that when he came nearer Don Quixote noticed that a ragged suede jerkin he was wearing was perfumed with ambergris, further confirmation that a person wearing such clothes couldn't be of low rank.

The young man came up and greeted them in a hoarse, discordant voice, but with great courtesy. Don Quixote replied no less politely and, dismounting from Rocinante, walked with graceful elegance to embrace him, and held him for some moments in his arms, as if he knew him from distant times. The young man, whom, just as Don Quixote was the Knight of the Sorry Face, we can call the Ragged Knight of the Miserable Face, submitted to the embrace and then pushed Don Quixote a little away, gazing at him with his hands on the other man's shoulders as if trying to recognize him, perhaps no less astonished to see Don Quixote's face, figure and armour than Don Quixote had been to see him. In the end the first one to speak after this embrace was the Ragged Knight, and he said what will be recorded in the next chapter.

CHAPTER XXIV

In which the adventure in the Sierra Morena is continued

The history says that Don Quixote listened with rapt attention to the ill-dressed and ill-starred Knight of the Sierra, who continued:

'Most certainly, sir, whoever you are, for I do not know you, I thank you for your expressions of civility, and I wish I were in a position to serve you with more than my goodwill in return for that which you have shown me in the warm reception which you have extended to me; but my fortune does not allow me anything with which to respond to the kindnesses done me, other than the sincere desire to repay them.'

'Mine,' replied Don Quixote, 'is to serve you; so much so, that I had resolved not to leave this sierra until I had found you and discovered from you whether there was any remedy for the grief that, to judge from your extraordinary life here, afflicts you; and if it were necessary to go in search of such a remedy, to do so with the utmost possible diligence. And if your misfortune were of the sort that keeps the doors tight shut to all solace, it was my intention to join you, as best I could, in your tears and lamentations, for it is always a consolation in disaster to find someone who is sympathetic. And if my good intentions deserve to be acknowledged with any kind of courtesy, I beg you, sir, in the name of the abundance of that quality that I can see you possess, and I entreat you in the name of whomsoever in this life you love or have loved the best, to tell me who you are and what has brought you to live and die in this wilderness like a brute animal, because your dress and person show how alien to you is this present life of yours. And I swear,' added Don Quixote, 'by the order of chivalry that I, although unworthy and a sinner, have received, and by the profession of knight errant, that if you comply with this request, sir, I shall serve you with that earnestness to which I am obliged by being who I am, either by remedying your misfortune, if indeed it has a remedy, or by assisting you to bewail it, as I have promised.'

When the Knight of the Forest heard the Knight of the Sorry Face speak in this way, he only stared at him, and stared at him again, and stared at him once more from head to foot; and once he'd had a good stare, he said:

'If you people have anything to eat, let me have it, for God's sake, and once I've eaten I'll do everything you say, to express my gratitude for the kind intentions you've expressed.'

They immediately produced some food, Sancho from his saddle-bag and the goatherd from his pouch, and the Ragged Knight satisfied his hunger, eating what he was given like a man in a daze, so fast that there was no space between one mouthful and the next, because he didn't so much swallow them as shovel them down; and while he ate, neither he nor those watching him spoke a word. Once he'd finished, he signalled to them to follow him, which they did, and he took them to a green meadow behind a rock not far away. On reaching it he stretched himself out on the grass, and the others did the same, all without a word being spoken by anyone until the Ragged Knight, once he'd made himself comfortable, said:

'If you wish me, gentlemen, to tell you in a few words about the immensity of my misfortunes, you must promise that you won't interrupt the thread of my sad story with any question or any other intervention, because the instant you do so my narrative will end.'

These words brought into Don Quixote's memory the story that his squire had told him, when he'd failed to keep count of how many goats had crossed the river, and the story had been left unfinished. But to return to the Ragged Knight, he continued:

'I give you this warning because I'd like to pass quickly over the story of my misfortunes, since bringing them back to my memory only adds to them, and the fewer questions you ask the sooner I'll be finished; but I shan't leave anything important out, because I want to satisfy all your wishes.'

Don Quixote promised in the name of the whole company that he would not be interrupted, and with this assurance the Ragged Knight began:

'My name is Cardenio; I'm from one of the finest cities in Andalusia; my family's noble; my parents are wealthy; and my misfortune's so great that my parents must have wept and my family grieved over it, unable with all their wealth to remedy it, for the greatest of fortunes can do little to relieve the misfortunes sent by heaven. There lived on this earth a heaven in which love had placed all the glory that I could ever wish for: such is the beauty of Luscinda, a maiden as noble and wealthy as I, but luckier, and less constant than my honourable intentions deserved. This Luscinda I loved, worshipped and adored from my tenderest and earliest years, and she loved me too, with the simple affection and eagerness of youth. Our parents knew of our feelings, and they weren't opposed to them, because they could see that if they continued they could only lead to marriage, something almost required by the equality of our lineage and wealth. Our love increased as we grew up, and Luscinda's father thought himself obliged by good form to refuse me entry to his house, imitating the parents of that Thisbe so celebrated by poets.[1] This ban only added flame to flame and desire to desire because, although our tongues had been silenced, it was impossible to silence our pens, which tell the loved one more freely than do tongues about the hidden secrets of the soul; for the presence of the beloved often confuses and silences the most determined intention and the boldest tongue. Heavens, how many letters I wrote her! What delicate and modest replies I received! How many songs I composed, how many verses of love, in which my soul declared and revealed its feelings, depicted its burning desires, cherished its memories and relived its passion! Eventually, at my wit's end and with my soul consumed by desire to see her, I decided to put into effect once and for all what I thought was the most effective means to gain my longed-for and deserved prize, which was to ask her father for her as my lawful wife, and I did this; he replied that he was grateful to me for wanting to honour him and seeking to honour myself with his precious treasure, but that, since my own father was still alive, it was he who should by rights make the request, because Luscinda was not a woman to be taken or given in an underhand way without his full permission and approval.

'I thanked him for his kindness, thinking that he was right, and that if I told my father about my proposal he would agree to it; so I immediately went to inform him of my wish. When I walked into his room, I found him with a letter open in his hand, and before I could speak he gave it to me and said:

' "You will see from this letter, Cardenio, the favour that Duke Ricardo wishes to do you."

'This Duke Ricardo, as you must already know, gentlemen, is a grandee of Spain, whose estate lies in the best part of Andalusia. I took and read the letter, which was so insistent that I myself would have objected if my father had failed to do what it asked of him, which was to send me immediately to the Duke: he wanted me as a companion, not a servant, for his elder son, and he would undertake to situate me in accordance with the high opinion he had of me. I read the letter and was dumbfounded, even more so when I heard my father saying:

' "In two days' time you will depart, Cardenio, to do as the Duke wishes; and give thanks to God for opening a way for you to what I know you well deserve."

'To this he added some more pieces of fatherly advice.

'The moment of my departure approached, I spoke by night with

Luscinda, I told her all that had happened and I told her father as well, and begged him to wait a few days and postpone settling her marriage until I found out what Ricardo wanted of me; he promised to do so, and she confirmed his promise with a thousand vows and a thousand swoons. So away I went to join Duke Ricardo. I was so well received and treated by him that envy immediately started to do its work and to possess his servants, for they thought that all the signs he gave of favouring me would be to their detriment. But the person who was most delighted at my arrival was the Duke's younger son, Fernando, a charming, attractive young man, of generous and amorous disposition, who soon wanted me to be such a close friend that everybody was gossiping about it; and although the elder son liked me and treated me well, he didn't go to Don Fernando's extremes of attention and affection.

'Now as there are no secrets between friends, and as the favour that Don Fernando showed me stopped being mere favour and turned into friendship, he told me all his thoughts, and in particular one relating to love that was worrying him somewhat. He loved a wealthy farmer's daughter, one of his father's tenants, and she was so beautiful, modest, intelligent and virtuous that nobody who knew her could decide which of these excellent qualities was most outstanding in her. And they raised Don Fernando's desires to such a pitch that he decided that to have his way with her and conquer her virginity he'd give her his word of marriage,[2] because to have tried any other approach would have been to attempt the impossible. Prompted by our friendship, I tried, with the best arguments I knew and the most eloquent examples I could find, to dissuade him and turn him aside from this course, but seeing that it was all in vain I decided to put the matter before Duke Ricardo, his father; Don Fernando, however, cunning and intelligent as he was, suspected and feared that I might do this, knowing that I was obliged, as a loyal servant, not to conceal something so prejudicial to the honour of my lord the Duke; and to mislead and deceive me he told me that he couldn't think of anything to take his mind off the beauty which had so captivated him other than going away for a few months, that he wanted to achieve this by staying with me at my father's house, and that the excuse the Duke would be given was that he was going to inspect and buy some excellent horses in my city, which breeds the best horses in the world.

'Moved by my own love, I should have welcomed his decision as soon as I heard it as one of the best imaginable, even if his motivation had been less laudable – because I could see what an excellent opportunity it gave me to see my dear Luscinda again. With this thought in mind I supported his ideas and encouraged his plan, advising him to carry it out as soon as possible, because absence was bound to have its effect, in spite of the strongest feelings. By the time he told me all this he had already, as later became apparent, enjoyed the girl's favours as her husband, and was looking for an opportunity to reveal all without having to pay the consequences, fearful as he was of what the Duke his father would do when he found out about his folly.

'It happened, then, that since love in young men is usually not love at all, but lust, which, since gratification is its sole aim, ceases to exist as soon as it is satisfied, and what had looked like love turns back because it cannot go any further than the limits fixed for it by nature, which does not establish any limits for true love . . . what I'm trying to say is that as soon as Don Fernando had his way with the farmer's daughter his desires abated and his ardour cooled, and, if at first he'd pretended to want to leave so as to cure his desires, now he really did want to leave so as not to put them into effect. The Duke gave his permission and told me to go with him. We arrived in my city, my father accorded him the reception due to his rank, I went to see Luscinda, my passion was revived (although it had never been dead or even dormant) and I was unwise enough to tell Don Fernando of it, because I thought that the great friendship he professed for me forbad me to keep anything from him. I praised Luscinda's beauty, grace and intelligence, and my praise aroused in him a desire to contemplate a maiden adorned with such fine qualities. For my own misfortune I fulfilled his desire by letting him see her one night, by the light of a candle, at a window where we used to talk. He saw her in a chemise and forgot all the beauties he'd ever seen before. He was struck dumb, he lost his senses, he was spellbound and, in short, he fell as hopelessly in love as you'll see in the course of this tale of my misfortune. And the more to inflame his passion (which he hid from me and revealed to the heavens when he was alone) he happened one day to find a letter written by her, asking me to ask her father for her hand in marriage, which was so well expressed, so modest and so tender that he told me Luscinda brought together in herself the beauty and understanding that was shared among all the other women in the world.

'I do have to confess that, although I could see how justified Don Fernando's praises were, I disliked hearing them in his mouth, and I began to grow fearful and suspicious of him, because there was never a moment when he didn't want us to be talking about Luscinda, and he was always dragging her up as a subject for conversation; and this awoke a strange jealousy in me – not that I was worried that Luscinda's fidelity and virtue might crumble, yet her very assurances did make me fear for my future. Don Fernando always contrived to read the letters I sent Luscinda and also her replies, on the grounds that he derived great pleasure from the good sense we both showed. It happened, then, that Luscinda asked me for a book of chivalry to read, one that she was very fond of, *Amadis of Gaul* . . .'

No sooner had Don Quixote heard the words 'book of chivalry' than he said:

'If you had said at the beginning of your story that the lady Luscinda was fond of books of chivalry, no other praise would have been necessary to make me appreciate the sublimity of her understanding; for it would not have been as fine as you, sir, have said if she had lacked a taste for such palatable reading-matter: and so, as far as I am concerned, there is no need to employ any more words in describing her beauty, worth and understanding, for knowledge of her reading alone is enough to make me confirm her as the most beautiful and intelligent woman in the world. And I should have wished, sir, that you had sent to her with *Amadis of Gaul* the good *Sir Rugel of Greece*,[3] because I know that the lady Luscinda would have much enjoyed Daraida and Geraya, and the wise words of the shepherd Darinel, and his admirable bucolics, sung and performed by him with such grace, good sense and assurance. But a time may come when that omission can be remedied; and indeed the remedy will be delayed no longer than it takes you to be so kind as to come with me to my village, for there I shall be able to lend you a goodly number of books, my soul's dearest treasure and my life's delight; although it is my belief that I no longer possess any books at all, thanks to the wickedness of evil and envious enchanters. And you must forgive me for having broken our promise not to interrupt your discourse, but as soon as I hear anything about chivalry and knights errant it is as much in my power not to talk about them as it is in the power of sunbeams not to warm us or in the power of moonbeams not to moisten us.[4] So do forgive me, and please continue, for that is of most importance to us at present.'

While Don Quixote had been saying all this, Cardenio's head had slumped upon his breast, a sign that he was engrossed in thought. And although Don Quixote twice asked him to continue his history, he neither raised his head nor spoke a word in reply; but after some time he did look up and say:

'One thing I cannot get out of my head, and there is nobody in the world who can get it out of there, nor is there anyone who can make me believe otherwise, and anyone who does believe otherwise is a fool – that poxy scoundrel Master Elisabat was sleeping with Queen Madásima.'[5]

'No, never, by God!' replied Don Quixote in fury, with his usual oaths, 'and that is a most malicious or more precisely villainous thing to say! Queen Madásima was a most noble lady, and it is not to be believed that so great a monarch would take some quack as a lover; and whoever maintains otherwise lies like an arrant scoundrel. And I will force him to admit it, on foot or on horseback, armed or unarmed, by night or by day, or howsoever he pleases.'

Cardenio was peering at Don Quixote: a fit of madness had come over him and he was in no state to continue his history, nor would Don Quixote have heard it even if he had, so enraged was he by those allegations about Madásima. It was a strange business – Quixote stood up for her just as if she really were his own true lady, such was the state that his unholy books had put him into! I was about to say that since Cardenio had gone mad, and had heard himself called a liar and a villain and other such insults, he didn't appreciate the joke and picked up a stone that he found by his side, and struck Don Quixote such a blow on the chest that he tumbled over backwards. Sancho Panza, seeing his master sprawling on the ground, took his fist to the madman, and the Ragged Knight received him with a punch that left him spread-eagled at his feet, and then jumped on to him and trampled his ribs to his heart's content. The goatherd went to Sancho's defence and suffered the same fate. And once the madman had thrashed them all, he withdrew with elegant composure into his mountain thickets.

Sancho got up and, furious at his undeserved beating, went to avenge himself on the goatherd, claiming that he was the one to blame, for not warning them that the man went mad every so often – because if they'd known this, they'd have been on their guard and taken the necessary precautions. The goatherd replied that he had told them this, and if they hadn't been listening it wasn't his fault. Sancho made his reply to this, and the goatherd replied to Sancho, and all this replying ended up with them grabbing each other by the beard and exchanging such punches that if Don Quixote hadn't pacified them they'd have thumped each other to pieces. And as Sancho grappled with the goatherd he was saying:

'Please let me take him on, Sir Knight of the Sorry Face – he's just a peasant like me and he's never been knighted, so it's all right for me to get my own back in a good fisticuff fight, like a man of honour, for all the wrong he's done me.'

'That is true,' said Don Quixote, 'but I know that he is not to blame for what has happened.'

With this he pacified them, and then he again asked the goatherd if it would be possible to find Cardenio, because he was anxious to hear the end of the story. The goatherd repeated what he'd said at the beginning, which was that he didn't know exactly where Cardenio's lair was, but that if Don Quixote kept wandering about the area he was bound to come across him sooner or later, sane or mad.

CHAPTER XXV

Concerning the strange things that happened to the brave knight of La Mancha in the Sierra Morena, and his imitation of the penance of Beltenebros

Don Quixote took his leave of the goatherd and, remounting Rocinante, told Sancho to follow him, which Sancho did, with his donkey and with bad grace. They were slowly entering the craggiest part of the sierra, and Sancho was dying to talk to his master and longing for him to start the conversation, so as not to disobey orders. But unable to bear so much silence he broke out:

'Don Quixote sir, please give me your blessing and my discharge – I want to go back home to my wife and children, because with them at least I'll be able to chatter away to my heart's content, and expecting me to traipse along with you through all these God-forsaken places by day and by night without speaking to you when I feel like it is the same as burying me alive. If fate had let animals talk, as they did in the times of that Hyssop character, it wouldn't be so bad, because then I could chat as much as I wanted with my donkey, and grin and bear it like that, because it's a hard business, and more than a man's patience can take, to go about looking for adventures your whole life long and only find kicks and blanket-tossings, brickbats and punches, and then on top of it all you've got to keep your mouth tight shut without daring to say what's inside your heart, as if you were dumb.'

'I understand you, Sancho,' replied Don Quixote. 'You are dying for me to lift the ban that I have placed on your tongue. Well, you can consider it lifted, and you can speak as much as you like, on condition that the lifting only lasts for as long as does our wandering about this sierra.'

'Agreed,' said Sancho. 'I'll speak now, and God's decided what'll happen later, and so to start to make use of my safe conduct, what I say is why were you so concerned to stick up for that queen with bad asthma, or whatever you said? And what did it matter whether that abbot was her lover or not? If you'd let it pass, because you weren't being her judge or anything, to my mind that madman would have gone on telling his story, and we'd have been spared the stone, and the kicks, and more than half-a-dozen backhanders as well.'

'Upon my soul, Sancho,' replied Don Quixote, 'if you knew, as I know, what an honourable and noble lady Queen Madásima was, I am certain you would say that I showed great forbearance in not dashing to pieces the mouth that uttered such blasphemies. For it is a very great blasphemy indeed to say or even think that a queen could take a sawbones to her bed. The truth about the story is that the Master Elisabat whom the madman mentioned was a very prudent man and wise counsellor, and he was the Queen's tutor and physician; but to think that she was his mistress is an absurdity worthy of the severest punishment. And to realize that Cardenio did not know what he was saying you have only to observe that he had lost his reason by the time he made that claim.'

'That's just what I'm saying,' said Sancho, 'there wasn't any need to bother about the ravings of a madman, and if good fortune hadn't come to your aid, and had made the stone hit your head instead of your chest, a fine state we'd have been in now, for sticking up for her ladyship, God damn her. And I bet Cardenio would have got off scot-free for being mad!'

'Against sane men and madmen alike it is every knight errant's duty to defend the honour of all women, whoever they may be, and even more so if they are queens of such high degree and worth as was Queen Madásima, for whom I feel a particular affinity because of her excellent qualities: apart from being beauteous, she was also very prudent and long-suffering in her calamities, of which there were many; and the advice and the company of Master Elisabat were of great benefit and comfort to her, to help her to bear her trials with prudence and patience. And this was what induced the ignorant, malicious rabble to think and say she was his mistress. And they lie, I tell you, they lie two hundredfold, all those who say or think such a thing!'

'I'm not saying it or thinking it,' replied Sancho. 'That's up to them, and it's their own lookout. Whether they were lovers or not, they'll have answered to God for it by now. I've got other fish to fry, and I just don't want to know, I'm not fond of prying into other people's lives. Him that buys and denies, his own purse belies. What's more, naked was I born, and naked I remain, so neither lose nor gain. And if they were, so what? It's no skin off my nose. There are those that think they'll find bacon where there isn't so much as a hook to hang it from. Till you cage in the sky, the sparrows will fly. And if they gossiped about God, who won't they gossip about?'

'And God save us all!' said Don Quixote. 'What a string of absurdities you have come out with now, Sancho! What connection is there between what we are discussing and all those proverbs you have just threaded together? For goodness sake, Sancho, do keep quiet, and from now on concern yourself with putting spurs to your ass rather than with putting your nose into what is no business of yours. And understand, with all your five senses, that whatever I have done, am doing and shall do is totally reasonable and in conformity with the rules of chivalry, for I have a better knowledge of them than any knight who has ever professed them.'

'But, sir,' replied Sancho, 'is it a good rule of chivalry for us to be wandering about aimlessly, lost in these here mountains, looking for a madman who when we find him is as likely as not to take it into his head to finish off what he started? And I don't mean his story, but the smashing of your head and my ribs!'

'Be quiet, Sancho, I tell you,' said Don Quixote. 'And let me inform you that what brings me to these parts is not only my wish to find the madman, but also my desire to perform here a deed with which I shall gain perpetual renown all over the face of the earth, and it will be such as to set the seal on everything that can make a knight errant perfect and famous.'

'And is this deed a very risky one?' asked Sancho Panza.

'No,' replied the Knight of the Sorry Face, 'although the dice could roll in such a way that we score a double one rather than a double six. But it all depends upon your diligence.'

'My diligence?' said Sancho.

'Yes,' said Don Quixote, 'because if you return quickly from where I am going to send you, my grief will quickly end and my glory will as quickly start. And because it is not right to keep you any longer in suspense, waiting to see where my words are leading, I want you to know, Sancho, that the famous Amadis of Gaul was one of the most perfect knights errant there ever was. No, I was wrong to say "one of": he was the only one, the first, unique, the lord of all the knights in the world in his day. A fig's end for Don Belianis and for all those who say that he was in any way the equal of Amadis, because I swear they are mistaken. Let me add that when a painter wants to become famous for his art, he tries to copy originals by the finest artists he knows. And this same rule holds good for nearly all the trades and professions of importance that serve to adorn a society; and so what a man must do and what a man does if he wishes to achieve a reputation for prudence and long-suffering, is to imitate Ulysses, in whose person and labours Homer painted for us a living portrait of these two qualities, just as Virgil showed us in the person of Aeneas the courage of a dutiful son and the sagacity of a brave and able captain, not describing or revealing them as they were but as they should have been, to leave models of their virtues for future generations. In this same way Amadis was the pole star, the morning star, the sun of brave and enamoured knights, and we who serve under the banner of love and chivalry should all imitate him. If, then, this is so, as it is, I consider, friend Sancho, that the knight errant who best imitates Amadis will be the closest to attaining perfection in chivalry. And one of the ways in which this knight best demonstrated his prudence, resolve, courage, long-suffering, steadfastness and love was when he withdrew, disdained by the lady Oriana, to do penance on Peña Pobre, after changing his name to Beltenebros, a name most certainly significant and suited to the life that of his own free will he had chosen. And it is easier for me to imitate him like this than by cleaving giants asunder, beheading serpents, slaughtering monsters, crushing armies, routing fleets and breaking spells. Since this place is so suitable for such a purpose, there is no good reason to allow opportunity to slip by, now that she so conveniently offers me her forelock.'

'So what is it, then,' asked Sancho, 'that you're planning to do in this God-forsaken place?'

'Have I not already told you,' replied Don Quixote, 'that I intend to imitate Amadis, and to act the desperate, foolish, furious lover so as also to imitate the valiant Orlando, when he found signs by a spring that the fair Angelica had disgraced herself with Medoro,[1] and the grief turned him mad, and he uprooted trees, sullied the waters of the clear springs, slew shepherds, destroyed flocks, burned cottages, tore down houses, dragged away mares and performed a hundred other excesses, worthy to be recorded on the tablets of eternal fame? And although I do not intend to imitate Orlando, or Roland, or Rotolando (for he had all these three names) step by step in each and every one of the mad things he did, said and thought, I shall act out a résumé, as best I can, of those that seem most relevant. And it could even be that I might settle for imitating Amadis alone, because his madness did not involve doing any damage, but just weeping and being heartbroken, and he achieved as much fame as the best of them.'

'But to my mind,' said Sancho, 'the knights who did all that were pushed into it and had their reasons for their antics and their penances, but what reason have you got for going mad? What lady has scorned you, what signs have you found that the lady Dulcinea del Toboso has been up to tricks with some Moor, or some Christian for that matter?'

'That is the whole point,' replied Don Quixote, 'and therein lies the beauty of my enterprise. A knight errant going mad for a good reason – there is neither pleasure nor merit in that. The thing is to become insane without a cause and have my lady think: if I do all this when dry, what would I not do when wet? Besides, my long absence from my ever-beloved lady Dulcinea del Toboso provides me with abundant motivation, for, as you heard that shepherd fellow Ambrosio say, the absent lover feels and fears every ill. So, Sancho my friend, do not waste your time advising me not to perform such a rare, happy and unprecedented imitation. I am mad, and mad I shall remain until you return with the reply to a letter that I intend to send by you to my lady Dulcinea; and should that reply be such as is due to my fidelity, then my folly and my penance will be at an end; and should it be otherwise, I shall go truly mad, and feel nothing. So however she replies I shall be free of the conflict and travail in which you will leave me: either sane, and enjoying the bliss you bear, or mad, and oblivious to the misery you bring. But tell me, Sancho: have you been looking after Mambrino's helmet with due care? I saw you picking it up after that ungrateful fellow had tried to smash it to smithereens. But he could not do so, and that is an indication of the excellence of its temper.'

To which Sancho replied:

'In God's own name, Sir Knight of the Sorry Face, I just can't stand some of these things you come out with, making me think that everything you tell me about chivalries, and winning kingdoms and empires, and giving islands away and doing other favours and great deeds, as knight errants do, must all be empty lies, and a fraction or a friction or whatever it is you call it. Because anyone who hears you saying that a barber's basin is Mambrino's helmet, and sticking to your story for days on end – what's he going to think except that the man who says things like that must be queer in the head? Yes, I've got the basin in my saddle-bag, well dented, and the reason I've got it there is to take it home and mend it for trimming my beard, if God's good enough to let me see my wife and children again some day.'

'Look here, Sancho,' said Don Quixote, 'I swear to you by the same oath you have just sworn to me that you are the most dim-witted squire there ever was. Is it possible that in all the time you have been with me you have failed to realize that all things appertaining to us knights errant seem like chimeras, follies and nonsenses, because they have all been turned on their head? Not because that is their real state, but because we are always attended by a crew of enchanters who keep transforming everything and changing it into whatever they like, according to whether they have a mind to help us or destroy us; and so what looks to you like a barber's basin looks to me like Mambrino's helmet and will look like something else to another person. And the sage who is on my side showed rare foresight in making everyone take what is really and truly Mambrino's helmet for a barber's basin, because Mambrino's helmet is so highly esteemed that everyone would otherwise have pursued me to try to take it from me, but since they see that it is only a barber's basin they do not bother about it, as was clearly shown when that youth tried to shatter it and left it on the ground; to be sure, if he had recognized it he would never have left it behind. You can keep the helmet, my friend, because for the moment I have no need of it; on the contrary, I am going to remove all this armour, and be left as naked as the day I was born, if the urge takes me to imitate Orlando in my penance rather than Amadis.'

That evening they reached the very heart of the Sierra Morena, where Sancho thought they could spend the night, and even a few days more, at least as many as their rations lasted. And so they slept between two crags and among many cork-oaks. But destiny, which, in the opinion of those who lack the light of the true faith, guides, fashions and disposes everything as it wishes, decreed that Ginés de Pasamonte, the famous liar and thief who'd escaped from the chain thanks to Don Quixote's madness, impelled by fear of the Holy Brotherhood (of which he had good reason to be afraid), decided to hide in those mountains, and fortune and fear led him to the same spot where they'd led Don Quixote and Sancho Panza, early enough in the evening for him to recognize them and late enough for them to be settling down to sleep. And since the wicked are always ungrateful, and necessity makes men do what they ought not to do, and the needs of the moment take precedence over thoughts for the future, Ginés, who was neither grateful nor well-intentioned, decided to steal Sancho Panza's ass, not bothering with Rocinante, a creature that it would have been as impossible to pawn as to sell. Sancho Panza slept, Ginés stole his donkey and long before morning it was much too far away to be found. Dawn broke, bringing joy to the earth and grief to Sancho Panza when he missed his precious dun, and he began to make the most doleful lamentation in the world, awaking Don Quixote with his cries:

'O child of my bowels, born in my very house, my children's treasure, my wife's delight, the envy of my neighbours, the ease of my burdens and, lastly, the half of my maintenance, because the twenty-six maravedís a day that you earned did cover half my expenses!'

On seeing Sancho's tears and learning the cause, Don Quixote consoled him with the best words he could think of, begged him to be patient and promised to give him a warrant on presenting which Sancho would be given three donkeys of the five that Don Quixote had left at home. This comforted Sancho, who dried his tears, restrained his sobs and thanked Don Quixote for the favour.

As they discussed these matters they reached a high mountain that stood out among the many hills surrounding it, almost as if it had been hewn from the living rock. At its foot a gentle stream flowed, and all around this stream a meadow spread forth, so green and lush that it was a joy to behold. There were many woodland trees and some plants and flowers to add to the delights of the spot, which the Knight of the Sorry Face chose for his penance; and so, as soon as he saw it, he began to proclaim, as if he were mad:

'This is the place, O heavens, that I hereby choose and select to lament the misfortune into which you have plunged me. This is the place where the humours of my eyes will swell the waters of this stream, and where my profound and incessant sighs will never stop stirring the leaves of these woodland trees, in testimony and token of the grief that harasses my hapless heart. O you rustic deities, whosoever you may be, dwelling in this uninhabited place, give ear to the laments of this ill-starred lover, brought by a long absence and imagined jealousy to weep among these craggy wastes and to complain of the hard heart of that beauteous ingrate, the sum and perfection of all human loveliness! O you wood nymphs and dryads, who are wont to dwell in the depths of the forest: may the fickle and lascivious satyrs, by whom you are loved, although in vain, never perturb your sweet repose; and help me to lament my misfortune, or at least do not weary of hearing about it! O Dulcinea del Toboso, day of my night, glory of my grief, goal of my journeying, star of my fortune: may the heavens grant you prosperity in all that you ask of them; and consider the place and the state to which absence from you has brought me, and grant me the reward that my fidelity deserves! O lonely trees, who from this day will accompany my solitude, show in the gentle movement of your branches that my presence is not disagreeable to you! O you, my squire, pleasant companion in my most prosperous and my most adverse eventualities, impress on your memory what you will see me do here, so that you can relate and recite it to the sole cause of it all!'

And so saying he dismounted from Rocinante and stripped him of bridle and saddle; and slapping him on the haunches, he said:

'He who lacks liberty gives you yours, O steed as excellent for your exploits as you are unfortunate in your fate! Go hence where'er you please, for on your forehead it is written that neither Astolfo's hippogryph nor the renowned Frontino, who cost Bradamante so dear, was your equal in fleetness of foot.'[2]

When Sancho saw this he said:

'And hurray for whoever it is that's just saved us the trouble of taking the pack-saddle off my dun! To be sure it wouldn't have gone without its slaps on the back or its praises, either. But if it had been here I wouldn't have let anyone take its pack-saddle off, because there wouldn't have been any reason to – it wasn't a witness to a desperate lover's goings-on, because its master, in other words me when it so pleased the Lord, never was one of that sort. And to tell you the truth, Sir Knight of the Sorry Face, if my journey and your madness are going to be for real, it'll be better to saddle Rocinante again to make up for the lack of my dun, and save time in my travels – if I go on foot I just can't tell when I'll get there or when I'll get back, because the truth is I'm a very bad walker.'

'What I say, Sancho,' replied Don Quixote, 'is that you must do as you please, for your idea does not seem a bad one; and I also say that you shall depart three days from now, because I want you to spend this time witnessing what I do and say for her sake, so that you can tell her about it.'

'And what else have I got to see,' asked Sancho, 'apart from what I've seen already?'

'You are well informed about these matters, I must say!' Don Quixote retorted. 'Now I must tear my garments, scatter my armour and dash my head against these rocks, and perform other similar actions that will amaze you.'

'For God's sake,' said Sancho Panza, 'do be careful how you go around dashing your head, because you could pick on such a rock and hit it in such a place that you put paid to the whole penance business with the very first knock you gave it. And if you really think head-dashing's essential and this job can't be done without it, to my mind you ought to be content, since it's all make-believe, a fake and a sham, to dash your head against the water, or something soft like cotton, and leave the rest to me – I'll tell my lady you were knocking it against a jutting crag, harder than diamonds.'

'I am grateful to you for meaning well, friend Sancho,' replied Don Quixote, 'but I would have you know that I am doing all these things not in jest but very much in earnest; for to behave otherwise would be to contravene the commands of chivalry, which instruct one never to tell a lie, on pain of being punished as a recidivist; and to do one thing instead of another is the same as lying. So my blows on the head must be real, firm and effective, with no element of the sophistical or the fantastic about them. And you will have to leave me some lint to cure my wounds, for fate has left us without our balsam.'

'Losing the ass was worse,' replied Sancho, 'because the lint and all was lost with it. And I'd ask you very kindly not to bring that damned potion up again – just hearing it mentioned turns not only my stomach but my very soul inside-out. And I'd also ask you, as regards those three days you allocated for watching the crazy things you're going to do, to make believe they're over and done with, because I'll be happy to take them for granted as if seen and approved, and I'll tell my lady wonders. So you write your letter and then send me packing, because I'm longing to come back and get you out of this purgatory where I'm leaving you.'

'Purgatory you call it, Sancho?' said Don Quixote. 'You would do better to call it hell, or worse, if there is anything worse.'

'In hell,' replied Sancho, '*nulla est retentio*, so I've heard say.'[3]

'I do not understand what you mean by *retentio*,' said Don Quixote.

'*Retentio* means,' replied Sancho, 'that people in hell never get out, and can't get out. It'll be the reverse with you, though, so long as I get my heels working, if I'm wearing spurs to make Rocinante move, that is – and you just wait till I reach El Toboso, and come before my lady Dulcinea, and then I'll tell her such stories about the acts of madness and stupidity, which comes to the same thing, that you've done and are doing as will make her as sweet as a nut, even if she's as hard as a cork-oak when I start work on her. And I'll come back through the air like a sorcerer with her honeyed answer, and I'll rescue you from this purgatory that seems like hell but isn't, because there's a hope of getting out of it, which people in hell haven't got, as I've just said, and I don't suppose you'll want to disagree with that.'

'True,' said the Knight of the Sorry Face, 'but how are we going to manage to write that letter?'

'And that donkey-warrant,' added Sancho.

'It will all be included,' said Don Quixote, 'and, since we have no paper, it would be appropriate to write it, as the ancients did, on leaves from the trees, or on tablets of wax; yet it would be as difficult to find these now as paper itself. But I have just thought of a good place, indeed an excellent one, to write it: the notebook that used to belong to Cardenio, and you must take care to have it copied in a clear hand on to a sheet of paper in the first village with a schoolmaster, or else any sexton will copy it for you; but do not ask a clerk to copy it, because they use a corrupt and degenerate hand that Satan himself would not be able to read.'

'And what's to be done about your signature?' asked Sancho.

'The letters of Amadis are never signed,' replied Don Quixote.

'That's as may be,' replied Sancho, 'but the warrant must be signed, and if it's copied out they'll say the signature's a fake and I'll be left without my donkeys.'

'The warrant will be signed in the notebook, and when my niece sees it she will not raise any objections about complying with it. And as regards the love-letter, you will have it signed: "Yours until death, The Knight of the Sorry Face". It will matter little that it is signed in another hand, because as far as I remember Dulcinea cannot read or write, and she has never seen a letter written by me, because the love between us has always been platonic, never going beyond a modest glance. And even this has been so occasional that I can truly swear that, in the twelve years I have loved her more than the light of these eyes that the earth will one day devour, I have not seen her as many as four times; and it is possible that on those four occasions she has not even once noticed that I was looking at her, such is the reserve and seclusion in which her father Lorenzo Corchuelo and her mother Aldonza Nogales have brought her up.'

'Oho!' said Sancho. 'So Lorenzo Corchuelo's daughter is the lady Dulcinea del Toboso, also known as Aldonza Lorenzo, is she?'

'She is,' said Don Quixote, 'and she it is who deserves to be the mistress of the entire universe.'

'I know her well,' said Sancho, 'and let me tell you she pitches a bar as far as the strongest lad in all the village. Good God, she's a lusty lass all right, hale and hearty, strong as an ox, and any knight errant who has her as his lady now or in the future can count on her to pull him out of the mire! The little baggage, what muscles she's got on her, and what a voice! Let me tell you she climbed up one day to the top of the church belfry to call to some lads of hers who were in a fallow field of her father's, and even though they were a good couple of miles off they could hear her just as if they'd been standing at the foot of the tower. And the best thing about her is she isn't at all priggish, she's a real courtly lass, enjoys a joke with everyone and turns everything into a good laugh. And now I can say, Sir Knight of the Sorry Face, that not only is it very right and proper for you to get up to your mad tricks for her sake – you've got every reason to give way to despair and hang yourself, too, and nobody who knows about it will say you weren't justified, even if it does send you to the devil. And I wish I was on my way already, just to take a look at her, because I haven't seen her for days, and she must be changed by now, because women's faces get spoiled by always being out in the fields, in the sun and the wind. And I must be honest with you, Don Quixote sir – until now I've been completely mistaken, because I really and truly believed that the lady Dulcinea must be some princess you were in love with, or at least someone who deserved all those fine gifts you've sent her, that Basque and those convicts, and lots of others that there must have been, too, considering how many victories you must have won before I became your squire. But all things considered, what will the lady Aldonza Lorenzo I mean the lady Dulcinea del Toboso care whether the knights you defeat and send to her get down on their bended knees before her? Because when they turn up she might be combing flax or threshing wheat in the yard, and then they'd be all embarrassed and she'd burst out laughing and turn up her nose at the gift.'

'I have often told you before now, Sancho,' said Don Quixote, 'that you are a chatterbox and that, although you are a dim-witted fellow, you often try to be too clever by half; but, so that you can see how stupid you are and how intelligent I am, I want you to listen to a little story. There was once a widow who was beautiful, young, unattached, rich and, above all, carefree, and who fell in love with a certain lay brother, a well-fleshed, corpulent young man; his superior found out, and said to the good widow one day, by way of friarly reprehension:

' "I am surprised, madam, and not without good reason, that a woman of your quality, as beautiful and as wealthy as you are, should have fallen in love with such a low, vulgar and ignorant fellow, when in this house there are so many bachelors, masters and doctors of divinity among whom you could have chosen as among pears at a fruit-stall, saying: 'I'll have this one; no, not that.' "

'But she replied to him with wit and dash:

' "You are much mistaken, sir, and very old-fashioned in your ideas, if you think I have made a bad choice, however stupid he may seem to you; because for what I want of him he knows as much philosophy as Aristotle, and more."

'And so, Sancho, for what I want of Dulcinea del Toboso, she is as good as the most exalted princess in the world. Yes indeed, for not all poets who praise ladies under a name that they choose for them really have any such mistresses at all. Do you really believe that the Amaryllises, Phyllises, Sylvias, Dianas, Galateas, Alidas and others that fill books, ballads, barbers' shops and theatre stages were real ladies of flesh and blood, and the mistresses of those that praise and have praised them? No, of course not, the poets themselves invent most of them, to have something to write their poetry about, and to make people think that they are in love and that they have it in them to be lovers. And so it is enough for me to be convinced that the good Aldonza Lorenzo is beautiful and virtuous, and the question of lineage is not very important, because nobody is going to be enquiring into it to see whether she is entitled to robes of nobility, and for me she is the greatest princess in the world. For I would have you know, Sancho, if you do not know it already, that there are just two qualities that inspire love more than any others, and these are great beauty and good repute, and these two qualities are to be found in abundance in Dulcinea, because no woman can equal her in beauty, and few can approach her in good repute. And to put it in a nutshell, I imagine that everything I say is precisely as I say it is, and I depict her in my imagination as I wish her to be, both in beauty and in rank, and Helen cannot rival her, nor can Lucretia[4] or any other of the famous women of past ages, whether Greek, Barbarian or

Roman, equal her. And people can say what they like, because if I am reproached by the ignorant for this, I shall not be punished by even the most severe judges.'

'And I say you're right as right can be,' replied Sancho, 'and I'm an ass – but I don't know why I'm talking about asses, because you don't mention ropes in the house of the man that hanged himself. Let's have the letter, though, and then I'll be off.'

Don Quixote took out the notebook and, drawing a little aside, he began with great deliberation to write the letter; and as he finished he called Sancho and said that he was going to read it aloud, so that Sancho could learn it by heart, in case he lost it on the way, because with his bad luck anything could happen. To which Sancho replied:

'You just write it down two or three times in the book and then let me have it, and I'll take good care of it – it's madness to think I'm going to learn it by heart, because my memory's so bad I often forget my own name. But read it to me all the same, I'll enjoy listening to it, because it must be a beauty.'

'Listen, then; it goes like this,' said Don Quixote.

Letter from Don Quixote to Dulcinea del Toboso

Sovereign and noble lady,

One sore-wounded by the dart of absence and lacerated to the very fabric of his heart, O sweetest Dulcinea del Toboso, wishes you the good health that he does not enjoy. If your beauteousness scorns me, if your worth does not favour me, if your disdain is my humiliation, I shall ill be able, albeit I am well furnished with longanimity, to suffer a grief that is not merely intense but protracted. My good squire Sancho will render you a full account, O lovely ingrate, O beloved enemy of mine, of the state to which I am reduced for your sake. If it be your wish to succour me, I am yours, and if not, do what you will, for by ending my life I shall satisfy your cruelty and my desire.

Yours until death,
THE KNIGHT OF THE SORRY FACE

'By my dear father's bones!' cried Sancho. 'That's the very finest thing I ever did hear! Damn it all, how well you say everything you want to say, and how well it all suits the signature "The Knight of the Sorry Face"! To be sure you're the very devil, there isn't anything you don't know!'

'Everything is needed,' replied Don Quixote, 'in the profession that I follow.'

'Come on, then,' said Sancho, 'turn over the page and write the warrant for the three donkeys, and sign it clear as clear, so they know your signature as soon as they see it.'

'Very well,' said Don Quixote.

And once he'd written it he read it out:

On receipt of this my first donkey-warrant, please order that three of the five that I left at home in your charge be given to my squire Sancho Panza. Which three donkeys I hereby order to be delivered to him and duly paid for, in return for the like number received from him here; and this bill, together with his receipt, will be sufficient for this transaction. Given in the heart of the Sierra Morena on the twenty-second of August of the current year.

'That's good,' said Sancho. 'Now sign it.'

'There is no need for me to sign it,' said Don Quixote. 'All I have to do is to append my flourish, which counts as a signature, and that is sufficient for three asses, and even for three hundred.'

'I'll believe you,' replied Sancho. 'Now let me go and saddle Rocinante, and you get ready to give me your blessing, because I'm leaving straight away, without waiting to see any of these antics you're going to get up to, though I'll tell her I saw you do so many of them that she'll be more than satisfied.'

'At least, Sancho, I want you, because it is essential – what I mean to say is that I want you to see me naked, performing a dozen or two dozen mad deeds, which will only take me half an hour, so that having seen them with your own eyes you can safely swear to any others that you may care to add; and I can assure you that you will not tell her of as many as I intend to perform.'

'For the love of God, sir, don't make me see you naked, I'll feel so sorry for you I shan't be able to help crying. And my head's in such a state after crying so much last night for my dun that I'm in no condition for any more tears, so if you want me to see some of your antics, do them with your clothes on – quick antics, just the most relevant ones. What's more, there isn't any need for all this as far as I'm concerned, and, as I said, it would mean I'd come back all the sooner with the news that you want and deserve to hear. If not, the lady Dulcinea had better look out, because if she doesn't reply as she ought to, I take my solemn oath that I'll kick and punch the right answer out of her guts. Because who can put up with a famous knight errant like you going mad, without any reason at all, for a . . . ? And the lady had better not make me say it, or else by God I'll upset the apple cart, and hang the consequences! And I can! She doesn't know what I'm like! If she did, she'd stand in fear of me, she would!'

'And so, Sancho,' said Don Quixote, 'it seems that you are no saner than I am.'

'No, I'm not as mad as you,' said Sancho, 'but I am angrier. Leaving all that aside, though, what are you going to eat while I'm away? Are you going to waylay goatherds and steal your food, like Cardenio?'

'You must not worry about that,' replied Don Quixote, 'for even if I had any food, all I should eat would be whatever herbs and other fruit of the land this meadow and these trees provide; for the beauty of my plan lies precisely in not eating and in other equivalent mortifications. And so goodbye.'

'But do you know what I'm scared of? Not finding the way back here where I'm leaving you, because it's so secluded.'

'You take good note of the landmarks, and I shall try not to move far off,' said Don Quixote, 'and I shall even take the precaution of climbing the highest of these crags here to see if I can spot you when you return. In addition, your surest way of not getting lost and missing me will be to cut some of this broom growing so abundantly hereabouts, and to drop a branch every so often until you reach the plain, and they will serve as guide-marks on your return, like the thread in Perseus's labyrinth.'[5]

'That's what I'll do,' replied Sancho Panza.

He cut some broom, asked his master for his blessing and, not without many tears on both sides, said goodbye. And climbing on to Rocinante, whom Don Quixote warmly entrusted to Sancho's safe-keeping, with the instruction to take as good care of him as of his own person, he headed off towards the plain, scattering broom-branches every so often, as his master had advised. And so he rode away, even though Don Quixote was still insisting that he should watch a couple of his wild deeds, at least. But Sancho hadn't gone a hundred steps when he turned and came back and said:

'I think you were right, sir, and to be able to swear with a clear conscience that I've seen you doing mad deeds, I'd better see one of them at least, although I must say I've seen a big enough one already – you staying here.'

'Did I not tell you so?' said Don Quixote. 'Just wait a minute, Sancho, I shall perform them in the saying of a creed.'

And pulling down his breeches as fast as ever he could, he stood there in his shirt and then did two leaps in the air followed by two somersaults, revealing things that made Sancho turn Rocinante so as not to have to see them again; and he felt fully satisfied that he could swear his master was mad. And we shall allow him to go his way until his return, which was speedy.

CHAPTER XXVI

❖

In which a further account is given of the dainty deeds performed by the lover Don Quixote in the Sierra Morena

And turning back to what the Knight of the Sorry Face did once he was alone, the history says that when Don Quixote had finished his somersaults or handsprings naked from the waist down and clothed from the waist up, and had seen Sancho depart without caring to witness any more antics, he climbed to the top of a high crag, and again turned his thoughts to what had often occupied them without ever having led him to a decision: which would be better and more suitable, imitating Orlando and his outrageous madness, or Amadis and his melancholy madness? And he said to himself:

'If Orlando was such an excellent knight and as brave as everybody says he was, what is so surprising about that? After all, he was enchanted, and nobody could kill him except by stabbing a penny pin into his big toe, and he always wore shoes shod with seven iron soles.[1] Yet these tricks were of no avail against Bernardo del Carpio, who saw through them all and squeezed him to death at Roncesvalles. But leaving his courage aside, let us consider his going mad, which he most certainly did, because of the signs he found by the spring and the news given him by the shepherd that Angelica had enjoyed more than a couple of siestas with Medoro, a young Moor with curly hair, Agramante's page-boy. And if he believed that this was true and that his lady had played him false, it was a normal enough reaction to go crazy. Yet how can I imitate his mad deeds if I do not imitate their cause? I would venture to swear that my Dulcinea del Toboso has never seen a real Moor in real Moorish clothes in all her life, and that she is today as intact as the mother who bore her; and I should be doing her a manifest wrong if, imagining something different, I went mad after the fashion of Orlando Furioso. Furthermore, I can see that Amadis of Gaul, without going insane or performing any crazy deeds, achieved as much renown as a lover as the best of them; because, according to his history, all he did when scorned by his lady Oriana, who told him not to appear in her presence until she commanded it, was to withdraw to Peña Pobre with a hermit, and there he wept and commended himself to God to his heart's content until heaven came to his aid in the midst of his greatest tribulation. And if this is true, as indeed it is, why should I take the trouble to strip naked or torment these trees that have never done me any harm? Nor have I any need to sully the clear waters of these streams, which will provide for me when I am thirsty. Long live the memory of Amadis, and let him be imitated as well as is possible by Don Quixote de la Mancha, of whom it shall be said what was said of another: if he did not achieve great things, he died in the attempt. And if I am not rejected or scorned by Dulcinea del Toboso, it is enough, as I have said, to be separated from her. So now to work! Come to my memory, O exploits of Amadis, and show me how my imitation must commence! Yet I well know that what he most did was to pray and commend himself to God; but what can I use as a rosary, not having one on me?'

As he said this an idea came into his head for making one, and he tore a long strip from his shirt-tail hanging down behind him, and he tied eleven knots in it, one of them bigger than the others, and this he used as a rosary² all the time he was there, during which he said a million Ave Marias. And what was a great worry to him was not finding thereabouts any hermit who could confess and console him. So he amused himself by taking strolls around the meadow, and carving in the bark of the trees and tracing in the fine sand of the stream a great number of verses, all of them expressive of his sadness, and some of them in praise of Dulcinea. But the only complete and legible poem that was discovered after he had been found was this:

> You trees, you herbs, you plants that show
> Your splendour in this pleasant site
> And tall and green and plenteous grow:
> Although my ills give no delight,
> Pray listen to my tale of woe.
>   And let my grief disturb you not
> Although you could not ever see a
> Lover pay you on the dot
> Or suffer like poor Don Quixote,
> Who weeps here for his Dulcinea
>   del Toboso.
>
>   Here, in this green and pleasant mead,
> The truest lover ever known
> Hides from his lady, in dire need:
> He has been made to grieve and groan,
> Not knowing whence his ills proceed.
>   Love keeps him always on the trot,
> A very wicked sort is he – ah!
> Enough to fill the biggest pot
> Are tears of doleful Don Quixote,
> Who weeps here for his Dulcinea
>   del Toboso.
>
>   He sought adventures as he pined
> Among these crags and rocks and stones,
> And cursed what made his maid unkind:

But this poor wretch, sad to his bones,
Could only misadventures find.
     Love laid his lash upon him hot:
No gentle thong – the very idea!
And when it touched his tender spot
Tears flowed from doleful Don Quixote,
Who weeps here for his Dulcinea
     del Toboso.

The addition of 'del Toboso' to the name of Dulcinea raised some giggles among those who found these verses, because they imagined that Don Quixote must have imagined that if, when he named Dulcinea, he didn't also say 'del Toboso', the stanza wouldn't be understood – and they were right, as he later confessed. He wrote many other lines of poetry but, as has been said, these three verses were all that was found complete and could be deciphered. In this, and in sighing, and in calling out to the fauns and sylvans of those woods, to the nymphs of the rivers, and to moist and mournful Echo,[3] to reply to him, comfort him and listen to him, he passed the time, and also in seeking herbs on which to live until Sancho's return; and had this taken three weeks instead of the three days it did take, the Knight of the Sorry Face would have been so ravaged that the very mother who'd borne him wouldn't have known him.

And it will be as well now to leave him wrapped in his sighs and his verses, so as to relate what happened to Sancho Panza on his mission. When he reached the highway he went in search of the road to El Toboso, and the next day he arrived at the inn where he'd suffered the mishap with the blanket; and no sooner had he glimpsed the place than he imagined himself flying through the air again, and he couldn't bring himself to go in, even though he'd come at an hour when he could and should have done so, for it was dinner-time and he was longing for something hot to eat, having had nothing but cold food for many days.

This craving forced him to approach the inn, still wondering whether to enter it or not. As he hovered there, two men came out and recognized him. And one of them said to the other:

'Look, reverend father, that man on the horse – isn't it Sancho Panza, the fellow our adventurer's housekeeper said had gone off with her master as his squire?'

'So it is,' said the priest, 'and that's our dear Don Quixote's horse.'

They recognized them immediately, being the priest and the barber of his own village, the two men who had carried out the interrogation and auto-da-fé of the books. Anxious for news of Don Quixote, they went up to him and the priest called him by his name:

'My dear friend Sancho Panza, where is your master?'

Sancho Panza recognized them at once, and decided to conceal the place and the circumstances in which he'd left his master; and so he replied that his master was busy in a certain place on a certain matter which was very important to him, and which he couldn't reveal, not for the very eyes in his head.

'No, no, Sancho Panza,' said the barber. 'If you don't tell us where he is we're going to imagine, as we already do, that you've murdered and robbed him, since you're riding his horse. You really must lead us to the nag's master, or it'll be the worse for you.'

'There isn't any need to come to me with your threats, I'm not one to go robbing or murdering people: let each man be killed by his own fate say I, or by the God that made him. My master's doing penance in the middle of these mountains, and loving every minute of it.'

And he reeled off an account of the state his master was in, the adventures he'd had and the letter to the lady Dulcinea del Toboso, Lorenzo Corchuelo's daughter, who he was up to his neck in love with.

They were both amazed at what Sancho Panza was telling them, because although they knew that Don Quixote was mad and they knew what sort of madness it was, whenever they heard about it again they were amazed again. They asked Sancho Panza to show them the letter he was taking to the lady Dulcinea del Toboso. He told them that it was written in a notebook, and that his master's orders were to have it copied on to a sheet of paper at the first village he came to; at which the priest asked to see it, saying that he would copy it out himself in a very good hand. Sancho Panza felt for the notebook inside his shirt, but he couldn't find it, and he wouldn't have found it if he'd kept searching for it to this day, because Don Quixote hadn't given him it, and he hadn't remembered to ask for it.

When Sancho realized that he couldn't find the notebook, a look of mortal horror crept over his face; and running his hands all over his body again, he confirmed that the notebook wasn't there, and then he clenched his hands and clutched at his beard and tore half of it out and gave himself half-a-dozen punches on the nose and the face, bathing them in blood. At this sight the priest and the barber asked him what had happened to make him treat himself so roughly.

'What do you think has happened?' said Sancho. 'Only that at one foul swoop and in a single instant I've been and gone and lost three donkeys as fine as three castles, that's all!'

'How can that be?' replied the barber.

'I've lost the notebook,' answered Sancho, 'with the letter for Dulcinea and a warrant signed by my master ordering his niece to give me three of the four or five donkeys he's got at home.'

And he went on to tell them about the theft of his dun. The priest comforted him, saying that as soon as he found Don Quixote he'd make him confirm the order and draw the warrant up again on a separate sheet of paper, as was the usual custom, because warrants written in notebooks were never accepted or honoured. This consoled Sancho, and he said that in that case he wasn't too concerned about the loss of Dulcinea's letter, because he had almost all of it in his memory, from where they could make a copy wherever and whenever they wanted.

'Let's hear it, Sancho,' said the barber, 'and then we'll make the copy.'

Sancho Panza dismounted to scratch his head and bring the letter back into his memory, balancing first on one foot and then on the other; sometimes he gazed at the ground, sometimes at the sky, and, after gnawing off half a finger-tip while those waiting to hear the letter stood there in suspense for an eternity, he said:

'By God, reverend father, the devil take all I can remember of the letter, though at the beginning it did say, "Noble and slobbered-on lady".'

'No, it won't have said slobbered-on lady,' said the barber, 'but sovereign lady, or maybe supreme lady.'

'That's it,' said Sancho. 'Then, if I remember rightly, it went on . . . , if I remember rightly, "One lastrated and well-finished with not sleeping and sore-wounded kisses your hands, beautiful and unknown ingrate", and then it said something about health and an illness he was sending her, and it went on and on and on like this, until it ended up, "Yours until death, The Knight of the Sorry Face".'

The two men were much amused by Sancho Panza's splendid memory and they praised it to the skies and asked him to recite the letter another couple of times so that they in their turn could commit it to memory and write it down in due course. Sancho went through it another three times, and on each occasion he came out with a further three thousand absurdities. He went on to relate his master's doings, but he didn't say a word about the blanket-tossing in that inn which he refused to enter. He also told them how, as soon as he brought his master good tidings from the lady Dulcinea del Toboso, his master was going to set out to try to become an emperor or at least a monarch, and that was what they'd agreed between the two of them, and he could easily manage it, considering the worth of his person and the might of his arm – and as soon as this happened, his master was going to find a wife for him, because he'd be a widower by then, he couldn't fail to be, and his master would marry him to the empress's lady-in-waiting, the heiress to a big, rich estate on dry land – no islands or such-like for him, he didn't have any use for those any more.

Sancho said all this with such calm assurance, every so often wiping his nose with the back of his hand, and it was all so absurd, that both men were again struck with amazement as they considered how powerful Don Quixote's madness was, carrying this poor man's wits along with it. They decided not to give themselves the trouble of trying to persuade him of his error because, as they believed, it did no harm to his conscience and so it was better to leave him be; and anyway it would be jolly good fun to listen to all his nonsense. So they told Sancho to pray to God for his master's well-being because it was possible and indeed extremely likely that with the passing of time he might become an emperor, just as he had said, or at least an archbishop or some equivalent dignitary. To which Sancho replied:

'If fortune changed everything, sirs, and my master got the urge not to be an emperor but an archbishop, what I'd like to know next is what archbishop errants give their squires.'

'Usually,' replied the priest, 'they give them some benefice, with or without cure of souls, or they make them sextons, which yields a good fixed income, quite apart from the surplice fees, which are usually reckoned at as much again.'

'For that,' Sancho replied, 'the squire will have to be a single man, and know how to help at mass, at least, and in that case – unhappy me, married as I am and not knowing so much as the first letter of the ABC! What will become of me if my master takes it into his head to be an archbishop rather than an emperor, which is what's normal with knight errants?'

'Don't distress yourself, friend Sancho,' said the barber. 'The reverend father and I shall ask your master, and indeed advise him, and even put it to him as a case of conscience, to be an emperor and not an archbishop – this will be easier for him, because he is more brave than studious.'

'That's what I've always thought, too,' replied Sancho, 'though let me tell you he can turn his hand to anything. What I'm going to do for my part is to pray to our Lord to give him whatever job does him the most good and lets him do me the most favours.'

'You speak like a wise man,' said the priest, 'and you'll be acting like a good Christian. But what must be done now is to work out how to extricate your master from that pointless penance that you say he's doing; and so, to think how we're going to set about it, and to have our dinner, for it's high time we did that, we'd better go into this inn.'

Sancho said that they could go in and he'd wait outside, and later he'd tell them why it didn't suit him to enter, but please would they bring out something hot for him to eat and also some barley for Rocinante. They went in and left him, and a little later the barber brought him out some food. Then, when the pair put their heads together to work out the best way of achieving their aim, the priest thought of a plan that was ideally suited to Don Quixote's tastes and to the goal they had in mind. And he told the barber that his idea was that he himself would dress up as a maiden errant, and the barber would try his best to make himself look like a squire, and then they would go off like that to see Don Quixote, pretending that she was a damsel in need and distress come to beg a boon of him, which he, as a brave knight errant, could not refuse to grant. And the boon was to be that he should go with her whither she should carry him, to redress an injury done her by a wicked knight, entreating him likewise that he would not desire her to divest herself of her mask, nor enquire anything further concerning her, until he should have done her justice upon that wicked knight – and he could rely on Don Quixote doing every single thing he was asked, and in that way they'd get him out of there and take him back to the village, where they'd see if there was any remedy for his strange madness.

CHAPTER XXVII

About how the priest and the barber achieved their aim,
and other matters worthy of being recounted in this
great history

The priest's plan didn't seem a bad one to the barber – indeed he thought it so splendid that they put it into action without delay. They asked the innkeeper's wife for a frock and a head-dress, leaving as security a new cassock of the priest's. The barber made a long beard from a pale red ox tail in which the innkeeper used to stick his comb. His wife asked them what they wanted these things for. The priest gave her a brief account of Don Quixote's madness, and told her that the disguise was needed to get him out of his present quarters in the sierra. And then the innkeeper and his wife realized that this madman was their former guest, the man with the balsam, the master of the blanket-tossed squire, and they told the priest everything that had happened, including what Sancho had been so concerned to omit. So the innkeeper's wife dressed the priest and left him looking as pretty as a picture: she fitted him out with a woollen frock, covered with black bands of slashed velvet, as broad as your hand, and bodices of green velvet with white satin trimmings; and they must have been made – both the bodices and the frock – in the times of King Wamba.[1] The priest wouldn't let them touch his head, but instead donned his quilted cotton nightcap and bound his forehead with a black taffeta garter, and he used another garter as a travelling-mask to conceal his face and beard. He rammed his hat, which was so big it could have served as a parasol, on to his head, wrapped himself in his cape and mounted his mule side-saddle, and the barber climbed on to his own mule, with his beard down to his waist – a pale red beard, as described, made out of the tail of a sorrel ox. They said goodbye to everyone, including the good Maritornes, who promised to say a rosary, sinner though she was, so that God would give them success in the difficult Christian task they'd set themselves.

But the priest had hardly left the inn when a thought struck him: it was improper to have rigged himself out like that, indecent for a man of the cloth to dress in that way, even if so much did depend on it; and he said so to the barber and asked him to exchange clothes, because it was more appropriate for the latter to appear as the maiden in distress, and he himself would act the part of the squire, which was less of a profanation of his office – and if the barber wasn't agreeable to this, the priest was resolved to have nothing more to do with the affair, and to let the devil take Don Quixote.

And now Sancho appeared, and when he saw the two of them dressed like that his mirth was uncontrollable. The barber agreed to all the priest's demands, and they changed their plans and the priest instructed him on his demeanour, and on the words with which he was to try to persuade Don Quixote to come away with them and give up his occupation of the place he'd chosen for his vain penance. The barber replied that he didn't need any lessons to handle the affair to perfection. He didn't want to get dressed yet, not until they came close to where Don Quixote was, so he folded up his clothes and the priest put his beard away, and they rode on with their guide Sancho Panza, who told them all about what had happened with the madman they'd found in the sierra, keeping quiet, however, about the discovery of the travelling bag and what was in it: the servant might have been stupid, but he did have his fair share of greed.

The next day they reached the place where Sancho had strewn the branches to help him find his master again, and, once he recognized the spot, he told the other two that this was the way in, so they could get dressed if that was what was needed for the rescue. Because they had earlier told him that wearing those disguises was of vital importance for extricating his master from the bad life he'd chosen, so would he please be careful not to tell him who they were or even that he knew them; and if Don Quixote asked, which he would, whether Sancho had given Dulcinea the letter, he should say that he had but that, as she couldn't read, she'd replied verbally ordering Don Quixote, on pain of incurring her displeasure, to go and visit her forthwith, this being a matter of the utmost importance to her – and what with this and the things that they themselves intended to say to him they were sure he could be led back to a better life, and made to set out to become an emperor or a monarch, and there wasn't any need to worry about that plan to become an archbishop.

Sancho listened to all of this, and took it into his memory with meticulous care, and gave them hearty thanks for deciding to advise his master to be an emperor and not an archbishop, because to his mind, when it came to doing favours to their squires, emperor errants had more clout than archbishop errants. He added that it would be best if he went on ahead to look for his master and give him his lady's reply, because this alone would be enough to make him leave that place, without any need for them to go to so much trouble. They liked Sancho Panza's idea, and decided to wait until he returned with the news that he'd found his master.

Sancho rode off into the mountain ravines, leaving the other two men in another ravine through which flowed a gentle little stream in the cool, pleasant shade of the rocks and trees surrounding it. It was a hot August day, and August is hot indeed in those parts; it was three o'clock in the afternoon; and all this made the spot even more delightful, inviting them to await Sancho's return there, which they did.

As they rested in the shade, they heard a voice that, unaccompanied by any other instrument, was sweet and melodious; and they were astonished, this not seeming to be a place to come across someone singing so well – because although it's often said that shepherds with fine singing voices are to be found in the woods and fields, this is more an exaggeration of poets than a sober truth. And they were even more amazed when they realized that what they could hear being sung were verses not of rustic herdsmen but of intelligent courtiers. This was confirmed by the fact that the verses they heard were the following:

> What puts my patience to the test?
> Absence's jest.
> What aggravates my misery?
> Fierce jealousy.
> What turns my happiness to pain?
> Unkind disdain.
> If this is so, there is no cure
> For torments that I now endure,

Since every hope of mine is slain
By absence, jealousy, disdain.

And what repels my happiness?
Fortune's duress.
What is the cause of such dire throes?
Love's cruel blows.
And what confirms my misery?
Heaven's decree.
If this is so, the sole release
Is death, from such a strange disease,
Since all unite to harrow me:
Fortune, and love, and heaven's decree.

What can release me from my sadness?
No less than madness.
Where shall I find a speedy cure?
Cold death is sure.
What gains love's joys most readily?
Inconstancy.
If this is so, it makes no sense
From such attacks to seek defence,
Since there's no better remedy
Than madness, death, inconstancy.

The time of day, the weather, the solitude, and the voice and the skill of the singer combined to astonish and delight the two listeners, who sat still, hoping to hear some more; but as the silence dragged on they decided to go in search of the man who sang so well. Just as they were about to do so, the same voice held them back as it reached their ears, singing this sonnet:

SONNET

O sacred Friendship, who in urgent flight,
And leaving here on earth your guileful ghost,
Exultant soared to that empyrean height

To dwell in glory with the heavenly host,
  From there to show us, when you think it best,
Behind a veil that peace for which we long
– A veil that other times betrays a zest
For doing good, which then does vicious wrong:
  Come back from heaven, Friendship: don't agree
To the destruction of sincere intent
When Fraudulence parades your livery;
For if his base charade has your consent
Grim-visaged war will win the world again
And dark primeval anarchy will reign.

The singing ended in a deep sigh, and the two men waited attentively to see if it would be resumed; but when they heard that the music had dissolved into sobs and pitiful groans they agreed to go and discover who was this sad man with a voice as superb as his moans were sorrowful. They hadn't walked far when, as they came round a boulder, they saw a man who looked exactly like the one described by Sancho Panza when he told them about Cardenio's story; and when this man saw them he didn't seem frightened but stayed still with his head bowed over his breast like someone lost in his thoughts, not raising his eyes again to look at them after his first glance when they'd appeared so suddenly.

The priest, who was a man of ready speech and knew about Cardenio's misfortune because he'd recognized him from Sancho's description, went up to him and with brief but judicious words begged and advised him to abandon that wretched existence so as not to die in that place, which would be the greatest of all misfortunes. Cardenio was enjoying a spell of sanity, free of the fury that often drove him out of his mind, and he was surprised to see two men in clothes so very different from the ones worn by those who wandered about these lonely places, and even more surprised to hear his private life being discussed as if it were common knowledge – because this was the impression given by the priest's words. So Cardenio replied like this:

'I can clearly see, gentlemen, whoever you are, that heaven, which takes care to succour the virtuous and even the wicked as well, has sent to me, unworthy though I am, here into these remote places so far from all human society, people who, by placing a diversity of powerful arguments before me to show me how unreasonable it is to live as I do, seek to take me away from this existence to a better one; but since they do not know, as I do, that if I escape from this affliction it will only be to plunge into another still greater one, it may be that they take me for a man of little sense or even what would be worse, one deprived of all reason. And this would not be surprising, because I am aware that the recollection of my misfortunes is so intense and has such power to destroy me that, without my being able to do anything to prevent it, I sometimes become as void of all sense and awareness as a stone; and I realize that this is so when people tell me and show me proof of the things I do when in the grips of those terrible fits, and all I can do then is express a futile regret for what has happened and utter fruitless curses on my fate, and offer as an excuse for my mad deeds an account of their cause to any who will hear me; because once reasonable people know the cause they will not wonder at the effects, and, if they cannot cure me, at least they will not blame me, and their annoyance at my impudence will turn to pity for my misfortunes. And if, gentlemen, you have come with the same intentions as others, I beg you, before you proceed with your judicious persuasion, to listen to the endless story of my misfortunes because, once you have heard it, perhaps you will save yourselves the trouble of trying to console me for an affliction that puts me beyond all consolation.'

The two men, who wanted nothing better than to hear the cause of his grief from his own mouth, asked him to tell them about it and assured him that in any attempts they might make to cure or comfort him they wouldn't do anything against his will; and so this sad gentleman began his piteous history, with almost the same words and events as when he'd narrated it to Don Quixote and the goatherd a few days earlier, and, on account of Master Elisabat and of Don Quixote's punctiliousness in maintaining the decorum of chivalry, the story had been left unfinished, as related in this history. But this time, fortunately, the fit of madness was suspended and he was able to tell his story to its conclusion; and so, when he reached the point at which Don Fernando found a letter among the pages of *Amadis of Gaul*, Cardenio said that he could remember it well, and that it went like this:

Luscinda to Cardenio

*Each day I discover in you qualities that oblige and compel me to hold you in
even higher esteem; and so, if you should wish to relieve me of this obligation
without causing me to forfeit my honour, you can easily do so. I have a father
who knows you and loves me, and who will not be going against my wishes
when he accedes to those which you may justly have, if you esteem me, as you
say and I believe.*

'This letter encouraged me to ask for Luscinda's hand in marriage, as
I've already told you, and it was also what established her in Don Fernando's
opinion as one of the most sensible and intelligent women of the day; and
it was this letter, too, that awoke in him the desire to destroy me, before
my own desire could be fulfilled. I told Don Fernando of Luscinda's father's
observation that it was my own father who should make the request, and
that I didn't dare mention it to him, fearing that he'd refuse to do so, not
because he wasn't well aware of Luscinda's rank, goodness, virtue and
beauty, or of the fact that her qualities were sufficient to ennoble any family
in Spain, but because I realized that he didn't want me to marry yet, not
until it became clear what Duke Ricardo had in store for me. In short, I
told him that I didn't dare tell my father about the matter, because of both
this obstacle and many others that discouraged me, although I didn't know
exactly what they were: all I did know was that it was looking as if what I
so desired could never be achieved.

'To all this Don Fernando replied that he'd take it upon himself to speak
to my father and persuade him to speak to Luscinda's father. Oh you
ruthless Marius, you cruel Catiline, you wicked Sulla, you deceitful Ganelon,
you treacherous Vellido, you vengeful Julián, you covetous Judas![2] Treacherous, cruel, vengeful, deceitful – what deeds of disloyalty had ever been
committed by this poor man who so frankly revealed to you the joys and
secrets of his heart? In what ways had I ever offended you? What words
did I ever speak to you, what advice did I ever give you, but that which
was designed to increase your honour and prosperity? Yet what am I
complaining about, miserable wretch that I am? It's certain that when
misfortune is brought by the movements of the stars, it comes crashing

down from on high with such fury and violence that there's no power on earth that can stop it, no human contrivance that can hold it back. Who could have imagined that Don Fernando, an illustrious and intelligent gentleman, indebted to me for my services and powerful enough to secure for himself whatever his amorous inclinations desired, would sully his conscience, as they say, by stealing from me one ewe lamb, which was not even yet mine?[3] But let's leave these considerations aside, because they're vain and fruitless, and take up the broken thread of my tale of woe.

'I was going to say, then, that Don Fernando, finding my presence an obstacle to the execution of his false and evil plan, decided to make me go to his elder brother to ask for money to pay for six horses that, with the sole object of sending me away so that he could more readily carry out his perverse scheme, he bought on the same day that he offered to talk to my father. So I was to go for the money. Could I have foreseen this treachery? Could I even have imagined it? No, of course not: on the contrary, I most willingly offered to leave at once, delighted with the excellent bargain he'd made. That night I spoke with Luscinda and told her what I'd agreed with Don Fernando, and how she should firmly trust that our good and just desires would be fulfilled. Suspecting Don Fernando's treachery as little as I did, she told me to try to come back soon, because she believed that the accomplishment of our wishes would be delayed by no longer than our fathers' conversation. I don't know why, but when she finished saying this her eyes filled with tears and a knot seemed to form in her throat, stopping her from speaking any more of the very many words that she appeared to want to say to me.

'I was astonished at this strange faltering, because it had never happened before and, whenever good fortune and my diligence had allowed us to talk, we'd done so with great joy, without any tears, sighs, jealousy, suspicion or fear. I would dwell on my good fortune, because heaven had given her to me as my lady; I would extol her beauty, marvel at her merit and her understanding. She would return the compliments with interest, praising in me that which seemed to her, as a woman in love, worthy of praise. And we would tell each other a hundred thousand tales and pieces of gossip about our friends and neighbours, and the most I ever dared to do was to take, almost by force, one of her lovely white hands and press it to my lips as well as the close bars separating us would allow. But on the night before the sorrowful day of my departure she wept, sighed and moaned, and went away leaving me confused and fearful at having seen these sad new signs of deep grief in her; yet, so as not to dash my own hopes, I put it all down to the strength of her feelings for me and the pain that absence causes in those who are in love.

'So I left, dejected and sunk in thought, with my soul loaded down with suspicions and imaginings, yet not knowing what it was that I suspected and imagined: clear signs of the sad event and the misfortune reserved for me. I reached the town to which I'd been sent, I gave the letters to Don Fernando's brother, I was well received but my business was not well attended to, because he told me to wait, much to my displeasure, for a week, where the Duke could not find me, as his brother had written asking him to send money without his father's knowledge; and this was all part of the treacherous Don Fernando's plan, because this brother of his had the money and could have sent me back with it immediately. This was an order that I was very close to disobeying, because it seemed impossible to endure life for so long without Luscinda, particularly since I had left her in the state that I've described; but in spite of all that I obeyed as a dutiful servant, although I could see that it would be at the cost of my well-being.

'But four days after I'd arrived a man came for me with a letter, and by the address I could tell it was from Luscinda, because it was in her handwriting. I opened it in fear and trembling, for it had to be a serious matter to make her write when I was far away – she seldom wrote even when I was near. Before I read it I asked the man who had given it to him and how long it had taken him to come. He told me that he'd happened to be walking down a street in his city at midday when a very beautiful lady called out to him from a window, with her eyes full of tears, and blurted:

'"Brother, if you're a Christian, as you seem to be, I beg you for the love of God to make sure that this letter reaches without delay the place and the person to whom it's addressed – they're both well-known enough; and you'll be doing a great service to our Lord, and, so that you don't lack the means to do so, please accept the contents of this handkerchief."

'"And so saying she threw me a handkerchief out of the window, and tied into it were these hundred reals and this gold ring I have here, together with the letter I've just given you. And without waiting for a reply she moved back from the window, though not before watching me pick up the letter and the handkerchief and make signs that I would indeed do as she had asked. Because seeing that I was so well paid for whatever trouble it could give me to bring it, and seeing from the address that it was for you – I know about you, sir, very well – and compelled, too, by that beautiful lady's tears, I decided not to entrust it to anybody else but to bring it myself, and in the sixteen hours that have elapsed since I was given it I have made the journey here – some sixty miles, as you know."

'As the grateful special messenger was telling me all this, I was hanging on his every word and my legs were shaking so much that I could hardly stand. I opened the letter and read the following:

The promise that Don Fernando made you, to persuade your father to speak to mine, has been kept, but more for his gratification than for your benefit. You must know, sir, that he has asked for my hand in marriage, and my father, persuaded that Don Fernando will be a better match, has given his consent so eagerly that the wedding is to take place two days from now, in such secret that the only witnesses will be the heavens and some of the household. My present state is something that you can imagine for yourself; whether it is in your interest to come is something that you must decide for yourself; and whether I love you or not is something that the outcome of this affair will demonstrate to you. God grant that this may reach your hand before mine is joined with that of one who keeps his promises so badly.

'This, then, was what the letter said, and this is what made me set off straight away, without waiting any longer for a reply or for money; because I could clearly see that it had been the purchase not of horses but of his pleasure that had led Don Fernando to send me to his brother. My indignation and my fear of losing the treasure that I had won by so many years of service and desire lent me wings, and the next day I was back in my town at the hour when I could speak to Luscinda, almost as if I'd flown there. I rode in unobserved, I left my mule at the house of the fellow who'd brought me the letter, and it was my good fortune to find Luscinda at her window, behind the grating that was the witness to our love. Luscinda recognized me and I recognized her, but not as we should have recognized each other. Yet who in this world can claim to have penetrated and understood the confused mind and fickle nature of a woman? Nobody, nobody. I was about to say that as soon as Luscinda saw me she said:

'"Cardenio, I'm wearing my wedding dress: the treacherous Don Fernando and my covetous father are waiting in the hall with others who will be witnesses rather of my death than of my marriage. Don't be upset, my dear, but do make sure that you're present at this sacrifice: if my words can't prevent it, a dagger I have hidden on me can resist the strongest forces by putting an end to my life and a beginning to your understanding of my love for you."

'In my confusion I made a hurried reply, afraid that I might run out of time:

'"Let your actions, madam, make good your words; for if you carry a dagger to vouch for you, I carry a sword to defend you or kill myself, if fortune proves adverse to us."

'I don't believe she could have heard all I said, because urgent voices were calling out to her that the bridegroom was waiting. And the night of my sadness came, and the sun of my happiness set: there was no light left in my eyes, no sense left in my brain. I couldn't enter her house – I couldn't move; but then I reminded myself how important it was for me to be present because of what might happen, I nerved myself as best I could and went in; and since I knew all the ways in and out, and the house was in its secret upheaval, nobody noticed me; so I was able to slip unobserved into the recess formed by a window in the hall, covered by the borders of two tapestries, between which I could see, without being seen, everything that happened.

'Who could describe the fluttering of my heart as I stood there, the thoughts that came into my mind, the calculations that I made? There were so many of them, and they were of such a nature, that I can't describe them, nor would it be right to do so. Suffice it to say that the bridegroom walked into the hall wearing nothing finer than his everyday clothes. His best man was one of Luscinda's cousins, and the only other people in the hall were the servants.

'A little afterwards Luscinda came out of a side room accompanied by her mother and two maids, and she was as richly dressed and adorned as her rank and beauty deserved, the perfection of elegance and courtly poise. My amazement and trepidation didn't allow me to observe the details of her dress; I only noticed its colours, crimson and white, and the glinting of the jewels in her hair and on her clothes, all of it surpassed by the singular beauty of her lovely blond hair to such an extent that, in competition with the precious stones and the light of four torches that were burning in the hall, her light was the one that offered most brilliance to the eyes. O memory, the mortal foe of my repose! Why bring before me now the incomparable beauty of that adored enemy of mine? Won't it be better, cruel memory, to recall and picture to me what she did next so that, moved by such a manifest affront, I can at least, since vengeance is impossible, put an end to my life?

'Try not to be bored, gentlemen, by these digressions of mine: my tale of woe is not one of those that can or should be told in a few words, because each aspect of it seems to demand a full explanation.'

To this the priest replied that not only were they not bored listening to him but they were deriving great pleasure from all the details he was providing, because they shouldn't be passed over in silence and indeed merited as much attention as the main thread of his story.

'I was about to say, then,' Cardenio continued, 'that the people were standing there in the hall and the parish priest came in and took each by the hand to do what had to be done, and when he said, "Will you, Luscinda, take Don Fernando, here present, to be your lawful wedded husband, as our Holy Mother the Church commands?", I thrust my head and neck out between the two tapestries to listen, with straining ears and soul in turmoil, to Luscinda's reply, knowing that it would be either my death sentence or the confirmation of my life. Oh, why didn't I rush out, crying, "Luscinda, Luscinda! Think what you're doing, consider what you owe me, remember you're mine and can't be another's! Remember that your saying 'I will' and the end of my life will be one and the same thing. O treacherous Don Fernando, thief of my glory, death of my life! What do you want? What do you seek? Bear in mind that there is no Christian way in which you can satisfy your desires, because Luscinda is my wife and I am her husband."

'What madness! Now that I'm far removed from the danger, I'm saying that I should have done what I didn't do! Now that I've allowed my dear one to be stolen, I curse the thief, on whom I could have taken revenge if I'd had the courage to do so, as I have for complaining! In short, I behaved then like a fool and a coward; no wonder that I'm dying now ashamed, repentant and mad.

'The priest was waiting for Luscinda's reply, and she was taking a long time to give it, and just when I thought that she was going to draw her dagger and allow it to speak for her, or else loosen her tongue to undeceive them all and help my cause, I heard her whisper "I will", and Don Fernando said the same thing and gave her the ring, and they were joined in an indissoluble bond. The bridegroom went to embrace his bride, and she clutched her hand to her heart and fell fainting into her mother's arms. It only remains for me to say how I felt as I saw, in her consent, that my hopes were shattered, that all Luscinda's words and promises had been false, and that it would be impossible ever to recover the treasure that I had lost in an instant. I was left not knowing what to do, forsaken, as it seemed to me, by all heaven: the earth that supported me had become my enemy, air denied itself to me for my sighs, water for my tears, and only fire grew, so that all burned in fury and jealousy.

'Everyone was thrown into confusion by Luscinda's fainting fit, and, when her mother loosened her bodices, a folded piece of paper was discovered there, which Don Fernando snatched up and started to read by the light of one of the torches; and once he'd finished reading he sat on a chair and put his hand to his cheek like a man lost in his thoughts, not going to help with the attempts that were being made to bring his bride round from her swoon. With everyone in such a commotion I plucked up my courage and left, not caring whether I was seen or not, and determined that, if I was, I'd do such a desperate deed that they'd all learn from my punishment of the false Don Fernando or even of the fickle, swooning traitress how just was my indignation. But my fate, which must have reserved me for even worse evils (if there can be any worse), decreed that I should then have full use of an understanding that has since failed me; so I didn't take my revenge on my greatest enemies (which would have been easy, for all thought of me was far from their minds) but decided to give myself the punishment that they deserved, and perhaps an even more severe one than I'd have given them had I killed them, because with sudden death the suffering is soon over, whereas torture endlessly protracts the life that it's doing away with.

'So I left that house and returned to the one where I'd left the mule; I told the man to saddle it and, without stopping to take my leave of him, I mounted it and rode out of the city, not daring to look back, like another Lot;[4] and once I found myself alone in the countryside, with the darkness of the night hiding me and its silence inviting me to voice my complaints without fear of being overheard or recognized, I bellowed out curse after curse on Luscinda and Don Fernando, as if this were satisfaction for the wrong they'd done me. I called her cruel, ungrateful, false, thankless, but above all covetous, because my enemy's wealth had closed the eyes of her affection, taking it away from me and giving it to one with whom fortune had been more bountiful and generous; but even as I was most furiously cursing and abusing her I was also making excuses for her, saying that it wasn't surprising that a young girl, immured in her parents' house, accustomed to obeying them always, should have decided to fall in with their wishes, because they were giving her as a husband a gentleman who was so eminent, so rich and so noble that, if she'd refused him, it could have been thought either that she was out of her mind or that she had another lover, which would have been so prejudicial to her good name and honour.

'Then I'd change my tune and say that, even if she had declared that she and I were married, they'd have seen that her choice hadn't been such a bad one that they couldn't forgive her, because before Don Fernando put himself forward they themselves couldn't have wanted a better husband for their daughter, if they'd kept their expectations within reasonable limits; and that, rather than making that last fatal move, giving her hand to Don Fernando, she could easily have said that I'd already given her mine, because I'd have confirmed whatever story she'd made up for the occasion.

'So I concluded that a lack of true love and of good sense, and an excess of ambition and of thirst for grandeur, had made her forget the words with which she'd deceived, kept alive and sustained my firm hopes and honourable desires. Shouting and agonizing in this way I rode on through what was left of the night, and at daybreak I came to a pass leading into this sierra, through which I wandered aimlessly for another three days until I reached some meadows somewhere among these mountains and asked some herdsmen where the wildest parts lay. They sent me in this direction. I headed for this place at once, intending to end my life here, and as I reached it my mule dropped dead from exhaustion and starvation or, as I rather believe, to be rid of so useless a burden. So I was left on foot, at the mercy of nature, perishing with hunger, with nobody to help me and no thoughts of looking for help.

'I lay like that for some time, I don't know how long, and then I stood up, now not feeling at all hungry, and found some goatherds there who must have been the people who'd satisfied my needs, because they told me how they'd found me raving in such a way that it was clear I'd lost my reason; and since then I've realized that I'm not always in full possession of it, but so deranged at times that I perform a thousand mad actions, tearing my clothes, bellowing in these solitudes, cursing my fortune and vainly repeating my beloved enemy's name, with no other thought or plan than to end my life in screams; and then when I come back to my senses I feel so weak and exhausted that I can hardly move. My usual dwelling-place is the hollow of a cork-oak, large enough to shelter this miserable carcass of mine. The cowherds and goatherds who roam over these mountains, moved by charity, provide me with sustenance, placing food by the paths and rocks where they think I might pass and find it; and when I do, even at times when I've lost my reason, natural instinct makes me recognize the food and awakes in me the desire to go and fetch it and the will to take it up. When they come across me in my senses they tell me that at other times I waylay the herdsmen carrying food up from the village to the folds and take it from them by force, even though they're happy to give it to me.

'This is how I'm spending the last days of my wretched existence, until heaven is pleased to put an end either to it or to my memory, so that I do not remember Luscinda's beauty and treachery or the wrong done me by Don Fernando; for if heaven does this without ending my life, I'll turn my thoughts to a better course; if not, all that can be done is to beg heaven to have infinite mercy on my soul, because I don't feel in myself the strength or vigour to rescue my body from these desperate straits to which I've chosen to reduce it.

'This, gentlemen, is the dismal story of my misfortune: you tell me now whether it would have been possible to tell it with less emotion than I've shown – and don't trouble to advise or try to persuade me to do what your reason suggests as a remedy for me, because that would be as much use to me as the medicine prescribed by a famous doctor for the patient who refuses to take it. I don't want well-being without Luscinda and, since she has seen fit to belong to another, although she is or should be mine, let me give myself up to misfortune, although I could have been given up to happiness. She wished, with her fickleness, to make my ruin permanent; by seeking my own ruin I'll satisfy her wishes, and this can show posterity that I alone have lacked what other unfortunates possess in abundance; for to them the impossibility of being consoled is in itself a consolation, whereas it only brings me still greater misery, because I believe that my wretchedness will not be ended by my death.'

Here Cardenio ended his long discourse and his tale of love and sorrow; and as the priest was preparing to speak some words of comfort, he was checked by a voice that reached his ears, saying in plaintive tones what will be set down in the fourth part of this narration, because at this point the wise and circumspect historian Cide Hamete Benengeli put an end to the third.

Fourth Part of
the Ingenious Hidalgo
DON QUIXOTE
de la Mancha

❋❋❋❋

CHAPTER XXVIII

※

*Concerning the unusual and agreeable adventure
undergone by the priest and the barber in the
Sierra Morena*

Most happy and fortunate were the times when that most daring knight
Don Quixote de la Mancha appeared on this earth, because it is thanks to
his honourable determination to revive and restore to the world the lost
and indeed almost defunct order of knight-errantry that we can now enjoy,
in this age of ours, so much in need of amusing entertainments, not only
the delights of his true history but also the stories and episodes inserted
into it, for in some ways they are no less agreeable or imaginative or true
than the history itself; which, resuming its thread (duly dressed, spun and
wound), relates that as the priest was preparing himself to comfort Cardenio,
he was checked by a voice that said in mournful tones:

'Oh God, is it possible that I've at last found a place that can serve as a
hidden tomb for the heavy burden of this body of mine, which I so
unwillingly bear? Yes, it is, if the solitude promised by these sierras doesn't
deceive me. Oh unhappy me, how much more agreeable company these
crags and thickets will be for my thoughts – since they'll give me the
opportunity to bewail my fate and tell heaven of my misery – than that of
any human being, because there isn't one on this earth from whom one can

expect advice in perplexity, comfort in lamentation or remedy in distress!'

When the priest and those with him heard these words they realized that the voice wasn't far away and stood up to go and look for the speaker, and they hadn't gone twenty paces when they saw, sitting behind a rock at the foot of an ash tree, a lad in farmer's clothes whose face they couldn't see, because his head was bent over a stream that flowed there, in which he was bathing his feet; and they approached him so quietly that he didn't notice them, being so engrossed in bathing his feet, which looked like nothing so much as two pieces of white crystal lying among the other stones there. They were astonished at the whiteness and the beauty of those feet, which didn't look as if they were accustomed to treading the clods or trudging behind the plough and the oxen, as the lad's clothes indicated they were.

And so, seeing that they hadn't been noticed, the priest, who'd gone on ahead, motioned to the other two to crouch down and hide behind some rocks, which they did, watching every movement made by the lad, who was wearing a pale-brown rustic cape, tied tight round his waist with a strip of white towelling. He was also wearing pale-brown woollen breeches and gaiters, and a cap of the same colour. He'd hitched his gaiters halfway up his legs, which, of course, resembled the purest alabaster. He finished washing those beautiful feet and then dried them with a kerchief that he untied from under his cap; and as he did so he raised his face and the onlookers saw such peerless beauty that Cardenio whispered to the priest:

'Since this isn't Luscinda, it's no human creature but a divine one.'

The lad removed his cap and, as he shook his head from side to side, hair that the sun itself might have envied began to flow down and spread out. This made them realize that the person who'd seemed to be a farmer was a woman, and a well-favoured one at that, indeed the most beautiful woman that two of them had ever seen, and that Cardenio would have ever seen if he hadn't seen Luscinda, because he later affirmed that only Luscinda's beauty could match hers. Her long blond hair didn't just cover her shoulders but spread all around her, and so lush and abundant was it that only her feet could be seen. And now she combed it with her hands, and, if her feet in the water looked like pieces of crystal, her hands in her hair looked like pieces of firm snow. All this increased the astonishment of the three men and their desire to know who she was.

So they decided to show themselves and, as they stood up, the beautiful young woman raised her head and, parting her hair from her eyes with both hands, looked to see what was making the noise; as soon as she saw them she sprang to her feet, and without stopping to put on her shoes or tie up her hair, she snatched up a bundle lying beside her, which looked as if it contained clothes, and began to run away in confusion and alarm. But she hadn't taken half-a-dozen steps when her delicate feet, unable to bear the roughness of the stones, failed her and she fell to the ground. The three men stepped forward, and the priest was the first to address her:

'Stop, madam, whoever you are: those whom you see before you desire only to serve you. Please do not attempt to make so inopportune an escape, for neither will your feet withstand it nor will we allow it.'

In her bewilderment she made no reply. So they went up to her and the priest took her hand and continued:

'What your clothes deny, madam, is betrayed by your hair: a clear sign that it can have been no trivial reason that led you to disguise your beauty in such an unworthy habit and that brought you into such a lonely place, where it has been a stroke of good fortune to find you – if not to remedy your ills, at least to give advice, for no ill can be so oppressive or so extreme that, while life lasts, the sufferer refuses to listen to well-meant counsel. And so, my dear lady, or my dear sir, whichever you prefer to be, do dismiss the fears that seeing us has caused you, and tell us about your good or evil fortune; for in all of us together, or in each separately, you'll find sincere sympathizers.'

As the priest was speaking, the disguised girl seemed as if she had lost her senses, gazing at them all without moving her lips or saying a word, like the rustic villager who's suddenly shown strange objects that he's never seen before. But the priest said some more words to the same effect, and she breathed a deep sigh and broke her silence:

'Since the solitude of these sierras hasn't been sufficient to hide me, and the loosening of my dishevelled hair won't allow my tongue to lie, it would be futile to maintain a pretence that could only be accepted out of politeness. In view of this, gentlemen, I thank you for your offer, which has placed me under an obligation to comply with your request, even though I fear that the tale I shall tell of my misfortunes will cause you not only pity but grief, because you won't be able to find any cure to remedy them, or any consolation to alleviate them. But in spite of all this, and to dispel any doubts you might be entertaining about my honour now that you know I'm a woman and have seen me young, alone and in these clothes – circumstances that coming together or even taken separately would be enough to demolish any reputation – I feel bound to tell you what I'd rather keep secret if I could.'

The newly discovered beauty said all this with such a fluent tongue and in such a calm voice that they were as amazed at her intelligence as at her looks. And after further offers had been made, together with further requests to do as she'd promised, she made any more coaxing unnecessary by putting on her shoes with all due modesty, tying up her hair, sitting on a rock with the three men around her, trying to suppress the tears that welled into her eyes and in a clear, serene voice commencing her life history:

'There is in Andalusia a town from which a certain duke takes his title, and which makes him one of those known here in Spain as grandees. He has two sons: the elder is the heir to his estate and, so it seems, to his virtuous habits, and the younger is the heir to I don't know what, unless it's the treachery of Vellido and the deceit of Ganelon. My parents are tenants of this duke, of humble stock but so rich that if nature had been as generous with their pedigree as fortune has been with their wealth, they could have nothing more to desire and there would have been no risk of my finding myself in my present predicament; because it may be that my bad luck is born of theirs, in not having been born aristocratic. It's certainly true that they're not so low-born as to feel affronted by their rank, but neither are they so exalted as to rid my head of the thought that my disaster derives from their modest station. In short they're farmers, simple folk, of pure blood unmixed with that of any ill-sounding races and, as it's often put, dyed-in-the-wool old Christians – but so rich that thanks to their wealth and generosity they're beginning to be regarded as hidalgos and even as nobles. But their greatest wealth and nobility was, for them, having me as a daughter, and, both because they had no other heir and because they were loving parents, I was one of the most indulged of children. I was the mirror in which they contemplated themselves, the staff of their old age and the goal towards which they guided, under the direction of heaven, all their desires, which were so worthy that mine never diverged one iota from them. And I was the mistress not only of their affections but of all they owned. I was in charge of hiring and dismissing the servants, I controlled all the sowing and harvesting, and the olive-presses, the wine-presses, the size of the herds and flocks, even the quantity of beehives. In short, I managed everything that a very wealthy farmer like my father can and does possess, and I was both the stewardess and the mistress of it all, with so much diligence on my part and so much satisfaction on his that I couldn't begin to say how splendid everything was.

'The moments of each day that were left to me after I'd paid the shepherds, foremen and day labourers, I spent on occupations that are both proper and necessary for young ladies, such as those provided by the needle and the pincushion and often the distaff; and if I occasionally put these activities aside in search of some recreation, I would entertain myself by reading a book of devotion, or playing a harp, because experience showed me that music settles the distressed mind and eases the troubles that are born of the spirit. This, then, was the life I led in my parents' house, and I've described it in such detail not to boast or to demonstrate that I'm a wealthy woman, but so that you can see how little I deserved to fall from that happy state into my present misery.

'As I spent my life, then, with so much to keep me busy, and in a seclusion which could be compared to that of a nunnery, and unseen, or so I thought, by anyone except the servants, because when I went to mass it was so early in the morning, and I was so closely attended by my mother and other maidservants and so carefully veiled and withdrawn that my eyes hardly glimpsed anything other than the ground I trod . . . – but, despite all these precautions, loving eyes or, more accurately, idle eyes, which the eyes of the lynx cannot rival, did see me: the eyes of the importunate Don Fernando, for this is the name of the younger son of the duke of whom I spoke.'

The storyteller had no sooner named Don Fernando than the colour of Cardenio's face changed and he broke into a sweat, in such violent perturbation that when the priest and barber noticed it they feared he was about to have one of the fits of madness that they'd been told he suffered every so often. But Cardenio only sat there perspiring and gaping at the farmer's daughter and imagining who she was; and she, not noticing Cardenio's response, continued her story:

'And the moment those eyes of his caught sight of me (as he later said), he fell as deeply in love as his demonstrations of it were to indicate. But to shorten the true story of my woes, I'll pass in silence over the measures that Don Fernando took to declare his love to me. He bribed all the servants in my house, he gave presents and offered favours to my relations. Every day was a happy fiesta day in my street, and at night nobody slept, with all the serenades. The love-letters that came into my hands by unknown means were countless, full of words of passion and promises, and containing more offers and vows than signs of the alphabet. All of which not only failed to weaken my resistance, but steeled me, as if he were my mortal enemy and everything he did to win me over were done with the opposite intention; not that I disliked Don Fernando's gallantry, or thought him too importunate, because it gave me a very special thrill of happiness to be loved and esteemed by such an eminent gentleman, and I wasn't sorry to read his praises in his letters: however ugly a woman is, it seems she always likes to hear herself called beautiful.

'But my sense of virtue did object, and so did my parents, who kept giving me their advice – by now they knew all about Don Fernando's passion, because he didn't care if everybody knew about it. My parents would tell me that their honour and reputation depended upon my virtue and goodness alone, and that I must consider the difference in rank between Don Fernando and me, and that this would make me see that his intentions, even if he said otherwise, had more to do with his pleasure than with my welfare; and also that if I would erect some kind of obstacle to make him desist from his unjust pretensions, they would marry me without delay to any man I chose among the most eminent men in our town and those near by, because with their great wealth and my good name anything was possible. My parents' firm promises and the truths they were telling me strengthened my resolve, and I never replied to Don Fernando with a single word that could have given him the remotest hope of fulfilling his desire.

'All this reserve of mine, which I suppose he took for disdain, must have had the effect of arousing his lust to an even higher pitch – this is the name I must give to his passion, which, had it been what it should have been, you wouldn't be hearing about now, for there wouldn't have been any occasion to tell you of it. In the end Don Fernando found out that my parents were looking for a match for me, so as to make him lose his hopes of possessing me, or at least to provide me with more guards to watch over me; and this information, or suspicion, was the reason why he did what you will now hear. One night I was in my room accompanied only by a maid, with all the doors locked for fear that any carelessness might in some unimagined way endanger my virtue, and in the midst of all these defences and precautions, in the solitude of this silence and seclusion, I found him standing there before me, and the sight of him so shocked me that I lost my sight and my power of speech. So I couldn't shout out, and anyway I don't believe he'd have let me, because he hurried over to me, took me in his arms (as I've said, I was so shocked I had no strength left with which to defend myself) and began to say such things to me – I just don't know how it's possible for duplicity to possess such skill in constructing lies that they seem like evident truths. The traitor produced tears to support his words and sighs to vouch for his passion. I, poor thing, alone in my own house, unprepared for such a situation, began – I don't quite know how – to take all these falsehoods for truths, but his tears and sighs didn't move me to anything more than honest compassion. And so, once I'd recovered from the initial shock, I began to regain some of my lost vital spirits, and with more energy than I thought there was in me I said:

' "If, sir, as I am in your grip, I were in that of some fierce lion, and I could gain my freedom by doing or saying something to the prejudice of my chastity, it would be as possible for me to say it or to do it as it is for that which has been to cease to have been. For if you hold my body in your arms, I keep my soul secure in the purity of my intentions, which are very different from yours, as you will soon realize if you try to carry them into effect by force. I am your tenant but I am not your slave, and the nobility of your blood should not and does not give you the authority to despise and dishonour the humility of mine; and I hold myself, a lowly farmer's daughter, in quite as much esteem as you, a lord and gentleman, hold yourself. All your violence will have no effect on me, all your wealth will be powerless, all your words will not deceive me, all your sighs and tears will not move me. If the man my parents give me as a husband were to prevail upon me in this way, I should bow to his will, and my will would not exceed the bounds of his; so, if my honour were secured in this way, even if my pleasure were not, I should willingly surrender to you what you are striving so hard to attain. I have said all this because it is unthinkable that any man who is not legitimately married to me can gain anything from me."

' "If that's all you're concerned about, lovely Dorotea," (for this is the name of the hapless woman you see before you) the dutiless gentleman exclaimed, "look here, I'll give you my hand in marriage, and let the witnesses be heaven, from which nothing's hidden, and this image of our Lady you've got here." '

When Cardenio heard her say that her name was Dorotea, he showed fresh agitation as he found his original suspicions confirmed, but he didn't interrupt her story, being anxious to hear the ending, which he almost knew already.

'Dorotea is your name, madam? I have heard of another Dorotea who, perhaps, has suffered similar misfortunes. Please continue, and in due course I shall tell you of things that will amaze you as much as they will arouse your compassion.'

Dorotea considered Cardenio's words and his strange, ragged clothes, and asked him, if he had any information about her affairs, to tell her immediately, because if fortune had allowed her to retain one good quality it was her determination to face up to any disaster that could befall her, in the certain belief that none could make matters any worse than they already were.

'I would not omit to tell you, madam,' replied Cardenio, 'what I think, were I certain that it is the truth; but the opportunity to do so still remains, and you do not need to know quite yet.'

'Be that as it may,' replied Dorotea, 'what happens next in my story is that Don Fernando picked up a holy image that I had in my room and made it the witness of our wedding. With persuasive words and extraordinary vows he gave me his word of marriage even though, before he finished speaking, I told him to think what he was doing and consider how angry his father would be when he discovered that he was married to a peasant girl, one of his tenants; I told him not to be blinded by my beauty, such as it was, for it wasn't sufficient to provide an excuse for his blunder; I told him that if he wished to do me a kindness, because of his love for me, he should allow my life to run a course appropriate to my rank, because such uneven matches never retain for long the happiness of their first days.

'I put all these arguments to him, and many others that I don't remember, but they were powerless to make him change his mind: the man who never intends to pay isn't worried about any problems when he strikes his bargain. Then I reasoned to myself like this:

'"All right then, I shan't be the first girl to rise by means of marriage from humble to high estate, nor will Don Fernando be the first man to be led by beauty or, more likely, by blind desire, into taking a wife beneath his rank. Well, since I'm not going to be changing the world or creating some new custom, it'll be best to accept this honour that fortune's offering me, even if the love this man professes does last no longer than it takes him to have his way – for, after all, in God's eyes I'll be his wife. And if I scorn and reject him, I can see he's in such a state that he'll ignore his obligations and use violence, and I'll be dishonoured and left without the excuses that anyone who doesn't know how innocently I have come to this pass would otherwise have made for me. Because what arguments will be powerful enough to persuade my parents and others that this gentleman entered my room without my consent?"

'I turned all these diverse considerations over in my mind in an instant, but what most affected me and pushed me towards what was, although I didn't realize it, my ruin were Don Fernando's vows, the witnesses he invoked, the tears he shed and, in general, his gentlemanly behaviour, which, accompanied by so many signs of true love, would have conquered any heart as fancy-free and over-protected as mine. I called out to my maid, to have a witness on earth as well as the heavenly ones. Don Fernando repeated and confirmed his oaths yet again; he added a few more saints to his list of witnesses; he called down a thousand curses on himself if he failed to carry out his promises; he again moistened his eyes and deepened his sighs; he pressed me tighter in his arms, from which he'd never released me. And then my maid left, and I stopped being one, and he started being a deceiver and a traitor.

'The day after the night of my undoing didn't come as soon as I think Don Fernando wanted, because once lust has been satisfied the greatest pleasure is to escape from the scene of the fun. I say this because Don Fernando was in a great hurry to leave, and with the help of my maid – she was the one who'd let him in – he was out in the street before daybreak. And when he said goodbye he also said (though with less ardour and vehemence than at the beginning) that I should feel certain of his faithfulness, and that his oaths were firm and true; and as further confirmation of his words he took a fine ring from his finger and put it on mine. So off he went, and I was left feeling I don't know whether sad or happy, but what I do know is that I was confused and pensive and almost beside myself at what had just happened; and I didn't have the heart, or it didn't occur to me, to scold my maid for her treachery in letting Don Fernando into my room, because I still couldn't decide whether what had just happened to me was good or bad. When he left I told him that he could come to me on other nights in the same way, until he wanted our marriage to be made public, for I was now his. But he only returned once more, on the following night, and I never set eyes on him for over a month, either in the street or at church – it was in vain that I searched and searched for him, even though I knew he was in town and went hunting (a sport he was very fond of) nearly every day.

'I well remember those were dismal days and wretched hours, and I also remember that I then began to doubt and even disbelieve Don Fernando's faithfulness, and I remember, too, that my maid did then hear the words of reproof for her effrontery that she hadn't heard before; and I remember that I had to control my tears and the looks on my face, so that my parents wouldn't ask me why I was unhappy and force me to invent a lie. But all this came to a sudden end as the moment arrived when the proprieties were cast aside and all thoughts of honour were abandoned, and when patience ran out and the secrets of my heart were revealed. And this happened because a few days later news spread through town that in a nearby city Don Fernando had married a young woman of great beauty and noble family, although not so very wealthy that her dowry could have led her to aspire to such a fine match. It was said that her name was Luscinda, and that all sorts of amazing things had happened at her wedding.'

When Cardenio heard Luscinda's name his only reaction was to hunch his shoulders, bite his lips, arch his eyebrows and, a few seconds later, let two springs of tears well from his eyes. But this didn't stop Dorotea from continuing her story and saying:

'When this sad news reached my ears, I could hardly say that it chilled my heart – on the contrary, my heart burned in such rage and fury that I was close to running out into the street to proclaim the evil treachery that had been done me. But the fury abated for the time being when I had the idea of doing what I did that very night: I dressed in these clothes, given me by a herdboy – as farmers call them – in my father's service, whom I told of my misfortune and asked to go with me to the city where I believed my enemy was to be found. Once he'd reproached me for my rashness and censured my decision and seen that I was resolute, he offered to go with me to the end of the world, as he put it. I immediately packed some of my clothes into a cotton pillow-case, together with jewels and money, to provide for any eventuality. And in the silence of that night, without saying anything to my treacherous maid, I left home, accompanied by my new servant and by many anxious thoughts, and I started out on foot for the city, lent wings by my need to be there, if not to prevent what I assumed was already done, then at least to make Don Fernando tell me how his conscience had allowed him to do it.

'In two and a half days I was there, and on the outskirts of the city I asked the way to Luscinda's parents' house, and the first man I asked replied with more details than I should have liked to hear. He told me where the house was and he told me everything that had happened at the wedding, an event of such notoriety in the city that groups of gossips had formed throughout it to discuss the details. He told me that on the night when Don Fernando married Luscinda, she fell into a deep faint after saying "I will", and, when her husband went to unbutton her bodices to give her air, he found a note written in her own hand, in which she declared that she couldn't be Don Fernando's wife, because she was already married to Cardenio, who the man told me was a noble gentleman of that city; and that if she'd agreed to be Don Fernando's wife, it was only so as not to disobey her parents. In short, he said that the note made it clear that she'd intended to kill herself once the ceremony was over, and set out her reasons for doing so, all of which is said to be confirmed by a dagger found in her clothing. When Don Fernando read the note he concluded that Luscinda had deceived and slighted and mocked him, and he fell upon her while she was still unconscious and tried to stab her with the dagger they'd found on her, and would have done so if her parents and the others hadn't stopped him. I was told more: Don Fernando left straight away, and Luscinda didn't recover from her faint until the following day, when she told her parents that she was truly married to that fellow Cardenio I mentioned before.

'I discovered still more: the said Cardenio, they claimed, had been present at the wedding, and once he'd seen Luscinda married, something he hadn't been expecting, he went from the city in despair, leaving her a letter in which he spoke of the wrong she'd done him and said he was going where no one could find him. Everybody in the city knew all about it, and everybody in the city was talking about it, and their tongues wagged even faster when it became known that Luscinda had gone missing from her parents' house and from the city, and wasn't anywhere to be found, and her parents were out of their minds with worry, and didn't know what they could do to trace her. This knowledge revived my hopes, and I thought it was better not to have found Don Fernando than to have found him properly married, because it meant that the door to reparation hadn't slammed on me; and it occurred to me that it might have been heaven that had put this impediment in the way of the second marriage, to make him remember his obligation to the first one and realize that he was a Christian and should have more regard for his soul than for mere human concerns. I turned all these ideas over in my imagination and tried to comfort myself by inventing feeble, distant hopes to sustain a life that I now abhor.

'So there I was in the city, not knowing what to do, because I couldn't find Don Fernando, when I heard a town-crier announcing a large reward for anyone who found me, stating my age and describing the clothes I was wearing. I heard someone saying it was rumoured I'd eloped with the lad who'd come with me, and this cut me to the quick, showing how low my credit had fallen – as if it weren't bad enough to have lost it by running away, everybody knew whom I'd run away with, someone so mean and unworthy of my affections. As soon as I heard the announcement I left the city with my servant, who was beginning to show signs of wavering in the loyalty he'd promised me; and that night, fearful of being discovered, we took refuge in the most densely wooded part of this sierra.

'But it's often said that misfortunes never come singly, and that the end of one is often the beginning of another still worse; and that's what happened to me, because once we were in these wilds my worthy servant, until then faithful and reliable, tried to take advantage of the opportunity that he thought these lonely places offered him, and, prompted more by his own wickedness than by my beauty, and bereft of all shame, fear of God and respect for me, he asked me for my love; and when he found that I responded to his insolence with just contempt, he abandoned the entreaties with which he'd thought he'd have his way, and turned to violence. But righteous heaven, which seldom if ever fails to watch over and favour good intentions, favoured mine, and with the little strength I have, and yet with little difficulty, I pushed him over a precipice, where I left him, whether dead or alive I don't know. And then, faster than could have been expected from my consternation and exhaustion, I made my way into these mountains, with no other thought or plan than to hide here from my father and from those whom he'd sent to look for me.

'I don't know how many months ago it was that I arrived here with this idea and came across a herdsman who took me as his servant to a village in the depths of the sierra, and I've been working for him as a herdboy all this time, always trying to stay out in the open so as to hide these locks of mine that have now so unexpectedly betrayed me. But all my cunning and all my precautions were futile, because my master found out that I'm not a man, and was seized with the same wicked desire as my servant; and since fortune doesn't always send the evil complete with its remedy, I couldn't find any precipice or ravine where I could put my master out of his misery, as I had my servant; and what seemed to be the lesser evil was to run away and hide once more in these wilds, rather than try my strength or my pretexts against him. So, as I said, I took to the forest again to look for a spot where I could, unhindered, implore heaven with sighs and tears to take pity on my plight, and grant me help and strength either to escape from it or to end my life in this wilderness, so that no memory remains of an unhappy creature who, through no fault of her own, must have provided grist for gossip in the place where she lives, and all around.'

CHAPTER XXIX

Concerning the beautiful Dorotea's intelligence and other delightful and entertaining matters

'This, gentlemen, is the true history of my tragedy. Now you must judge whether you mightn't have expected even more sighs than you have listened to, even more words than you have heard, even more tears than have fallen from my eyes; and, if you consider the nature of my misfortune, you'll see that consolation is futile, because there is no possible remedy. All I beg of you – and it's something that you can easily do, and should do – is to tell me where I can spend my life without being tormented by my dread of being found by those who are looking for me; because although I know that my parents' deep love is an assurance of a kind welcome from them, I'm filled with such shame just to think that I must appear before them so different from how they had taken me to be, that I prefer to banish myself for ever from their sight rather than look them in the face in the knowledge that they see me deprived of the purity that they must have expected me to defend.'

She fell silent, and her face was suffused with a colour that showed the suffering and the shame in her soul. Those who had been listening to her felt in their own souls as much pity as amazement at her misfortune, and, although the priest was about to console and counsel her, Cardenio took the initiative and said:

'And so you're the lovely Dorotea, the only daughter of wealthy Clenardo?'

Dorotea was astonished to hear her father's name spoken by such a low fellow – Cardenio's dress has already been described. So she said:

'And who might you be, my good man, to know my father's name? If I remember rightly, I have not mentioned it once in the whole course of my tale of woe.'

'I, madam,' replied Cardenio, 'am that unfortunate man to whom, as you have told us, Luscinda said she was married. I am the unhappy Cardenio, whom the villainy of the person who has reduced you to your present state has left as you can see me, clothed in rags, half naked, deprived of all human consolation and, what is worst of all, deprived of my reason, because I only enjoy its use when heaven sees fit to let me have it for a while. I, Dorotea, am the man who witnessed the wrong done me by Don Fernando, the man who stopped to hear Luscinda say "I will." I am the man who lacked the courage to wait to see how her fainting fit ended, or what were the consequences of the discovery of the note in her bodice, because my heart couldn't bear so much misfortune all at once; and so I abandoned patience and I abandoned her house, and I left a letter with someone with whom I'd often stayed, asking him to place it in Luscinda's hands, and I came away to these empty places, intending to end my life, which I hated from that moment as my mortal enemy. But fate wouldn't deprive me of it, and was content to deprive me of my senses, perhaps to save me for the good fortune of meeting you; because if everything that you have said is true, as I believe it is, it might even be that heaven has in store for us a happier ending to our misfortunes than we think. For given that Luscinda can't marry Don Fernando, because she's mine, and he can't marry her, because he's yours, as she has made perfectly clear, we can well hope that heaven will restore to us what is ours, because it's all still valid, it hasn't been alienated or damaged. And since we do have this consolation, not born of remote hopes, nor founded on wild imaginings, I entreat you, madam, to reconsider your original decision, as I shall mine, and prepare yourself to expect better fortune; for I swear by the faith of a gentleman and a Christian that I won't forsake you until I see you married to Don Fernando, and that, if I can't persuade him with arguments to acknowledge what he owes you, I will make use of the privilege to which every gentleman is entitled, and demand satisfaction for the wrong he has done you, setting aside the injuries he has done me, the avenging of which I leave to heaven so as to be able to attend to yours here on earth.'

Cardenio's words completed Dorotea's amazement and, not knowing how to thank him for such generous offers, she tried to seize his feet and kiss them, but he wouldn't allow it, and the priest replied on her behalf as well as his own and praised Cardenio's good thinking; and he particularly begged, advised and encouraged them to return with him to his village, where they would be able to stock up with all they needed, and where a method could be devised for finding Don Fernando, or restoring Dorotea to her parents, or doing whatever seemed best. Cardenio and Dorotea thanked him and accepted his kind offer. The barber, who had remained in silent bewilderment throughout, also spoke some fine words and offered with no less goodwill than the priest to serve them in whatever way he could. He went on to give them a brief account of what had brought him and his friend there, of Don Quixote's strange madness, and of how they were waiting for his squire, who'd gone in search of him. Cardenio recalled, as if from a dream, his fight with Don Quixote, and told the others about it, but he couldn't say what the cause of their disagreement had been.

And now they heard a shout and realized that it came from Sancho Panza, who, not finding them where he'd left them, was calling out to them. They went to meet him and in answer to their enquiries about Don Quixote he said he'd found him dressed only in his shirt, skinny, pale and half dead with hunger, and sighing for his lady Dulcinea; and that although he'd told him that she'd ordered him to leave that place and go back to El Toboso, where she was waiting for him, he'd replied that he was resolved not to appear before her beauteousness until such time as he should have performed such exploits as would render him worthy of her favour. And if all that palaver went on much longer, he was running the risk of never getting to be an emperor, as he damn well should, or even an archbishop, which was the least you could expect. So they had to put a scheme together to get him out of there.

The priest replied that Sancho mustn't worry – they would indeed get him out of there, whether he liked it or not. Then the priest told Cardenio and Dorotea about the plan for curing Don Quixote, or at least taking him back home. To which Dorotea replied that she could play the damsel in distress better than the barber, and, what was more, she had with her some clothes for making her performance totally convincing, and they could trust her to play the role precisely as was necessary for success in their plans, because she'd read lots of books of chivalry and knew exactly how damsels in distress turned their hands to begging favours of knights errant.

'Well, all we have to do now,' said the priest, 'is to put the plan into action without delay: fortune's clearly on my side, because a door has begun to open so unexpectedly to a solution to your problems, my friends, and the door that we needed has also been provided.'

Dorotea now took out of her pillow-case a frock of fine camlet and a bright green shawl, and out of a casket a necklace and other jewels, and in an instant she put them on and looked like a rich, fine lady. She said she'd brought all this and more from home, to provide for any eventuality, but hadn't needed to use it yet. They were all charmed by her grace, elegance and loveliness, and convinced that Don Fernando was a man of little judgement to reject such a beauty. But the person who was most amazed was Sancho Panza, because he thought, and he was right, that in all the days of his born life he'd never seen such a lovely creature; so he begged the priest to tell him who that very beauteous lady was, and what she was looking for in those God-forsaken parts.

'This beautiful lady, brother Sancho,' replied the priest, 'is no less a personage than the heiress in the direct male line of the great kingdom of Micomicón, and she's come in search of your master to beg a boon of him: that he would redress a wrong and grievance done unto her by an evil giant; and, attracted by the fame as an excellent knight that your master has conquered over the entire face of the earth, this princess has travelled here all the way from Guinea to find him.'

'That's good searching and good finding,' Sancho Panza interrupted, 'and even better if my master's lucky enough to redress that grievance and right that wrong by killing that bastard of a giant you just mentioned, and he will kill him if he catches up with him, so long as he isn't a ghost that is, because my master can't cope with ghosts. But there's just one thing I'd like to ask you to do, reverend sir, among others, so as to stop my master from getting the urge to become an archbishop, which is what I'm most frightened of – advise him to marry this here princess straight away, and then he won't be allowed to take archbishop's orders and then it'll be easy for him to get his empire and for me to get everything I want, because I've looked into it and I've worked out that it won't suit me for my master to be an archbishop, because I'm useless to the Church, being as I am married, and to go getting dispensations to let me have a living, with a wife and children and all, would be an endless job. So you see, sir, everything hangs on my master marrying that lady right away – nobody's told me what her name is yet, so I can't call her by it.'

'Her name,' replied the priest, 'is the Princess Micomicona, as indeed it would be, seeing that her kingdom is called Micomicón.'

'You're right there,' replied Sancho, 'because I've often known people to take their surnames from the towns where they were born, and call themselves Pedro de Alcalá, Juan de Úbeda, Diego de Valladolid and the like, and they must do the same in Guinea – queens taking their names from their kingdoms, I mean.'

'That must indeed be so,' said the priest, 'and as for your master's marrying, I shall do everything in my power to bring it about.'

This left Sancho as content as the priest was amazed at his simplicity and at the hold his master's nonsenses had taken of his imagination, because Sancho really did believe that Don Quixote was going to become an emperor.

By now Dorotea had mounted the priest's mule and the barber had stuck the ox-tail beard on to his face, and they told Sancho to lead them to Don Quixote, and warned him not to reveal that he knew the priest or the barber, because his master's becoming an emperor depended on his not recognizing them. But neither the priest nor Cardenio would go with them, because Cardenio didn't want Don Quixote to remember their fight, and the priest's presence wasn't needed yet. So they sent the others on ahead and followed slowly on foot. The priest didn't omit to tell Dorotea what she had to do, to which she replied that they needn't worry, everything would be done exactly right, just as the chivalry books described and demanded.

They'd have gone a couple of miles when they caught sight of Don Quixote amidst a maze of rocks, wearing his clothes now but not his armour; and as soon as Dorotea saw him and was informed by Sancho who he was, she whipped her palfrey onwards, followed by the bushy-bearded barber. When they reached Don Quixote, the squire sprang from his mule and ran to help Dorotea to dismount, and she did so most gracefully and fell on her knees before the knees of Don Quixote; and although he was striving to bring her to her feet she remained kneeling, and spake thus:

'I will not arise from this spot, O valorous and redoubtable knight, until your benevolence and courtesy vouchsafe me a boon that will redound to the honour and glory of your person and to the weal of the most disconsolate and aggrieved damsel that ever the sun beheld. And if it be that the strength of your formidable arm is correspondent to the voice of your immortal fame, you are obliged to favour this unhappy damsel who comes from far distant lands, attracted by the odour of your celebrated name, to seek from you a remedy for her woes.'

'I will not answer you one word, most beauteous lady,' answered Don Quixote, 'nor will I hear one circumstance more of your affairs, until you arise from the ground.'

'I will not arise, sir,' replied the damsel in distress, 'ere of your courtesy the boon I crave is first vouchsafed me.'

'I do indeed vouchsafe and grant it you,' replied Don Quixote, 'provided that it does not lead me to act to the detriment or disservice of my king, my country or her who holds the key of my heart and my liberty.'

'It is not to the detriment or disservice of any of those you've just mentioned, my good sir,' replied the doleful damsel.

And at this point Sancho Panza sidled up to his master and muttered in his ear:

'You can easily grant her this here boon she's craving, sir, it isn't anything special, only killing some enormous giant, and this here woman craving it is the high-up princess Micomicona, the queen of the great kingdom of Micomicón in Ethiopia.'

'Whosoever she may be,' replied Don Quixote, 'I will do my duty, as my conscience dictates, in conformity to what I have professed.'

And turning to the damsel, he said:

'Arise, arise, most beauteous lady, for I vouchsafe whatever boon you may wish to crave of me.'

'Well, what it is I'm craving,' said the damsel, 'is that your magnanimous person will come with me right now to where I'm going to take you, and will promise not to get involved in any other adventure or similar activity until you've taken vengeance for me on a traitor who, flouting all human and divine law, has usurped my kingdom.'

'I repeat that I do vouchsafe it,' replied Don Quixote, 'and so you can, my lady, from this day forward, dispel the melancholy that oppresses you, and allow your fainting hopes to gain fresh strength and vigour; for, with God's help and that of my arm, you shall soon see yourself restored to your kingdom and seated on the throne of your ancient and high estate, in spite and in defiance of all the wretches who would gainsay it. And let us set to work forthwith; for, as the saying goes, delays are dangerous.'

The damsel in distress strove and struggled to kiss his hands, but Don

Quixote, always a gallant and courteous knight, would by no means consent to this; on the contrary, he brought her to her feet and embraced her with great courtesy and gallantry, and he ordered Sancho to check Rocinante's girths and to arm him without a moment's delay. Sancho took the armour down from the tree on which it was hanging like some trophy, checked the nag's girths and in an instant slipped the armour on to his master, who said:

'Let us go from hence in God's name to succour this great lady.'

The barber was still on his knees, at great pains to smother his laughter and to stop his beard from falling off, which could have put paid to all their fine plans; and seeing that the boon had been granted and that Don Quixote was preparing so diligently to go and keep his word, he stood up and offered his free hand to his lady, and the two men helped her on to the mule. Then Don Quixote climbed on to Rocinante, and the barber settled himself on his mount, and Sancho was left on his feet, a predicament that renewed his grief for the loss of his dun; but he bore it all with good cheer because he considered that his master was at last well on the way to being an emperor, indeed right on the verge of it, because he was definitely going to marry that princess and become, at the very least, the King of Micomicón. He was only worried by the thought that this kingdom was in the land of negroes and that all the people he was going to be given as vassals would be black, but his imagination soon worked out a good solution, as he said to himself:

'Who cares if my vassals are negroes? All I'll have to do is ship them over here to Spain, sell them for hard cash, buy myself a title or some official position or other, and live at my ease for the rest of my days. Oh yes, I'm going to be caught napping, I am, and I won't have the wit or the savvy to see to things and sell thirty or ten thousand vassals in the twinkling of an eye, I won't! By God I'll shift them, as a job lot or however I can, and they can be as black as they like, I'll soon turn them into yellow gold and white silver! Come on, come on, I'm an innocent little thumb-sucker, I am!'

He was so engrossed in these thoughts, and so happy with them, that he forgot all about the distress of having to walk.

Cardenio and the priest were watching this scene from behind some bushes, wondering how they could contrive to join company with the others, but the priest was a great schemer and soon thought of a way: he took a pair of scissors out of their case and whipped Cardenio's beard off, and dressed him in a pale brown cape that the priest had been wearing, and also gave him his black cloak, which left the priest in his doublet and hose; and the transformation of Cardenio was such that he wouldn't have known himself if he'd looked in a mirror. Although the others had ridden on while Cardenio and the priest had been disguising themselves, it was easy for these two to reach the highway first, because the undergrowth and the uneven surface made the progress of riders slower than that of walkers. So they waited on the plain where it joins the sierra and, as soon as Don Quixote and his companions emerged, the priest stood gazing at him, indicating that he thought he knew him, and after a good long look he hurried over with open arms, crying:

'Well met, well met, O mirror of chivalry, my good neighbour Don Quixote de la Mancha, the very flower of politeness, the succour of the needy, the quintessence of knights errant!'

While he said this he was embracing the left knee of Don Quixote, who, astonished at what he was seeing and hearing the man say and do, peered down at him and eventually recognized him, and was full of wonder when he did so, and struggled to dismount; but the priest wouldn't let him, which led Don Quixote to say:

'Pray permit me to alight, sir, for it is not fit that I should be on horseback while so reverend a person as you is on foot.'

'I will by no means consent to that,' said the priest. 'You stay on your horse, for on your horse you carry out the greatest exploits and adventures that our age has ever beheld, and for me, although an unworthy priest, it will be enough to get up behind one of these gentlemen riding with you on their mules, if it isn't too much trouble for them. And it will even seem to me as if I'm prancing along on the steed Pegasus, or on the zebra or warhorse of the famous Moor Muzaraque, who lies to this day enchanted on the great hill of Zulema, not far from the splendid town of Compluto.'[1]

'That solution had not occurred to me, reverend sir,' replied Don Quixote, 'and I know that my lady the princess will, for my sake, be glad to order her squire to accommodate you on the saddle of his mule, and he shall ride behind you, so long as the mule can withstand it.'

'Yes, it can, I think,' replied the princess, 'and I know that I shan't need to order my dear squire to do this, because he's so courteous, not to say courtly, that he won't allow a man of the cloth to walk when he can ride.'

'Quite right,' replied the barber.

And alighting in an instant he offered his saddle to the priest, who accepted it without having to be asked a second time. But the problem was that as the barber was clambering up on to the crupper, the mule, a hired one, which is the same as saying a bad one, reared its hind quarters and sent its back legs flying in the air, and if it had sent them at Master Nicolás's chest or head he'd have sent Don Quixote and their trip to fetch him to the devil. Master Nicolás was so frightened that he tumbled to the ground, taking so little care of his beard that it fell off, and when he noticed his beardlessness all he could think of doing was to clutch both hands to his face and cry out that his teeth had been kicked in. When Don Quixote saw that hank of beard-hair, bloodlessly detached from its jaw and lying far from the fallen squire, he said:

'Good God, this is indeed a great miracle! The mule has plucked his beard clean from his face, just as if it had been shaved off!'

The priest, seeing that his plot was at risk of being discovered, snatched up the beard, hurried with it to where Master Nicolás lay still moaning, clasped the barber's head to his breast and stuck the beard back in place as he muttered some words that he described as a certain spell for beard-reattachment, as they would soon see; and having performed this operation he stepped aside, and the squire was as whole and as bearded as before, which astonished Don Quixote, who begged the priest to teach him the spell as soon as he had a moment to spare, for he reasoned that its power must extend beyond beard-reattachment since it was obvious that where a beard had been ripped off the flesh must be left torn and raw: so, since the spell had brought about a complete cure, it followed that it wasn't only good for beards.

'Quite right,' said the priest, and then promised to teach it to him at the earliest opportunity.

They all agreed that the priest would ride the mule to begin with and that the three of them would take turns on it until they reached the inn, which must be a half-a-dozen miles away. So with three of them mounted (Don Quixote, the princess and the priest) and three of them on foot (Cardenio, the barber and Sancho Panza) Don Quixote said to the damsel:

'My lady: Your Highness must direct us whithersoever it most pleases you to go.'

Before she could reply, the priest said:

'Towards which kingdom does Your Excellency wish to direct us? Is it, perchance, the kingdom of Micomicón? I think it must be, or else I am a poor judge of kingdoms.'

She knew what she was doing and understood that it was up to her to agree, so she said:

'Yes, sir, my way lies towards that kingdom.'

'If that's the case,' said the priest, 'we shall pass through my home town, and from there you must head towards Cartagena, where you can embark, all being well; and if there's a favourable wind, a calm sea and no storms, in a little less than nine years you might be in sight of the great Urinals I mean Urals, which are slightly more than one hundred days' journey on this side of Your Highness's kingdom.'

'No, you are mistaken, my dear sir,' she said, 'because I left there not two years ago and I haven't really had any fine weather at all; but despite all that, I have succeeded in seeing what I so longed to see – Don Quixote de la Mancha, the news of whose deeds reached my ears as soon as I set foot in Spain and encouraged me to come in search of him to commend myself to his courtesy and commit my just cause to the might of his invincible arm.'

'That is quite enough: no more praise of me,' said Don Quixote, 'for I hate all flattery and, even if this is not flattery, such talk still offends my chaste ears. What I can say, my lady, is that whether I am mighty or not, such might as I do or do not possess shall be employed in your service even unto death; and now, leaving all that aside until later, I would beg you, reverend sir, to tell me what has brought you into these parts alone, without servants, and so lightly clad that you quite alarm me.'

'My reply will be brief,' the priest replied. 'You must know, sir, that I was on my way with Master Nicolás, our friend and barber, to Seville to collect some money sent me by a relative who settled in South America many years ago – no inconsiderable sum, in fact it was more than sixty thousand pesos in pure silver bars, worth double that amount once alloyed and coined; and yesterday, as we were riding through these parts, four highwaymen waylaid us and literally fleeced us; and so, finding himself without a beard, the barber thought it better to wear a false one, and they even left this young fellow here' (pointing to Cardenio) 'in the state in which you see him. And the best part of it is that everybody in these parts is saying that the men who attacked us were from a chain-gang that's said to have been released, almost on this very spot, by a man who's so brave that, in spite of the sergeant and the guards, he freed them all; and there can't be the slightest doubt that the fellow must be out of his mind, or perhaps he's another villain as bad as them, or someone without a soul or a conscience, letting the wolf loose among the sheep, the fox among the chickens, the fly among the honeycombs. He has defrauded justice and flown in the face of his king and natural lord, because he has flouted his king's just commands. He has, furthermore, robbed the galleys of their engines and disturbed the Holy Brotherhood, which had been reposing for many years. And he has done a deed that will lose him his soul and gain nothing for his body.'

Sancho had told the priest and the barber all about the adventure of the convicts, brought to such a glorious conclusion by his master, and this was why the priest had now laid it on so thick, to see what Don Quixote would do and say: his colour changed with every word, but he didn't dare admit that he had been those good people's liberator.

'These, then,' said the priest, 'were the men who robbed us. May God in his infinite mercy forgive whoever it was that prevented them from being taken to the punishment that they deserved.'

CHAPTER XXX

✣

Concerning the amusing and ingenious plan to extricate our enamoured knight from the cruel penance that he had imposed upon himself

The priest had hardly finished speaking when Sancho said:

'Well by my faith, reverend sir, the one who did that there deed was my master, and not for any want of me warning him to be careful what he was getting up to, and telling him it was a sin to set them free, because they were all there for being terrible villains.'

'You blockhead!' exploded Don Quixote. 'It is not the responsibility of knights errant to discover whether the afflicted, the enchained and the oppressed whom they encounter on the road are reduced to these circumstances and suffer this distress for their vices, or for their virtues: the knight's sole responsibility is to succour them as people in need, having eyes only for their sufferings, not for their misdeeds. I came across a rosary of angry, wretched men, I did with them what my religion requires of me, and nothing else is any concern of mine; and to anyone who thinks ill of it – saving, reverend sir, your holy dignity and honourable person – I say that he is no judge of matters of chivalry, and that he is lying like a bastard and a son of a whore, and I swear by my gospel-oath that I will make him acknowledge this with my sword, at length and in extenso.'

As he said this he steadied himself in his stirrups and pulled his steel cap down tight, because the barber's basin, which in his reckoning was Mambrino's helmet, was hanging from the pommel of his saddle, awaiting repair after its maltreatment by the convicts. Dorotea was sharp-witted and full of fun, she knew all about Don Quixote's strange turns and that everyone was teasing him except Sancho Panza, and she didn't want to be left out, so seeing that he was in a temper she said:

'Sir knight, pray remember the boon that you have granted me and remember, too, that by its terms you cannot become involved in any other adventure, however urgent it may be; so calm your breast, for if the priest had known that it was your unconquered arm that freed the convicts, he would have put three stitches through his lips and would even have bitten his tongue three times rather than utter a single word that redounded to your disparagement.'

'I swear that's true,' said the priest, 'and I'd have pulled half my moustache off as well.'

'I will be silent, my lady,' said Don Quixote, 'and repress the just indignation that had risen in my breast, and I will ride with you in the utmost peace and quiet until I have accomplished the promised boon; but in return for my firm resolve I entreat you to tell me, if it is not too grievous for you, what is your woe and how many, who and of what sort are the people on whom I am, on your behalf, to take due, sufficient and complete revenge.'

'I'll be happy to do so,' replied Dorotea, 'so long as it doesn't bother you to hear about afflictions and misfortunes.'

'Not at all, my lady,' replied Don Quixote.

To which Dorotea answered:

'That being so, will you all give me your attention, please?'

She hadn't finished saying this when Cardenio and the barber hurried to her side, eager to hear how this quick-witted woman would go about making up her story, and so did Sancho, as fully taken in by her as his master. And once she'd made herself comfortable in her saddle and prepared herself by coughing and taking other preliminary precautions, she began to make merry:

'First of all, I'd like you to know, gentlemen, that my name is . . .'

And here she hesitated, because she'd forgotten the name with which the priest had christened her; but realizing what the trouble was he came to the rescue and said:

'It is no wonder, my lady, that Your Highness should be overcome by confusion and embarrassment as you relate your misfortunes, for their ravages often deprive victims of their memory to such an extent that they cannot even remember their own names, as has just happened to Your Majesty, who has forgotten that your name is Princess Micomicona, the legitimate heiress to the great kingdom of Micomicón; and with the help of this prompting Your Highness will now, no doubt, be able to recall to your buffeted memory everything you wish to tell us.'

'Right you are,' replied the damsel, 'and I don't think any more prompting's going to be needed for me to sail the flagship of my true history to a safe harbour. My father, the King, whose name was Tinacrio the Sage,[1] was very learned in what are named the magic arts, and he divined that my mother, whose name was Queen Jaramilla, was going to die before him, and that a little after that he too would depart this life and I'd be left an orphan. But he used to say that this didn't worry him as much as having discovered for a certain fact that an enormous giant, the lord of a big island almost bordering on our kingdom, whose name is Pandafilando of the Grim Visage, because it's a well-known fact that, although his eyes are perfectly normal, he always looks at you skew-whiff, as if he was cross-eyed, and he does this out of spite and to strike fear and terror into those he's looking at . . . I was saying that my father found out that as soon as this giant knew I was an orphan he was going to invade my kingdom at the head of a great army and take it from me, without leaving me so much as a tiny village to retire to, but that I could avoid all this ruin and disaster if I agreed to marry him; yet my father's understanding of the matter was that I would never agree to so ill-assorted a match, and in this he was quite right, because it has never even occurred to me to marry that giant, or any other, however vast and enormous he might be. My father also said that when, after his death, I saw that Pandafilando was beginning to invade my kingdom, I shouldn't stay to defend it, because that would be my ruin, but that I should let him have it without offering any resistance, if I wanted to avoid the death and total destruction of my good and loyal subjects, because I wasn't going to be able to defend myself against the giant's diabolical power. Instead I should set out immediately with a few followers for Spain, where I'd find the solution to my troubles as soon as I found a knight errant whose fame would have extended by this time over the whole kingdom and whose name would be, if I remember rightly, Don Biscuit, or Don Fixit, or Don Riskit.'

'Don Quixote he must have said, lady,' Sancho interrupted, 'also known as the Knight of the Sorry Face.'

'Right you are,' said Dorotea. 'And my father said something else, too: that this knight would be tall and thin-faced and that on the right side of his body under his left shoulder-blade, or thereabouts, he'd have a brown mole with long stiff hairs growing out of it.'

When Don Quixote heard this he said to his squire:

'Here, Sancho my son, help me to undress – I want to see if I am the knight that the wise king prophesied.'

'But why get undressed?' asked Dorotea.

'To see whether I bear the mole to which your father referred,' replied Don Quixote.

'There isn't any need for you to get undressed,' said Sancho, 'I know you've got a mole just like that halfway down your backbone, the sign of a strong man.'

'That's enough for me,' said Dorotea, 'there isn't any call to bother about such trifles among friends, and who cares whether it's on his shoulder or on his backbone – he's got a mole, and that's all that matters, wherever it is, because it's all the same flesh; and it's clear that my good father was right in everything he prophesied, and that I am right to put myself in the hands of Don Quixote, who is definitely the man my father said, because his face, at least, exactly matches what is trumpeted about this knight not only in Spain but throughout the length and breadth of La Mancha – no sooner had I landed at Osuna than I heard accounts of so many deeds of his that my heart told me straight away that this was the very man I was looking for.'

'But how could you have landed at Osuna, my lady?' asked Don Quixote. 'Osuna is not on the sea.'

Before Dorotea could reply, the priest stepped in:

'The Princess must mean that after she had landed at Malaga, the first place where she heard about you was Osuna.'

'Yes, that's what I meant,' said Dorotea.

'And that's more like it,' said the priest, 'and do continue, Your Majesty.'

'There's nothing more to say,' replied Dorotea, 'except that now I've had the great good fortune to find Don Quixote, I already look upon myself as queen and mistress of all my kingdom, for he, in his courtesy and magnificence, has granted me my boon and will go with me wherever I take him, and that will be to where he'll find himself face to face with Pandafilando of the Grim Visage, so that he can kill him and restore to me what has been so wrongfully usurped; and all this is going to work out to a T, because it's what my good father Tinacrio the Sage prophesied, and he also left it written in Chaldean or Greek letters that I can't read that if this knight in his prophecy, once he'd slit the giant's throat, wanted to marry me, I must immediately and without demur submit to be his lawful wife, and give him possession of my kingdom and my person.'

'What do you think now, friend Sancho?' Don Quixote exclaimed. 'Did you hear that? Did I not tell you so? You see, now we have our kingdom to reign over and our queen to marry!'

'I should damn well say so,' said Sancho, 'and the devil take the bugger that wouldn't marry her as soon as old Pandoflando's gullet's slit! And she's a bit of all right, she is, the Queen! I wouldn't complain if the fleas in my bed were like her!'

And as he said this he showed how delighted he was by leaping into the air a couple of times and slapping his shoe as he did so, and then he grasped the reins of Dorotea's mule to make it stop, threw himself to his knees before her and begged her to let him kiss her hands to show that he accepted her as his queen and mistress. How could the onlookers have failed to laugh as they witnessed the madness of the master and the simplicity of the servant? Dorotea held out her hands and promised to make him a great lord in her kingdom, as soon as heaven was so benevolent as to put her back in possession of it. Sancho expressed his thanks in words that sent them into fresh fits of laughter.

'This, gentlemen,' Dorotea continued, 'is my history. It only remains for me to tell you that of all the attendants I brought with me from my kingdom I have none left except this well-bearded squire, because the others drowned in a violent storm that overtook us within sight of harbour, and by some miracle he and I reached shore on a couple of planks; and indeed the whole of my life has been one great miracle or mystery, as you all must have noticed. And if I have been in any way immoderate, or have been less exact than I might, you must blame that on what the priest said at the beginning of my story: continual and extraordinary travails affect the memory of the person suffering them.'

'Mine will not be affected, O great and worthy lady,' said Don Quixote, 'by whatever travails I undergo in your service, however severe and unprecedented they may be; and so I again confirm the boon that I have vouchsafed you, and I promise to go with you to the end of the world until I confront your fierce enemy, whose haughty head, by the help of God and this arm, I shall cut off with the blade of this . . . I cannot say good sword, thanks to Ginés de Pasamonte, who stole mine from me.'

He muttered these last few words to himself, and continued:

'And after I have cut it off and restored you to the peaceful possession of your realm, it shall be left to your own will to dispose of your person according to your pleasure; because so long as my memory is pervaded, my will enslaved, my understanding enthralled, by that . . . I say no more . . . , it is impossible for me even to contemplate marriage, even if it were to the Phoenix itself!'[2]

Sancho was so outraged by what Don Quixote had just said about not marrying that he cried out in fury:

'Damn and confound it all, Don Quixote sir, you can't be in your right mind! How can you have any doubts about marrying a high-up princess like this one? Do you think fortune's going to be offering you a stroke of luck like this round every corner you turn? Is my fine lady Dulcinea better-looking by any chance? No, of course she isn't, not by a long chalk, and I'd even go so far as to say that she can't hold a candle to this lady here. A fat chance I have of getting my earldom if you go reaching for the stars like that. Get married, get married as soon as you can, in the name of Satan, and grab that kingdom that's falling into your hands without you having to lift a finger, and once you're king make me a marquis or a governor – and then the whole show can go to the devil!'

Don Quixote couldn't bear to hear such blasphemies uttered against his lady Dulcinea and without one word of warning he raised his pike and dealt Sancho two blows that flattened him; and if Dorotea hadn't cried out to him to stop, he'd have ended his squire's life there and then.

'Do you imagine, you villainous wretch,' he said after a while, 'that you can always be cocking a snook at me, sir, and that we shall go on for ever like this with you misbehaving and me forgiving? Well, do not imagine it, you damned rogue; and indeed you are damned, for defaming the peerless Dulcinea. And do you not realize, you layabout, you miscreant, you brute, that if it were not for the might that she infuses into my arm I should not have the strength to kill a flea? Tell me, you viper-tongued scoffer, what do you think has conquered this kingdom and cut off this giant's head and made you into a marquis (I take all this for granted as if seen and approved, of course) but the might of Dulcinea, using my arm as the instrument for its exploits? In me she does battle and conquers, and in her I live and breathe and have my being.[3] O you villain, you bastard, what ingratitude you show: you find yourself raised up from the dust of the earth to be made a titled lord, and you repay such kindness by maligning your benefactress!'

Sancho's beating hadn't been severe enough to prevent him from hearing everything his master said, and he got up rather nimbly and positioned himself behind Dorotea's palfrey, from where he added:

'Just you tell me this, sir: if you've decided not to marry this great princess, it's clear the kingdom won't be yours, and if the kingdom isn't yours what favours can you do me? That's all I'm concerned about. Marry the queen, marry the queen, do, now that we've got her here heaven-sent out of the blue, and then afterwards you can go back to my lady Dulcinea – there must have been kings before now who've had a bit on the side. As for their beauty, I won't poke my nose into that, but to tell you the truth, if I've got to, they both seem all right to me, though I've never seen the lady Dulcinea.'

'How can you say that you have never seen her, you blasphemous traitor?' said Don Quixote. 'Have you not just brought me a message from her?'

'I mean I've never examined her so very closely,' said Sancho, 'as to see in detail how lovely she is, and size up her fair features one by one. But she looks all right to me, on the whole.'

'Now I can excuse you,' said Don Quixote, 'and you must forgive me for the annoyance I have caused you: man's first impulses are beyond his control.'

'I can see that all right,' replied Sancho, 'and as for me, my first impulse is always to talk, and I can't help saying, once over at least, whatever comes into my head.'

'All the same,' said Don Quixote, 'you had better be careful what you say, Sancho, because the pitcher goes so often to the well . . . I need say no more.'

'All right,' said Sancho, 'but God's up there in heaven, and he sees what we get up to, and he'll be the judge of who's worse – me for not being careful what I say, or you for not being careful what you do.'

'That's enough of that, now,' said Dorotea. 'Come on, Sancho, kiss your master's hand, and beg his forgiveness, and from now on do try to be more judicious with your praise and your condemnation; and don't speak ill of that lady Tobosa, of whom all I know is that I am her humble servant, and place your faith in God, who won't fail to provide you with an estate on which you can live like a prince.'

Sancho went up to his master with his head bowed and asked for his hand, which his master gave him with tranquil solemnity, and after Sancho had kissed it his master blessed him and said that he would like the two of them to move on a little ahead of the others, because he had some matters of great importance to ask about and discuss. Sancho did as he was told and the pair went on a short way in front, and Don Quixote said:

'I have not had an opportunity since your return to enquire about many interesting particulars concerning your mission and the reply that you brought back; and, now that fortune has granted us that opportunity, do not refuse to give me the happiness that your good news can bring me.'

'You go ahead and ask whatever you like,' replied Sancho, 'I found my way in and I'll find my way out. But please, sir, don't be so vindictive from now on.'

'Why do you say that, Sancho?' asked Don Quixote.

'I say that,' Sancho replied, 'because the beating you just gave me had more to do with the quarrel that the devil sparked off between us the other night than with what I said about my lady Dulcinea, who I love and revere like a relic although of course she's nothing of the sort, just because she's yours.'

'For goodness sake do not harp on that conversation, Sancho,' said Don Quixote. 'It is very upsetting for me. I have forgiven you for all that, but you know the saying: for a new sin a new penance.'

As they talked they saw a man riding a donkey towards them along the road, and when he came closer they thought he was a gipsy. Whenever Sancho Panza saw a donkey he riveted his eyes and soul on it; so as soon as he could take a good look at this man he realized that it was Ginés de Pasamonte; and putting two and two together he concluded that it was his own dun that Pasamonte was riding – and he was right. To avoid recognition and to sell the ass, the convict had dressed himself in gipsy clothes, because he could speak Romany, as he could speak many other languages, like a native. But Sancho did recognize him, as soon as he saw him, and he cried:

'Hey, Ginesillo, you thief! Leave my dearest alone, free my heart's content, unload the comfort of my life, leave my donkey be, leave my beauty alone! Clear off you bugger, go away you robber and give up what isn't yours!'

There wasn't any need for so many insults, because as soon as Ginés heard the first of them he jumped off the donkey and departed at a lively trot that might almost have been taken for a gallop, and in an instant he was far away.

Sancho went to his dun, and as he embraced it he said:

'And how have you been, my sweet, my darling dun, my boon companion?'

And he kissed it and caressed it as if it were a human being. The ass quietly accepted the kisses and the caresses without offering a word in reply. The others came and congratulated Sancho on finding his dun, in particular Don Quixote, who added that this wouldn't cause him to revoke his warrant for the three donkeys. Sancho thanked him for his generosity.

While the two of them were talking away like this, the priest told Dorotea that she'd put on an intelligent performance in the way she'd invented the story, kept it brief and made it follow the pattern of the books of chivalry. She said that she'd often whiled away the time reading such books, but didn't know where the different provinces and seaports were, and that was why she'd had to guess the bit about landing at Osuna.

'That's what I thought,' said the priest, 'and why I butted in to say what I did, and put things right. But isn't it extraordinary how this unfortunate hidalgo believes all these lies and fictions, just because they imitate the style and manner of the nonsense in his books?'

'Yes, it is strange,' said Cardenio, 'and the whole business is so weird and wonderful that I can't believe that if anyone wanted to invent such a story he'd be clever enough to do it.'

'And there's something else, too,' said the priest. 'If we leave aside the absurdities that the good hidalgo comes out with concerning his mania, in conversations on other subjects he talks with great good sense, and shows himself to have a clear and balanced judgement. So long as you don't get him going on his chivalry, nobody would say that he wasn't a man of excellent understanding.'

While they were engaged in this conversation, Don Quixote was continuing his with Sancho:

'Friend Panza, we must let bygones be bygones and forget about our quarrels, and now do tell me, leaving aside all anger and resentfulness: where, how and when did you find Dulcinea? What was she doing? What did you say to her? What did she reply? What look was on her face as she read my letter? Who copied it out for you? And tell me, too, everything else that you consider worth knowing, asking and answering; and you must not add anything or tell any lies to increase my pleasure, still less omit anything to detract from it.'

'To tell you the honest truth, sir,' replied Sancho, 'nobody copied the letter out, because I didn't have it on me.'

'Yes, it is just as you say,' replied Don Quixote, 'because two days after you had left I found the notebook in which I had written the letter, which caused me great sorrow because I did not know what you would do when you missed it; and I must say I thought you would return to me as soon as you did miss it.'

'And that's just what I would have done, too,' said Sancho, 'if I hadn't learned it by heart when you read it to me, so I repeated it to a sexton, who took it down from my memory so exactly that he said he'd never seen or read such a pretty letter in all the days of his born life, even though he'd read out lots and lots of letters of excommunication.'

'And do you still retain my letter in your memory, Sancho?' asked Don Quixote.

'No, sir,' replied Sancho, 'because once I'd said it to the sexton I could see it wasn't going to be of any more use, so I turned my mind to forgetting it. If there's anything I do remember it's that bit about your slobbered-on I mean sovereign lady and the ending, "Yours until death, The Knight of the Sorry Face". And in between I stuck more than three hundred darlings, dear hearts and lights of my eyes.'

CHAPTER XXXI

About the delectable conversation between Don Quixote
and his squire Sancho Panza, and other events

'All this does not displease me; do continue,' said Don Quixote. 'So you arrived; and what was that queen of beauty doing? No doubt you found her stringing pearls, or embroidering some emblem in gold thread for this her hapless knight.'

'All I found her doing,' said Sancho, 'was sieving a bushel or two of wheat in a yard.'

'Then you may well suppose,' said Don Quixote, 'that the grains of wheat became grains of pearl when touched by her hands. And did you look, my friend, to see whether it was white wheat or spring wheat?'

'Just buckwheat,' replied Sancho.

'Yet I can assure you,' said Don Quixote, 'that, sieved by her hands, it produced the finest white bread. But continue: when you gave her my letter, did she kiss it? Did she press it to her brow? Did she perform some similar ceremony worthy of such a letter, or what did she do?'

'When I went over to give it to her,' said Sancho, 'she was busy shaking a great sieveful of wheat, and she said: "Put the letter on top of that sack, love, I can't read it till I've done with this lot." '

'A wise lady!' said Don Quixote. 'That would have been so as to read it at her leisure, and savour it. Continue, Sancho: while she was about her task, what conversation passed between you? What did she ask you about me? And what did you reply to her? Come on, tell me everything, and do not omit the smallest detail.'

'She didn't ask any questions,' said Sancho, 'but I told her how as you were doing penance to serve her, naked from the waist up and stuck in these sierras like a savage, sleeping on the ground and ne'er at table eating bread or combing your beard, and crying, and cursing your fate.'

'You were wrong to say that I was cursing my fate,' said Don Quixote, 'because, on the contrary, I bless it and shall bless it all the days of my life, for having made me worthy to love so lofty a lady as Dulcinea del Toboso.'

'Yes,' replied Sancho, 'and she's so lofty I'll swear she's a good hands-breadth taller than me.'

'How do you know that, Sancho?' said Don Quixote. 'Did you measure yourself against her?'

'Yes,' said Sancho, 'and it happened like this – I went to help her load a sack of wheat on to a donkey, and we got so close to each other I could see she was more than a handsbreadth above me.'

'And truly,' exclaimed Don Quixote, 'the stature of her person is accom-panied and graced by a thousand million spiritual gifts! But you will not deny me one thing, Sancho: when you approached her did you not notice a certain Sabaean[1] perfume, an aromatic fragrance, some undefinable sweetness that I cannot find words to express? I mean some sort of odour that might have made you think you were in a shop in which expensive gloves were being sold?'

'All I can say,' said Sancho, 'is that I noticed a mannish kind of smell, and it must have been that she was working so hard she'd got a bit runny like, a bit sweaty.'

'No, it would not have been that,' replied Don Quixote. 'Rather you must have had a cold in the head, or have been smelling yourself, for I well know the aroma of that rose among thorns, that lily of the field, that liquid ambergris.'

'You could be right,' said Sancho. 'I've often noticed that same smell I thought was coming out of her highness the lady Dulcinea coming out of me, but that's no wonder, one devil's much the same as another.'

'Well then,' continued Don Quixote, 'she has finished sifting her wheat and sending it off to the mill. What did she do when she read the letter?'

'She didn't read the letter at all,' said Sancho, 'because she said she couldn't read or write, and instead she tore it up into little bits and told me she didn't want anyone to read it to her and have her secrets known all over the village, and it was enough with what I'd mentioned about your love and the special penance you were doing for her sake. And she ended up by telling me to tell you that she sent her kind regards, and was keener to see you than to write to you and, having received yours of this inst., she begged and ordered you to leave these wastelands and stop playing the fool and set off straight away for El Toboso, if nothing else of greater importance happened, because she wanted to see you so much. She had a good laugh when I told her you were called the Knight of the Sorry Face. I asked her if that Basque had gone to see her, and she said he had, and he was a decent enough sort. I asked her about the convicts, too, but she said she hadn't seen any of those yet.'

'So far so good,' said Don Quixote. 'But now tell me this: what jewel did she give you when you bade her farewell, to reward you for the news you had borne her from me? For it is a common and ancient custom among knights and ladies errant to make to squires, dwarfs and damsels – the ladies to the former and the knights to the latter – a gift of some rich jewel, in gratitude for their errand.'

'I don't doubt it for a moment, and it seems like a good idea to me. But it must have been in times gone by when they did that, and all they give nowadays must be a hunk of bread and cheese, because that's what my lady Dulcinea gave me, over the yard wall, when I said goodbye to her. And what's more it was sheep's cheese.'

'She is a most generous lady,' said Don Quixote, 'and if she did not give you a jewel set in gold it must have been because she did not have one on her at the time. But better late than never: I shall see her about it, and all will be put right. Do you know what it is that astonishes me, Sancho? It is that you seem to have flown there and back, because it has taken you little more than three days to go to El Toboso and return here, and El Toboso is more than a hundred miles away. Which leads me to believe that the wise sorcerer who is in charge of my affairs and who is on my side – because there is one, there has to be one, on pain of my not being a good knight errant – this sorcerer, I say, must have helped you on your way without your realizing it; for there are sages of this sort who take a knight errant sleeping in his bed and, without the faintest idea how it has happened, he wakes up the following morning more than three thousand miles away from where he fell asleep. And if it were not for this, knights errant would not be able to assist each other when in danger, as they do, all the time. One might be fighting in the mountains of Armenia with some monster or fierce ogre, or with another knight, having the worst of the battle and about to be killed, and when one least expects it – hey presto, along on a cloud or a chariot of fire comes another knight, one's friend, who had been in England a moment earlier, to help one and save one from certain death, and by nightfall he is back at his inn, enjoying his supper; and the one place is usually eight or ten thousand miles away from the other. And all this is achieved by the cunning and the wisdom of these wise enchanters who look after these worthy knights. And so it is, friend Sancho, that I do not find it difficult to believe that in so short a time you have travelled to El Toboso and back again because, as I said, some friendly sage must have swept you through the air without your knowing it.'

'I expect you're right,' said Sancho, 'because, upon my soul, old Rocinante moved as if he was a gipsy's donkey with quicksilver poured into his ears!'

'Quicksilver, you say!' exclaimed Don Quixote. 'And a legion of devils besides, because they can move and make others move, without tiring, as fast as they like. But leaving all this aside, what do you think I should do now about this matter of my lady's command to go and see her? For although I appreciate that I am obliged to obey her, I also appreciate that I am prevented from doing so by the boon I have vouchsafed to the princess who is travelling with us; and the law of chivalry obliges me to put my promise before my pleasure. On the one side, I am pursued and hounded by my desire to see my lady; on the other, I hear the call of the faith I have pledged and of the glory I shall acquire in this undertaking. But what I intend to do is to hurry to wherever this giant is to be found, and when I arrive I shall cut off his head and restore the princess to the peaceful possession of her realm, and then I shall immediately return to behold the light that lightens my senses, and I shall present to her such excuses as will make her approve of my delay, for she will see that it all redounds to her greater glory and fame; because all the fame and glory I have achieved, do achieve and shall achieve by force of arms in this life springs from the succour that she affords me and from my being hers.'

'Oh dear me!' said Sancho. 'You really have gone off your head, haven't you just! Look here, sir – do you seriously intend to make this journey for nothing, and let a noble and money-spinning match like this one slip through your fingers? As a dowry you'll get a kingdom that I've heard, honestly, is more than seventy thousand miles round, and is full of everything needed to support human life, and is bigger than Portugal and Castile put together. Stop your nonsense, for God's sake, you ought to be ashamed of yourself – take my advice, if you'll kindly forgive me for speaking, and get married in the first village where there's a priest, or else make use of the one we've got with us, he'll do a very good job. I'm old enough by now, you know, to give advice, and this advice I'm giving you here is just what the doctor ordered, and a bird in the hand is worth two in the bush, because when the pig's offered you must poke open the hold.'

'Look here, Sancho,' replied Don Quixote, 'if you are advising me to marry so that once I have killed the giant and become king I shall be in a position to do you favours and give you what I have promised you, I would have you know that it will be easy for me to fulfil your desire without marrying; for before I go into battle I shall require as a further condition that once I am victorious, if I do not marry, I am to be presented with a part of the kingdom, so that I can give it to whomever I please; and, when I do receive it, to whom do you expect me to give it, if not to you?'

'Right you are,' replied Sancho, 'but just make sure you pick somewhere by the seaside so that if I don't like the way of life I can load up my black vassals and do with them what I said I would. And don't bother to visit my lady Dulcinea for the time being, go and kill the giant and get it over and done with – I've got a hunch, by God, that it'll bring us plenty of honour and profit.'

'And I say, Sancho,' said Don Quixote, 'that you are right, and that I shall accept your advice about going away with the princess before I visit Dulcinea. And let me warn you not to tell anyone, not even our companions here, about what we have been discussing: since Dulcinea is so modest that she does not want her feelings known, it would not be right for me, or anyone else because of me, to reveal them.'

'Well, if that's the way it is,' said Sancho, 'why do you make all those defeated by your mighty arm go and present themselves before my lady Dulcinea, when that's like signing a statement to the effect that you love her and you're her sweetheart? And seeing as how you force them all to get down on their bended knees in her presence and say they've come on your behalf to swear obedience, how can you expect to hide what's going on between you?'

'Oh what a dunderhead, what a nincompoop you are!' said Don Quixote. 'Can you not see, Sancho, that all this redounds to her greater glory? For I would have you know that in this our way of chivalry it is a great honour for a lady to have many knights errant serving her without any other ambition than to serve her, merely because she is who she is, and without expecting any other reward for their manifold good services than the knowledge that she is content to accept them as her knights.'

'That's the kind of love,' said Sancho, 'that I've heard in sermons we're supposed to feel for our Lord – for his own sake, without being moved by hopes of glory or fears of punishment. Though I must say I'd prefer to love him and serve him for what he can do for me.'

'The devil take you, you peasant!' said Don Quixote. 'What good sense you sometimes speak! Anyone would think you'd been to university!'

'Well, I promise you I can't so much as read,' replied Sancho.

As they talked, Master Nicolás shouted out to them to wait a minute, because the company wanted to stop and have a drink at a nearby spring. Don Quixote stopped, and Sancho wasn't sorry about the interruption, being exhausted by all that lying and scared that his master might catch him in the net of his questions because, although he knew that Dulcinea was a peasant girl from El Toboso, he'd never seen her in his life.

By this time Cardenio had put on the clothes that Dorotea had been wearing when they found her, and although they weren't very good clothes they were a great improvement on those which they'd replaced. They all dismounted by the spring and, with the provisions that the priest had acquired at the inn, they did something, although not very much, about the ravenous hunger afflicting them all. As they sat there a lad happened to come along the road, and he stopped and stared at the people by the spring; and after a moment he charged at Don Quixote and hugged his legs and burst into tears and said:

'Oh, my lord! Don't you recognize me? Take a good look at me, I'm that lad Andrés you freed from the evergreen oak where I was tied.'

Don Quixote did recognize him, and taking him by the hand he turned to the others and said:

'So that you can see how important it is that there be knights errant in the world to redress the wrongs and outrages committed by the wicked and insolent men who live in it, I would have you know that some time ago I was riding through a wood when I heard cries and piteous shouts as of one afflicted and in distress; I hastened, as was my duty, to where I thought the sad sounds were coming from, and I found, tied to an evergreen oak, this lad you see before you, whose presence fills my soul with joy because he is a witness who will confirm everything that I say. He was tied to the evergreen oak, then, naked from the waist up, and a peasant, who I later learned was his master, was flaying him alive with the reins of his mare; and as soon as I saw this I enquired into the reason for this terrible flogging, and the brute replied that he was whipping the boy because he was his servant and a certain lack of care on his part had more to do with thieving than with simple-mindedness. Upon which the boy said:

'"Sir, the only reason he's flogging me is because I asked for my wages."

'His master replied with all kinds of bluster and excuses, to which I listened but which I did not accept. The end of the matter was that I made his master untie him and swear that he would take him away and pay him every single real he owed him, and with brass knobs on, too. Is this not all true, Andrés, my son? Did you not see how imperiously I issued my command, and how humbly he promised to carry out everything I ordered and specified and required? Speak up; do not be embarrassed or hesitant; tell these people what happened, so that it can be seen and understood that the presence of knights errant on the road is as beneficial as I say it is.'

'Everything you've said is very true,' replied the lad, 'but it all ended up the opposite of what you think.'

'What do you mean, the opposite?' replied Don Quixote. 'Did the peasant not pay you, then?'

'Not only that,' replied the lad, 'but as soon as you were out of the wood and we were left on our own again he tied me back to the same oak tree and gave me a fresh flogging, and I was left skinned like another St Bartholomew. And each time he hit me he cracked a joke about how he was making a fool of you, and if I wasn't in such pain I'd have had a really good giggle at the things he said. To cut a long story short, he left me in such a state that I've been in hospital ever since, getting over the injuries he did me, that evil peasant. And you're to blame for it all, because if you'd gone on your way and hadn't come poking your nose into other people's business, my master would have been content to hit me a dozen or a couple of dozen times, and then he'd have untied me and paid me what he owed me. But since you threw all those pointless insults at him and called him all those names he got into a temper, and since he couldn't take it out on you he loosed his storm on me as soon as we were alone – and I don't think I'll be the same again as long as I live.'

'The trouble was,' said Don Quixote, 'that I departed, which I should not have done until he had paid you; for I should have known, from long experience, that no peasant keeps his word if he thinks that breaking it will profit him. But no doubt you remember, Andrés, that I swore that if he did not pay you I should go in search of him and that I should find him, even if he hid in the belly of the whale.'²

'That's true enough,' said Andrés, 'but it didn't do any good at all.'

'Now you will see whether it does any good or not,' said Don Quixote. And as he said this he sprang to his feet and told Sancho to bridle Rocinante, who was grazing while they ate. Dorotea asked Don Quixote what he was planning to do. He replied that he was going in search of that peasant to punish him for his wicked behaviour, and to see that Andrés was paid to the last maravedí, in spite of all the peasants in the world. To which she replied that he must remember that, according to the vouchsafed boon, he couldn't be involved in any other enterprise until he'd completed hers, and as he knew this better than anybody he'd do well to calm down until he'd finished his business in her kingdom.

'That is true,' replied Don Quixote, 'and Andrés will have to be patient until I return, as you say, my lady; and I again swear to him and I promise him once more that I will not stop until I have seen him avenged and paid.'

'I don't believe all those oaths of yours,' said Andrés. 'At the moment I'd rather have what's needed to get me to Seville than all the vengeance in the world – so give me something to eat and something to take with me, if you've got anything, and God be with you and all knights errant. And I hope all their errantry does them every bit as much good as it's done me.'

Sancho took a hunk of bread and a lump of cheese from his supply and gave them to the lad with the words:

'Here you are, brother Andrés, each one of us has a share in your misfortune.'

'And what's your share, then?' asked Andrés.

'This share of bread and cheese I'm giving you,' replied Sancho. 'God in heaven knows whether I'm going to feel the want of it, because I'll have you know, my friend, that we knight errants' squires must face up to a lot of hunger and bad luck, as well as other things it's better not to talk about.'

Andrés grabbed his bread and cheese and, seeing that nobody was giving him anything else, bowed his head and, as they say, made himself scarce. It has to be added that as he left he addressed Don Quixote:

'Look here, mister knight errant, if you ever come across me again, even if you can see that I'm being torn to pieces, for God's sake don't come to my rescue – just leave me alone with my troubles, because they can't possibly be so great that your help won't make them much worse. And God's curses on you and on every single knight errant that ever was born.'

Don Quixote was rising to punish him, but he scampered away at such a pace that nobody tried to follow. Don Quixote was plunged into embarrassment by Andrés's tale, and the others had to stifle their laughter so as not to complete his discomfiture.

CHAPTER XXXII

❉

Concerning what happened to Don Quixote and his gang at the inn

The banquet was over, they saddled their mounts and nothing else worth mentioning happened until on the following day they reached the inn that was the dread and terror of Sancho Panza; and reluctant though he was to go in, he couldn't avoid doing so. The innkeeper and his wife and daughter and Maritornes saw Don Quixote and Sancho coming, and went out to receive them with a great show of contentment, and Don Quixote accepted their welcome with solemn gravity, and told them to prepare a better bed than last time; to which the innkeeper's wife replied that if he paid for it better than last time she'd give him one fit for a king. Don Quixote said he would, so they made up a tolerable bed for him in the attic where he'd slept before, and he retired immediately because he was both exhausted and upset. No sooner had he locked the door than the innkeeper's wife descended on the barber and, seizing him by the beard, exclaimed:

'By all that's holy, you aren't using my tail as a beard any more, you've got to give it back to me, it's shameful how my husband's thingummy's bandied about all over the place nowadays – I mean his comb that I used to stick into my fine tail!'

The barber wouldn't part with it, however hard she tugged, until the priest told him to let her have it back: the disguise wasn't necessary any longer, he could show himself as he really was, and tell Don Quixote that when the convicts had stripped him he had fled to the inn, and if Don Quixote asked about the princess's squire he could be told that she'd sent him on ahead to warn the people in her kingdom that she was on her way there with the liberator of them all. So the barber willingly gave the innkeeper's wife back her tail, and they also returned all the other accessories she'd lent them for the freeing of Don Quixote. Everyone at the inn was astonished by Dorotea's beauty and by the good looks of the herdboy Cardenio. The priest ordered whatever food there was in the house to be prepared, and the innkeeper, in hope of better payment, did his very best to cook a passable meal; and all this time Don Quixote slept on, and they thought it better not to awake him, because it would do him more good to sleep than to eat.

The conversation after the meal, with the innkeeper, his wife, his daughter, Maritornes and all the guests sitting round the table, was about Don Quixote's strange madness and how he had been found. The innkeeper's wife related the events involving the muleteer, and, after looking around to see if Sancho was present and not finding him there, she told them all about the blanket-tossing, which gave them no little merriment. And the priest's observation that the books of chivalry which Don Quixote had read had turned him mad prompted the innkeeper to say:

'I don't understand how that can be so, because to my mind there isn't a better read anywhere in the world – I've got two or three of them back there, with some other papers, and I can truly say they've given me new life, and plenty of other people besides. At harvest time, you see, lots of the reapers come in here on rest-days, and there are always some who can read, and one of them picks up one of these books, and more than thirty of us gather around him, and we enjoy listening so much that it takes all our worries away. Speaking for myself, at least, when I hear him describing all those furious and terrible blows that the knights deal one another I feel like doing the same thing myself, and I could go on listening day and night.'

'And so do I,' said the innkeeper's wife, 'because the only time I get any peace and quiet in this place is when you're sitting there listening – you're in such a stupor you forget all about yelling at me for a while.'

'You're right there,' said Maritornes, 'and I can tell you I love hearing about all those goings-on, they're wonderful, especially when it's about a lady lying under orange trees in her knight's arms, and this duenna standing guard over them, dying of envy and scared out of her wits. It's lovely, it really is.'

'And what about you, young lady, what do you think?' the priest asked the innkeeper's daughter.

'I don't know, sir, I'm sure,' she replied. 'I listen, too, and the honest truth is that even though I don't understand it, I do enjoy it. I don't enjoy those fights that my father likes, mind you, but the knights' laments when they're separated from their ladies – to tell you the truth they sometimes make me cry out of sheer pity for them.'

'So would you do something to put them out of their misery, young lady,' asked Dorotea, 'if it was you they were crying for?'

'I really don't know what I'd do,' the girl replied. 'All I do know is that some of those ladies are so cruel that their knights call them tigers and lions and thousands of other nasty names. Good Lord, I can't imagine how they can be so heartless, so remorseless, letting an honest man die or go mad rather than look at him! I can't see why they're so bashful – if it's for their virtue's sake, they can just get married, that's what the men are after.'

'Hush, my girl,' said the innkeeper's wife, 'you seem to be very well-informed about these matters – it isn't right for young women to know or say so much.'

'This gentleman here asked me the question,' her daughter replied, 'so I had to give him an answer.'

'And now,' said the priest, 'bring me those books, landlord, I want to see them.'

'Very well,' he replied.

He went into his room and came back carrying an old case, fastened with a chain, which he unlocked to reveal three large books and some manuscript papers written in an excellent hand. When the priest opened the first book he saw it was *Don Cirongilio of Thrace*, and the next was *Felixmarte of Hyrcania*, and finally the *History of the Great Captain Gonzalo Fernández de Córdoba, together with the Life of Diego García de Paredes*.[1] As the priest read the first two titles he turned to the barber and said:

'What we need here and now is my friend's housekeeper, and his niece.'

'No, we don't,' replied the barber, 'because I'm just as good as they are at carting books off to the yard – or to the fireplace, there's a good fire burning there.'

'Do you want to burn still more books?' said the innkeeper.

'Just these two,' said the priest. '*Don Cirongilio* and *Felixmarte*.'

'Are my books heretics, then, or phlegmatics,' said the innkeeper, 'to make you want to burn them?'

'You mean schismatics, my friend,' said the barber, 'not phlegmatics.'

'All right, then,' replied the innkeeper. 'But if you want to burn a book, burn this one about the Great Captain and that Diego García fellow. I'd sooner allow one of my children to be burned than either of the other two.'

'My dear friend,' said the priest: 'those two books are full of lies, absurdities and nonsense. But this other one about the Great Captain is a true history, because it narrates the deeds of Gonzalo Fernández de Córdoba, universally known for his many splendid exploits as the Great Captain, a famous and illustrious title, earned only by him; and Diego García de Paredes was an eminent gentleman from the city of Trujillo in Extremadura, a most courageous soldier and so strong that with one finger he could stop a millstone turning at top speed; and armed with a two-handed sword he stood at the approach to a bridge and prevented a vast army from crossing it. And he performed so many other feats of this kind that if, instead of recounting them himself with all the modesty of a gentleman who is his own chronicler, someone else had done so with dispassionate objectivity, his deeds would have relegated those of the likes of Hector, Achilles and Roland to oblivion.'

'Pooh, so that's all he did, is it?' said our innkeeper. 'Fancy getting all het up about somebody stopping a millstone! For God's sake, you ought to read about what Felixmarte of Hyrcania got up to – with just one back-stroke he cut five giants clean through the middle, as if they were those friar-dolls that children make out of bean-pods! And another time he charged at an enormous powerful army and defeated more than one million six hundred thousand soldiers all in armour from head to foot, and he routed the lot of them as if they were flocks of sheep. And what do you think about good old Don Cirongilio of Thrace, who was as brave and daring as you'll read he was in the book, where it says that once when he was sailing down a river a serpent of fire came out of the midst of the water and as soon as he saw it he flung himself on top of it and sat astride its scaly back and squeezed its throat so hard with both hands that the serpent realized it was being strangled and had no choice but to sink to the bottom of the river with the knight sitting on top of it because he wouldn't let go? And when they got to the bottom he found himself among such lovely palaces and gardens that they were wondrous to behold, and then the serpent turned into an old old man who told him such things, you couldn't possibly imagine them. Come, say no more, sir – if all this was read out to you, you'd go mad with pleasure. A fig for the Great Captain and another for that Diego García character!'

When Dorotea heard this she whispered to Cardenio:

'Our host could almost play second lead to Don Quixote.'

'I agree,' replied Cardenio, 'because all the signs are he's convinced that everything in those books happened exactly as they say, and a churchful of discalced friars couldn't make him believe otherwise.'

'Look here, my friend,' the priest resumed, 'there never was any Felixmarte of Hyrcania or Don Cirongilio of Thrace or any of those other knights in those books of chivalry of yours, because it's all make-believe, fiction invented by idle minds for the purpose you've just mentioned, passing the time of day as your reapers do when they sit listening to it. I solemnly swear that such knights never existed and that such deeds or rather such nonsenses never took place.'

'You can go and throw that bone to another dog!' the innkeeper retorted. 'As if I didn't know how many beans make five, or where my own shoe pinches! Don't you come trying to feed me with pap – I wasn't born yesterday, by God! A fine thing it is for you to come telling me that everything in these good books is stuff and nonsense, when they were all published with their proper licences from the gentlemen on the Royal Council – as if those were the kind of people who'd allow a pack of lies to be printed, and all those battles and enchantments that fair turn you crazy!'

'I have already told you, my friend,' replied the priest, 'that this is only done to while away our idle moments; and just as in well-ordered societies such games as chess, tennis and billiards are permitted for the amusement of those who do not, should not and cannot work, so permission is also granted for the publication of such books, in the justified belief that there can't be anybody so ignorant as to read them as if they were true histories. And if it were timely to do so, and if those here present were to request it, I'd say a few words now about the qualities that books of chivalry need in order to be good books; and some people might find my words useful or even enjoyable. But I expect that a time will come when I can convey my ideas to a person in a position to do something about such matters; and meanwhile, landlord, you take me at my word, and here are your books – now you can find your own way among their lies and their truths, and much good may they do you, and God grant that you don't end up lame in the same leg that your guest Don Quixote halts on.'

'Don't you worry,' replied the innkeeper, 'I'm not so mad as to become a knight errant, and it's clear enough to me that things are different now from what they were then, when all those famous knights are supposed to have roamed about all over the world.'

Sancho appeared in the middle of this conversation and was plunged into thought and confusion when he heard that knight errants had fallen out of fashion and that books of chivalry were a pack of arrant lies; and he decided that he'd better wait and see how this latest trip of his master's turned out, and if it didn't turn out as well as expected, he'd leave him and go back home to his wife and his children and his everyday labours.

The innkeeper was taking his case away with the books in it when the priest said:

'Wait a minute, I want to have a look at those papers, they're written in such a fine hand . . .'

The innkeeper took them out and handed them over to the priest, who found eight folios and on the title-page the words, printed large: 'The Tale of Inappropriate Curiosity.' He read three or four lines to himself, and said:

'I must say this tale has rather a good title: I have a mind to read it through.'

To which the innkeeper replied:

'Well, you go ahead and do so, your reverence, because I can tell you some of our guests have read it and enjoyed it enormously, and begged me to let them take it away. But I wouldn't part with it, because I intend to return it to the man who left this case behind with these books and those papers – he might well come back for it some day and, although I know I'm going to miss the books, I'll hand them over to him all right. I might be an innkeeper, but I'm still a Christian.'

'That's very right and proper, my friend,' said the priest. 'If I like the tale, however, you must allow me to copy it out.'

'Most willingly,' replied the innkeeper.

While the two men had been talking, Cardenio had picked up the story and begun to peruse it, and, reaching the same conclusion as the priest, he asked him to read it aloud so that they could all hear.

'I'd be most happy to,' said the priest, 'except that our time would be better spent sleeping than reading.'

'It'll be wonderfully relaxing for me,' said Dorotea, 'to while away the time by listening to a story, because I haven't calmed down enough yet to be able to get to sleep.'

'Well, in that case,' said the priest, 'perhaps I will read it, if only out of curiosity. Who knows, maybe it'll prove curiously entertaining.'

Master Nicolás also urged him to do so, as did Sancho; the priest realized that he could give them all some pleasure, and receive some himself, and said:

'If that's so, pay attention all of you. The tale begins like this:'

CHAPTER XXXIII

※

Which tells the Tale of Inappropriate Curiosity

'In Florence, that rich and famous Italian city in the province of Tuscany, there once lived two wealthy and eminent gentlemen called Anselmo and Lotario, who were so close that all their acquaintances referred to them by way of antonomasia as "the two friends". They were bachelors, young men of the same age and the same habits, which is enough to explain the friendship that bound them together. It is true that Anselmo was somewhat more inclined towards amorous dallying than Lotario, whose favourite pastime was hunting; but when the occasion arose, Anselmo put his own interests aside and pursued those of Lotario, and Lotario did the same for Anselmo; and in this way their inclinations were so concordant that no clock could have been better regulated.

'Anselmo was madly in love with a beautiful young lady of high rank from the same city, the daughter of such excellent parents and so excellent, too, in her own right that he decided (after consulting Lotario, because he never did anything without Lotario's consent) to ask them for her hand in marriage, and this he did; the man entrusted with the mission was Lotario, who carried it out so much to his friend's satisfaction that he soon found himself in possession of the object of his desires, and Camila was so happy to have gained Anselmo as her husband that she never stopped thanking heaven and Lotario, whose mediation had brought her such joy.

'A wedding celebration is a time of happiness, so for the first few days Lotario continued to frequent his friend Anselmo's house, doing all he could to honour, regale and delight him; but once the celebrations were over and the congratulatory visits had abated, Lotario began to be careful to neglect to go to see Anselmo, because it seemed to him (as it would to any person of good sense) that a man shouldn't haunt his friends' houses once they're married as he used to do in their bachelor days; for although good, true friendship must be above all suspicion, the honour of a married man is so delicate that even a brother, it seems, let alone a friend, can damage it.

'Anselmo noticed the falling-off in Lotario's visits and made heated complaints about it, saying that if he'd known getting married was going to erect a barrier between them he would never have taken such a step; and that if their closeness as bachelors had earned them that fine reputation as "the two friends", Lotario mustn't allow a circumspection that was quite unnecessary and gratuitous to destroy such a famous and agreeable title; and that he therefore begged Lotario, if the use of such a word between them could be justified, to treat his house as his own again, and to come and go as before, with the assurance that his wife Camila had no pleasure or desire other than those that he wanted her to have; and that, knowing as she did how fond they were of each other, she couldn't understand why he had become so elusive.

'To all these and many other arguments that Anselmo used to persuade Lotario to visit him as often as he had before, Lotario replied with such prudence, good sense and sound judgement that Anselmo was convinced that his friend had the best of intentions, and they agreed that Lotario would go to dine with him just twice a week and on holy days; in spite of this, however, Lotario decided to do only what he considered was best for his friend's honour, which he held in higher esteem than his own. He would say, with good reason, that the man to whom heaven had granted a beautiful wife should be as careful over what friends of his he invited home as over supervising what friends of hers she talked to, because that which isn't arranged and indeed put into effect at market-places, churches, public festivities and devotions (which husbands can't always keep their wives away from), is arranged and put into effect in the houses of the wife's most trusted friends and relatives.

'Lotario would also say that every married man needs to have a friend to warn him about the shortcomings in his behaviour, because the great love a husband has for his wife can lead him not to want to annoy her and therefore not to tell her to do or refrain from doing certain things that can honour or shame him; and with the friend to warn him he can easily deal with this problem. But where can one find a friend as wise, loyal and true as Lotario had in mind? I certainly don't know, unless it was Lotario himself, who watched over his friend's honour with the greatest care and vigilance, and contrived to pare and whittle down the number of visiting-days agreed upon, to prevent the idle vulgar herd with their wandering, malicious eyes from gossiping about the visits of a well-born young gentleman with the qualities he believed he possessed to the house of a woman as beautiful as Camila; for although her worth and her virtue were enough to silence any wagging tongue, he still didn't want to put her good name or that of his friend at risk, and he found other occupations and activities, which he claimed were unavoidable, for most of the agreed visiting-days. And so it was that much of each day was spent in complaints on the one side and excuses on the other.

'Now it happened that once, when they were strolling in a meadow outside the city, Anselmo addressed the following words to Lotario:

' "No doubt you think, my good friend Lotario, that, given the favours which God has bestowed upon me in making me the son of such parents as mine and in heaping upon me what are known as the blessings of nature and the gifts of fortune, it is impossible for me to respond with a gratitude that equals the good I have received or exceeds that which he granted me in providing me with you as a friend and Camila as a wife, two treasures that I value, if not as much as I should, then as much as I can. Well, in spite of all these gifts, which are enough to fill most people with happiness, I'm the angriest and bitterest man in the world, because for I don't know how long now I've been assailed and tormented by a desire that's so peculiar and so unusual that I'm astonished at myself, and accuse and scold myself when alone, and try to stifle it and hide it from myself; but I've been as successful in repressing it as if my intention had been to tell the whole world about it. And since it must be revealed, I want this to happen in the total secrecy that I can expect from you, trusting that in this secrecy, and thanks to the care that you, as my true friend, will devote to relieving me,

I shall soon be free of this anguish, and your concern will bring me as much joy as my madness has brought me misery."

'Anselmo's words bewildered Lotario, who couldn't imagine where such a long prelude or preamble was leading, and although he tried to imagine what desire this was that so disturbed his friend, he was always very wide of the mark; and to ease the agony of the suspense Lotario said it was offensive to their close friendship for Anselmo to search for roundabout ways to convey his most secret thoughts, because he well knew that he could count on his friend for either advice to dissipate them or help to put them into action.

' "You're right," replied Anselmo, "and with that assurance I can tell you, dear Lotario, that this desire that so disturbs me is the urge to find out whether my wife Camila is as virtuous and perfect as I think she is; and I can't convince myself of this truth except by putting her to the test in such a way as to reveal the purity of her virtue, as fire reveals the purity of gold. Because it's my belief, dear friend, that a woman is good only in proportion as she is or is not tempted, and that the only virtuous woman is the one who doesn't give in to promises, gifts, tears and all the advances of persistent suitors. For what thanks are due to a woman for being good," he went on, "if nobody is asking her to be bad? What merit is there in all her reserve and reticence, if she isn't given any opportunity to go astray, and if she knows that she has a husband who'll kill her if he catches her cutting loose even once? So I can't have the same regard for the woman who's virtuous out of fear or lack of opportunity as I'd have for the one who's tempted and pursued and emerges wearing the crown of victory. And for these reasons, and many others that I could give you to support and reinforce my ideas, I want my wife Camila to be put to this test, and to be proved and assayed in the flames of enticement and temptation by a man worthy to make her the object of his desires; and if she emerges from this battle with the palm of victory, as I believe she will, I shall account myself the luckiest of mortals. I shall be able to say that the cup of my desires is full; I shall say that the virtuous woman, of whom the wise man says 'Who can find her?'[1] has fallen to my lot. And if the outcome is the opposite of what I anticipate, the pleasure of seeing that I was right will enable me to bear without feeling it the pain that such a costly experiment could be expected to cause. And since no objections that you can raise to this desire of mine will prevent me from putting it into practice, I want you, my good friend Lotario, to make yourself ready to be the instrument that will carry into effect this plan on which I've set my heart; I shall provide you with the opportunities for doing so and ensure that you lack nothing that I consider necessary for seducing a virtuous, honourable, modest and high-principled woman. And what moves me, among other considerations, to entrust this arduous enterprise to you is the knowledge that if you do overcome Camila's resistance your triumph won't be carried to the ultimate extreme, but will simply consist, because of your respect for me, in establishing that you could have taken it that far; and in this way I shall only be wronged in the intention, and the offence will remain hidden in your virtuous silence, which I well know will be as eternal as the silence of death, in any affair of mine. So if you want me to enjoy a life worthy of the name, you must enter now into this battle of love, not in any half-hearted or dilatory way but with all the determination and diligence that my decision demands, and with the resolve of which I am assured by our friendship."

'This was what Anselmo said, and Lotario listened so attentively that he didn't open his lips until his friend had finished, except to say the few words recorded earlier; and when Lotario saw that he had nothing more to say, he stood staring at him for a while, as if staring at something he'd never seen before, at something that amazed and terrified him, and then he spoke:

'"I can't persuade myself, my dear friend Anselmo, that what you've just said isn't a joke; and if I'd believed you were in earnest I shouldn't have allowed you to say as much as you did, and by refusing to listen I'd have cut short your lengthy harangue. I'm convinced that either you don't know me or I don't know you. And yet I do know that you're Anselmo, and you know that I'm Lotario; the trouble is that I don't think you're the Anselmo you used to be, and you must have thought that I'm not the Lotario I ought to be, because what you've just said doesn't come from my friend Anselmo, and what you've asked me to do can't be asked of the Lotario you know. Good friends should verify their friendship and help each other *usque ad aras*, as the poet put it;[2] which means that they mustn't use their friendship for purposes that are offensive to God. Now if this is what a pagan thought about friendship, how much more intensely must a Christian believe in the same principle, because he knows that the love of God mustn't be lost for the sake of any human love? And if a friend does go so far as to set aside his duty to heaven to attend to the duties of friendship, this mustn't be for petty, trivial matters, but for matters involving his friend's honour and his life. Now you tell me this, Anselmo: which of these two is in danger, to make me take the risk of trying to please you by doing this detestable thing you're asking of me? Neither of them, of course; on the contrary, what you're asking me, as far as I can see, is to do all I can to deprive you of your honour and your life, and to deprive myself of them at the same time. Because if I try to deprive you of your honour, it's clear that I shall also be depriving you of your life, since a man without honour is worse than a dead man; and if I'm the instrument, as you want me to be, of so much harm to you, am I not dishonoured too and, by the same logic, dead? No, no, listen to me, Anselmo, and have the patience not to reply until I've finished telling you how I feel about what this desire of yours is urging you to do, and there will be plenty of time afterwards for you to reply and for me to hear you out."

' "Very well," said Anselmo, "say what you like."

'And Lotario continued:

' "It seems to me, Anselmo, that your mind is in the same state as the minds of Moors, who can't be made to understand the error of their sect with references to Holy Scripture or with arguments involving intellectual speculation or based on articles of faith, but must rather be confronted with examples that are palpable, straightforward, easy to understand, demonstrable, indisputable – with mathematical proofs that can't be denied, such as 'If equal parts are taken from equal parts, the remainders are also equal'; and if they can't follow the verbal reasoning, as indeed is the case, they must be shown it all using one's fingers, and have it placed in front of their eyes, and even so nobody can persuade them of the truths of our holy religion. And I shall have to use the same approach and method with you, because this desire that has developed in you is so misguided and so far from any semblance of rationality that I believe I shall be wasting my time if I try to make you understand how silly you're being – for the moment I shall call it that; and I'm even inclined to abandon you to your folly, as a punishment for that evil desire of yours; but my friendship won't allow me to be so severe or leave you in such manifest danger of destroying yourself.

' "And to make it all clear to you, tell me, Anselmo, haven't you urged me to entice a woman who's modest, inveigle a woman who's virtuous, bribe a woman who's high-principled, court a woman who's prudent? Indeed you have. Now if you know that you have a wife who's modest, virtuous, high-principled and prudent, what more do you need to know? And if you believe she'll emerge victorious from all my attacks, as indeed she will, what finer names do you intend to call her afterwards than she already deserves, and in what way will she be a better woman than she already is? Either you don't believe her to be what you say she is, or you don't know what you're asking for. If you don't believe her to be what you say she is, why do you want to test her instead of dealing with her as you think best and as befits a wicked woman? But if she's as good as you say she is, it's inappropriate to go performing experiments on truth itself, because it can't have a greater value afterwards than it had in the first place. And so the conclusion we must reach is that to attempt things that are more likely to do us harm than good is an action of rash, unstable minds, even more so if we aren't forced into them and it's perfectly clear that it's madness to attempt them.

' "Difficult tasks are attempted for God's sake, or for the world's sake, or for both at the same time: those that are attempted for God's sake are the actions of saints, who try to live lives of angels in human bodies; those that are attempted for the world's sake are the actions of the men who pass across great expanses of water, through vast varieties of climates and among a bewildering diversity of peoples in order, as it is said, to make their fortunes; and the tasks that are attempted for the sake of both God and the world are the actions of brave soldiers, who no sooner see in the enemy's ramparts the small breach that a single cannon-ball can make than, casting all fear aside, without thinking, or paying any heed to the evident perils threatening them, carried forward on the wings of their desire to fight for their faith, their country and their king, they hurl themselves fearlessly into the midst of a thousand different deaths awaiting them. These are the tasks that men attempt, and it is honourable, glorious and beneficial to attempt them, even though they are full of difficulties and dangers; but the task that you say you want to carry out won't gain you the glory of God, or make you a fortune, or give you fame among men, because even if you do achieve what you seek you won't be any grander, richer or more honourable than you already are, and if you don't achieve what you seek you'll be left as wretched as it's possible for a man to be: it won't help to tell yourself that nobody knows about the calamity that has befallen you, because merely knowing about it yourself will be enough to torment and destroy you. As a confirmation of this truth let me quote a stanza from the end of the first part of the famous poet Luigi Tansillo's *Le lacrime di San Pietro*:[3]

> The grief is greater, greater is the shame
> In Peter once he sees the light of day
> And though he is alone he takes the blame
> And knows he's left the straight and narrow way:
> An upright, honest spirit feels the same
> Repentance, even if not seen to stray:
> The heart is filled with shame and misery
> When only heaven and earth are there to see.

'"So you won't avoid grief by keeping it secret; on the contrary, you won't stop weeping, if not tears of water from your eyes, then tears of blood from your heart, like that simple-minded doctor who, as the poet tells us, made the trial of the magic cup, which the prudent Reynald more wisely refrained from doing;[4] for although this is a poetic fiction it contains a hidden moral that should be observed and understood and imitated. All the more so since what I'm about to tell you will convince you once and for all that you're about to make a very great mistake.

'"Tell me this, Anselmo: if heaven or fortune had made you the lawful owner of a superb diamond, and every expert who examined it was convinced of its quality and value, and they all with one voice proclaimed that it attained the utmost perfection possible in such a stone, and you yourself were certain of this without a shadow of doubt – would it be reasonable to take it into your head to place that diamond between an anvil and a hammer and there, by the brute force of one blow after another, test it to see if it was as hard and excellent as everybody said? Wouldn't it be even less reasonable to put this desire into effect? For even if the stone could resist such an absurd test it wouldn't thereby gain in value or repute, and if it were destroyed, which is something that could well happen, all would be lost, wouldn't it? Yes, of course it would, and the diamond's owner would be left looking a fool in everybody's eyes. Now think of

Camila, Anselmo my friend, as a superb diamond, in your opinion and in everybody else's, and think whether it's reasonable to expose her to the risk of destruction, because even if she does remain intact, she won't then be worth any more than she is now; and if she falters and can't withstand the trial, consider how you'd feel without her, and how justly you'd reproach yourself for having been the cause of her downfall and your own as well. Remember that there's no jewel in the world as valuable as a chaste and honourable woman, and that women's honour lies exclusively in their good reputations; and since your wife's reputation couldn't be better, as you know, why do you insist on calling this truth into question? Remember, too, my friend, that woman is an imperfect animal, and that obstacles shouldn't be placed before her to make her stumble and fall, but rather removed to free her way of pitfalls so that she can run on unhindered to achieve the perfection she needs, that of being virtuous.

'"Naturalists tell us that the ermine is a little animal with pure white fur, and that when huntsmen want to catch it they use the following stratagem: they trace its tracks and its haunts, and daub them over with mud, and then they frighten it into running in that direction, and as soon as the ermine reaches the mud it stops and allows itself to be caught rather than run over the mud and sully and lose its whiteness, which it treasures more than its liberty and its life. The pure, chaste woman is an ermine, and the virtue of chastity is whiter and purer than snow, and the man who wants her not to lose it, but on the contrary to keep and preserve it, shouldn't do as huntsmen do with ermine – he shouldn't place before her the mud of insistent suitors' gifts and offers, because it's possible or, more accurately, it's certain that she has insufficient natural strength and virtue to be able to overcome such obstacles unaided, and it's necessary to remove them for her, and place before her the purity of virtue and the beauty that good repute contains within itself.

'"A good woman is also like a mirror of clear, shining glass, but any breath that touches this mirror will cloud and dim it. She should be treated like a holy relic, adored but not touched. She should be guarded and prized like a beautiful garden full of roses and other flowers, whose owner doesn't allow anybody to walk in it or touch the blooms; it's enough for the visitors to enjoy their beauty and fragrance from afar, from behind its iron railings. And to summarize I'd like to recite some lines of poetry that I've just remembered and that I heard in a modern play, because they seem relevant to what we're discussing. A wise old man is advising another, a young woman's father, to keep her securely locked up at home, and among other reasons he adduces these:

> One never should experiment
> On Woman, who is made of glass,
> To see if she will break or not,
> For anything could come to pass.
>   A breakage being probable,
> It's equally absurd and vain
> To put at such excessive risk
> What never can be joined again.
>   To this belief let all assent,
> And reason strengthens what I say:
> Wherever there's a Danae
> A shower of gold will find its way.[5]

'"Everything I've said so far, Anselmo, relates to your part in all this, and now I ought to say something concerning my own interests in the matter; if I do so at some length you'll have to forgive me, because it's made necessary by the labyrinth into which you've strayed and from which you want me to extricate you. You consider me your friend, but you want to deprive me of my honour, something that flies in the face of all friendship; and not only that, but you want me to deprive you of your honour, too. That you want to deprive me of my honour is clear, because when Camila sees that I'm trying to seduce her, as you desire, it's obvious that she'll take me for a man without honour or scruple, because I shall be attempting and indeed doing something so contrary to the obligations of my breeding and your friendship. That you want me to deprive you of your honour is beyond doubt, because when Camila sees that I'm trying to seduce her she'll think that I've noticed some fickleness in her that encourages me to reveal my evil intentions to her, and in considering herself disgraced her dishonour will extend to you, as a part of her. And from this springs what so often happens: even though the adulterous woman's husband doesn't know that his wife isn't what she ought to be, hasn't given her any motives for being unfaithful, has never had it in his power to prevent his misfortune and hasn't contributed to it by any neglect or lack of precautions, he is nonetheless called by a vile and shameful name, and those who know about his wife's wickedness regard him with a certain contempt instead of compassion, even though they can see that it isn't his fault but his wayward companion's lust that has caused him such misfortune.

'"Now I'm going to tell you why a wicked woman's husband is justly dishonoured, even if he doesn't know that she's wicked, and isn't to blame, and hasn't contributed to her sin, and hasn't given her any motives for it. And don't grow tired of listening to me, because it's all for your own good.

'"When God created our first father in the earthly paradise, Holy Scripture says that he made Adam fall asleep and took one of the ribs from his left side, from which he created our mother Eve; and when Adam awoke and saw her he said, 'This is flesh of my flesh and bone of my bone.' And God said, 'For this cause a man shall leave his father and his mother, and they two shall be one flesh.'[6] And at that moment the divine sacrament of matrimony was instituted, with such bonds as only death can untie. And this miraculous sacrament has such power that it makes two different people into one flesh; and it does even more when two good people marry, because although they have separate souls they have only one will. It follows that, since the wife's flesh is the same as the husband's, anything that blemishes it, any defects it acquires, affects his flesh too, even if he hasn't, as I said, given her any cause to misbehave. For just as a pain in the foot or anywhere else is felt all over the body, because it's all the same flesh, and the head feels the pain in the ankle without having caused it, so the husband shares his wife's dishonour, because he and she are one and the same. And since all the honour and dishonour in the world springs from human flesh and blood, and this includes the disgrace of a bad wife, the husband is bound to share it and to be regarded as a man without honour even if he doesn't know about it.

'"So you can see, Anselmo, the danger in which you are placing yourself by seeking to disturb the tranquillity that your good wife enjoys; you can see how vain and inappropriate is the curiosity that leads you to want to stir up the passions that now lie quiet in her breast; you can see that you're giving yourself the chance of gaining very little, and that what you'll lose is so very much that I shan't attempt to assess it, for there are no words to express its value. But if everything I've said isn't enough to dissuade you from your wicked plan, you can go and look for another instrument to bring about your misfortune and disgrace, because I don't intend to do it, even if it means losing your friendship, the greatest loss I can imagine."

'The virtuous and wise Lotario stopped speaking, and Anselmo was left so confused and sunk in thought that for a while he couldn't reply; but finally he said:

' "I've been listening attentively, Lotario, as you've observed, to everything you've said, and in your arguments, examples and comparisons I've confirmed how much good sense you're blessed with, and what a true friend you are; and I do see and confess that if I don't agree with your opinions and I adhere to my own I'll be shunning good and pursuing evil. I acknowledge this, but you must consider that I'm suffering from the disease that sometimes affects women and makes them want to eat earth, plaster, coal and even worse things, disgusting to look at, let alone to eat; so some plan has to be devised to cure me, and this could easily be done by your beginning, in a half-hearted and make-believe way, to court Camila, who can't be so frail as to allow her virtue to collapse at the first encounter; and with this beginning I shall rest content, and you'll have done what's due to our friendship, by not only restoring me to good health but also persuading me not to strip myself of honour. And you have a duty to do this for one reason alone, which is that, since I'm resolved to carry out this test, you can't allow me to reveal my foolishness to anybody else, because that would be to place at risk the honour that you don't want me to lose; and if your honour isn't all it should be in Camila's opinion when she realizes that you're making advances to her, that's of little or no importance because very soon, once you encounter the firm resistance we expect, you'll be able to tell her the truth about our plan and your good name will be restored. And since you can give me so much happiness by risking so little, please don't fail me, however many objections you can see, because, as I've said, if you'll only make a beginning I shall regard the matter as concluded."

'Lotario realized that Anselmo had made up his mind, couldn't think of any other examples or arguments with which to dissuade him and saw that he was threatening to tell others about this evil desire of his, so he decided to keep him happy and prevent a greater ill by doing as he asked, with the intention of managing the affair so as to satisfy Anselmo without disturbing Camila's peace of mind; so he told him not to reveal his thoughts to anybody else, because he was going to take the matter in hand and make a beginning whenever Anselmo wished. Anselmo gave him a fond and tender embrace and thanked him for his offer, as if his friend had done him some great favour, and the two of them agreed that Lotario would set to work on the very next day. Anselmo would give him an opportunity to speak to Camila alone, and would provide him with money to offer her and jewels to give her. He advised him to serenade her and to write poetry praising her, and said that if Lotario didn't want to go to so much trouble he'd write it himself. Lotario agreed to everything, but not with the intention that Anselmo supposed. Having reached this understanding they returned to Anselmo's house, where they found Camila anxiously awaiting her husband, because he was later than usual that day.

'Lotario went home, leaving Anselmo as contented as he himself was troubled, wondering how he was going to manage to bring that inappropriate enquiry to a satisfactory conclusion. But that night he thought of a way to deceive Anselmo and not offend Camila, and on the following day he went for lunch with his friend and was made welcome by Camila, who always gave him a cordial reception, knowing how fond her husband was of him.

'They finished the meal, the table was cleared and Anselmo asked Lotario to stay with Camila while he went off on urgent business from which he said he'd return in an hour and a half. Camila begged him not to go, and Lotario offered to accompany him, but it was all to no avail; on the contrary, Anselmo insisted that Lotario must stay and wait for him, because they had to talk about a matter of the greatest importance. He also told Camila not to leave Lotario by himself while he was away. In short, he was so successful in feigning that heedless, needless need to absent himself that nobody would have realized that it was feigned. So Anselmo departed, and Camila and Lotario were left alone at table, because all the servants had gone away to their own meal. And Lotario found himself entering the lists, as his friend had planned, and facing an enemy who could have vanquished a whole squadron of knights in armour with her beauty alone. Lotario had good reason to fear her!

'But what he did was to lean his elbow on the arm of his chair and his cheek on his open hand, ask Camila to forgive his manners and say that he'd like to rest for a while, until Anselmo returned. Camila replied that he'd rest more comfortably on the cushions in the estrade than at the dining-table, and asked him to go in there to sleep. Lotario declined, and dozed where he sat until the return of his friend, who found Camila in her room and Lotario asleep and assumed that, since he'd been away so long, the two had had plenty of time to talk and even to nap; and he was longing for Lotario to wake up, so anxious was he to go out with him and ask what had happened.

'Everything fell out as he wished: Lotario woke up, they left the house together, Anselmo asked his questions and his friend replied that it hadn't seemed wise to be too blatant on the very first occasion, so he had only praised Camila's beauty and told her that nobody was talking in the whole city about anything other than her fine looks and her intelligence, because this had seemed an appropriate way to start gaining her confidence and making her ready to lend a willing ear the next time, using the trick that the devil uses when he wants to deceive those who are on their guard: he turns himself from an angel of darkness into an angel of light, presents a specious appearance of virtue, and finally reveals himself and achieves what he wants, so long as his deceit isn't discovered at the outset. Anselmo was well pleased, and said that he'd provide the same opportunity every day even if he didn't leave home, because he'd find things to do about the house in such a way that Camila wouldn't suspect their plot.

'Many days went by and Lotario didn't say a word to Camila, yet assured Anselmo that he'd talked to her and couldn't elicit the smallest hint of an agreement to do anything untoward, or make her give him the slightest shadow of hope – on the contrary, she'd threatened to tell her husband if he didn't give up his wicked designs.

' "Very well," said Anselmo. "So far Camila has resisted words, and now we must see how she resists deeds: tomorrow I shall give you two thousand gold escudos for you to offer or even give her, and another two thousand to buy jewels to tempt her, because women, particularly beautiful ones, are fond of dressing well and looking smart, however virtuous they are. And if she resists this temptation I shall rest satisfied and shan't trouble you any more."

'Lotario replied that now he'd started out on that business he'd see it through, even though he knew he was going to end up exhausted and defeated. On the next day he received the four thousand escudos, and with them four thousand headaches, because he couldn't think how he could lie his way out of this new predicament; but in the end he decided to tell Anselmo that Camila was as impervious to gifts and promises of gifts as she was to words, and that there wasn't any point in wearing himself out any more, because it was all a waste of time.

'But fortune, which had other plans, ordained that once Anselmo had left Lotario and Camila alone as usual, he should lock himself into a side room and watch and listen through the keyhole, and discover that in over half an hour Lotario didn't direct a single word at Camila, and wouldn't have done so if he'd sat there for a century; and Anselmo realized that everything his friend had told him about Camila's replies had been fiction and falsehoods. And to confirm his suspicion he walked out of the room, called Lotario to one side and asked him what news there was and what state Camila was in. Lotario replied that he wasn't going to address her on the subject ever again, because her answers were so brusque and surly that he wouldn't have the courage to say another word to her.

'"O Lotario, Lotario," cried Anselmo, "how badly you fulfil your duty and repay all the trust I've placed in you! I've been watching you through this keyhole and I've seen that you haven't said a word to Camila, from which I conclude that your very first words to her have yet to pass your lips; and if this is so, as I'm sure it is, why do you deceive me, why do you plot to deprive me of the means of carrying this desire of mine into effect?"

'Anselmo said no more, but he had said enough to cover Lotario with shame and confusion; and, as if he took being caught in this lie as a blemish on his honour, he swore that from that moment on he'd take the utmost care to do exactly as he was told and never lie again, as Anselmo would be able to corroborate if he spied on his every move, although he wouldn't need to put himself to any such trouble, because of the pains Lotario would take to raise himself above all suspicion. Anselmo believed Lotario and, to smooth his path and remove all risk of interruption, he decided to absent himself from home for a week by going to visit a friend who lived in a village not far from the city; and he persuaded this friend to summon him urgently, to provide Camila with an excuse for his departure.

'Unfortunate, ill-advised Anselmo! What are you doing? What are you plotting? What are you trying to bring about? Look here: you're doing yourself great harm, you're plotting your own dishonour and you're bringing about your own destruction. Your wife Camila is a good woman; you possess her in peace and security; nobody interrupts your contentment; her desires don't venture beyond the walls of her house; you're her heaven on earth, the goal of her desires, the fulfilment of her joys and the rule by which she measures her will, always adjusting it to your will and that of heaven. So if the mine of her honour, beauty, virtue and modesty yields up to you, without even needing to be worked, all the riches that it contains and that you can desire, why do you want to dig still deeper in search of yet more veins of new and unseen treasure, risking the collapse of the whole structure, which is supported only on the feeble props of her frail nature? Remember that the man who seeks the impossible may justly be denied the possible, or, as the poet expressed it better:

> I look to death in quest of life;
> I seek health in infirmity
> And freedom in captivity;
> I search for rest in bitter strife
> And faithfulness in treachery.
> But fortune always was unkind:
> I know that it has been designed
> By adverse fate and heaven's decree
> That, since I seek what cannot be,
> What can be I shall never find.[7]

'The next day Anselmo went off to the village, after telling Camila that Lotario would come to look after the house and dine with her while he was away, and that she should take care to treat Lotario as she would her own husband. Camila, being a sensible and honourable woman, was distressed by these orders, and asked him to bear in mind that it wasn't right for anybody to take his place at table while he was away, and that, if he was doing it because he was uncertain of her ability to manage the household affairs, he should give her this one chance to show him that she could cope with this and much greater problems. Anselmo replied that he'd made up his mind, and that she just had to bow her head and obey him. Camila said that she would do so, but much against her will.

'Anselmo left, and on the following day Lotario came to the house, where Camila gave him a warm but correct welcome. She avoided places where he might find her alone, seeking always to be attended by her servants, in particular a maidservant called Leonela of whom she was very fond, because the two of them had been brought up together in Camila's parents' house and, when she'd married Anselmo, Leonela had come with her. For the first three days Lotario didn't say a word to Camila, even though he had an opportunity to do so whenever the table was cleared and the servants went away for a hasty meal, as she had ordered. And Leonela had even received instructions to dine before Camila did, and then never to leave her side; but the maidservant's thoughts were intent on other matters concerning her own pleasures, and she needed time for her amusements, so she didn't always obey her mistress's orders, but left the two alone, as if that were what she'd been told to do. But Camila's modest manner, her gravity of expression and the composure of her person were enough to curb Lotario's tongue.

'Whatever good was done by Camila's virtues in silencing Lotario was outweighed, however, by the harm they did in other ways, because even if his tongue was stilled, his feelings were not, and he had the opportunity to gaze in awe at each one of Camila's perfections of goodness and beauty, which were enough to make a marble statue fall in love, let alone a human heart.

'Lotario would be looking at her when he should have been speaking to her, and he would be thinking how lovable she was, and this idea slowly began to make inroads on his consideration for Anselmo, and a thousand times he decided to leave the city and go where Anselmo would never see him again, nor he Camila; but he was held back by the delight he derived from looking at her. He struggled and struggled with himself to repress the pleasure that forced him to keep looking at Camila. When he was alone he condemned his folly; he called himself a false friend and even a bad Christian; he argued with himself and drew up comparisons between himself and Anselmo, and the conclusion was always that Anselmo's madness and rashness were worse than his own breach of trust, and that if what he was planning to do was as excusable before God as it was before men, he needn't fear any punishment for his sin.

'And so it was that Camila's beauty and goodness, together with the opportunity that her stupid husband had placed in his hands, overthrew all Lotario's loyalty; and, after three days during which he fought a continuous battle against his desires, he made his first pass at Camila without a thought for anything other than his pleasure, and in such a fluster and with such words of love that all she could do in her bewilderment was to come to her feet and walk to her room in silence. But this rebuttal, far from stifling Lotario's hopes, because love and hopes are always born together, only strengthened his feelings. Camila, for her part, had found in Lotario what she had never suspected was there, and she didn't know what to do. Considering it unsafe and improper to give him any more opportunities to talk to her, she decided to send a servant to Anselmo that very night with a letter in which she wrote:

CHAPTER XXXIV

※

In which the Tale of Inappropriate Curiosity is continued

Just as it is commonly said that an army is in a bad way without its general and a castle without its warden, so I say that a young married woman is very much worse off without her husband, unless the most pressing of reasons forces him to be absent. I am in such a bad way without you, and so unable to bear your absence, that if you do not come home soon I shall have to go and stay for a while at my parents' house, even though that would leave yours unguarded; because the guard whom you left me, if that is what he is meant to be, seems more concerned with his own pleasure than with your interest; and since you are an intelligent man I need say no more, nor would it be right for me to do so.

'When Anselmo received this letter he realized that Lotario had begun the campaign, and that Camila must have responded as he'd hoped she would; and, delighted with the news, he didn't write back but told the messenger to tell Camila on no account to leave the house, because he'd soon return. Camila was amazed at Anselmo's reply, which threw her into even greater confusion, because she didn't dare stay at home, still less go to her parents' house, since if she stayed her virtue was imperilled and if she left she would be disobeying her husband.

'She eventually decided to do what was the worst thing she could have done – to stay at home and not to avoid Lotario, so as not to give her servants food for gossip; and she was already regretting having written to her husband, worried that he might think Lotario had noticed some levity in her conduct that had encouraged him to abandon the respect he owed her. But she trusted her own virtue and put her faith in God and in her determination to resist all Lotario's advances in silence, without mentioning the matter again to her husband, so as not to create any trouble or conflict for him. And she was even searching for some way in which she could exonerate Lotario when Anselmo asked what had prompted her to write that letter.

'On the following day, armed with these resolutions, more honourable than wise or effective, she sat listening to Lotario, who was so insistent that her steadfastness began to weaken, and her modesty had to struggle to come to the rescue of her eyes and prevent them from betraying the loving compassion that Lotario's words and tears had awoken in her breast. Lotario observed all this, and it inflamed him even more. The moment arrived when he decided that he must intensify his siege of this fortress while the opportunity provided by Anselmo's absence lasted; so he attacked her pride by praising her beauty, because there's nothing that can demolish the fortified towers of a beautiful woman's vanity sooner than that vanity itself when deployed by flattery. And he mined away at the fort of Camila's integrity with such charges that even if she'd been made of bronze she'd have come toppling down. Lotario wept, he begged, he promised, he flattered, he insisted and he feigned with such feeling, with such shows of sincerity, that he overcame Camila's modesty and won the victory that he'd least expected and most desired.

'She surrendered; Camila surrendered; but what wonder, if Lotario's friendship didn't stand firm? A clear example showing that love can only be conquered by fleeing from it, and that nobody should engage with such a powerful enemy, because its human strength can only be defeated by divine might. Leonela alone knew about her mistress's frailty, because the two false friends and new lovers couldn't keep it from her. Lotario didn't see fit to tell Camila about Anselmo's scheme and reveal that he was the one who'd provided the opportunity for what had happened, wanting her not to disparage his love but to believe that his advances had been spontaneous, uncontrollable, unpremeditated.

'A few days later Anselmo returned to his house and didn't notice what was missing there: what he'd taken least care of, yet had most valued. He went at once to see Lotario, and found him at home; the two embraced each other, and one of them asked for the news that meant life or death for him.

' "The news I have for you, my dear friend Anselmo," said Lotario, "is that you have a wife worthy to be an example and a pattern for all good women. My words to her have gone with the wind; my promises have been disdained; my gifts have been rejected; she has mocked my crocodile tears. In short, just as Camila is the epitome of beauty, so she also is the treasure-house of chastity, propriety, and modesty and all the virtues that can make an honourable woman fortunate and praiseworthy. Here you are, my friend, take back your money: I haven't needed to touch it, because Camila's integrity doesn't yield to such wretched things as gifts and promises. Be satisfied with this, Anselmo, don't make any further trials, and, now that you've navigated unscathed the gulf of all the suspicions that can be and are entertained about women, don't venture again on to the deep sea of yet more problems, don't engage another pilot to test the soundness and strength of the ship that heaven has sent you for your passage across the ocean of this life, but rather consider yourself safe in harbour, and moor your ship to the anchors of proper respect, and stay there until you have to pay the debt that not even the noblest of mortals are exempt from paying."

'Anselmo was delighted with what Lotario had said, and he believed every word of it as if some oracle had been speaking. But this didn't prevent him from begging his friend not to abandon the campaign, even if only for the sake of curiosity and amusement, and using less urgent methods than hitherto; all Anselmo wanted Lotario to do now was to write some poetry praising Camila and calling her Chloris, because then he would tell her that their friend was in love with a lady to whom he'd given that name so that he could sing her praises with the propriety due to her good character. And if Lotario didn't want to take the trouble to write the verses, he would do so himself.

'"That won't be necessary," said Lotario, "because the muses aren't so hostile to me that they don't pay me occasional visits. Tell Camila about my love and her false name, just as you've suggested, and leave me to see to the verses, which will be the very best that I can manage, even if not as good as their subject deserves."

'This was what the inappropriately curious husband and his treacherous friend agreed; and when Anselmo returned home he asked Camila what she was astonished he hadn't asked already: to tell him what had prompted her to write that letter. Camila replied that Lotario had seemed to be rather freer with his looks than when Anselmo was present, but that she'd later realized she'd been mistaken: it must all have been in her imagination, because Lotario always avoided seeing her and being alone with her. Anselmo told her that she could indeed dismiss her suspicions, because he knew that Lotario was in love with one of the high-born young ladies of the city, whose praises he sang using the name Chloris; and that, even if he weren't in love with Chloris, Camila could have nothing to fear, given Lotario's uprightness and the close friendship that united the two men. If Camila hadn't been warned by Lotario that this love for Chloris was a pretence and that he'd told Anselmo all this so that he could while away the time writing in praise of Camila herself, she'd have fallen into the snare of despairing jealousy; but, being forewarned, she didn't so much as bat an eyelid.

'The next day, as the three sat round the table after dinner, Anselmo asked Lotario to recite some of those verses that he'd written about his beloved Chloris: since Camila didn't know her, he could safely say whatever he pleased.

'"Even if Camila did know her," replied Lotario, "I wouldn't keep anything back, because when a lover praises his lady for her beauty and reproaches her for her cruelty he can't do her good name any harm. But, be that as it may, I can tell you that yesterday I wrote a sonnet about my Chloris's ingratitude, and it goes like this:

SONNET

In the quiescence of the silent night,
As others dream in comforting repose,
To heaven and to Chloris I recite
The mean account of my abundant woes.
    And as Aurora rises and displays
On eastern balconies her rosy face
I sigh and stammer as I try to raise
My protest and submit my plaintive case.
    And then, as Phoebus, from his starry throne,
Casts down his rays upon the burning soil,
With aggravated grief I weep and moan.
And night's return renews my sorrow's toil.
But never, as I madly persevere,
Will heaven listen, or will Chloris hear."

'Camila liked the sonnet, but Anselmo liked it even more, and he praised it and declared that the woman who didn't respond to such evident truths was too cruel. To which Camila replied:

' "So everything that lover-poets say is true, is it?"

' "No, as poets they don't tell the truth," said Lotario, "but what they say as lovers is as understated as it is, indeed, truthful."

' "There's no doubt of that," replied Anselmo, to press Lotario's feelings on Camila, who was as unaware of Anselmo's stratagem as she was in love with Lotario.

'And so, since she took such delight in everything Lotario did, and even more because she knew that his verses and his desires were directed at her and that she was the real Chloris, she asked him to recite another sonnet or any other poem of his, if he could remember one.

' "Yes, I can," replied Lotario, "though I don't think it's as good or, rather, as tolerable as the first one. But you can judge for yourselves, because here it is:

SONNET

I know you're killing me! And I repeat,
Since, thankless beauty, you still doubt it's true,
You'll sooner see me dying at your feet
Than giving up my reverence for you.
    Then I'll be gone from human memory,
Bereft of glory, honour, life and grace,
And on my opened breast the gods shall see
The image of your captivating face.
    This is a relic that I shan't forsake
In that most desperate and dreadful strait
In which I'll be, for obstinacy's sake,
Made, by your rigour, still more obstinate.
Unhappy he who sails through storm-tossed night
And rock-strewn seas without a guiding light!"

'Anselmo praised this second sonnet as he had the first one; and so he went on adding link after link to the chain with which he was shackling himself and securing his own dishonour, because the more Lotario dishonoured him the more he told him that his honour was assured; and, in this way, every step Camila took down into the depths of disgrace was, as her husband saw it, a step that she climbed up towards the pinnacles of virtue and good repute.

'Once when Camila was alone with her maidservant, she said:

'"I feel ashamed, Leonela, when I consider how little I've valued myself, because I didn't even make Lotario spend any time to buy full possession of the favours I so quickly granted him. I fear he'll only remember how eagerly and easily I gave in to him, and not bear in mind the pressure he exerted to make himself irresistible."

'"You shouldn't worry about that, my lady," replied Leonela. "The value of a gift neither rises nor falls as a result of giving it quickly, so long as the gift is a good one and of value in itself. Indeed it's often said that she who gives quickly gives twice."

' "And it's also said," said Camila, "that what's cheaply bought is little valued."

' "But that doesn't apply to you," replied Leonela, "because love, I've heard, sometimes flies and sometimes walks, rushes along with one person and dawdles with another, cools some people down and heats some others up, wounds this one and slaughters that, ends the race of passion just about as soon as he's started it, lays siege to a fortress in the morning and overruns it in the evening, because there's no force that can resist him. And this being so, what is it that alarms you, what have you got to fear? Because this is what Lotario must have felt, too, once love had taken my master's absence as his instrument for overcoming both of you. And it was inevitable that, while Anselmo was away, what love had already made up his mind about was going to happen, without giving Anselmo time to return and curtail love's work, because love has no better minister to carry out his desires than opportunity: he makes use of opportunity in all his actions, particularly at the beginning. I know all this very well, more from experience than from hearsay, and one day I'll tell you all about it, ma'am, because I'm young, too, and made of flesh and blood.

' "What's more, my lady Camila, you didn't give in so soon that you couldn't first see Lotario's soul revealed in his eyes, in his sighs, in his words and his promises and his gifts – and you also saw there and in his virtues how worthy he was of your love. Now this being so, don't you go bothering your head with all those finicky and prudish scruples, just be assured that Lotario thinks as much of you as you do of him, and be thankful and happy that, given that you've fallen into the snare of love, your captor's a worthy and honourable man. He's sensible, solitary, solicitous and secretive, so he's got the four S's they say all good lovers must have – not only that, though, he's got a whole alphabet of qualities, and if you don't believe me you just listen and you'll soon hear how I reel it off! If I judge right he's appreciative, benevolent, chivalrous, dutiful, enamoured, firm, gallant, honourable, illustrious, judicious, kind, loyal, manly, noble, onest, princely, quantious, rich, the four S's of the saying, and then tacit, unattached, veracious, well-born, the X doesn't suit him because it's a rough old letter, the Y I've already done and as for the Z he's really zealous for your honour."

'Camila laughed at her maidservant's alphabet, and thought that she was more practised in matters of love than she'd admitted; and the girl confessed as much, revealing that she was seeing a well-born young man of that city, which worried Camila, who feared that this could put her own honour at risk. She insisted on being told whether the relationship had gone beyond words, and her maid replied without a blush that it had gone beyond words. It's clear that a lady's failings rob her maids of their shame, and when they see their mistress trip and fall they think nothing of stumbling – and letting her know all about it.

'All Camila could do was ask Leonela not to breathe a word about her mistress's affair to the man she said was her lover, and to manage her own affair in the utmost secrecy so that neither Anselmo nor Lotario found out about it. Leonela agreed, but the way in which she kept her promise confirmed Camila's fear that her servant was going to bring about the loss of her good name. Because once that brazen hussy Leonela became aware of the change in her mistress's behaviour, she had the effrontery to bring her own lover into the house, safe in the knowledge that even if her mistress saw him there she wouldn't dare expose him. The sins of any lady give rise to this evil, among many others: she becomes her own servants' slave, and has to cover up for their immorality and depravity, as did Camila, who realized dozens of times that Leonela was with her young man in a room in the house, yet not only didn't dare scold her but provided her with opportunities to let him in, and removed all obstacles from his path, to prevent her husband from seeing him. But she couldn't remove them successfully enough to prevent Lotario from seeing the young man as he left one day at dawn. At first, not recognizing him, Lotario thought he was a ghost, but when he saw him walk away muffling himself up with studied care, he abandoned that absurd notion for another which would have been the ruin of them all if Camila hadn't found a remedy. It didn't occur to Lotario that the man he'd seen leaving Anselmo's house at such an unseemly hour might have gone there for Leonela – Lotario didn't even remember that Leonela existed. All that came to his mind was that Camila had been an easy and rapid conquest for another man, just as she had been for him. These are the consequences of a sinning woman's behaviour. Her reputation is lost in the eyes of the man to whom she has surrendered after all his pleading and persuasion; and then he thinks that she will surrender to other men even more readily, and he is ready to believe every suspicion that finds its way into his mind. And at this point, it seems, all Lotario's good sense deserted him and all sound reasoning abandoned his head, because without pausing for a single judicious or even sane thought, blinded by the rage of jealousy gnawing at his entrails, and determined to avenge himself on Camila, who had done him no wrong, he ran to see Anselmo, who was still in his bed, and said:

'"I must inform you, Anselmo, that for many days now I have been battling with myself, struggling to avoid telling you something that it's neither possible nor right for me to conceal any longer. I must inform you that the fortress of Camila's virtue has surrendered, and that I can do with her as I please; and if I have been slow to reveal this truth to you, it's only because I wanted to see if it was merely some passing whim of hers, or if she was perhaps behaving as she was to test me and discover whether the advances I was making to her with your permission were seriously intended. I also believed that, if she was the woman she should be and we both thought she was, she would have told you about my approaches by now; but her delay forces me to recognize that she was telling the truth when she promised me that the next time you leave home she'll meet me in the garderobe where you keep your personal effects." (This was, indeed, their rendezvous.) "I don't want you to rush into taking your vengeance, because the sin is as yet committed only in thought, and, between now and the time of committing it in deed, Camila may change her mind and repent. And so, since you've always followed my advice at least in part, do take the advice I'm going to give you now so that you can, with a clear and cautious judgement unimpaired by error, decide on the best course of action to take. Pretend to go away for two or three days, as you sometimes do, and then conceal yourself in the garderobe – the tapestries and other hiding places there will make this easy; and then you'll see with your own eyes, and I shall see with mine, what is in Camila's mind, and if it's the wickedness that's to be feared rather than to be expected, you can inflict silent, prudent and judicious punishment for the wrong done you."

'Anselmo was left in stunned and bewildered amazement by Lotario's revelation, because it came when he was least expecting it: convinced as he was by now of Camila's triumph over Lotario's sham assaults on her virtue, he was beginning to enjoy the glory of victory. He remained silent for some moments, gazing at the floor without moving so much as an eyelash, until at length he said:

' "You have done everything, Lotario, that I expected of your friendship; I shall follow your advice; do as you please, but keep this secret as carefully as you can understand is necessary in this unexpected situation."

'Lotario promised to do so, but as soon as he left he realized how stupidly he'd acted, and repented of everything he'd said, because he could have taken revenge on Camila himself, and in a less cruel and dishonourable way. He cursed his lack of judgement, condemned his reckless action and racked his brains to find some way to undo what he'd done, or to save the situation. In the end he decided to make a clean breast of it all to Camila; there was no lack of opportunity for this, and he found her alone that same day; but when she saw that there was a chance to speak she was the one who did so:

' "I must tell you, my dear Lotario, that there's a grief so intense in my heart that it seems to be about to burst in my breast, and it will be a wonder if it doesn't; because Leonela's brazenness has reached such a pitch that every night she lets her lover into this house and he stays with her until morning, at great cost to my good name if anyone sees him leaving at such an unusual hour and reaches the obvious conclusion. And what most infuriates me is that I can't scold or punish her, because her knowledge of our affair stills my tongue and forces me to keep quiet about her affair, and I fear some harm will come of all this."

'At first Lotario thought this was a trick to persuade him that the man he'd seen leaving the house wasn't her lover; but her grief and her tears and her pleas for help made him see the truth, and this completed his confusion and remorse. Yet he replied to Camila that she shouldn't worry, because he would take measures to put an end to Leonela's insolence. He also told Camila what, in his jealous rage, he'd said to Anselmo, and how it had been agreed that Anselmo would hide in the garderobe and witness her infidelity for himself. Lotario begged her forgiveness for his folly and asked for her advice about how to put things right and extricate himself from the tortuous labyrinth into which his thoughtlessness had led him.

'Camila was appalled and infuriated by what Lotario had told her, and with many heated and well-chosen words she rebuked him and reviled his foul suspicions and his stupid action; but as women are naturally more quick-witted, for both good and evil, than men, though not when it comes to constructing coherent arguments, Camila hit there and then upon a way in which to solve such an apparently insoluble dilemma, and told Lotario to make Anselmo hide the next day where he'd said he would, and then she'd contrive to ensure that in future they'd be able to take their pleasure together without fear of interruption; and, without revealing any more of her plans, she instructed him, once Anselmo had hidden, to come as soon as Leonela called and to reply to everything she said exactly as he would reply if he didn't know that Anselmo was listening. Lotario pressed her to explain her scheme in full, so that he could make sure to do whatever he saw was necessary.

'"I'm telling you," said Camila, "that you have nothing to do except answer my questions," because she didn't want to forewarn him about her intentions, fearful that he might be unwilling to co-operate in the plan that seemed so excellent to her, and that he might develop other less effective plans of his own.

'Off went Lotario, and the next day Anselmo produced his excuse about going into the country to see his friend, made his departure, and returned to hide in the garderobe, which was easy for him to do because Camila and Leonela made it so. Anselmo lurked in his hiding-place with the trepidation of one waiting to see the bowels of his own honour torn to shreds, and on the brink of losing the supreme good that he'd once believed he possessed in his beloved Camila. Once Camila and Leonela were certain that Anselmo was installed, they walked into the garderobe, and no sooner had Camila set foot in it than she heaved the deepest of sighs and said:

'"Oh, my dear Leonela! Would it not be better, before I put into execution what I will not inform you of, so that you do not attempt to hinder me, if you took this dagger of Anselmo's, which I have just asked you to give me, and transfixed this infamous breast of mine with it? But no, no, do not do that; because it would not be right for me to receive the punishment for another's crime. First I must know what it was that Lotario's audacious and licentious eyes saw in me to make him dare to disclose his evil desire, both scorning his friend and dishonouring me. Go to that window, Leonela, and call him; he must be waiting out there, hoping to carry out his wicked design. But first mine, cruel yet honourable, will be put into effect."

'"Oh, my lady!" replied the wily and well-rehearsed Leonela. "What are you going to do with this dagger? Do you perhaps intend to take your own life, or to take Lotario's? Either of these actions will lead to the loss of your good name and reputation. It will be better to dissemble your wrong, and not give this wicked man the opportunity to enter this house and find us here alone. Remember, my lady, that we are weak women, and he is a man, and a determined one; and since he comes with that wicked intention, blinded by passion, perhaps before you can do whatever it is you have in mind he may do what would be worse for you than death itself. A plague upon my master Anselmo for giving this cutthroat such a free rein in his house! And when you have killed him, my lady, as I think you intend, what shall we do with him once he's dead?"

'"Do with him?" replied Camila. "Oh, we'll leave him for Anselmo to dispose of, because it's only right that he should enjoy the restful toil of burying his own infamy. Come now, call the man here, for every moment I delay my just revenge I seem to be failing in the loyalty I owe my husband."

'As Anselmo listened, his feelings changed with every word that Camila spoke. But when he heard that she was determined to kill Lotario, he made up his mind to come out and show himself, to avert such a disaster; he was held back, however, by his desire to see where all these brave words and virtuous sentiments would lead, and he decided to emerge later, in time to forestall any mischief.

'And now Camila was overcome by a violent fainting-fit and, as she threw herself on to a nearby bed, Leonela began to weep bitter tears and say:

'"Oh, woe is me that I should be so unhappy as to see dying here between my arms the flower of the world's chastity, the pick of pure women, the pattern of feminine virtue," and more to the same effect, and nobody could have heard her and not taken her for the most loyal and heart-broken maidservant in the world, and her mistress for another persecuted Penelope.[1]

'It wasn't very long before Camila came out of her fainting-fit, and as she did so she said:

'"Why do you not go, Leonela, to call the most faithful friend that the sun ever saw or the night ever hid? Come now, be quick, hurry, fly, lest the delay dampens the fire of my wrath, and the just revenge that I await is dissipated in threats and curses."

'"Yes, I am going to call him now, my lady," said Leonela, "but first you must give me that dagger, to prevent you from doing, while I am away, that which would leave all those who love you mourning for the rest of their lives."

' "Go, Leonela my friend, I assure you that I shall not do any such thing," replied Camila, "because even though it might be rash and stupid of me, in your eyes, to defend my honour, I am not going to be as rash and stupid as that Lucretia of whom it is said that she killed herself without having done anything blameworthy, and without first killing the man who caused her misfortune. I shall die if I have to, but I shall die revenged of him who made me come to this place to bewail his audacity, which sprang from no misconduct of mine."

'Leonela had to be coaxed again and again before she would go and call Lotario; but she went in the end, and while she was away Camila spoke, as if talking to herself:

' "God help me! Would it not have been better to send Lotario away, as I have on so many other occasions, than make him think, as must now be the case, that I am a loose and wicked woman, even if only until I correct him? Yes, it would, there is no doubt; but I should not achieve my revenge, and my husband's honour would not be upheld, if Lotario were allowed to stroll away unscathed from where his evil intentions have brought him. Let the traitor pay with his life for what his lust has led him to attempt. Let the whole world know (if it finds out) that Camila not only kept faith with her husband but avenged him on the man who presumed to offend him. Yet I do think, all the same, that it would be better to tell Anselmo about this; but then I tried to do so in that letter I sent him, and I suppose that the reason why he did nothing about the trouble to which it referred must have been because he is so good and trusting that he would not or could not believe that the breast of such a firm friend housed any feelings that went against his honour; and I myself did not believe it, either, for very many days, and would never have believed it if his insolence had not grown so great that his blatant gifts and splendid promises and never-ending tears made it plain. But why try to reason it all out now? Does a brave decision stand in need of arguments? No, of course not. Begone, then, traitors! Draw nigh, revenge! Let the cheat enter, approach and die, come what may! I was pure when I came into the possession of the man that heaven gave me as my husband, and pure I shall be when I cease to be his; or, at worst, I shall be bathed in my own chaste blood and in the foul blood of the falsest friend the world has ever seen."

'As she talked she paced about the room brandishing the dagger, taking such enormous and irregular strides and making such gestures that she seemed to have lost her senses, and she looked more like some desperate villain than a gentle lady. Anselmo, hiding behind the tapestries, was watching it all in utter amazement, thinking that what he'd seen and heard was quite enough to refute even worse suspicions, and wishing that Lotario's part in the test could be avoided, because he feared a sudden disaster. He was about to emerge and embrace his wife and tell her the truth, yet he stayed where he was because he saw Leonela return leading Lotario by the hand; and when Camila saw him she drew a long line on the floor in front of her with the dagger, and said:

' "Lotario, listen to what I am going to say: if you should venture to cross this line or even approach it, as soon as I see what you are doing I shall plunge this dagger I hold deep into my breast. No, no, before you reply you must hear me out, and then you can say what you please. First of all, Lotario, I want you to tell me whether you know my husband Anselmo, and what you think of him; and then I want you to tell me whether you know me. Answer now, and do not be embarrassed or start weighing your words, because my questions are not difficult ones."

'Lotario wasn't so foolish that he hadn't realized, as soon as she'd told him to make Anselmo hide, what she was going to do; and he played along with such skill and good timing that the two of them could have persuaded anyone that their lie was more truthful than truth itself. He replied:

' "I did not suspect, lovely Camila, that you had summoned me to ask questions so far removed from the purpose that has brought me here. If you have done this to delay granting me the favour that you have promised me, you could have achieved that without making me come, because the nearer the prospect of possession the more eager we are to enjoy the desired good. But, so as not to be accused of refusing to answer your questions, let me say that I do know your husband Anselmo, and we have known each other since our tenderest years, and I will not say what you know only too well about our friendship, because I do not wish to bear witness to the offence that I am being forced to commit against it by love, a potent excuse for even greater sins. I do know you, too, and I hold you as dear as your husband does; or else I should not, for lesser charms than yours, be acting so contrary to my duty as a gentleman and to the holy laws of true friendship, which I have now violated and broken at the instigation of an enemy as dauntless as is love."

' "If you confess to that," replied Camila, "you mortal enemy of everything that truly deserves to be loved, how can you dare appear before the woman you know is the mirror into which gazes a man whom you should use as your mirror so that he could show you how little excuse you have for wronging him? But ah! unhappy me! now I realize what it was that led you to forget yourself: it must have been some indiscretion of mine – I will not call it immodesty, because it cannot have been deliberate, but rather one of those slips that we women are prone to make when we believe that we do not need to be on our guard. Or else just tell me this, O traitor! When did I ever respond to your appeals with any word or hint that could have awoken the slightest shadow of a hope of gratifying your infamous desires? When were your words of love not rejected and reproved with words of the harshest severity? When were your many promises ever believed, your even more abundant gifts ever accepted? And yet it is my belief that no man can persevere in his quest for love unless he is sustained by some glimmer of hope; so I shall blame myself for your insolence, because some thoughtlessness of mine must have kept your hopes alive, and I shall inflict on myself the punishment that you deserve. And so that you can see that if I am going to be so cruel to myself I cannot fail to treat you in the same way, I have brought you here to witness the sacrifice that I am going to offer to the offended honour of my most honourable husband, whom you have wronged to the utmost of your power, and whom I too have wronged by not taking sufficient care to avoid giving you the impression, if this is what I did, that I welcomed and applauded your wicked designs. I repeat that what most distresses me is my suspicion that it was some carelessness on my part that spawned such wild feelings in you, and this is what I most wish to punish with my own hand, because if another executioner did so my guilt might become public; but I shall die killing, and take with me the one who will satisfy my desire for the vengeance that I long for – nay, now enjoy! – so that I can see, wherever it may be, the punishment that impartial, unbending justice metes out to the man who has reduced me to this desperate plight."

'As she spoke these words she sprang upon Lotario with unbelievable violence and agility, brandishing the dagger in such a show of determination to bury it in his chest that he himself almost wondered whether she was pretending or not, because he had to have recourse to all his strength and dexterity to prevent Camila from wounding him. She acted out her strange, unworthy deceit to such perfection that to make it even more realistic she decided to colour it with her own blood, and realizing, or pretending to realize, that she couldn't wound Lotario, she said:

' "Though fate denies me a full satisfaction of my just desires, at least it will not prevent me from satisfying them in part."

'And wresting the hand holding the dagger from Lotario's grasp she placed the point of the weapon where it could only make a shallow wound and slid it into her armpit, under her left shoulder, and then dropped to the floor as if she had fainted. Leonela and Lotario stood astonished at this development, still wondering whether what they were witnessing could be true, as Camila lay there on the floor, bathed in her own blood. Breathless with terror, Lotario ran to pull the dagger out, but when he saw how slight the wound was the fear that till then had possessed him was dispelled, and he was struck anew with amazement at the lovely Camila's cunning, prudence and quick wits; and, continuing to play his part, he began to make a long, sorrowful lament over her, as if she were dead, cursing not only himself but also the man who had put him in this position. And since he knew that his friend Anselmo was listening, his lamentations were such that anyone who heard him would have felt much sorrier for him than for Camila, even supposing her to be dead.

'Leonela took her up in her arms and laid her on the bed, entreating Lotario to go and bring someone who could look after her in secret. She also asked him for his advice about what they could tell Anselmo concerning her mistress's wound if he returned before it healed. Lotario replied that they could say whatever they liked, because he was in no state to give advice that would be of any use; he only told her to try to stop the bleeding, because he was going where nobody could find him. And with a show of enormous grief he left the house, and once he was alone where nobody could see him he crossed himself over and over again in wonder at Camila's ingenuity and Leonela's role-playing. He reflected on how convinced Anselmo must be that he had a second Portia for a wife,[2] and he couldn't wait to see his friend to rejoice together over the most perfectly dissembled lie and truth that could ever be imagined.

'So Leonela staunched the bleeding, which was no more copious than was necessary to lend credibility to the performance, washed the wound with a little wine and bound it up as best she could, uttering while she did so such words as, even if nothing had been said before, would have been enough to convince Anselmo that in Camila he possessed a pattern of chastity. Leonela's words were accompanied by others from Camila, as she called herself a spineless coward for having lacked courage when she most needed it, to take that life of hers that she held in such abhorrence. She asked for her maid's advice about whether she should tell her dear husband all about the incident, and her maid advised her not to, because that would compel him to avenge himself on Lotario, which he couldn't do without great risk, and it was the good wife's duty not to give her husband reasons to fight, but rather to keep him out of trouble as much as possible. Camila replied that this was sound advice and that she would follow it, but that at all events they were going to have to find some explanation for her wound, because Anselmo was bound to notice it; to which Leonela replied that she was incapable of telling a lie, even in jest.

'"And how capable do you think I am, my dear?" replied Camila. "I should not dare to invent or maintain a falsehood even if my life depended on it. So if we can think of no escape from this difficulty, it will be better to make a clean breast of it than have him catch us telling lies."

'"Do not worry, my lady," replied Leonela. "By tomorrow I shall have thought of something to tell him, and maybe, with the wound being where it is, it can be covered up so that he does not notice; and heaven will see fit, I am sure, to favour our just and honourable cause. Do calm down, my lady, and try to control your feelings, so that master does not realize that you are upset when he returns – and leave all the rest to me and to God, who always comes to the help of well-intentioned people."

'Anselmo had been watching and listening, with rapt attention, to the tragedy of the death of his honour, as it was performed by the players with such unusual and effective feeling that they seemed to have been transformed into the very characters they were acting. He was longing for night to come to give him the chance to slip away from home and go to see his good friend Lotario and rejoice with him over the precious pearl[3] that he'd discovered in the revelation of his wife's virtue. The two women took good care to give him an easy opportunity to escape, and he accepted it and slipped away, and went straight to look for Lotario; he found him, and words can't describe his embraces, his expressions of joy and his praise of Camila. Lotario listened to it all, unable to produce any expressions of joy at all, because he couldn't help thinking how deluded his friend was, and how inexcusable was his own treachery. And although Anselmo noticed that Lotario wasn't at all happy, he supposed that it was because Camila had been left bleeding on the floor and he had been the cause. And so, among other arguments, Anselmo told his friend not to worry about Camila – the wound was clearly not such a serious one, since the two women had agreed to keep it hidden, and this showed that there was nothing to fear, and they could rejoice and celebrate together; because thanks to Lotario's ingenious mediation Anselmo had been raised to the highest happiness that he'd ever dared to desire for himself, and the only pastime he wanted now was writing poems in praise of Camila to make her eternal in the memory of future generations. Lotario praised his friend's good intentions and said that he, for his part, would help to erect so glorious an edifice.

'This left Anselmo the most splendidly bamboozled man that the world had ever seen: he led home by the hand the man who had ruined his good name, believing that what he was taking there was the instrument of his glory. Camila greeted him with a grimace on her face and a smile in her heart. This deception lasted for some while until, a few months later, fortune turned her wheel, the artfully concealed intrigue was revealed and Anselmo's inappropriate curiosity cost him his life.'

CHAPTER XXXV

❀

Which brings the Tale of Inappropriate Curiosity to an end

Not much more of the tale remained to be read when Sancho Panza came running in a frenzy from the loft where Don Quixote had gone to bed, crying:

'Come on, come on, all of you, come and help my master, he's got himself into the roughest and toughest battle I've ever set eyes on. Great God, he's just taken his sword to that giant who's my lady Princess Micomicona's enemy, and he's topped him like a turnip!'

'What do you mean, my dear friend?' said the priest, putting aside what was left of the tale. 'Are you in your right mind, Sancho? How the devil can what you say be right, when the giant's a good seven thousand miles away?'

They heard a great uproar in the loft, and Don Quixote bellowing:

'Stay, robber, scoundrel, poltroon; I have you at last; and your scimitar shall not save you!'

It sounded as if he was slashing the walls. Sancho said:

'Don't just stand around listening, get in there and pull them apart, or give my master a helping hand, though that won't be needed any more, because the giant's dead by now, for certain, and answering to God for his evil past – I saw his blood flowing all over the floor, and his head cut off and lying on its side, and it's as big as an enormous wineskin.'

'I'll be hanged,' interjected the innkeeper, 'if Don Quixote or Don Devil hasn't been slashing at those skins of red wine I keep behind that bed, and the wine he's spilled must be what this character took for blood.'

And he burst into the loft, and the others followed him, and they found Don Quixote wearing the strangest outfit in the world. He was in his shirt, which wasn't long enough in front to cover his thighs, and was some six inches shorter behind; his legs were long and scrawny, hairy and none too clean; on his head he had a greasy red nightcap belonging to the innkeeper.

Round his left arm he had wound the blanket from his bed, against which Sancho bore such a grudge, for reasons well known to himself; in his right hand he grasped his sword, with which he was letting fly in all directions as he shouted out as if he really were fighting with a giant. And the best part of it all is that his eyes were tight shut, because he was asleep and dreaming that he was battling against the giant: so intensely had he lived in his imagination the adventure in which he was going to be triumphant that he was dreaming he'd reached the kingdom of Micomicón and was at grips with the enemy. And he'd given the wineskins so many slashes, thinking he was slashing the giant, that the loft was flooded with wine. This sight so enraged the innkeeper that he flew at Don Quixote and began to rain so many punches on him that, if Cardenio and the priest hadn't dragged him away, he'd have put an end to the adventure of the giant there and then; yet the poor knight still didn't wake up, until the barber brought a large bucketful of cold water from the well and drenched him from head to toe, and then he did awaken, but not fully enough to be aware of his situation.

In view of Don Quixote's short and scanty apparel, Dorotea didn't care to go in to watch the battle between her protector and her adversary. Sancho was looking all over the floor for the giant's head and, not finding it, he said:

'Now I know that everything about this house is enchanted – last time, here, where I'm standing now, I got a good hiding and I never knew who gave it to me, and I never even saw anyone, and this time I can't find that head I saw cut off with my own two eyes, and the blood was gushing from the body like a fountain.'

'Blood and fountain my foot, you enemy of God and all his holy saints!' said the innkeeper. 'Can't you see, you idiot, that your blood and your fountain are none other than these wineskins here all full of holes and this red wine we're swimming in? And I'd like to see the soul of the man who spilled it all swimming too – swimming in hell!'

'I don't know anything about that,' replied Sancho, 'all I know is that I'm going to be so unlucky that just because I can't find this head my earldom's going to melt away like salt in water.'

And Sancho awake was worse than his master asleep, so besotted was he with his master's promises. The innkeeper was in despair at the squire's apathy and his master's handiwork, and swore it wasn't going to be like last time when they got away without paying – all the privileges of his chivalry weren't going to let him off coughing up for the two of them, right down to the cost of the patches for the perforated wineskins.

The priest was holding on to Don Quixote by his hands, and he, thinking that the adventure was over now and that he was standing before Princess Micomicona, fell to his knees in front of the priest, saying:

'O great and famous lady, Your Highness can from this day forward rest assured that this ill-born creature can do you no further harm, and from this day forward, too, I am released from the promise I made you, for, with the help of God on high and through the favour of her for whom I live and breathe, I have fulfilled it to perfection.'

'Didn't I tell you so?' said Sancho when he heard this. 'It's true, it's true, I wasn't drunk – my master's done for the giant good and proper! We're having a fiesta after all, my earldom's on its way!'

Who could have failed to laugh at the nonsense of these two, master and servant? And laugh they did, all except the innkeeper, who was cursing himself to the devil. But at length the barber, Cardenio and the priest managed to force Don Quixote down on to the bed, where, exhausted, he fell asleep. They left him there and went out into the porch to console Sancho Panza for not having found the giant's head, but it was a harder job to pacify the innkeeper, who was reduced to despair by his wineskins' sudden death. And his wife was screaming:

'In an evil hour that knight errant came into my house, and I wish I'd never set eyes on him, he's turned out so expensive. The last time he went off owing me for the night, supper, bed, straw and barley for him and his squire and a nag and a donkey, saying that he was a knight adventurer, and I hope God sends him plenty of misadventures, him and all the adventurers in the world, and he said that being one made him exempt from paying, because this was written up on all the knight-errantry price-lists. And then, thanks to him, this other character came and took my tail away, and he's given it back with more than half-a-real's damage, all the hair gone, and now it's no good for what my husband wants it for. And on top of all that, hacking my wineskins to pieces and spilling all my wine – I'd like to see all his blood spilled, I can tell you that much. Well, they aren't getting away with it – by the bones of my father and the eternal glory of my mother I swear they're going to pay me back, every single maravedí they owe me, or my name isn't what it is and I'm not my father's daughter!'

The innkeeper's wife went on railing away like this, with her good servant Maritornes seconding her. Her daughter kept quiet, and every so often she smiled. The priest calmed everyone down, promising to make good their losses as best he could – both the wineskins and the wine, and above all the tail, which they evidently held so dear. Dorotea consoled Sancho Panza by promising him that so long as it was confirmed that his master had indeed cut the giant's head off, and once her kingdom was restored to peace, she'd give him the very best earldom in her gift. Sancho took comfort from this, and he assured the princess that she could be dead certain he really had seen the giant's head and that if she wanted any more details he'd got a beard that went right down to his middle, and if the head didn't turn up it was because all the goings-on in that place were enchanted, as he'd found the other time he'd stayed there. Dorotea said she believed he was right, and he shouldn't worry, everything would go well and turn out to his heart's content.

Now that peace was restored, the priest thought it would be a good idea to finish reading the tale, because he could see that not much was left. Cardenio, Dorotea and all the others begged him to do so. He was eager to please everyone, and was enjoying the reading himself, so he continued:

'So Anselmo, convinced of Camila's virtue, led a happy and carefree life, and Camila took good care to glower at Lotario whenever she saw him, so that Anselmo should believe her feelings for him to be the opposite of what they were, and to provide even more confirmation Lotario begged leave not to return, because it was clear how upset Camila was by his visits; but the deluded Anselmo replied that by no manner of means should he absent himself. And so in a thousand different ways Anselmo was manufacturing his own dishonour in the belief that he was creating his own happiness.

'Meanwhile, Leonela's satisfaction at finding her love affair officially approved was such that she brushed all other considerations aside and pursued her pleasure with abandon, safe in the knowledge that her mistress was covering up for her and even advising her on how she could enjoy herself with little fear of detection. But finally, one night Anselmo heard footsteps in Leonela's room, and, when he tried to go in to see who it was, he found that the door was being held against him, which made him even more determined to open it; he forced it open and broke in to see a man jumping out of the window into the street, and, as he ran over to catch him or at least see who he was, Leonela prevented him from doing either by clinging on to him and crying:

' "Calm down, sir, don't get excited, don't follow him out of the window – it's my own affair, indeed he's my husband."

'Anselmo wouldn't believe her, and instead, in a blind rage, he drew his dagger and threatened her, saying that if she didn't tell him the truth he'd kill her. She was so terrified that she didn't know what she was saying when she said:

' "Don't kill me, sir, I'll tell you something more important than you can imagine."

' "I want to hear it now," said Anselmo. "If not, you're dead."

' "I can't, not now," said Leonela, "I'm too upset. Give me till tomorrow, and then I'll tell you something that'll amaze you. And believe me, the person who jumped out of the window is a local young man who's given me his hand in marriage."

'With this Anselmo regained his composure and agreed to the postponement, not suspecting that he was going to hear anything against Camila, about whose virtue he was so convinced; and so he left the room and locked Leonela into it, telling her that she wouldn't be allowed out until she said what she had to say.

'He went straight to Camila to inform her about what had happened and about the maid's promise of revelations of the utmost importance. There's no need to describe Camila's perturbation, for her fear was so great – believing, as she did and as she had every reason to, that Leonela was going to tell Anselmo all she knew about her mistress's infidelity – that she didn't have the courage to wait and see whether her suspicions were justified; and that very night, once she saw Anselmo was asleep, she collected together her finest jewels and some money and slipped unnoticed from the house and went to Lotario's and told him what had happened, imploring him to find a safe hiding-place for her or to run away with her to where Anselmo couldn't catch up with them. Camila's words plunged Lotario into such confusion that he couldn't reply, still less decide what to do. At length he resolved to remove Camila to a convent where one of his sisters was prioress. Camila agreed, and with all the urgency demanded by the circumstances Lotario took her to the convent and left her there, and departed from the city without telling anybody.

'At dawn the next day, Anselmo was so anxious to learn what Leonela had to tell him that he didn't notice that Camila was missing from his side when he got up and walked to the room into which he'd locked their servant. He opened the door and went in, but Leonela wasn't there; all he found were some sheets knotted together and hanging from the window, a sure sign of how she'd escaped. He went sadly back to tell Camila and was astonished not to find her in bed or anywhere in the house. He asked his servants where she was, but nobody could give him an answer.

'As he was searching for Camila he came across her jewel-boxes open and most of the jewels gone, and this made him realize the full extent of his misfortune and appreciate that Leonela wasn't the one to blame. He went off, still only half-dressed, lost in thought and stricken with grief, to tell his friend Lotario about the disaster. When he couldn't find him either, and Lotario's servants said he had departed that night and had taken all his money with him, Anselmo thought he'd go mad. And as the last straw, he returned home and found not one of his servants there, just an empty, deserted house.

'He didn't know what to think, say or do, and he was slowly losing his sanity. He found himself deprived at one blow of his wife, his friend and his servants, abandoned by the heavens above and, worst of all, dishonoured, because in Camila's disappearance he could see his own undoing.

'Eventually he decided to go to the village where his friend lived, and where he himself had stayed to make it possible to contrive this whole disaster. He shut up his house, mounted his horse and started out with a heavy heart; but he'd hardly gone halfway when, besieged by his own thoughts, he had to dismount and tie his horse by the reins to a tree, at the foot of which he dropped to the ground, breathing piteous sighs of sorrow; and there he lay until close to nightfall, when he saw a man coming on horseback from the city, and, after greeting him, he asked what was the news from Florence. The man from the city replied:

' "It's the strangest news that's been heard there for many a long day; because it's reported that Lotario, the great friend of rich Anselmo, who used to live in the San Giovanni area, ran away last night with Camila,

Anselmo's wife, who's nowhere to be found. Camila's maidservant told the whole story, after being discovered last night by the Governor letting herself down by a sheet from a window in Anselmo's house. The fact is I don't know exactly what happened, all I do know is that the whole city is astonished, because this wasn't something to be expected from the close friendship between the two men, which is said to have been so remarkable that everyone called them 'the two friends'."

' "Is it known, by any chance," asked Anselmo, "which way Lotario and Camila went?"

' "Nobody knows that," said the man from Florence, "even though the Governor has ordered the most thorough searches to be made."

' "God be with you, sir," said Anselmo.

' "And with you," said the other, and rode away.

'This terrible news brought Anselmo to the verge of losing not only his reason but his life as well. He struggled to his feet and rode on to his friend's house; his friend didn't yet know about the disaster but, seeing Anselmo arrive looking pale, gaunt and haggard, he realized that something awful had happened. Anselmo asked to be put to bed and provided with writing materials. This was done, and he was left there by himself, for this was what he wanted, and he even asked for the door to be locked. Once he was alone all the details of the disaster crowded in on his brain and he knew he was dying, so he decided to leave an account of the reasons for his strange death; and he began to write but, before he could finish setting down all he wanted, he breathed his last and left his life in the hands of the grief that his inappropriate curiosity had brought upon him.

'When the master of the house saw that it was getting late and that Anselmo remained silent, he decided to go in to find out if he was any worse, and discovered him lying face down with half his body on the bed and half on the writing-tray, a paper with writing on it open in front of him and the pen still in his hand. He called out to his guest, then ran over and took his hand and, finding that there was no response and that he was cold, knew that he was dead. He was overcome by amazement and grief, and summoned his servants to come and see what a disaster had befallen Anselmo; and then he read the paper written, as he could see, in Anselmo's own hand:

A stupid and inappropriate desire has taken my life. If news of my death reaches Camila's ears, I want her to know that I forgive her, because she was under no obligation to work miracles, nor had I any need to expect her to; and since I manufactured my own dishonour, there is no cause to . . .

'This was all Anselmo had written, showing that here his life had ended, before his letter could. On the following day Anselmo's friend sent news of his death to his relatives, who already knew of his misfortune, as well as to the convent where Camila was very close to accompanying her husband on that unavoidable journey, not because of the news of her husband's death but because of what she'd heard about her missing lover. It's said that although she was now a widow she would neither leave the convent nor take the veil until, not long afterwards, she received news that Lotario had died in a battle waged by Monsieur de Lautrec against the Great Captain Gonzalo Fernández de Córdoba in the kingdom of Naples,[1] where the tardily repentant friend had ended up; and then Camila did take the veil, and died shortly afterwards at the unforgiving hands of sadness and melancholy. These were the ends that the three of them came to, arising from such ridiculous beginnings.'

'This,' said the priest, 'seems like a pretty good tale to me, but I can't believe it's true; and if it's invented the author hasn't done his job in a very convincing way, because I can't believe there could ever be a husband so stupid as to want to carry out such a costly experiment. If it were presented as involving a lover and his mistress it might pass, but with a man and his wife it approaches the impossible. Yet the way in which it's told doesn't displease me at all.'

CHAPTER XXXVI

✤

*Concerning the fierce and prodigious battle that Don
Quixote fought against some skins of red wine, and other
things that happened to him at the inn*

And now the innkeeper, standing by the door, said:

'Here's a fine troop of customers on their way – if they stop, we're going
to have ourselves a party.'

'Who are they?' asked Cardenio.

'Four men,' replied the innkeeper, 'on horseback – short stirrups Arab-
style, lances and leather shields, black travelling-masks – and with them a
woman in white – high saddle complete with back and arms, face covered
too – and two servants on foot.'

'Are they very near?' asked the priest.

'They're so very near,' replied the innkeeper, 'that here they are.'

When Dorotea heard this she veiled her face, and Cardenio disappeared
into Don Quixote's room; and they hardly had time to do so before all the
people described by the innkeeper came in. The four on horseback, who
looked and behaved like men of breeding, dismounted and went to help
the lady down from her high saddle; and one of them took her into his
arms and sat her in a chair by the entrance to the room in which Cardenio
had hidden. Neither she nor they had removed their travelling-masks or
uttered a word; as the woman sank into the chair she only exhaled a deep
sigh and let her arms drop to her side, like someone who was weak and ill.
The foot-servants took the horses to the stable. The priest wanted to know
what people these were who appeared in such garb and such silence, and
he went to see the two servants and put his question to one of them, who
replied:

'By God, sir, I can't tell you who they are, all I know is that they seem
to be very high-up, specially that one who went over to take the lady in
his arms, and I say this because all the others are full of respect for him and
nothing ever gets done unless he says so.'

'And who is the lady?' asked the priest.

'I couldn't tell you that, either,' replied the servant, 'because I haven't set eyes on her face all the way here. I've heard her sigh all right, lots and lots of times, and groan away as if she was about to give up the ghost each time she groaned. And you mustn't wonder about us not knowing any more than this, because we haven't been with them for more than a couple of days – they came across us on the road and persuaded us to go with them to Andalusia and promised to pay us very good wages.'

'And have you heard any of their names?' asked the priest.

'No, never,' replied the servant, 'because they all ride along in such silence you wouldn't believe it, nothing to be heard except the poor lady sighing and sobbing, which makes us feel very sorry for her; and we're both convinced she's being forced to go wherever she's being taken, and as far as you can tell from her clothes she's a nun, or about to become a nun, which is more likely, and maybe it's because she isn't becoming a nun of her own free will that she's as sad as she seems to be.'

'That may well be the case,' the priest declared.

And he left them and went back to Dorotea who, moved by natural compassion when she heard the masked woman's sighs, drew near to her and said:

'What's wrong with you, my lady? If it's something that another woman might be able to help you with, I'll do so with the best will in the world.'

But the grieving lady didn't answer, and although Dorotea repeated her offer with even greater insistence, she stayed silent; and then the masked man, the one whom the servant said the others obeyed, came over and said to Dorotea:

'Don't waste your time, madam, making this woman any offers, because it isn't her way to be thankful for what's done for her; and don't attempt to make her reply, unless you want to hear a falsehood.'

'I have never told lies,' the silent woman burst out. 'It's precisely because I'm so honest and incapable of lying that I'm so wretched now; and I call you as a witness to that, since it's my total truthfulness that forces you to lie and to cheat.'

Cardenio heard these words clearly, being so close to the speaker, because only the door of Don Quixote's room separated them, and he cried:

'Good God! What is this I hear? Whose voice is ringing in my ears?'

The lady looked round in alarm and, not seeing who could have shouted, stood up and went to enter the room; observing which the gentleman grasped her and prevented her from taking a step. In her agitation the taffeta travelling-mask slipped down, revealing a face of incomparable and miraculous beauty, although pale and terrified, as her eyes ranged all round the room so eagerly that she looked like a madwoman – behaviour that mystified Dorotea and the others, and filled them with pity. The gentleman was gripping the lady by the shoulders and was so concerned to hold on to her that he couldn't attend to his mask as it slipped down his face and eventually fell off; Dorotea, with her arms round the lady, looked up and saw that the man also holding her was her husband Don Fernando, and a sigh rose from the deepest depths of her being as she toppled over backwards – and if the barber hadn't been standing near by to catch her, Dorotea would have fallen to the floor.

The priest ran over to remove her veil and sprinkle water on her face, and as he did so Don Fernando recognized her and was thunderstruck, not that this made him release Luscinda, for she it was who was trying to struggle free from him, having in her turn recognized Cardenio from his cries, as he had her. And Cardenio had heard Dorotea's sigh as she'd fainted, and, in the belief that it was his Luscinda, he rushed in terror out of the loft, and what he first saw was Don Fernando with Luscinda in his arms. Don Fernando also recognized Cardenio, and the three of them, Luscinda, Cardenio and Dorotea, were struck dumb with amazement, hardly knowing what had happened to them. Speechless, they all gazed at each other: Dorotea gazed at Don Fernando, Don Fernando at Cardenio, Cardenio at Luscinda and Luscinda at Cardenio. The first to break the silence was Luscinda, who said to Don Fernando:

'Don Fernando: because of what you owe yourself as a gentleman, if no other duty sways you, you must allow me to go and cling to that wall on which I am the ivy, and lean on that support from which you have never been able to separate me with all your insistence, your threats, your promises and your gifts. See how heaven, working in ways strange and mysterious to us, has placed my true husband before me. And you know very well, from a thousand costly experiences, that only death would be strong enough to erase him from my memory. So let those lessons in disillusionment teach you, if you aren't capable of anything better, to turn love into rage, desire

into murderous vindictiveness, and take my life, because if I yield it up in
the presence of my dear husband I shall consider it well spent: maybe my
death will convince him that I have remained faithful until the very last
moments of my existence.'

In the meantime Dorotea had recovered consciousness and had been
listening to everything Luscinda had said, from which she deduced who
she was; and seeing that Don Fernando was still not releasing Luscinda or
replying to her, Dorotea struggled to her feet and went to kneel before
him and, as lovely, pitiful tears flowed from her eyes, she began:

'Unless, my lord, the rays of that sun that you are holding eclipsed in
your arms have dazzled and blinded you, you will have perceived that the
woman kneeling here at your feet is Dorotea, luckless and wretched for
as long as you are pleased to have it so. Yes, I am that humble farmer's
daughter whom you chose, out of your kindness or for your pleasure, to
raise to the eminence of calling herself yours. I am the woman who,
enclosed within the bounds of virtue, lived a contented life until she
responded to the insistent calls of what seemed like true love, opened the
doors of her chaste seclusion and handed you the keys of her freedom, a
gift you thought very little of, as is made clear by my being reduced to the
circumstances in which you find me, and by your being in the situation in
which I find you. Yet in spite of all that I shouldn't wish you to imagine
that I have come here driven by my dishonour: it is only the deep sorrow
of being forgotten by you that has brought me. You wanted me to be yours
and you were so successful that, even if you now want me to stop being
yours, you can't stop being mine.

'Bear in mind, my lord, that my matchless love for you can be a
compensation for the beauty and nobility of the woman for whom you
want to desert me. You can't be lovely Luscinda's, because you're mine,
and she can't be yours, because she's Cardenio's. And, if only you think
about it, it will be easier for you to force yourself to love the woman who
adores you than to persuade the woman who hates you to love you. You
laid siege to my unsuspecting heart; you importuned my integrity; you
were not unaware of my rank; you well know the circumstances in which
I gave in to your desires: you can't claim that you were deceived into our
bond. And if all this is so, as it is, and you are a Christian as you are a
gentleman, why are you using all this evasion to delay making me as happy

331

in the sequel as you did in the beginnings? And if you don't want me as what I am, your true and lawful wife, at least accept me as your slave, because so long as I'm in your power I shall consider myself a fortunate woman. Don't abandon me for the gossips to huddle together in their little groups and destroy my honour; don't give my parents such an unhappy old age, because it isn't what they deserve for the loyal services that, as good tenants, they've always rendered your parents.

'And if you believe that you'll destroy your blood if you mix it with mine, bear in mind that there are few, if any, noble families in the world who haven't travelled down this road, and that the women's blood is not what counts in illustrious pedigrees; what's more, true nobility consists in virtue, and if you forfeit that by denying me my just rights, I shall be left with better claims to nobility than you. And finally, sir, let me say that whether you like it or not I am married to you; your own words are witnesses, and they cannot and must not be false ones, if you pride yourself on possessing what you despise me for lacking; the signature you put on the document will be a witness, and so will heaven, because you called on heaven to be a witness to what you were promising me. And if all this doesn't move you, your own conscience won't fail to raise its silent voice in the midst of your joys, defending this truth that I've laid before you, and disturbing all your finest moments of pleasure.'

The afflicted Dorotea spoke these and other words with such feeling and accompanied by such tears that even the men with Don Fernando joined all the others in weeping with her. Don Fernando listened in silence until she stopped speaking and started sighing and sobbing so sorrowfully that only a heart of brass could have remained unmoved. Luscinda stood gazing down at her, no less afflicted by her grief than amazed by her beauty and good sense, and, although she wanted to hurry to her side with some words of comfort, Don Fernando was still holding her tight and preventing her from moving. He stood there staring at Dorotea in bewilderment and alarm, and after a while he opened his arms to release Luscinda and said:

'You've won, lovely Dorotea, you've won: nobody could have the heart to deny such an assemblage of truths.'

When Don Fernando released Luscinda she swooned and would have slumped to the floor, but Cardenio was close at hand, having placed himself behind Don Fernando so as not to be recognized, and he set fear aside and ventured all as he hurried to support Luscinda, and taking her into his arms he said:

'If merciful heaven is minded to grant you some repose at last, my steadfast, faithful and beautiful lady, I believe that nowhere can you rest more safely than in these arms that hold you now and held you once before, when fortune was pleased to let me call you mine.'

At these words Luscinda looked up at Cardenio, at first recognizing him by his voice and then confirming with her eyes that it was he; almost beside herself, and with no regard for the proprieties, she threw her arms around his neck and, pressing her face to his, said:

'You, my dearest, you are the true master of this your slave, however much adverse fate tries to prevent it, and however many threats are made against this life of mine, which depends on yours.'

This was a strange sight for Don Fernando and all the others, who stood in wonder at such an unusual occurrence. It seemed to Dorotea that Don Fernando had paled and was about to avenge himself on Cardenio, because she saw his hand moving towards his sword; and as soon as this idea struck her she clasped his legs and kissed them and held on to him, and as her tears flowed on down her cheeks she said:

'Don Fernando, my one and only refuge: what is it that you have in mind to do in this unexpected predicament? At your feet is your wife, and the woman you want to make your wife is in her husband's arms. Ask yourself whether it will be right or even possible to undo what heaven has done, or whether it will be better to raise up and make your equal the woman who, overcoming all obstacles and confirmed in her faithfulness and constancy, is gazing into your eyes and bathing in loving tears the face and breast of her lawful husband. For the good Lord's sake I beg you, for your own sake I implore you, not to allow this stark revelation of the truth to increase your wrath, but rather to quell it so that you can bring yourself in your tranquillity to allow these two lovers to enjoy peace together without any interference from you for as long as heaven sees fit to grant it to them; and in so doing you will be showing the generosity of your illustrious and noble breast, and all the world will be able to see that reason has more power over you than passion.'

As Dorotea was saying this, Cardenio continued to hold Luscinda in his arms, but he didn't take his eyes off Don Fernando, determined as he was that if he saw any hostile movement he'd defend himself and attack as best he could anyone who attacked him, even if it cost him his life. But now Don Fernando's friends, and the priest and the barber, who'd been present throughout, together with the good Sancho Panza, surrounded Don Fernando and entreated him to heed Dorotea's tears and, if what she'd said was true, as they believed it was, not to allow her legitimate hopes to be frustrated. He should reflect that it wasn't by chance, as it might appear, but by a special disposition of Providence, that they had all come together where nobody could have anticipated such a meeting. And the priest told him that only death could part Luscinda from Cardenio, and that even if they were separated by the blade of a sword, they'd count that a happy death; and that in these irremediable circumstances his wisest course would be to control and conquer himself and show a generous heart by allowing these two, of his own free will, to enjoy the happiness that heaven had now granted them; and he should also contemplate Dorotea's beauty, and he'd see that few if any women could equal let alone surpass it, and he should add to her beauty her humility and the great love she felt for him, and above all bear in mind that, if he prized himself on being a gentleman and a Christian, he had no alternative but to keep the promise that he'd made her; and that in this way he would be doing his duty to God and what was right in the eyes of all men of good sense, who well know that it's one of the prerogatives of beauty, even in a woman of low birth, so long as her beauty is united with virtue, to be capable of being raised to any height, without any disparagement to the man who thus raises it to equality with himself; and nobody can be blamed for responding to the powerful promptings of pleasure, so long as no sin is involved.

And to these words all those present added others, so many of them and so well chosen that Don Fernando's worthy heart – nourished, after all, with illustrious blood – relented and gave in to the truth, which he couldn't have denied even if he'd wanted to; and the sign he gave of having surrendered and accepted the excellent advice he'd been offered was to stoop down and embrace Dorotea, saying:

'Rise, my lady: it isn't right for the woman I hold in my heart to be kneeling at my feet, and if I've been slow to demonstrate that I believe this, perhaps it has been ordered by heaven, so that on seeing the constancy with which you love me I should be brought to hold you in the esteem you deserve. What I beg of you is that you don't reprimand me for my bad behaviour and my neglect, because the same force that impelled me to accept you as mine drove me to try to avoid being yours. And for proof that what I say is true, turn round and look into the eyes of Luscinda here, happy at long last, and in them you'll find an excuse for all my errors; and since she has found and achieved all that she desired, and I have found in you what I deserve, may she live secure and contented for many happy years with her Cardenio, and I shall pray heaven to allow me the same happiness with my Dorotea.'

And as he said this he embraced her again and pressed his face to hers with such warmth of feeling that he had to exercise great self-control to prevent his tears from giving final proof of his love and his repentance. But it wasn't so with Luscinda and Cardenio and indeed most of those present, because they began to shed so many tears, some for joy on their own account and some on the account of others, that anyone would have thought some awful disaster had befallen them all. Even Sancho Panza was weeping, although he was later to say that this was only because he could see that Dorotea wasn't Queen Micomicona, from whom he'd been expecting so many favours, as he'd thought she was. Their tears and their amazement took some time to dissipate, and then Cardenio and Luscinda went to kneel before Don Fernando and thank him for the favour he'd done them, in such courteous words that Don Fernando didn't know how to reply, so he brought them to their feet and embraced them with every mark of affection and courtesy.

He asked Dorotea how she'd come to that place, so far from her home. In a few, well-chosen words she told him what she'd earlier told Cardenio, and Don Fernando and his men so enjoyed what she said that they wished the tale had gone on longer, because she spoke so entertainingly about her misfortunes. And once she'd finished, Don Fernando described what had happened to him in the city after he'd found among Luscinda's bodices the paper declaring that she was Cardenio's wife and couldn't marry Don Fernando. He said that he'd meant to kill her and would have done so if her parents hadn't stopped him, and that he'd left the house in embarrassment and fury, determined to take his revenge at a more convenient moment; and the next day he'd learned that Luscinda had gone missing from her parents' house, and no one knew where she was, and finally, some months later, he'd been told she was in a convent, with the intention of staying there for the rest of her life if she couldn't share it with Cardenio; and he'd immediately picked those three men and ridden with them to the convent, but hadn't tried to speak to her because of his fear that if it was known he was there the guard would be redoubled; so one day he waited until the porter's lodge was left unmanned, and posted two of his men at the door as he went in with the other in search of Luscinda, whom they found in the cloister talking to a nun; and they seized her without giving her a chance to resist and took her to a place where they provided themselves with everything they needed for their journey. It had all been simple for them, because the convent was in the middle of fields, a long way from the city. On finding herself in his hands Luscinda had fainted, and even after recovering consciousness all she'd done was weep and sigh, without speaking a word; and so, accompanied by silence and tears, they'd arrived at the inn, which for Don Fernando was the same as arriving in heaven, where all the wretchedness of this earth comes to an end.

CHAPTER XXXVII

✤

Which continues the history of the famous Princess Micomicona, together with other amusing adventures

Sancho had been listening with a grieving heart as he saw all his hopes of an earldom going up in smoke, and the lovely Princess Micomicona turning into Dorotea before his very eyes, and the giant becoming Don Fernando, and his master still fast asleep and not in the slightest concerned about what was happening. Dorotea couldn't be certain that the happiness she'd attained wasn't all a dream. Cardenio was thinking the same thoughts, as was Luscinda. Don Fernando was thanking heaven for the benefit it had bestowed upon him in extricating him from that tortuous maze in which he'd been on the brink of forfeiting both his good name and the salvation of his soul; and everyone at the inn was rejoicing at this happy solution to such a convoluted and seemingly irremediable quandary.

The priest was speaking a few timely words, as the sensible man that he was, and congratulating them on the happiness they'd attained; but the most contented and delighted of them all was the innkeeper's wife, because of the promise made by Cardenio and the priest to pay all damages, plus all interest accruing, for losses sustained at the hands of Don Quixote. Only Sancho, as has been said, was heart-broken and grief-stricken, and so, with a woebegone look on his face, he went for his master, who had just woken up, and said:

'Yes, you can carry on sleeping, Sir Sorryface, as much as you like, and not bother your head about killing any giants or getting the princess's kingdom back for her – it's all over and done with.'

'I am certain you are right,' replied Don Quixote, 'because I have just been fighting against that giant in the most atrocious and dreadful battle that I ever expect to wage in all the days of my life, and with one backstroke, swish! – I sent his head flying to the ground, and so much blood came gushing out that it ran all over the earth like water from rivers.'

'Like red wine, you'd do better to say,' replied Sancho, 'and I want you to know, if you don't know it already, that the dead giant is a wineskin all full of holes, and the blood is twenty gallons of red wine he had in his belly, and the head you chopped off is the whore that brought me into this world, and the devil take the giant and all the rest of it!'

'What are you saying, you madman?' exclaimed Don Quixote. 'Can you be in your right mind?'

'Well, you get up,' said Sancho, 'and you'll see for yourself what a fine mess you've made and we've got to pay for, and you'll also see the queen changed into a private individual called Dorotea, and other doings that'll leave you dumb-struck, if you happen to understand what's going on.'

'That would not surprise me in the least,' replied Don Quixote, 'because, if you remember, that other time we were here I told you that everything that happens in this place is brought about by enchantment, and it would be no wonder if it were so now.'

'I'd believe every word you say,' replied Sancho, 'if my blanket-tossing had been like that, but it wasn't, it was the real thing all right, and I saw the very same innkeeper who's here today holding one corner of the blanket, and he was sending me up into the sky for all he was worth and enjoying himself too, laughing as hard as he was heaving. And when you start recognizing people it's my opinion, simpleton and sinner though I am, that it isn't an enchantment at all, but real bruises and real misery.'

'Well, well, God will provide a remedy,' said Don Quixote. 'Help me dress and I shall go out there, for I want to see these doings and transformations to which you refer.'

Sancho helped him dress and, while he was doing so, the priest told Don Fernando and the others about Don Quixote's escapades and the trick they'd used to extract him from Peña Pobre, where he'd imagined that his lady's disdain had taken him. The priest also recounted most of the adventures narrated by Sancho, which amazed and amused them no end, because they were of the same opinion as everybody else: this was quite the weirdest sort of madness that could attack a disordered brain. The priest added that, since Dorotea's happy resolution of her problems prevented them from going ahead with their scheme, they'd have to dream up another way to get him back to his village. Cardenio offered to continue what they'd started, with Luscinda taking over the part played by Dorotea.

'No,' said Don Fernando, 'you mustn't do that: I want Dorotea to carry on with her impersonation, and so long as the village where this worthy knight lives isn't too far away, I shall be delighted if there's something that can be done for him.'

'It's no more than two days' journey from here.'

'Well, even if it were further off, I'd be happy to go, for such a good cause.'

And now Don Quixote emerged, in full panoply, with Mambrino's helmet, battered as it was, on his head, his little round infantryman's shield on his arm, and leaning on his branch, or pike. Don Fernando and his party were astounded at the extraordinary figure he presented: his face, gaunt and pale and as long as a wet week, his ill-matching arms and armour, his sober demeanour. They waited in silence to see what he was going to say until, with great gravity and composure, and fixing his eyes on the beautiful Dorotea, he spoke:

'I am informed, lovely lady, by my squire here, that Your Highness has been annihilated and your being destroyed, because from the queen and great lady that you used to be you have been turned into a private individual.

If this has been done by order of your father, the sorcerer king, because he feared that I should not give you the due and necessary assistance, I can only say that the man did not and does not know what he is talking about, and has little acquaintance with histories of chivalry; because if he had read and reread them as slowly and carefully as I have, he would have discovered on every page how other knights, of less renown than I, have brought more difficult enterprises to a successful conclusion; and killing some paltry giant, however proud he may be, poses few problems, for it was only a few hours ago that I tackled him, and . . . yet I had better keep quiet, so as not to be accused of lying; but time, the revealer of all things, will tell, when we are least expecting it.'

'What you tackled was two wineskins not a giant,' put in the innkeeper.

Don Fernando told him to be quiet and on no account to interrupt Don Quixote's speech again, and he continued:

'I say, then, exalted and disinherited lady, that if it is for the reason I have mentioned that your father has performed this metamorphosis in your person, you must not believe what he says, for there is no peril on earth that my sword cannot brush aside, and with it, casting your enemy's head to the ground, I shall soon place the crown of your country upon yours.'

Don Quixote stopped speaking and waited for the princess to reply, and, in view of Don Fernando's determination to press on with the deceit until they took Don Quixote back home, she answered with waggish gravity:

'Whosoever told you, O worthy Knight of the Sorry Face, that I had been altered and transformed, did not tell you the truth, for I am the same woman that I was yesterday. It is the case, indeed, that some modification has been worked within me by certain strokes of good fortune which have brought the greatest happiness I could desire, but I have not stopped being who I was before, or continuing to hope, as always, that I can verily avail myself of the valour of your valorous and invenerable arm. And so, my dear sir, you must let the father who begot me have his honour back, and look upon him as a man of sagacity and foresight, because he used his great knowledge to find such a sure and straightforward way to remedy my misfortune – I do believe that if it were not for you, sir, I should never have attained the happiness I now enjoy, and when I say this I tell a truth to which most of those here present can stand as witnesses. All that remains is to set out tomorrow, because we would not be able to travel far in what is left of today, and as for the rest of what needs to be done to achieve the happy outcome I expect, I shall leave that to God and to the worth of your heroic breast.'

So spoke the quick-witted Dorotea, and when Don Quixote heard her words he turned in high fury to Sancho and said:

'Now let me tell you, Sancho you wretch, that you are the greatest little villain in the whole of Spain. Have you not just been claiming, you good-for-nothing rogue, that this princess had been turned into a private individual called Dorotea and that the head I believe I cut off a giant was the whore that brought you into this world, and other nonsenses that plunged me into the greatest bewilderment I have known in all the days of my life? By . . . ,' – and he raised his eyes to heaven and gritted his teeth – 'I have a good mind to work such havoc on you as will force some sense into the brainpans of all the lying squires of knights errant from now until the end of time!'

'Calm down, sir,' replied Sancho. 'I might have been mistaken about the alteration to my lady the Princess Micomicona, but as for the giant's head or rather the cutting-up of wineskins, and the blood that's really red wine, I'm not making any mistakes, as God's my witness, because the skins are there to be seen, all wounded at the head of your bed, and the red wine's turned the room into a lake, and if you don't believe me the proof of the pudding's in the eating – what I mean to say is you'll soon see, when our friend the innkeeper here charges you for all the damage. And as for the rest, about my lady the queen being just as she always has been, it warms the cockles of my heart, because I've got a stake in that, as much as any other father's son.'

'All I can say, Sancho,' said Don Quixote, 'is that you are a fool, and forgive me, and enough said.'

'Enough said, indeed,' said Don Fernando, 'and now let's drop the subject. And since my lady the princess says we should set off tomorrow, because it's too late today, so be it, and we can while away the night in pleasant conversation until dawn arrives, when we shall all accompany Don Quixote, for we want to witness the splendid and unheard-of deeds that he will perform in the course of this grand enterprise that he has undertaken.'

'I am the one who must serve and accompany all of you,' replied Don Quixote, 'and I am deeply grateful for the favour you are doing me and for the good opinion you have of me, which I shall attempt to justify, else it will cost me my life, and even more, if such a thing is possible.'

Many courteous words and offers of service were exchanged between Don Quixote and Don Fernando, but they were brought to an end by the sudden arrival of a traveller whose dress indicated that he was a Christian recently returned from the lands of the Moors, for he was wearing a blue woollen doublet with short tails, half sleeves and no collar; his cotton breeches were also blue, as was his cap; he had date-brown riding-boots and a scimitar was hanging from a broad strap that crossed his chest. Behind him, on a donkey, came a woman dressed in the Moorish style: a veil over her face, a brocade cap on her head and a cloak from her shoulders to her feet. The man had a fine, robust physique; he was a little over forty, swarthy, with a long moustache and a good beard; and his agreeable presence showed that if he hadn't been wearing the uniform of a slave of the Moors he'd have been considered a well-born person of high rank. As he walked in he asked for a private room, and when he was told that there weren't any available he seemed concerned, and went over to the woman who appeared from her dress to be Moorish, and lifted her down. Luscinda, Dorotea, the innkeeper's wife and daughter and Maritornes, attracted by the novelty of her clothes, the like of which they'd never seen before, surrounded her, and Dorotea, always charming, courteous and sensible, and seeing that both she and the man seemed troubled by the want of a room, said to her:

'Try not to be too worried, my lady, by the lack of comfort here, because that's what you must expect at any roadside inn; but, all the same, if you'd like to accept our company' – motioning towards Luscinda – 'you may find that you've met with worse welcomes in the course of your journey.'

The veiled woman didn't reply, but only rose from her seat and, with her hands crossed over her chest and her head bowed, leaned forward to indicate her gratitude. Her silence confirmed that she must be Moorish and couldn't speak Spanish. The former captive, who'd been busy with other matters, joined them, and, when he saw that they were all standing round his companion and that she wasn't replying to anything they said, he told them:

'Ladies, this young woman hardly understands our language and can only speak her own, and this is why she won't have answered and isn't answering your questions.'

'All we're asking her,' replied Luscinda, 'is whether she'd like to accept our company for the night and share our sleeping quarters with us, because we'll make her as comfortable as ever we can, with all the goodwill due to foreigners in need of help, particularly women.'

'On her behalf and my own,' replied the captive,' I kiss your hands in gratitude, madam, and highly prize, as I am bound to, the favour you have offered – in such circumstances, and coming from such people as you show yourselves to be, it must evidently be a very great one.'

'Tell me, sir,' said Dorotea, 'is this lady Christian or Moorish? Because her clothes and her silence are making us think that she's what we'd prefer her not to be.'

'Her clothes and her body are Moorish, but her soul is devoutly Christian, because she has the most fervent desire to become one.'

'So she hasn't been baptized?' asked Luscinda.

'There hasn't been an opportunity since she left Algiers, where she comes from,' replied the former captive, 'and she hasn't yet been in such danger of imminent death as to make it necessary for her to be baptized without first receiving instruction in all the ceremonies that our Mother the Holy Church requires; but, if it pleases God, she will soon be baptized with all the formalities due to someone of her rank, which is higher than her clothes and mine suggest.'

These words made all those who heard them eager to know who the Moorish woman and the former captive were, but nobody cared to ask them yet, this being more a time for helping them to rest than for asking them to recount their life histories. Dorotea took her by the hand and sat her by her side, and asked her to remove her veil. She looked towards the captive, as if to ask what they were saying and what she should do. He told her in Arabic that she was being asked to remove her veil, and that she should do so; she removed it, revealing a face so lovely that Dorotea thought her more beautiful than Luscinda, Luscinda thought her more beautiful than Dorotea and all the others thought that if any face could be compared to Dorotea's and Luscinda's it was the Moorish woman's, and there were even those who found hers somewhat superior. And since beauty enjoys the privilege and prerogative of reconciling hearts and attracting affections, they all surrendered forthwith to the desire to serve and cherish the beautiful Moor.

Don Fernando asked the former captive what her name was, and he replied that it was Lela Zoraida; but as soon as she heard his answer she realized what the question had been, and in a flurry of delightful distress she blurted:

'No, Zoraida no: María, María!'

These words and the warm feeling with which they were spoken drew tears from some of those listening, especially the women, by nature tender and compassionate. Luscinda gave her a loving embrace and said:

'Yes, yes, María, María.'

To which the Moor replied:

'Yes, yes, María: *Zoraida makanshe!*' – meaning 'not Zoraida'.

Night was now falling, and by order of Don Fernando's men the innkeeper had taken the utmost pains to prepare the very finest meal of which he was capable. Suppertime arrived, and they all sat down at a long table like the ones servants eat at, because there wasn't a round or square one in the house. They sat Don Quixote at the head of it, in spite of his protestations, and he asked Princess Micomicona to sit beside him, since he was her protector. Next to her, Luscinda and Zoraida took their places, and opposite them Don Fernando and Cardenio, and then the former captive and the other gentlemen, and on the ladies' side the priest and the barber. And there they enjoyed their supper, and their pleasure was even greater when they saw Don Quixote stop eating, moved by an impulse similar to the one that had led him to discourse at such length after the supper with the goatherds, and begin to address them:

'In truth, ladies and gentlemen, if we reflect upon it, those who belong to the order of knight-errantry behold the most extraordinary and wondrous sights. Or else who in the whole wide world coming in now through the gates of this castle and seeing us sitting here would believe that we are who we are? Who could tell that this lady at my side is the great queen we all know her to be, or that I am that Knight of the Sorry Face who is so celebrated by the voice of fame? It is no longer possible to doubt that this profession of mine surpasses all those ever invented by mankind, and that it should be held in even higher esteem for being exposed to more dangers.

Away with anyone who gives letters the preference over arms, for I say to him, whoever he may be, that he does not know what he is talking about. The argument that such people usually adduce and depend upon is that brain-work is superior to physical work, and that the exercise of arms involves the body alone, as if it were the business of market-porters, which needs nothing more than brute strength; or as if acts of fortitude requiring a keen intelligence were not involved in what we fighters call soldiership; or as if the warrior who is in charge of an army or the defence of a besieged city did not labour with his mind as much as with his body. Or else you tell me how mere bodily strength can enable one to assess the enemy's intentions, tactics and stratagems, size up the difficulties, and forestall the dangers – because all these are acts of the understanding, in which the body plays no part.

'Since it is the case, then, that arms need brains as much as letters do, let us go on to see which of the two brains, that of the scholar or that of the warrior, has more work to do. And this can be determined by the goal to which each is directed, because the intention that has the nobler goal in view must be more highly regarded. The goal of letters . . . and I do not now refer to sacred letters, whose goal is to conduct souls to heaven, for to an end as endless as this no other can be compared; I refer to human learning, the goal of which is to organize distributive justice and give to every man according to his deserts: to interpret and enforce the law. This is a goal that is certainly noble and generous and praiseworthy, but less so than the goal that arms have before them, which is peace, the greatest good to which men can aspire in this life. And so it was that the first good news the world and men received was proclaimed by the angels on that night which was our day, when they sang in the heavens "Glory to God in the highest, and on earth peace to men of good will;"[1] and the greeting that the greatest master on earth and in heaven taught his followers and disciples to give when they entered any house was "Peace be to this house;"[2] and on many other occasions he said to them "My peace I give unto you; my peace I leave with you; peace be unto you,"[3] like a precious jewel left us by him as a gift: a jewel without which there can be no well-being on earth or in heaven. This peace is the true goal of war; and war and arms are all one. Given, then, this truth, that the goal of war is peace, and that this is nobler than the goal of letters, let us now consider the bodily hardships of the man of letters and the man of arms, and see which are greater.'

Don Quixote was developing his arguments in such an orderly and lucid way that for the time being none of those listening to him could believe that he was a madman. On the contrary, since most of them were gentlemen and therefore much concerned with arms, they were delighted to sit there listening as he continued:

'I should say that the hardships of the student are these: above all poverty – not that they are all poor, but I am putting the strongest possible case for them; and having said that the student suffers poverty it seems to me that there is nothing more to add concerning his troubles, because he who is poor lacks everything that is good. He suffers this poverty in each of its facets: now hunger, now cold, now nakedness, now all of them together; but in spite of that, his hunger is never so great that he goes without eating, even if he does so a little later than other people, even if he eats leftovers from the tables of the rich, for it is the student's greatest suffering to beg his bread, as they themselves term it; and there is always somebody who will let them in to sit at the fireside or by the brazier, which, if it does not warm them, at least takes the edge off the cold, and they always sleep under a roof at night. I shall not descend to other details such as their lack of shirts or shortage of shoes, their thin and threadbare clothes, or how they gorge themselves with such gusto when good fortune sets a banquet before them.

'Along this road that I have described, rough and difficult, stumbling here and falling there, struggling to their feet and falling again, they gain the degree to which they aspire; and once they attain this, many are those we see who, having sailed over these shoals and between these Scyllas and Charybdises [4] as if borne on the wings of favourable fortune, govern and rule the world from an armchair, with their hunger turned into satiety, their pinching cold into cool comfort, their nakedness into finery and regalia, their nights shivering on rush mats into repose between holland-cloth and damask, the just reward for their virtue. But if their hardships are compared and contrasted with those of the militiaman or warrior, they fall very far short, as I shall now demonstrate.'

CHAPTER XXXVIII

Concerning Don Quixote's curious discourse about arms and letters

Don Quixote continued:

'Since, in discussing the student, we began with his poverty and its different facets, let us now see if the soldier is any richer. And we shall observe that he is the very poorest of the poor, because he depends on his paltry pay, which he receives late or not at all, or on what he can loot at grave risk to his life and his conscience. And sometimes he is so short of clothes that a slashed jerkin has to serve him as both uniform and shirt, and in mid-winter he is often all too aware of the inclemency of heaven when he is out in the open field with nothing to warm him but his breath, which issues from an empty space and must therefore, I am sure, emerge cold, contrary to all the laws of nature. And now let us contemplate him waiting for night to arrive so that he can recover from all these discomforts in the bed that is ready for him and that will not be a painfully narrow one unless he has done something to deserve it: he will be able to measure out as much ground as he likes, and turn over and over to his heart's content, without a moment's worry about the sheets riding up.

'And then come the day and the time for his degree ceremony – a battle day, when he will have a doctor's cap placed on his head, made of lint to dress a bullet wound in the temple, unless he has received some other injury disabling a leg or an arm. And if this does not happen, if merciful heaven keeps him alive and whole, he might still be left as poor as ever, and it will need one engagement after another, one battle after another, and him triumphing in all of them, to make some improvement in his situation; but such miracles seldom occur.

'But tell me now, ladies and gentlemen, if you have ever considered it: how many men have been rewarded by war, compared with all those who have perished in it? You will have to reply that there is no comparison, and there is no counting those who have died, while those alive and rewarded can be reckoned in three figures. It is the very opposite with men of letters, because on their salaries, let alone the payments on the side, they can make ends meet well enough. So although the soldier's hardships are greater, his reward is much smaller. But to this it can be replied that it is easier to reward two thousand men of letters than thirty thousand soldiers, because the former are rewarded with jobs that have to be given to men of their profession, whereas the latter can only be rewarded from the property of the master they serve; and this fact only strengthens my case.

'But let us set all this aside, for it is a maze from which it is very difficult to find a way out, and return to the pre-eminence of arms over letters, a controversy that has yet to be decided, because the arguments on both sides are strong ones; and in addition to those I have mentioned, letters say that arms could not exist without them, because war too has its laws and is subject to them, and laws are the province of men of letters. To which arms reply that laws could not exist without them, because arms are responsible for defending nations, preserving kingdoms, guarding cities, keeping highways safe, clearing seas of pirates; and, in short, if it were not for arms, all states, kingdoms, monarchies, cities and journeys over land and sea would be subject to the cruelty and turmoil that war brings with it for as long as it lasts and is free to make use of its privileges and powers.

'And it is a proven truth that what costs most is and should be most valued. To become eminent in letters costs time, sleepless nights, hunger, nakedness, dizzy spells, indigestion and other related problems, some of which I have already mentioned. But to go through the various stages necessary to become a good soldier costs everything that it costs to be a student to such a greater degree that there is no comparison between the two, because at every step one is on the point of losing one's life. And what dread of poverty and want can afflict the student as much as the dread that the soldier feels when, on sentry duty on a ravelin of some besieged fortress, he realizes that the enemy is mining towards the place where he stands, and he cannot on any account abandon his post or flee from the danger that so imminently threatens him? All he can do is inform his captain of what is happening so that the situation may be remedied with a countermine, and stand his ground, wondering in fear when the moment will suddenly come for him to fly up to the clouds without wings and descend to the depths against his will. And if this seems but a trifling danger, let us consider whether it is equalled or surpassed when two galleys ram each other in the middle of the open sea, and once they are grappled together the soldier has no more room for his charge than the two-foot wide timber at the prow; and despite this, and seeing before him as many ministers of death threatening him as there are guns being aimed not a lance's length from him, and knowing that one slip of his feet will send him down to visit the depths of Neptune's dominions, he still, with an undaunted heart and sustained by the honour that inspires him, makes himself a target for all those harquebuses and tries to storm his way across such a narrow bridge into the enemy vessel. And what is even more astonishing is that as soon as one soldier falls, never to rise until doomsday, another takes his place; and, if this one also falls into the sea that awaits him like one more enemy, another and another replace him without a moment's pause between their deaths: the finest example of courage and daring to be found in all the extremities of war.

'A blessing on those happy ages that did not know the dreadful fury of these devilish instruments of artillery, whose inventor is, I feel sure, being rewarded in hell for his diabolical creation, by which he made it possible for an infamous and cowardly hand to take away the life of a brave knight as, in the heat of the courage and resolution that fires and animates the gallant breast, a stray bullet appears, nobody knows how or from where – fired perhaps by some fellow who took fright at the flash of the fiendish contraption, and fled – and in an instant puts an end to the life and loves one who deserved to live for many a long age. And when I think about this I am tempted to say that it grieves me to the depths of my soul that I ever took up this profession of knight-errantry in such a detestable age as this one in which we are living, because even though there is no danger that can strike fear into me I am concerned when I think that gunpowder and lead might deprive me of the opportunity to make myself famous all over the face of the earth by the might of my arm and the blade of my sword. But let heaven do what it pleases, for I shall be more highly esteemed, if I accomplish my aim, for having exposed myself to dangers greater than were ever faced by knights errant of centuries past.'

Don Quixote gave voice to this long digression while the others were eating their supper, yet he didn't remember to lift a single morsel to his mouth, even though Sancho Panza told him several times to eat up, there'd be plenty of time later to talk as much as he wanted. Those who'd been listening to him were again moved to pity on seeing that a man who seemed to have a good brain, and could argue clearly about everything he discussed, so totally lost his senses as soon as the talk turned to his detestable and damnable chivalry. The priest told him that he'd been quite right in everything he'd said in favour of arms and that, although he himself was a man of letters and a graduate, he shared his beliefs.

They finished their supper and the table was cleared, and, while the innkeeper's wife and daughter and Maritornes were tidying Don Quixote de la Mancha's attic, where it had been decided that only the women would sleep, Don Fernando begged the captive to tell them the story of his life, because it was bound to be unusual and entertaining, to judge from the first sample of it, his arrival there with Zoraida. To which the captive replied that he'd willingly do so, only he feared that they weren't going to like his tale as much as he'd wish; but, in spite of all that, so as not to appear disobliging, he would tell it. The priest and all the others expressed their thanks and added their entreaties. And, in the face of such unanimity, the captive said that they didn't need to beg what they could command.

'So listen carefully, and you'll hear a true story that could never, perhaps, be equalled by any of those fictional ones that people compose with such care and skill.'

This made them all settle down in total silence, and, once the captive saw that they were quiet and waiting to hear what he had to say, he began to speak in a calm and pleasant voice:

CHAPTER XXXIX

✠

In which the captive tells the story of his life and adventures

'My family had its origins in one of the villages in the mountains of León, and was always more favoured with the blessings of nature than with the gifts of fortune, although in the general poverty of those parts my father had the reputation of being rich, and really would have been, if he'd been as good at looking after what he owned as he was at spending it. Being free with his money was a consequence of a youth as a soldier, because a soldier's life is a school in which the niggardly learn to be generous, and the generous to be prodigal; and if there are any miserly soldiers, they're like monsters that one seldom sees. My father exceeded the bounds of liberality and was close to being a spendthrift, which is of no benefit at all to a married man with children to inherit his name and his position. He had three grown-up sons. Since he realized that he couldn't cope with his character, as he put it, he decided to deprive himself of what was both the instrument and the cause of his prodigality, in other words to rid himself of his property, without which Alexander himself would have seemed tight-fisted. So one day, calling all three of us aside into a room, he spoke to us along the following lines:

'"My sons, to assure you that I love you dearly, no more needs to be known and said than that you are my sons; but for you to think that I don't love you at all, no more is needed than to observe that I'm not managing to cope with my character so as to keep your inheritance intact for you. Well, to make it clear that I do love you like a father, and that I don't want to destroy you like a stepfather, I intend to put into effect something that I've been thinking about for some time and have decided upon after careful consideration. You've all reached the age at which you should settle down in life, or, at any rate, choose a career that, with the passing of the years, will bring you honour and profit. And what I've decided to do is to divide all I own into four parts, and I shall give three of them to you, each receiving his due and no more, and I shall keep the fourth to live on for as long as heaven is pleased to spare me. But after you've taken possession of your shares, I should like each of you to take one of the paths I'm going to indicate. We have a proverb here in Spain, in my opinion a very true one, as they all are, being brief maxims arising from the wisdom of long experience; and this proverb says 'The church, the sea or the palace of the king', or, to spell it out more clearly, 'Whoever wants to prosper and be rich should either enter the church, or take up trading and go to sea, or serve a king in his palace', because, as they also say, 'Better the king's crumb than the lord's boon'. I say all this because what I want is for one of you to study to become a man of letters, another to go into commerce and the third to serve the king in his wars, since obtaining a position in his palace is difficult, and even though war doesn't bring much wealth, it does greatly increase one's worth and one's good name. In a week's time I shall give each of you his share in cash, not withholding a single maravedí, as you will see for yourselves. Now, tell me whether you are willing to follow the advice I'm offering you."

'He called on me, as the eldest, to reply first, and after I'd protested that he shouldn't part with his possessions but spend as much as he liked, because we were old enough to make our own fortunes, I concluded by saying that I'd do as he wished, and that my choice would be to follow the profession of arms, and serve God and my king in that way. My younger brother made a similar protest and chose to sail to America with merchandise that he'd buy with his share. The youngest, and, I think, the most sensible of us, said that he wanted to enter the Church, or go and complete his studies at Salamanca University. As soon as we'd reached this agreement and chosen our ways of life, my father embraced us; and he fulfilled his promise as quickly as he said he would, giving each of us his share, which was, as I remember, three thousand ducats, because an uncle of ours bought the entire estate and paid for it in cash, to keep it in the family, and on that same day all three of us said goodbye to our dear father; and thinking it inhuman to leave him in his old age with so little to live on, I made him take back two thousand of my three thousand ducats, because the rest was quite enough to provide me with all a soldier needs. My two brothers were moved by my example to give him a thousand ducats each. So my father was left with four thousand ducats in cash and three thousand more, which was, it seems, the value of the estate that fell to his share and that he didn't want to sell and had kept as land. In short, we said goodbye to him and to our uncle, with the tears of sorrow rolling down our cheeks, and they urged us to send them our news, whether good or bad, whenever we had a chance. We promised that we would, our father hugged and blessed us, and one son set out for Salamanca, another for Seville, and I left for Alicante, having heard that a Genoese ship was in that part loading wool for Genoa.

'It's twenty-two years now since I left my father's house, and in all this time, even though I've written letters, I haven't received any news about him or my brothers. And now I'll tell you briefly what has happened to me during these years. I embarked in Alicante, I had a good trip to Genoa, from there I went to Milan, where I equipped myself with arms and military clothing, and from there I decided to go to Piedmont to enlist; I was on my way to Alessandria when I heard that the great Duke of Alba was marching to Flanders.[1] I changed my plans, went to join him, served him in his campaigns, was present at the executions of Count Egmont and Count Hoorne,[2] rose to be an ensign under a famous captain from Guadalajara called Diego de Urbina,[3] and, a little after I reached Flanders, news arrived of the alliance that His Holiness Pope Pius V, of happy memory, had made with Venice and Spain against the common enemy, the Turk, whose fleet had just taken the famous island of Cyprus, which had been under the rule of Venice: a lamentable, disastrous loss.[4] It became known that His Serene Highness Don John of Austria, our good king Don Philip's half-brother, was to be the general in command of the allied armies. News spread of the massive preparations for war that were being made, and all this inflamed my desire to fight in the great battle that lay ahead; and even though I'd been given hints and almost firm promises that I was going to be promoted to captain at the earliest opportunity, I decided to drop everything and go back to Italy. And as my good fortune would have it, Don John of Austria had just reached Genoa on his way to Naples to join the Venetian fleet, which he later did at Messenia.[5] So, to be brief, I fought in that glorious battle,[6] having already been made a captain in the infantry, to which honourable rank I rose more by luck than through merit. And on that day, so happy for all Christendom, because it was when all the nations in the world learned how wrong they'd been to believe the Turks invincible at sea, on that day when Ottoman pride was dashed to pieces, among all the happy men there – because the Christians who died were even happier than those who survived victorious – I alone was wretched: instead of the naval crown that I could have expected if these had been Roman times, I found myself on the night following that famous day with my feet fettered and my hands manacled.

'And it happened like this: after Alouk Ali, the King of Algiers, a bold and successful privateer, had rammed and overpowered the Maltese flagship and only three Knights of Malta were left alive on it, all badly wounded, Giovanni Andrea Doria's flagship, on which I was serving with my company, went to the rescue; and doing what was my duty at such a juncture I leapt aboard the enemy galley, which then sheered off from the galley ramming her, thus preventing my soldiers from following me and leaving me alone among my enemies – so many of them that I couldn't resist for long and was overpowered, covered in wounds. And as you'll have heard, gentlemen, Alouk Ali escaped with his entire squadron, so I ended up a captive in his power, the only sad man on a day when so many rejoiced, the only prisoner on a day when so many were set free, for on that day fifteen thousand Christians rowing in the Turkish fleet gained the liberty they'd been longing for. I was taken to Constantinople, where the Grand Turk Selim promoted my captor to admiral for having done his duty in the battle and having carried off, as proof of his bravery, the standard of the Knights of Malta.

'In the second year of my captivity, which was seventy-two, I was at Navarino,[7] rowing in the admiral's flagship with its three lanterns. I was a witness to the opportunity that was lost to catch the whole Turkish fleet in harbour – all the Turkish sailors and soldiers were convinced that they were going to be attacked there, and had their clothes and their passamackeys, or shoes, ready to flee over land without waiting for the assault, such was the terror that our fleet had inspired in them. But heaven decreed otherwise, not through any fault or negligence of our general but because of Christendom's sins and because it is God's will that there shall always be scourges to chastise us. And Alouk Ali took refuge on Modon, an island near Navarino, disembarked his troops, fortified the harbour entrance and waited there until Don John went away. In this campaign the galley called *The Prize*, whose captain was a son of the famous privateer Barbarossa, was captured by the flagship of Naples, called *The She-Wolf*, commanded by that thunderbolt of war, that father to his soldiers, that happy and never-defeated captain Don Álvaro de Bazán, the Marquis of Santa Cruz. And I don't want to pass over the events associated with the taking of *The Prize*. Barbarossa's son was so cruel and treated his captives so badly that as soon as the galley-men saw that *The She-Wolf* was closing in on them they all dropped their oars, pulled him down from the awning-bollard where he stood screaming at them to row faster and passed him along from bench to bench, from the stern to the prow, biting him all the way so viciously that he'd gone little further than the mast before his soul had gone down to hell, such was their hatred for him because of his ill-treatment.

'We returned to Constantinople, and the next year, seventy-three, news

reached the city that Don John had taken Tunis and won the whole
kingdom of Tunisia from the Turks,[8] and had handed it over to Muley
Hamet, putting an end to the hopes that Muley Hamida, the cruellest and
bravest Moor there's ever been, had cherished of regaining his throne. The
Grand Turk felt this loss keenly and, with the sagacity characteristic of all
his dynasty, he made peace with the Venetians, who wanted it much more
than he did, and in the following year of seventy-four he attacked the
Goletta and the fort that Don John had left half-built just outside Tunis.[9]
In all these actions I was at the oar, without any hope of liberty; at least I
didn't have any hopes of being ransomed, because I'd decided not to send
news of my misfortune to my father.

'Both the Goletta and the fort eventually fell, in the face of seventy-five
thousand regular Turkish soldiers and more than four hundred thousand
Moors and Arabs from all Africa, and this vast army was supplied with all
the munitions they could ever have needed, and with so many sappers that
they could have buried the Goletta and the fort using their bare hands. The
Goletta, until then believed impregnable, was the first to fall, through no
fault of its garrison, which did everything that could and should have been
done to defend it, but because it was easy, as the event proved, to throw
earthworks up in that desert sand: in normal conditions water would be
struck a spit deep, yet the Turks could dig down six feet without being
hampered by it; and so, by piling up sandbags, they made the earthworks
so high that they commanded the walls of the Goletta and the attackers
could fire down at the defenders, which made it impossible for any of these
to hold his ground or put up a defence.

'There was a widespread belief that our troops shouldn't have shut
themselves up in the Goletta, but should rather have gone out to meet the
enemy as it landed; those who say this are speaking from a safe distance
and with little experience of such matters, because if there were hardly
seven thousand soldiers in the Goletta and the fort, how could so few, no
matter how valiant, have both taken the field and held the two fortresses
against so many? And how is it possible not to lose a fortress that's never
relieved, particularly when it's besieged by so many determined enemies in
their own country? But many people thought, as I did, that it was a special
favour granted by heaven to Spain to allow the destruction of that seedbed
and cloak of iniquity, that glutton, that sponge, that canker consuming the

endless money that was squandered there and that served no other purpose than to preserve the memory of its conquest by the most invincible Emperor Charles V of most happy memory, as if the support of all those stones were necessary to make his name eternal, as it is and always will be.

'The fort fell too, but the Turks had to take it inch by inch, because the soldiers defending it put up such a brave and fierce resistance that they killed more than twenty-five thousand of the enemy in twenty-two general assaults. Not one of the three hundred survivors was captured uninjured, clear and certain proof of their strength and resolution and of how well they'd defended themselves and maintained their positions. A small fort or tower in the middle of the lagoon, commanded by Don Juan Zanoguera, a gentleman from Valencia and a famous soldier, surrendered on the enemy's conditions. Don Pedro Puertocarrero, the commander of the Goletta, who'd done everything he could to defend it, was taken prisoner; he felt the loss so deeply that he perished of grief on the way to Constantinople. They also captured the commander of the fort, who was called Gabrio Cervellón, a gentleman from Milan, a great engineer and a brave soldier. Many people of note died in these two fortresses, among them Pagán Doria, a Knight of Malta and a generous man, as he showed in his liberality to his brother the famous Giovanni Andrea Doria; and what made his death all the more lamentable was that he perished at the hands of Arabs whom he had trusted when he saw the fort was lost, and who had offered to take him in Moorish clothes to Tabarca, an anchorage and station of Genoese coral-fishers; and these Arabs cut off his head and took it to the admiral of the Turkish fleet, who applied to them our Castilian proverb that says "Love the treason but hate the traitor", and so it is said that the admiral ordered the gift-bearers to be hanged for not having brought a live gift.

'Among the Christians captured in the fort was one called Don Pedro de Aguilar,[10] an ensign from somewhere in Andalusia, a soldier of distinction and a very clever man; he had a special gift for that business they call poetry. I mention him because he happened to be sent to my galley and my bench, and to be my own master's slave, and before we left the port this gentleman composed two sonnets in the style of epitaphs, one for the Goletta and the other for the fort. And I really must recite them, because I know them by heart and I think they won't displease you – you might even enjoy them.'

The moment the captive named Don Pedro de Aguilar, Don Fernando glanced at his companions, and all three of them smiled; and when he spoke of the sonnets, one of them said:

'Before you continue, please would you tell me what became of that Don Pedro de Aguilar you mentioned?'

'All I know,' replied the captive, 'is that after two years in Constantinople he disguised himself as an Albanian and escaped with a Greek spy, and I don't know whether he gained his freedom, but I think he did, because a year later I saw the Greek in Constantinople, though I couldn't ask him about the outcome of their journey.'

'No, Don Pedro wasn't recaptured,' the gentleman replied, 'because he's my brother, and he's alive and well in our village, wealthy and married with three children.'

'Thanks be to God for all the mercies he has shown him,' said the captive, 'because in my opinion there's no happiness on earth to compare with regaining one's liberty.'

'And what's more,' the gentleman went on, 'I know the sonnets my brother composed.'

'You recite them, then,' said the captive, 'you'll do it better than me.'

'Very well,' replied the gentleman. 'The one about the Goletta goes like this:'

CHAPTER XL

In which the captive's tale is continued

SONNET

'O happy souls, delivered and set free
By heroes in a sacrosanct campaign
From the dark prison of mortality
To soar aloft to heaven's supreme domain:

Your breasts with noble zeal and fury glowed,
Your tireless sinews braved prodigious toil,
Your blood with that of Turks and Arabs flowed
To stain the sea and drench the dusty soil.
  Your earthly lives but not your courage failed
In bodies from which all the strength had flown,
Victorious though defeated and bewailed
On perishing between cold steel and stone;
Because for such a death before such foes
Its fame the world, its glory heaven bestows.'

'That's exactly the version I know,' said the captive.

'The one about the fort, if I remember rightly,' said the gentleman, 'goes like this:

SONNET

And from these ruins on the desert plain,
These scattered clods that heap this bloody site,
Three thousand soldiers' souls, alive though slain,
To happier regions winged their joyous flight,
  Yet not before they vainly had essayed
The vigour of their arms with dauntless zeal
Until, outnumbered and fatigued, they laid
Down their young lives to scimitars of steel.
  This is the place, and this the dismal ground,
That for men's hopes has offered but a tomb,
Through past and present centuries renowned
For evils spawned in its unloving womb.
From braver bodies never could there rise
Such saintly souls from earth to gain the skies.'

The company thought the sonnets weren't too bad, and the captive was cheered by the news of his companion. He continued his tale:

'Once the Goletta and the fort had fallen, the Turks set about demolishing the Goletta, because there was nothing left of the fort to knock down, and to save time and labour they mined it in three places; but they couldn't blow up what seemed to be the weakest part, the old walls, although all of what was left standing of the new fortifications built by Friar Puck[1] came down without any trouble whatsoever. To cut a long story short, the fleet returned to Constantinople triumphant and victorious, and a few months later my master Alouk Ali died – he was known as Alouk Ali Fartach, which in Turkish means "The Scabby Renegade", because he suffered from ringworm, and it's a custom among the Turks to name people after some defect or quality of theirs. And this is because there are only four families with their own surnames, all of them descended from the house of Ottoman, and everyone else, as I've just said, takes his name and surname from bodily defects or moral qualities. And this Scabby Renegade had rowed as a slave of the Grand Turk for fourteen years and, at the age of thirty-four, enraged at having his face slapped by a Turk while he was at the oar, had abandoned his faith so as to be able to avenge himself; and he was such an able man that, without resorting to the vile methods used by most of the Grand Turk's favourites to rise, he'd become the King of Algiers and then the Admiral of the Fleet, which is the third most important position in that empire. He was from Calabria, an upright man and very kind to his captives, and he amassed three thousand of them, who were divided after his death, as he'd ordered in his will, between his renegades and the Grand Turk, who counts as a son and heir of anyone who dies, and shares his wealth with the other sons; and I fell to the lot of a Venetian renegade who'd been captured by Alouk Ali when he was a deckhand and was so well-loved by him that he became one of his most pampered pages, and then turned into one of the cruellest renegades there ever was. He was called Hassan Aga, and he became very rich and rose to be King of Algiers; and I was quite happy to come with him from Constantinople because it brought me so close to Spain – not that I was going to write to anyone about my sad lot, but I did hope that fortune might be kinder to me in Algiers than in Constantinople, where I'd tried a thousand different ways of escaping, without ever having any luck; and it was my intention to seek in Algiers other means of achieving what I so desired, because the hope of gaining my freedom never forsook me, and whenever what I dreamt up and put into practice didn't have the intended result I would immediately, without despairing, seek out or invent some other grounds for hope, however feeble they might be, to sustain me.

'This was how I whiled the time away, shut up in a prison or rather a kind of compound called a *bagnio*, where they keep Christian captives belonging to the king and to private individuals, as well as those they call slaves of the Almazen, in other words those belonging to the town council and employed on public works and other similar jobs; and it's next to impossible for these captives to gain their freedom, because they're public property and have no single master, so there's nobody with whom they can agree their ransom, even if they can get the money. In these bagnios, as I said, private individuals often keep their captives, particularly those who are to be ransomed, because they can have them safely waiting there without working, until the money comes. The king's captives who are to be ransomed don't go out to work with the slave-gang, either, except when the money takes a long time to appear; in which case, to make them write asking for it with greater urgency, they are forced to work and go collecting firewood with all the others, and that's no laughing matter.

'I was classed as a ransomable captive: since it was known that I was a captain, even though I told them about my lack of means and my small chances of raising money, nothing could prevent them from placing me on the list of gentlemen-slaves to be ransomed. They put a chain on me, more as a mark of this than to secure me, and so I spent my time in that bagnio with many other gentlemen and important people chosen to be held for ransom. And although hunger and lack of clothes might have distressed us at times – in fact, nearly always – nothing afflicted us as much as hearing and seeing, all the time, my master's unimaginable cruelty to the Christians. Every day he hanged one, impaled another, cut the ears off a third, and all for such petty causes, or without any cause at all, so that the Turks knew he did it for its own sake and because he was by nature a mass murderer. The only man who emerged unscathed from his hands was a Spanish soldier called something Saavedra,[2] who performed exploits that will stay in the memory of those people for many years, all for the sake of gaining his liberty, yet Hassan Aga never beat him or ordered him to be beaten, or even spoke a harsh word to him; and for the very least of his many doings we all feared that he was going to be impaled, and so did he, more than once, and if we weren't short of time I'd tell you of this soldier's exploits, and they would entertain and amaze you much more than my own story.

'I should mention that our prison yard was overlooked by the windows of a house belonging to a rich and eminent Moor – as is normal in Moorish houses, they were more like little holes than windows, and even so they were covered by dense and impenetrable grilles. And one day, when I was with three companions on a roof terrace in the prison, whiling away the time by seeing who could jump the furthest in our chains – we were alone because all the other Christians had gone out to work – I happened to look up and I saw a cane being poked out of one of those little latticed windows, and tied to the end of it there was a handkerchief, and the cane was being waved up and down as if to signal to us to go and take it. We considered the situation and one of the men with me went to stand under the cane to see if the person holding it dropped it, or what would be done with it; but when he went the cane was raised and waved from side to side like someone shaking their head. My companion rejoined us, and the cane was lowered again with the same movements as before. Another of my companions walked over to the cane, with the same result. Finally the third one went, and was similarly dismissed. Seeing all this, I wanted to try my luck as well, and as soon as I stationed myself under the cane it was dropped into the bagnio, at my feet. The handkerchief had been tied into a knot and I made haste to undo it, and inside I found ten zianyis, Moorish coins of gold alloy each worth ten of our reals. There's no need to tell you how happy I was with this windfall: my joy was matched only by my amazement as I wondered who could have sent that gift to us, or more precisely to me, because the fact that the cane had been dropped for me alone showed for whom the present was meant. I took the welcome cash, broke the cane into little pieces, returned to the roof terrace, looked up at the window and saw there a pure white hand being rapidly opened and closed. This gave us to understand or imagine that it must have been a woman living in that house who'd made us that gift, and to indicate our gratitude we made salaams in the Moorish way, lowering our heads and bowing with our arms held over our chests. A little after that a small cross made of cane appeared for an instant at the same window. This sign made us think that a Christian woman must be a captive in that house, and that it was she who had favoured us; but the whiteness of that hand and the bracelets it displayed soon dispelled this notion, though we did then imagine that she might be a Christian renegade, for these are often taken as wives by their masters, who even consider it a stroke of good fortune to be able to do so, because they hold Christian women in higher esteem than women of their own race.

'In all our speculations we were very far from the truth; and so from that day on we had no other pastime than to gaze up at that horizon or window at which the north star or cane had appeared, but for a good fortnight we didn't see it, or the hand, or any other sign. And although we did all we could during those days to find out who lived in that house and whether there was any renegade Christian woman in it, all we learned was that a rich and important Moor called Hajji Murad lived there, and that he'd been governor of Al-Batha,[3] a position of great importance. But when we were least expecting it to rain more zianyis, we saw the cane suddenly appear, and another handkerchief on it, tied into a bigger knot; and this happened at a time when the bagnio was, as before, empty except for us. We did as we had the first time, each of the three others going up before I did, but the cane was only surrendered to me, being dropped when I walked up. I undid the knot and found forty Spanish gold escudos and a piece of paper with Arabic writing on it, with a large cross drawn at the end of the text. I kissed the cross, I took the escudos, I went back to the roof terrace, we all performed our salaams, the hand appeared again, I signalled my intention to read the paper, the window was shut. We were all left bewildered and happy, and since none of us understood Arabic, our desire to know what the paper said was very great, but our difficulty in finding someone to read it for us was even greater.

'In the end I made up my mind to confide in a renegade from Murcia who considered himself a close friend of mine and had given me certain pledges of his loyalty that forced him to keep any secret I entrusted to him. Some renegades who want to return to Christian lands take with them documents signed by important captives in which these captives certify as best they can that the renegade in question is an upright man who has always treated Christians well, and that it's his wish to escape at the very first opportunity to do so. Some of them procure these affidavits with honest intentions, and others to make opportunistic use of them in emergencies: if they happen to be shipwrecked or captured on their way to a raid into Christian territory, they produce their affidavits and say that these papers prove their real reason for coming was to stay behind in Christian lands, and that's why they're in the corsair with the Turks. In this way they're

spared their captors' initial fury, and are readmitted to the Church, and
nobody does them any harm; and as soon as they see their chance they go
back to Barbary to be what they were before. There are others who procure
these papers with good intentions and do stay in Christian lands. Well, one
such renegade was this friend of mine, who had documents signed by all
the captives in which we vouched for him in the highest terms, and if the
Moors had found these papers they would have burned him alive. I
discovered that he had an excellent knowledge of Arabic, written as well
as spoken; before I took him fully into my confidence, however, I asked
him to read me a paper that I'd found in a hole in my hut. He unfolded it,
and spent some time examining and construing it, muttering to himself as
he did so. I asked him if he understood it. He said that he did, perfectly,
and that if I wanted an exact translation I should give him pen and ink to
facilitate his task. This we did, and he worked his way through the paper,
and once he'd finished he said:

'"What I've written here in Spanish, omitting not so much as a single
letter, reproduces what is contained in this Moorish document, and please
note that where it says *Lela Marien* it means 'Our Lady the Virgin Mary'."

'We read the paper, which went like this:

*When I was a little girl, my father had a female slave who taught me Christian
worship in my own language and told me many things about Lela Marien.
The Christian slave died, and I know that it wasn't to the fire that she went
but to Allah, because since then I have seen her twice, when she told me to go
to the land of the Christians to see Lela Marien, who loved me very much. I
don't know how I can go. Many Christians have I seen through this window,
and none but you has seemed a gentleman. I'm very beautiful, and young, and
I have much money to take with me. See if you can find a way for us to go,
and there you'll be my husband if you want, and if you don't want I don't
mind, because Lela Marien will give me a husband. I've written this myself;
be careful whom you allow to read it: don't trust any Moor, because they're
all treacherous. I'm very worried about this, and please don't tell anyone,
because if my father finds out he'll throw me down a well and cover me over
with stones. I shall fasten a thread on to my cane; you tie your answer to it;
and if there isn't anybody to write Arabic for you, answer me in sign language,
and Lela Marien will make me understand you. May she and Allah keep you,*

and this Cross that I kiss again and again, because it is what the slave told me
to do.

'Consider, ladies and gentlemen, whether our wonder and delight at the
contents of this letter were justified; and both were so evident that the
renegade realized it hadn't been found by chance, but had been written to
one of us; and so he asked us, if his suspicions were correct, to trust him
and tell him the truth, because he would risk his life to give us our liberty.
As he said this he drew a metal crucifix from inside his shirt, and with
copious tears he swore by the God that the image represented, in whom
he, though a wicked sinner, faithfully and devotedly believed, to be loyal
to us and keep whatever secrets we entrusted to him, because he imagined
and could almost guarantee that with the help of the woman who had
written that letter both he and we would be freed, and he would achieve
what he so desired: to be restored to the bosom of our Holy Mother
Church, from which like a gangrenous limb he had been cut off because
of his ignorance and sinfulness. The renegade said this with so many tears
and such signs of repentance that we all agreed to reveal the truth to him;
and we told him the whole story, not keeping anything back. We showed
him the window at which the cane kept appearing, and he took note of
the house and undertook to spare no effort to discover who lived there.
We also agreed that we ought to reply to the Moorish woman's letter; and,
since we had someone there who could do so, the renegade wrote down
what I dictated to him, and I can give you the exact words, because not
one of the material circumstances of that affair has faded from my memory,
nor shall I forget them as long as I live. The reply to the Moorish woman
went like this:

> *May the true Allah keep you, my lady, and also that blessed Marien who is*
> *the true Mother of God and has filled your heart with the desire to go to the*
> *lands of the Christians, because she loves you dearly. Pray to her to reveal*
> *how you can carry out what she has commanded, because she is so good that*
> *she will respond. For myself and all the other Christians here with me I can*
> *say that we will do everything we can for you, and die if necessary. Do not*
> *fail to write to me and tell me what you intend to do, because I will never fail*
> *to answer your letters: the great Allah has sent us a Christian captive who can*

speak and write your language well, as you can see from this letter. So you
can, without fear, tell us anything you want. As for what you say about
becoming my wife if you reach the lands of the Christians, I promise you as a
good Christian that this shall be so; and remember that Christians keep their
word better than Moors. May Allah and Marien, his mother, protect you, my
lady.

'After this letter had been written and folded I waited two days for the
bagnio to be left empty, as before, and then I went to the usual place on
the roof terrace to see if the cane appeared, which it wasn't long in doing.
As soon as I saw it, even though I couldn't see who was holding it, I held
up my letter to indicate that the thread should be fastened to the cane; but
it was already there, and I tied my letter to it, and a little after that our star
showed again, with the white flag of peace – the knotted handkerchief. It
was dropped into the bagnio, I picked it up, and inside I found more than
fifty escudos in all kinds of gold and silver coinage, which multiplied our
joy fifty times over and confirmed our hopes of gaining our freedom.

'That same night our renegade returned, and told us he'd discovered
that the Moor we'd been told about, Hajji Murad, did indeed live there,
that he was a man of unimaginable wealth, and had an only daughter, the
heiress to all his estate, who was in the opinion of everyone in the city the
most beautiful woman in all Barbary; that many of the viceroys who had
served there had asked for her hand, but that she had never wanted to
marry; and he'd also discovered that she'd once had a Christian slave, now
dead. All of this agreed with the contents of the letter. We had a discussion
with the renegade about how we could rescue the Moorish woman from
her house and escape to Christian territory, and we finally agreed to wait
for a second letter from Zoraida, because that was the name of the woman
who now wants to be called María: we could well see that she and nobody
else was the one who could find a solution to all our problems. After we'd
decided on this, the renegade told us not to worry – he would set us free
or die in the attempt.

'The bagnio was full for the next four days, and so there were no signs
of the cane; then the bagnio emptied again and the handkerchief appeared,
so very pregnant that it promised a most happy delivery. The cane and
handkerchief bowed before me, and in it I found another piece of paper

and one hundred escudos, all of gold. The renegade was there with us, and we returned to the seclusion of our hut and gave him the paper, which he translated as follows:

I don't know, sir, how to arrange for us to go to Spain, and Lela Marien hasn't told me, even though I've asked her; what can be done is for me to send you through this window many, many gold coins; then ransom yourself and your friends, and one of you go to Christian lands and buy a boat and come back for the others; and I shall be in my father's villa by the Bab Azzun gate, next to the seashore, where I must spend all the summer with my father and my servants. From there, at night, you'll be able to take me to the boat without fear of discovery; and don't forget that you are to be my husband, because otherwise I shall pray to Lela Marien to punish you. If there is no one you can trust to go for the boat, ransom yourself and go, because I know that you're more likely to come back than anybody else, since you're a gentleman and a Christian. Try to find out where the villa is, and when you walk about the roof terrace I shall know that the bagnio is empty and I shall give you lots of money. May Allah keep you, sir.

'This was what the second letter said, and on hearing it each of my companions offered to be the man ransomed, and promised to go to Spain and return exactly as agreed, and I made the same offer as well; but the renegade opposed all these suggestions, saying that he wouldn't allow anyone to go free until we all went together, because experience had taught him how remiss freed men were in keeping promises made in captivity – captives who were important men had often tried this remedy, ransoming someone who was to go to Valencia or Majorca with money to equip a boat and return for those who'd ransomed him, and not one of these had ever come back; because the new freedom and the fear of losing it erased from their memories all the obligations in the world. And as confirmation that what he said was true he briefly told us about what had happened not long before to some Christian gentlemen, the strangest affair that had ever occurred even there, where the most dreadful and amazing events are witnessed every day. His conclusion was that what could and should be done was for him to be given the money provided for the ransom, and he would buy a boat in Algiers itself, on the pretext that he was becoming a merchant and was going to trade in Tetuan and along the coast; and once he was the boat's owner it would be easy for him to find a way to get them all out of the bagnio and on to the boat. Even more so if the Moorish woman, as she had promised, provided enough money to ransom all of them, because once they were free it would be the simplest matter to embark, even at midday; but the biggest problem was that the Moors don't allow any renegade to buy or own a boat unless it's a large vessel for privateering, because they're afraid that he'd only want it to go back to Christian territory, particularly if he's Spanish; yet this renegade would overcome the difficulty by taking a Tagarene Moor as his trading partner, and with this blind he would become the boat's real owner, and the rest would be as good as done. And even though my companions and I had thought it preferable to send to Majorca for the boat, as the Moorish woman had suggested, we didn't dare contradict him for fear that if we didn't do as he said he might inform on us, and put our lives at risk, if he revealed our agreement with Zoraida, for whose life we would all have sacrificed our own; so we decided to place ourselves in God's hands and in those of the renegade, and we immediately replied to Zoraida saying that we'd do everything she suggested, because she'd advised us as well as if Lela Marien had told her what to say, and it was in her hands whether to delay the plan or put it into action straight away. I repeated my promise to marry her, and the next day, when the bagnio happened to be deserted, she used the cane and the handkerchief several times to send us two thousand escudos of gold, and a letter in which she said that on the following Juma, in other words Friday, she was going away to her father's villa, that before she went she would let us have some more money, and if it wasn't enough we should tell her so and she would give us as much as we needed, because her father was so wealthy that he wouldn't miss it, particularly since she held all the keys.

'We immediately gave the renegade five hundred escudos to buy the boat; I ransomed myself for eight hundred, handing the money over to a Valencian merchant who was in Algiers at the time and who ransomed me from the King by promising to pay the money on the arrival of the first ship from Valencia, because if he'd paid up straight away it would have made the King suspect that my ransom-money had been in Algiers for some time and that the merchant had kept quiet about it in order to speculate with it. And my master was so mistrustful that I didn't dare, on any account, have the money handed over immediately. On the day before the Friday when the lovely Zoraida was to go away to the villa she gave us another thousand escudos, told us of her departure and begged me, if I was ransomed, to locate the villa immediately and, come what might, to find an opportunity to go and see her there. I hurried to assure her that I would, and told her to take care to commend us to Lela Marien in all those prayers that the captive had taught her. Next, procedures were set in motion for the ransoming of my three companions, both to make it easier for us to leave the bagnio and in case seeing me ransomed and themselves not, although we had the money, made them alarmed and the devil put it into their heads to do something that could endanger Zoraida; for even though their breeding might have been a guarantee against this fear, I still didn't want to take any risks; so I had them ransomed by the same method that I'd used for ransoming myself, giving the merchant all the money so he could stand surety for them with certainty and confidence. But we never revealed our plan or our secrets to him, because that would have been too dangerous.

CHAPTER XLI

In which the captive gives us still more of his tale

'Within a fortnight our renegade had bought an excellent boat, with room for more than thirty people in it; and for the sake of greater credibility and security he decided to make a trip to a town called Cherchell, which is some sixty miles from Algiers going towards Oran, and does an extensive trade in dried figs. He made this journey two or three times with that Tagarene I mentioned. In Barbary they call the Moors of Aragon *Tagarenes*, and those of Granada *Mudéjares*, and in the kingdom of Fez they call the Mudéjares *Elches*, and these are the men most used by that king in his wars. Well, each time the renegade went by in his boat he cast anchor in a cove not a couple of bowshots from the villa where Zoraida was waiting, and there he would either, with great deliberation, set about performing his daily devotions with the young Moors who were rowing for him, or try out as if in jest what he was planning to do later in earnest, by going to Zoraida's villa and asking for fruit, and her father would give him some without knowing who he was; and although he would have liked to speak to Zoraida, as he later informed me, and tell her that he was the man who, on my orders, was going to take her away to the lands of the Christians, and that she could feel happy and safe with him, he was unable to do so, because a Moorish woman will never appear before a Moor or a Turk unless her husband or father tells her to. They don't mind Christian slaves keeping them company and talking to them, even more than might seem proper; and I must say I'd have been concerned if he had talked to her, because it could have raised all sorts of fears to find renegades discussing her affairs. But God had decided otherwise and didn't give the renegade any opportunities to put his good intentions into effect. Seeing that he could travel to and from Cherchell in complete safety and anchor whenever and wherever and however he pleased, and that his partner the Tagarene had no will of his own, and that I had by now been ransomed, and that it only remained to find some Christians to row the boat, he told me to consider which of these I wanted to take with me, apart from the ransomed ones, and to engage them for the following Friday, when he decided that we should set out. So I spoke to twelve Spaniards, all excellent oarsmen and free to leave the city whenever they pleased; and it was no small achievement to have found so many of them, because twenty vessels were out privateering and had taken all the rowers with them, and I wouldn't have found the men I did find if their master hadn't stayed behind that summer to finish a galliot in the shipyard. All I told them was that on the following Friday evening they should steal out of the city one by one, make their way towards Hajji Murad's villa, and wait for me there. I gave each man these instructions separately and told him that if he saw other Christians he shouldn't say anything other than that I'd instructed him to wait for me there.

'Once I'd seen to this, one more move remained to be made, the most important of them all: to let Zoraida know how matters stood so that she was forewarned and prepared and didn't become alarmed if we suddenly appeared before she imagined that the Christian boat could have had time to come. So I decided to visit the villa and see if I could speak to her, and a few days before our departure I went there pretending to be collecting wild salad leaves, and the first person I met was her father, who asked me in a language that's spoken between captives and Moors all over Barbary and even in Constantinople, and that's neither Arabic nor Castilian nor the tongue of any other country but a mixture of them all, and we all manage to understand each other using it – anyway, he asked me in this strange language what I was looking for on his property, and who was my master. I replied that I was one of Arnaute Mami's slaves[1] (I said this because I knew very well that these two men were close friends) and that I was looking for any leaves that would be suitable for a salad. Then he asked me whether I was up for ransom or not, and how much my master was asking for me. While we were busy with these questions and answers, the beautiful Zoraida, who'd been watching me for some time, wandered out of the house, and since, as I've said, Moorish women aren't particular about showing themselves to Christians and aren't at all coy with them, she didn't have any scruples about coming to where we stood; indeed, when her father saw her hesitant approach he called her over.

'I couldn't begin to describe Zoraida's beauty and grace or her rich and elegant attire when she came before me; all I will say is that there were more pearls hanging from her lovely neck, ears and tresses than hairs on her head. On her ankles, which, in the Moorish fashion, were bare, she was wearing two karkashes (that's what they call ankle-rings in Arabic) of the purest gold and set with so many diamonds that she later told me her father put their value at ten thousand doubloons, and her bracelets were worth the same amount. She was wearing all those superb pearls because for any Moorish woman they are the most splendid finery to be had, and this is the reason why there are more pearls and seed-pearls in Moorish hands than among all the other peoples in the world put together; and Zoraida's father had the reputation of possessing great numbers of the best pearls in Algiers, as well as two hundred thousand Spanish escudos. And all this was hers, then – and now all she has is me.

'You can imagine her beauty in prosperous times and when thus adorned from what remains of it now, after so much toil and trouble. Because we all know that some women's beauty has its days and its seasons, that circumstances can increase or diminish it and that it's natural for intense emotions to alter it for better or for worse, though they more often destroy it. As I was saying, then, at that moment she was so magnificently attired and so very beautiful that she seemed to me the loveliest woman that I'd ever seen, and when on top of this I considered how indebted I was to her, she seemed to me like a goddess from heaven who had come down to earth for my delight and deliverance. When she reached us her father told her in their language that I was a captive belonging to his friend Arnaute Mami and that I'd come to look for salad leaves. She took up the conversation and asked in that mixture of languages I've just described whether I was a gentleman and why I hadn't ransomed myself. I replied that I had, and that my master's esteem for me could be judged from the price I'd paid, one thousand five hundred sultanins. To which she replied:

' "To tell you the truth, if you belonged to my father I wouldn't let him part with you for twice as much, because you Christians never stop lying and pretending that you're poor, to cheat us Moors."

' "That might well be so, dear lady," I replied, "but the truth is that I dealt honestly with my master, as I deal and shall always deal with everybody."

' "And when are you leaving?" asked Zoraida.

' "Tomorrow, I believe," said I, "because there's a French ship here that sets sail tomorrow, and I intend to go in her."

' "Wouldn't it be better," replied Zoraida, "to wait for ships to come from Spain and go in one of those, rather than with the French, who are no good friends of you Spaniards?"

' "No," I replied, "although if the news I've heard that a Spanish vessel is on its way turns out to be true I'll wait for it – but it's more likely that I'll leave tomorrow, because my longing to be back in my own country with the people I love is so great that it won't allow me to wait long for another passage, however preferable it might be."

' "You must be a married man," said Zoraida, "and that's why you're so keen to go back, to be with your wife again."

' "No, I'm not married," I replied, "but I have given my word to marry as soon as I reach Spain."

' "And is the lady you've promised to marry very beautiful?" Zoraida asked.

' "She's so very beautiful," I replied, "that to convey how lovely she is I can only say that she looks just like you."

'At this her father burst out laughing and said:

' "By Allah, Christian, she must be beautiful indeed if she looks like my daughter, because my daughter is the most beautiful woman in this whole kingdom. If you do not believe me take a good look at her, and then you will see that I am telling the truth."

'Zoraida's father acted as interpreter for most of this conversation because, although she spoke in the hybrid language that, as I've said, is used there, she expressed herself more in gestures than in words, and he was more fluent in it. While we were engaged in this conversation, a Moor ran up and shouted that four Turks had climbed over the wall and were picking the fruit even though it wasn't yet ripe. This alarmed the old man, as it did Zoraida, because the fear that Moors feel of Turks is widespread and almost instinctive, and especially their fear of Turkish soldiers, who are so insolent and tyrannical to any Moors subjected to them that they treat them worse than slaves. So Zoraida's father said to her:

' "Return to the house, daughter, and lock yourself in, while I go and talk to these dogs; and you, Christian, can pick your salad and depart in peace, and may Allah bear you safely to your own country."

'I bowed, and he went to look for the Turks, leaving me alone with Zoraida, who made a show of doing as her father had ordered. But as soon as he'd disappeared among the trees in the garden, she turned to me with her eyes full of tears, and said:

' "*Ameshi*, Christian, *ameshi?*" – which means, "Are you going away, Christian, are you going away?"

'I replied:

' "Yes, dear lady, but most certainly not without you: expect me tomorrow, *Juma*, and don't be alarmed when you see us, because we're going to the lands of the Christians, I assure you."

'This I said in such a way that she understood everything I'd been telling her, and putting her arm over my shoulder she began to walk with faltering steps towards the villa; and as fortune would have it (with disastrous results, if heaven hadn't decreed otherwise), as we went along like this, her father, on his way back after sending the Turks away, saw how we were walking, and we saw that he'd seen us; but Zoraida, alert and quick-witted, didn't withdraw her arm but rather came closer to me, went limp at the knees and leaned her head on my chest to give a clear indication that she was fainting, while I, for my part, acted as if I were being forced to support her. Her father ran up to us and, seeing his daughter's distress, asked her what was wrong, but she didn't reply and he said:

'"The fright those dogs coming in here gave her must have made her faint."

'And taking her from me he held her to his breast, and she, sighing and with her eyes not yet dry from her tears, repeated:

'"*Ameshi*, Christian, *ameshi*!" – this time meaning, "Go away, Christian, go away!"

'To which her father replied:

'"There is no need for the Christian to go, daughter, he has not done you any harm, and the Turks have left. Do not be alarmed, there is nothing to be frightened of: as I said, the Turks went by the same way they came as soon as I told them to."

'"It was they who alarmed her, sir, as you thought," I said to her father. "But she's telling me to go away, and I don't want to upset her: peace be with you, and with your permission I shall come back here for salad leaves if I need them again, because my master says that there are none better to be found anywhere."

'"You can come whenever you like," replied Hajji Murad. "My daughter did not speak as she did because she dislikes you or any other Christian: she really meant to tell the Turks to go away, or maybe she thought it was time for you to go to look for your salad leaves."

'With this I said goodbye to them both, and she went off with her father looking as if her soul was being torn out of her; and under the pretence of searching for leaves I walked all round the grounds at my leisure. I studied the ways in and out, and the strengths and weaknesses of the house, and everything that could be exploited to expedite our plan. Then I went back and told the renegade and my companions what had happened, and looked forward with impatience to the time when I could enjoy untroubled the happiness that fortune was offering me in the lovely Zoraida.

And in this way the time went by and the day that we had all been longing for arrived; and, since everyone put into practice with great precision the plans that we had so often and in such careful detail thrashed out, we achieved the success for which we had hoped; because the Friday after the day I spoke to the lovely Zoraida outside the villa, our renegade anchored his boat at nightfall almost directly opposite it. The Christians who were going to row the boat were ready and hiding in different places near by. They were awaiting me with anxious joy, eager to attack the boat they had before their eyes, because they didn't know the renegade's plan and thought they were going to have to fight for their freedom and kill the Moors who were on board. So as soon as my companions and I showed ourselves they all came out of their hiding-places and approached us. By this time the city gates had been shut, and there was nobody to be seen in that area of open country. Once we were all together, we wondered what it would be better to do first, go to fetch Zoraida or overpower the Moorish sailors who were the oarsmen in the boat. As we stood there hesitating, our renegade appeared and asked what we were waiting for – it was time to get moving and all his Moors were off guard, most of them asleep. We told him what we were undecided about, and he said that we should first take control of the boat, which could easily and safely be done, and then we could go for Zoraida. We all thought this was good advice and so, without further delay, he led us to the boat, climbed on board, drew his scimitar and shouted in Arabic:

' "None of you must move an inch unless you want to die."

'By this time most of the Christians were aboard. The Moors were a poor-spirited lot, and when they heard their captain speaking like that they were terror-stricken; not one of them reached for his weapon (hardly any of them had a weapon, anyway), and without making a sound they allowed their wrists to be bound by the Christians, who did so at speed as they threatened the Moors that if any one of them spoke so much as a single word they would all be put immediately to the sword.

'Once this had been achieved, half our number stayed to guard the Moors, and the rest of us, still led by the renegade, hastened to Hajji Murad's villa, and were lucky enough to find that when we went to force the gate in the wall it swung open as readily as if it hadn't been locked at all, and so we reached the house in tranquil silence and unnoticed by anyone. The lovely Zoraida was waiting for us at a window, and as soon as she heard people in the garden below she asked in a whisper if we were *Nizarani*, in other words if we were Christians. I replied that we were, and asked her to come down. She recognized me and didn't hesitate for an instant, but came down without a word and opened the door, revealing herself to all of us so beautiful and so wonderfully dressed that I couldn't begin to describe her. When I saw her I took her hand and kissed it, and the renegade did the same, and so did my two companions; and all the others, who didn't know what was happening, copied us, because they could see that we were thanking and acclaiming her as our liberator. The renegade asked her in Arabic if her father was in the house. She replied that he was, asleep.

'"We're going to have to wake him up," said the renegade, "and take him with us, and everything of value in this lovely villa."

'"No," she replied. "No one, no one is to touch my father, and there's nothing in this house except what I'm bringing with me, which is quite enough to make you all rich and happy. Just wait and see."

'And she went back into the villa saying she'd return in a moment and we must stay still and not make any noise. I asked the renegade what they'd been saying to each other, and he told me, and then I told him that nothing must be done unless Zoraida agreed to it; she was already approaching with a coffer full of so many gold coins that she could hardly carry it, but meanwhile her father had unfortunately awakened, heard the noise in the garden, hurried to his window and realized that all the men below were Christians; at which he began to bellow in Arabic:

'"Christians, Christians! Thieves, thieves!"

'These cries threw us all into the greatest confusion and trepidation. But the renegade, seeing the danger we were in and the importance of completing this operation undetected, rushed up to Hajji Murad's room followed by a few others – I didn't dare leave Zoraida, who'd fainted in my arms. To be brief, the men who'd entered the house did their job so well that in an instant they came down with Hajji Murad, bound and gagged, warning him that any further attempt to cry out would cost him his life. When his daughter saw him she covered her eyes to shut the sight out, and he was horror-struck, not knowing how willingly she had placed herself in our hands. But it was our feet that we needed to use, and we ran back to the boat, where those who'd remained on board were anxious for our return, fearing for our safety.

'We were all on the boat before two hours of the night had elapsed, and Zoraida's father's hands were untied and the gag was taken out of his mouth; but the renegade repeated the threat that he'd be killed if he uttered a single word. Seeing his daughter there he began to breathe piteous sighs, redoubled when he noticed that I was holding her tight and that she lay motionless in my arms, without making any attempts to resist or to protest or to struggle free; but he kept quiet, fearful that the renegade might put his many threats into effect. Finding herself on board, and the boat about to set off, and her father and the other Moors lying there with their ankles bound, Zoraida told the renegade to ask me to do her the favour of releasing them all, and her father with them, because she'd sooner throw herself overboard than have a father who'd loved her so dearly carried off as a captive in her presence and because of her. The renegade told me what she'd requested, and I replied that I gladly agreed. But he said that this would be unwise, because if we left them behind they'd immediately raise the alarm in the city and throughout the country, and then fast frigates would be sent out after us, leaving us nowhere to go on land or sea and making escape impossible; and he added that what we could do was to set them free on the first Christian territory we reached. We all agreed to this, and informed Zoraida of our decision and our reasons for not doing as she wished, and she was satisfied with the arrangement; and in a joyful silence and with a happy diligence each of our lusty rowers took his oar, and, commending ourselves to God with all our hearts, we began our journey to the Balearic Islands, the nearest Christian lands. But since a moderate northwester was blowing and the sea was choppy, it was impossible to keep a straight course for Majorca, and we had to coast in the direction of Oran, with heavy hearts because we feared we might be spotted from Cherchell, sixty miles from Algiers along that coast. We were also afraid that we might come across some galliot returning with merchandise from Tetuan, although each of us felt such confidence in himself and in the whole group that we were sure that if we did meet one of them, so long as it wasn't equipped for privateering, not only would we resist being taken but acquire a vessel in which to complete our journey in greater safety. As we pursued our course, Zoraida kept her head buried in my hands to avoid seeing her father, and I heard her calling on Lela Marien to help us.

'We would have gone a good thirty miles by the time dawn came, and we found ourselves about three musket-shots from land, which we could see was deserted, so nobody was going to detect us yet; but just to be on the safe side we rowed further out to sea, because it was now a little calmer, and after five or six miles the order was given to row by turns so that everyone could have a bite to eat, because the boat was well supplied with food; but the oarsmen said this was no time to be resting, and those who weren't rowing could feed them, because they certainly weren't going to abandon their oars. That's what we did, but then a strong crosswind began to blow, forcing us to hoist the sails, and stop rowing, and head for Oran, because it was impossible to steer any other course. This all happened very quickly, and once we were under sail we careered along at more than eight knots, fearing nothing except an encounter with some privateer. We fed the Moorish sailors, and the renegade offered them some comfort by telling them that they weren't being taken captive, and would be freed as soon as possible. Zoraida's father was given the same assurance, and he replied:

' "I could expect any other kindness from your liberality and courtesy, my Christian friends, but do not think me so stupid as to imagine that you are going to hand me my liberty: you did not take such risks to deprive me of it only to give it back so generously, knowing who I am and how much money you can make by selling it. And if you name your price, I will give you whatever you want for me and this unfortunate daughter of mine, or else for her alone, the greater and better part of my soul."

'As he said this he began to cry so bitterly that we all felt for him, and Zoraida couldn't help stealing a glance at him; and the sight of her father weeping so moved her that she rose from where she was sitting at my feet and went to hug him and, with their cheeks pressed together, they both wept with such loving tenderness that many of the rest of us shed tears with them. But when her father realized that she was wearing her finest clothes and so many jewels, he said in Arabic:

' "What does this mean, daughter? Yesterday evening, before this disaster overtook us, I saw you wearing your everyday indoor clothes; and now, even though you have not had time to change, and I have not brought you any good news to be celebrated by putting on finery and jewels, here you are sporting the very best clothes I was capable of giving you when fortune most favoured us. Let me hear your answer, because this astonishes and perturbs me even more than the predicament in which I find myself."

'The renegade told us what the Moor had said to his daughter, who offered not one word in reply. But when in a corner of the boat he saw her jewel-coffer, which he was certain she'd left in Algiers and hadn't taken to the villa, he was even more bewildered, and asked her how it had found its way into our hands, and what was in it. To which the renegade replied, before Zoraida could:

'"Don't weary yourself, sir, asking your daughter Zoraida so many questions, because by answering just one of them I can answer them all: let me tell you, then, that she's a Christian, and that she's the one who has broken our chains and freed us from captivity. She's here of her own free will, and she's as happy, I imagine, to find herself in this position as is anyone emerging from darkness to light, from death to life and from grief to glory."

'"Is what this man says true, daughter?" the Moor asked.

'"Yes, it is," replied Zoraida.

'"So you are a Christian," the old man said, "and you are responsible for putting your own father into his enemies' power?"

'To which Zoraida replied:

'"Yes, I am a Christian, but I am not responsible for putting you in this predicament, because it was never my intention to do you harm, only to do myself good."

'"And what is this good that you have done yourself, daughter?"

'"That," she replied, "is something you should ask Lela Marien, because she can tell you better than I could."

'As soon as the Moor heard this he hurled himself with extraordinary agility head first into the sea, where he would have drowned if his long, cumbersome robes hadn't kept him afloat. Zoraida cried out to us to rescue him and we all rushed to his aid and, seizing hold of his haik, hauled him out of the water half drowned and unconscious, and Zoraida was so distressed that she burst into a tender and sorrowful lament over him, as if he were dead. We turned him face downwards; he brought up a great quantity of water; he regained consciousness two hours later, during which time the wind changed and we had to go back inshore and then ply our oars to avoid running aground; but we were fortunate enough to come to a creek next to a small headland that the Moors call the Cape of *La Cava Rumia*, which means "the wicked Christian woman"; and there is a tradition among the Moors that *la Cava*, through whom Spain was lost,[2] is buried there, because in their language *cava* means "wicked woman" and *rumia* means "Christian"; and they look on it as a bad omen to be forced to anchor there – they'll never do so unless they have to, although for us it wasn't so much a wicked woman's haven as the safe anchorage of our salvation, so rough had the sea become. We posted sentries on shore, and the oars weren't relinquished for a moment as we ate what the renegade had provided, and prayed to God and our Lady with all our hearts to favour us and help us to bring to a happy conclusion what we'd so successfully started. At Zoraida's request we considered releasing her father and all the other Moors who were tied up in the boat, because her tender heart could no longer bear seeing him bound and her countrymen prisoners. We promised to do this when we set off again, since it wouldn't be dangerous to leave them in that uninhabited place. Our prayers weren't in vain: heaven heard them and turned the wind in our favour and calmed the sea, inviting us to resume our voyage in good heart. So we untied the Moors and put them ashore one by one, to their astonishment; but when we came to Zoraida's father, by now fully recovered, he said:

'"Why do you think, Christians, that this evil woman is so pleased to see me set free? Do you think that it is out of pity? No, not at all: it is only because my presence would be a hindrance as soon as she wants to gratify her wicked desires. And do not imagine that what has led her to change religions is any belief that yours is better than ours: it is only the knowledge that promiscuity is more freely practised in your country than in ours."

'And turning to Zoraida, while another Christian and I held his arms to prevent him from doing something desperate, he added:

'"Oh, you misguided girl, you infamous creature! Where do you think you are going, in your blindness and stupidity, and in the clutches of these dogs, our natural enemies? Accursed be the hour when I begot you, accursed be the delights and the luxuries among which I reared you!"

'I could see that he was intending to go on like this for some time, so I hustled him on to the beach and from there he continued screaming out his curses and his lamentations, calling on Muhammad to call on Allah to confound us and destroy us and exterminate us; and even when we had set sail and could no longer hear what he was saying, we could see what he was doing as he tore at his beard and hair and writhed on the sand. But at one point he shouted so loud that we could hear:

'"Come back, my darling daughter, come back to land, I forgive you for everything! Let those men have the money, for it is theirs now anyway, and come back to comfort your sorrowing father, who will die here on these empty sands if you forsake him!"

'Zoraida was listening, and grieving, and weeping, and all she could answer was:

'"May it please Allah, dear father, to have Lela Marien, who turned me into a Christian, comfort you in your grief. Allah knows that I couldn't have done otherwise, and that these Christians don't have to feel indebted to me for any particular goodwill towards them, because even if I hadn't wanted to come with them, but to stay at home, that would have been impossible, with my soul so eager to perform a deed that is as righteous in my opinion, beloved father, as it is wicked in yours."

'But when Zoraida said all this, her father couldn't hear her and we couldn't see him; and, as I comforted her, we all turned our attention to our voyage, now assisted by a favourable wind, so that we felt certain that by dawn the next day we'd be on the Spanish coast. But good seldom or never comes pure and simple, unaccompanied by some evil to throw it into disarray, and as our fortune would have it – or perhaps it was the curses that the Moor had hurled at his daughter, because any father's curses are to be feared – when we were well out at sea, and almost three hours of the night had elapsed, and we were racing along under full sail with our oars held at the ready because the favourable wind saved us the trouble of using them, we saw by the light of the clear moon a square-rigged vessel also in full sail, steering almost directly into the wind and across our bows, so close that we had to shorten sail to avoid a collision, while they clapped their helm a-starboard to give us room to pass. They'd gathered on the deck to ask us who we were, where we were going and where we'd come from, but since the questions were put in French, our renegade muttered:

'"Don't reply, any of you – these must be French privateers, and they plunder everything that comes their way."

'Thus warned, none of us said a word; but after we'd drifted a little further on and left their ship leeward of us, they suddenly fired two cannon, both of which must have been loaded with chainshot, because one cut our mast off and dumped it and the sail in the sea, and the other, seconds later, hit our boat amidships and staved her in without doing any further damage. We could see that we were sinking and we all began to shout for help, begging the men in the ship to take us on board because we were going under. They shortened sail and launched the skiff, in other words the ship's boat, and about a dozen well-armed Frenchmen climbed into it complete with their harquebuses and glowing fuses; they drew alongside and saw how few of us there were and how our boat was sinking, and they took us in, saying that all this had happened to us for not having had the courtesy to reply to them. When no one was looking, our renegade picked up Zoraida's jewel-coffer and dropped it into the sea.

'So we all joined the Frenchmen who, having extracted from us all the information they wanted, stripped us of everything we owned as if we were their mortal enemies, even taking Zoraida's ankle-rings. But I was less concerned about Zoraida's distress than about my fear that they might proceed from taking her exquisite and priceless jewels to depriving her of the most valuable jewel of them all, the one she prized above all the others. But those people's desires don't extend beyond money, and their lust for it is never satisfied, and it was then at such a pitch that they would even have stripped us of our captives' uniforms if they had been worth anything to them. There were those among them who thought that we should all be tied up in a sail and thrown overboard, because it was their intention to trade in Spanish ports pretending to be Bretons, and if they let us live and took us with them their theft would be discovered and they'd be punished. But the captain, the man who'd robbed my beloved Zoraida, said that he was happy with the prize he'd taken and didn't intend to call at any Spanish port, but slip through the Straits of Gibraltar by night, or in any way he could, and make for La Rochelle, from where they had set out. So they agreed to let us have the skiff and whatever else we needed for the short voyage that remained, as they did the following day, within sight of the Spanish coast; and as soon as we saw it we forgot all about our troubles and our hardships, as if they'd never happened – such is the joy of recovering lost liberty.

'It must have been about midday when they put us in the skiff with two barrels of water and some ship's biscuit; and the captain, moved by strange compassion, gave the lovely Zoraida forty gold escudos as she embarked, and stopped his men from taking these clothes she's wearing now. We climbed down into the skiff and thanked them for their kindness, showing that our gratitude outweighed our resentment; they sailed on towards the Straits; we rowed so hard, guided only by the shore before us, that by dusk we were near enough, we thought, to be able to land before the night was far advanced; but there was no moon, and the sky was dark, and we didn't know where we were, so it didn't seem safe to run the skiff ashore as many of us wanted, arguing that we should do so even though we might hit rocks and be far from any town, because in this way we should be relieved of the fear we naturally felt of the prowling vessels of the Tetuan corsairs, who leave Barbary at dusk, reach the Spanish coast at dawn, take some prize and go back home to bed; we resolved the difference of opinion by agreeing to approach the shore slowly and land wherever we could if the sea was calm enough to permit it. This we did, and it would have been a little before midnight when we arrived at the foot of a towering hill, which didn't fall quite so sheer into the sea but that it left us a little room to land in comfort. We ran the skiff on to the sand, climbed out, kissed the ground and with tears of infinite joy thanked the Lord God for his incomparable goodness. We took the provisions out of the skiff, hauled it up the beach and then climbed far up the hill; because even though we were where we were, we still couldn't calm the fears in our breasts, or persuade ourselves that it was Christian soil beneath us.

'Dawn came later, I think, than we'd have liked. We climbed to the top of the hill to see if we could make out any village or herdsmen's huts, but however hard we looked we couldn't spot any settlement, or human being, or road, or path. But we decided to press on inland, because we were bound before very long to come across somebody who could tell us where we were. What most pained me was seeing Zoraida trudging along over that rough ground, because although I took her on my back once or twice, my weariness was more wearisome to her than her rest was restful, and she wouldn't let me carry her any more, and on she walked, patient and looking happy, holding my hand. After nearly a mile the sound of a sheep-bell reached our ears, telling us that a flock wasn't far away, and as we all looked around for it we saw a shepherd-boy sitting at the foot of a cork-oak calmly whittling away at a stick. We called out to him and he looked up and jumped to his feet, and, as we later learned, the first people he saw were the renegade and Zoraida; and since they were in Moorish dress he thought that the whole of Barbary had come for him, and he sprinted into the wood with the loudest screams ever heard in this world:

'"Moors, the Moors have come! Moors, Moors! To arms, to arms!"

'Bewildered by these cries, none of us knew what to do; but realizing that the shepherd-boy's shouts would alarm the whole area and that the coastguards would soon come to see what was up, we agreed that the renegade should take off his Turkish robes and put on the captive's doublet that one of my companions handed him, even though that left him in his shirtsleeves; and, commending ourselves to God, we took the path we'd seen the shepherd-boy take, expecting the coastguards to appear at any moment. And our assumptions weren't mistaken, because before two hours had elapsed, when we'd emerged from the woodland on to an open plain, we saw about fifty coastguards galloping towards us; we stopped and waited for them, and, when they came up and, instead of the Moors they were looking for, only found a bunch of poor Christians, they were puzzled; and one of them asked us if we were by any chance the people who had caused a shepherd-boy to raise the alarm.

'"Yes," I said, and as I was starting to explain what had happened, and where we'd come from and who we were, one of the Christians with us recognized the horseman who'd asked the question and interrupted me:

'"Praise be to God, gentlemen, for bringing us to so fine a place. Because if I'm not mistaken this soil we're treading belongs to Vélez Málaga, and if my years of captivity haven't impaired my memory, you, sir, asking us these questions, are Pedro de Bustamante, my uncle."

'Hardly had the Christian captive finished speaking when the coastguard leapt from his horse and ran to embrace the young man, crying:

'"My dear, dear nephew, I can recognize you now: how I've wept for you, believing you dead, and my sister your mother too, and all your family – they're all still alive, and God has been pleased to spare them to give them the joy of seeing you again. We knew you were in Algiers, and judging from your clothes and those of your companions here, I can see you've had a miraculous deliverance."

'"Yes, we have," replied the young man, "and there'll be plenty of time to tell you all about it."

'As soon as the horsemen realized that we were Christian captives they dismounted and offered us their animals for the journey to the city of Vélez Málaga, about five miles away. We told them where we'd left the skiff, and some of them went to take it to the city; each of the others sat one of us behind him, and Zoraida rode behind our companion's uncle. The whole town came out to welcome us, because one of the coastguards had gone on ahead to spread the news of our arrival. They weren't surprised to see either Christian slaves who'd escaped or Moors who'd been captured, because everyone along that coast is used to seeing both, but what did astonish them was Zoraida's beauty, which at that time was in its full perfection, because the fatigue of the journey and the happiness of being at last on Christian soil without any fear of recapture had brought such a glow to her cheeks that, unless my love was deceiving me, I'd venture to say that there was no more beautiful creature in the whole world – not, at least, that I had ever seen.

'We went straight to church to thank God for the mercies we'd received, and as Zoraida walked in she said that there were faces there that looked like Lela Marien's faces. We told her that they were images, and the renegade explained as best he could what they signified, so that she could worship them as if each one really were the very same Lela Marien who'd spoken to her. Zoraida has a good mind and a clear and ready understanding, and immediately grasped what she was told about the images. From there we were taken to be lodged in various houses in the town, and our companion who lived there took the renegade, Zoraida and me to stay with his parents, who had their fair share of the good things of life, and they treated us with as much love as they did their own son.

'We stayed for six days in Vélez Málaga, at the end of which the renegade, having made his formal declaration of intentions to the authorities, went to the city of Granada to be restored to the sacred bosom of the Church through the good offices of the Holy Inquisition, all the other freed captives went their various ways and Zoraida and I were left alone, possessing only the escudos that the courteous Frenchman had given her. I used them to buy this donkey that she's riding, and with me acting so far as her father and her squire rather than as her husband, we're going to see if my own father is still alive and if either of my brothers has had better luck than I have – though since heaven has made me Zoraida's companion, I don't believe there's any other stroke of good fortune that I could ever prize more highly. She is enduring the discomforts of poverty with such patience, and is so determined to become a Christian, that I'm filled with amazement, and resolved to serve her all the days of my life, although the happiness of knowing that I am hers and she is mine is marred by not knowing whether I shall find any corner back home where we can find shelter, or whether time and death have made such changes in the fortunes and lives of my father and brothers that, if they are no longer in this world, there will hardly be anyone left who knows me.

'There's nothing more to tell you, gentlemen, and I'll leave it to your discernment to judge whether my story's an entertaining and curious one; all I can say is that I wish I could have been briefer, although my concern not to bore you has led me to omit several episodes.'

CHAPTER XLII

Concerning further events at the inn, and many other particulars worth knowing about

The captive stopped speaking, and Don Fernando said:

'Truly, captain, the way in which you have narrated these strange events has been every bit as extraordinary as the events themselves. The whole tale is curious, and surprising, and full of incidents that astonish the listener. And it has given us such pleasure that we'd be happy to hear it all over again, even if it took you until tomorrow morning to tell it.'

And then Cardenio and all the others offered to help the captain in every way they could, in such affectionate and sincere words that he was left in no doubt about their goodwill. In particular, Don Fernando said that if the captain would like to go with him he'd persuade his brother the Marquis to be godfather at Zoraida's baptism, and that for his own part he'd equip him to appear in his own town with all the dignity and decorum that was due to his person. The captain gave Don Fernando the most courteous thanks, but declined his generous offers.

The evening had moved on, and as night fell a coach drew up at the inn, accompanied by some men on horseback. They asked for a lodging, but the innkeeper's wife replied that there wasn't an inch of room left in the house.

'Well, even if that is true,' said one of the horsemen, who had entered the inn, 'some room will have to be found for His Honour the Judge.'

When she heard this title the innkeeper's wife became flustered and said:

'What I meant to say, sir, is that I haven't any beds; if His Honour has one with him, as I'm sure he must, he's more than welcome, and me and my husband will give up our own room for him.'

'That'll do,' said the squire.

By this time a man had alighted from the coach, and his clothes proclaimed the position he occupied: his long robe with loose slashed upper sleeves showed him to be a judge, as his servant had said. He led by the hand a girl who seemed about sixteen years old, dressed in travelling clothes, and so marvellously beautiful and graceful that everyone was dazzled by the sight of her and, if they hadn't seen Dorotea, Luscinda and Zoraida at the inn, they'd have believed it next to impossible to find another comparable beauty. Don Quixote was still sitting there when the judge and the girl walked in, and on seeing them he said:

'You can safely enter this castle, sir, and take your ease in it because, although it is cramped and uncomfortable, there is nowhere in the world so lacking in space and comfort that it does not make room for arms and letters, especially if arms and letters have beauteousness as their guide and leader, as letters, represented by you, sir, do in this beauteous maiden, before whom not only should castles open their doors and humble themselves, but rocks should split asunder, and mountains should gape and bow to welcome her in. Enter, sir, I say, into this paradise, because here you will find stars and suns for the heaven you bring with you: here you will find arms at their zenith and beauty in its prime.'

The judge was amazed at Don Quixote's speech, and looked him up and down, and was no less amazed at his appearance than at his words; and not finding any with which to reply, he was amazed yet again when he saw before him Luscinda, Dorotea and Zoraida, who, on hearing about the new guests and being given by the innkeeper's wife an account of the girl's beauty, had come to have a look at her and welcome her. Don Fernando, Cardenio and the priest greeted the judge with more normal and straightforward courtesies. So he entered the house in some bewilderment, both at what he saw and at what he heard, and the beauties at the inn welcomed the latest beauty to arrive. It was easy for the judge to tell that all the people at the inn were of high rank, but Don Quixote's figure, face and bearing bemused him; and after they'd all exchanged the usual courtesies, and questions had been asked and answered about the accommodation, what had previously been decided was decided again: all the ladies would sleep in the loft we know about, and the men would stay outside it on guard, as it were. And the judge was happy for his daughter to go with the other ladies, which she was very willing to do. And on a part of the innkeeper's narrow bed, and a half of the bed that the judge had brought with him, the ladies were more comfortable that night than they'd thought they'd be.

As soon as the captive saw the judge his heart throbbed with the suspicion that this was his brother, and he asked one of the servants who he was and where he was from. The servant replied that the judge was called Juan Pérez de Viedma, MA, and that he'd heard he was from a village in the mountains of León. This news, together with what the captive had seen, confirmed that the man who'd just arrived was indeed his brother, the one who, following their father's advice, had studied to be a man of letters; overjoyed, he called Don Fernando, Cardenio and the priest aside, saying he was certain the judge was his brother. The servant had also said that his master was on his way to take up an important position in America, in the Supreme Court of Mexico; and that the girl was the judge's daughter, that her mother had died in giving birth to her and that the judge was a very wealthy man thanks to the fortune that his wife had settled on the child. The captive asked for their advice about how to reveal his identity, and how to find out first whether his brother, when he saw how poor he was, would feel affronted or welcome him back with open arms.

'Let me be allowed to discover that,' said the priest. 'But it's inconceivable, captain, that you won't be warmly welcomed, because the resolve and the wisdom that your brother reveals in his impressive presence don't make him seem at all like an arrogant man or one who disregards his obligations, or one who won't be able to relegate the vicissitudes of fortune to their proper place.'

'In spite of all that,' said the captain, 'I'd prefer not to make myself known to him all of a sudden, but in a roundabout way.'

'I've already told you,' replied the priest, 'that I'll manage it so that we're all happy with the outcome.'

By now supper was ready and they all sat down at the table except the captive and the ladies, who ate in their own room. Halfway through the meal the priest said:

'A companion of mine in Constantinople, where I was a captive for some years, had the same surname as you, Your Honour, and he was one of the best soldiers and captains in the whole of the Spanish infantry. But he was as unfortunate as he was resolute and valiant.'

'And what was the captain's name, my dear sir?' asked the judge.

'His name,' replied the priest, 'was Ruy Pérez de Viedma, and he was from a village in the mountains of León; and he told me a story about his father, his brothers and himself that, if he weren't such an honest man, I'd have taken for one of those tales that old wives tell each other round the fire in wintertime. He said that his father had divided all he had among his three sons and had given them better advice than Cato himself could have given. And let me tell you that the son who chose to become a soldier started out so well that in only a few years, thanks to his courage and determination, and without any patron other than his great virtue, he rose to be a captain in the infantry, and was on the very verge of being promoted to field officer. But fortune turned against him, because just when he might have expected to enjoy her favour she withdrew it from him, and he lost his liberty on that glorious day when so many others gained theirs, at the battle of Lepanto. I lost mine at the Goletta, and circumstances brought us together in Constantinople. From there he went to Algiers, where I know he had one of the strangest experiences that anyone could ever have had.'

The priest continued the tale, and provided the judge with a summary of his brother's adventures with Zoraida. The judge was all ears – never had he heard any case as attentively as he did this one. The priest stopped at the point where the French stripped the Christians in the skiff of all their possessions and left his companion and the beautiful Moorish woman in such dire poverty, and said that he didn't know what had happened to them after that – whether they'd made it to Spain or the French had taken them off to France. The captain was standing some distance away, listening to every word that the priest uttered and watching every movement made by his brother, who, seeing that the story had ended, sighed from the depths of his soul and said, as his eyes brimmed with tears:

'Oh, sir, if only you knew how very concerned I am about this news that you've brought me – I can't help showing it in these tears I'm shedding, in spite of all my cleverness and self-restraint! This brave captain about whom you've been talking is my elder brother, who, being stronger and more high-minded than my younger brother or I, chose the honourable and meritorious profession of arms, one of the three ways proposed to us by our father, as your companion told you in what you thought was an old wives' tale. I chose letters, and God and my own exertions have brought me to the position in which you find me. The younger of my brothers is in Peru and is such a wealthy man that with what he has sent back to my father and me he has more than repaid the money he was given, and provided plenty more for my father to indulge his natural generosity, and for me to pursue my studies in a more respectable and dignified way, and reach my present position. My father is still alive, but dying to receive news of his eldest son, and never ceasing to pray to God that death does not close his eyes until they have gazed upon those of that son. What does surprise me in a man of his good sense is that neither in his times of toil and trouble nor in his prosperity did he ever see fit to send his father any news; if we'd known what was happening, my brother wouldn't have had to wait for the miracle of the cane to obtain his ransom. But what I'm worried about now is whether those Frenchmen have released him, or killed him to cover up their robbery. And this means that I can't continue my journey joyfully, as I began it, but in deep grief. Oh, my beloved brother, how I wish I knew where you are now: I'd go and rescue you from all your troubles, whatever it cost me! Oh, how I wish I could take our dear old father the news that you're alive, even if in the deepest dungeons of Barbary – because his wealth and my brother's and mine would soon get you out of there! Oh, lovely and generous Zoraida, how I wish I could repay you for what you've done for my brother! How I wish I could be present at the rebirth of your soul, and at your wedding, both of which would give us all such great joy!'

The judge spoke these and many other similar words, so moved by the news about his brother that all who heard him joined him in manifestations of their tender concern for his sorrow. So the priest, seeing that he'd achieved what he and the captain wanted, decided not to keep these people in distress any longer, and he rose to his feet and walked into the ladies' room and returned holding Zoraida by the hand, followed by Luscinda, Dorotea and the judge's daughter. The captain was waiting to see what the priest was going to do next, and what he did was to go and take him by the hand, too, and walk with both of them to where the judge and the other men were sitting, and say:

'You can stop crying now, Your Honour, and enjoy the culmination of all your most cherished desires, because here before you stand your beloved brother and your dear sister-in-law. This man you see here is Captain Viedma, and this woman is the lovely Moor who did him such good. Those Frenchmen left them as poor as you see them so that you could show the generosity of your noble heart.'

The captain sprang forward to embrace his brother, who, however, kept him at arm's length with his hands on his shoulders to take a proper look at him; but once he'd recognized him he clutched him so tight and shed such tender tears of happiness that most of those present couldn't help weeping with him. The words the two brothers exchanged and the emotion they showed can, I think, hardly be imagined, let alone put down in writing. They exchanged brief accounts of their adventures; they demonstrated the finest brotherly feeling; the judge embraced Zoraida; he offered her all he possessed; he told his daughter to embrace her; and then the beautiful Christian and the lovely Moor caused everybody's tears to spring forth yet again. Don Quixote sat there watching, uttering not one word, pondering over such extraordinary events and putting them down to the chimeras of knight-errantry. It was agreed that the captain and Zoraida would go with the judge to Seville and tell their father about how he'd regained his freedom and been found, so that the old man could come as soon as possible to be present at the wedding and at Zoraida's baptism, since the judge had to press on with his trip, because he'd been given news that a fleet was leaving Seville in a month's time for Mexico and it would be most inconvenient to miss it.

So everyone was delighted with the happy ending to the captive's tale, and since by now almost two-thirds of the night had elapsed, they agreed to retire and rest for what was left of it. Don Quixote offered to mount guard over the castle to prevent attacks by giants and other villainous wretches, greedy for the precious treasure of beauty that it contained. Those who knew him thanked him for his kindness, and informed the judge about Don Quixote's whimsy, which he thought most amusing. Only Sancho Panza was unhappy, as he despaired of ever turning in, and only he made himself really snug afterwards, on his donkey's tackle – which was to cost him dear, as will be seen in due course. The ladies had retired to their room, the men settled down with as little discomfort as they could manage and Don Quixote marched out of the inn to his sentry duty, as he'd promised.

A little before dawn the ladies heard a voice which was so fine and tuneful that they all had to listen, particularly Dorotea, who was already awake and by whose side Doña Clara de Viedma, the judge's daughter, was fast asleep. None of them could imagine who it was singing so well, and unaccompanied. Sometimes the voice seemed to be coming from the courtyard, at other times from the stables; and as they lay there listening in bewilderment Cardenio came to their door and said:

'If any of you are awake, do listen and you'll hear a young footman singing. It's the most gorgeous sound: enchanting chanting, one might say.'

'We're already trying to listen, sir,' Dorotea replied.

So Cardenio crept away, and Dorotea, listening as hard as she could, heard that what was being sung was the following:

CHAPTER XLIII

Which relates the agreeable history of the footman,
together with other strange events at the inn

A mariner of love am I
Who, far from any strand,
Sails on, although without a hope
Of ever reaching land.

My eyes are on a distant star
That serves me as a guide,
More beautiful and bright than all
That Palinurus[1] spied.

    I don't know where she's leading me,
And so, bemused, I steer,
My heart intent on watching her,
Careless and full of care.

    And her unkindly bashfulness
And undue modesty
Are clouds that hide her from my eyes,
The girl I long to see.

    O Clara, clear and shining star,
I fade beneath your light,
And if you hide your beams from me
I'll die in darkest night.

When the singer reached this point in his song, Dorotea thought it would be a pity if Clara missed hearing such a good voice, so she shook her awake and said:

'Forgive me for waking you up, my child, but I did it so that you can enjoy the finest voice perhaps you've ever heard.'

Clara was still half-asleep and couldn't at first make out what Dorotea was saying, so she asked her, and Dorotea repeated her words, and Clara began to listen. But hardly had she heard the next two lines of the song when she was seized with a strange trembling, as if she were having a violent attack of malaria, and clinging to Dorotea she said:

'Oh, my dear, dear lady, why did you wake me up? The greatest good that fortune could have done me was to have kept my eyes and ears shut, so as not to see or hear that unhappy singer.'

'What are you saying, my child? I'm told he's a mere footman, you know.'

'No, on the contrary, he's the lord of many manors,' replied Clara, 'and he's so securely in possession of the manor of my heart that so long as he doesn't give it up he'll never be ejected from it.'

Dorotea was amazed at the girl's passionate words, which seemed to indicate an intelligence far in excess of her years. She said:

'You talk in such a way, Doña Clara, that I cannot understand you: please explain yourself and tell me what you mean about your heart and manors and this singer whose song disturbs you so. But don't tell me anything yet, I'm not going to let worrying about your nervous turns deprive me of the pleasure of listening to him – he's starting up again, I think, with different words and a different melody.'

'Just as you wish,' replied Clara.

And to avoid hearing him she pressed both hands over her ears, which also surprised Dorotea, who listened avidly as the singer continued:

> O sweetest hope of mine,
> Breaking through all the barriers of despair
> To keep the firm straight line
> That you yourself imagine and prepare:
> Don't be dismayed to see
> That every step has death for company.
>
> No sluggard ever gained
> Triumphs or laurels to adorn his brow,
> And joy won't be attained
> By those who, faced by Fortune, tamely bow
> And yield their feeble arms
> To Indolence's comfortable charms.
>
> Love's glory's dear: that's fair
> And only as it should be, honest trade;
> For there's no gift as rare
> As one that has been properly assayed.
> What easy joy is prized?
> What's cheaply bought is soon to be despised.
>
> But Love will persevere
> And sometimes do what never can be done,
> And though I often fear
> I'm striving for the stars and for the sun,
> My hope is still to rise
> Impossibly from earth to gain the skies.

Here the song ended and Clara's sobs began afresh, all of which made Dorotea even more curious to know the cause of such sweet singing and such sad weeping. So she again asked the girl what she'd meant by what she'd said before. Clara, afraid that Luscinda might be listening, hugged Dorotea tight, brought her lips close to her new friend's ear so as to speak without fear of being overheard, and whispered:

'The singer, my lady, is the son of an Aragonese gentleman, the lord of two manors, who lives across the road from my father's house in the capital. And although my father covered the windows with oilcloths in the winter and lattices in the summer, I really don't know how it happened but this young man, who was a student, saw me, maybe in church or somewhere like that. And he fell in love with me, and told me so from the windows of his house with such signs and tears that I ended up believing him, and even loving him back, not knowing who I was in love with. Among the signs he made to me was one where he clasped his hands together to say that he wanted to marry me, and even though I'd have been very happy with that, I was motherless and alone and didn't know who to talk to about it, so I didn't make any response except, when both our fathers were out, to lift the oilcloth or the lattice a little and let him see me, which made him show such delight that it looked as if he was going mad.

'The time came for my father to leave, and the young man found out about it – not from me, though, because there wasn't any way I could tell him. I believe he fell ill with grief, so on the day we left home I couldn't see him to say goodbye, not even with my eyes. But two days after we'd set out, when we were going into an inn in a village a day's journey from here, I saw him standing by the door dressed as a footman, looking so much the part that if his features hadn't been engraved on my memory I could never have recognized him. But I did recognize him and I was astonished and delighted; and he stole glances at me when my father wasn't looking, and he always hides from him when we meet on the lanes and at the inns; and since I know who he is, and I believe it's for love of me that he's walking all this way and putting up with all this hardship, I'm heartbroken for him, and watch over every step he takes. I don't know what he's hoping to achieve, or how he could have run away from his father, who loves him deeply because he hasn't any other heir and because he deserves it, as you'll agree when you meet him. And I'll tell you something else: everything he sings comes out of his own head, because I've heard he's an excellent student and poet. And what's more, whenever I see him and whenever I hear him sing, I tremble all over and become so alarmed, because I'm frightened my father might recognize him and find out about our feelings for each other. I've never spoken to him, yet I love him so much that I'm not going to be able to live without him. And this is all I can tell you, my lady, about this singer whose voice you liked so much – and just by listening to it you can tell he's no mere footman, as you say, but a lord of manors and a lord of hearts, as I say.'

'Say no more, Doña Clara,' Dorotea broke in as she kissed her over and over again. 'Say no more, only wait for tomorrow to come, because it is my hope that with God's help I'll be able to set your affairs on course for the happy ending that such a virtuous beginning deserves.'

'But, madam,' said Doña Clara, 'how can it end, if his father's so high-up and so rich that he won't think me fit to be his son's servant-girl, let alone his wife? And getting married behind my father's back – I won't do that for anything in the world. All I want is for this lad to leave me alone and go back home – maybe with not seeing him and the great distance we're going to travel, this grief I'm feeling would ease off, though I must say this remedy I'm imagining isn't going to do me much good. I just don't know what the devil's happened or how this love I feel for him can have got into me – I'm still so young and he is, too, I do believe we're both the same age, and I'm not sixteen yet, because my father says I'll be sixteen come Michaelmas.'

Dorotea couldn't help laughing as she heard Clara's childish talk, and she said:

'Let's rest now, young lady, for what little is left of the night, and tomorrow will be another day, and things will improve – if I have anything to do with it.'

They settled down again, and there was silence throughout the inn. The only ones not asleep were the innkeeper's daughter and her servant Maritornes, who, knowing Don Quixote's weakness, and knowing that he was outside the inn mounting guard in armour and on horseback, decided to play a trick on him or, at any rate, to pass the time listening to his nonsense.

Now the fact is that there wasn't any outward-looking window in all the inn, except a large hole in a hay-loft for taking in the straw. The two demi-virgins posted themselves behind this hole and saw that Don Quixote was sitting on his horse, leaning on his pike and from time to time heaving such huge, mournful sighs that each one of them seemed as if it would tear his very soul out of his body. And they heard him saying in soft, delicate, loving tones:

'O my lady Dulcinea del Toboso, the perfection of all beauty, the acme and pinnacle of intelligence, the treasury of the finest wit, the depository of virtue and, in short, the exemplar of all that is beneficial, pure and delightful in this world! And what might you be doing now? Might you, perchance, be thinking of this your hapless knight, who to so many perils, only to serve you, voluntarily exposes himself? Bring me tidings of her, O three-faced luminary![2] Perhaps you are even now gazing down at her in envy as she strolls along a gallery beside her sumptuous chambers or, leaning over a balcony, considers how, without detriment to her chastity and nobility, she can calm the storm that this my aching heart endures for her own sake, and thinks what glory she can bestow on my sufferings, what rest on my cares, and, in short, what life on my death and what reward on my services. And you, O sun, hastening no doubt to harness your steeds and sally forth betimes to behold my lady: I entreat you, as soon as you behold her, to greet her on my behalf, but pray take care that when you do behold and greet her you do not kiss her on the face, for if you did so I should be more consumed by jealousy than you were when that wanton ingrate made you sweat on the plains of Thessaly or by the banks of Peneus – I cannot remember exactly where it was that you ran on that occasion, consumed by jealousy and love.'[3]

As Don Quixote reached this point in his pitiful monologue, the inn-keeper's daughter began to psst him and to whisper:

'Hey, sir, do come over here, if you wouldn't mind.'

This summons made Don Quixote turn his head, and, by the light of the moon, shining at that moment at its brightest, he saw someone beckoning to him from the hole that he took for a window with the golden bars that any castle as splendid as this one must have on its windows; and then his wild imagination made him see that yet again, just like the last time, the beauteous maiden, the daughter of the lord of that castle, overwhelmed by her love, was making up to him; and so, not wanting to appear unmannerly or ungrateful, he turned Rocinante's head and rode up to the hole, and when he saw the two girls there he said:

'My heart goes out to you, beauteous lady, for having directed your amorous inclinations towards a quarter where it is not possible that they should find the response due to your great merit and grace; for which you should not blame this wretched knight errant, prevented by love from being able to yield his heart to any other than her whom, at the very moment when he first saw her, he made absolute mistress of his soul. Forgive me, good lady, and retire to your room, and do not, by insisting on your requests, oblige me to appear still more ungrateful; and if the love that you feel for me can find in me anything, other than love itself, with which I can satisfy you, pray command it, for I swear by that absent sweet enemy of mine that I shall give it you forthwith, even were you to ask me for one of Medusa's ⁴ tresses, all of which were serpents, or indeed the very rays of the sun itself enclosed within a vial.'

'No, my mistress won't be needing any of all that, sir,' Maritornes interrupted.

'And what is it that your mistress does need, wise duenna?' Don Quixote replied.

'One of your lovely hands, that's all,' said Maritornes, 'so she can use it to relieve the immense desire that's brought her to this hole, putting her honour at such risk that if her father had heard her she'd have been lucky to get off minus an ear.'

'I should like to see him try!' replied Don Quixote. 'But he will take good care not to do any such thing, unless he wishes to meet the wretchedest end that any father in this world ever did meet, for laying hands on the tender extremities of his love-stricken daughter.'

Maritornes felt sure that Don Quixote was going to give her the hand that he'd been asked for, and, making up her mind what she must do, she climbed down from the hole and hurried to the stable, where she grabbed Sancho Panza's donkey's halter and then ran back to her hole, in time to find Don Quixote standing on Rocinante's saddle so as to reach the gold-barred window at which he believed the love-lorn maiden was pining; and as he gave her his hand he said:

'Take, dear lady, this hand, or rather this scourge of the malefactors of the world; take this hand, I say, which has never been touched by that of any woman, nay not even by her who has complete possession of my entire body. I do not present it for you to kiss, but rather for you to observe the structuring of its sinews, the conformation of its muscles, the size and prominence of its veins, from all of which you will be able to deduce the might of the arm to which such a hand belongs.'

'We'll soon see about that,' Maritornes muttered.

And she made a running knot in the halter, which she slipped round his wrist, and then she climbed down from the hole and tied the other end of the halter to the bolt on the hay-loft door. When Don Quixote felt the roughness of the rope on his wrist he said:

'You appear, madam, to be grating rather than greeting my hand; do not maltreat it so, for it is not to blame for the ill that my heart does you, nor is it right that such a small part of me should bear the whole brunt of your wrath. Pray consider that true love does not wreak such cruel revenge.'

But nobody was listening to Don Quixote any more, because as soon as Maritornes had tied him up she and the other girl had run away, bursting with laughter and leaving him so well-secured that it was impossible for him to release himself. So there he was, standing on Rocinante, with the full length of his arm thrust through the hole, tied by his wrist to the bolt on the hay-loft door and terrified by the thought that if Rocinante took just one step in any direction he'd be left hanging by his arm; so he didn't dare make the slightest movement, even though Rocinante was such a patient and sedate creature that he could well have been expected to stand there for a century without budging an inch.

So finding himself strung up in this way, without any sign of the ladies, Don Quixote assumed that it had all happened by magic, just like that other time when the enchanted Moor or muleteer had thrashed him in that same castle; and he cursed his own lack of sense and judgement in venturing into it again after having come off so badly the first time, because it's a precept among knights errant that if they are unsuccessful in an adventure this is a sign that it is not meant for them, but for others, and so they are not required to attempt it again. He did try a few tugs with his arm to see if he could free himself, but he was so well-lashed that all his attempts were in vain. It is true that his tugs were only tentative ones, so as to keep Rocinante from moving, and however much he longed to sit in his saddle he had to stay standing – unless he tore his hand off.

And then did he wish for Amadis's sword, against which no enchantment had any power; and then did he curse his ill fortune; dwell on how sorely his presence would be missed in the world for as long as he remained enchanted, as he had by now convinced himself he was; think again of his beloved Dulcinea del Toboso; call for his trusty squire Sancho Panza, who, buried in sleep and stretched out on his donkey's pack-saddle, hadn't a thought for anyone, not even the mother who'd borne him; call on the sages Lirgandeo[5] and Alquife to help him; invoke his good friend Urganda to rescue him: and eventually morning came and found him so desperate and bewildered that he was bellowing like a bull, because he didn't have any hope that day would relieve his plight, which he considered to be eternal, since he was enchanted. He was confirmed in this opinion by the fact that Rocinante never budged an inch, and he believed that he and his horse would remain in that position, without eating or drinking or sleeping, until the malign influence of the stars should have dissipated, or until another wiser enchanter should have disenchanted him.

But in this he was much mistaken, because just as day was dawning four well-dressed and well-equipped men on horseback arrived at the inn, their muskets resting on their saddle-bows. They banged on the inn door, which was still shut, whereupon Don Quixote shouted in imperious tones from where he remained on sentry duty:

'Knights, or squires, or whatever you are: you have no business to be knocking on the castle door, for it is evident that at such an hour those inside are either asleep or not in the habit of opening the fortifications until the sun's rays are extended over the surface of the earth. Draw back and wait outside until day comes, and then we shall see whether it is appropriate to open to you.'

'What bloody fortification or castle is this,' said one of them, 'to make us go through such ceremonies? If you're the innkeeper, just tell them to open up – we're on a long journey and only want to feed our horses and continue on our way, because we're in a hurry.'

'Do you really believe, sirs, that I look like an innkeeper?' retorted Don Quixote.

'I don't know what you look like,' replied the other, 'but I do know you're talking nonsense when you call this inn a castle.'

'A castle it is,' replied Don Quixote, 'and one of the finest in the province, too; and it houses one who has had a sceptre in her hand and a crown on her head.'

'It'd be better the other way round,' said the traveller. 'The sceptre in her head and the crown in her hand. But what's more likely is that there's some company of strolling players lodging in there, they often mess around with these crowns and sceptres you're on about – because in a place as small and dead as this I can't believe that anyone with a right to a real crown and sceptre can be lodging.'

'You know little of the world,' replied Don Quixote, 'because you are ignorant of events that are common in knight-errantry.'

The other travellers were growing tired of their companion's conversation with Don Quixote, and they renewed their banging on the door so furiously that the innkeeper awoke, as did everyone else, and got up to find out who it was. While this was going on, one of the travellers' horses happened to trot over to Rocinante to smell him as he stood there motionless, sorrowful and with drooping ears, supporting his lofty master; and since Rocinante was, after all, made of flesh and blood, even if he did seem to be carved out of a solid block of wood, he couldn't help weakening and repaying the compliment to the one who'd come to caress him; and he'd hardly moved an inch when both Don Quixote's feet slipped off the saddle, and he'd have tumbled to the ground if he hadn't been left hanging by his arm, which caused him such pain that he thought that either his hand was being severed or his arm was being torn off, because he was left dangling so close to the ground that he could just touch it with the tips of his toes, which made matters even worse because, feeling how near he was to being able to put his feet down, he stretched and struggled to do so, just like those who are tortured on the pulley and left with their toes similarly brushing the floor, and who increase their own agony in their determination to stretch, deluding themselves with the hope that by stretching just a little further they'll make it to the ground.

CHAPTER XLIV

✠

In which a further account is given of the singular events at the inn

And Don Quixote made such a commotion that the innkeeper flung open the doors and rushed out in alarm to go and see who it was bawling away like that, and the men outside ran over to him as well. The din had also awoken Maritornes, who, guessing what had happened, hurried across to the hay-loft without anyone seeing her and untied the halter from which Don Quixote was dangling; and this sent him sprawling to the ground in front of the innkeeper and the travellers, who went up to him and asked what was the matter to make him shout so loud. He answered not one word, but removed the rope from his wrist, rose to his feet, mounted Rocinante, seized his shield, couched his pike, rode off to take up his position a good distance away and then cantered back with the words:

'If anyone claims that I was rightfully enchanted, I hereby – provided that my lady the Princess Micomicona gives me leave to do so – declare that he lies and is a traitor, and challenge him to single combat!'

The newcomers were astonished at these words, but the innkeeper dispelled their astonishment by telling them that this was Don Quixote, and they mustn't take any notice of him, because he was mad. They then asked the innkeeper whether a lad of about fifteen had by any chance turned up there dressed as a footman, and gave a description that fitted Doña Clara's admirer. The innkeeper replied that there were so many people at the inn that he hadn't noticed the one they were asking about. But one of the four had spotted the coach in which the judge had arrived, and said:

'Yes, he must be here, because this is the coach that he's said to be following. One of us will stay by the door and the others go in and look for him – it'll be better, though, if someone else rides round the outside of the inn to stop him from getting away over the yard wall.'

'That's what we'll do,' replied another.

Two of them went in, one stayed at the door and the other started off round the inn; as the innkeeper watched all this he couldn't imagine why these men were taking such measures, although he did realize that they must be looking for the lad they'd described. It was getting lighter by now and, both because of this and because of the row that Don Quixote had made, everyone was awake and getting up, the first among them Doña Clara and Dorotea, neither of whom had slept much that night, one from her excitement at knowing that her admirer was so close and the other from her eagerness to see what he looked like. Don Quixote, observing that none of these four travellers paid him the slightest attention or responded to his challenge, was seething with indignation and fury, and if he'd discovered in his chivalry statutes that a knight errant could legitimately undertake another venture after he'd given his word not to do so until he'd completed the one to which he was already pledged, he'd have charged the lot of them and forced an answer out of them. But since he considered that it wouldn't be right or proper to start out on a fresh enterprise until he'd restored Micomicona to her kingdom, he felt obliged to hold his tongue, stay where he was and wait to see the result of the travellers' search: one of them found the lad for whom he was looking, asleep beside a footman and little suspecting that anyone was searching for him, still less that they had found him. The traveller grasped the lad by the arm and said:

'I must say, Don Luis, the clothes that you are wearing are most suitable for your rank, and the bed in which I find you lying accords splendidly with the luxury amidst which your mother raised you!'

The lad wiped his sleepy eyes, stared up at the man holding him and soon realized that this was one of his father's servants; which gave him such a shock that he was speechless for a good while; and the servant continued:

'There's nothing for it, Don Luis, but for you to be patient and come back home, unless you want to send my master your father to his last home; because no other outcome is to be expected from the grief into which your absence has plunged him.'

'And how,' asked Don Luis, 'did my father find out that I was coming this way and that I was wearing these clothes?'

'From a student whom you told of your plans,' replied the servant. 'He was the one who gave you away, moved to pity by your father's laments when he found you'd gone. So he sent us four servants off to look for you, and here we all are at your service, happier than anyone could imagine at being able to return with such good news and restore you to his loving arms.'

'That'll be if I say so, or if heaven decrees,' retorted Don Luis.

'What can you say, and what can heaven decree, except that you're coming back with us? There's no other possible outcome.'

The footman lying beside Don Luis overheard this conversation and went away to find Don Fernando and Cardenio and the others, who were dressed by now, and to tell them what had happened, and how the man had called the lad *Don*, and all about the conversation they'd had, and how the man wanted to take him back to his father's house and the lad didn't want to go. And this, and what they knew about him, and the fine singing voice that God had given him, made them all long to find out exactly who he was, and even to help him if he was threatened with violence; so they walked over to where he was still talking and arguing with his servant. At that moment Dorotea was emerging from her room followed by Doña Clara in the utmost confusion, and Dorotea called Cardenio aside and summarized the history of Doña Clara and the singer, and then Cardenio told Dorotea about what had happened when the lad's father's servants had come for him, but didn't speak quietly enough to prevent Clara from overhearing, which made such an impact on her that she'd have slumped to the floor if Dorotea hadn't hurried to support her. Cardenio told Dorotea to take Clara back into their room and he'd try to sort everything out, and off the ladies went.

By now all the four men who'd come for Don Luis were inside the inn and had surrounded him to try to persuade him not to delay a moment longer but to return home to comfort his father. He replied that on no account could he do so until he'd settled a matter that involved his life, his honour and his soul. The servants insisted that they would not return without him – they were going to take him back whether he liked it or not.

'You'll do no such thing,' replied Don Luis, 'unless you carry me back dead – though whichever way you take me, I'll have lost my life.'

By now nearly everyone at the inn had come to listen to the argument, in particular Cardenio, Don Fernando, his companions, the judge, the priest, the barber and Don Quixote, who considered that there was no further need to mount guard over the castle. Cardenio, knowing the lad's history, asked the men who wanted to take him away why they were determined to do so against his will.

'To save his father's life,' said one of the four. 'This young gentleman going missing has put him in danger of losing it.'

At this Don Luis said:

'You haven't any business to be discussing my private affairs here. I'm free to do as I please, and I'll go back if I feel like it, and if I don't feel like it none of you is going to force me.'

'Reason will make you go back,' the man replied, 'and if that isn't enough for you, it's quite enough for us, and we'll do what we've come to do and what it's our duty to do.'

'Let's get to the root of all this,' put in the judge.

The man recognized him as a neighbour, and replied:

'Don't you know this young gentleman, Your Honour? He's your neighbour's son, and he's run away from home in clothes that are quite unworthy of his rank, as you can well see.'

The judge looked at the lad more closely, recognized him and embraced him, saying:

'What pranks are these, Don Luis, and what motive can have been powerful enough to make you come here like this, wearing clothes so unsuitable for someone in your position?'

Tears flooded into the lad's eyes and he couldn't reply. The judge told the four men to calm down, because a satisfactory solution would be found; and taking Don Luis by the hand he went to one side with him and asked what it was that had impelled him to come to the inn.

While he was putting this question and others, shouts came from the inn door, and the reason was that two guests who'd stayed there overnight, seeing everyone so busy finding out what the four men wanted, had tried to leave without paying their bill; but the innkeeper, more mindful of his own business than of other people's, grabbed them as they sidled out, and demanded his money, and reproached them for their wicked intentions with words that moved them to reply with their fists; and they started to give him such a thrashing that the poor man had to shout for help. His wife and daughter couldn't see anyone who wasn't too busy to help except Don Quixote, and the daughter said to him:

'Oh, sir knight, please use the mighty power God gave you, to help my poor father – two wicked men are beating the living daylights out of him.'

To which Don Quixote replied with leisurely composure:

'Beauteous maiden, I cannot at present grant your petition, because I am prevented from involving myself in another adventure until I have brought the one to which I have already pledged myself to a happy conclusion. But what I can do to serve you is what I shall now inform you of: you should run and tell your father to hold his own in this battle as best he can, and on no account to be vanquished, while I go to beg for Princess Micomicona's permission to succour him in his plight; and if she concedes it, you can rest assured that I shall rescue him.'

'God bless my sinning heart!' Maritornes broke in. 'By the time you get this permission of yours my master'll have gone to kingdom come!'

'Allow me, my lady, to obtain the permission to which I have referred,' replied Don Quixote, 'and, once I have done so, it will matter little that he has gone to kingdom come, for I will bring him back from there even if that whole kingdom opposes me; or, at the very least, I will wreak such vengeance upon those who will have sent him there that you will be more than moderately satisfied.'

And without another word he went to kneel before Dorotea and beg her in knightly and errantical terms that Her Highness would be pleased to concede him permission to aid and succour the lord of that castle, who was in a most grievous pass. The princess graciously granted it, and he took up his shield and drew his sword and marched to the inn door, where the two guests were still beleaguering the innkeeper; but when he arrived he stopped and stood there aghast, despite all the demands of Maritornes and the innkeeper's wife to know why he was holding back and wasn't running to help their master and husband.

'I am holding back,' said Don Quixote, 'because it is not licit for me to draw my sword against squirely characters; but summon my own squire Sancho, for this defence and revenge is a task for him to perform.'

As this discussion proceeded at the inn door, so did the punching and the pounding, much to the disadvantage of the innkeeper and the displeasure of Maritornes and the innkeeper's wife and daughter, who were in despair at

Don Quixote's cowardice and the sufferings of their master, husband and father. But let's leave him there, because someone's bound to come to his rescue sooner or later – and if not, let him suffer in silence for biting off more than he can chew; and let's walk fifty paces into the inn to find out what Don Luis said in reply to the judge, whom we left standing aside with the boy and asking him why he'd come here on foot and in such disgraceful clothes. The lad, seizing the judge's hands, as if to indicate that his heart was oppressed by some great sorrow, and with the tears pouring from his eyes, replied:

'Oh, sir, all I can say is that from the very moment when heaven decreed and our being neighbours made it possible that I should set eyes on Doña Clara, your daughter and my lady, I made her the mistress of my heart; and if you, my true lord and father, don't prevent it, we shall be married this very day. For her I left home, for her I put on these clothes, to follow her wherever she went, as the arrow seeks its target and the sailor the North Star. All she knows of my passion is what she might have deduced from sometimes seeing at a distance my eyes full of tears. You know, sir, of my parents' wealth and nobility, and you know that I am their only heir; if you believe that these are motives enough for you to venture to make me a perfectly happy man, accept me now as your son; and if my father has plans of his own for me and doesn't approve of this happiness I have found, time has more power to undo and change things than the human will.'

With this the young lover fell silent, and the judge was left bewildered, bemused and amazed, both at the intelligent way in which Don Luis had expressed his feelings and at finding himself with no idea how to react in such a sudden and unexpected situation; so he made no reply except to tell the lad to calm down and to procrastinate with his servants so that they didn't take him back that day, leaving time to consider what was best for all parties. Don Luis seized and kissed his hands and even bathed them in tears, which would have melted a heart of stone, let alone the heart of the judge, who was shrewd enough to have realized immediately how advantageous this marriage would be for his daughter; though, if possible, he wanted it to be done with the consent of Don Luis's father, who, he knew, was hoping to acquire a title for his son.

By now the two guests had made peace with the innkeeper because, thanks to Don Quixote's persuasion and fine words rather than any threats, they'd paid their bill in full, and Don Luis's servants were awaiting the outcome of the confabulation with the judge and the decision of their master, when the devil, who never sleeps, brought into the inn that barber from whom Don Quixote had taken Mambrino's helmet and Sancho Panza the ass's trappings that he'd exchanged for his own; and as the barber was taking his donkey to the stable he caught sight of Sancho Panza, who was mending something on the pack-saddle, and immediately recognized him, and made bold to charge at him, crying:

'Hey, you thief, I've got you now! You give me back my basin and my pack-saddle and all the rest of the tackle you stole off me!'

Sancho, finding himself so suddenly attacked and hearing such abuse being hurled at him, grabbed the pack-saddle with one hand and with the other delivered to the barber's mouth a punch that bathed his teeth in blood; but this didn't make the barber loosen the grip he'd taken on the pack-saddle – on the contrary he raised such an outcry that everyone flocked over to watch the new fight, as he yelled:

'Help, help, in the King's name, justice! First he steals my property and now he wants to kill me, the thief, the highwayman!'

'You liar!' Sancho rejoined. 'I'm no highwayman, my master Don Quixote won these spoils in a just war.'

Don Quixote had reached the scene by now, and was delighted to see how well his squire was defending himself and attacking the enemy; and from that moment on he deemed him a man of mettle, and he took the decision to knight him at the earliest opportunity, for he truly deserved to be received into the order of chivalry. The barber said many things in the course of the disagreement, among them:

'Look, all of you, this pack-saddle's as much mine as is the death I owe God, and I know it as well as if I'd given birth to it, and my ass over there in the stable will confirm my story, because if you don't believe me just try the pack-saddle on its back, and if it doesn't fit like a glove you can call me all the names you like. Not only that, the day it was stolen they also stole a brand-new brass basin, never used, worth a whole escudo.'

Don Quixote could contain himself no longer, and thrusting himself between the two to keep them apart, and depositing the pack-saddle on the floor in safe-keeping until the truth should be made manifest, he declared:

'Here you can perfectly clearly see for yourselves how mistaken this fellow is, calling a basin what was, is and shall be Mambrino's helmet, which I won from him in a just war and of which I thus became the true and lawful owner! With regard to the pack-saddle I shall not interfere: all I can say about that is that my squire Sancho requested my permission to remove the caparisons from this vanquished coward's horse and to adorn his own with them; I gave it, he took them, and if the caparisons have been converted into a pack-saddle I can only give the usual explanation, that these transformations do occur in the affairs of chivalry; for confirmation of which, Sancho my son, hurry and fetch the helmet that this fellow says is a basin.'

'By God, sir,' said Sancho, 'if we haven't got any better proof to support us than that, Malino's helmet is as much a barber's basin as this character's comparisons are a pack-saddle!'

'Go and do what I told you to do,' replied Don Quixote. 'Not everything in this castle can be governed by enchantment.'

Sancho went and fetched the basin, and as soon as Don Quixote saw it he took it into his hands and said:

'Consider, ladies and gentlemen, the sheer impudence of this squire in claiming that this is a basin and not the helmet I have specified; and I swear by the order of chivalry which I profess that this helmet is the same helmet I won from him, and I have not added or removed any part.'

'There isn't any doubt about that,' Sancho put in, 'because from the time my master won it up to now he's only fought one battle wearing it, when he freed those poor wretches in chains, and if it hadn't been for this here basinelmet he'd have had a bad time of it, because there was lots of stonethrowing on that occasion.'

CHAPTER XLV

✠

*In which the doubts about Mambrino's helmet, about
the pack-saddle and about other adventures are
finally resolved*

'Now you all tell me,' said the barber, 'what you think about these fine gentlemen still insisting this isn't a basin but a helmet!'

'And I will make whoever says anything different,' said Don Quixote, 'admit, if he is a knight, that he is a liar, and if he is a squire, that he is a liar a thousand times over.'

Our own barber, having been present throughout these exchanges and being well acquainted with Don Quixote's disposition, decided to give his folly some encouragement and spin the joke out so that everyone could have a good laugh, and so he addressed the other barber:

'Mister barber or mister whoever you are: I'll have you know that I'm in the same line of business as you, and I've had my certificates these twenty years or more, and I know the tools of the trade, every one of them; on top of all that, as a young man I was a soldier, so I know what a helmet is, and I know what a morion is, and I know what a sallet is, and other matters concerning the militia, in other words the arms and armour used by soldiers; and what I'm saying, with all due respect of course and do correct me if I'm wrong, is that this object here before us in the hands of this good gentleman not only is not a barber's basin but is as far from being a barber's basin as black is from being white and as truth is from being falsehood; but I do also have to say that although it is a helmet it isn't a complete one.'

'No, of course not,' said Don Quixote, 'because half of it, the beaver, is missing.'

'That is indeed so,' said the priest, who'd realized what his friend the barber was up to. Cardenio and Don Fernando and his men backed him up, and, if the judge hadn't been so concerned with the Don Luis affair, he, too, would have done his bit to advance the joke; but the serious matters on his mind so preoccupied him that he was paying little or no attention to these pleasantries.

'Good God!' exploded the bantered barber. 'How can it be possible for all these respectable people to be saying that this here isn't a basin but a helmet? It's enough to confound an entire university, however brainy it might be! All right then: if this here basin's a helmet, then this here pack-saddle must be a horse's caparisons, just as the gentleman said.'

'To me it looks like a pack-saddle,' said Don Quixote, 'but then I have already stated that this is an affair in which I shall not interfere.'

'Whether it's a pack-saddle or a caparison,' said the priest, 'is something that only Don Quixote can decide, because in matters of chivalry all these gentlemen, and I too, bow to his superior knowledge.'

'By God, sirs,' said Don Quixote, 'so very many strange things have happened to me in this castle on the two occasions when I have lodged here that I dare not give a clear answer to any question about anything in it, because I imagine that everything that occurs here is carried out by enchantment. The first time I was much harassed by an enchanted Moor who lives here, and Sancho did not fare too well in an encounter with some of his henchmen, and last night I hung by this arm for nearly two hours, without the faintest idea how I came to suffer such a misfortune. So to start giving my opinion now about such a perplexing matter would be to commit the sin of making a rash judgement. As regards some people's opinion that this is a basin and not a helmet, I have already given my answer; but as for declaring whether this is a pack-saddle or a caparison, I dare not give a definitive decision: I can only leave it to your own good judgement. It is possible that, since you have not been knighted, as I have, the enchantments in this place do not affect you, and that your understanding is unclouded, and that you can form judgements about the affairs of this castle as they really and truly are, rather than as they appeared to me.'

'There's no doubt,' Don Fernando replied, 'that Don Quixote has just spoken most judiciously – it's up to us to reach a decision in this case; and, to ensure that our decision is a well-founded one, I shall now take a secret vote among these ladies and gentlemen, and give you all a full and clear account of the result.'

All this had those who knew about Don Quixote's foibles splitting their sides with laughter; but to those who didn't know about them it just seemed extremely silly – in particular to Don Luis's four servants and Don Luis himself, and to another three travellers who'd turned up at the inn and who looked like officers of the Holy Brotherhood, as indeed they were. But one man had been plunged into the deepest depths of despair, and that was the barber, whose basin, there before his very eyes, had turned into Mambrino's helmet, and whose pack-saddle, he was sure, was about to turn into the splendid caparisons of some handsome steed; but both those who were in the know and those who weren't chortled as they saw Don Fernando going from one person to the next, collecting votes and whispering into ears to obtain secret declarations as to whether the treasure that had been the cause of such strife was a pack-saddle or a caparison. And after taking the votes of those who knew Don Quixote, he declared:

'The fact is, my dear fellow, that I'm tired of sounding out so many opinions, because there isn't a single person I ask who doesn't say it's the height of absurdity to claim that this is a donkey's pack-saddle rather than a horse's caparison – and a thoroughbred's at that; so you'll just have to grin and bear it because, in spite of you and your ass, this is a caparison and not a pack-saddle, and you have pleaded and presented your case very poorly indeed.'

'May I never be presented in heaven,' cried the extra barber, 'if you aren't wrong, the whole lot of you, and as sure as I hope my soul will appear before God this looks to me like a pack-saddle and not a caparison, but then it's the lords that make the laws, and I'll say no more – and I'm not drunk, honestly I'm not, because I haven't had my breakfast yet and there's nothing inside me but my sins.'

This nonsense spoken by the barber caused no less mirth than the absurdities voiced by Don Quixote, who remarked:

'All that can be done now is for each to take what belongs to him, and may St Peter bless what God has given.'

One of Don Luis's four servants said:

'Unless this is some practical joke, I just can't fathom how men of good understanding, as these here present are or seem to be, can have the gall to keep saying that this isn't a basin and that that isn't a pack-saddle; but since this is exactly what they are saying, all I can suppose is that something mysterious is afoot when people insist on what's so contrary to what we can see with our own eyes to be the case; because I swear by . . .' – and the oath was a rich one – 'nobody in the whole wide world is going to tell me that this isn't a barber's basin and that that isn't a jackass's pack-saddle.'

'It could be a she-ass's,' said the priest.

'That doesn't matter,' said the servant. 'That isn't the point at issue – the point at issue is whether this is a pack-saddle or, as you all say, it isn't.'

When one of the newly arrived officers of the Holy Brotherhood, who had been listening to the argument, heard this, he cried in a blind fury:

'If that isn't a pack-saddle then my father isn't my father, and anyone who says anything different must be half-seas over.'

'You lie like a base villain,' Don Quixote replied.

And raising his pike, which was never out of his hands, he aimed such a blow at the officer's head that, if he hadn't ducked, it would have stretched him out at full length. The pike shattered on the ground and the other peace-officers, seeing their comrade assaulted, cried out demanding assistance for the Holy Brotherhood. The innkeeper, who was also a peace-officer, hurried to fetch his staff of office and his sword, and stationed himself by his comrades' side; Don Luis's servants surrounded the lad to prevent him from escaping in the confusion; the barber took advantage of the turmoil to grab his pack-saddle, and so did Sancho; Don Quixote drew his sword and attacked the officers; Don Luis was shouting at his servants to leave him be and go to help Don Quixote and also Cardenio and Don Fernando, both of whom had gone to Don Quixote's assistance; the priest was shouting, the innkeeper's wife was screaming, her daughter was moaning, Maritornes was weeping, Dorotea was bewildered, Luscinda was astonished and Doña Clara was fainting. The barber was pounding away at Sancho; Sancho was hammering away at the barber; Don Luis gave a servant who dared to seize one of his arms to prevent him from running away a punch that bathed his teeth in blood; the judge was defending the servant; Don Fernando had a peace-officer under his feet and was trampling away to his heart's content; the innkeeper cried out again demanding help for the officers of the Holy Brotherhood. So the inn was all tears, shouts, screams, confusion, fear, alarm, disasters, flashing knives, flying fists, flailing cudgels, pounding feet and flowing blood. And in the midst of this chaos, this labyrinth, this edifice of mischief, Don Quixote took it into his head that he was in the thick of the turmoil in King Agramante's camp,[1] and he cried in a voice that thundered throughout the inn:

'Stay still everyone; everyone sheathe his sword; everyone be calm; listen everyone, if you value your lives!'

At these stentorian commands everybody froze, and Don Quixote continued:

'Did I not tell you, sirs, that this castle is enchanted, and that some legion of devils must inhabit it? As proof of which I call on you to behold with your own eyes how the turmoil in King Agramante's camp has been transported into our midst. See how they are fighting there for the sword, here for the horse, there for the eagle, here for the helmet, and every one of us is fighting, and every one of us is at odds with his neighbour. Come then, Your Honour, and come, Your Reverence, and one of you can be King Agramante, and the other King Sobrino, and make peace among us because, by God Almighty, it is sheer villainy for such eminent personages as us to be killing each other for such petty causes.'

The men of the Holy Brotherhood, who didn't understand Don Quixote's diction and were having little success in their tussle with Don Fernando, Cardenio and friends, weren't ready to be pacified; but the barber was, because both his beard and his pack-saddle had been destroyed in the struggle; Sancho obeyed his master's slightest word like a good servant; and Don Luis's four servants also stopped in their tracks, seeing that it wouldn't be a good idea not to. Only the innkeeper was insisting that this madman must be punished for his effrontery, throwing the whole house into an uproar every five minutes. So the din died down for the time being, the pack-saddle was left as a caparison until judgement day, and the basin remained as a helmet and the inn as a castle in Don Quixote's imagination.

With peace restored and everyone friends again thanks to the judge and the priest, Don Luis's servants insisted yet again that he must return home; and while he was busy with them the judge consulted Don Fernando, Cardenio and the priest about what he should do, and told them what Don Luis had told him. It was finally decided that Don Fernando would reveal his identity to the servants and tell them that he'd like Don Luis to go with him to Andalusia, where he'd receive from Don Fernando's brother the marquis the welcome to which his quality entitled him, because it had become clear that Don Luis was determined to allow himself to be torn limb from limb rather than return so soon to his father's arms. When the four servants were informed about Don Fernando's rank and Don Luis's resolution, they decided that three of them would go back and tell his father how matters stood, and that the fourth would stay to serve Don Luis and not leave his side until the others returned or his father's orders were known.

And so that edifice of dispute was pacified, by the authority of Agramante and the wisdom of King Sobrino; but the enemy of concord and adversary of peace, finding himself scorned and outwitted, and seeing how little it had benefited him to embroil them all in that labyrinth of confusion, decided to try his luck again by reviving old quarrels and disturbances.

What happened was that the peace-officers calmed down on overhearing the rank of the men who'd been fighting against them, and withdrew from the conflict realizing that whatever the result they were going to get the worst of it; but one of them, the one who'd been trampled and kicked by Don Fernando, recalled that among the warrants he had on him for the arrest of various criminals there was one for Don Quixote, whom the Holy Brotherhood had ordered to be detained for setting the convicts free, as Sancho had so rightly feared. With this in mind, the peace-officer decided to check whether the description of Don Quixote fitted the man before him, and he pulled a parchment folder out of his shirt and found the warrant he was looking for, and began to peruse it with the utmost deliberation, not being very good at reading, and looked up at Don Quixote at every word to compare his face with the description in the warrant, and found that this was most certainly his man. Once he'd reached this conclusion he put his folder away, took the warrant in his left hand, with his right hand seized Don Quixote so tight by the collar that he couldn't breathe, and cried:

'Help, help the Holy Brotherhood! And to see that I really mean it, just read this warrant, where it says that this highwayman must be arrested.'

The priest took the warrant and saw that the peace-officer was telling the truth and that the description did match Don Quixote, who, finding himself so roughly handled by that base caitiff, and at the highest pitch of fury, and with every bone in his body creaking, grabbed the officer by the throat with both hands and with all the strength he could muster; and if the officer's companions hadn't gone to his aid he'd have given up the ghost before Don Quixote had given up his prey. The innkeeper, obliged to assist a fellow officer, also ran to help him. The innkeeper's wife, seeing her husband involved in yet another fight, raised her voice again, and their daughter and Maritornes provided accompaniment as the three of them begged heaven and all those present for help. In view of what was going on, Sancho remarked:

'Good God, it's true what my master says about this castle being enchanted – you don't get a moment's peace and quiet in here!'

Don Fernando prised the peace-officer and Don Quixote apart and, much to the relief of both of them, unhooked their hands, one from a tabard collar and the other from a throat; but this didn't make the officers stop claiming their prisoner and demanding the assistance of the company, who were to tie him up and deliver him to their charge, as required in the service of the King and of the Holy Brotherhood, in whose name they repeated their demand for aid in detaining that thief and highway robber. But Don Quixote only laughed at these words, and declared with supreme composure:

'Look you here, you wretched and low-born rabble: is highway robbery your name for the liberation of those who are in chains, the release of prisoners, the succour of the unfortunate, the raising of the fallen, the relief of the needy? You infamous crew: your vile and paltry minds make you unworthy that heaven should reveal to you the worth that is in knight-errantry, or make you understand your sinfulness and ignorance in not revering the shadow, let alone the presence, of any knight errant! Look you here, you who are not officers of the law but officers of lawlessness, footpads licensed by the Holy Brotherhood: tell me, who was the ignoramus that signed a warrant of arrest against such a knight as I am? Who was it that did not know that knights errant are independent of all judicial authority, and that their law is their sword, their decrees are their prowess and their edicts are their will? Who was the numbskull, I repeat, who was unaware that there is no patent of nobility with as many privileges and prerogatives as the one that a knight errant acquires the very day he is dubbed and gives himself over to the rigorous exercise of chivalry? What knight errant ever paid tallage, excise, royal subsidies, septennial levies, tolls or ferry taxes? What tailor ever presented him with a bill for his labours? What lord of a castle ever made him pay for his sojourn? What king ever failed to sit him at his own table? What maiden ever failed to fall in love with him and give herself up to his will and pleasure? And, in short, what knight errant of the past, the present or the future would not have the spirit to deal four hundred cudgellings to any four hundred peace-officers confronting him?'

CHAPTER XLVI

❈

About the notable adventure of the peace-officers, and the ferocity of our good knight Don Quixote

While Don Quixote was saying all this, the priest was explaining to the peace-officers that the knight was out of his senses, as they could see from his deeds and his words, and that it was futile to press the matter any further, since even if they did arrest him and take him away, he'd be released immediately as a madman; to which the one with the warrant retorted that it wasn't his job to judge whether Don Quixote was mad or not, but to carry out his superior's orders, and once he'd arrested him they could let him go three hundred times over for all he cared.

'All the same,' said the priest, 'I'm sure you'll let him off just this once – and anyway I don't think he'd allow anyone to arrest him, so far as I can tell.'

And the priest spoke so many fine words and Don Quixote performed so many mad deeds that the officers would have been even madder than he was if they hadn't acknowledged his weakness; and so they thought it best to calm down and even act as peacemakers between the barber and Sancho Panza, who were still wrangling away for all they were worth. As officers of justice, therefore, they mediated in the case and arbitrated to such effect that both parties were left if not completely content then at least reasonably satisfied, because pack-saddles were exchanged but not girths or headstalls. And as regards Mambrino's helmet, the priest, surreptitiously and behind Don Quixote's back, let the barber have eight reals for the basin, and the barber made out a receipt and a written promise not to claim that he'd been unfairly treated, now and for ever and ever, amen.

Now that these two disputes, the most serious ones, had been settled, it only remained for Don Luis's servants to agree that three of them would return home and the other one would accompany him to where Don Fernando wanted to take him; and since good luck and even better fortune had begun to smile on the lovers and the brave men at the inn and to smooth away obstacles for them, it decided to finish the job and produce a happy outcome for everyone, because the servants agreed to everything Don Luis wanted, which made Doña Clara so happy that nobody could see her face and not know of the joy in her soul. Although Zoraida didn't fully understand what was going on, she was vaguely sad or glad according to the looks she saw on people's faces, and in particular on the face of her Spanish man, on whom her eyes were fixed, and her heart and soul as well. The innkeeper, who hadn't failed to spot the priest making the barber his compensatory gift, demanded payment for Don Quixote's stay, together with the damage to his wineskins and the loss of his wine, swearing that neither Rocinante nor Sancho's donkey would leave the inn until he'd been paid to the last maravedí. The priest appeased the innkeeper and Don Fernando paid him, even though the judge had also hastened to offer the money; and they were all left in tranquillity and harmony, so that the inn no longer bore any resemblance to the turmoil in King Agramante's camp, as Don Quixote had claimed, but rather recalled the peace and calm of Octavian's time;[1] and it was the general opinion that they owed thanks for all this to the priest's goodwill and eloquence and to Don Fernando's incomparable generosity.

Now that Don Quixote was rid of all those disputes, both his squire's and his own, he thought it would be a good idea to continue the journey that he had begun, and conclude that great adventure for which he had been chosen and called; and so he advanced with firm and resolute tread to kneel before Dorotea, who wouldn't let him utter a word until he'd come to his feet; and, obeying her, he rose and said:

'It is a well-known proverb, beauteous lady, that diligence is the mother of good fortune, and in many grave matters experience has shown that the assiduity of the negotiator can bring a difficult dispute to a happy conclusion; but nowhere is this truth more evident than in war, in which speed and alacrity forestall the enemy's plans, and bring victory before he can defend himself. I say all this, eminent and lovely lady, because I believe that our stay in this castle is no longer beneficial, and indeed could cause us very great harm, as one day we might discover; for who knows whether your enemy the giant has, from diligent and hidden spies, discovered that I am on my way to destroy him and, in his own good time, is fortifying his position in some impregnable castle or fortress against which all my efforts and the might of my indefatigable arm would be of little avail? And so, my lady, let us forestall his plans, as I have suggested, by our diligence, and depart immediately in search of good fortune: Your Highness's finding it as you desire will take no longer than it takes me to confront your adversary.'

Don Quixote fell silent and waited in serene silence for the beauteous princess's reply: with a royal bearing, to match Don Quixote's style, she replied as follows:

'I am obliged to you, sir knight, for the desire that you express to succour me in my great necessity, like the true knight you are, whose care and concern it is to assist orphans and the distressed; and may heaven grant that your desire and mine may be fulfilled, so that you may see that there are women on this earth who are capable of gratitude. And as regards my departure, let it be immediate, for I have no other will than yours: pray dispose of me according to your will and pleasure, for she who has once entrusted to you the defence of her person, and has placed in your hands the restoration of her domains, will not contradict whatever your wisdom may decree.'

'God's will be done,' said Don Quixote. 'And since a lady humbles herself thus before me, I will not let slip the opportunity of raising her up and placing her upon the throne that she inherited. Let us leave forthwith, for that expression about there being danger in delay is putting spurs to my desire to be on the road. And since heaven has never created nor has hell ever seen any danger that can strike fear into me, go, Sancho, and saddle Rocinante and make your donkey and the Queen's palfrey ready, let us take our leave of the lord of the castle and these other gentlemen, and be on our way.'

Sancho, who had been present all the time, shook his head and said:

'Oh, sir, there's more going on in the village than folks know about – with all due respect to your hard feelings, ma'am.'

'What can be going on in any village or in all the cities in the world that can be known about to my discredit, you peasant?'

'If you're going to get cross, now,' replied Sancho, 'I'll keep quiet about what it's my duty as a good squire to tell you, and what any good servant ought to tell his master.'

'You may say whatever you please,' replied Don Quixote, 'so long as it is not the intention of your words to strike fear into me; for if you are frightened, you are acting like the man you are, and if I am not frightened, I am acting like the man I am.'

'It isn't that, God bless my sinful heart!' replied Sancho. 'What it is, is that I know for a certain fact that this lady who's said to be the queen of the great kingdom of Micomicón is no more a queen than my mother was, because if she was what she says she is, she wouldn't go slobbering over a certain person whenever she gets a chance and thinks nobody's looking.'

Sancho's words brought Dorotea's face out in a blush, because it was true that her husband Don Fernando had occasionally, unseen by other eyes, taken with his lips a part of the prize gained by his love, and Sancho had spotted them and considered that this brazenness was more appropriate to a courtesan than to a queen of such a great kingdom; and Dorotea couldn't and wouldn't say a word in reply, but allowed Sancho to continue with his tirade:

'I'm only saying this, sir, because if after all that plodding on and on and on down highways and up byways, and putting up with bad nights and worse days, a certain person who spends his time having fun at the inn is going to come and gather the fruit of our toils, there isn't any reason for me to be in such a hurry to saddle Rocinante, put the pack-saddle on the donkey or get the palfrey ready – we'd better both sit on our backsides, and let the whores get on with their work, while we eat!'

God save us! How mighty was Don Quixote's anger when he heard his squire's disrespectful words! It was so great, I say, that his voice shook and his tongue faltered and fire darted from his eyes as he cried:

'Oh, you villainous peasant, lout, jackanapes, ignoramus, gibberer, foul-mouth, malapert, backbiter, scandal-monger! How dare you speak such words in my presence and in that of these illustrious ladies, or allow such insolent indecencies into your disordered imagination? Begone from my presence, you monster of nature, depository of lies, storehouse of deceit, silo of knavery, inventor of evil, proclaimer of nonsense, enemy of the respect that is due to royal persons! Begone, get out of my sight, under pain of incurring my wrath!'

And as he said this he arched his eyebrows, blew out his cheeks, glared around in all directions and gave a great stamp on the ground with his right foot, all of which showed how mighty was the wrath in his bowels. In the face of these words and these furious gestures Sancho was so abashed and terror-stricken that he'd have been happy for the earth to open up at his feet and swallow him. And all he could think of doing was turning round and removing himself from his master's raging presence. But to temper his fury the quick-witted Dorotea, who by now knew Don Quixote's character so well, said:

'Be not wrathful, Sir Knight of the Sorry Face, at the absurdities uttered by your worthy squire; for perhaps he does not speak them without some cause, and a man with his good understanding and Christian conscience cannot be suspected of bearing false witness; so we must assume, indeed there can be no doubt about it, that since everything in this castle, as you yourself, sir, have said, proceeds by means of enchantment, it could be the case, I believe, that Sancho did see, by these diabolical means, what he says he saw, so much to the detriment of my virtue.'

'I swear by almighty God,' Don Quixote exclaimed, 'that Your Highness has hit the mark, and that some evil vision was placed before this sinner Sancho, which made him see what he could never possibly have seen by any means other than enchantment; for I know all about the goodness and innocence of this poor unfortunate, who is quite incapable of bearing false witness.'

'You're absolutely right there,' said Don Fernando, 'and so, Don Quixote, you must forgive him now and restore him to the bosom of your favour, *sicut erat in principio*,[2] before those visions turned his brain.'

Don Quixote replied that he did indeed forgive him, and the priest went to fetch Sancho, who returned in abject humility and, falling to his knees, asked his master for his hand; and his master acceded, allowed it to be kissed, blessed him and said:

'Now you must finally realize, Sancho my son, that what I have so often told you is true, and that everything that happens in this castle takes place by way of enchantment.'

'I believe you,' said Sancho, 'except for the blanket business – that definitely happened in the ordinary way.'

'You must not think that,' replied Don Quixote, 'for if it were the case, I should have avenged you then, and would even avenge you now; but neither then nor now has it been possible for me to do so, nor have I ever identified anybody on whom I could take vengeance for the injury done you.'

They asked what this blanket business had been all about, and the innkeeper gave them a meticulous account of Sancho's aerial acrobatics, which provided them with a hearty laugh and would have provided Sancho with as much embarrassment if his master hadn't assured him yet again that it had been a magic spell; though Sancho was never simple-minded enough to believe that it wasn't the absolute and verified truth, unadulterated by any trickery whatsoever, that he'd been blanket-tossed by men of flesh and blood and not by ghosts that he'd dreamed up and imagined, as his master believed and asserted.

That illustrious company had now been at the inn for two days, and, since they thought it was time they were leaving, they conceived a scheme that obviated the need for Dorotea and Don Fernando to go with Don Quixote to his village under the pretence of the restoration of Queen Micomicona, and made it possible for the priest and the barber to take him back, as they wanted, to try to cure his madness at home. And what they did was to agree with a man with an ox-cart who happened to come that way to carry Don Quixote off in the following manner: they constructed a cage with wooden bars, large enough to hold him comfortably, and then Don Fernando and his companions, Don Luis's servants, the peace-officers and the innkeeper, all taking their orders from the priest, masked their faces and disguised themselves, some in one way and some in another, to make Don Quixote think that they weren't the same people he'd seen at the inn. Then they all tiptoed in to where he lay recovering his strength after the recent skirmishes. They crept up to him, fast asleep and oblivious to what was going on, seized him and bound him hand and foot, so that when he awoke with a start he couldn't move or do anything other than gaze in bewilderment at all those deformed faces before him. And he believed what his tireless and delirious imagination was telling him, that all those figures were the ghosts of that enchanted castle and that he himself was obviously enchanted again, since he couldn't move or defend himself: exactly as the priest, the designer of the scheme, had thought would happen. Only Sancho, of all those present, was both in his right mind and in his right clothes, and, although he wasn't far from suffering from his master's disease, this didn't prevent him from recognizing the men through their disguises; but he didn't dare to part his lips until he saw what came of the attack and arrest of his master, and the victim didn't utter a word, either, as he, too, waited to see the upshot of this latest misfortune; and the upshot was that the masked figures brought in the cage and shut him up in it and nailed it down so firmly that it wasn't going to be broken open in a hurry. They hoisted it on to their shoulders, and as they marched out of the room a fearful voice was heard, or at least one as fearful as the barber – not the saddle-bag barber, the other one – could make it, and it was saying:

'O Knight of the Sorry Face! Be not abashed by the captivity to which you have been reduced, which is needful for the more speedy accomplishment of the adventure in which your valour has engaged you. And it will be accomplished when the livid lion of La Mancha shall lie with the white dove of El Toboso, once their lofty necks have been humbled by the gentle yoke of matrimony; from which unique coupling shall come into the light of the world brave cubs that will emulate the rampant claws of their valiant sire. And this will come to pass before the bright pursuer of the fugitive nymph shall have twice performed his round of visits to the luminous signs in his natural and rapid course.[3] And you, the most noble and obedient squire that ever had a sword in his belt, a beard on his face and a smell in his nose, be not dismayed or grieved to see the flower of knight-errantry thus borne away before your eyes; for ere long, if it so please the Fabricator of this world, you will find yourself so ennobled and exalted that you will not recognize yourself, and you will not be defrauded of the rewards promised you by your noble lord. And I assure you, on behalf of the sage Mentironiana,[4] that your wages will be paid, as you will duly see; so follow in the footsteps of the valiant and enchanted knight, for it is necessary that you travel together to the end of your journey. And because I am not permitted to say any more, God be with you. I am returning now to I know where.'

And as he reached the end of the prophecy he raised his voice and then lowered it again in such tender tones that even those who knew that it was all a joke were close to believing what they'd heard. The prophecy was a great comfort to Don Quixote, because he at once grasped its full meaning, and understood that it promised that he would be joined in holy and lawful matrimony with his beloved Dulcinea del Toboso, from whose fortunate womb would issue the cubs, in other words his sons, for the everlasting glory of La Mancha; and in this firm and steadfast belief he heaved a profound sigh and cried:

'O you, whoever you may be, who have prophesied such good for me! I beg that you will, on my behalf, ask the wise enchanter who is in charge of my affairs not to permit me to perish in this prison in which I am being borne away, until I have seen the fulfilment of the joyful and incomparable promises that have here been made me; for if this is granted, I shall consider the griefs of my captivity as glories, the chains that bind me as comforts, and these boards on which I am made to lie not as a hard battlefield but as a soft and happy nuptial couch. And as regards your consolation of my squire Sancho Panza, I trust that his goodness and integrity will not allow him to leave me, in prosperity or adversity. For if it so falls out that, because of his or my bad fortune, I cannot give him the island that I have promised him, or something equivalent, he will, at least, not lose his wages, since in my will I have declared what is to be given him, not I fear proportionate to his many good services, but rather to my own possibilities.'

Sancho Panza made him a bow expressive of deep respect and kissed both his hands, it being impossible to kiss only one of them, because they were tied together. The visions hoisted the cage back on to their shoulders, and then fixed it on top of the ox-cart.

CHAPTER XLVII

❈

About the strange way in which Don Quixote was enchanted, and other famous events

Finding himself caged on a cart, Don Quixote said:

'Many weighty histories of knights errant have I read, but never have I read, or seen, or heard of enchanted knights being carried off in this way or as slowly as these heavy, slothful beasts promise; for knights are always borne through the air, at extraordinary speed, wrapped in some dark, grey cloud, or on some chariot of fire, or on some hippogryph or similar beast; but for me to be carried off now on an ox-cart does, as God is good, throw me into the greatest confusion! Yet maybe the chivalry and the enchanting of these times of ours follow different paths from those of earlier days. And it could also be that, since I am a new knight in the world, and the first to resuscitate the forgotten exercise of knight-errantry, new forms of enchantment and other ways of carrying off the enchanted have been invented. What do you think, Sancho my son?'

'I don't know what I think,' replied Sancho, 'not being as well-read as you are in errantry writings – all the same I must say I haven't got much faith in these here visions.'

'Faith? Goodness gracious me!' replied Don Quixote. 'How could you have faith in them when they are all demons who have assumed fantastic bodies to come and do this to me and reduce me to this situation? And if you want to see that I am right, just touch them and feel them, and you will find that their bodies are only air, nothing but outward appearance.'

'I have touched them, sir, so help me God,' replied Sancho, 'and this devil that's fussing about here is as plump as a dumpling, and there's something else about him that's very different from what I've heard about demons – it's said they all stink of sulphur and other such muck, but this one reeks of ambergris from a couple of miles away.'

Sancho was referring to Don Fernando, who, being of such high rank, must have smelled of what Sancho said.

'You must not wonder at that, friend Sancho,' replied Don Quixote, 'because I can tell you, devils are crafty characters, and even if they carry smells with them, they themselves do not smell, because they are spirits, and if they do smell of anything it can never be pleasant, but foul and noxious. And the reason is that since they take hell with them wherever they go, and since they cannot receive any kind of relief from their torments, and since a good smell is pleasing and delightful, it is not possible for them to smell of anything wholesome. So if you think that demon to which you referred smells of ambergris, either you are deceiving yourself or he wants to deceive you and make you believe that he is not a demon.'

As master and servant conversed, Don Fernando and Cardenio, fearing that Sancho might tumble to their scheme, since he was on the very verge of doing so, decided to hasten their departure; and, calling the innkeeper aside, they told him to saddle Rocinante and put the pack-saddle on Sancho's donkey, which he hurried to do. In the meantime the priest had arranged for the peace-officers to accompany them back to the village for a daily payment. Cardenio hung the shield from one end of Rocinante's saddle-tree and the basin from the other, signalled to Sancho to mount his ass and take Rocinante's reins, and positioned two peace-officers with their muskets on either side of the cart. But before the cart moved off, the innkeeper's wife and daughter and Maritornes came out to say goodbye to Don Quixote, pretending to be shedding tears of grief at his misfortune, and Don Quixote addressed them:

'Weep not, good ladies; for all these calamities are the lot of those who profess what I profess, and if these disasters did not befall me I should not consider myself a famous knight errant: such things do not happen to knights of small repute, because nobody ever bothers about them. They happen to valiant knights, because their resolve and courage is envied by many men of high rank and by many other knights, who attempt by evil means to destroy these good men. But in spite of all that, virtue is so mighty that it will, unaided, and despite all the sorcery that the very first sorcerer, Zoroaster,[1] ever knew, emerge triumphant from every predicament, and give its light to the world as the sun gives its light to the sky. Forgive me, beauteous damsels, if, quite inadvertently, I have done you any mischief, for I have never harmed anyone wilfully or consciously; and pray to God that he deliver me from this captivity, to which some ill-intentioned enchanter has reduced me; for if I am one day freed, the favours you have done me at this castle will not escape my remembrance, that I may acknowledge, requite and repay them as they deserve.'

While the damsels of the castle were busy with Don Quixote, the priest and the barber said goodbye to Don Fernando and his companions, to the captain and his brother and to all the contented ladies, particularly Dorotea and Luscinda. They all embraced each other and agreed to keep in touch, and Don Fernando let the priest have his address so that he could write and tell him what happened to Don Quixote, as there would be no greater pleasure for him, he said, than to be informed about this; and Don Fernando in his turn would let the priest have any news that might interest him, about his wedding and Zoraida's baptism and the Don Luis affair and Luscinda's return home. The priest promised to do exactly as he was asked. They embraced again, and made each other some more promises. The innkeeper approached the priest and gave him a bundle of papers, saying that he'd found it in a pocket in the case where the 'Tale of Inappropriate Curiosity' had been discovered, and that since its owner hadn't come back the priest could have it, because not being able to read he didn't have any use for it himself. The priest thanked him, opened the bundle and saw written at the top of the first page: *The Tale of Rinconete and Cortadillo*;[2] from which he gathered that this was another work of fiction and that, since the 'Tale of Inappropriate Curiosity' had been a good one, perhaps this was too, because they might both be by the same author; so he put it in a safe place, intending to read it when he had an opportunity.

He mounted, and so did his friend the barber, both wearing their masks to prevent Don Quixote from recognizing them, and they started out behind the cart. And the procession set off as follows: first went the cart, led by its owner; on either side of it went the peace-officers, as we have said, with their muskets; then Sancho Panza on his ass, leading Rocinante by the reins. Bringing up the rear came the priest and the barber on their powerful mules, with their faces covered in the way described, and their bearing grave and sedate, since they couldn't ride any faster than the oxen would permit. Don Quixote was sitting in the cage with his hands tied and his legs stretched out in front of him, leaning against the bars, and his silence and his patience were such that he seemed more like a stone statue than a man of flesh and blood.

They rode on in this ponderous silence for half-a-dozen miles until they reached a valley that seemed to the carter like a good place to let his oxen rest and graze; but when he said so to the priest, the barber thought it would be better to ride on a little further, because he knew that behind a hill they could see not far away there was a valley with more and better grass than there was where they were thinking of stopping. The barber's advice was followed, and so they plodded on. As they did so, the priest looked back and saw approaching them some six or seven men, well dressed and equipped, who soon caught up with them because they weren't riding at the sedate and imperturbable pace of oxen but on canons' mules, and were anxious to reach the next inn, which could be seen only a couple of miles ahead, before the sun was intolerably hot. The speedy duly overtook the slow, and courteous greetings were exchanged; and one of the newcomers, who turned out to be a canon of Toledo and the man in charge of the group, on seeing the well-organized procession of cart, peace-officers, Sancho, Rocinante, priest and barber, and Don Quixote caged and imprisoned, couldn't resist asking why they were taking that man along in that way, although he'd already guessed from the peace-officers' insignia that he must be a wicked highwayman or some other delinquent for whose punishment the Holy Brotherhood was responsible. One of the officers, to whom the question had been put, replied:

'Sir, why this knight is being taken along in this way is something he'll have to tell you himself, because we haven't the faintest idea.'

Don Quixote overheard the conversation and said:

'Are you gentlemen by any chance versed and skilled in the matter of knight-errantry? If you are, I shall communicate my misfortunes to you, but if you are not, it would be pointless for me to bother to do so.'

By now the priest and the barber, seeing that the travellers were talking to Don Quixote de la Mancha, had ridden over to provide answers that wouldn't betray their scheme. The canon replied to Don Quixote:

'The fact of the matter, my dear friend, is that I know more about books of chivalry than about Villalpando's *Summaries*.[3] So if that's the only problem, you can safely communicate whatever you like to me.'

'God's will be done,' replied Don Quixote. 'And in that case I should like you to know, sir knight, that I am travelling in this cage under a spell, because of the envy and deceit of evil enchanters, for virtue is more persecuted by the wicked than it is beloved by the righteous. I am a knight errant, not one of those whose names fame has never been concerned to perpetuate in her memory, but one who, in spite of envy itself, and of all the magicians Persia ever bred, all the Brahmans of India, and all the Gymnosophists of Ethiopia,⁴ shall write his name in the temple of immortality to serve for future ages as a pattern and example, by which knights errant will know the steps that they must follow if they wish to reach the peak and honourable summit of arms.'

'Don Quixote de la Mancha is speaking the truth,' the priest inserted here, 'for he is indeed travelling on this cart under a spell, not for his crimes and sins but because of the ill will of those who are annoyed by virtue and infuriated by valour. This, sir, is the Knight of the Sorry Face, of whom you may perhaps have heard, and whose valiant exploits and mighty deeds shall be engraved in durable bronze and eternal marble, however much envy may toil to obscure them and malice may labour to conceal them.'

When the canon heard both the prisoner and the free man speaking in this way, he was so amazed that he almost crossed himself, unable to imagine what had happened; and all those with him were similarly astonished. And Sancho Panza, who'd come over to listen to the conversation, said, just to add the finishing touch:

'Look here, sirs, I expect I'll make myself unpopular with what I'm going to say but the plain truth is my master Don Quixote's about as bewitched as my mother is: he's in his right mind and he eats and drinks and does his business just like anybody else, the same as yesterday before they put him in a cage. So how can anyone try and tell me he's enchanted? Because I've heard lots of people say that when you're enchanted you don't eat or sleep or talk, yet my master'll talk more than thirty lawyers if someone doesn't stop him.'

And turning to face the priest, he continued:

'Oh father, father! Did you think I don't recognize you, do you imagine I can't see where all these latest enchantments are leading? Well, let me tell you that I do recognize you, however much you cover up your face, and I can see through you, too, however much you try to cover up your tricks. But there we are, where envy rules virtue can't survive, and where meanness is king there isn't any room for generosity. Hell and damnation! If it wasn't for your reverence, my master would be married to Princess Micomicona by now and I'd be a count at least, because I couldn't expect anything less than that, what with my master of the Sorry Face being so kind and my services being so first-rate. But now I can see it's right what they say – the wheel of fortune goes round faster than a mill-wheel, and there you were up at the top yesterday and here you are down on the floor today. I'm sorry for the wife and for the children, because they could and should have expected to see their father walk in through the door as the governor of some island or the viceroy of some kingdom, and all they're going to see is a stable-boy. I've only said this, father, to urge your reverence to have second thoughts about this bad treatment of my master – and you'd better watch out in case God takes you to task in the next life for locking my master up like this, and makes you answer for all the rescues and other good deeds he's being prevented from carrying out all this time he's being held prisoner.'

'Strike a light!' the barber interrupted. 'Do you belong to your master's fraternity as well, Sancho? As God is good, I can see you're going to be keeping him company in his cage, and be as enchanted as he is, because of what you've caught of his character and his chivalry! An evil hour it was when you allowed yourself to be seduced by his promises, and an evil hour it was when the idea of that island you're so set on found its way into your brain-box.'

'I haven't been seduced by anyone,' retorted Sancho, 'and I'm not the sort of man to let himself be seduced, not even by the king himself, and I might be poor but I'm of old Christian stock, and I don't owe anybody anything, and if I'm set on islands others are set on worse, and deeds make the man, and being as I am a man I can get to be pope let alone governor of an island, and even more so with a master who's going to conquer so many of them that he'll run out of people to hand them out to. You be careful what you say, mister barber, there are other things in life than shaving beards, and each man's a little bit different from the next. I'm only saying this because we all know one another, and nobody's going to play against me with loaded dice. And as for this enchanting of my master, God knows the truth, and let's leave it at that, because the more you stir it the worse it gets.'

The barber didn't reply to Sancho, concerned as he was that any more absurdities might reveal what he and the priest were striving so hard to conceal; and this same fear had made the priest suggest to the canon that the two of them might ride a little ahead so that he could explain the mystery of the caged man and other matters that the canon would enjoy. The canon agreed and, after going on in front with his servants and with the priest, listened to everything the priest told him about Don Quixote's standing, life, madness and habits, as he provided a brief account of the beginnings and the cause of his folly, and of everything that had happened to him until they'd put him in the cage, and of their plan to take him back home to see if they could find some cure for his madness. The canon and his servants were again struck with amazement as they listened to the extraordinary history of Don Quixote, and when it was finished the canon said:

'The truth is, my dear sir, that I myself consider these so-called books of chivalry to be prejudicial to the public good. And although my idleness and poor taste have led me to start reading most of those that have been printed, I've never managed to reach the end of a single one, because it seems to me that they're all more or less the same as each other, without any important differences between them. In my opinion this kind of writing comes under the heading of Milesian tales,[5] which are absurd stories, concerned only to amuse and not to instruct, unlike apologues, which amuse and instruct at the same time. And even though the main aim of such books is to amuse, I don't know how they can succeed when they're full of so many monstrous absurdities, because the soul can only take delight in the beauty and harmony that it sees or contemplates in what the eyes or the imagination places before it, and nothing that contains ugliness or disorder can give us any pleasure. Because what beauty can there be, what proportion of the parts to the whole, or of the whole to the parts, in a book or story in which a sixteen-year-old lad slashes at a giant as tall as a tower and slices him in two as if he were made of marzipan, or in which a battle is described and after we've been told that there are a million warriors on the enemy's side we have to accept, like it or not, so long as the book's hero is opposing them, that this knight gains the victory by the valour of his mighty arm alone? And what can one say about the readiness with which a queen or empress-to-be falls into the arms of some unknown errant knight? What mind that isn't totally barbarous or uneducated can derive any pleasure from reading that an enormous tower full of knights sails on through the sea, like a ship with a favourable wind, and that tonight it's in Lombardy and tomorrow morning it's in Prester John's land in the Indies, or somewhere else never described by Ptolemy or seen by Marco Polo? [6]

'And if someone replies that the authors of such books write them as fictions and are therefore under no obligation to bother with subtleties or truths, I'd answer by saying that the more a lie looks like the truth the better a lie it is, and the more feasible it is the more it pleases us. Fictional stories should suit their readers' understanding and be written in such a way that, by making impossibilities seem easy and marvels seem straightforward and by enthralling the mind, they amaze and astonish, gladden and entertain, so that wonder and pleasure go hand in hand; and none of this can be achieved by the writer who forsakes verisimilitude and imitation, because the perfection of all writing consists in these two qualities.

'I've never seen a book of chivalry that could be regarded as a whole body complete with all its members, and in which the middle corresponds with the beginning and the end with the beginning and the middle; on the contrary, their authors give them so many members that their intention seems more to produce a chimera or a monster than a well-proportioned figure. Apart from this, their style is harsh, their adventures are incredible, their loves are licentious, their civilities are uncouth, their battles are endless, their speeches are absurd, their journeys are preposterous, and, in short, there's no ingenious artifice about them, so they deserve to be thrown out of a Christian society as useless wastrels.'

The priest had been listening to the canon with rapt attention, and thought him a man of sound understanding who was making very good sense; so he told him that, being of the same opinion and sharing his dislike for books of chivalry, he had burned the whole of Don Quixote's large collection of them. And he described the scrutiny he'd made of them, and the ones he'd condemned to the flames and the ones he'd spared, at which the canon chortled heartily and then said that despite all his strictures on such books he did find one positive quality in them: they provided subject matter with which a good intelligence could express itself, because they made available a broad and spacious canvas on which the pen could wander unhindered, describing shipwrecks, storms, skirmishes and battles; portraying an exemplary captain with all the necessary characteristics –

prudent in anticipating his enemies' tricks, an eloquent orator in persuading or dissuading his soldiers, mature in his decisions, quick to act, courageous both in awaiting an attack and in launching one; depicting now a lamentable and tragic event, now a happy and unexpected one, there a lovely lady, virtuous, intelligent and demure, here a Christian knight, brave and courteous, there a reckless braggart of a barbarian, here a worthy, polite and considerate prince; representing goodness and loyalty in vassals, grandness and generosity in lords. The author can show himself to be an astrologer, a skilled cosmographer, a musician, knowledgeable about affairs of state, and perhaps he will even have an opportunity to show himself to be a magician, if he so wishes. He can portray the wiles of a Ulysses, the piety of an Aeneas, the courage of an Achilles, the misfortunes of a Hector, the treachery of a Sinon, the friendship of a Euryalus, the generosity of an Alexander, the resolve of a Caesar, the clemency and honesty of a Trajan, the fidelity of a Zopyrus,[7] the wisdom of a Cato, and, in short, all the faculties that contribute to the perfection of an illustrious man, whether he unites them all in one hero or distributes them among several.

'And if all this is done in an agreeable style and with ingenious inventiveness, and comes as close as possible to the truth, it will most certainly weave a web of beautiful and varied threads which, once complete, will display such perfection and loveliness that it will attain the highest goal to which writing can aspire: giving instruction and pleasure together, as I have said. Because the openness of such books allows the author to display his talent for the epic, the lyric, the tragic and the comic, together with all the qualities of the sweet and pleasing arts of poetry and oratory; for epic can be written in prose as well as in verse.'

CHAPTER XLVIII

�֎

In which the canon continues on the subject of books of chivalry and on other matters worthy of his mind

'It's just as you say, sir,' said the priest, 'and this makes those who've written such books all the more blameworthy, disregarding all sound reasoning and all the rules of art, by which they could have been guided and helped to become famous for their prose, as the two princes of Greek and Latin poetry[1] are for their verse.'

'I myself,' replied the canon, 'have been tempted to write a book of chivalry, observing all those points I've just been making, and to tell the truth I've written more than a hundred pages of it. And to find out how accurate my own opinion of it was, I gave it to men who like reading such books and who are learned and intelligent, and also to others who are ignorant and only concerned with the pleasure they derive from reading nonsense, and I'm pleased to say that all of them have expressed their approval; in spite of that, however, I haven't written any more, both because it seems rather inappropriate to my profession and because I'm aware that there are more fools than wise men in the world and, although the praise of the wise few is more important than the mockery of the foolish many, I'm not willing to subject myself to the indiscriminate judgement of the fickle mob, the principal readers of such books. But what most made me put it aside and indeed put the idea of finishing it out of my head was an argument that I derived from those plays that are always being performed nowadays, and I said to myself:

'"If it's no secret that all or at least most of these fashionable plays, both the purely fictional ones and those based on historical fact, are so much stuff and nonsense, higgledy-piggledy hodgepodges, and yet the masses love them, and think they're splendid creations when they're the very opposite, and the authors who write them and the actors who perform them say that it can't be otherwise because that's how people want them and they wouldn't have them any other way, and that plays which are properly structured and plotted as art demands are only good for the half-a-dozen intelligent people who understand them, and all the rest are left in the dark about their subtleties, and that it's better to earn a living from the many than approval from the few – then all of that is exactly what would happen with my book, and after burning the midnight oil to make sure I observed all those rules I've been mentioning I'd end up like that proverbial tailor who sewed for nothing and provided the thread himself."

'And although on occasions I've tried to persuade the impresarios that they're wrong about all this, and that they'd attract larger audiences and gain more credit by putting on works of art rather than balderdash, they're so wedded to their own opinions that no amount of argument or evidence can make them change their minds. I recall that one day I said to one of these stubborn people:

'"You tell me this: don't you remember that a few years ago three tragedies written by a famous Spanish poet were performed in this country, and that they were so good they delighted, surprised and amazed all those who went to see them, both the simple-minded and the wise, both the riff-raff and the élite, and that those three plays alone made more money for the players than the best thirty that have been produced since?"

'"I'm sure you must be referring," said the impresario, "to *Isabella, Phyllis* and *Alexandra*."[2]

'"Yes, they're the ones I mean," I replied, "and you just tell me whether they observed the rules of art, and whether this prevented them from showing themselves to be the excellent works they are, or from pleasing everyone. So it isn't the masses who are to blame for demanding rubbish, but rather those who aren't capable of providing them with anything else. Yes, indeed: *Ingratitude Revenged* wasn't rubbish, nor was there any in *Numancia*, nor did anybody find any in *The Merchant Lover*, still less in *The Friendly Enemy*[3] or a few others written by a handful of skilled poets who in this way added both to their own renown and to the profits of the players."

'I added some further considerations in my attempt to make him see how wrong he was, and I thought they left him somewhat bemused, though not convinced.'

'The subject you've broached, sir,' the priest interrupted, 'has awoken my old loathing for these fashionable plays, which is as great as my loathing for books of chivalry, because whereas drama should, as Cicero puts it,[4] be a mirror of human life, an exemplar of customs and an image of truth, these modern plays are just mirrors of absurdity, exemplars of folly and images of lewdness. Because what greater absurdity can there be in the theatre than having a baby in nappies appear in the first scene of the first act, who by the second scene has become a grown man with a beard? Or than presenting us with an old man who's courageous and a young one who's a coward, a lackey who's a great orator, a page who's a counsellor, a king who's a porter and a princess who's a cleaning-woman? And what can I say about their notion of how the actions they represent can or could be distributed into acts, except that I've seen a play in which the first act began in Europe, the second in Asia, the third ended up in Africa, and if there had been four acts the last would have finished in America, and so it would have been set in all four quarters of the globe? And if imitation is the principal feature expected of a play, how can anyone with the slightest intelligence be content with this other one I'm going to describe? The action is set in the times of King Pepin and Charlemagne, yet the protagonist is the Emperor Heraclius, who carries the Cross into Jerusalem and recovers the Holy Sepulchre, like Godfrey of Bouillon,[5] when in reality a whole age separated one event from the other; and although the play is based on fictitious actions, historical veracity is claimed for it, and bits and pieces of other histories involving different people and periods are mixed in, and without any attempt at verisimilitude, either, but with obvious mistakes that are quite inexcusable. And what's worst of all is that there are people ignorant enough to say that this is sheer perfection, and that to expect anything better is to ask for the moon and the stars.

'And what about plays on religious subjects? How many false miracles they invent, how many apocryphal and misunderstood events, with the miracles of one saint attributed to another! And even in the plays that aren't religious they make bold to insert miracles, without any respect or consideration – their only thought is that such and such a miracle or special effect, as they call them, would do very nicely there, to fill the ignorant rabble with amazement and persuade more of them to come and see the play; and all this works to the detriment of truth and to the prejudice of history, and even to the discredit of Spanish writers, because foreigners, who are most meticulous in obeying the rules of drama, consider us to be barbarous and ignorant when they see the absurdities and nonsenses in our plays.

'And it isn't a sufficient excuse to say that the main reason why well-ordered societies allow the public performance of plays is to entertain the community with some harmless recreation, and to keep at bay the bad temper that idleness sometimes produces, and that, since this end is achieved with any play, good or bad, there's no need to make laws or oblige those who write and perform plays to do so in the proper way because, as I said before, any old play will do the job. To this I'd reply that this end would be far, far better achieved with good plays than with bad ones, because the audience that has gone to see an ingenious and well-crafted play comes out at the end cheered by its jests, instructed by its truths, amazed at its action, wiser thanks to its speeches, warned by its roguery, shrewder for its examples, incensed against vice and enamoured of virtue; for a good play will provoke all these reactions in anyone who watches it, including the most slow-witted of yokels, and it's absolutely impossible for a play possessing these qualities not to cheer and entertain, satisfy and please far more than one that lacks them, as do nearly all of those performed nowadays.

'And the blame for this doesn't lie with their authors, because some of them know very well where they're going wrong and what they should be doing; but, since plays have been turned into goods for sale, playwrights say, and they speak the truth, that the players wouldn't buy them if they weren't of the kind I've described; so the writer tries to meet the demands of the impresario who's going to pay him for his work. The truth of what I'm saying can be seen in many, indeed countless plays written by a brilliant Spanish genius,[6] with such panache and wit, in such elegant verses, containing such excellent speeches and weighty maxims, and, in short, so rich in eloquence and loftiness of style, that he has filled the world with his fame; yet his urge to comply with the actors' taste has meant that not all his plays have reached the required pitch of perfection, although some certainly have. Others write their plays so thoughtlessly that the actors have to run away and hide after performances for fear of being punished, as they often have been, for scenes that insult kings or dishonour families.

'Now all these problems, and many others that I haven't mentioned, would be solved if there were some intelligent and sensible person in the capital to scrutinize all plays before they're performed, not only there but anywhere in Spain, and if no local authorities could permit the production of any play without his approval, seal and signature; and then the actors would make sure to send their plays off to the capital so as to be able to perform them safely, and the playwrights would devote much more care to their work because of their fear of this rigorous examination by someone who knew what he was doing; and in this way good plays would be written and their goals splendidly attained: not only the amusement of the people but also the good reputation of Spanish writers, the livelihood and security of the actors and the avoidance of the trouble of punishing them.

'And if another person, or even the same one, were given the job of scrutinizing any new books of chivalry that were written, some of these might well show the perfection that you've specified, enriching our language with the delightful, precious treasure of eloquence, eclipsing old books in the light of the new ones published for the innocent amusement not only of the idle but also of the busy, because the bow can't always be bent, nor can our frail human nature subsist without some honest recreation.'

As the canon and the priest reached this point in their conversation, the barber rode up to them and said to the priest:

'This is the place, sir, that I said would be a good one for us to rest while the sun is high and for the oxen to enjoy plenty of lush pasture.'

'I agree with you,' replied the priest.

He told the canon of their plans, and the canon decided to stay with them, attracted by the sight of a beautiful valley that opened up before them. So to enjoy the view and the priest's conversation, which he was growing to like, and to find out in more detail about Don Quixote's exploits, he told some of his servants to ride on to the inn, which wasn't far away, and to bring back all the food to be had there, so that everybody could eat, because he intended to take his rest where he was; to which one of his servants replied that their supply-mule, which must by then have reached the inn, had sufficient provisions, and all they'd need from the inn itself was barley.

'In that case,' said the canon, 'take all the animals on to the inn, and bring the supply-mule back here.'

While all this was happening Sancho saw his opportunity to speak to his master without those suspicious characters the priest and the barber breathing down his neck, for once, and he sidled up to his master's cage and muttered:

'Look, sir, I want to unburden my conscience and tell you what's what concerning this enchantment of yours – those two over there with their faces all covered up are the village priest and the barber, and I expect they've decided to carry you off like this because they're bursting with envy at you getting in ahead of them at doing famous deeds. Now if I'm right you aren't under a spell at all, but just a fool with the wool pulled over your eyes. And to prove it I'm going to ask you one question, and if you answer as I think you will, you'll rumble their trick for yourself and see you're more bamboozled than enchanted.'

'You ask whatever you wish, Sancho my son,' replied Don Quixote, 'and I shall do as you ask and give all the answers that you require. And as regards what you said about those two men riding hither and thither being the priest and the barber, our friends from the village, it may well be that they look like them; but you should not believe by any manner of means that they really are them. What you should believe and understand is that if they look like our friends, as you say they do, what must have happened is that those who have enchanted me have assumed their likenesses; because it is easy for enchanters to take on whatever appearance they please, and they must have taken on the appearance of our friends to make you think what you are thinking, and lead you into a maze of conjectures from which you would not be able to extricate yourself even if provided with the thread of Theseus. And they must also have done it to befuddle my understanding so that I cannot fathom from where this harm has come; because if on the one hand you tell me that the village priest and barber are accompanying me and, on the other, I find myself in a cage and I know full well that no mere human powers, only supernatural ones, would be sufficient to put me here, what can you expect me to say or think except that the manner of my enchantment is more extraordinary than all those about which I have ever read in all the histories dealing with knights errant who have been enchanted? So you can rest assured and be certain that they are not who you say they are: if they are the priest and the barber, I am a Turk. And as regards your desire to ask me a question, ask away, Sancho, and I shall answer, even if your interrogation lasts from now until tomorrow.'

'God save us all and his Holy Mother too!' Sancho exclaimed. 'How can you be so thick-skulled and empty-headed that you can't see that what I'm saying is the plain truth, and that it's more through roguery than enchantment that you're in this mess and in this cage? But since that's the way it is I'm going to give you clear proof that you aren't enchanted. Just you tell me, then, as you'd have God save you from this pickle, and as you'd have my lady Dulcinea take you into her arms when you're least expecting it . . .'

'You needn't exorcize me,' said Don Quixote, 'just ask me your question. I have already said that I shall give you a complete and honest answer.'

'That's all I'm asking for,' replied Sancho, 'and what I want to know is for you to tell me, without adding anything or taking anything away, but giving me the whole truth, as can rightly be expected from all those who profess arms, as you profess them, with the title of knight errants . . .'

'I tell you I do not intend to lie,' replied Don Quixote. 'Do put your question to me; I really am beginning to grow tired of all these salvos, prayer-bells and preparatives, Sancho.'

'And I tell you I'm sure my master's a good and honest man, and so, being as it is very much to the point, what I'm asking, with all due respect, is whether maybe, in the time you've been shut up and, as you think, enchanted here in this cage, you've ever felt the need or urge to do number one or number two, as some people put it.'

'I do not understand what you mean by "doing numbers", Sancho; you must be more explicit if you wish me to give you a clear answer.'

'How can you not know about doing number one and number two? It's the very first thing you learn at school. Look, what I'm asking is if you've felt the urge to do what you've got to do.'

'Oh, now I understand you, Sancho! Yes, yes, often; indeed I am feeling it at this very moment. Do save me from my plight, for things in here are none too clean!'

CHAPTER XLIX

✠

*Which concerns the intelligent conversation that Sancho
Panza had with his master Don Quixote*

'Oho!' said Sancho. 'Now I've caught you! That's what I wanted to know,
with all my heart and soul. Look here sir: can you deny that when someone's
off colour people often say, "I don't know what's wrong with him, he
won't eat or drink or sleep, or give a proper answer when you ask him a
question, anyone would think he'd been bewitched"? You can see from
this that people who don't eat or drink or sleep or answer the call of nature
as I said before are enchanted, but not people who feel the urges you're
feeling and who drink when they're given a drink, and eat when there's
food to be had, and reply to everything they're asked.'

'What you say is true, Sancho,' replied Don Quixote, 'but I have already
told you that enchantment can take many different forms, and it could be
that these have changed in the course of time, so that what happens
nowadays is that the enchanted do all the things that I do, even though
formerly they did not. So one cannot either argue against the customs of the
times, or draw any conclusions from them. I know for certain that I am
enchanted, and this is enough for the comfort of my conscience; because my
remorse would be great indeed if I thought that I am not enchanted and that
I am sitting here in this cage like an idler and a coward, depriving so many
distressed and needy people of the succour I could be giving them, when they
must at this very moment be in extreme need of my aid and protection.'

'All that's as may be,' said Sancho, 'but what I'm saying is that just to
make doubly sure it'd be a good idea if you tried to get out of this prison,
and what I'll do for my part is help you as much as I can, and even rescue
you myself, and then you could try to get up on good old Rocinante –
you'd think he's enchanted, too, he's so dejected and miserable. And once
we'd done that we could try our luck at looking for more adventures, and
if things didn't go well we'd be in plenty of time to come back to the cage,
and I give you my word as a good and loyal squire that I'd lock myself up

in it with you if you were so unlucky or I was so stupid that I couldn't do what I've said I'll do.'

'I am content to do as you say, brother Sancho,' replied Don Quixote, 'and, as soon as you spot an opportunity to contrive my release, I shall obey your every command; but you will see, Sancho, how mistaken you are in your assessment of my misfortune.'

The knight errant and his errant squire chatted away like this until they caught up with the priest, the canon and the barber, who'd dismounted and were waiting for them. The carter unyoked his oxen and set them free to wander in that green and pleasant place, whose coolness was an open invitation, not to enchanted people like Don Quixote, but to those as wide-awake and quick-witted as his squire, who asked the priest to let his master out of the cage for a while, because if he didn't it was going to end up less spick and span than was required for a respectable knight like his master. The priest understood his meaning, and said he'd most willingly do as asked if he weren't afraid that once Don Quixote found himself free he'd get up to his old tricks again and take himself off to where nobody could ever find him.

'I'll guarantee he won't run away,' replied Sancho.

'And so shall I,' said the canon, 'particularly if he gives me his word as a knight that he won't go anywhere unless we say so.'

'I do indeed give my word,' said Don Quixote, who'd been listening to the conversation, 'and in any case, a person who is enchanted, as I am, is not at liberty to dispose of his person as he wishes, because the man who enchanted him can prevent him from moving for three centuries on end, and if he flees he will bring him back in the twinkling of an eye.' And this being so they could well release him, since it would be to everyone's advantage, and if they didn't he could assure them that he wouldn't be able to help offending their noses, unless they kept their distance.

The canon took him by the hand, even though it was tied to the other one, and, after he'd given them his word of honour they uncaged him, and he was overcome by joy and delight to find himself out of the cage. And what he first did was to have a good stretch, and then he went over to Rocinante, gave him a couple of slaps on the haunches and said:

'I still trust in God and his Blessed Mother, O flower and mirror of steeds, that we two shall soon be as we would wish to be: you with your master on your back, and I mounted upon you, practising the profession for which God sent me into this world.'

And so saying, Don Quixote retired with Sancho to a far distant spot, from where he returned much eased and comforted, and with increased desires to put into execution whatever his squire should order him to do. The canon was gazing at Don Quixote and wondering at this strange, great madness of his, and at how he showed a fine understanding in all his remarks and replies, only taking leave of his senses, as has already been pointed out, when chivalry was the subject under discussion. And so, after everybody had sat down on the green grass to wait for the provisions, the canon, moved by pity, said to him:

'Can it really be possible, my dear hidalgo, that reading all those useless and pernicious books of chivalry has had such an effect on you as to make you mad enough to believe you're enchanted, and other such stuff and nonsense that's as far from being true as is falsehood itself? And how can any human understanding persuade itself that the world has ever contained such an infinity of different Amadises, and such a mob of so many famous knights, so many Emperors of Trebizond, all those Felixmartes of Hyrcania, all those palfreys, and maidens errant, and serpents, and monsters, and giants, and unique adventures, and enchantments of every kind, and battles, and terrible combats, and splendid costumes, and lovelorn princesses, and squires who become counts, and funny dwarfs, and love-letters, and amorous compliments, and valiant women and, in short, all those absurdities to be found in books of chivalry? Speaking for myself I can say that when I read them they give me some pleasure so long as I overlook the fact that they're all folly and falsehood; but as soon as I remember what they are, I dash the best of them against the wall, and I'd even hurl it into the fire if there were one handy, because they all deserve this punishment for being cheats and impostors and beyond the pale of common nature, for inventing new sects and a new way of life, and for inducing the ignorant rabble to accept as truths all the absurdities they contain. And such is their audacity that they even dare to unsettle the wits of intelligent and well-born hidalgos, as is clear from what they've done to you, because they've reduced you to such a state that it has proved necessary to shut you up in a cage and transport you on top of an ox-cart, as people wheel a lion or a tiger from one village to the next to exhibit it for money.

'Come now, Don Quixote, take pity on yourself, and restore yourself to the bosom of good sense, and make use of the generous amount of it that heaven has been kind enough to give you, by applying your splendid gifts of mind to different reading matter that will benefit your conscience and increase your honour! And if, following your natural inclinations, you still want to read books of adventure and chivalry, take the Scriptures and read the Book of Judges, and there you will find great truths and deeds as authentic as they are brave. Portugal had its Viriatus, Rome its Caesar, Carthage its Hannibal, Greece its Alexander, Castile its Count Fernán González, Valencia its Cid, Andalusia its Gonzalo Fernández, Extremadura its Diego García de Paredes, Jerez its Garci Pérez de Vargas, Toledo its Garcilaso and Seville its Don Manuel de León;[1] and reading about their meritorious deeds can entertain, teach, delight and amaze the finest minds. Now this would be reading matter worthy of your excellent understanding, my dear Don Quixote, and it will make you knowledgeable about history, enamoured of virtue, instructed in goodness, improved in your habits, brave but not rash; and all for God's greater glory, for your own benefit and for the renown of La Mancha, from where, I've been told, you hail.'

Don Quixote had been listening with profound attention to the canon's words, and when he realized that he'd finished, he sat staring at him for some time; and then he said:

'It seems to me, my dear hidalgo, that your speech was intended to give me to understand that there never have been any knights errant in the world, and that all books of chivalry are false, full of lies, harmful and of no use to society, and that I have done wrong in reading them, and worse in believing them, and worse still in imitating them and setting out to follow the rigorous profession of knight-errantry that they teach; and you deny that there ever were any Amadises, of Gaul or of Greece, in this world, or any of the other knights of whom the writings are full.'

'Yes, that is precisely what I meant,' said the canon.

To which Don Quixote replied:

'You went on to say that such books had done me great harm, inasmuch as they had made me take leave of my senses and had confined me to a cage, and that it would be better for me to mend my ways and change my reading, turning to other more truthful books that amuse and instruct more effectively.'

'Indeed I did,' said the canon.

'Well, for my part,' replied Don Quixote, 'I consider that it is you who are out of your senses and under some spell, for you have taken it upon yourself to utter such blasphemies against what has been so well received in the world and so widely accepted as the truth that anyone who denies it, as you do, deserves the same punishment that you say you inflict on books that annoy you when you read them. Because trying to persuade anyone that Amadis and all the other knights adventurers that pack the histories never existed is like trying to persuade him that the sun does not give out light, and that ice is not cold, and that the earth does not sustain us. For what mind can there be in the entire world capable of convincing another that there is no truth in the story about Princess Floripes and Guy of Burgundy, or about Fierabras at the Bridge of Mantible,[2] an event that took place in Charlemagne's time, and I swear is as true as that it is now daytime? And if that is a lie, it must also be a lie that there ever was a Hector, or an Achilles, or a Trojan War, or the Twelve Peers of France, or King Arthur of England, who still wanders about today transformed into a raven and is expected in his realms at any moment. And no doubt they will also attempt to persuade us that the history of Guerrino Il Meschino is false, and so is the quest for the Holy Grail, and that the loves of Sir Tristan and Queen Iseult and of Guenevere and Lancelot are apocryphal, even though there are people alive who almost remember seeing the duenna Quintañona, the best server of wine there ever was in the whole of Great Britain.[3] And the truth of this is shown by the fact that I remember my grandmother on my father's side saying, whenever she saw some aged duenna go by in her weeds: "That one over there, my boy, she could be old duenna Quintañona herself." From which I conclude that my grandmother must have known her, or at least have contrived to see some portrait of her. And who could deny that the history of Pierres and the fair Magalona is a true one, for to this very day one can see in the royal armoury the peg with which the brave Pierres guided the wooden horse as he rode through the air, and it is a little bigger than a cart-pole.[4] And next to the peg is Babieca's saddle, and Roland's horn is at Roncesvalles, the size of a large beam, from all of which we can deduce that the Twelve Peers did exist, that Pierres did exist, that the Cid and other such knights did exist

And went, as people say,
Adventuring their way.

'Or else let them try to tell me that it is not true that the brave Portuguese Juan de Merlo was a knight errant who went to Burgundy and did battle in the city of Arras with the famous lord of Charny called Monseigneur Pierres and later, in the city of Basle, with Monseigneur Henri de Remestan, emerging victorious and crowned with honour and glory from both exploits; and let them try to deny the adventures and challenges, also in Burgundy, of those courageous Spaniards Pedro Barba and Gutierre Quixada (from whose stock I am descended in the direct male line), who defeated Count St Pol's sons. They might as well also deny that Don Fernando de Guevara ever went to Germany in search of adventures, and fought against Messire George, a knight of the Duke of Austria's household. And let them claim that the jousts of Suero de Quiñones by the Honourable Pass never happened, and nor did the exploits of Monseigneur Louis de Falces against the Castilian knight Don Gonzalo de Guzmán, and many other deeds performed by Christian knights of these and foreign realms, all of which are so true and authentic that I repeat that anyone who denied them would be devoid of all reason and good sense.'[5]

The canon was amazed to hear the mixture that Don Quixote had concocted of real events and fictional ones, and to discover how well informed he was about everything connected with the exploits of his precious knight-errantry; and he replied:

'I can't deny, Don Quixote sir, that some of what you've said is true, particularly concerning Spanish knights errant; and I'll also concede that the Twelve Peers of France did exist, but I can't believe they did everything that Archbishop Turpin says they did, because the truth of the matter is that they were knights chosen by the kings of France, and were called peers because they were all equals in worth, rank and courage – or at least if they weren't they should have been – and it was like a religious order after the style of the present-day orders of Santiago and Calatrava, the members of which we presume are, or should be, worthy, courageous and high-born knights; and just as nowadays people refer to a knight of St John, or of Alcántara, in those times they used to talk about a knight of the Twelve Peers, because there were always twelve equals who'd been chosen for this military order. As regards the existence of the Cid, there can't be any doubt about that, or about Bernardo del Carpio, but there are very great doubts about whether they performed the exploits ascribed to them. And as for that other matter of Count Pierres' peg, which you say is next to Babieca's saddle in the royal armoury, I must confess my sin: I'm so ignorant, or so short-sighted, that although I've seen the saddle I've never spotted the peg, even though you say it's so big.'

'Yet it is most definitely there,' replied Don Quixote, 'and furthermore it is said to be kept in a calfskin cover to prevent it from becoming mouldy.'

'That's as may be,' replied the canon, 'but I'm as sure that I've never seen it as I am that I'm a priest. And even if I did concede that it is there, this wouldn't oblige me to believe the histories of so many Amadises or of that great mob of knights in the stories people tell; nor is it right for a man like you, honourable and talented and intelligent, to give any credit to the extravagant nonsense that's written in those ridiculous books of chivalry.'

CHAPTER L

*About the intelligent dispute between Don Quixote and
the canon, and other matters*

'Now that is a good one!' Don Quixote retorted. 'Books printed with licences from kings and with the approval of those to whom they have been submitted, read with universal delight and praised by great and small, poor and rich, the educated and the ignorant, plebeians and gentlemen, in short by all kinds of people of all ranks and circumstances – are they likely to be lies, above all when they bear such an appearance of truth, telling us about the father, mother, country, kindred, time, place and deeds, detail by detail and day by day, performed by the knight or knights in question? Hold your tongue, sir, and do not voice such blasphemies, and believe me, I am advising you now to act as a man of good sense should; only read them, and you will find out for yourself how much pleasure they afford you. Or else tell me this: can there be any greater delight than to see, as it were, here and now before us a vast lake of bubbling pitch, and swimming about in it vast numbers of serpents, snakes and lizards and many other kinds of fierce and fearsome animals, while from the lake comes a plaintive voice:

'"You, O knight, whosoever you may be, beholding this dread lake: if you wish to attain the good hidden beneath these black waters, you must show the resolve of your dauntless breast and cast yourself into the midst of its dark, burning liquid, else you will not be worthy to see the mighty marvels contained in the seven castles of the seven fairies that lie beneath its murky surface"?

'And what of our delight when the knight, almost before the fearful voice has ceased, without giving his situation a second thought, without stopping to consider the peril to which he is exposing himself, or even shedding the burden of his heavy armour, commends himself to God and to his lady and hurls himself into the boiling lake and, all of a sudden when he least knows where he is bound, finds himself amidst flowery meadows, far finer than the Elysian fields themselves? Here it seems to him that the skies are clearer, and that the sun shines with a different brightness; and here his gaze is regaled with a pleasant glade of such green and leafy trees that his eyes rejoice at the sight of them, and his ears are delighted by the sweet, artless song of the innumerable little brightly coloured birds that flit to and fro in the maze of branches. Here he espies a brook whose cool waters, like liquid crystal, lap over fine sand and white pebbles that resemble gold dust and perfect pearls; there he sees a cunningly wrought fountain of many-coloured jasper and smooth marble; in another place he finds another fountain adorned in the grotesque style, in which tiny clam shells and the curling yellow and white dwellings of sea-snails, placed in disordered order and mingling with pieces of glittering crystal and imitation emeralds, form so varied a composition that art, imitating nature, seems here to surpass it. And over there he suddenly beholds a mighty castle or splendid palace, with walls of solid gold, battlements of diamond and doors of jacinth; yet it is so admirably built that, although it is made of nothing less than diamonds, carbuncles, rubies, pearls, gold and emeralds, its workmanship is even more praiseworthy.

'And what more splendid sight, after seeing all this, than a bevy of damsels emerging from the castle gate, wearing such elegant and splendid apparel that if I started now to describe it as the histories do, I should never finish? And then she who appears to be the most important damsel takes the hand of the bold knight who cast himself into the boiling lake, and walks with him, without a word, into the sumptuous castle or palace, and has him strip as naked as the day he was born, and bathes him in warm waters, and then anoints his whole body with aromatic balsams and dresses him in a shirt of the finest sendal, perfumed and sweet-smelling, and another damsel comes and throws over his shoulders a cloak that is said to be worth at least as much as a city if not more! And is it not a marvellous sight when we are told that after all this he is taken to another hall where he finds tables laid with such orderly elegance that he is dazzled and amazed? And seeing him sprinkle his hands with the essence of ambergris and perfumed flowers? And then to see him seated on a chair of ivory? Seeing him being served by all the damsels in a wonderful silence? Being brought such a variety of foods, so exquisitely cooked, that the appetite is at a loss which to choose? Hearing the song that sounds as he eats, not knowing whence it comes or who is singing it? And then when, once the meal is over and the tables have been cleared, as the knight lolls in his chair picking his teeth, as is the custom, through the door suddenly comes another damsel much more beautiful than any of the others, who sits by his side and begins to tell him what castle this is, and how she lives there under a spell, and other matters that amaze the knight and astonish the readers of his history?

'I shall not enlarge any further on this subject, because from what I have said it is clear that any passage from any history of a knight errant is bound to delight and amaze anyone who reads it. Only believe me and, as I said before, read these books, and you will soon see how they banish any melancholy you might be feeling, and improve your disposition, if it is a bad one. Speaking for myself, I can say that ever since I became a knight errant I have been courageous, polite, generous, well-bred, magnanimous, courteous, bold, gentle, patient and long-suffering in the face of toil, imprisonment and enchantment; and although so short a time ago I found myself locked into a cage like some madman, it is my intention, by the might of my arm, if heaven favours me and fortune does not oppose me, to become within a few days the king of some kingdom where I shall be able to demonstrate the gratitude and liberality contained in my breast. Because on my faith, sir, the poor man is prevented from showing the virtue of liberality towards anyone, even if he possesses it to a degree; and gratitude that is restricted to good intentions is as dead as faith without works. For this reason I do wish that fortune would soon offer me some opportunity to become an emperor, so that I can show my true nature by doing good to my friends, especially poor Sancho Panza here, my squire, who is the salt of the earth, and I should love to give him an earldom that I promised him a long time ago, except that I fear he will not have what it takes to govern his estate.'

Sancho overheard these last few words, and he said to his master:

'You set to work, Don Quixote sir, and get that earldom you've been promising me and I've been waiting for all this time, and what I can promise you is that I won't be found wanting in what it takes to govern it. And if I am found wanting, I've heard there are men that rent lords' estates from them, and give these lords money every year and govern the estates themselves, and the lord sits about with his feet up all day long having a good time on the rent he's paid and not worrying about anything at all – and that's what I'll do, and I won't bother to bargain, I'll just hand the whole lot over and enjoy my rent like a duke, and everyone else can go and get stuffed.'

'That, brother Sancho,' said the canon, 'might apply to enjoying the revenues, but the lord of the estate must concern himself with the administration of justice, and this is where his ability and good judgement come into play, and above all his honest determination to do what is right, because if this isn't present from the very beginning, things will go wrong in the middle and at the end; and that is why God favours the good intentions of the simpleton as much as he obstructs the evil intentions of the clever man.'

'I don't know about all that philosopherizing,' replied Sancho Panza, 'all I do know is that I wish I was as sure that I'm going to lay my hands on that earldom as I am that I've got what it takes to govern it – I have as much of a soul as the next man, and as much of a body as the best of them, and I'd be as good a king of my estate as anyone else, and that being so I'd be doing as I liked, and doing as I liked I'd be doing what I wanted to do, and doing what I wanted to do I'd be happy, and if you're happy you can't ask for more than that, and if I couldn't ask for more there's nothing more to say, and let's have my estate, and goodbye and I hope we'll be seeing each other soon, as one blind man said to the other.'

'That isn't bad philosophizing, as you put it, Sancho; all the same, there's a great deal more that could be said on the subject of earldoms.'

To which Don Quixote replied:

'I am not so sure that there is any more to be said: I am simply guided by the example given me by the great Amadis of Gaul, who made his squire the Count of the Firm Isle; and so I can make Sancho Panza a count without any qualms of conscience, because he is one of the best squires that any knight errant ever had.'

The canon was astounded at the concerted nonsense spoken by Don Quixote, at his evocation of the adventure of the Knight of the Lake, at the effect on him of the premeditated lies in the books he'd read, and also at Sancho's simplicity and his longing to possess the earldom that his master had promised him.

The canon's servants were by now approaching with the supply-mule that they'd fetched from the inn; and turning a carpet they had with them and the green grass of the meadow into a table in the shade of some trees, they all sat and ate there so that the carter's oxen could continue to enjoy the advantages of the spot. As they were eating they suddenly heard a loud rustling and the clanking of a tin bell in a thicket of brambles near them, and at the same instant a handsome black, brown and white goat broke out of the thicket, followed by a goatherd who was calling to her in goatherds' language to stop or go back to the herd. The runaway, panic-stricken goat trotted over to the picnickers as if to implore their protection, and then halted. The goatherd followed her, seized her by the horns and addressed her as if she could understand his words:

'Oh Dapple, Dapple, you wild gadabout, how footloose you have become! What wolves are you running away from, my dear? Won't you tell me what's up, my beauty? But what can it be except that you're a female and can't settle down – and the devil take those ways of yours and the people you've copied them from! Come back, come back with me, my sweet, you'll be safer, even if you aren't as happy, in your fold or in the herd with your friends – and if you who are meant to be keeping order among them are so out of order yourself, what are they going to end up by doing?'

The goatherd's words delighted all those who heard them, especially the canon, who said:

'Do please calm down a little, my friend, and don't be in such a hurry to return the goat to her herd – since she's a female, as you put it, she's going to follow her natural instincts whatever you do to try to stop her. Have a bite to eat and a drop to drink, and that will make you simmer down, and in the meantime the goat can have a rest.'

And as he said this he speared a quarter of a cold rabbit on his knife and offered it to him. The goatherd took it and thanked him; he drank wine and calmed down, and said:

'I wouldn't like any of you to think me a simpleton because I spoke to this animal so seriously – the truth is that my words were a little strange. I may be a rustic, but not so much of one that I don't know the difference between talking to a human being and talking to a beast.'

'I don't doubt that,' said the priest, 'because I have found out for myself that mountains breed scholars and herdsmen's huts house philosophers.'

'Or at least, sir,' replied the goatherd, 'they give shelter to men who've learned from bitter experience; and so that you can see for yourselves how true this is, even though I might seem to be forcing myself on you, I shall – so long as it isn't tiresome, gentlemen, and you're willing to lend me your ears for a while – tell you a true story that will confirm what this gentleman' – pointing to the priest – 'and I have just said.'

To this Don Quixote replied:

'Seeing that this seems to have some suspicion of a chivalry adventure about it, I for my part am most willing to listen to you, my friend, and so are all these gentlemen, for they are intelligent people and are keen to hear anything new and curious that amazes, delights and captivates the mind, as I am sure your story will. You may begin, my friend, for we shall all listen.'

'You can count me out,' said Sancho, 'I'm off to that stream over there with this pie I've got here, and I'm going to stuff myself enough to last me for three days, because I've heard my master Don Quixote say that a knight errant's squire must eat whenever he gets a chance to, until he can't eat any more, since what often happens is that they wander into such a thick forest that it takes them more than six days to find their way out, and if the squire wasn't full at the beginning, and his saddle-bags weren't full either, he might not get out at all, as often does happen, and be left there to turn into a mummy.'

'You are quite right, Sancho,' said Don Quixote. 'You go wherever you like, and eat as much as you can; I am fully satisfied already, and only need refection for my spirit, which I shall obtain by listening to this good fellow's story.'

'And that's what we'll all do,' said the canon.

And he asked the goatherd to do as he'd promised. He gave the goat, which he was still holding by the horns, a couple of slaps on the back with the words:

'You lie down here next to me, Dapple – there's plenty of time to go back to the herd.'

The goat seemed to understand him, because as her master sat down she quietly stretched herself out by his side, and looking up into his face she indicated that she was paying attention to what he was saying; and he began his story like this:

CHAPTER LI

Concerning what the goatherd told Don Quixote's kidnappers

'Ten miles from this valley there's a village which, though small, is one of the richest hereabouts, and in it there lived a farmer of great renown who, although honour always goes with money, was even more highly regarded for his goodness than for his wealth. But what made him happiest of all, he said, was having a daughter of such exquisite beauty, rare intelligence, elegance and virtue that anyone who knew her and beheld her was amazed to see the extraordinary qualities with which heaven and nature had endowed her. As a child she was pretty, and she continued to grow in beauty, so that by the age of sixteen she was lovely. The fame of her loveliness began to spread throughout the nearby villages – but why do I leave it at the nearby ones, when it spread to distant cities and even reached the halls of royal palaces and the ears of all kinds of people who came from every part to see her, as if she were some strange curiosity or miracle-working image?

'Her father stood guard over her virtue, and she stood guard over it herself, too, because there are no keys, locks or bolts that can protect a maiden better than her own modest reserve. The father's wealth and the daughter's beauty moved many men, both from the village and from elsewhere, to ask for her hand in marriage; but given the task of disposing of such a precious jewel, he was perplexed and couldn't decide which of the countless men who pestered him he should entrust her to. Among all those with this honourable intention I was one, and I was given great hopes of success by the knowledge that her father knew me to be of good family, from the same village, of pure Christian blood, in the prime of life, rich in worldly goods, and no less so in intelligence. Another man from the village, with the same qualities, also asked for her hand; and so her father couldn't make up his mind, because he felt that either of us would be a good match for her; and to resolve this difficulty he decided to refer the matter to Leandra herself (that's the name of the lady of fortune who has reduced me to wretchedness), because he realized that since there was nothing to choose between us it would be best to let his beloved daughter make up her own mind, an example that could well be followed by all parents in search of spouses for their children. I'm not saying that they should allow their children to choose among evil or base suitors, but that they should propose several good ones and give them a free choice among these. I don't know which was Leandra's choice; all I do know is that her father put us off with talk about how young she was and with generalities that neither put him under any obligation nor released us from ours. My rival is called Anselmo and I'm Eugenio, so now you know the names of the people involved in this tragedy, which hasn't ended yet, although it's plain enough that the ending is going to be calamitous.

'At about this time one Vicente de la Rosa, the son of a poor farmer from the village, returned from Italy and various other parts of the world where he'd been serving as a soldier. He'd gone off at the age of about twelve with a company that happened to come our way, and he returned twelve years after that, dressed as all soldiers like to dress, in a thousand different colours, covered in glass trinkets and little steel chains. One day he'd be wearing one piece of finery and the next another, all of them flimsy, artificial, tawdry, worthless. Village people, who are naturally malicious, and who with time on their hands turn into malice personified, took due note of this, started counting all his baubles and gewgaws, one by one, and found that he owned just three suits of clothes, of different colours, each with its garters and hose; but he rang the changes on his finery in such a way that if his clothes hadn't been counted anyone would have sworn that he'd displayed more than ten suits and more than twenty plumes. And don't imagine that what I'm telling you about his clothes is irrelevant or gratuitous, because they play an important part in this story.

'He used to sit on a stone bench under the great poplar tree in our village square, and we'd all sit around him with our mouths agape, hanging on the exploits he was telling us about. There wasn't a land in the world he hadn't been to, not a battle he hadn't fought in; he'd slaughtered more Moors than there are in Morocco and Tunis, had taken part in more single combats, according to him, than Gante y Luna,[1] Diego García y Paredes and thousands of others he named, and had been victorious in every one of them, without ever having been made to shed a single drop of blood. And then he'd show us scars that we couldn't see but that he said were from gunshot wounds received in various skirmishes and raids. And he had the unparalleled effrontery to address equals, and even those who knew what he was, as if they were inferiors, and declare that his arm was his father, that his deeds were his pedigree and that, being a soldier, he was second to nobody, not even the King himself. In addition to all this bravado, he had a smattering of music and could strum a guitar, and there were those who said that he could make it talk; and his talents didn't end here, because he could also write poems, and produced five-mile-long ballads about every single trifling incident in the life of the village.

'Now this soldier I've described, this Vicente de la Rosa, this hero, this man of fashion, this musician, this poet, was often seen and indeed gazed upon by Leandra from a window in her house that overlooked the square. She fell in love with his gaudy clothes; she was captivated by his ballads – he distributed twenty copies of every one; she heard all about the feats he claimed to have performed; and in the end – it must have been the devil's own work – she fell in love with the man himself, before he had the presumption to try his luck with her. And since in no affair of the heart do events proceed more smoothly than when the initiative comes from the woman, it was easy for Leandra and Vicente to reach an understanding, and before any of her suitors had the slightest inkling of her infatuation she had satisfied it by leaving the house of the father she loved so much (she has no mother) and running away with the soldier, who carried this venture to a more triumphant conclusion than any of the others to which he had laid claim.

'This event astonished the whole village and indeed all who heard about it; it left me dumbfounded, Anselmo thunderstruck, her father wretched, her relatives humiliated, the authorities alerted, the officers of the Holy Brotherhood astir: the roads were patrolled, the woods were searched, the whole countryside was scoured, and after three days they found the flighty Leandra in a mountain cave, wearing only a chemise, and all the money and the valuable jewels that she'd taken from the house had disappeared. They returned her to her forlorn father; they asked her what had brought about this disaster; she confessed without any coercion that Vicente de la Rosa had deceived her, promising to marry her and persuading her to run away from home: he was going to take her to the richest and most luxurious city in the whole world, Naples, and she'd been ill-advised and beguiled enough to believe him; after robbing her father she'd placed herself in the soldier's hands that same night when she'd gone missing; and then he'd taken her to a rocky mountain and shut her up in the cave where she'd been found. She also told them that the soldier had plundered her of everything she possessed except her honour, had left her in the cave and had gone away; and this detail was a cause of fresh amazement for everyone. It was hard to believe that the young man had been so restrained, yet she insisted on this earnestly enough to console her disconsolate father, who wasn't concerned about the riches that had been stolen, since his daughter had been allowed to keep that jewel which once lost can never be retrieved.

'The very same day that Leandra reappeared her father made her disappear again, taking her away to shut her up in a convent in a town not far from here, in the hope that time might efface a part of the bad reputation that she'd earned for herself. Leandra's tender years were some excuse for her lapse, at least in the eyes of those who had no personal interest in whether she was a good girl or not; yet those who knew just how clever and intelligent she was didn't put her sin down to ignorance but to her pertness and to the natural propensity of her sex for reckless impetuosity.

'Once Leandra had been locked away, Anselmo lost his sight – or at least was left with nothing to look at that could give him any joy; and I was plunged into darkness – for there was no light to guide me towards any pleasant goal. Leandra's absence increased our sorrow, wore away at our patience, made us curse the finery of the soldier and abominate the negligence of Leandra's father. In the end Anselmo and I agreed to leave the village and come to this valley, where he grazes a large flock of his sheep and I pasture a great herd of my goats, and we spend our time among these trees relieving our passions by together singing the praises or dispraises of the lovely Leandra and separately sighing and confiding our complaints to heaven. Many of Leandra's other suitors have copied us and have come to these rugged mountains with their animals, and there are so many of them that anyone would think the place has been converted into the pastoral Arcadia,² teeming with shepherds and goatherds and their folds, and there's no part of it where the name of the lovely Leandra can't be heard. This man fulminates against her and calls her flighty, fickle and wanton; that man condemns her forwardness and levity; a third absolves and pardons her, a fourth judges and condemns her; another praises her beauty, another rails at her wicked ways, and in short they all vilify her, and they all adore her, and the madness that affects them all is so great that there are those who bewail her disdain without ever having spoken to her, and others who complain of being afflicted by the raging disease of jealousy, when she can never have made anyone jealous because, as I said, her sin was discovered before anyone knew where her fancies lay. There's not a hollow in a rock, or the bank of a stream, or a shade under a tree that isn't taken up by some shepherd telling the air all about his misfortunes; wherever an echo can sound it repeats Leandra's name: "Leandra" the mountains ring out, "Leandra" murmur the streams, and Leandra has us all in suspense and under her spell, hoping against hope and fearing without knowing what it is that we fear.

'Among all these lunatics, the one who shows the least and at the same time the most sense is my rival Anselmo, who has so much to complain about yet only complains of her absence; and to the sound of his fiddle, which he plays admirably, he voices his laments in verses that display his great ability. I take an easier and, I think, the wisest course, which is to revile women's fickleness, their inconstancy, their double-dealing, their worthless promises, their broken faith and, in short, their lack of judgement in bestowing their affections. And this is the explanation, gentlemen, of the way in which I spoke to this goat earlier: since she's a female I don't have a very high opinion of her, even though she's the best goat in my herd.

'This is the story that I promised to tell you; and if I've been long-winded in the telling I shan't give you short shrift in hospitality – my fold isn't far away, and there I have fresh milk, delicious cheese and all kinds of ripe fruit no less pleasing to the eye than to the palate.'

CHAPTER LII

※

About Don Quixote's fight with the goatherd, and the singular adventure of the penitents, which he brought to a happy conclusion by the sweat of his brow

The goatherd's tale delighted all those who heard it, particularly the canon, who paid special attention to the way in which he told it, making him seem less like a rustic herdsman than a sharp-witted courtier; and so the canon declared that the priest had been quite right to say that mountains breed scholars. They all offered Eugenio their services, but the one who did so with the most expansive generosity was Don Quixote, who said:

'In truth, brother goatherd, if I were in a position to be able to embark on another adventure, I should without a moment's delay set about bringing yours to a happy conclusion; for I should rescue Leandra from the convent (where she is most certainly being held against her will) in spite of the abbess and of anybody else who attempted to prevent me, and I should place her in your hands so that you could deal with her exactly as you wished, always obeying, however, the laws of chivalry, which command that no mischief whatsoever be done to any damsel; yet I trust that by the grace of our Lord God the powers of an evil enchanter are not so great that they cannot be overridden by those of another better-disposed one, and I promise to give you all my assistance as soon as that should come about, as required by my profession, which is none other than to succour the needy and helpless.'

The goatherd looked at Don Quixote, and finding him such a sorry sight he asked the barber – who was sitting next to him – in some bewilderment:

'Who is this man, sir, that cuts such a figure and speaks in such a way?'

'Who should he be,' answered the barber, 'but the famous Don Quixote de la Mancha, the redresser of injuries, the righter of wrongs, the protector of damsels, the terror of giants and the victor in battles?'

'That sounds to me,' replied the goatherd, 'like what you read in books about knights errant, who used to do all those things you said this man does, but it's my opinion that either you're joking or some of the rooms in this character's upper storey are empty.'

'You are a villainous wretch,' Don Quixote burst out, 'and you are the one who is empty and a fool, and I am fuller than the whore of a bitch who bore you ever was.'

And with these words he snatched up a loaf and hurled it at the goatherd's face with such furious force that he flattened his nose; and the goatherd, who couldn't take a jest and found himself being assaulted in earnest, disregarded the carpet and the tablecloths and all the people who were eating, and leapt upon Don Quixote, seized him by the throat with both hands and wouldn't have hesitated to throttle him if Sancho Panza hadn't rushed over, grabbed the goatherd by the shoulders and flung him down on the table, breaking plates, smashing cups and overturning and scattering everything else. As soon as Don Quixote found himself free he jumped on top of the goatherd, who, bloody-faced and pounded by Sancho's feet, was crawling over the tablecloths in search of a knife with which to take some gory revenge, but the canon and the priest were making sure this couldn't happen; and then the barber intervened to enable the goatherd to climb on top of Don Quixote, at whom he flailed away until as much blood was pouring from the poor knight's face as from his own. The canon and the priest were laughing fit to burst, the peace-officers were jumping with joy, everyone was cheering the two men on as dogs are cheered on when they're fighting; only Sancho Panza was in despair, because he couldn't wriggle free of the grasp of one of the canon's servants who was preventing him from going to help his master.

In short, just when everyone was enjoying this festival of fun, except the two battered, scratching warriors, they heard a trumpet call, so mournful that it made them all turn towards where it seemed to be coming from; but the man who was most affected by the sound was Don Quixote who, although he was under the goatherd, much against his will and most severely mauled, said to him:

'Brother devil, for that is what you must be, since you have found the resolve and the strength to overpower me: I request that we agree on a truce for just one hour, because the sorrowful sound of that trumpet which we can hear appears to be summoning me to a new adventure.'

The goatherd, who by now was tired of thumping and being thumped, climbed off without more ado, and Don Quixote stood up and looked with the others in the direction of the sounds, and as he did so a horde of men dressed as penitents in white suddenly came into sight as they descended one of the sides of the valley. What had happened was that the clouds had withheld their moisture from the earth that year, and processions, public prayers and acts of penitence were being organized in all the villages in the area to entreat God to open the hands of his mercy and send down some rain; and to this end the people from a nearby village were coming in a procession to a holy chapel on one side of the valley. Don Quixote, seeing the processionists' strange dress, and not pausing to remember that he must have seen such penitents many times before, imagined that this was the subject for an adventure, and that it was his task alone, as a knight errant, to undertake it; and he was further confirmed in this belief when he saw a holy image swathed in mourning that they were carrying, and thought it was some eminent lady whom those arrant and insolent knaves were bearing off against her will; and no sooner had this idea found its way into his head than he charged over to where Rocinante was grazing, unhooked both the horse's bit and his own shield from the pommel, put the bit in its place in the twinkling of an eye, told Sancho to give him his sword, mounted Rocinante, took up his shield and cried to all present:

'And now, O doughty company, you shall perceive how important it is that knights who profess the order of knight-errantry should exist in the world; now, I say, you shall perceive, in the freeing of that good lady who is being carried away captive, whether or not knights errant are worthy of esteem.'

And as he said this he put thighs to Rocinante, because he wasn't wearing any spurs, and at a canter, because we don't read anywhere in this true history that Rocinante ever ventured on a full gallop, he advanced on the penitents, despite all the efforts of the priest and the canon and the barber to stop him; but it was impossible, and Sancho couldn't do anything to dissuade him, either, by yelling:

'What are you going to do now, Don Quixote sir? What demons have you got inside your breast egging you on against our holy Catholic faith? I'll be damned – look, look, that's a penitents' procession, and that lady they're carrying on the platform is the blessed image of the immaculate Virgin. Be careful, sir, what you're doing – this time I'm really sure it isn't what you think it is.'

But Sancho laboured in vain, because his master was so set on confronting the men in white and freeing the lady in black that he didn't hear a word; and even if he had heard one he wouldn't have turned back, not if it had been the King himself ordering him. So on he cantered towards the procession and then he halted Rocinante, who was by now ready to take a rest, and he cried in a hoarse and agitated voice:

'O you who hide your faces, perchance because you are evil: pay attention and listen to what I have to say to you.'

The first to stop were the men carrying the image, and one of the four priests chanting the litanies took one look at Don Quixote's strange figure, Rocinante's thinness and other ludicrous aspects of the knight's appearance, and replied with the words:

'If you want to say something to us, my good man, say it quickly, because our brethren here are tearing their flesh to shreds, and we cannot and must not stop to listen to anything unless it's brief enough to be said in a couple of words.'

'I shall say it all in one word,' replied Don Quixote, 'and it is this: you must at this very instant set free that beautiful lady, whose tears and sorrowful face are clear proof that you are bearing her off against her will and that you have done her some very great mischief; and I, who came into this world to redress such injuries, will not permit you to take one step forward unless you give her the liberty that she desires and deserves.'

These words made all those who heard them realize that Don Quixote must be some madman, and they burst into hearty laughter, which was like pouring gunpowder on to the fire of Don Quixote's wrath: without another word he drew his sword and charged at the platform. One of the men carrying it left his companions holding it up, came out to meet Don Quixote brandishing the forked prop on which he helped to support it whenever they paused for a rest, used this prop to ward off a mighty sword-stroke that the knight aimed at him and that cut it in two and then, with the part left in his hand, delivered such a blow to the shoulder of his enemy's sword arm, which the shield couldn't protect against brute strength, that poor Don Quixote tumbled to the ground in dire straits. Sancho Panza, who came puffing after his master, saw him fall and cried out to his demolisher not to hit him again, he was only a poor enchanted knight who'd never done anyone any harm in all the days of his born life. But what stopped the peasant wasn't Sancho's shouts but seeing that Don Quixote wasn't stirring, not so much as a hand or a foot; and so, in the belief that he'd killed him, he hoisted his tunic up to his waist and ran away across the fields like a deer.

And now Don Quixote's companions arrived on the scene, as did the other processionists, who saw their opponents come running up with the peace-officers clutching their crossbows, feared the worst and swarmed around the holy image with their hoods raised from their faces, brandishing their scourges while the priests wielded their great processional candlesticks, awaiting the assault in the determination to defend themselves and even attack their assailants if they could; but fortune treated them better than they'd thought it would, because all Sancho did was to throw himself upon his master's body and pour over him the most piteous and laughable lament ever heard, in the belief that he was dead. Our priest was recognized by one of the priests in the procession, and this calmed the fears that had developed in both squadrons. The first priest gave the second one a brief account of Don Quixote, and then he went with the throng of penitents to see whether the poor knight was dead, and they all heard Sancho Panza saying, with tears in his eyes:

'O flower of chivalry, whose well-spent life just one thump with a cudgel has done for! O pride of your family, honour and glory of all La Mancha and all the world – now that you've gone from it, it'll fill up with evil-doers who won't be frightened of being punished for their wicked ways! O you who were more open-handed than all the Alexanders, because for only eight months' service you said you'd give me the best island that ever had the sea all round it! O you who were humble to the haughty and haughty to the humble, tackler of dangers, taker of insults, in love without a cause, imitator of the good, scourge of the wicked, enemy of villains – in a word, knight errant, and that says it all!'

Sancho's cries and groans revived Don Quixote, and what he first said was:

'He who lives absent from you, sweetest Dulcinea, is subject to even greater calamities than this. Help me, dear Sancho, to climb on to the enchanted cart: I am no longer in any fit state to burden Rocinante's saddle, for this shoulder of mine has been smashed to smithereens.'

'I'll do that with a will, sir,' replied Sancho, 'and let's go back to our village with these gentlemen, who only want what's best for you, and there we'll work out a way to make another sally that'll bring us more profit and renown.'

'You are speaking sound sense,' replied Don Quixote, 'and it will be wise indeed to wait for the presently prevailing malign influence of the stars to dissipate.'

The canon and the priest and the barber told him that he would be quite right to do as he'd said; and so, having been most wonderfully entertained by Sancho Panza's absurdities, they put Don Quixote back on the cart. The religious procession formed up again, and went on its way. The goatherd said goodbye to everyone. The peace-officers refused to go any further, and the priest paid them what he owed them. The canon asked the priest to let him know what happened to Don Quixote, whether he recovered from his madness or continued in the same state, and then begged their leave to continue his journey.

And so the party split up and each followed his own road, leaving the priest and the barber, Don Quixote and Panza and the good Rocinante, as patient as his master in the face of everything he'd undergone. The carter yoked his oxen, put Don Quixote on top of a truss of hay, followed with his usual sedateness the route indicated by the priest; and six days later they reached their village, which they entered at noon, and as it happened to be a Sunday everybody was in the square, through the middle of which the cart trundled on its way. Everyone went over to see what was in the cart, and when they recognized their neighbour they were astonished, and a lad ran to tell the housekeeper and the niece that their master and uncle had come back, thin and pale, and lying on top of a pile of hay in an ox-cart. It was pitiful to hear the cries these two good ladies let loose, the slaps they gave themselves, the curses they again directed at those damned books of chivalry; all of which they renewed when they saw Don Quixote coming in through the door.

At the news of Don Quixote's arrival Sancho Panza's wife hurried to his house, because she had discovered that her husband had gone away with him as his squire, and when she saw Sancho the first thing she asked was whether the ass was well. Sancho replied that the ass was better than its master was.

'Thanks be to God for his great goodness to me,' she replied. 'And now tell me, husband, what have you got out of all this squiring of yours? How many fine skirts have you brought back for me? How many pairs of shoes for your children?'

'I haven't brought any of all that, wife,' said Sancho. 'But I've got other stuff that's much more special and important.'

'I'm very pleased to hear it, too,' his wife replied. 'Now show me this stuff that's so much more important and special, husband – I'd love to see it to cheer up this heart of mine that's been so sad and out of sorts all these ages that you've been away.'

'I'll let you see it when we get home,' said Panza, 'and meantime you can count yourself lucky, because if it's God's will for us to go off again in search of adventures you'll soon see me made an earl or the governor of an island, and not any old island either but the very best island there is.'

'May heaven grant it, husband, we need it badly enough. But tell me, what's all this about islands? I don't understand you.'

'Honey wasn't made for the mouths of asses,' Sancho retorted. 'You'll see in due course, wife, and you'll get a surprise, I can tell you, when you hear all your vassals calling you your ladyship.'

'What's this you're saying, Sancho, about ladyships, islands and vassals?' replied Juana Panza, for this was the name of Sancho's wife, not that they were blood relations but because it's the custom in La Mancha for women to take their husbands' surnames.

'Don't you be in such a hurry, Juana, to know about all these things; I'm telling you the truth, and that's enough for you, so shut up. All I will say, since I'm on the subject, is that there's nothing better in life than being an honest man who's the squire of a knight errant who goes in search of adventures. It is true that most of the adventures you find don't turn out as well as what you'd like them to, because out of a hundred you come across ninety-nine usually go skew-whiff. I know that from experience, because I've ended up blanket-tossed in some and beaten black and blue in others. But in spite of all that, it's great to be waiting to see what's going to happen next as you ride across mountains, explore forests, climb crags, visit castles and put up at inns as and when you like, and not the devil a farthing to pay.'

While Sancho Panza and his wife Juana Panza chatted away like this, Don Quixote's housekeeper and niece welcomed their master, undressed him and laid him on his ancient bed. He was peering at them through unfocused eyes, and couldn't fathom where on earth he was. The priest told the niece to make sure to pamper her uncle and have him watched so that he didn't escape again, and described what they'd had to do to bring him back home. And then the two women again raised the roof with their outcry; again they renewed their cursing of the books of chivalry; again they implored heaven to cast the authors of all those lies and absurdities into the depths of the bottomless pit. All this left them bewildered and fearful that as soon as their master and uncle felt a little better they'd lose him again; and that was indeed what happened.

But although the author of this history has searched with the most meticulous care for an account of the deeds performed by Don Quixote during his third sally, he hasn't been able to find any information about them, not at least in writings by reputable authors; tradition alone has preserved, in the memory of La Mancha, the belief that the third time Don Quixote left home he went to Saragossa, where he took part in some famous jousts and underwent experiences worthy of his courage and intelligence. But the author could not discover any information about how Don Quixote met his end, nor would he ever have even known about it if good fortune had not sent him an aged doctor who had in his possession a lead casket which, he said, had been found among the foundations of an old, ruined chapel that was being rebuilt. In this casket there were some parchments with texts written in Roman letters but in Castilian verse, describing many of his exploits and giving accounts of Dulcinea del Toboso's beauty, Rocinante's looks, Sancho Panza's loyalty and Don Quixote's grave, in various epitaphs and eulogies about his life and works. And those that could be read and understood have been set down here by the trustworthy author of this original and matchless history, who only asks from his readers, in recompense for the immense trouble that he has taken to scrutinize and explore all the archives in La Mancha so as to be able to bring it to the light of day, that they give it the same credit that people of good sense give to books of chivalry, so highly prized by all; and this will make him feel well rewarded and satisfied, and encourage him to search out other histories, perhaps less authentic than this one but no less ingenious or entertaining.

The first words written on the parchment found in the lead casket were these:

THE ACADEMICIANS OF ARGAMASILLA, A VILLAGE IN LA MANCHA, DURING THE LIFE AND DEATH OF THE BRAVE DON QUIXOTE DE LA MANCHA[1]

HOC SCRIPSERUNT[2]

SAMBO, A MEMBER OF THE ACADEMY OF ARGAMASILLA, TO THE GRAVE OF DON QUIXOTE

Epitaph

This thunderpate who decked La Mancha's plain
With trophies more than Jason gave to Crete; [3]
This solid judgement of a weathervane
– And spindly, too, where potency was meet;
    This arm so lengthened by its own vast might,

Extending to Gaeta from Cathay; [4]
This ugliest and wisest muse to write
A verse on sheet of bronze or slab of clay;
  This man who left Amadis in his wake,
And thought but little of proud Galaor;
Who even made brave Belianis quake
And, faced by love and valour, stand in awe:
He who on Rocinante erring went
Lies here, beneath this cold stone monument.

FLUNKEY,
A MEMBER OF THE ACADEMY OF ARGAMASILLA

IN LAUDEM DULCINEAE DEL TOBOSO

SONNET

  She whom you gaze on here, this moon-faced dame,
Big-breasted and of energetic mien,
Was once Don Quixote de la Mancha's flame,
Fair Dulcinea, El Toboso's Queen.
  For her alone he wandered far and wide
Across Sierra Morena (that Brown Hill),
To Montiel Plain, and grassy fields beside
Aranjuez, all on foot, and tired, and ill.
  The fault was Rocinante's. O black doom
Of this Manchegan dame and errant knight
Unconquered, in his prime, her tender bloom!
For death destroyed her beauty at its height
And, though hard bronze records his every deed,
He never from love's wrath and wiles was freed.

FLIGHTY,
A WISE MEMBER OF THE ACADEMY OF
ARGAMASILLA, IN PRAISE OF ROCINANTE,
DON QUIXOTE DE LA MANCHA'S HORSE

SONNET

Upon his proud and diamond-studded throne,
Where mighty Mars once pressed his bloody heel,
The hero from La Mancha sits alone
And brandishes his flag with frenzied zeal.

He hangs up all his armour, hangs his swords
With which he used to ravage, hack and hew:
Unprecedented deeds! But Art accords
To champions that are new a style that's new.

And if Amadis is the pride of Gaul
And his brave sons have heightened Greece's fame,
Bellona now crowns Quixote in her hall
And, more than either, Mancha loves his name.
Forgotten, never: even Rocinante
Makes Brillador's and Bayard's verve ⁵ seem scanty.

DECEIVER,
AN ARGAMASILLAN ACADEMICIAN,
TO SANCHO PANZA

SONNET

Here Sancho Panza lies, in body small,
In courage great – a miracle most rare;
The simplest and most guileless squire of all
That ever trod this earth, I vow and swear.

A count or earl he surely would have been,
Had not this wicked world conspired, alas,
To wound him with its insolence and mean
Contempt. It will not even spare an ass,

On which he rode (forgive this lowly word),
A meek, mild squire who plodded on behind
The mild steed Rocinante and his lord.
How vain are all the hopes of humankind!
How sweet our promises of comfort seem,
And yet they end in shadow, smoke and dream!

HOBGOBLIN,
A MEMBER OF THE ARGAMASILLA ACADEMY,
ON THE GRAVE OF DON QUIXOTE

Epitaph

Here lies a knight, a man of pluck,
Rich in thumpings, poor in luck,
Who, perched on Rocinante's back,
Rode up this path and down that track.
And Sancho Panza is the dolt
Who lies beside him in this vault:
The loyallest man in our empire
Who ever earned the name of squire.

DING-DONG,
A MEMBER OF THE ARGAMASILLA ACADEMY,
ON THE GRAVE OF DULCINEA DEL TOBOSO

Epitaph

Fair Dulcinea here is laid
And though she was a meaty maid
Death turned her into dust and clay
In his horrendous, dreadful way.
Of a true breed she surely came,
She was the great Don Quixote's flame,
She wore with style a lady's gown:
The glory of Toboso town.

These were the verses that were legible; since the others were worm-eaten, they were handed to an academician for him to decipher. It is reported that he has done so, after long vigils and much toil, and that he intends to publish them, as we await Don Quixote's third sally.

Forsi altro canterà con miglior plectio.[6]

FINIS

NOTES

PART I

PROLOGUE

1. *St Thomases*: St Thomas Aquinas (1225–74), the great Italian philosopher and theologian.

2. *Xenophon and Zoilus or Zeuxis*: The Greek historian, writer and military leader (*c.* 435–*c.* 354 BC); the Greek grammarian (*c.* 400–*c.* 320 BC) chiefly known for the acerbity of his attacks on Homer; and the Greek painter who flourished in the late fifth century BC.

3. *Prester John . . . Trebizond*: Legendary medieval Christian king of Asia, and one of the four parts into which the Byzantine Empire was divided in the early thirteenth century, often mentioned in books of chivalry; it fell to the Turks in 1461.

4. *Non . . . venditur auro*: 'Freedom should not be sold for all the gold in the world', from the version by Walter Anglicus (twelfth century) of Aesop's fable of the dog and the wolf.

5. *Pallida . . . Regumque turres*: 'Pale Death with impartial foot knocks at the doors of poor men's hovels and of kings' palaces' (Horace, *Odes*, I, 4b).

6. *Ego . . . diligite inimicos vestros*: 'But I say unto you, Love your enemies' (Matthew 5. 44). (Here and below the Authorized Version is quoted.)

7. *De . . . cogitationes malae*: 'Out of the heart proceed evil thoughts' (Matthew 15. 19).

8. *Donec . . . solus eris*: 'When you are happy you have many friends, but if the weather becomes cloudy you are alone' (Ovid, *Tristia*, I, 9). Cervantes replaces Ovid's (not Cato's) *sospes* with its synonym *felix*, possibly a sly allusion to the

dramatist Lope Félix de Vega Carpio, known as Lope de Vega (1562–1635), whom he attacks in this prologue and elsewhere (see note 21 below).

9. *where you'll find it written*: 1 Samuel 17. The passage is in the Book of Kings in the Vulgate, the Latin Bible of the Roman Catholic Church.

10. *Cacus*: Legendary son of Vulcan, who stole oxen from Hercules and was killed by him.

11. *Bishop . . . and Flora*: In one of his *Epístolas familiares*, Antonio de Guevara, the Bishop of Mondoñedo (1480–1545), tells the story of these three ladies.

12. *Medea . . . Circe*: Medea, the legendary enchantress who helped Jason to escape with the Golden Fleece by killing the boy Apsyrtus and cutting his body into pieces, and later caused various other gory deaths (Ovid, *Metamorphoses*, VII). Calypso, the legendary daughter of Atlas who lived on the island of Ogygia and became Odysseus's mistress after he was wrecked there (Homer, *Odyssey*, X). Circe, the sorceress who lived on the island of Aeaea and became Odysseus's mistress, and turned his men into pigs, after he was cast ashore there (Virgil, *Aeneid*, VII).

13. *a thousand Alexanders*: In Plutarch's *Parallel Lives*. Alexander the Great (356–323 BC), the Macedonian warrior and empire-builder.

14. *Leone Ebreo . . . full measure*: Real name is Judah Abarbanel (c. 1460–c. 1521); his seminal *Dialoghi d'Amore* (1535) expounds the neoplatonic theory of love.

15. *On the Love of God*: Cristóbal de Fonseca, *Tratado del amor de Dios* (1592).

16. *St Basil . . . Cicero*: An early Doctor of the Church (c. 330–79), and the famous Roman statesman, orator and writer (106–43 BC).

17. *the Plain of Montiel*: The plain, in the present-day provinces of Ciudad Real and Albacete, on which Don Quixote's village stands.

18. *Urganda the Unknowable*: Benevolent enchantress, the friend of the famous knight Amadis of Gaul, who was the hero of the most famous and influential Spanish romance of chivalry, immensely popular throughout Europe in the sixteenth century. The earliest known edition of *Amadís de Gaula*, a version by Garci Rodríguez de Montalvo, dates from 1508. Urganda is unknowable because of her frequent self-transformations.

These verses are in a form that enjoyed some transitory popularity in Spain at the time of writing, with the last unstressed syllable of each line omitted, for the reader to fill it in (*versos de cabo roto*). Only the final stressed vowels rhyme, in the pattern abbaaccddc (the *décima*).

19. *In Béjar*: Cervantes dedicated Part I of *Don Quixote* to the Duke of Béjar.

20. *Ladies and arms, loves and knights e—*: The opening line of *Orlando Furioso* (1532), a reworking of the Charlemagne legends, by Ludovico Ariosto (1474–1533).

21. *on your fine scu—*: Lope de Vega, with whom Cervantes was not on good terms, was fond of including elaborate shields of arms in the frontispieces of his books, as well as prefacing them with arrays of complimentary sonnets and including many shows of erudition. See also n. 8 above.

22. *Álvaro de Lu— . . . Dame Fortune's stu—*: Don Álvaro de Luna (1390–1453), the favourite of Juan II, held absolute power at court for thirty years until he was disgraced and beheaded. After Hannibal saw his immense power collapse he killed himself in 183 BC. Francis I of France was captured by the Spaniards at the battle of Pavia (1525), and held captive in Spain.

23. *Juan Lati—*: Juan Latino (d. *c.* 1573), humanist and son of an African slave.

24. *Peña Pobre's rugged face*: A desolate island to which Amadis retreated after a tiff with his lady Oriana.

25. *so long . . . in the fourth sphere*: In terms of Greek mythology, so long as the sun comes out each day. The universe was believed to consist of a number of concentric spheres.

26. *Sir Belianis of Greece*: Irascible protagonist of the romance of chivalry *Don Belianís de Grecia* (1547 and 1579), by Jerónimo Fernández.

27. *The Lady Oriana*: Mistress and later secret wife of Amadis of Gaul, who lived in Miraflores Palace, two leagues from London, where she became pregnant and shunned all company.

28. *Villadiego . . . is divi—*: In Act XII of Fernando de Rojas's *Tragicomedia de Calisto y Melibea* (1502), popularly known as *La Celestina*, the cowardly servant Sempronio tells his colleague Pármeno to 'put on Villadiego's breeches', in other words to flee, a proverbial expression referring to some now lost comic tale about a man who fled in such a hurry that he did not stop to put his breeches on.

29. *the great Babie—*: Babieca was the horse of the legendary eleventh-century Castilian hero Rodrigo Díaz de Vivar, El Cid, immortalized in the epic *Poema de mio Cid* (1207?).

30. *Lazari— . . . to his blind ma—*: The first picaresque novel, *La vida de Lazarillo de Tormes* (1554), by an unknown author; in the first chapter Lazarillo's wary blind master clutches the jar of wine, but the boy uses a straw to drink some.

31. *harried By sweet Angelica*: In Ariosto's *Orlando Furioso*, Angelica, the Princess of Cathay, sends the hero mad, by her preference for the young Moor Medoro.

32. *Moor and . . . Scythian foe*: Moors and Scythians were legendary for their fierceness in battle.

33. *The Knight of Phoebus*: One of the protagonists of the chivalry romance *Espejo de príncipes y caballeros* (1555), by Diego Ortúñez de Calahorra. In it, Claridiana is the daughter of the Emperor of Trebizond.

34. *Solisdán*: Not found in any of the chivalry books, and presumably Cervantes's invention.

CHAPTER I

1. *as many of them as he could find*: The popularity of romances of chivalry and other prose fiction was considered a very grave social and moral problem. A petition to Charles I and V at the Valladolid parliament of 1555 complains about the damage done to 'men, youths and girls and other kinds of people' by 'books of lies and nonsense like Amadis and all its imitations', because youngsters of both sexes become so absorbed in these fictional accounts of deeds of arms and love that 'when something similar presents itself to them in real life they give themselves over to it in a more unbridled way than if they had not read about it'. The petitioner requested that such books be burned, so that young people would be 'left with no alternative but to read religious books to edify their souls and reform their bodies'. (*Cortes de los antiguos reinos de León y de Castilla* (Madrid: Real Academia de la Historia, 1903), V, pp. 687–8.) The king took the petition seriously, replying that a decree had been drawn up to remedy the problem and would soon be published. What is curious is that Cervantes was behind the times (or maybe this is part of the joke): by the early seventeenth century the romances of chivalry were no longer fashionable or therefore seen as a threat. And it was young women, not old men like Don Quixote, who had been regarded as being most at risk from their influence.

2. *Feliciano de Silva*: Notorious hack (1492?–1558?), who wrote various romances of chivalry. See note 4.

3. *Sigüenza . . . Palmerin of England*: A very small minor university 120 kilometres north-east of Madrid, and Palmerin of England is the protagonist of the *Libro del muy esforzado caballero Palmerín de Inglaterra* (1547), the Spanish translation of a Portuguese chivalry romance by Francisco de Moraes Cabral.

4. *Knight of the Burning Sword*: Amadis of Greece, the protagonist of one of de Silva's efforts, *The Ninth Book of Amadis of Gaul* (1530).

5. *Bernardo del Carpio . . . with a bear-hug*: Bernardo del Carpio was a legendary Castilian hero, who, in a Spanish continuation (1555) of Ariosto's *Orlando Furioso* by Nicolás Espinosa, defeats Roland at Roncesvalles. Antaeus, in Greek legend, was a Libyan giant, the son of Poseidon, invincible at wrestling until overcome by Hercules.

6. *giant Morgante . . . well-mannered*: The protagonist of the poem *Morgante maggiore* by Luigi Pulci (1432–84), in which he is converted to Christianity by Roland.

7. *Reynald of Montalban*: Hero of French epic and Spanish ballads. Spanish legend has him participate in the events at Roncesvalles.

8. *the traitor Ganelon in the dust*: According to Carolingian legend, he caused the disaster at Roncesvalles.

9. *Gonella's . . . ossa fuit*: Pietro Gonella was the Marquis of Ferrara's court jester in the fifteenth century, often appearing in sixteenth-century joke-books. The Latin means 'was all skin and bone' (Plautus, *Aulularia*, III, 6, 28).

10. *Caraculiambro*: Strong overtones of 'Arse-face'.

CHAPTER II

1. *My arms . . . the bloody fray*: Opening lines of a popular Spanish ballad of the time. The innkeeper completes the stanza.

2. *the Playa district of Sanlúcar*: A notorious centre of Spanish picaresque life.

3. *And never . . . whose name*: Opening lines of a popular Spanish ballad about Lancelot, with appropriate alterations.

CHAPTER III

1. *Percheles . . . and Ventillas in Toledo*: List of disreputable districts in various Spanish towns and cities.

2. *Doña Tolosa*: Only members of the aristocracy were entitled to affix the titles 'Don' and 'Doña' to their names. Quixote himself, as a mere hidalgo, has no business to do so, and drops the title as soon as he regains his sanity. In Part II, chapter XVI, Diego de Miranda is another pompous hidalgo who calls himself 'Don'.

CHAPTER IV

1. *You dare to use that word in my presence*: The mention of the verb 'to lie' was considered an insult not just to the one accused but to any high-ranking person who was present, particularly if he had taken the side of the accused.

2. *St Bartholomew*: Apostle said to have been flayed alive in Armenia.

3. *Guadarrama spindle*: The Sierra de Guadarrama is a mountain range to the north of Madrid. Nobody has been able to explain why Don Quixote claims that spindles made there are particularly straight.

CHAPTER V

1. *the story of Baldwin . . . forest*: Don Quixote again remembers a popular Spanish ballad rather than a chivalry book. It relates the killing by Carloto, Charlemagne's son, of the Marquis de Mantua's nephew Baldwin.

2. *Diana*: The first pastoral romance, written in Spanish by its Portuguese author, and published in 1558 or 1559.

3. *the Twelve Peers . . . the Nine Worthies as well*: The Twelve Peers of France were a body of the most famous knights at the court of Charlemagne. The Nine Worthies were three Christians (King Arthur, Charlemagne and Godfrey of Bouillon), three Jews (Joshua, David and Judas Maccabeus) and three Gentiles (Alexander, Hector and Julius Caesar).

4. *Barabbas*: The robber whom Pilate released from prison to the Jews instead of Christ (John 18. 40), traditionally regarded as hardly less evil than the devil himself.

5. *the famous sage Squiffy*: The enchanter Alquife is the husband of Urganda the Unknowable in *Amadis of Gaul*.

CHAPTER VI

1. *hyssop*: A small bushy aromatic herb used for sprinkling holy water.

2. *the very first chivalry romance . . . Spain*: Although it was the most influential one, *Amadis* (see Prologue, note 18) was not the first, which was *Tirant lo Blanc* (see note 14).

3. *The Exploits of Esplandian*: *Las sergas de Esplandián*, also by Garci Rodríguez de Montalvo, and published in 1510.

4. *of that same family*: The success of *Amadis of Gaul* provoked many continuations by other hands.

5. *Don Olivante de Laura*: (1564) by Antonio de Torquemada. His *Jardín de flores curiosas* was published in 1570.

6. *Florismarte of Hyrcania*: *Primera parte de la grande historia del muy animoso y esforzado príncipe Felixmarte de Yrcania y de su estraño nascimiento* (1556) by Melchior de Ortega. The protagonist, called both Florismarte and Felixmarte, is born on a mountain.

7. *The Knight Platir*: *Crónica del muy valiente y esforzado caballero Platir, hijo del Emperador Primaleón* (1533), its author unidentified.

8. *The Knight of the Cross*: Probably *La Crónica de Lepolemo, llamado el Caballero de la Cruz, compuesta en arábigo por Xartón y trasladada en castellano por Alonso de Salazar* (1521). The claim that his book had been 'composed in Arabic . . . and translated into Castilian' could have given Cervantes the idea for the developments in chapter IX.

9. *The Mirror of Chivalry . . . true historian Turpin*: *Primera, segunda y tercera parte de Orlando Enamorado. Espejo de Caballerías* (1586), a prose adaptation of *Orlando Innamorato*, by Matteo Boiardo (1441–94), which inspired Ariosto to write *Orlando Furioso*. Turpin was Archbishop of Rheims in the eighth century, and a prominent figure in the French epics about Charlemagne. He was claimed to be the author of the twelfth-century Latin chronicle about the exploits of Charlemagne and Roland that came to be known as the pseudo Turpin.

10. *turning it into Castilian*: The first of the sixteenth-century Spanish translations of *Orlando Furioso* was by Captain Jerónimo de Urrea, published in 1549.

11. *Bernardo del Carpio*: *Historia de las hazañas y hechos del invencible caballero Bernardo del Carpio* (1585), by Agustín Alonso: see also chapter I, note 5.

12. *Roncesvalles*: *El verdadero suceso de la famosa batalla de Roncesvalles* (1555), by Francisco Garrido Villena.

13. *Palmerin of Oliva*: *Libro del famoso y muy esforzado caballero Palmerín de Oliva*, the first in this popular series, was published in 1511, and widely believed to have been written by King John II or III of Portugal.

14. *Tirante the White*: *Tirant lo Blanc* (1490), the Catalan romance of chivalry by Johanot Martorell and Johan de Galba, first published in Spanish translation in 1511.

15. *enchanted water*: Lovers with problems went to the enchantress Felicia, who gave them a potion the consumption of which led to new pairings.

16. *the second part . . . Gil Polo*: Continuations of *Diana*: *Segunda parte de la Diana de Jorge de Montemayor* (1564), by Alonso Pérez, and *Diana enamorada* (1564), by Gaspar Gil Polo, of considerable literary quality.

17. *Lofraso, a Sardinian poet*: Another pastoral romance, *Los diez libros de Fortuna de Amor* (1573).

18. *The Shepherd of Iberia . . . The Undeceptions of Jealousy*: Three more pastoral romances: *El pastor de Iberia* (1591), by Bernardo de la Vega; *Primera parte de las ninfas y pastores de Henares* (1587), by Bernardo González de Bobadilla; and *Desengaño de celos* (1586) by Bartolomé López de Enciso. The first is the most recently published book mentioned in this chapter.

19. *The Shepherd of Filida*: *El pastor de Fílida* (1582), by Luis Gálvez de Montalvo.

20. *The Treasury of Divers Poems*: *Tesoro de varias poesías* (1580), by Pedro de Padilla.

21. *López Maldonado's Book of Songs*: *Cancionero* (1586), including two poems by Cervantes. López Maldonado, Padilla and Gálvez de Montalvo were friends of Cervantes.

22. *Galatea . . . Cervantes*: The *Primera parte de la Galatea* (1585), his own pastoral romance; he kept promising a second part, but never produced it.

23. *Araucana . . . Monserrate*: Three works of heroic poetry: *La Araucana* (three parts, 1569–89), *La Austríada* (1584) and *El Monserrate* (1587).

24. *The Tears of Angelica*: *Primera parte de la Angélica* (1586), by Luis Barahona de Soto; it continues the story of Angelica and Medoro from *Orlando Furioso*. The same author's *Acteón* paraphrases Ovid's *Metamorphoses*.

CHAPTER VII

1. *Carolea . . . Luis de Ávila*: The two parts of *La Carolea* (1560), a heroic poem by Jerónimo Sempere about the exploits of Charles I and V; *La Primera y Segunda Parte de El León de España* (1586), a similar poem by Pedro de la Vecilla. Luis de Ávila wrote a factual prose chronicle about Charles's deeds (1584), *Comentarios . . . de la guerra de Alemaña, hecha de Carlos V*, published in Venice in 1548, but no poem; Luis Zapata did, however, write one, *Carlo famoso* (1566).

2. *Frestón*: The enchanter in *Don Belianís de Grecia* is Fristón.

CHAPTER VIII

1. *the giant Briareus*: A Titan in Greek and Roman mythology, Briareus had fifty heads and a hundred arms.

2. *Diego Pérez de Vargas . . . many Moors*: At the battle of Jerez, 1233.

3. *Agrages*: Character in *Amadis of Gaul*, fond of menacing people with these words.

CHAPTER IX

1. *Who go . . . their way*: Probably from some old ballad, now lost. Quoted again in chapter XLIX.

2. *Platir*: The exploits of the hero of *The Knight Platir* are presented as having been recorded by the sage Galtenor.

3. *better and older language*: Hebrew.

4. *Cide Hamete Benengeli*: Cide is a title, meaning 'My Lord'; Hamete is the Spanish

version of the Arabic personal name Hamed, meaning 'he who praises'; and Benengeli is a comic invention suggesting the idea of 'aubergine-eater', via the Spanish *berenjena*, 'aubergine', popularly considered at the time to be the favourite food of the people of Toledo.

5. *Azpetia*: Present-day Azcoitia, in the province of Guipúzcoa.

CHAPTER X

1. *the Holy Brotherhood*: La Santa Hermandad, the rural police, who were invested with the power to judge and punish those they arrested. They had a reputation for cruelty, corruption and cowardice.

2. *the Chaldeans*: In the Old Testament, feared enemies of the Israelites (Jeremiah 32. 28–9, 43. 3).

3. *the Balsam of Fierabras*: In Carolingian legend, a balsam, in which Christ had been embalmed, with miraculous healing properties when drunk. It was stolen in two barrels by the Saracen giant Fierabras when he conquered Rome (in another version, Jerusalem) and later returned to Rome by Charlemagne.

4. *Mambrino's helmet, which cost Sacripante so dear*: In Boiardo's *Orlando Innamorato* (see chapter VI, note 9), Mambrino is a Moorish king whose enchanted helmet Reynald of Montalban wins in battle. In Ariosto's continuation *Orlando Furioso* it is Dardinel, not Sacripante (Angelica's lover), who is defeated and killed by Reynald, thanks to the helmet.

5. *fell upon Albracca to carry off the fair Angelica*: In *Orlando Innamorato*. Agricane besieges the castle of Albracca, where Angelica is being held by her father, with an army of twenty-two hundred thousand knights.

6. *the kingdom of Soliadisa*: There is a Princess Soliadisa in *Clamades y Carmonda* (1562), and a kingdom of Sobradisa in *Amadis of Gaul*.

CHAPTER XI

1. *he that humbleth himself shall be exalted*: Luke 18. 14.

2. *another Cretan labyrinth*: Don Quixote refers to the labyrinth constructed, according to legend, at Knossos in Crete to house the Minotaur.

CHAPTER XII

1. *the mystery plays for Corpus Christi*: *Autos sacramentales*, plays on religious themes, were traditionally performed as part of the celebrations that took place during the week following Corpus Christi (the commemoration of the Eucharist on the Thursday after Easter Sunday).

CHAPTER XIII

1. *Quintañona*: Spanish addition to Arthurian myth.
2. *Let no man . . . their lord*: Ariosto, *Orlando Furioso*, canto 24.
3. *Augustus Caesar . . . Mantuan poet ordered in his will*: Virgil is said to have ordered his *Aeneid* to be burned, because he had not been able to perfect it. Augustus Caesar refused to heed Virgil's will, and ordered the poem to be published.

CHAPTER XIV

1. *the much-envied owl*: In popular belief, birds of prey attacked owls' eyes out of envy for their size and beauty.
2. *Father Tagus' banks . . . Betis'*: The Tagus, rising in the mountains of eastern Spain and reaching the Atlantic near Lisbon, is the longest river in the Iberian peninsula; Betis is the Roman name for the Guadalquivir, the great Andalusian river that flows by Cordoba and Seville, through the Tartesian plains, to reach the Atlantic near Cadiz.
3. *Tantalus . . . you sisters toiling night and day*: The Danaids, like Tantalus, Sisyphus, Tityus and Ixion, were figures from classical mythology, each with his or her own special torment in Hades. The Danaids had to fill a leaky jar with water.
4. *three-faced guardian of the dreadful gate*: Cerberus, the monstrous watchdog with three heads, who stood guard over the gate to hell.
5. *ride roughshod . . . her father Tarquin*: Tullia's father, over whom she drove her chariot, was Servius Tullius, not Tarquin, who was her husband.

CHAPTER XV

1. *after the Knight of the Sun had been caught in a trap*: This curious incident is Don Quixote's creation. It is not narrated in any of the romances of chivalry about the Knight of the Sun.

2. *Silenus, the tutor . . . on a handsome ass*: Bacchus's tutor rode into the Thebes in Boeotia, not the Thebes in Egypt (the city of the hundred gates).

CHAPTER XVI

1. *an Asturian lass*: Asturias is a region in north-west Spain, whose inhabitants had in earlier times a reputation for being wild and uncouth.

2. *muleteers of Arévalo*: Most muleteers were Moriscos. It is not known why a special mention is made here of Arévalo, a town near Ávila, in central Spain.

3. *Tablante de Ricamonte . . . deeds of Count Tomillas*: *La corónica de los nobles caballeros Tablante de Ricamonte y de Jofre hijo del conde Donason* (1513), a translation of a French chivalry romance; and *Historia de Enrique Fi de Oliva* (1498), a version of a French epic poem, in which Count Tomillas is a secondary character.

CHAPTER XVII

1. *in the Vale of Staffs*: The narrator refers to the beating by the men from Yanguas by quoting from an old ballad about the Cid.

2. *the Heria quarter in Seville*: Places of ill repute.

CHAPTER XVIII

1. *the great island of Taprobana*: Sri Lanka. Alifanfarón and most of the other warriors are Don Quixote's inventions, as well as some of the places that they come from.

2. *King of the Garamantes*: In ancient times the Garamantes were a barbarous and ferocious African people.

3. *Xanthus*: Don Quixote moves from his fantasy chivalresque heroes to real peoples, first of Asia and Africa and then of Spain, mostly identified by the rivers flowing through their territories, as in Homer and Virgil and some

romances of chivalry. The Xanthus was a river in Troy; the Massilian fields were in Africa; Arabia Felix was one of the three Arabias (Happy, Desert and Stony) mentioned above; the Thermodon was a river in Cappadocia (Turkey); the Pactolus was a river in Lydia, in Asia Minor, said to be rich in gold because Midas had bathed in it. The Genil runs by Granada; the Elysian Fields were thought by some ancient writers to be near Jerez de la Frontera; the Pisuerga, the old boundary between León and Castile, has its source in Palencia and flows into the Duero near Valladolid; the Guadiana flows through La Mancha, some of the way underground.

4. *Dr Laguna's magnificent edition*: Andrés Laguna (1499?–1560) was a famous doctor, whose heavily annotated translation of the Greek physician's treatise on the medicinal properties of over six hundred plants was published in 1555.

5. *sends his rain on the just and on the unjust*: Cf. Matthew 5. 45.

CHAPTER XIX

1. *I've come from . . . his home town*: They are on a long and difficult journey: Baeza is 290 kilometres to the south of Madrid, Segovia is 70 kilometres to the north of it. Alcobendas is a town near Madrid.

2. *the Knight of the Sorry Face*: A knight in the chivalry romance *Don Clarian de Landanis* (1524) is called 'El Caballero de la Triste Figura', because the face of a beautiful weeping damsel appears on his shield.

3. *Knight of the Burning Sword . . . Knight of Death*: The titles assumed by Amadis of Greece, Belianis of Greece, Florandino of Macedonia, Florarlan of Thrace, the Count of Arenberg (who lived during the reign of Philip II) and, again, Amadis of Greece.

4. *Si quis suadente diabolo, etc.*: The bachelor of arts quotes a canon approved at the Council of Trent, excommunicating 'according to where it says anyone who, persuaded by the devil', attacks a priest or a monk.

5. *Cid Ruy Díaz . . . honourable and valiant knight*: Incident narrated in one of the ballads of the Cid cycle.

CHAPTER XX

1. *the Mountains of the Moon*: It was believed in ancient times that the source of the Nile was in the Mountains of the Moon, in Ethiopia.

2. *danger loved is death won*: Ecclesiasticus 3. 27.

3. *Cato the Senseless of Rome*: Cato the Censor, since medieval times considered an authoritative source of maxims and proverbs.

CHAPTER XXI

1. *the beaver . . . being hunted for*: Allusion to an old myth about the beaver, hunted for the medicinal qualities of the castor in its genital organs.

2. *piece of eight . . . maravedí*: The maravedí was the smallest coin in common use; 68 maravedís were worth 1 silver real, 1 piece of eight was 8 silver reals and 5 silver reals were worth 1 escudo. A ducat was a gold coin, worth approximately the same as an escudo. Sancho says, in chapter XXV, that his daily maintenance costs him 52 maravedís (and, in Part II, chapter XXVIII, that he earned two ducats a month plus food when he worked as a farm labourer).

3. *the god of forges . . . the god of battles*: Vulcan and Mars.

4. *Greeks . . . the rape of Helen*: In Greek mythology, the abduction of Helen, the wife of Menelaus and the most beautiful woman in the world, by the Trojan prince Paris led to the ten-year siege of Troy and its sacking by the Greeks.

5. *mutatio capparum*: The Easter ceremony at which the cardinals exchanged their winter capes of fur for summer ones of silk.

6. *jupon*: Tight-fitting tunic worn under body armour.

CHAPTER XXII

1. *civil death, more or less*: The removal of all rights.

2. *Ginesillo de Parapilla*: The diminutive endings add a derogatory shade of meaning.

3. *Lazarillo de Tormes*: The picaresque novel, see Prologue, note 30.

4. *the flesh-pots of Egypt*: A life of abundance: see Exodus 16. 3.

CHAPTER XXIII

1. *twelve tribes of Israel . . . Castor and Pollux*: The brothers of the twelve tribes of Israel were Jacob's sons (Genesis 49); the killing of the seven Maccabees is narrated in 2 Maccabees; in classical mythology, Castor and Pollux were the twin sons of Leda.

CHAPTER XXIV

1. *that Thisbe so celebrated by poets*: In Roman mythology a Babylonian girl, the lover of Pyramus. (The sonnet in Part II, chapter XVIII tells their story).

2. *give her his word of marriage*: Secret marriages by oral or written pact had been forbidden by the Council of Trent, yet the practice still continued, and there are several examples of it in *Don Quixote.*

3. *Sir Rugel of Greece*: *Crónica del muy excelente príncipe don Florisel de Niquea, en la cual trata de las grandes hazañas de los excelentísimos príncipes don Rogel de Grecia y el segundo Agesilao* (1535), by Feliciano de Silva, the eleventh of the Amadis romances.

4. *to moisten us*: The moon was believed to be a humid planet.

5. *Queen Madásima*: There are three Madásimas in *Amadis of Gaul,* none a queen and none involved with Elisabat.

CHAPTER XXV

1. *Medoro*: *Orlando Furioso*, cantos 19 and 23.

2. *Astolfo's hippogryph . . . in fleetness of foot*: Astolfo's winged horse is in *Orlando Furioso,* canto 4, and Frontino, which belonged to the female warrior Bradamante, is in canto 23.

3. *nulla est retentio, so I've heard say*: Sancho garbles a line from the burial service, *Quia in inferno nulla est redemptio* (He who is in hell cannot be redeemed).

4. *Lucretia*: In Roman legend, the wife of Lucius Tarquinius Collatinus. Her rape by Sextus Tarquinius led to her suicide and the founding of the Roman republic.

5. *Perseus's labyrinth*: It should be Theseus's labyrinth, where he killed the Minotaur, finding his way out with the aid of the thread. Later editions make the correction. For Perseus, see chapter XXXIII, note 5.

CHAPTER XXVI

1. *seven iron soles*: Don Quixote confuses Orlando with his enemy the giant Ferragut, who wore seven iron plates over the only place where he could be wounded, his navel. He goes on to say that Medoro was Agramante's page, but he was Dardinel's.

2. *from his shirt-tail . . . a rosary*: From the second edition onwards, this passage is amended so that Don Quixote makes his rosary out of oak galls. Nobody knows

who decided that Cervantes's disrespect for Roman Catholic ritual had gone too far this time.

3. *moist and mournful Echo*: Because of the tears she sheds when rejected by Narcissus.

CHAPTER XXVII

1. *King Wamba*: Proverbial king of the Goths in Spain.

2. *Marius . . . Judas*: Gaius Marius was a Roman general and statesman, ever thirsty for power; Lucius Sergius Catilina led a life of conspiracy and intrigue; Lucius Cornelius Sulla, as absolute master of Rome and Italy, imposed a reign of terror; Vellido Dolfos treacherously killed King Sancho II of Castile at the siege of Zamora; Count Don Julián was blamed in legend for the loss of Spain to the Moors (see chapter XLI, note 2); Judas Iscariot was the apostle who betrayed Christ to the Jewish authorities in return for thirty pieces of silver.

3. *Stealing from me . . . was not even yet mine*: Reference to the parable in 2 Samuel 12, with which the prophet Nathan upbraids David for taking Uriah's wife.

4. *not daring to look back, like another Lot*: Genesis 19. When Lot and his family were allowed to escape from the destroyed city of Sodom, his wife disobeyed orders and looked back. She was turned into a pillar of salt.

CHAPTER XXIX

1. *Pegasus . . . town of Compluto*: Pegasus is the famous winged horse of Greek mythology. Muzaraque seems to be Cervantes's own invention, although Zulema Hill exists, near Alcalá. Compluto is the Latin name for Alcalá de Henares, near Madrid, where Cervantes was born.

CHAPTER XXX

1. *Tinacrio the Sage*: Enchanter who appears in various romances of chivalry. All the other names in the story are invented ones.

2. *the Phoenix itself*: Mythical bird, the only one of its kind, which burns itself on a funeral pyre and rises from the ashes to live again.

3. *and in her . . . have my being*: Very reminiscent of Paul's words, referring to God, in Acts 17. 28.

CHAPTER XXXI

1. *Sabaean*: From Saba or Sheba, in Arabia.
2. *in the belly of the whale*: Reference to the prophet Jonah, who tried to disobey God's command to preach in Nineveh by escaping in a boat, was thrown overboard and swallowed by a great fish.

CHAPTER XXXII

1. *Don Cirongilio . . . Diego García de Paredes*: *Los cuatro libros del valeroso caballero don Cirongilio de Tracia* (1545), by Bernardo de Vargas. The third book is not a chivalry romance but an account of the exploits of the Great Captain, a famous Spanish general of the early sixteenth century. It was published in 1559, but the first edition to include the life of the valiant soldier García de Paredes came out in 1580.

CHAPTER XXXIII

1. *the wise man . . . her*: See Proverbs 31. 10.
2. *usque . . . as the poet put it*: Plutarch ascribes the phrase ('as far as the altar') not to a poet but to the orator Pericles.
3. *Le lacrime di San Pietro*: Religious poem, first published in 1585, and in Spanish translation in 1587.
4. *simple-minded doctor . . . refrained from doing*: Lotario fuses two incidents in Ariosto's *Orlando Furioso* (cantos 42 and 43) involving a magic cup that spills its contents if the drinker's wife has been unfaithful to him.
5. *a modern play . . . find its way*: The play has not been identified. In Greek mythology, Danae was the daughter of Acrisius, king of Argos, imprisoned by him in a tower in an attempt to evade a prediction that she would bear a son who would kill him. But Zeus visited her in the form of a shower of gold and she conceived Perseus, who was to kill Acrisius by accident.
6. *For this . . . one flesh*: Cf. Genesis 2. 23.
7. *I look . . . shall never find*: The poem and poet have not been identified.

CHAPTER XXXIV

1. *Penelope*: In Greek mythology, Odysseus's wife, beset by unsuccessful suitors when her husband did not return after the fall of Troy. A symbol of wifely fidelity.

2. *Portia for a wife*: Wife of Marcus Brutus, who killed herself by swallowing red-hot coals when her husband died.

3. *the precious pearl*: See Matthew 13. 45–6.

CHAPTER XXXV

1. *battle waged . . . in the kingdom of Naples*: Probably the battle of Cerignola, 1503.

CHAPTER XXXVII

1. *Glory to God . . . good will*: Cf. Luke 2. 14.

2. *Peace to be this house*: Luke 10. 5; see also Matthew 10. 12.

3. *My peace . . . peace be unto you*: Cf. John 14. 27, and see also John 20. 19.

4. *Scyllas and Charybdises*: In Greek mythology, Scylla was a sea monster who devoured sailors when they tried to navigate the narrow channel between her cave and the whirlpool Charybdis. In later legend they were identified with two dangerous rocks on either side of the Strait of Messina.

CHAPTER XXXIX

1. *Duke of Alba was marching to Flanders*: The Duke of Alba, Fernando Álvarez de Toledo, arrived in Brussels with ten thousand men on 22 August 1567, having marched from Alessandria, a city some 80 kilometres south-west of Milan.

2. *the executions of Count Egmont and Count Hoorne*: In Brussels, 5 June 1568.

3. *Diego de Urbina*: Under whom Cervantes fought at Lepanto. The captive's tale is based on Cervantes's own experiences as a soldier and slave – but when he returned to Spain he was not accompanied by a Moorish woman.

4. *the alliance . . . a lamentable, disastrous loss*: In 1570–71. The alliance was the Holy League, formed 25 May.

5. *Don John of Austria . . . later did at Messenia*: He reached Genoa, from Barcelona,

on 26 July 1571, and Messenia, in the south of the Peloponnese, on 23 August.

6. *that glorious battle*: The naval battle of Lepanto, 7 October 1571, in which an alliance of Mediterranean Christian states defeated a large Turkish fleet, and Cervantes lost the use of his left hand.

7. *Navarino*: Port in the Gulf of Messenia.

8. *taken Tunis . . . from the Turks*: 11 October 1573.

9. *the Goletta . . . just outside Tunis*: The Goletta, the fort at the mouth of the bay of Tunis, was taken by the Turks on 23 August 1574. It had been occupied by a Spanish garrison since Charles V and I had captured it in 1535.

10. *Don Pedro de Aguilar*: A fictional creation, unlike the other people mentioned in the captive's tale.

CHAPTER XL

1. *Friar Puck*: 'El fratín', the nickname given to the Italian engineer Giacome Paleazzo.

2. *something Saavedra*: I.e. Miguel de Cervantes Saavedra.

3. *Hajji Murad . . . Al-Batha*: An important Moor of this name (a renegade, in fact) who was living in Algiers at this time, and a fortress near Oran, on the Mediterranean coast of Algeria.

CHAPTER XLI

1. *Arnaute Mami's slaves*: Arnaute Mami was the Albanian renegade who captured Cervantes in September 1575.

2. *La Cava Rumia . . . Spain was lost*: According to medieval legend, Count Julián, the governor of Ceuta (see chapter XXVII, note 2), allowed the Moors to conquer Spain to avenge himself on King Rodrigo, who had seduced Count Julian's daughter Florinda, 'la Cava'.

CHAPTER XLIII

1. *Palinurus*: Pilot of Aeneas's fleet.

2. *three-faced luminary*: The moon, in classical tradition. The faces are waxing, full and waning.

3. *wanton ingrate . . . consumed by jealousy and love*: In Greek mythology, the nymph Daphne fled from Apollo (the sun) over the plains of Thessaly, and the river Peneus, her father, turned her into a laurel bush to save her from him.

4. *Medusa*: In Greek mythology, one of the Gorgons, three sisters with snakes for hair, who had the power to turn anyone who looked at them to stone.

5. *Lirgandeo*: Enchanter, the mentor of the Knight of Phoebus (see Prologue, note 33).

CHAPTER XLV

1. *the turmoil in King Agramante's camp*: In *Orlando Furioso*, canto 27, Agramante is the chief of the Moors who besiege Charlemagne in Paris. The Archangel Michael sends discord into the Moorish camp, but Agramante and Sobrino restore order.

CHAPTER XLVI

1. *the peace and calm of Octavian's time*: The proverbial peace enjoyed by Rome under its first emperor (63 BC–AD 14).

2. *sicut erat in principio*: 'As it was in the beginning', from the *Gloria Patri*.

3. *the bright pursuer . . . in his natural and rapid course*: Before Apollo or the Sun, the pursuer of Daphne (see chapter XLIII, note 3) has twice visited all the signs of the zodiac; in other words within two years.

4. *the sage Mentironiana*: Not taken from any chivalry book or classical myth. The name has implications of 'liar'.

CHAPTER XLVII

1. *Zoroaster*: Or Zarathushtra, the Persian king who reformed his country's religion in about 800 BC, but who came to be popularly regarded as the inventor of magic.

2. *Tale of Rinconete and Cortadillo*: Story by Cervantes in the picaresque tradition, published as one of his *Novelas ejemplares* in 1613. They are a collection of twelve short tales loosely modelled on the Italian *novelle* of the fifteenth and sixteenth centuries, and their subject matter ranges from adventure and intrigue to realistic studies of contemporary low life.

3. *Villalpando's Summaries*: Gaspar Cardillo de Villalpando, *Summa summularum* (1557), a university textbook.

4. *the Gymnosophists of Ethiopia*: The Greeks' and Romans' name for the Brahmans of India.

5. *Milesian tales*: A classification developed in antiquity; such tales were associated with the city of Miletus, in Asia Minor.

6. *Ptolemy . . . Marco Polo*: The famous Greek astronomer and geographer of the second century, and the Italian explorer of the East (*c.* 1254–*c.* 1324).

7. *Sinon . . . Zopyrus*: Sinon persuaded the Trojans to take the wooden horse into their city; Euryalus was a Greek warrior famous for his friendship with Nisus (Virgil, *Aeneid*, V, 286–361); Zopyrus was a Persian nobleman who mutilated himself as a trick to enable his king Darius to capture a besieged city.

CHAPTER XLVIII

1. *the two princes of Greek and Latin poetry*: Homer and Virgil.

2. *Isabella, Phyllis and Alexandra*: La Isabela, La Filis and La Alejandra, by Lupercio Leonardo de Argensola, thought to have been written between 1581 and 1584.

3. *Ingratitude Revenged . . . The Friendly Enemy*: La ingratitud vengada, by Lope de Vega; La Numancia, by Cervantes; El mercader amante, by Gaspar de Aguilar; La enemiga favorable, by Francisco Agustín Tárrega, all plays written in the late sixteenth or early seventeenth centuries.

4. *as Cicero puts it*: According to Donatus in his commentaries on Terence, V, 1.

5. *King Pepin . . . Godfrey of Bouillon*: Pepin was Charlemagne's father, and reigned until 768; Charlemagne reigned until 814. Heraclius, the Byzantine Emperor, reigned from 610 to 641. Godfrey of Bouillon was the leader of the first crusade, and won Jerusalem in 1099.

6. *a brilliant Spanish genius*: Lope de Vega.

CHAPTER XLIX

1. *Viriatus . . . Don Manuel de León*: Viriatus was a Portuguese hero in the resistance against the Romans; Count Fernán González fought in the tenth century for the independence of Castile; for Gonzalo Fernández (or Hernández), the Great Captain (see chapter XXXII, note 1); Diego García de Paredes fought under the Great Captain and was a hero in the Naples campaign against the French (see

the same note); Diego García Pérez de Vargas fought heroically under Fernando III at the siege of Seville (1248); Garcilaso de la Vega is not the soldier-poet of the early sixteenth century but one of his fifteenth-century ancestors, a knight who fought in the taking of Granada from the Moors; Manuel Ponce de León was another hero in the war of Granada, a legendary figure in the ballads.

2. *Princess Floripes . . . Bridge of Mantible*: An episode from Carolingian legend: Floripes was the sister of the good giant Fierabras (see chapter X, note 3) and the wife of Guy of Burgundy, a nephew of Charlemagne and one of the Twelve Peers; the Bridge of Mantible was defended by the ferocious giant Galafre but carried by Charlemagne with the help of Fierabras.

3. *Guerrino il Meschino . . . of Great Britain*: Guerrino il Meschino is the hero of the Carolingian romance by Andrea de Barberino (c. 1370–c. 1431), which was published in Spanish translation in 1527; the Grail, Tristan and Iseult, Guenevere and Lancelot all belong to Arthurian myth, with the Spanish addition of Quintañona.

4. *Pierres . . . a cart-pole*: The wooden horse does not appear in the story of these lovers, the *Historia de la linda Magalona, hija del Rey de Nápoles, y de Pierres, hijo del Conde de Provenza* (1519, translated from the French), but in another popular love story, *La historia del muy valiente y esforzado caballero Clamades, hijo del rey de Castilla, y de la linda Clarmonda, hija del rey de Tuscana* (1521, also from a French original).

5. *of all reason and good sense*: In this paragraph Don Quixote has moved on to list some real Spanish knights of the early fifteenth century, whose exploits are recorded in the *Crónica del Rey Juan II*. The jousts of the Honourable Pass (1434) were among the most famous chivalric exploits of the Middle Ages. Suero de Quiñones, a Leonese knight, had sworn to wear an iron ring round his neck every Thursday in honour of his lady. To free himself of this promise he undertook to hold the bridge of Órbigo, between León and Astorga, with nine followers, for thirty days. Sixty-eight knights presented themselves and three hundred lances were broken.

CHAPTER LI

1. *Gante y Luna*: Not traced.

2. *the pastoral Arcadia*: The mountainous region of the Peloponnese, the pastoral paradise for classical and Renaissance writers, most notably Jacopo Sannazzaro (1458–1530), whose prose romance *Arcadia* was first published in 1504, and in Spanish translation in 1547.

CHAPTER LII

1. *ARGAMASILLA . . . DE LA MANCHA*: There are two villages in La Mancha with this name, Argamasilla de Alba and Argamasilla de Calatrava. It has traditionally been assumed that one of these, or the two fictionally fused, is the village that the narrator claims not to remember in the famous first sentence of the novel: amateur poets are fond of writing poems in praise of the local celebrity; furthermore, *argamasa* means 'mortar, plaster' and *masilla* means 'putty' (just as *mancha* means 'stain'), so it would not be surprising if the narrator conveniently forgot that his hero came from a place with such humble connotations.

2. *HOC SCRIPSERUNT*: Latin: 'wrote this'.

3. *than Jason gave to Crete*: In Greek mythology, Jason was a hero from Thessaly, not Crete, who led the Argonauts in their quest for the Golden Fleece.

4. *Gaeta . . . Cathay*: Port near Naples, and the name by which China was commonly known in the Middle Ages.

5. *Bellona . . . Brillador's and Bayard's verve*: Bellona was the Roman goddess of war; Brigliadoro was Orlando's horse; Bayard was Reynald's horse.

6. *Forsi . . . miglior plectio*: *Orlando Furioso*, canto 30, l. 16: 'perhaps another will sing with a better plectrum'.

Miguel de Cervantes Saavedra (*c.* 1547–1616) published the first part of *Don Quixote* in 1605, which brought him immediate popularity. The second part of *Don Quixote* (not included in this volume) was published in 1615. He also wrote plays (sixteen of which survive), a pastoral novel, *La Galatea* (1585), and *Exemplary Stories* (1613).

John Rutherford is a Fellow of The Queen's College, Oxford, where he teaches Spanish, Spanish-American and Galician language and literature.

Seven Wonders of the World

The Aeneid	VIRGIL
Anna Karenina	LEO TOLSTOY
Don Quixote Part One	CERVANTES
Faust Part One	JOHANN WOLFGANG VON GOETHE
Hell	DANTE ALIGHIERI
Madame Bovary	GUSTAVE FLAUBERT
The Odyssey	HOMER